THE
JOHN
VARLEY
READER

THE JOHN VARLEY READER

Thirty Years of Short Fiction

JOHN VARLEY

ACE BOOKS, NEW YORK

THE BERKLEY PUBLISHING GROUP
Published by the Penguin Group
Penguin Group (USA) Inc.
375 Hudson Street, New York, New York 10014, USA
Penguin Group (Canada), 10 Alcorn Avenue, Toronto, Ontario M4V 3B2, Canada
(a division of Pearson Penguin Canada Inc.)
Penguin Books Ltd., 80 Strand, London WC2R 0RL, England
Penguin Group Ireland, 25 St. Stephen's Green, Dublin 2, Ireland (a division of Penguin Books Ltd.)
Penguin Group (Australia), 250 Camberwell Road, Camberwell, Victoria 3124, Australia
(a division of Pearson Australia Group Pty. Ltd.)
Penguin Books India Pvt. Ltd., 11 Community Centre, Panchsheel Park, New Delhi—110 017, India
Penguin Group (NZ), Cnr. Airborne and Rosedale Roads, Albany, Auckland 1310, New Zealand
(a division of Pearson New Zealand Ltd.)
Penguin Books (South Africa) (Pty.) Ltd., 24 Sturdee Avenue, Rosebank, Johannesburg 2196,
South Africa

Penguin Books Ltd., Registered Offices: 80 Strand, London WC2R 0RL, England

First edition: September 2004

Library of Congress Cataloging-in-Publication Data

Varley, John, 1947 Aug. 9–
    The John Varley reader : thirty years of short fiction / John Varley.— 1st ed.
        p. cm.
    ISBN 0-441-01195-0
    1. Science fiction, American. I. Title.

PS3572.A724A6 2004
813'.54—dc22

                                                                        2004050349

PRINTED IN THE UNITED STATES OF AMERICA

10   9   8   7   6   5   4   3   2   1

CONTENTS

INTRODUCTION TO
The John Varley Reader

On January 20, 2002, at 2:30 in the afternoon, a fire broke out in the big, abandoned fruit and vegetable market and warehouse covering the two blocks between SE 10th and 11th, Belmont and Taylor, in Portland, Oregon. By the time the fire department arrived there was little they could do but try to keep the fire from spreading to adjacent buildings. In less than half an hour a fourth alarm was called in. At peak, 125 firefighters were involved. Eventually the fire reached the north end of the warehouse, which abutted the building that used to contain the Monte Carlo restaurant, where Lee and I spent some pleasant years in one of the two great old apartments above.

It is very strange to look at the gutted remains of a place you used to call home.

Only the edges of the tiled roof survived. Some of the huge old attic beams still stood, though the fire had eaten deeply. In back, the roof and the attic floor had fallen and taken the walls and floors of our bedroom and offices with them. A tiny portion of the south wall of Lee's office was visible, one of the walls with the decorative sponge painting job she had been so proud of.

Taking the good with the bad, the Monte Carlo was a pretty cool place to live. On a coolness scale of 1 to 10, with Leavenworth Prison being a 1, San Simeon a 10, and Travis McGee's "Busted Flush" houseboat a 9, the Monte Carlo was an 8.

The apartment looked out on downtown Portland from across the river. On the fourth of July, Cinco de Mayo, and half a dozen festivals each year we could watch the fireworks from our windows. The restaurant itself was a hangout for half the elderly Italian population of Portland. Lots of guys who looked like Don Corleone showed up most days. They made the best minestrone in town. While we were there it became the hot nightspot for Reed College students, doing some disco revival thing, then went back to its old slumber again as fashion moved on to a new spot.

We knew it was a firetrap. Only one stairway, made of old dry wood. It was the only place I ever lived that was plumbed for beverages. Flexible plastic tubes led from pressurized bottles in the basement, up our stairs, and through a wall into the bar be-

low. I figured if a fire got started I'd cut a pipe and drown the blaze with 7-Up or Coke. I'd have to be careful not to confuse it with the other pipes, which were full of vodka, Scotch, and gin. I thought of splicing into one, like stealing cable service, but decided it wasn't worth it for bar whiskey.

Many people go through their entire lives without ever living in an 8, and I've lived in three. The first was 1354 Haight Street, San Francisco, a block and a half from the Center of the Universe. You could almost see the Haight & Ashbury sign from there. Across the street was a head shop, the floor above was a notorious crank house where we once saw Janis Joplin going in to score, and down at the corner was Magnolia Thunderpussy, probably the coolest ice cream parlor in America. I feel very lucky to have lived there for a year, and to have survived, as we were all experimenting with various drugs at the time.

I've been lucky about many things.

This year, 2004, marks the thirtieth anniversary of my first publication of a science fiction story. That strikes me as a pretty good time for a retrospective. Such a thing ought to have an introduction.

I didn't always feel that way. When I started out as a writer, I was very uncomfortable with interviews, radio, and television. In fact, I still hate to do self-promotion. I felt the stories ought to speak for themselves. So my first story collection, The Persistence of Vision, *had a very flattering introduction by Algis Budrys, because my publisher insisted on it, and the next two,* The Barbie Murders *and* Blue Champagne, *had nothing at all; just a table of contents and the stories.*

I'm not saying I'm an exceptionally private person. I've gone to conventions, sat on panels discussing my works and science fiction in general. My phone number has always been a listed one, and I've only regretted that once. And I've recently gone public in a big way, for me, by opening a website where I post my thoughts (what they call blogs these days) and odd items I write that I don't feel are likely to sell.

But re-reading these stories, thinking about them and about the recent fire and the transience of things and of life itself, realizing that since I don't build things, haven't founded any corporations, and am not likely to revolutionize science with a stunning new discovery anytime soon, my most important legacy will be these stories. And while I still believe they must stand on their own with no explanations from me, that they must speak for themselves . . . it strikes me that telling a little about where I was, what I was doing, and who I was when I wrote them might be of interest to readers.

It is probably as close to an autobiography as I will ever get. I don't propose to write one here, and I don't intend to put it all up front in one indigestible lump,

*either. Instead, I will scatter it through the book in introductions to the individual sto-
ries. If you aren't interested in stuff like that, feel free to skip to the stories themselves,
which is what this volume is all about, anyway. But if you do enjoy the introductions
you are invited to join me at www.varley.net for lots more.*

INTRODUCTION TO

"*Picnic on Nearside*"

The Monte Carlo fire was not the first time a place I had recently lived in burned. 1735 Waller Street in San Francisco was a 6 on the cool-places-to-live scale. Maybe a 6.5. It would have scored higher because the location was great—half a block away from Golden Gate Park, one block from Haight Street—but this was the early seventies, and the Haight-Ashbury had come down a bit since the "golden age" of the hippies. In fact, the streets were littered with the wreckage of those people whose experiments in mind expansion had not stopped with marijuana and LSD, but had moved on to the joys of crank and heroin. Many of the storefronts were empty, and most of the old Victorian houses were firetraps.

Go back there now and you will see that gentrification has hit the neighborhood like a gold-plated hammer. Everything has been rehabilitated and repainted and the people living there are urban professionals. They are the only ones who can afford it. I doubt that I could rent a closet at 1735 for the $175/month that I used to pay for the whole four-bedroom second-floor flat. There's a McDonald's on the corner of Haight and Stanyan. The old Straight Theater is gone, replaced by an upscale Goodwill store. Most of the rest of the businesses deal in antiques.

I have to confess I liked it better in the seventies, even though I might have died there.

There was an ex–Jehovah's Witness named Teardrop who lived in a room below us. He was one of the sweetest guys I've ever met, but he had one bad habit: he smoked in bed. That would have been dangerous enough, but he was also epileptic. One night he had a seizure, and in minutes his room was an inferno. I stumbled downstairs with my family in a torrent of smoke, virtually blind.

The SFFD is very quick; they arrived while I was still coughing, and had the fire out before much damage was done. We were all safe, Teardrop didn't even have a minor burn, but I was always nervous about the place after that.

With good reason. One month after we moved to Eugene, Oregon, fire gutted the place. It was empty for years, but has now been restored.

* * *

It was while living in this flat that I first got the idea that I might try to write and sell science fiction stories. The reason was simple. I needed the money.

I had left southeast Texas on a National Merit Scholarship to Michigan State, mostly because on the list of schools which had accepted me and whose tuition and room and board the scholarship would cover, MSU was the most distant from Texas. I began as a physics major, then saw how hard and how little fun that was going to be, switched to English, found that to be rather dry, and hit the road in the footsteps of Jack Kerouac. I thought of myself as a beatnik until I got to the Haight during the Summer of Love, where I first heard the word hippie.

Within a few hours of our arrival my traveling companion, Chris, and I found ourselves in San Francisco sitting on the floor of an empty storefront on Stanyan Street with a few dozen others, a place run by people called The Diggers, feasting on free chicken necks and chanting some Hindu mantra with Allen Ginsberg playing a hand organ about the size of Schroeder's piano.

So just what do hippies do? *we wanted to know. Write angry poetry? Sit around coffee shops? Plot to overthrow the government with force and violence? Well, no, mostly we sing and dance to groups like the Grateful Dead, Jefferson Airplane, and Big Brother and the Holding Company (while sneering at groups from Los Angeles and New York), smoke or ingest various psychedelic substances, and just generally groove on life. Oh, yeah, and we are in favor of peace and free love, which means we screw a lot.*

Your basic sex, drugs, and rock 'n' roll.

Works for me.

We had been squeaking by for years on nothing much. I think it may have been easier in those days than it is today to exist with no visible means of support. There was a feeling of community, even in the drug-ravaged streets of the Haight. We never even considered illegal activities, never stole anything, never dealt in drugs. We never had to. If people had stuff, they shared.

That's not to say it was easy. Standing in line at St. Anthony's Mission downtown for their daily (and surprisingly good) free lunch was fun. Standing outside the Lucky market on Stanyan Street panhandling got old quickly. In fact, after about five years on the roads between LA and New York and San Francisco and Berkeley, dodging the draft board all the way, it was all *starting to get old.*

In all my meanderings I had never held an actual job for more than a few weeks. I washed dishes. I worked in a warehouse wrapping packages. I lasted for three days as a "flyboy" at the end of a printing press, gathering up advertising circulars still wet with ink in stacks of fifty, always falling behind as the press spit out paper faster than I could pick it up, until I realized one night I was becoming part of the machine, and the least efficient part of it, at that. I bused tables (and to this day will not bus my own table at fast-food places). That was about the extent of my labor skills. That is still about the extent of my skills.

So what did I have that people would pay money for? A handful of credits toward a B.A. in English, one creative writing class which I seldom attended after I heard the lame assignments the teacher was giving out, and an extensive background in science fiction. Reading it, not writing it.

I'd been doing it since Mr. Green, the librarian at my junior high school, handed me a copy of Red Planet, by Robert A. Heinlein, and said I might enjoy it, very much as a street-corner dealer in heroin will give you a free sample.

Could I write this stuff? Could I write it well? Would people pay me for it? I didn't know the answers to any of these questions, but with the optimism of youth I decided it couldn't hurt anything to try, between stints of bumming spare change. What's the worst that could happen? Rejection slips. Believe me, standing outside the Lucky market you quickly get a very thick skin when it comes to rejection.

I sat down at a little desk at 1735 Waller Street and started to write a novel.

I wrote it in ballpoint pen, on ruled notebook paper, just like I had in high school. It was called Gas Giant, and it was pretty bad. (I still like the title; maybe I'll use it someday.) I taught myself to type—badly, I still look at the keyboard—on an electric Smith-Corona that I bought for $5 at a thrift store. Then I sent the novel out and started collecting the well-deserved rejection slips. It began to seem that Hugo and Nebula awards for this book were just an idle dream, not to mention the New York Times bestseller list and that screenwriting Oscar.

But I didn't give up. To stay busy I wrote the following short story, "Picnic on Nearside." Actually, it was a novelette, but I didn't even know that term at the time. It was 12,563 words long . . . by actual count. (I later learned that you could count three representative pages and average them. Who knew?) I sent it out to Ed Ferman at The Magazine of Fantasy and Science Fiction, and a few months later I got back a nice letter. Mr. Ferman said he liked the story a lot, but he'd like it a lot better if it was 10,000 words. I spent all of five minutes raging about idiot editors, then sat down and started crossing stuff out. I declared war on modifiers, clauses, sentences, entire paragraphs that had snuck in there when I wasn't looking. I got it down to pretty much exactly 10,000 words . . . and discovered that I had accidentally improved the story tremendously. I sent it back, and a few months later got a check for $200.

That was a whole month's rent, with $25 left over to buy records!

I decided this was the life for me.

PICNIC ON NEARSIDE

THIS IS THE story of how I went to the Nearside and found old Lester and maybe grew up a little. And about time, too, as Carnival would say.

Carnival is my mother. We don't get along well most of the time, and I think it's because I'm twelve and she's ninety-six. She says it makes no difference, and she waited so long to have her child because she wanted to be sure she was ready for it. And I answer back that at her age she's too far away from childhood to remember what it's like. And she replies that her memory is perfect all the way back to her birth. And I retort . . .

We argue a lot.

I'm a good debater, but Carnival's a special problem. She's an Emotionalist; so anytime I try to bring facts into the argument she waves it away with a statement like, "Facts only get in the way of my preconceived notions." I tell her that's irrational, and she says I'm perfectly right, and she meant it to be. Most of the time we can't even agree on premises to base a disagreement on. You'd think that would be the death of debate, but if you did, you don't know Carnival and me.

The major topic of debate around our warren for seven or eight lunations had been the Change I wanted to get. The battle lines had been drawn, and we had been at it every day. She thought a Change would harm my mind at my age. *Every*body was getting one.

We were all sitting at the breakfast table. There was me and Carnival, and Chord, the man Carnival has lived with for several years, and Adagio, Chord's daughter. Adagio is seven.

There had been a big battle the night before between me and Carnival. It had ended up (more or less) with me promising to divorce her as soon as I was of age. I don't remember what the counterthreat was. I had been pretty upset.

I was sitting there eating fitfully and licking my wounds. The argument had been inconclusive, philosophically, but from the pragmatic standpoint she had won, no question about it. The hard fact was that I couldn't get a Change until she affixed her personality index to the bottom of a sheet of input, and she said she'd put her brain in cold storage before she'd allow that. She would, too.

"I think I'm ready to have a Change," Carnival said to us.

"That's not fair!" I yelled. "You said that just to spite me. You just want to rub it in that I'm nothing and you're anything you want to be."

"We'll have no more of that," she said, sharply. "We've exhausted this subject, and I will not change my mind. You're too young for a Change."

"Blowout," I said. "I'll be an adult soon; it's only a year away. Do you really think I'll be all that different in a year?"

"I don't care to predict that. I hope you'll mature. But if, as you say, it's only a year, why are you in such a hurry?"

"And I wish you wouldn't use language like that," Chord said.

Carnival gave him a sour look. She has a hard line about outside interference when she's trying to cope with me. She doesn't want anyone butting in. But she wouldn't say anything in front of me and Adagio.

"I think you should let Fox get his Change," Adagio said, and grinned at me. Adagio is a good kid, as younger foster-siblings go. I could always count on her to back me up, and I returned the favor when I could.

"You keep out of this," Chord advised her, then to Carnival, "Maybe we should leave the table until you and Fox get this settled."

"You'd have to stay away for a year," Carnival said. "Stick around. The discussion is over. If Fox thinks different, he can go to his room."

That was my cue, and I got up and ran from the table. I felt silly doing it, but the tears were real. It's just that there's a part of me that stays cool enough to try and get the best of any situation.

Carnival came to see me a little later, but I did my best to make her feel unwelcome. I can be good at that, at least with her. She left when it became obvious she couldn't make anything any better. She was hurt, and when the door closed, I felt really miserable, mad at her and at myself, too. I was finding it hard to love her as much as I had a few years before, and feeling ashamed because I couldn't.

I worried over that for a while and decided I should apologize. I left my room and was ready to go cry in her arms, but it didn't happen that way. Maybe if it had, things would have been different and Halo and I would never have gone to Nearside.

Carnival and Chord were getting ready to go out. They said they'd be gone most of the lune. They were dressing up for it, and what bothered me and made me change my plans was that they were dressing in the family room instead of in their own private rooms where I thought they should.

She had taken off her feet and replaced them with peds, which struck me as foolish, since peds only make sense in free-fall. But Carnival wears them every chance she gets, prancing around like a high-stepping horse because they are so unsuited to walking. I think people look silly with hands on the ends of their legs. And naturally she had left her feet lying on the floor.

Carnival glanced at her watch and said something about how they would be late for the shuttle. As they left, she glanced over her shoulder.

"Fox, would you do me a favor and put those feet away, please? Thanks." Then she was gone.

* * *

An hour later, in the depths of my depression, the door rang. It was a woman I had never seen before. She was nude.

You know how sometimes you can look at someone you know who's just had a Change and recognize them instantly, even though they might be twenty centimeters shorter or taller and mass fifty kilos more or less and look nothing at all like the person you knew? Maybe you don't, because not everyone has this talent, but I have it very strong. Carnival says it's an evolutionary change in the race, a response to the need to recognize other individuals who can change their appearance at will. That may be true; she can't do it at all.

I think it's something to do with the way a person wears a body: any body, of either sex. Little mannerisms like blinking, mouth movements, stance, fingers; maybe even the total kinesthetic gestalt the doctors talk about. This was like that. I could see behind the pretty female face and the different height and weight and recognize someone I knew. It was Halo, my best friend, who had been a male the last time I saw him, three lunes ago. She had a big foolish grin on her face.

"Hi, Fox," she said, in a voice that was an octave higher and yet was unmistakably Halo's. "Guess who?"

"Queen Victoria, right?" I tried to sound bored. "Come on in, Halo."

Her face fell. She came in, looking confused.

"What do you think?" she said, turning slowly to give me a look from all sides. All of them were good because—as if I needed anything else—her mother had let her get the full treatment: fully developed breasts, all the mature curves—the works. She had been denied only the adult height. She was even a few centimeters shorter than she had been.

"It's fine," I said.

"Listen, Fox, if you'd rather I left . . ."

"Oh, I'm sorry, Halo," I said, giving up on my hatred. "You look great. Fabulous. Really you do. I'm just having a hard time being happy for you. Carnival is never going to give in."

She was instantly sympathetic. She took my hand, startling me badly.

"I was so happy I guess I was tactless," she said in a low voice. "Maybe I shouldn't have come over here yet."

She looked at me with big brown eyes (they had been blue, usually), and I started realizing what this was going to mean to me. I mean, Halo? A female? Halo, the guy I used to run the corridors with? The guy who helped me build that awful eight-legged cat that Carnival wouldn't let in the house and looked like a confused caterpillar? Who made love to the same girls I did and compared notes with me later when we were alone and helped me out when the gang tried to beat me up and cried with me and vowed to get even? Could we do any of that now? I didn't know. Most of my best friends were male, maybe because the sex thing tended to make matters too complicated with females, and I couldn't handle both things with the same person yet.

But Halo was having no such doubts. In fact, she was standing very close to me and practicing a wide-eyed innocent look that she knew did funny things to me. She knew it because I had told her so, back when she was a boy. Somehow that didn't seem fair.

"Ah, listen, Halo," I said hastily, backing away. She had been going for my pants! "Ah, I think I need some time to get used to this. How can I . . . ? You know what I'm talking about, don't you?" I don't think she did, and neither did I, really. All I knew was I was unaccountably mortified at what she was so anxious to try. And she was still coming at me.

"Say!" I said, desperately. "Say! I have an idea! Ah . . . I know. Let's take Carnival's jumper and go for a ride, okay? She said I could use it today." My mouth was leading its own life, out of control. Everything I said was extemporaneous, as much news to me as it was to her.

She stopped pursuing me. "Did she really?"

"Sure," I said, very assured. This was only a half lie, by my mother's lights. What had happened was I had meant to ask her for the jumper, and I was sure she would have said yes. I was logically certain she would have. I had just forgotten to ask, that's all. So it was almost as if permission had been granted, and I went on as if it had. The reasoning behind this is tricky, I admit, but as I said, Carnival would have understood.

"Well," Halo said, not really overjoyed at the idea, "where would we go?"

"How about to Old Archimedes?" Again, that was a big surprise to me. I had had no idea I wanted to go there.

Halo was really shocked. I jolted her right out of her new mannerisms. She reacted just like the old Halo would have, with a dopey face and open mouth. Then she tried on other reactions: covering her mouth with her hands and wilting a little. First-time Changers are like that; new women tend to mince around like something out of a gothic novel, and new men swagger and grunt like Marlon Brando in *A Streetcar Named Desire*. They get over it.

Halo got over it right in front of my eyes. She stared at me, scratching her head.

"Are you crazy? Old Archimedes is on the Nearside. They don't let anybody go over there."

"Don't they?" I asked, suddenly interested. "Do you know that for a fact? And if so, why not?"

"Well, I mean everybody knows . . ."

"Do they? Who is 'they' that won't let us go?"

"The Central Computer, I guess."

"Well, the only way to find out is to try it. Come on, let's go." I grabbed her arm. I could see she was confused, and I wanted it to remain that way until I could get my own thoughts together.

"I'd like a flight plan to Old Archimedes on the Nearside," I said, trying to sound as grownup and unworried as possible. We had packed a lunch and reached the field in ten minutes, due largely to my frantic prodding.

"That's a little imprecise, Fox," said the CC. "Old Archimedes is a big place. Would you like to try again?"

"Ah . . ." I drew a blank. Damn all computers and their literal-mindedness! What did I know about Old Archimedes? About as much as I knew about Old New York or Old Bombay.

"Give me a flight plan to the main landing field."

"That's better. The data are . . ." It reeled off the string of numbers. I fed them into the pilot and tried to relax.

"Here goes," I said to Halo. "This is Fox-Carnival-Joule, piloting private jumper AX1453, based at King City. I hereby file a flight plan to Old Archimedes' main landing field, described as follows . . ." I repeated the numbers the CC had given me. "Filed on the seventeenth lune of the fourth lunation of the year 214 of the Occupation of Earth. I request an initiation time."

"Granted. Time as follows: thirty seconds from mark. Mark."

I was stunned. "That's all there is to it?"

It chuckled. Damn maternalistic machine. "What did you expect, Fox? Marshals converging on your jumper?"

"I don't know. I guess I thought you wouldn't allow us to go to the Nearside."

"A popular misconception. You are a free citizen, although a minor, and able to go where you wish on the lunar surface. You are subject only to the laws of the state and the specific wishes of your parent as programmed into me. I . . . Do you wish me to start the burn for you?"

"Mind your own business." I watched the tick and pressed the button when it reached zero. The acceleration was mild, but went on for a long time. Hell, Old Archimedes is at the antipodes.

"I have the responsibility to see that you do not endanger yourself through youthful ignorance or forgetfulness. I must also see that you obey the wishes of your mother. Other than that, you are on your own."

"You mean Carnival gave me permission to go to the Nearside?"

"I didn't say that. I have received no instruction from Carnival *not* to permit you to go to Nearside. There are no unusual dangers to your safety on Nearside. So I had no choice but to approve your flight plan." It paused, significantly. "It is my experience that few parents consider it necessary to instruct me to deny such permission. I infer that it's because so few people ever ask to go there. I also note that your parent is at the present moment unreachable; she has left instructions not to be disturbed. Fox," the CC said, accusingly, "it occurs to me that this is no accident. Did you have this planned?"

I *hadn't*! But if I'd known . . .

"No."

"I suppose you want a return flight plan?"

"Why? I'll ask you when I'm ready to come back."

"I'm afraid that won't be possible," it said, smugly. "In another five minutes you'll be out of range of my last receptor. I don't extend to the Nearside, you know. Haven't in decades. You're going out of contact, Fox. You'll be on your own. Think about it."

I did. For a queasy moment I wanted to turn back. Without the CC to monitor us, kids wouldn't be allowed on the surface for *years*.

Was I that confident? I know how hostile the surface is if it ever gets the drop on you. I thought I had all the mistakes trained out of me by now, but did I?

"How exciting," Halo gushed. She was off in the clouds again, completely over her shock at where we were going. She was bubble-headed like that for three lunes after her Change. Well, so was I, later, when I had my first.

"Hush, numbskull," I said, not unkindly. Nor was she insulted. She just grinned at me and gawked out the window as we approached the terminator.

I checked the supply of consumables; they were in perfect shape for a stay of a full lunation if need be, though I had larked off without a glance at the delta-vee.

"All right, smart-ass, give me the data for the return."

"Incomplete request," the CC drawled.

"Damn you, I want a flight plan Old Archimedes–King City, and no back talk."

"Noted. Assimilated." It gave me that data. Its voice was getting fainter.

"I don't suppose," it said, diffidently, "that you'd care to give me an indication of when you plan to return?"

Ha! I had it where it hurt. Carnival wouldn't be happy with the CC's explanation, I was sure of that.

"Tell her I've decided to start my own colony and I'll never come back."

"As you wish."

Old Archimedes was bigger than I had expected. I knew that even in its heyday it had not been as populated as King City is, but they built more above the surface in those days. King City is not much more than a landing field and a few domes. Old Archimedes was chock-a-block with structures, all clustered around the central landing field. Halo pointed out some interesting buildings to the south, and so I went over there and set down next to them.

She opened the door and threw out the tent, then jumped after it. I followed, taking the ladder since I seemed elected to carry the lunch. She took a quick look around and started unpacking the tent.

"We'll go exploring later," she said, breathlessly. "Right now let's get in the tent and eat. I'm hungry."

All right, all right, I said to myself. I've got to face it sooner or later. I didn't think she was really all that hungry—not for the picnic lunch, anyway. This was still going too fast for me. I had no idea what our relationship would be when we crawled out of that tent.

While she was setting it up, I took a more leisurely look around. Before long I was wishing we had gone to Tranquillity Base instead. It wouldn't have been as private, but there are no spooks at Tranquillity. Come to think of it, Tranquillity Base used to be on the Nearside, before they moved it.

About Old Archimedes:

I couldn't put my finger on what disturbed me about the place. Not the silence. The race has had to adjust to silence since we were forced off the Earth and took to growing up on the junk planets of the system. Not the lack of people. I was accustomed to long walks on the surface where I might not see anyone for hours. I don't know. Maybe it was the Earth hanging there a little above the horizon.

It was in crescent phase, and I wished uselessly for the old days when that dark portion would have been sprayed with points of light that were the cities of mankind. Now there was only the primitive night and the dolphins in the sea and the aliens—bogies cooked up to ruin the sleep of a child, but now I was not so sure. If humans still survive down there, we have no way of knowing it.

They say that's what drove people to the Farside: the constant reminder of what they had lost, always there in the sky. It must have been hard, especially to the Earthborn. Whatever the reason, no one had lived on the Nearside for almost a century. All the original settlements had dwindled as people migrated to the comforting empty sky of Farside.

I think that's what I felt, hanging over the old buildings like some invisible moss. It was the aura of fear and despair left by all the people who had buried their hopes here and moved away to the forgetfulness of Farside. There were ghosts here, all right: the shades of unfulfilled dreams and endless longing. And over it all a bottomless sadness.

I shook myself and came back to the present. Halo had the tent ready. It bulged up on the empty field, a clear bubble just a little higher than my head. She was already inside. I crawled through the sphincter, and she sealed it behind me.

Halo's tent was a good one. The floor was about three meters in diameter, plenty of room for six people if you didn't mind an occasional kick. It had a stove, a stereo set, and a compact toilet. It recycled water, scavenged CO_2, controlled temperature, and could provide hydroponic oxygen for three lunations. And it all folded into a cube thirty centimeters on a side.

Halo had skinned out of her suit as soon as the door was sealed and was bustling about, setting up the kitchen. She took the lunch hamper from me and started to work.

I watched her with keen interest as she prepared the food. I wanted to get an insight into what she was feeling. It wasn't easy. Every fuse in her head seemed to have blown.

First-timers often overreact, seeking a new identity for themselves before it dawns on them there was nothing wrong with the old one. Since our society offers so little differentiation between the sex roles, they reach back to where the differences are so vivid and startling: novels, dramas, films, and tapes from the old days on Earth and the early years on the moon. They have the vague idea that since they have this new body and it lacks a penis or vagina, they should behave differently.

I recognized the character she had fallen into; I'm as interested in old culture as the next kid. She was Blondie and I was supposed to be Dagwood. The Bumsteads, you know. Typical domestic nineteenth-century couple. She had spread a red-and-white-checkered tablecloth and set two places with dishes, napkins, washbowls, and a tiny electric candelabra.

I had to smile at her, kneeling at the tiny stove, trying to put three pans on the same burner. She was trying so hard to please me with a role I was completely uninterested in. She was humming as she worked.

After the meal, I offered to clean up for her (well, *Dagwood* would have), but Blondie said no, that's all right, dear, I'll take care of everything. I lay flat on my back, holding my belly, and watched the Earth. Presently I felt a warm body cuddle up, half beside me and half on top of me, and press close from toenails to eyebrows. She had left Blondie over among the dirty dishes. The woman who breathed in my ear now was—Helen of Troy? Greta Garbo?—someone new, anyway. I wished fervently that Halo would come back. I was beginning to think Halo and I could screw like the very devil if this feverish creature that contained her would only give us a chance. Meantime, I had to be raped by Helen of Troy. I raised my head.

"What's it like, Halo?"

She slowed her foreplay slightly, but it never really stopped. She propped herself up on one elbow.

"I don't think I can describe it to you."

"Please try."

She dimpled. "I don't really know what it's *all* like," she said. "I'm still a virgin, you know."

I sat up. "You got *that, too?*"

"Sure, why not? But don't worry about it. I'm not afraid."

"What about making love?"

"Oh, Fox, Fox! Yes, yes. I . . ."

"No, no! Wait a minute." I squirmed beneath her, trying to hold her off a little longer. "What I meant was, wasn't there any problem in making the shift? I mean, do you have any aversion to having sex with boys now?" It was sure a stupid question, but she took it seriously.

"I haven't noticed any problem so far," she said, thoughtfully, as her hand reached down and fumbled, inexpertly trying to guide me in. I helped her get it right, and she poised, squatting on her toes. "I thought about that before the Change, but it sort of melted away. Now I don't feel any qualms at all. Ahhhhh!" She had thrust herself down, brutally hard, and we were off and running.

It was the most unsatisfactory sex act I ever had. It was not entirely the fault of either of us; external events were about to mess us up totally. But it wasn't very good even without that.

A first-time female Changer is liable to be in delirious oblivion through the entire first sex act, which may last all of sixty seconds. The fact that she is playing the game from the other court with a different set of rules and a new set of equipment does not handicap her. Rather, it provides a tremendous erotic stimulus.

That's what happened to Halo. I began to wonder if she'd wait for me. I never found out. I looked away from her face and got the shock of my life. There was someone standing outside the tent, watching us.

Halo felt the change in me and looked at my face, which must have been a sight, then looked over her shoulder. She fainted; out like a light.

Hell, I almost fainted myself. Would have, but when she did, it scared me even more, and I decided I couldn't indulge it. So I stayed awake to see what was going on.

It looked way too much like one of the ghosts my imagination had been walking through the abandoned city ever since we got there. The figure was short and dressed in a suit that might have been stolen from the museum at Kepler, except that it was more patches than suit. I could tell little about who might be in it, not even the sex. It was bulky, and the helmet was reflective.

I don't know how long I stared at it; long enough for the spook to walk around the tent three or four times. I reached for the bottle of white wine we had been drinking and took a long pull. I found out that's an old movie cliché; it didn't make anything any better. But it sure did things for Halo when I poured it in her face.

"Get in your suit," I said, as she sat up, sputtering. "I think that character wants to talk to us." He was waving at us and pointing to what might have been a radio on his suit.

We suited up and crawled through the sphincter. I kept saying hello as I ran through the channels on my suit. Nothing worked. Then he came over and touched helmets. He sounded far away.

"What're you doin' here?"

I had thought that would have been obvious.

"Sir, we just came over here for a picnic. Are we on your land or something? If so, I'm sorry, and . . ."

"No, no." He waved it off. "You can do as you please. I ain't your ma. As to owning, I guess I own this whole city, but you're welcome to do as you please with most of it. Do as you please, that's my philosophy. That's why I'm still here. They couldn't get old Lester to move out. I'm old Lester."

"I'm Fox, sir," I said.

"And I'm Halo." She heard us over my radio.

He turned and looked at her.

"Halo," he said, quietly. "A Halo for an angel. Nice name, miss." I was wishing I could see his face. He sounded like an adult, but he was sure a small one. Both of us were taller than he was, and we're not much above average for our age.

He coughed. "I, ah, I'm sorry I disturbed you folks . . . ah." He seemed embarrassed. "I just couldn't help myself. I haven't seen any people for a long time—oh, ten years, I guess—and I just had to get a closer look. And I, uh, I needed to ask you something."

"And what's that, sir?"

"You can knock off the 'sir.' I ain't your pa. I wanted to know if you folks had any medicine?"

"There's a first-aid kit in the jumper," I said. "Is there someone in need of help? I'd be glad to take them to a hospital in King City."

He was waving his arms frantically.

"No, no, no. I don't want doctors poking around. I just need a little medicine. Uh, say, could you take that first-aid kit out of the jumper and come to my warren for a bit? Maybe you got something in there I could use."

We agreed, and followed him across the field.

He led us into an unpressurized building at the edge of the field. We threaded our way through dark corridors.

We came to a big cargo lock, stepped inside, and he cycled it. Then we went through the inner door and into his warren.

It was quite a place, more like a jungle than a home. It was as big as the Civic Auditorium at King City and overgrown with trees, vines, flowers, and bushes. It looked like it had been tended at one time, but allowed to go wild. There were a bed and a few chairs in one corner, and several tall stacks of books. And heaps of junk; barrels of leak sealant, empty O_2 cylinders, salvaged instruments, buggy tires.

Halo and I had our helmets off and were half out of our suits when we got our first look at him. He was incredible! I'm afraid I gasped, purely from reflex; Halo just stared. Then we politely tried to pretend there was nothing unusual.

He looked like he made a habit of going out without his suit. His face was grooved and pitted like a plowed field after an artillery barrage. His skin looked as tough as leather. His eyes were sunk into deep pits.

"Well, let me see it," he said, sticking out a thin hand. His knuckles were swollen and knobby.

I handed him the first-aid kit, and he fumbled with the catches, then got it open. He sat in a chair and carefully read the label on each item. He mumbled while he read.

Halo wandered among the plants, but I was more curious about old Lester than about his home. I watched him handle the contents of the kit with stiff, clumsy fingers. All his movements seemed stiff. I couldn't imagine what might be wrong with him and wondered why he hadn't sought medical help long ago, before whatever was afflicting him could go this far.

At last he put everything back in the kit but two tubes of cream. He sighed and looked at us.

"How old are you?" he asked, suspiciously.

"I'm twenty," I said. I don't know why. I'm not a liar, usually, unless I have a good reason. I was just beginning to get a funny feeling about old Lester, and I followed my instincts.

"Me, too," Halo volunteered.

He seemed satisfied, which surprised me. I was realizing he had been out of touch for a long time. Just how long I didn't know yet.

"There ain't much here that'll be of use to me, but I'd like to buy these here items, if you're willin' to sell. Says here they're for 'topical anesthesia,' and I could use some of that in the mornings. How much?"

I told him he could have them for nothing, but he insisted; so I told him to set his own price and reached for my credit meter in my suit pouch. He was holding out some rectangular slips of paper. They were units of paper currency, issued by the old Lunar Free State in the year 76 O.E. They had not been used in over a century. They were worth a fortune to a collector.

"Lester," I said, slowly, "these are worth more than you probably realize. I could sell them in King City for . . ."

He cackled. "Good man. I know what them bills is worth. I'm decrepit, but I ain't senile. They're worth thousands to one what wants 'em, but they're worthless to me. Except for one thing. They're a damn good test for findin' an honest man. They let me know if somebody'd take advantage of a sick, senile ol' hermit like me. Pardon me, son, but I had you pegged for a liar when you come in here. I was wrong. So you keep the bills. Otherwise, I'd a took 'em back."

He threw something on the floor in front of us, something he'd had in his hand and I hadn't even seen. It was a gun. I had never seen one.

Halo picked it up, gingerly, but I didn't want to touch it. This old Lester character seemed a lot less funny to me now. We were quiet.

"Now I've gone and scared you," he said. "I guess I've forgot all my manners. And I've forgot how you folks live on the other side." He picked up the gun and opened it. The charge chamber was empty. "But you wouldn't of knowed it, would you? Anyways, I'm not a killer. I just pick my friends real careful. Can I make up the fright I've caused you by inviting you to dinner? I haven't had any guests for ten years."

We told him we'd just eaten, and he asked if we could stay and just talk for a while. He seemed awfully eager. We said okay.

"You want some clothes? I don't expect you figured on visiting when you come here."

"Whatever your custom is," Halo said, diplomatically.

"I got no customs," he said, with a toothless grin. "If you don't feel funny naked, it ain't no business of mine. Do as you please, I say." It was a stock phrase with him.

So we lay on the grass, and he got some very strong, clear liquor and poured us all drinks.

"Moonshine," he laughed. "The genuine article. I make it myself. Best liquor on the Nearside."

We talked, and we drank.

Before I got too drunk to remember anything, a few interesting facts emerged about old Lester. For one thing, he really was old. He said he was two hundred and fifty-seven, and he was Earthborn. He had come to the moon when he was twenty-eight, several years before the Invasion.

I know several people in that age range, though none quite that old. Carnival's great-grandmother is two twenty-one, but she's moonborn, and doesn't remember the Invasion. There's virtually nothing left of the flesh she was born with. She's transferred her memories to a new brain twice.

I was prepared to believe that old Lester had gone a long time without medical care, but I couldn't accept what he told us at first. He said that, barring one new heart eighty years ago, he was unreconstructed since his birth! I'm young and naive—I freely admit it now—but I couldn't swallow that. But I believed it eventually, and I believe it now.

He had a million stories to tell, all of them at least eighty years old because that's how long he had been a hermit. He had stories of Earth, and of the early years on the moon. He told us about the hard years after the Invasion. Everyone who lived through that has a story to tell. I drew a blank before the evening was over, and the only thing I remember clearly is the three of us standing in a circle, arms around each other, singing a song old Lester had taught us. We swayed against each other and bumped foreheads and broke up laughing. I remember his hand resting on my shoulder. It was hard as rock.

The next day Halo became Florence Nightingale and nursed old Lester back to life. She was as firm as any nurse, getting him out of his clothes over his feeble protests, then giving him a massage. In the soberness of the morning I wondered how she could bring herself to touch his wrinkled old body, but as I watched, I slowly understood. He was beautiful.

The best thing to compare old Lester to is the surface. There is nothing older, or more abused, than the surface of the moon. But I have always loved it. It's the most beautiful place in the system, including Saturn's Rings. Old Lester was like that. I imagined he *was* the moon. He had become part of it.

Though I came to accept his age, I could still see that he was in terrible shape. The drinking had taken a lot out of him, but he wouldn't be kept down. The first thing he wanted in the morning was another drink. I brought him one, then I cooked a big breakfast: eggs and sausage and bread and orange juice, all from his garden. Then we were off and drinking again.

I didn't even have time to worry about what Carnival and Halo's mother might be thinking by now. Old Lester had plainly adopted us. He said he'd be our father, which struck me as a funny thing to say since who the hell ever knows who their father is? But he began behaving in the manner I would call maternal, and he evidently thought of it as *pa*ternal.

We did a lot of things that day. He taught us about gardening.

He showed me how to cross-fertilize the egg plants and how to tell when they were ripe without breaking the shells to see. He told us the secrets of how to grow breadfruit trees so they'd yield loaves of dark-brown, hard, whole wheat or the strangely different rye variety by grafting branches. I had never had rye before. And we learned to dig for potatoes and steakroots. We learned how to harvest honey and cheese and tomatoes. We stripped bacon from the surface of the porktree trunks.

And we'd drink his moonshine while we worked, and laugh a lot, and he'd throw in more of his stories between the garden lore.

Old Lester was not the fool he seemed at first. His speech pattern was largely affected, something he did to amuse himself over the years. He could speak as correctly as anyone when he wanted to. He had read much and remembered it all. He was a first-rate engineer and botanist, but his education and skills had to be qualified by this fact: everything he knew was eighty years out of date. It didn't matter much: the old methods worked well enough.

In social matters it was a different story.

He didn't know much about Changing, except that he didn't like it. It was Changing that finally decided him to separate himself from society. He said he had been having his doubts about joining the migration to Farside, and the sex-change issue had been the final factor. He shocked us more than he knew when he revealed that he had never been a woman. I thought his lack of curiosity must be monumental, but I was wrong. It turned out that he had some queer notions about the morality of the whole process, ideas he had gotten from some weirdly aberrant religion in his childhood. I had heard of the cult, as you can hardly avoid it if you know any history. It had said little about ethics, being more interested in arbitrary regulations.

Old Lester still believed in it, though. His home was littered with primitive icons. There was a central symbol he cherished above the others: a simple wooden fetish in the shape of a plus sign with a long stem. He wore one around his neck, and others sprouted like weeds.

I came to realize that this religion was at the bottom of the puzzling inconsistencies I began to notice about him. His "do as you please" may have been sincere, but he did not entirely live by it. It became clear that, though he thought people should have freedom of choice, he condemned them if the choice they made was not his own.

My spur-of-the-moment decision to lie about my age had been borne out, though I'm not sure the truth wouldn't have been better. It might have kept us out of the further lies we told or implied, and I always prefer honesty to deception. But I still don't know if old Lester could have been our friend without the lies.

He knew something of life on Farside and made it clear he disapproved of most of it. And he had deluded himself (with our help) that we weren't like that. In particular, he thought people should not have sex until they reached a "decent age." He never defined that, but Halo and I, at "twenty," were safely past it.

It was a puzzling notion. Even Carnival, who is a bit old-fashioned, would have been shocked. Granted, we speed up puberty now—I have been sexually potent since I was seven—but he felt that even *after* puberty people should abstain. I couldn't make any sense out of it. I mean, what would you *do*?

Then there was a word he used, "incest," that I had to look up when I got home to be sure I'd understood him. I had. He was against it. I guess it had a basis back in the dawn of time, when procreation and genetics were so tied up with sex, but how could it matter now? The only place Carnival and I get along at all is in bed; without that, we would have very little in common.

It went on and on, the list of regulations. Luckily, it didn't sour me on old Lester. All I disliked was the lies we had trapped ourselves into. I'm willing to let people have all sorts of screwball notions as long as they don't force them on me, like Carnival was doing about the Change. That I found myself expressing agreement with old Lester's ideas was my own fault, not his. I think.

The days went by, marred by only one thing. I had not broken any laws, but I knew I was being searched for. And I knew I was treating Carnival badly. I tried to figure out just how badly, and what I should do about it, but kept getting fogged up by the moonshine and good times.

Carnival had come to the Nearside. Halo and I had watched them from the shadows when old Lester's radar had picked them up coming in. There had been six or seven figures in the distance. They had entered the jumper and made a search. They had cast around at the edge of the field for our tracks, found them, and followed them to where they disappeared on concrete. I would have liked to have listened in, but didn't dare because they were sure to have detection apparatus for that.

And they left. They left the jumper, which was nice of them, since they could have taken it and rendered us helpless to wait for their return.

I thought about it, and talked it over with Halo. Several times we were ready to give up and go back. After all, we hadn't really set out to run away from home. We had only been defying authority, and it had never entered my head that we would stay as long as we had. But now that we were here we found it hard to go back. The trip to Nearside had acquired an inertia of its own, and we didn't have the strength to stop it.

In the end we went to the other extreme. We decided to stay on Nearside forever. I think we were giddy with the sense of power a decision like that made us feel. So we covered up our doubts with backslapping encouragement, a lot of giggling, and inflated notions of what we and old Lester would do at Archimedes.

We wrote a note—which proved we still felt responsible to *someone*—and taped it to the ladder of the jumper; then Halo went in and turned on the outside lights and pointed them straight up. We retired to a hiding place and waited.

Sure enough, another ship returned in two hours. They had been watching from close orbit and landed on the next pass when they noticed the change. One person got out of the ship and read the note. It was a crazy note, saying not to worry, we were all right. It went on to say we intended to stay, and some more things I'd rather not remember. It also said she should take the jumper. I was regretting that even as she read it. We must have been crazy.

I could see her slump even from so far away. She looked all around her, then began signaling in semaphore language.

"Do what you have to," she signaled. "I don't understand you, but I love you. I'm leaving the jumper in case you change your mind."

Well. I gulped, and was halfway up on my way out to her when, to my great surprise, Halo pulled me down. I had thought she was only going along with me to avoid having to point out how wrong I was. This hadn't been her idea; she had not been in her right mind when I hustled her over here. But she had settled down from all that lunes ago and was now as level-headed as ever. And was more taken with our adventure than I was.

"Dope!" she hissed, touching helmets. "I thought you'd do something like that. Think it through. Do you want to give up so easy? We haven't even tried this yet."

Her face wasn't as certain as her words, but I was in no shape to argue her out of it. Then Carnival was gone, and I felt better. It was true that we had an out if it turned sour. Pretty soon we were intrepid pioneers, and I didn't think of Carnival or the Farside until things *did* start to go sour.

For a long time, almost a lunation, we were happy. We worked hard every day with old Lester. I learned that in his kind of life the work was never done; there was always an air duct to repair, flowers to pollinate, machinery to regulate. It was primitive, and I could usually see ways to improve the methods but never thought of suggesting them. It wouldn't have fit with our crazy pioneer ideas. Things *had* to be hard to feel right.

We built a grass lean-to like one we had seen in a movie and moved in. It was across the chamber from old Lester, which was silly, but it meant we could visit each other. And I learned an interesting thing about sin.

Old Lester would watch us make love in our raggedy shack, a grin across his leathery face. Then one day he implied that lovemaking should be a private act. It was a sin to do it in front of others, and a sin to watch. But he still watched.

So I asked Halo about it.

"He needs a little sin, Fox."

"Huh?"

"I know it isn't logical, but you must have seen by now that his religion is mixed up."

"That's for sure. But I still don't get it."

"Well, I don't either, but I try to respect. He thinks drinking is sinful, and until we came along it was the only sin he could practice. Now he can do the sin of lust, too. I think he needs to be forgiven for things, and he can't be forgiven until he does them."

"That's the craziest thing I ever heard. But even crazier, if lust is a sin to him, why doesn't he go all the way and make love with you? I've been dead sure he wants to, but as far as I know, he's never done it. Has he?"

She looked at me pityingly. "You don't know, do you?"

"You mean he has?"

"No. I don't mean that. We haven't. And not because I haven't tried. And not because he doesn't want to. He looks, looks, looks; he never takes his eyes off me. And it isn't because he thinks it's a sin. He *knows* it's a sin, but he'd do it if he could."

"I still don't understand, then."

"What do you mean? I just told you. He *can't*. He's too old. His equipment won't function anymore."

"That's *terrible!*" I was almost sick. I knew there was a word for his condition, but I had to look it up a long time afterward. The word is crippled. It means some part of your body doesn't work right. Old Lester had been sexually crippled for over a century.

I seriously considered going home then. I was not at all sure he was the kind of person I wanted to be around. The lies were getting more galling every day, and now this.

But things got much worse, and still I stayed.

He was ill. I don't mean the way we think of ill; some petty malfunction to be cleared up by a ten-minute visit to the bioengineers. He was wearing out.

It was partly our fault. Even that first morning he was not very quick out of bed. Each lune—after a long night of drinking and general hell-raising—he was a little slower to get up. It got to where Halo was spending an hour each morning just massaging him into shape to stand erect. I thought at first he was just cannily malingering because he liked the massage and Halo's intimacy when she worked him over. That was not the case. When he did get up, he hobbled, bent over from pains in his belly. He would forget things. He would stumble, fall, and get up very slowly.

"I'm dying," he said one night. I gasped; Halo blinked rapidly. I tried to cover my embarrassment by pretending he hadn't said it.

"I know it's a bad word now, and I'm sorry if I offended you. But I ain't lived this long without being able to look it in the eye. I'm dying, all right, and I'll be dead pretty soon. I didn't think it'd come so sudden. Everything seems to be quittin' on me."

We tried to convince him that he was wrong and, when that didn't work, to convince him that he should take a short hop to Farside and get straightened out. But we couldn't get through his superstition. He was awfully afraid of the engineers on Farside. We would try to show him that periodic repairs still left the mind—he called it the "soul"—unchanged, but he'd get philosophical.

The next day he didn't get up at all. Halo rubbed his old limbs until she was stiff. It was no good. His breathing became irregular, and his pulse was hard to find.

So we were faced with the toughest decision ever. Should we allow him to die, or carry him to the jumper and rush him to a repair shop? We sweated over it all lune. Neither course felt right, but I found myself arguing to take him back, and Halo said we shouldn't. He could not hear us except for brief periods when he'd rouse himself and try to sit up. Then he'd ask us questions or say things that seemed totally random. His brain must have been pretty well scrambled by then.

"You kids aren't really twenty, are you?" he said once.

"How did you know?"

He cackled, weakly.

"Old Lester ain't no dummy. You said that to cover up what I caught you doin' so's I wouldn't tell your folks. But I won't tell. That's your business. Just wanted you to know you didn't fool me, not for a minute." He lapsed into labored breathing.

We never did settle the argument, unless by default. What I wanted to do took some action, and in the end I didn't have it in me to get up and do it. I wasn't sure enough of myself. So we sat there on his bed, waiting for him to die and talking to him when he needed it. Halo held his hand.

I went through hell. I cursed him for a vacuum-skulled, mentally defective, prehistoric poop, and almost decided to help him out in his pea-brained search for death. Then I went the other way; loving him almost like he loved his crazy God. I imagined he was the mother that Carnival had never really been to me and that my world would have no purpose when he was dead. Both those reactions were crazy, of course; old Lester was just a person. He was a little crazy and a little saintly, and hardly a person you should either love or hate. It was Death that had me going in circles: the creepy black-robed skeletal figure old Lester had told us about, straight out of his superstition.

He opened one bleary eye after hours of no movement.

"Don't ever," he said. "You shouldn't ever. You, I mean. Halo. Don't ever get a Change. You always been a girl, you always should be. The Lord intended it that way."

Halo shot a quick glance at me. She was crying, and her eyes told me: *Don't breathe a word. Let him believe it.* She needn't have worried.

Then he started coughing. Blood came from his lips, and as soon as I saw it, I passed out. I thought he would literally fall apart and rot into some awful green slime, slime that I could never wash off.

Halo wouldn't let me stay out. She slapped me until my ears were ringing, and when I was awake, we gave up. We couldn't make a meaningful decision in the face of *this*. We had to give it to someone else.

So twenty-five minutes later I was over the pole, just coming into range of the CC's outer transmitters.

"Well, the black sheep return," the CC began in a superior tone. "I must say you outlasted the usual Nearside stay, in fact . . ."

"Shut *up!*" I bawled. "You shut up and listen to me. I want to contact Carnival, and I want her *now,* crash priority, emergency status. Get on it!"

The CC was all business, dropping the *in loco parentis* program and operating with the astonishing speed it's capable of in an emergency. Carnival was on the line in three seconds.

"Fox," she said, "I don't want to start this off on a bad footing; so, first of all, I thank you for giving me a chance to settle this with you face-to-face. I've retained a family arbiter, and I'd like for us to present our separate cases to him on this Change you want, and I'll agree to abide by his decision. Is that fair for a beginning?" She sounded anxious. I knew there was anger beneath it—there always is—but she was sincere.

"We can talk about that later, Mom," I sobbed. "Right now you've got to get to the field, as quick as you can."

"Fox, is Halo with you? Is she all right?"

"She's all right."

"I'll be there in five minutes."

It was too late, of course. Old Lester had died shortly after I lifted off, and Halo had been there with a dead body for almost two hours.

She was calm about it. She held Carnival and me together while she explained what had to be done, and even got us to help her. We buried him, as he had wanted, on the surface, in a spot that would always be in the light of Old Earth.

Carnival never would tell me what she would have done if he had been alive when we got there. It was an ethical question, and both of us are usually very opinionated on ethical matters. But I suspect we agreed for once. The will of the individual must be respected, and if I face it again, I'll know what to do. I think.

I got my Change without family arbitration. Credit me with a little sense; if our case had ever come up before a family arbiter, I'm sure he would have recommended divorce. And that would have been tough, because difficult as Carnival is, I love her, and I need her for at least a few more years. I'm not as grownup as I thought I was.

It didn't really surprise me that Carnival was right about the Change, either. In another lunation I was male again, then female, male; back and forth for a year. There's no sense in that. I'm female now, and I think I'll stick with it for a few years and see what it's about. I was born female, you know, but only lasted two hours in that sex because Carnival wanted a boy.

And Halo's a male, which makes it perfect. We've found that we do better as opposites than we did as boyfriends. I'm thinking about having my child in a few years, with Halo as the father. Carnival says wait, but I think I'm right this time.

I still believe most of our troubles come from her inability to remember the swiftly moving present a child lives in. Then Halo can have her child—I'd be flattered if she chose me to father it—and . . .

We're moving to Nearside. Halo and me, that is, and Carnival and Chord are thinking about it, and they'll go, I think. If only to shut up Adagio.

Why are we going? I've thought about it a long time. Not because of old Lester. I hate to speak unkindly of him, but he was inarguably a fool. A fool with dignity, and the strength of his convictions; a likable old fool, but a fool all the same. It would be silly to talk of "carrying on his dream" or some of the things I think Halo has in mind.

But, coincidentally, his dream and mine are pretty close, though for different reasons. He couldn't bear to see the Nearside abandoned out of fear, and he feared the new human society. So he became a hermit. I want to go there simply because the fear is gone for my generation, and it's a lot of beautiful real estate. And we won't be alone. We'll be the vanguard, but the days of clustering in the Farside warrens and ignoring Old Earth are over. The human race came from Earth, and it was ours until it was taken from us. To tell the truth, I've been wondering if the aliens are really as invincible as the old stories say.

It sure is a pretty planet. I wonder if we could go back?

INTRODUCTION TO

"Overdrawn at the Memory Bank"

First stories by writers you admire can be an embarrassment. Isaac Asimov's first was not very good. Theodore Sturgeon's was okay, and hinted of greatness to come. But often the best thing you can say about them is that they show promise. Rarely does someone come along like Robert Heinlein, whose first story, "Lifeline," seems the work of a fully formed professional. I am not ashamed of the story you just read, but when I look at it now I see hundreds of things I wish I could do over. I think it is significant that no one has ever wanted to reprint it in an anthology.

I already mentioned that my first attempt at a novel, Gas Giant, was a disaster. That's okay; I just read Heinlein's unpublished first novel, soon to be in print, and it was even worse than mine. My chief regret is that Gas Giant was the basis for many of my stories to come. It told the tale of how alien beings from a giant planet like Jupiter invaded our solar system. Their purposes were mostly incomprehensible to us, but the one thing we did get was that these invaders viewed aquatic mammals like dolphins and whales as the only intelligent species on the third planet. Humans were despoiling their environment, thus it became necessary to evict and/or exterminate us. They killed billions, but couldn't be bothered to completely wipe us out, so humanity survived and eventually thrived on the junk planets like Mercury, Venus, Luna, and Mars.

At the outset I had very little idea that Gas Giant would become the basis for the stories I would eventually call "The Eight Worlds."

I had always been a compulsive reader, and I read mostly science fiction. I still am a compulsive reader, but during my hippie years I was not. I'm not sure why. Part of it was that I was sometimes too high to deal with words on paper, but I was not a steady or heavy drug user. We didn't watch TV, either. Didn't even own one for many years. I completely missed Star Trek, and have never regretted it. I read some of the standard texts by the gurus of the sixties, found them to be mostly dreck. My main artistic pursuit at the time was making films on an old Bolex 8 mm camera. The rest of my time was divided between scrambling for a living, dodging the draft, attending the occasional protest march in Berkeley (and always leaving when the tear gas started to fly), and just having fun. Being a hippie, somehow, was a full-time job.

Then one day while I was casting around for a means of livelihood that didn't involve holding my hand out to strangers, I found a secondhand copy of a book called Ringworld, *by Larry Niven. It blew me away. There had been some exciting changes in science fiction since I graduated high school in the Nederland, Texas, Class of '65.*

I had been aware of the New Wave in SF, enough to know that some of it was a pretentious waste of paper and some of it was very, very good. But I didn't think I could write that way. I found other books by Larry, and saw that he was following in a tradition I had first encountered in junior high: the "Future History" stories of Heinlein. Niven called his future history "Known Space," and it was populated with strange and inventive aliens, a history reaching back billions of years, and marvelous technological advances. It seemed wonderfully rigorous, and the stories were fun.

That led me to other writers working in the same area. I realized that, since the days of the "Golden Age" writers of the forties and fifties, there had been a blizzard of astronomical discoveries, from neutron stars to quasars to colliding galaxies way, way out there, to fundamental reversals of most of our best guesses right in our own neighborhood. Mercury didn't always keep one face turned to the sun. Venus was not a swamp planet. Mars had no canals. Jupiter had rings. There were so many exciting possibilities, and Larry Niven was taking advantage of them all to tell good old-fashioned thought-provoking tech stories.

I can't say that I immediately got to work mapping out a history and milieu for the Eight Worlds as I was reading the Niven stories. I had to get Gas Giant *out of my system first . . . so to speak. But when that was done, I began to think about what life might be like for the survivors of the alien invasion. What kind of stories could I write about them? What would life be like for them?*

First, I decided to begin about two hundred years after the invasion. The invasion itself I had set in the far, distant future. Say . . . oh, around 2005. The moon, Luna, was the center of civilization, so many stories would be set there. But I decided to write one story on each of the different planets that made up the Eight Worlds. (I haven't done that yet, haven't had the time. To make a living one must write novels.) Thus, my Mercury story became "Retrograde Summer," referring to the fact that on Mercury, the sun will sometimes set and then rise again, before finally setting for the "day," which is very long. My Venus story was "In the Bowl," inspired by the fact that the thickness of the atmosphere would distort light like a lens, making it appear that you were standing in a crater wherever you went.

All that was easy. Much harder was to decide what the people would be like. What new technologies would they have? How would these new things affect human behavior? What would it be like to know that we were not the smartest or most powerful species in the galaxy, that we weren't even a good second place?

It was from such premises that "Picnic on Nearside" grew. Other stories followed, including this one, which I now see as a sort of early take on virtual reality. It was filmed, starring Raul Julia, and shown on PBS. I don't think it was entirely successful, but I enjoyed it as it was the first of my works to be dramatized.

OVERDRAWN AT THE MEMORY BANK

I T WAS SCHOOLDAY at the Kenya disneyland. Five nine-year-olds were being shown around the medico section where Fingal lay on the recording table, the top of his skull removed, looking up into a mirror. Fingal was in a bad mood (hence the trip to the disneyland) and could have done without the children. Their teacher was doing his best, but who can control five nine-year-olds?

"What's the big green wire do, teacher?" asked a little girl, reaching out one grubby hand and touching Fingal's brain where the main recording wire clamped to the built-in terminal.

"Lupus, I told you you weren't to touch anything. And look at you, you didn't wash your hands." The teacher took the child's hand and pulled it away.

"But what does it matter? You told us yesterday that the reason no one cares about dirt like they used to is dirt isn't dirty anymore."

"I'm sure I didn't tell you exactly *that*. What I said was that when humans were forced off Earth, we took the golden opportunity to wipe out all harmful germs. When there were only three thousand people alive on the moon after the Occupation it was easy for us to sterilize everything. So the medico doesn't need to wear gloves like surgeons used to, or even wash her hands. There's no danger of infection. But it isn't polite. We don't want this man to think we're being impolite to him, just because his nervous system is disconnected and he can't do anything about it, do we?"

"No, teacher."

"What's a surgeon?"

"What's 'infection'?"

Fingal wished the little perishers had chosen another day for their lessons, but as the teacher had said, there was very little he could do. The medico had turned his motor control over to the computer while she took the reading. He was paralyzed. He eyed the little boy carrying the carved stick, and hoped he didn't get a notion to poke him in the cerebrum with it. Fingal was insured, but who needs the trouble?

"All of you stand back a little so the medico can do her work. That's better. Now, who can tell me what the big green wire is? Destry?"

Destry allowed as how he didn't know, didn't care, and wished he could get out of here and play spat ball. The teacher dismissed him and went on with the others.

"The green wire is the main sounding electrode," the teacher said. "It's attached to a series of very fine wires in the man's head, like the ones you have, which are implanted at birth. Can anyone tell me how the recording is made?"

The little girl with the dirty hands spoke up.

"By tying knots in string."

The teacher laughed, but the medico didn't. She had heard it all before. So had the teacher, of course, but that was why he was a teacher. He had the patience to deal with children, a rare quality now that there were so few of them.

"No, that was just an analogy. Can you all say analogy?"

"*Analogy,*" they chorused.

"Fine. What I told you is that the chains of FPNA are very much *like* strings with knots tied in them. If you make up a code with every millimeter and every knot having a meaning, you could write words in string by tying knots in it. That's what the machine does with the FPNA. Now . . . can anyone tell me what FPNA stands for?"

"Ferro-Photo-Nucleic Acid," said the girl, who seemed to be the star pupil.

"That's right, Lupus. It's a variant on DNA, and it can be knotted by magnetic fields and light, and made to go through chemical changes. What the medico is doing now is threading long strings of FPNA into the tiny tubes that are in the man's brain. When she's done, she'll switch on the machine and the current will start tying knots. And what happens then?"

"All his memories go into the memory cube," said Lupus.

"That's right. But it's a little more complicated than that. You remember what I told you about a divided cipher? The kind that has two parts, neither of which is any good without the other? Imagine two of the strings, each with a lot of knots in it. Well, you try to read one of them with your decoder, and you find out that it doesn't make sense. That's because whoever wrote it used two strings, with knots tied in different places. They only make sense when you put them side by side and read them that way. That's how this decoder works, but the medico uses twenty-five strings. When they're all knotted the right way and put into the right openings in that cube over there," he pointed to the pink cube on the medico's bench, "they'll contain all this man's memories and personality. In a way, he'll be in the cube, but he won't know it, because he's going to be an African lion today."

This excited the children, who would much rather be stalking the Kenya savanna than listening to how a multi-holo was taken. When they quieted down the teacher went on, using analogies that got more strained by the minute.

"When the strings are in . . . class, pay attention. When they're in the cube, a current sets them in place. What we have then is a multi-holo. Can anyone tell me why we can't just take a tape recording of what's going on in this man's brain, and use that?"

One of the boys answered, for once.

"Because memory isn't . . . what's that word?"

"Sequential?"

"Yeah, that's it. His memories are stashed all over his brain and there's no way to sort them out. So this recorder takes a picture of the whole thing at once, like a hologram. Does that mean you can cut the cube in half and have two people?"

"No, but that's a good question. This isn't that sort of hologram. This is something like . . . like when you press your hand into clay, but in four dimensions. If you chip off a part of the clay after it's dried, you lose part of the information, right? Well, this is sort of like that. You can't see the imprint because it's too small, but everything the man ever did and saw and heard and thought will be in the cube."

"Would you move back a little?" asked the medico. The children in the mirror over Fingal's head shuffled back and became more than just heads with shoulders sticking out. The medico adjusted the last strand of FPNA suspended in Fingal's cortex to the close tolerances specified by the computer.

"I'd like to be a medico when I grow up," said one boy.

"I thought you wanted to go to college and study to be a scientist."

"Well, maybe. But my friend is teaching me to be a medico. It looks a lot easier."

"You should stay in school, Destry. I'm sure your parent will want you to make something of yourself." The medico fumed silently. She knew better than to speak up—education was a serious business and interference with the duties of a teacher carried a stiff fine. But she was obviously pleased when the class thanked her and went out the door, leaving dirty footprints behind them.

She viciously flipped a switch, and Fingal found he could breathe and move the muscles in his head.

"Lousy conceited college graduate," she said. "What the hell's wrong with getting your hands dirty, I ask you?" She wiped the blood from her hands onto her blue smock.

"Teachers are the worst," Fingal said.

"Ain't it the truth? Well, being a medico is nothing to be ashamed of. So I didn't go to college, so what? I can do my job, and I can see what I've done when I'm through. I always did like working with my hands. Did you know that being a medico used to be one of the most respected professions there was?"

"Really?"

"Fact. They had to go to college for years and years, and they made a hell of a lot of money, let me tell you."

Fingal said nothing, thinking she must be exaggerating. What was so tough about medicine? Just a little mechanical sense and a steady hand, that was all you needed. Fingal did a lot of maintenance on his body himself, going to the shop only for major work. And a good thing, at the prices they charged. It was not the sort of thing one discussed while lying helpless on the table, however.

"Okay, that's done." She pulled out the modules that contained the invisible FPNA and set them in the developing solution. She fastened Fingal's skull back on and tightened the recessed screws set into the bone. She turned his motor control back over to him while she sealed his scalp back into place. He stretched and yawned. He always grew sleepy in the medico's shop; he didn't know why.

"Will that be all for today, sir? We've got a special on blood changes, and since you'll just be lying there while you're out doppling in the park, you might as well—"

"No, thanks. I had it changed a year ago. Didn't you read my history?"

She picked up the card and glanced at it. "So you did. Fine. You can get up now, Mr. Fingal." She made a note on the card and set it down on the table. The door opened and a small face peered in.

"I left my stick," said the boy. He came in and started looking under things, to the annoyance of the medico. She attempted to ignore the boy as she took down the rest of the information she needed.

"And are you going to experience this holiday now, or wait until your double has finished and play it back then?"

"Huh? Oh, you mean . . . yes, I see. No, I'll go right into the animal. My psychist advised me to come out here for my nerves, so it wouldn't do me much good to wait it out, would it?"

"No, I suppose it wouldn't. So you'll be sleeping here while you dopple in the park. Hey!" She turned to confront the little boy, who was poking his nose into things he should stay away from. She grabbed him and pulled him away.

"You either find what you're looking for in one minute or you get out of here, you see?" He went back to his search, giggling behind his hand and looking for more interesting things to fool around with.

The medico made a check on the card, glanced at the glowing numbers on her thumbnail and discovered her shift was almost over. She connected the memory cube through a machine to a terminal in the back of Fingal's head.

"You've never done this before, right? We do this to avoid blank spots, which can be confusing sometimes. The cube is almost set, but now I'll add the last ten minutes to the record at the same time I put you to sleep. That way you'll experience no disorientation, you'll move through a dream state to full awareness of being in the body of a lion. Your body will be removed and taken to one of our slumber rooms while you're gone. There's nothing to worry about."

Fingal wasn't worried, just tired and tense. He wished she would go on and do it and stop talking about it. And he wished the little boy would stop pounding his stick against the table leg. He wondered if his headache would be transferred to the lion.

She turned him off.

They hauled his body away and took his memory cube to the installation room. The medico chased the boy into the corridor and hosed down the recording room. Then she was off to a date she was already late for.

The employees of Kenya disneyland installed the cube into a metal box set into the skull of a full-grown African lioness. The social structure of lions being what it was, the proprietors charged a premium for the use of a male body, but Fingal didn't care one way or the other.

A short ride in an underground railroad with the sedated body of the Fingal-lioness, and he was deposited beneath the blazing sun of the Kenya savanna. He awoke, sniffed the air, and felt better immediately.

The Kenya disneyland was a total environment buried twenty kilometers beneath Mare Moscoviense on the far side of Luna. It was roughly circular, with a radius of two hundred kilometers. From the ground to the "sky" was two kilometers except over the full-sized replica of Kilimanjaro, where it bulged to allow clouds to form in a realistic manner over the snowcap.

The illusion was flawless. The curve of the ground was consistent with the curvature of the Earth, so that the horizon was much more distant than anything Fingal was used to. The trees were real, and so were all the animals. At night an astronomer would have needed a spectroscope to distinguish the stars from the real thing.

Fingal certainly couldn't spot anything wrong. Not that he wanted to. The colors were strange but that was from the limitations of feline optics. Sounds were much more vivid, as were smells. If he'd thought about it, he would have realized the gravity was much too weak for Kenya. But he wasn't thinking; he'd come here to avoid that.

It was hot and glorious. The dry grass made no sound as he walked over it on broad pads. He smelled antelope, wildebeest, and . . . was that baboon? He felt pangs of hunger but he really didn't want to hunt. But he found the lioness body starting on a stalk anyway.

Fingal was in an odd position. He was in control of the lioness, but only more or less. He could guide her where he wanted to go, but he had no say at all over in-stinctive behaviors. He was as much a pawn to these as the lioness was. In one sense, he *was* the lioness; when he wished to raise a paw or turn around, he simply did it. The motor control was complete. It felt great to walk on all fours, and it came as easily as breathing. But the scent of the antelope went on a direct route from the nostrils to the lower brain, made a connection with the rumblings of hunger, and started him on the stalk.

The guidebook said to surrender to it. Fighting it wouldn't do anyone any good, and could frustrate you. If you were paying to be a lion, read the chapter on "Things to Do," you might as well *be* one, not just wear the body and see the sights.

Fingal wasn't sure he liked this as he came downwind of the antelope and crouched behind a withered clump of scrub. He pondered it while he sized up the dozen or so animals grazing just a few meters from him, picking out the small, the weak, and the young with a predator's eye. Maybe he should back out now and go on his way. These beautiful creatures were not harming him. The Fingal part of him wished mostly to admire them, not eat them.

Before he quite knew what had happened, he was standing triumphant over the bloody body of a small antelope. The others were just dusty trails in the dis-tance.

It had been incredible!

The lioness was fast, but might as well have been moving in slow motion com-pared to the antelope. Her only advantage lay in surprise, confusion, and quick, all-out attack. There had been the lifting of a head; ears had flicked toward the bush he was hiding in, and he had exploded. Ten seconds of furious exertion and he bit down on a soft throat, felt the blood gush and the dying kicks of the hind legs under his paws. He was breathing hard and the blood coursed through his veins. There was only one way to release the tension.

He threw his head back and roared his bloodlust.

He'd had it with lions at the end of the weekend. It wasn't worth it for the few minutes of exhilaration at the kill. It was a life of endless stalking, countless fail-ures, then a pitiful struggle to get a few bites for yourself from the kill you had made. He found to his chagrin that his lioness was very low in the dominance or-der. When he got his kill back to the pride—he didn't know why he had dragged it back but the lioness seemed to know—it was promptly stolen from him. He/she sat back helplessly and watched the dominant male take his share, followed by the rest of the pride. He was left with a dried haunch four hours later, and had to con-test even that with vultures and hyenas. He saw what the premium payment was for. That male had it *easy*.

But he had to admit that it had been worth it. He felt better; his psychist had been right. It did one good to leave the insatiable computers at his office for a weekend of simple living. There were no complicated choices to be made out here. If he was in doubt, he listened to his instincts. It was just that the next time, he'd go as an elephant. He'd been watching them. All the other animals pretty much left them alone, and he could see why. To be a solitary bull, free to wander where he wished with food as close as the nearest tree branch . . .

He was still thinking about it when the collection crew came for him.

He awoke with the vague feeling that something was wrong. He sat up in bed and looked around him. Nothing seemed to be out of place. There was no one in the room with him. He shook his head to clear it.

It didn't do any good. There was still something wrong. He tried to remember how he had gotten there, and laughed at himself. His own bedroom! What was so remarkable about that?

But hadn't there been a vacation, a weekend trip? He remembered being a lion, eating raw antelope meat, being pushed around within the pride, fighting it out with the other females and losing and retiring to rumble to him/herself.

Certainly he should have come back to human consciousness in the disney-land medical section. He couldn't remember it. He reached for his phone, not knowing who he wished to call. His psychist, perhaps, or the Kenya office.

"I'm sorry, Mr. Fingal," the phone told him. "This line is no longer available for outgoing calls. If you'll—"

"Why not?" he asked, irritated and confused. "I paid my bill."

"That is of no concern to this department, Mr. Fingal. And please do not interrupt. It's hard enough to reach you. I'm fading, but the message will be continued if you look to your right." The voice and the power hum behind it faded. The phone was dead.

Fingal looked to his right and jerked in surprise. There was a hand, a woman's hand, writing on his wall. The hand faded out at the wrist.

"*Mene, Mene* . . ." it wrote, in thin letters of fire. Then the hand waved in irritation and erased that with its thumb. The wall was smudged with soot where the words had been.

"You're projecting, Mr. Fingal," the hand wrote, quickly etching out the words with a manicured nail. "That's what you expected to see." The hand underlined the word "expected" three times. "Please cooperate, clear your mind, and see what is *there,* or we're not going to get anywhere. Damn, I've about exhausted this medium."

And indeed it had. The writing had filled the wall and the hand was now down near the floor. The apparition wrote smaller and smaller in an effort to get it all in.

Fingal had an excellent grasp on reality, according to his psychist. He held tightly onto that evaluation like a talisman as he leaned closer to the wall to read the last sentence.

"Look on your bookshelf," the hand wrote. "The title is *Orientation in your Fantasy World*."

Fingal knew he had no such book, but could think of nothing better to do.

His phone didn't work, and if he was going through a psychotic episode he didn't think it wise to enter the public corridor until he had some idea of what was going on. The hand faded out, but the writing continued to smolder.

He found the book easily enough. It was a pamphlet, actually, with a gaudy cover. It was the sort of thing he had seen in the outer offices of the Kenya disneyland, a promotional booklet. At the bottom it said, "Published under the auspices of the Kenya computer; A. Joachim, operator." He opened it and began to read.

CHAPTER ONE

"Where Am I?"

YOU'RE probably wondering by now where you are. This is an entirely healthy and normal reaction, Mr. Fingal. Anyone would wonder, when beset by what seem to be paranormal manifestations, if his grasp on reality had weakened. Or, in simple language, "Am I nuts, or what?"

No, Mr. Fingal, you are not nuts. But you are not, as you probably think, sitting on your bed, reading a book. It's all in your mind. You are still in the Kenya disneyland. More specifically, you are contained in the memory cube we took of you before your weekend on the savanna. You see, there's been a big goof-up.

CHAPTER TWO

"What Happened?"

WE'D like to know that, too, Mr. Fingal. But here's what we do know. Your body has been misplaced. Now, there's nothing to worry about, we're doing all we can to locate it and find out how it happened, but it will take some time. Maybe it's small consolation, but this has never happened before in the seventy-five years we've been operating, and as soon as we find out how it happened this time, you can be sure we'll be careful not to let it happen again. We're pursuing several leads at this time, and you can rest easy that your body will be returned to you intact just as soon as we locate it.

You are awake and aware right now because we have incorporated your memory cube into the workings of our H-210 computer, one of the finest holomemory systems available to modern business. You see, there are a few problems.

CHAPTER THREE

"What Problems?"

IT'S kind of hard to put in terms you'd understand, but let's take a crack at it, shall we?

The medium we use to record your memories isn't the one you've probably used yourself as insurance against accidental death. As you must know, that system will store your memories for up to twenty years with no degradation or loss of information, and is quite expensive. The system we use is a temporary one, good for two, five, fourteen, or twenty-eight days, depending on the length of your stay. Your memories are put in the cube, where you might expect them to remain static and unchanging, as they do in your insurance recording. If you thought that, you would be wrong, Mr. Fingal. Think about it. If you die, your bank will immediately start a clone from the plasm you stored along with the memory cube. In six months, your memories would be played back into the clone and you would awaken, missing the memories that were accumulated in your body from the time of your last recording. Perhaps this has happened to you. If it has, you know the shock of awakening from the recording process to be told that it is three or four years later, and that you had died in that time.

In any case, the process we use is an *ongoing* one, or it would be worthless to you. The cube we install in the African animal of your choice is capable of adding the memories of your stay in Kenya to the memory cube. When your visit is over, these memories are played back into your brain and you leave the disneyland with the exciting, educational, and refreshing experiences you had as an animal, though your body never left our slumber room. This is known as "doppling," from the German *doppelganger*.

Now, to the problems we talked about. Thought we'd *never* get around to them, didn't you?

First, since you registered for a weekend stay, the medico naturally used one of the two-day cubes as part of our budget-excursion fare. These cubes have a safety factor, but aren't much good beyond three days at best. At the end of that time the cube would start to deteriorate. Of course, we fully expect to have you installed in your own body before then. Additionally, there is the problem of storage. Since these ongoing memory cubes are intended to be in use all the time your memories are stored in them, it presents certain problems when we find ourselves in the spot we are now in. Are you following me, Mr. Fingal? While the cube has already passed its potency for use in coexisting with a live host, like the lioness you just left, it *must* be kept in constant activation at all times or loss of information results. I'm sure you wouldn't want that to happen, would you? Of course not. So what we have done is to "plug you in" to our computer, which will keep you aware and healthy and guard against the randomizing of your memory nexi. I won't go into that; let it stand that randomizing is not the sort of thing you'd like to have happen to you.

CHAPTER FOUR
"So What Gives, Huh?"

I'M glad you asked that. (Because you *did* ask that, Mr. Fingal. This booklet is part of the analogizing process that I'll explain further down the page.)

Life in a computer is not the sort of thing you could just jump into and hope to retain the world-picture compatibility so necessary for sane functioning in this complex society. This has been tried, so take our word for it. Or rather, my word. Did I introduce myself? I'm Apollonia Joachim, First Class Operative for the DataSafe computer troubleshooting firm. You've probably never heard of us, even though you do work with computers.

Since you can't just become aware in the baffling, on-and-off world that passes for reality in a data system, your mind, in cooperation with an analogizing program I've given the computer, interprets things in ways that seem safe and comfortable to it. The world you see around you is a figment of your imagination. Of course, it looks real to you because it comes from the same part of the mind that you normally use to interpret reality. If we wanted to get philosophical about it, we could probably argue all day about what constitutes reality and why the one you are perceiving now is any less real than the one you are used to. But let's not get into that, all right?

The world will likely continue to function in ways you are accustomed for it to function. It won't be exactly the same. Nightmares, for instance. Mr. Fingal, I hope you aren't the nervous type, because your nightmares can come to life where you are. They'll seem quite real. You should avoid them if you can, because they can do you real harm. I'll say more about this later if I need to. For now, there's no need to worry.

CHAPTER FIVE
"What Do I Do Now?"

I'D advise you to continue with your normal activities. Don't be alarmed at anything unusual. For one thing, I can only communicate with you by means of paranormal phenomena. You see, when a message from me is fed into the computer, it reaches you in a way your brain is not capable of dealing with. Naturally, your brain classifies this as an unusual event and fleshes the communication out in unusual fashion. Most of the weird things you see, if you stay calm and don't let your own fears out of the closet to persecute you, will be me. Otherwise, I anticipate that your world should look, feel, taste, sound, and smell pretty normal. I've talked to your psychist. He assures me that your world-grasp is strong. So sit tight. We'll be working hard to get you out of there.

CHAPTER SIX
"Help!"

YES, we'll help you. This is a truly unfortunate thing to have happened, and of course we will refund all your money promptly. In addition, the lawyer for Kenya wants me to ask you if a lump sum settlement against all future damages is a topic worthy of discussion. You can think about it; there's no hurry.

In the meantime, I'll find ways to answer your questions. It might become unwieldy the harder your mind struggles to normalize my communications into things you are familiar with. That is both your greatest strength—the ability of your mind to bend the computer world it doesn't wish to see into media you are familiar with—and my biggest handicap. Look for me in tea leaves, on billboards, on holovision; anywhere! It could be exciting if you get into it.

Meanwhile, if you have received this message you can talk to me by filling in the attached coupon and dropping it in the mailtube. Your reply will probably be waiting for you at the office. Good luck!

Yes! I received your message and am interested in the exciting opportunities in the field of *computer living!* Please send me, without cost or obligation,

your exciting catalog telling me how I can *move up* to the big, wonderful world
outside!

NAME _____

ADDRESS _____

I.D. _____

_____

Fingal fought the urge to pinch himself. If what this booklet said was true—and he
might as well believe it—it would hurt and he would *not* wake up. He pinched
himself anyway. It hurt.

If he understood this right, everything around him was the product of his imagination. Somewhere, a woman was sitting at a computer input and talking to him in
normal language, which came to his brain in the form of electron pulses it could not
cope with and so edited into forms he was conversant with. He was analogizing like
mad. He wondered if he had caught it from the teacher, if analogies were contagious.

"What the hell's wrong with a simple voice from the air?" he wondered aloud.
He got no response, and was rather glad. He'd had enough mysteriousness for now.
And on second thought, a voice from the air would probably scare the pants off him.

He decided his brain must know what it was doing. After all, the hand startled
him but he hadn't panicked. He could *see* it, and he trusted his visual sense more
than he did voices from the air, a classical sign of insanity if ever there was one.

He got up and went to the wall. The letters of fire were gone, but the black
smudge of the erasure was still there. He sniffed it: carbon. He fingered the rough
paper of the pamphlet, tore off a corner, put it in his mouth and chewed it. It tasted
like paper.

He sat down and filled out the coupon and tossed it to the mailtube.

Fingal didn't get angry about it until he was at the office. He was an easygoing
person, slow to boil. But he finally reached a point where he had to say something.

Everything had been so normal he wanted to laugh. All his friends and ac-
quaintances were there, doing exactly what he would have expected them to be doing. What amazed and bemused him was the number and variety of spear carriers,
minor players in this internal soap opera. The extras that his mind had cooked up
to people the crowded corridors, like the man he didn't know who had bumped
into him on the tube to work, apologized, and disappeared, presumably back into
the bowels of his imagination.

There was nothing he could do to vent his anger but test the whole absurd setup. There was doubt lingering in his mind that the whole morning had been a fugue, a temporary lapse into dreamland. Maybe he'd never gone to Kenya, after all, and his mind was playing tricks on him. To get him there, or keep him away? He didn't know, but he could worry about that if the test failed.

He stood up at his desk terminal, which was in the third column of the fifteenth row of other identical desks, each with its diligent worker. He held up his hands and whistled. Everyone looked up.

"I don't believe in you," he screeched. He picked up a stack of tapes on his desk and hurled them at Felicia Nahum at the desk next to his. Felicia was a good friend of his, and she registered the proper shock until the tapes hit her. Then she melted. He looked around the room and saw that everything had stopped like a freeze-frame in a motion picture.

He sat down and drummed his fingers on his desk top. His heart was pounding and his face was flushed. For an awful moment he had thought he was wrong. He began to calm down, glancing up every few seconds to be sure the world really *had* stopped.

In three minutes he was in a cold sweat. What the hell had he *proved?* That this morning had been real, or that he really was crazy? It dawned on him that he would never be able to test the assumptions under which he lived.

A line of print flashed across his terminal.

"But when could you ever do so, Mr. Fingal?"

"Ms. Joachim?" he shouted, looking around him. "Where are you? I'm afraid."

"You mustn't be," the terminal printed. "Calm yourself. You have a strong sense of reality, remember? Think about this: even before today, how could you be sure the world you saw was not the result of catatonic delusions? Do you see what I mean? The question 'What is reality?' is, in the end, unanswerable. We all must accept at some point what we see and are told, and live by a set of untested and untestable assumptions. I ask you to accept the set I gave you this morning because, sitting here in the computer room where you cannot see me, my world-picture tells me that they are the true set. On the other hand, you could believe that I'm deluding myself, that there's nothing in the pink cube I see and that you're a spear carrier in *my* dream. Does that make you more comfortable?"

"No," he mumbled, ashamed of himself. "I see what you mean. Even if I am crazy, it would be more comfortable to go along with it than to keep fighting it."

"Perfect, Mr. Fingal. If you need further illustrations you could imagine yourself locked in a straitjacket. Perhaps there are technicians laboring right now to correct your condition, and they are putting you through this psychodrama as a first step. Is that any more attractive?"

"No, I guess it isn't."

"The point is that it's as reasonable an assumption as the set of facts I gave you this morning. But the main point is that you should behave the same whichever set is true. Do you see? To fight it in the one case will only cause you trouble, and in the other, would impede the treatment. I realize I'm asking you to accept me on faith. And that's all I can give you."

"I believe in you," he said. "Now, can you start everything going again?"

"I told you I'm not in control of your world. In fact, it's a considerable obstacle to me, seeing as I have to talk to you in these awkward ways. But things should get going on their own as soon as you let them. Look up."

He did, and saw the normal hum and bustle of the office. Felicia was there at her desk, as though nothing had happened. Nothing had. Yes, something had, after all. The tapes were scattered on the floor near his desk, where they had fallen. They had unreeled in an unruly mess.

He started to pick them up, then saw they weren't as messy as he had thought. They spelled out a message in coils of tape.

"You're back on the track," it said.

For three weeks Fingal was a very good boy. His co-workers, had they been real people, might have noticed a certain standoffishness in him, and his social life at home was drastically curtailed. Otherwise, he behaved exactly as if everything around him were real.

But his patience had limits. This had already dragged on for longer than he had expected. He began to fidget at his desk, let his mind wander. Feeding information into a computer can be frustrating, unrewarding, and eventually stultifying. He had been feeling it even before his trip to Kenya; it had been the *cause* of his trip to Kenya. He was sixty-eight years old, with centuries ahead of him, and stuck in a ferro-magnetic rut. Longlife could be a mixed blessing when you felt boredom creeping up on you.

What was getting to him was the growing disgust with his job. It was bad enough when he merely sat in a real office with two hundred real people, shoveling slightly unreal data into a much-less-than-real-to-his-senses computer. How much worse now, when he knew that the data he handled had no meaning to anyone but himself, was nothing but occupational therapy created by his mind and a computer program to keep him busy while Joachim searched for his body.

For the first time in his life he began punching some buttons for himself. Under slightly less stress he would have gone to see his psychist, the approved and perfectly normal thing to do. Here, he knew he would only be talking to himself.

He failed to perceive the advantages of such an idealized psychoanalytic process; he'd never really believed that a psychist did little more than listen in the first place.

He began to change his own life when he became irritated with his boss. She pointed out to him that his error index was on the rise, and suggested that he shape up or begin looking for another source of employment.

This enraged him. He'd been a good worker for twenty-five years. Why should she take that attitude when he was just not feeling himself for a week or two?

Then he was angrier than ever when he thought about her being merely a projection of his own mind. Why should he let *her* push him around?

"I don't want to hear it," he said. "Leave me alone. Better yet, give me a raise in salary."

"Fingal," she said promptly, "you've been a credit to your section these last weeks. I'm going to give you a raise."

"Thank you. Go away." She did, by dissolving into thin air. This really made his day. He leaned back in his chair and thought about his situation for the first time since he was young.

He didn't like what he saw.

In the middle of his ruminations, his computer screen lit up again.

"Watch it, Fingal," it read. "That way lies catatonia."

He took the warning seriously, but didn't intend to abuse the newfound power. He didn't see why judicious use of it now and then would hurt anything. He stretched, and yawned broadly. He looked around, suddenly hating the office with its rows of workers indistinguishable from their desks. Why not take the day off?

On impulse, he got up and walked the few steps to Felicia's desk.

"Why don't we go to my house and make love?" he asked her.

She looked at him in astonishment, and he grinned. She was almost as surprised as when he had hurled the tapes at her.

"Is this a joke? In the middle of the day? You have a job to do, you know. You want to get us fired?"

He shook his head slowly. "That's not an acceptable answer."

She stopped, and rewound from that point. He heard her repeat her last sentences backwards, then she smiled.

"Sure, why not?" she said.

Felicia left afterwards in the same slightly disconcerting way his boss had left earlier, by melting into the air. Fingal sat quietly in his bed, wondering what to do with himself. He felt he was getting off to a bad start if he intended to edit his world with care.

His telephone rang.

"You're damn right," said a woman's voice, obviously irritated with him. He sat up straight.

"Apollonia?"

"Ms. Joachim to you, Fingal. I can't talk long; this is quite a strain on me. But listen to me, and listen hard. Your navel is very deep, Fingal. From where you're standing, it's a pit I can't even see the bottom of. If you fall into it I can't guarantee to pull you out."

"But do I have to take *everything* as it is? Aren't I allowed some self-improvement?"

"Don't kid yourself. That wasn't self-improvement. That was sheer laziness. It was nothing but masturbation, and while there's nothing wrong with that, if you do it to the exclusion of all else, your mind will grow in on itself. You're in grave danger of excluding the external universe from your reality."

"But I thought there was no external universe for me here."

"Almost right. But I'm feeding you external stimuli to keep you going. Besides, it's the attitude that counts. You've never had trouble finding sexual partners; why do you feel compelled to alter the odds now?"

"I don't know," he admitted. "Like you said, laziness, I guess."

"That's right. If you want to quit your job, feel free. If you're serious about self-improvement, there are opportunities available to you there. Search them out. Look around you, explore. But don't try to meddle in things you don't understand. I've got to go now. I'll write you a letter if I can, and explain more."

"Wait! What about my body? Have they made any progress?"

"Yes, they've found out how it happened. It seems . . ." Her voice faded out, and he switched off the phone.

The next day he received a letter explaining what was known so far. It seemed that the mix-up had resulted from the visit of the teacher to the medico section on the day of his recording. More specifically, the return of the little boy after the others had left. They were sure now that he had tampered with the routing card that told the attendants what to do with Fingal's body. Instead of moving it to the slumber room, which was a green card, they had sent it somewhere—no one knew where yet—for a sex change, which was a blue card. The medico, in her haste to get home for her date, had not noticed the switch. Now the body could be in any of several thousand medico shops in Luna. They were looking for it, and for the boy.

Fingal put the letter down and did some hard thinking.

Joachim had said there were opportunities for him in the memory banks. She had also said that not everything he saw was his own projections. He was receiving, was capable of receiving, external stimuli. Why was that? Because he would

tend to randomize without them, or some other reason? He wished the letter had
gone into that.

In the meantime, what did he do?

Suddenly he had it. He wanted to learn about computers. He wanted to know
what made them tick, to feel a sense of power over them. It was particularly strong
when he thought about being a virtual prisoner inside one. He was like a worker
on an assembly line. All day long he labors, taking small parts off a moving belt
and installing them on larger assemblies. One day, he happens to wonder who puts
the parts on the belt. Where do they come from? How are they made? What happens after he installs them?

He wondered why he hadn't thought of it before.

The admissions office of the Lunar People's Technical School was crowded. He
was handed a form and told to fill it out. It looked bleak. The spaces for "previous
experience" and "aptitude scores" were almost blank when he was through with
them. All in all, not a very promising application. He went to the desk and handed
the form to the man sitting at the terminal.

The man fed it into the computer, which promptly decided Fingal had no talent for being a computer repairperson. He started to turn away when his eye was
caught by a large poster behind the man. It had been there on the wall when he
came in, but he hadn't read it.

**LUNA NEEDS
COMPUTER TECHNICIANS.
THIS MEANS YOU,
MR. FINGAL!**

Are you dissatisfied with your present employment? Do you feel you
were cut out for better things? Then today may be your lucky day.
You've come to the right place, and if you grasp this golden opportunity you will find doors opening that were closed to you.

Act, Mr. Fingal. This is the time. Who's to check up on you? Just
take that stylus and fill in the application any old way you want. Be
grandiose, be daring! The fix is in, and you're on your way to

BIG MONEY!

The secretary saw nothing unusual in Fingal's coming to the desk a second
time, and didn't even blink when the computer decided he was eligible for the accelerated course.

* * *

It wasn't easy at first. He really did have little aptitude for electronics, but aptitude is a slippery thing. His personality matrix was as flexible now as it would ever be. A little effort at the right time would go a long way toward self-improvement. What he kept telling himself was that everything that made him what he was, was etched in that tiny cube wired in to the computer, and if he was careful he could edit it.

Not radically, Joachim told him in a long, helpful letter later in the week. That way led to complete disruption of the FPNA matrix and catatonia, which in this case would be distinguishable from death only to a hair splitter.

He thought a lot about death as he dug into the books. He was in a strange position. The being known as Fingal would not die in any conceivable outcome of this adventure. For one thing, his body was going toward a sex change and it was hard to imagine what could happen to it that would kill it. Whoever had custody of it now would be taking care of it just as well as the medicos in the slumber room would have. If Joachim was unsuccessful in her attempt to keep him aware and sane in the memory bank, he would merely awake and remember nothing from the time he fell asleep on the table.

If, by some compounded unlikelihood, his body *was* allowed to die, he had an insurance recording safe in the vault of his bank. The recording was three years old. He would awaken in the newly grown clone body knowing nothing of the last three years, and would have a fantastic story to listen to as he was brought up to date.

But none of that mattered to *him*. Humans are a time-binding species, existing in an eternal *now*. The future flows through them and becomes the past, but it is always the present that counts. The Fingal of three years ago was *not* the Fingal in the memory bank. The simple fact about immortality by memory recording was that it was a poor solution. The three-dimensional cross section that was the Fingal of now must always behave as if his life depended on his actions, for he would feel the pain of death if it happened to him. It was small consolation to a dying man to know that he would go on, several years younger and less wise. If Fingal lost out here, he would *die,* because with memory recording he was three people: the one who lived now, the one lost somewhere on Luna, and the one potential person in the bank vault. They were really no more than close relatives.

Everyone knew this, but it was so much better than the alternative that few people rejected it. They tried not to think about it and were generally successful. They had recordings made as often as they could afford them. They heaved a sigh of relief as they got onto the table to have another recording taken, knowing that another chunk of their lives was safe for all time. But they awaited the awakening nervously, dreading being told that it was now twenty years later because they had died sometime after the recording and had to start all over. A lot can happen in twenty years. The person in the new clone body might have to cope with a child he or she had never seen, a new spouse, or the shattering news that his or her employment was now the function of a machine.

So Fingal took Joachim's warnings seriously. Death was death, and though he could cheat it, death still had the last laugh. Instead of taking your whole life from you, death now only claimed a percentage, but in many ways it was the most important percentage.

He enrolled in classes. Whenever possible, he took the ones that were available over the phone lines so he needn't stir from his room. He ordered his food and supplies by phone and paid his bills by looking at them and willing them out of existence. It could have been intensely boring, or it could have been wildly interesting. After all, it was a dream world, and who doesn't think of retiring into fantasy from time to time? Fingal certainly did, but firmly suppressed the idea when it came. He intended to get out of this dream.

For one thing, he missed the company of other people. He waited for the weekly letters from Apollonia (she now allowed him to call her by her first name) with a consuming passion and devoured every word. His file of such letters bulged. At lonely moments he would pull one out at random and read it again and again.

On her advice, he left the apartment regularly and stirred around more or less at random. During these outings he had wild adventures. Literally. Apollonia hurled the external stimuli at him during these times and they could be anything from The Mummy's Curse to Custer's Last Stand with the original cast. It beat hell out of the movies. He would just walk down the public corridors and open a door at random. Behind it might be King Solomon's mines or the sultan's harem. He endured them all stoically. He was unable to get any pleasure from sex. He knew it was a one-handed exercise, and it took all the excitement away.

His only pleasure came in his studies. He read everything he could about computer science and came to stand at the head of his class. And as he learned, it began to occur to him to apply his knowledge to his own situation.

He began seeing things around him that had been veiled before. Patterns. The reality was starting to seep through his illusions. Every so often he would look up and see the faintest shadow of the real world of electron flow and fluttering circuits he inhabited. It scared him at first. He asked Apollonia about it on one of his dream journeys, this time to Coney Island in the mid-twentieth century. He liked it there. He could lie on the sand and talk to the surf. Overhead, a skywriter's plane spelled out the answers to his questions. He studiously ignored the brontosaurus rampaging through the roller coaster off to his right.

"What does it mean, O Goddess of Transistoria, when I begin to see circuit diagrams on the walls of my apartment? Overwork?"

"It means the illusion is beginning to wear thin," the plane spelled out over the next half-hour. "You're adapting to the reality you have been denying. It could be trouble, but we're hot on the trail of your body. We should have it soon and get you out of there." This had been too much for the plane. The sun was down now, the brontosaurus vanquished and the plane out of gas. It spiraled into the ocean and the crowds surged closer to the water to watch the rescue. Fingal got up and went back to the boardwalk.

There was a huge billboard. He laced his fingers behind his back and read it.

"Sorry for the delay. As I was saying, we're almost there. Give us another few months. One of our agents thinks he will be at the right medico shop in about one week's time. From there it should go quickly. For now, avoid those places where you see the circuits showing through. They're no good for you, take my word for it."

Fingal avoided the circuits as long as he could. He finished his first courses in computer science and enrolled in the intermediate section. Six months rolled by.

His studies got easier and easier. His reading speed was increasing phenomenally. He found that it was more advantageous for him to see the library as composed of books instead of tapes. He could take a book from the shelf, flip through it rapidly, and know everything that was in it. He knew enough now to realize that he was acquiring a facility to interface directly with the stored knowledge in the computer, bypassing his senses entirely. The books he held in his hands were merely the sensual analogs of the proper terminals to touch. Apollonia was nervous about it, but let him go on. He breezed through the intermediate and graduated into the advanced classes.

But he was surrounded by wires. Everywhere he turned, in the patterns of veins beneath the surface of a man's face, in a plate of French fries he ordered for lunch, in his palmprints, overlaying the apparent disorder of a head of blonde hair on the pillow beside him.

The wires were analogs of analogs. There was little in a modern computer that consisted of wiring. Most of it was made of molecular circuits that were either embedded in a crystal lattice or photographically reproduced on a chip of silicon. Visually, they were hard to imagine, so his mind was making up these complex circuit diagrams that served the same purpose but could be experienced directly.

One day he could resist it no longer. He was in the bathroom, on the traditional place for the pondering of the imponderable. His mind wandered, speculating on the necessity of moving his bowels, wondering if he might safely eliminate the need to eliminate. His toe idly traced out the pathways of a circuit board incorporated in the pattern of tiles on the floor.

The toilet began to overflow, not with water, but with coins. Bells were ringing happily. He jumped up and watched in bemusement as his bathroom filled with money.

He became aware of a subtle alteration in the tone of the bells. They changed from the merry clang of jackpot to the tolling of a death knell. He hastily looked around for a manifestation. He knew that Apollonia would be angry.

She was. Her hand appeared and began to write on the wall. This time the writing was in his blood. It dripped menacingly from the words.

"What are you doing?" the hand wrote, and having writ, moved on. "I told you to leave the wires alone. Do you know what you've done? You may have wiped the financial records for Kenya. It could take *months* to straighten them out."

"Well, what do I care?" he exploded. "What have they done for me lately? It's *incredible* that they haven't located my body by now. It's been a full *year*."

The hand bunched up in a fist. Then it grabbed him around the throat and squeezed hard enough to make his eyes bulge out. It slowly relaxed. When Fingal could see straight, he backed warily away from it.

The hand fidgeted nervously, drummed its fingers on the floor. It went to the wall again.

"Sorry," it wrote, "I guess I'm getting tired. Hold on."

He waited, more shaken than he remembered being since his odyssey began. There's nothing like a dose of pain, he reflected, to make you realize that it *can* happen to you.

The wall with the words of blood slowly dissolved into a heavenly panorama. As he watched, clouds streamed by his vantage point and mixed beautifully with golden rays of sunshine. He heard organ music from pipes the size of sequoias.

He wanted to applaud. It was so overdone, and yet so convincing. In the center of the whirling mass of white mist an angel faded in. She had wings and a halo, but lacked the traditional white robe. She was nude, and hair floated around her as if she were under water.

She levitated to him, walking on the billowing clouds, and handed him two stone tablets. He tore his eyes away from the apparition and glanced down at the tablets:

> Thou shalt not screw around with
> things thou dost not understand.

"All right, I promise I won't," he told the angel. "Apollonia, is that you? Really you, I mean?"

"Read the Commandments, Fingal. This is hard on me." He looked back at the tablets.

> Thou shalt not meddle in the hardware systems of the
>   Kenya Corporation, for Kenya shall not hold him
>   indemnifiable who taketh freedoms with its property.
> Thou shalt not explore the limits of thy prison. Trust in
>   the Kenya Corporation to extract thee.
> Thou shalt not program.
> Thou shalt not worry about the location of thy body, for
>   it has been located, help is on the way, the cavalry has
>   arrived, and all is in hand.
> Thou shalt meet a tall, handsome stranger who will guide
>   thee from thy current plight.
> Thou shalt stay tuned for further developments.

He looked up and was happy to see that the angel was still there.

"I won't, I promise. But where is my body, and why has it taken so long to find it? Can you—"

"Know thou that appearing like this is a great taxation upon me, Mr. Fingal. I am undergoing strains the nature of which I have no time to reveal to thee. Hold thy horses, wait it out, and thou shalt soon see the light at the end of the tunnel."

"Wait, don't go." She was already starting to fade out.

"I cannot tarry."

"But . . . Apollonia, this is charming, but why do you appear to me in these crazy ways? Why all the pomp and circumstance? What's wrong with letters?"

She looked around her at the clouds, the sunbeams, the tablets in his hand, and at her body, as if seeing them for the first time. She threw her head back and laughed like a symphony orchestra. It was almost too beautiful for Fingal to bear.

"Me?" she said, dropping the angelic bearing. "Me? I don't pick 'em, Fingal. I told you, it's *your* head, and I'm just passing through." She arched her eyebrows at him. "And really, sir, I had no idea you felt this way about me. Is it puppy love?" And she was gone, except for the grin.

The grin haunted him for days. He was disgusted with himself about it. He hated to see a metaphor overworked so. He decided his mind was just an inept analogizer.

But everything had its purpose. The grin forced him to look at his feelings. He was in love, hopelessly, ridiculously, just like a teenager. He got out all his old letters from her and read through them again, searching for the magic words that could have inflicted this on him. Because it was *silly*. He'd never met her except under highly figurative circumstances. The one time he had seen her, most of what he saw was the product of his own mind.

There were no clues in the letters. Most of them were as impersonal as a text-book, though they tended to be rather chatty. Friendly, yes; but intimate, poetic, insightful, revealing? No. He failed utterly to put them together in any way that should add up to love, or even a teenage crush.

He attacked his studies with renewed vigor, awaiting the next communication. Weeks dragged by with no word. He called the post office several times, placed personal advertisements in every periodical he could think of, took to scrawling messages on public buildings, sealed notes in bottles and flushed them down the disposal, rented billboards, bought television time. He screamed at the empty walls of his apartment, buttonholed strangers, tapped Morse Code on the water pipes, started rumors in skid-row taprooms, had leaflets published and distributed all over the solar system. He tried every medium he could think of, and could not contact her. He was alone.

He considered the possibility that he had died. In his present situation, it might be hard to tell for sure. He abandoned it as untestable. That line was hazy enough already without his efforts to determine which side of the life/death dichotomy he inhabited. Besides, the more he thought about existing as nothing more than kinks in a set of macromolecules plugged into a data system, the more it frightened him. He'd survived this long by avoiding such thoughts.

His nightmares moved in on him, set up housekeeping in his apartment. They were a severe disappointment, and confirmed his conclusion that his imagination was not as vivid as it might be. They were infantile boogeymen, the sort that might scare him when glimpsed hazily through the fog of a nightmare, but were almost laughable when exposed to the full light of consciousness. There was a large, talkative snake that was crudely put together, fashioned from the incomplete picture a child might have of a serpent. A toy company could have done a better job. There was a werewolf whose chief claim to dread was a tendency to shed all over Fingal's rugs. There was a woman who consisted mostly of breasts and genitals, left over from his adolescence, he suspected. He groaned in embarrassment every time he looked at her. If he had ever been that infantile he would rather have left the dirty traces of it buried forever.

He kept booting them into the corridor but they drifted in at night like poor relations. They talked incessantly, and always about him. The things they knew! They seemed to have a very low opinion of him. The snake often expressed the opinion that Fingal would never amount to anything because he had so docilely accepted the results of the aptitude tests he took as a child. That hurt, but the best salve for the wound was further study.

Finally a letter came. He winced as soon as he got it open. The salutation was enough to tell him he wasn't going to like it.

Dear Mr. Fingal,

I won't apologize for the delay this time. It seems that most of my man-ifestations have included an apology and I feel I deserved a rest this time. I can't be always on call. I have a life of my own.

I understand that you have behaved in an exemplary manner since I last talked with you. You have ignored the inner workings of the computer just as I told you to do. I haven't been completely frank with you, and I will explain my reasons.

The hook-up between you and the computer is, and always has been, two-way. Our greatest fear at this end had been that you would begin inter-fering with the workings of the computer, to the great discomfort of everyone. Or that you would go mad and run amok, perhaps wrecking the entire data system. We installed you in the computer as a humane necessity, because you would have died if we had not done so, though it would have cost you only two days of memories. But Kenya is in the business of selling memories, and holds them to be a sacred trust. It was a mix-up on the part of the Kenya Corporation that got you here in the first place, so we decided we should do everything we could for you.

But it was at great hazard to our operations at this end.

Once, about six months ago, you got tangled in the weather-control sec-tor of the computer and set off a storm over Kilimanjaro that is still not fully under control. Several animals were lost.

I have had to fight the Board of Directors to keep you on-line, and sev-eral times the program was almost terminated. You know what that means.

Now, I've leveled with you. I wanted to from the start, but the people who own things around here were worried that you might start fooling around out of a spirit of vindictiveness if you knew these facts, so they were kept from you. You could still do a great deal of damage before we could shut you off. I'm laying it on the line now, with directors chewing their nails over my shoulder. Please stay out of trouble.

On to the other matter.

I was afraid from the outset that what has happened might happen. For over a year I've been your only contact with the world outside. I've been the only other person in your universe. I would have to be an extremely cold, hateful, awful person—which I am not—for you not to feel affection for me under those circumstances. You are suffering from intense sensory depriva-tion, and it's well known that someone in that state becomes pliable, sug-gestible, and lonely. You've attached your feelings to me as the only thing around worth caring for.

I've tried to avoid intimacy with you for that reason, to keep things firmly on a last-name basis. But I relented during one of your periods of despair. And you read into my letters some things that were not there. Remember, even in the printed medium it is your mind that controls what you see. Your censor has let through what it wanted to see and maybe even added some things of its own. I'm at your mercy. For all I know, you may be reading this letter as a passionate affirmation of love. I've added every reinforcement I know of to make sure the message comes through on a priority channel and is not garbled. I'm sorry to hear that you love me. I do not, repeat not, love you in return. You'll understand why, at least in part, when we get you out of there.

It will never work, Mr. Fingal. Give it up.

Apollonia Joachim

Fingal graduated first in his class. He had finished the required courses for his degree during the last long week after his letter from Apollonia. It was a bitter victory for him, marching up to the stage to accept the sheepskin, but he clutched it to him fiercely. At least he had made the most of his situation, at least he had not meekly let the wheels of the machine chew him up like a good worker.

He reached out to grasp the hand of the college president and saw it transformed. He looked up and saw the bearded, robed figure flow and writhe and become a tall, uniformed woman. With a surge of joy, he knew who it was. Then the joy became ashes in his mouth, which he hurriedly spit out.

"I always knew you'd choke on a figure of speech," she said, laughing tiredly.

"You're here," he said. He could not quite believe it. He stared dully at her, grasping her hand and the diploma with equal tenacity. She was tall, as the prophecy had said, and handsome. Her hair was cropped short over a capable face, and the body beneath the uniform was muscular. The uniform was open at the throat, and wrinkled. There were circles under her eyes, and the eyes were bloodshot. She swayed slightly on her feet.

"I'm here, all right. Are you ready to go back?" She turned to the assembled students. "How about it, gang? Do you think he deserves to go back?"

The crowd went wild, cheering and tossing mortarboards into the air. Fingal turned dazedly to look at them, with a dawning realization. He looked down at the diploma.

"I don't know," he said. "I don't know. Back to work at the data room?"

She clapped him on the back.

"No. I promise you that."

"But how could it be different? I've come to think of this piece of paper as something . . . real. Real! How could I have deluded myself like that? Why did I accept it?"

"I helped you along," she said. "But it wasn't all a game. You really did learn all the things you learned. It won't go away when you return. That thing in your hand is imaginary, for sure, but who do you think prints the real ones? You're registered where it counts—in the computer—as having passed all the courses. You'll get a real diploma when you return."

Fingal wavered. There was a tempting vision in his head. He'd been here for over a year and had never really exploited the nature of the place. Maybe that business about dying in the memory bank was all a shuck, another lie invented to keep him in his place. In that case, he could remain here and satisfy his wildest desires, become king of the universe with no opposition, wallow in pleasure no emperor ever imagined. Anything he wanted here he could have, anything at all.

And he really felt he might pull it off. He'd noticed many things about this place, and now had the knowledge of computer technology to back him up. He could squirm around and evade their attempts to erase him, even survive if they removed his cube by programming himself into other parts of the computer. He could do it.

With a sudden insight he realized that he had no desires wild enough to keep him here in his navel. He had only one major desire right now, and she was slowly fading out. A lap dissolve was replacing her with the old college president.

"Coming?" she asked.

"Yes." It was as simple as that. The stage, president, students, and auditorium faded out and the computer room at Kenya faded in. Only Apollonia remained constant. He held onto her hand until everything stabilized.

"Whew," she said, and reached around behind her head. She pulled out a wire from her occipital plug and collapsed into a chair. Someone pulled a similar wire from Fingal's head, and he was finally free of the computer.

Apollonia reached out for a steaming cup of coffee on a table littered with empty cups.

"You were a tough nut," she said. "For a minute I thought you'd stay. It happened once. You're not the first to have this happen to you, but you're no more than the twentieth. It's an unexplored area. Dangerous."

"Really?" he said. "You weren't just saying that?"

"No," she laughed. "Now the truth can be told. It *is* dangerous. No one had ever survived more than three hours in that kind of cube, hooked into a computer. You went for six. You *do* have a strong world picture."

She was watching him to see how he reacted to this. She was not surprised to see him accept it readily.

"I should have known that," he said. "I should have thought of it. It was only six hours out here, and more than a year for me. Computers think faster. Why didn't I see that?"

"I helped you not see it," she admitted. "Like the push I gave you not to question why you were studying so hard. Those two orders worked a lot better than some of the orders I gave you."

She yawned again, and it seemed to go on forever.

"See, it was pretty hard for me to interface with you for six hours straight. No one's ever done it before; it can get to be quite a strain. So we've both got something to be proud of."

She smiled at him but it faded when he did not return it.

"Don't look so hurt, Fingal. What *is* your first name? I knew it, but erased it early in the game."

"Does it matter?"

"I don't know. Surely you must see why I haven't fallen in love with you, though you may be a perfectly lovable person. I haven't had *time*. It's been a very long six hours, but it was still only six hours. What can I do?"

Fingal's face was going through awkward changes as he absorbed that. Things were not so bleak after all.

"You could go to dinner with me."

"I'm already emotionally involved with someone else, I should warn you of that."

"You could still go to dinner. You haven't been exposed to my new determination. I'm going to really make a case."

She laughed warmly and got up. She took his hand.

"You know, it's possible that you might succeed. Just don't put wings on me again, all right? You'll never get anywhere like that."

"I promise. I'm through with visions—for the rest of my life."

"In the Hall of the Martian Kings"

I sold half a dozen stories over the next year. Not enough to support myself and my family, but enough to make life a bit easier. But it was becoming clear that I was unlikely to make a living just selling short stories. I worked fast in those days, but never turned out more than two in any given month, and usually only one. If I sold them all, it wouldn't be enough. I started to think in terms of another novel.

Growing up, I had been aware that there was something called fandom, but it had never occurred to me that I might be a part of it. I know there are places more off the beaten track than Nederland, Texas, but growing up there it was hard to imagine them. We had a good football team, went to the state AAA finals a couple times. We had a great band, one of the best in the state, that had marched in John F. Kennedy's inaugural parade, in which I played trumpet, French horn, and baritone horn at various times. But academically we were only middling. The only other things Nederland had to brag about, wedged there between Beaumont and Port Arthur, were mosquitoes the size of P-51s, five big refineries within smelling distance, and the semiannual hurricane.

I was not a complete hick. I'd been to Dallas, and New Orleans, and knew that was the life for me. When I got my driver's license (you could get it at age fourteen in Texas), I used every opportunity I could find to wheedle the keys to Dad's big Mercury and tear down U.S. 90 to Houston, ninety miles away, seeing if that needle would still peg out at 120 mph. It always did, and so did the Pontiac, later (Sorry, Dad) . . . just to stare up at the big buildings. One was forty stories tall!

But so far as I knew no science fiction convention had ever been held within a thousand miles of me. Those things happened in New York, Los Angeles, Philadelphia, Denver.

Shangri-La, Neverland, El Dorado.

Then I became aware that something called Westercon was being held in Oakland, California. By then I was living in Eugene, Oregon, and driving the sort of car that the EPA is mostly keeping off the road these days. I didn't trust it to get much past Mount Shasta, and besides, my wife and children couldn't go, and they would need the car. By then I knew a few science fiction fans, including a couple who always went to Westercon. So we set off down I-5 in a car not a whole lot better than mine—I remember getting down to as low as 20 mph on some of the grades—and with some smiles from the gods of the highway, actually made it.

I didn't have enough money to join the convention and eat, too, so I lurked around the big, noisy place, knowing no one. But I had sold a story to David Gerrold for an anthology he was putting together, and saw he was on a panel. I sneaked in, waited around in the back when it was over, and approached him as he was on his way to the next event on the schedule of a busy professional writer who had written "The Trouble With Tribbles," the most popular Star Trek *episode of all time. David was cordial at first sight, as I have found most pros to be with fans, but when I introduced myself I first experienced something I had not expected: instant acceptance. David's enthusiasm at meeting me was not a fluke, not just because David is a sweet guy. All the writers I would meet that day were just as cordial, just as accepting. Apparently, in the world of science fiction writers, one sale was all you needed to be a member. I stood in awe of some of the people I met that day, tried not to show it too egregiously, and never felt a hint of condescension.*

David immediately swept me up to Valhalla, or as he called it, "the SFWA suite." I was too embarrassed to admit I didn't know what SFWA stood for. I later learned it was Science Fiction Writers of America. The pros. And I was welcomed there, even though I wasn't a member.

Hal Clement was there. John Brunner. Charles Brown, the editor of Locus, *the newsmagazine of SF. Larry Niven and Jerry Pournelle were there. (Larry Niven!) I talked to him for a while. It's hard to recall now just who all was in that room, since so many of them later became my friends, and I was still dazzled by the idea of them as colleagues.*

Colleagues!

Someone, probably David, wangled a membership for me and I could stop feeling like an illegal alien on the lookout for la migra. *I was hustled off to appear on a panel about breaking into the business. And soon I was having lunch with Donald Bensen from New York, who was involved in launching a new publishing line called Quantum SF. He asked me if I was thinking about writing a novel, and what it might be about. I came up with an idea, winging it, and soon had outlined* The Ophiuchi Hotline, *something I had made up in a recent story. Before long I had been put in contact with Jim Frenkel, who was later to guide me through the process of getting my first book in print.*

Each night I sneaked off and walked to the fleabag hotel almost a mile away where I was staying because I couldn't afford even one night at the convention hotel, and wondered if I had been dreaming it all.

Then I went back to Eugene to get to work on the novel.

* * *

The following story is one I wrote not long after that. It is not part of the Eight World series, or any series at all, though I have had some notion of using all or part of it as a segment of a novel. We'll see what develops from that.

"In the Hall of the Martian Kings" was given an award for best story of the year by an organization of teachers of science fiction. This delighted me more than I can say. Not just the award itself, but the very idea that there could be such an organization. These days, when 80 percent of the giant movie blockbusters have an SF or fantasy element, when the novels of Philip K. Dick are being butchered and making billions, it's hard to remember just how disreputable all that "spaceship stuff" used to be, right into the 1970s. Mr. Green, my librarian/pusher, had to have some real nerve to order hundreds of SF paperbacks, boxes and boxes of them, simply because I and a few of my friends couldn't get enough of them. These days, no big deal. Back then, back in that stronghold of Southern Baptists, he might have been brought up before the school board and burned alive on a pile of degenerate rock 'n' roll 45s.

IN THE HALL OF THE MARTIAN KINGS

I T TOOK PERSEVERANCE, alertness, and a willingness to break the rules to watch the sunrise in Tharsis Canyon. Matthew Crawford shivered in the dark, his suit heater turned to emergency setting, his eyes trained toward the east. He knew he had to be watchful. Yesterday he had missed it entirely, snatched away from it by a long, unavoidable yawn. His jaw muscles stretched, but he controlled this yawn and kept his eyes firmly open.

And there it was. Like the lights in a theater after the show is over: just a quick brightening, a splash of localized bluish-purple over the canyon rim, and he was surrounded by footlights. Day had come, the truncated Martian day that would never touch the blackness over his head.

This day, like the nine before it, illuminated a Tharsis radically changed from what it had been over the last sleepy ten thousand years. Wind erosion of rocks can create an infinity of shapes, but it never gets around to carving out a straight line or a perfect arc. The human encampment below him broke up the jagged lines of the rocks with regular angles and curves.

The camp was anything but orderly. No one would get the impression that any care had been taken in the haphazard arrangement of dome, lander, crawlers, crawler tracks, and scattered equipment. It had grown, as all human base camps seem to grow, without pattern. He was reminded of the footprints around Tranquillity Base, though on a much larger scale.

Tharsis Base sat on a wide ledge about halfway up from the uneven bottom of the Tharsis arm of the Great Rift Valley. The site had been chosen because it was a smooth area, allowing easy access up a gentle slope to the flat plains of the Tharsis Plateau, while at the same time only a kilometer from the valley floor. No one could agree which area was most worthy of study: plains or canyon. So this site had been chosen as a compromise. What it meant was that the exploring parties had to either climb up or go down, because there wasn't a damn thing worth seeing near the camp. Even the exposed layering and its archeological records could not be seen without a half-kilometer crawler ride up to the point where Crawford had climbed to watch the sunrise.

He examined the dome as he walked back to camp. There was a figure hazily visible through the plastic. At this distance he would have been unable to tell who it was if it weren't for the black face. He saw her step up to the dome wall and wipe a clear circle to look through. She spotted his bright red suit and pointed at him. She was suited except for her helmet, which contained her radio. He knew he was in trouble. He saw her turn away and bend to the ground to pick up her helmet, so she could tell him what she thought of people who disobeyed her orders, when the dome shuddered like a jellyfish.

An alarm started in his helmet, flat and strangely soothing coming from the tiny speaker. He stood there for a moment as a perfect smoke ring of dust billowed up around the rim of the dome. Then he was running.

He watched the disaster unfold before his eyes, silent except for the rhythmic beat of the alarm bell in his ears. The dome was dancing and straining, trying to fly. The floor heaved up in the center, throwing the black woman to her knees. In another second the interior was a whirling snowstorm. He skidded on the sand and fell forward, got up in time to see the fiberglass ropes on the side nearest him snap free from the steel spikes anchoring the dome to the rock.

The dome now looked like some fantastic Christmas ornament, filled with snowflakes and the flashing red and blue lights of the emergency alarms. The top of the dome heaved over away from him, and the floor raised itself high in the air, held down only by the unbroken anchors on the side farthest from him. There was a gush of snow and dust; then the floor settled slowly back to the ground. There was no motion now but the leisurely folding of the depressurized dome roof as it settled over the structures inside.

*   *   *

The crawler skidded to a stop, nearly rolling over, beside the deflated dome. Two pressure-suited figures got out. They started for the dome, hesitantly, in fits and starts. One grabbed the other's arm and pointed to the lander. The two of them changed course and scrambled up the rope ladder hanging over the side.

Crawford was the only one to look up when the lock started cycling. The two people almost tumbled over each other coming out of the lock. They wanted to *do* something, and quickly, but didn't know what. In the end, they just stood there, silently twisting their hands and looking at the floor. One of them took off her helmet. She was a large woman, in her thirties, with red hair shorn off close to the scalp.

"Matt, we got here as—" She stopped, realizing how obvious it was. "How's Lou?"

"Lou's not going to make it." He gestured to the bunk where a heavyset man lay breathing raggedly into a clear plastic mask. He was on pure oxygen. There was blood seeping from his ears and nose.

"Brain damage?"

Crawford nodded. He looked around at the other occupants of the room. There was the Surface Mission Commander, Mary Lang, the black woman he had seen inside the dome just before the blowout. She was sitting on the edge of Lou Prager's cot, her head cradled in her hands. In a way, she was a more shocking sight than Lou. No one who knew her would have thought she could be brought to this limp state of apathy. She had not moved for the last hour.

Sitting on the floor huddled in a blanket was Martin Ralston, the chemist. His shirt was bloody, and there was dried blood all over his face and hands from the nosebleed he'd only recently gotten under control, but his eyes were alert. He shivered, looking from Lang, his titular leader, to Crawford, the only one who seemed calm enough to deal with anything. He was a follower, reliable but unimaginative.

Crawford looked back to the newest arrivals. They were Lucy Stone McKillian, the redheaded ecologist, and Song Sue Lee, the exobiologist. They still stood numbly by the air lock, unable as yet to come to grips with the fact of fifteen dead men and women beneath the dome outside.

"What do they say on the *Burroughs*?" McKillian asked, tossing her helmet on the floor and squatting tiredly against the wall. The lander was not the most comfortable place to hold a meeting; all the couches were mounted horizontally since their purpose was cushioning the acceleration of landing and takeoff. With the ship sitting on its tail, this made ninety percent of the space in the lander useless. They were all gathered on the circular bulkhead at the rear of the life system, just forward of the fuel tank.

"We're waiting for a reply," Crawford said. "But I can sum up what they're going to say: not good. Unless one of you two has some experience in Mars-lander handling that you've been concealing from us."

Neither of them bothered to answer that. The radio in the nose sputtered, then clanged for their attention. Crawford looked over at Lang, who made no move to go answer it. He stood and swarmed up the ladder to sit in the copilot's chair. He switched on the receiver.

"Commander Lang?"

"No, this is Crawford again. Commander Lang is . . . indisposed. She's busy with Lou, trying to do something."

"That's no use. The doctor says it's a miracle he's still breathing. If he wakes up at all, he won't be anything like you knew him. The telemetry shows nothing like the normal brain wave. Now I've got to talk to Commander Lang. Have her come up." The voice of Mission Commander Weinstein was accustomed to command, and about as emotional as a weather report.

"Sir, I'll ask her, but I don't think she'll come. This is still her operation, you know." He didn't give Weinstein time to reply to that. Weinstein had been trapped by his own seniority into commanding the *Edgar Rice Burroughs,* the orbital ship that got them to Mars and had been intended to get them back. Command of the *Podkayne,* the disposable lander that would make the lion's share of the headlines, had gone to Lang. There was little friendship between the two, especially when Weinstein fell to brooding about the very real financial benefits Lang stood to reap by being the first woman on Mars, rather than the lowly mission commander. He saw himself as another Michael Collins.

Crawford called down to Lang, who raised her head enough to mumble something.

"What'd she say?"

"She said take a message." McKillian had been crawling up the ladder as she said this. Now she reached him and said in a lower voice, "Matt, she's pretty broken up. You'd better take over for now."

"Right, I know." He turned back to the radio, and McKillian listened over his shoulder as Weinstein briefed them on the situation as he saw it. It pretty much jibed with Crawford's estimation, except at one crucial point. He signed off and they joined the other survivors.

He looked around at the faces of the others and decided it wasn't the time to speak of rescue possibilities. He didn't relish being a leader. He was hoping Lang would recover soon and take the burden from him. In the meantime he had to get them started on something. He touched McKillian gently on the shoulder and motioned her to the lock.

"Let's go get them buried," he said. She squeezed her eyes shut, forcing out tears, then nodded.

It wasn't a pretty job. Halfway through it, Song came down the ladder with the body of Lou Prager.

* * *

"Let's go over what we've learned. First, now that Lou's dead there's very little chance of ever lifting off. That is, unless Mary thinks she can absorb everything she needs to know about piloting the *Podkayne* from those printouts Weinstein sent down. How about it, Mary?"

Mary Lang was lying sideways across the improvised cot that had recently held the *Podkayne* pilot, Lou Prager. Her head was nodding listlessly against the aluminum hull plate behind her; her chin was on her chest. Her eyes were half-open.

Song had given her a sedative from the dead doctor's supplies on the advice of the medic aboard the *E.R.B.* It had enabled her to stop fighting so hard against the screaming panic she wanted to unleash. It hadn't improved her disposition. She had quit, she wasn't going to do anything for anybody.

When the blowout started, Lang had snapped on her helmet quickly. Then she had struggled against the blizzard and the undulating dome bottom, heading for the roofless framework where the other members of the expedition were sleeping. The blowout was over in ten seconds, and she then had the problem of coping with the collapsing roof, which promptly buried her in folds of clear plastic. It was far too much like one of those nightmares of running knee-deep in quicksand. She had to fight for every meter, but she made it.

She made it in time to see her shipmates of the last six months gasping soundlessly and spouting blood from all over their faces as they fought to get into their pressure suits. It was a hopeless task to choose which two or three to save in the time she had. She might have done better but for the freakish nature of her struggle to reach them; she was in shock and half believed it was only a nightmare. So she grabbed the nearest, who happened to be Dr. Ralston. He had nearly finished donning his suit, so she slapped his helmet on him and moved to the next one. It was Luther Nakamura, and he was not moving. Worse, he was only half-suited. Pragmatically she should have left him and moved on to save the ones who still had a chance. She knew it now, but didn't like it any better than she had liked it then.

While she was stuffing Nakamura into his suit, Crawford arrived. He had walked over the folds of plastic until he reached the dormitory, then sliced through it with the laser he normally used to vaporize rock samples.

And he had had time to think about the problem of whom to save. He went straight to Lou Prager and finished suiting him up. But it was already too late. He didn't know if it would have made any difference if Mary Lang had tried to save him first.

Now she lay on the bunk, her feet sprawled carelessly in front of her. She slowly shook her head back and forth.

"You sure?" Crawford prodded her, hoping to get a rise, a show of temper, *anything.*

"I'm sure," she mumbled. "You people know how long they trained Lou to fly this thing? And he almost cracked it up as it was. I . . . ah, nuts. It isn't possible."

"I refuse to accept that as a final answer," he said. "But in the meantime we should explore the possibilities if what Mary says is true."

Ralston laughed. It wasn't a bitter laugh; he sounded genuinely amused. Crawford plowed on.

"Here's what we know for sure. The *E.R.B.* is useless to us. Oh, they'll help us out with plenty of advice, maybe more than we want, but any rescue is out of the question."

"We know that," McKillian said. She was tired and sick from the sight of the faces of her dead friends. "What's the use of all this talk?"

"Wait a moment," Song broke in. "Why can't they . . . I mean they have plenty of time, don't they? They have to leave in six months, as I understand it, because of the orbital elements, but in that time—"

"Don't you know anything about spaceships?" McKillian shouted. Song went on, unperturbed.

"I do know enough to know the *Edgar* is not equipped for an atmosphere entry. My idea was not to bring down the whole ship, but only what's aboard the ship that we need. Which is a pilot. Might that be possible?"

Crawford ran his hands through his hair, wondering what to say. That possibility had been discussed, and was being studied. But it had to be classed as extremely remote.

"You're right," he said. "What we need is a pilot, and that pilot is Commander Weinstein. Which presents problems legally, if nothing else. He's the captain of a ship and should not leave it. That's what kept him on the *Edgar* in the first place. But he did have a lot of training on the lander simulator back when he was so sure he'd be picked for the ground team. You know Winey, always the instinct to be the one-man show. So if he thought he could do it, he'd be down here in a minute to bail us out and grab the publicity. I understand they're trying to work out a heat-shield parachute system from one of the drop capsules that were supposed to ferry down supplies to us during the stay here. But it's very risky. You don't modify an aerodynamic design lightly, not one that's supposed to hit the atmosphere at ten-thousand-plus kilometers. So I think we can rule that out. They'll keep working on it, but when it's done, Winey won't step into the damn thing. He wants to be a hero, but he wants to live to enjoy it, too."

There had been a brief lifting of spirits among Song, Ralston, and McKillian at the thought of a possible rescue. The more they thought about it, the less happy they looked. They all seemed to agree with Crawford's assessment.

"So we'll put that one in the Fairy Godmother file and forget about it. If it happens, fine. But we'd better assume that it won't. As you may know, the *E.R.B.-Podkayne* are the only ships in existence that can reach Mars and land on it. One other pair is in the congressional funding stage. Winey talked to Earth and thinks there'll be a speedup in the preliminary paperwork and the thing'll start building in a year. The launch was scheduled for five years from now, but it might get as much as a year's boost. It's a rescue mission now, easier to sell. But the design will need modification, if only to include five more seats to bring us all back. You can bet on there being more modifications when we send in our report on the blowout. So we'd better add another six months to the schedule."

McKillian had had enough. "Matt, what the hell are you talking about? Rescue mission? Damn it, you know as well as I that if they find us here, we'll be long dead. We'll probably be dead in another year."

"That's where you're wrong. We'll survive."

"How?"

"I don't have the faintest idea." He looked her straight in the eye as he said this. She almost didn't bother to answer, but curiosity got the best of her.

"Is this just a morale session? Thanks, but I don't need it. I'd rather face the situation as it is. Or do you really have something?"

"Both. I don't have anything concrete except to say that we'll survive the same way humans have always survived: by staying warm, by eating, by drinking. To that list we have to add 'by breathing.' That's a hard one, but other than that we're no different than any other group of survivors in a tough spot. I don't know what we'll have to do, specifically, but I know we'll find the answers."

"Or die trying," Song said.

"Or die trying." He grinned at her. She at least had grasped the essence of the situation. Whether survival was possible or not, it was necessary to maintain the illusion that it was. Otherwise, you might as well cut your throat. You might as well not even be born, because life is an inevitably fatal struggle to survive.

"What about air?" McKillian asked, still unconvinced.

"I don't know," he told her cheerfully. "It's a tough problem, isn't it?"

"What about water?"

"Well, in that valley there's a layer of permafrost about twenty meters down."

She laughed. "Wonderful. So that's what you want us to do? Dig down there and warm the ice with our pink little hands? It won't work, I tell you."

Crawford waited until she had run through a long list of reasons why they were doomed. Most of them made a great deal of sense. When she was through, he spoke softly.

"Lucy, listen to yourself."

"I'm just—"

"You're arguing on the side of death. Do you want to die? Are you so determined that you won't listen to someone who says you can live?"

She was quiet for a long time, then shuffled her feet awkwardly. She glanced at
him, then at Song and Ralston. They were waiting, and she had to blush and smile
slowly at them.

"You're right. What do we do first?"

"Just what we were doing. Taking stock of our situation. We need to make a
list of what's available to us. We'll write it down on paper, but I can give you a general rundown." He counted off the points on his fingers.

"One, we have food for twenty people for three months. That comes to about
a year for the five of us. With rationing, maybe a year and a half. That's assuming
all the supply capsules reach us all right. In addition, the *Edgar* is going to clean the
pantry to the bone, give us everything they can possibly spare, and send it to us in
three spare capsules. That might come to two years, or even three.

"Two, we have enough water to last us forever if the recyclers keep going.
That'll be a problem, because our reactor will run out of power in two years. We'll
need another power source, and maybe another water source.

"The oxygen problem is about the same. Two years at the outside. We'll have to
find a way to conserve it a lot more than we're doing. Offhand, I don't know how.
Song, do you have any ideas?"

She looked thoughtful, which produced two vertical punctuation marks between her slanted eyes.

"Possibly a culture of plants from the *Edgar*. If we could rig some way to grow
plants in Martian sunlight and not have them killed by the ultraviolet . . ."

McKillian looked horrified, as any good ecologist would.

"What about contamination?" she asked. "What do you think that sterilization
was for before we landed? Do you want to louse up the entire ecological balance of
Mars? No one would ever be sure if samples in the future were real Martian plants
or mutated Earth stock."

"What ecological balance?" Song shot back. "You know as well as I do that this
trip has been nearly a zero. A few anaerobic bacteria, a patch of lichen, both barely
distinguishable from Earth forms—"

"That's just what I mean. You import Earth forms now, and we'll never tell the
difference."

"But it could be done, right? With the proper shielding so the plants won't
be wiped out before they ever sprout, we could have a hydroponics plant
functioning—"

"Oh, yes, it could be done. I can see three or four dodges right now. But you're
not addressing the main question, which is—"

"Hold it," Crawford said. "I just wanted to know if you had any ideas." He was secretly pleased at the argument; it got them both thinking along the right lines, moved them from the deadly apathy they must guard against.

"I think this discussion has served its purpose, which was to convince everyone here that survival is possible." He glanced uneasily at Lang, still nodding, her eyes glassy as she saw her teammates die before her eyes.

"I just want to point out that instead of an expedition, we are now a colony. Not in the usual sense of planning to stay here forever, but all our planning will have to be geared to that fiction. What we're faced with is not a simple matter of stretching supplies until rescue comes. Stopgap measures are not likely to do us much good. The answers that will save us are the long-term ones, the sort of answers a colony would be looking for. About two years from now we're going to have to be in a position to survive with some sort of life-style that could support us forever. We'll have to fit into this environment where we can and adapt it to us where we can't. For that, we're better off than most of the colonists of the past, at least for the short term. We have a large supply of everything a colony needs: food, water, tools, raw materials, energy, brains, and women. Without these things, no colony has much of a chance. All we lack is a regular resupply from the home country, but a really good group of colonists can get along without that. What do you say? Are you all with me?"

Something had caused Mary Lang's eyes to look up. It was a reflex by now, a survival reflex conditioned by a lifetime of fighting her way to the top. It took root in her again and pulled her erect on the bed, then to her feet. She fought off the effects of the drug and stood there, eyes bleary but aware.

"What makes you think that women are a natural resource, Crawford?" she said, slowly and deliberately.

"Why, what I meant was that without the morale uplift provided by members of the opposite sex, a colony will lack the push needed to make it."

"That's what you meant, all right. And you meant women, available to the *real* colonists as a reason to live. I've heard it before. That's male-oriented way to look at it, Crawford." She was regaining her stature as they watched, seeming to grow until she dominated the group with the intangible power that marks a leader. She took a deep breath and came fully awake for the first time that day.

"We'll stop that sort of thinking right now. I'm the mission commander. I appreciate your taking over while I was . . . how did you say it? Indisposed. But you should pay more attention to the social aspects of our situation. If anyone is a commodity here, it's you and Ralston, by virtue of your scarcity. There will be some thorny questions to resolve there, but for the meantime we will function as a unit, under my command. We'll do all we can to minimize social competition among the women for the men. That's the way it must be. Clear?"

She was answered by nods of the head. She did not acknowledge it but plowed right on.

"I wondered from the start why you were along, Crawford." She was pacing slowly back and forth in the crowded space. The others got out of her way almost without thinking, except for Ralston, who still huddled under his blanket. "A historian? Sure, it's a fine idea, but pretty impractical. I have to admit that I've been thinking of you as a luxury, and about as useful as the nipples on a man's chest. But I was wrong. All the NASA people were wrong. The Astronaut Corps fought like crazy to keep you off this trip. Time enough for that on later flights. We were blinded by our loyalty to the test-pilot philosophy of space flight. We wanted as few scientists as possible and as many astronauts as we could manage. We don't like to think of ourselves as ferry-boat pilots. I think we demonstrated during Apollo that we could handle science jobs as well as anyone. We saw you as a kind of insult, a slap in the face by the scientists in Houston to show us how low our stock had fallen."

"If I might be able to—"

"Shut up. But we were wrong. I read in your resume that you were quite a student of survival. What's your honest assessment of our chances?"

Crawford shrugged, uneasy at the question. He didn't know if it was the right time to even speculate that they might fail.

"Tell me the truth."

"Pretty slim. Mostly the air problem. The people I've read about never sank so low that they had to worry about where their next breath was coming from."

"Have you ever heard of Apollo Thirteen?"

He smiled at her. "Special circumstances. Short-term problems."

"You're right, of course. And in the only two other real space emergencies since that time, all hands were lost." She turned and scowled at each of them in turn.

"But we're *not* going to lose." She dared any of them to disagree, and no one was about to. She relaxed and resumed her stroll around the room. She turned to Crawford again.

"I can see I'll be drawing on your knowledge a lot in the years to come. What do you see as the next order of business?"

Crawford relaxed. The awful burden of responsibility, which he had never wanted, was gone. He was content to follow her lead.

"To tell you the truth, I was wondering what to say next. We have to make a thorough inventory. I guess we should start on that."

"That's fine, but there is an even more important order of business. We have to go out to the dome and find out what the hell caused the blowout. The damn thing should *not* have blown; it's the first of its type to do so. And from the *bottom*. But it did blow, and we should know why, or we're ignoring a fact about Mars that might still kill us. Let's do that first. Ralston, can you walk?"

When he nodded, she sealed her helmet and started into the lock. She turned and looked speculatively at Crawford.

"I swear, man, if you had touched me with a cattle prod you couldn't have got a bigger rise out of me than you did with what you said a few minutes ago. Do I dare ask?"

Crawford was not about to answer. He said, with a perfectly straight face, "Me? Maybe you should just assume I'm a chauvinist."

"We'll see, won't we?"

"What is that stuff?"

Song Sue Lee was on her knees, examining one of the hundreds of short, stiff spikes extruding from the ground. She tried to scratch her head but was frustrated by her helmet.

"It looks like plastic. But I have a strong feeling it's the higher life form Lucy and I were looking for yesterday."

"And you're telling me those little spikes are what poked holes in the dome bottom? I'm not buying that."

Song straightened up, moving stiffly. They had all worked hard to empty out the collapsed dome and peel back the whole, bulky mess to reveal the ground it had covered. She was tired and stepped out of character for a moment to snap at Mary Lang.

"I didn't tell you that. We pulled the dome back and found spikes. It was your inference that they poked holes in the bottom."

"I'm sorry," Lang said, quietly. "Go on with what you were saying."

"Well," Song admitted, "it wasn't a bad inference, at that. But the holes I saw were not punched through. They were eaten away." She waited for Lang to protest that the dome bottom was about as chemically inert as any plastic yet devised. But Lang had learned her lesson. And she had a talent for facing facts.

"So. We have a thing here that eats plastic. And seems to be made of plastic, into the bargain. Any ideas why it picked this particular spot to grow, and no other?"

"I have an idea on that," McKillian said. "I've had it in mind to do some studies around the dome to see if the altered moisture content we've been creating here had any effect on the spores in the soil. See, we've been here nine days, spouting out water vapor, carbon dioxide, and quite a bit of oxygen. Not much, but maybe more than it seems, considering the low concentrations that are naturally available. We've altered the biome. Does anyone know where the exhaust air from the dome was expelled?"

Lang raised her eyebrows. "Yes, it was under the dome. The air we exhausted was warm, you see, and it was thought it could be put to use one last time before we let it go, to warm the floor of the dome and decrease heat loss."

"And the water vapor collected on the underside of the dome when it hit the cold air. Right. Do you get the picture?"

"I think so," Lang said. "It was so little water, though. You know we didn't want to waste it; we condensed it out until the air we exhausted was dry as a bone."

"For Earth, maybe. Here it was a torrential rainfall. It reached seeds or spores in the ground and triggered them to start growing. We're going to have to watch it when we use anything containing plastic. What does that include?"

Lang groaned. "All the air lock seals, for one thing." There were grimaces from all of them at the thought of that. "For another, a good part of our suits. Song, watch it, don't step on that thing. We don't know how powerful it is or if it'll eat the plastic in your boots, but we'd better play it safe. How about it, Ralston? Think you can find out how bad it is?"

"You mean identify the solvent these things use? Probably, if we can get some sort of work space and I can get to my equipment."

"Mary," McKillian said, "it occurs to me that I'd better start looking for air-borne spores. If there are some, it could mean that the air lock on the *Podkayne* is vulnerable. Even thirty meters off the ground."

"Right. Get on that. Since we're sleeping in it until we can find out what we can do on the ground, we'd best be sure it's safe. Meantime, we'll all sleep in our suits." There were helpless groans at this, but no protests. McKillian and Ralston headed for the pile of salvaged equipment, hoping to rescue enough to get started on their analyses. Song knelt again and started digging around one of the ten-centimeter spikes.

Crawford followed Lang back toward the *Podkayne.*

"Mary, I wanted . . . Is it all right if I call you Mary?"

"I guess so. I don't think 'Commander Lang' would wear well over five years. But you'd better still *think* commander."

He considered it. "All right, Commander Mary." She punched him playfully. She had barely known him before the disaster. He had been a name on a roster, and a sore spot in the estimation of the Astronaut Corps. But she had borne him no personal malice, and now found herself beginning to like him.

"What's on your mind?"

"Ah, several things. But maybe it isn't my place to bring them up now. First, I want to say that if you're . . . ah, concerned, or doubtful of my support or loyalty because I took over command for a while . . . earlier today, well . . ."

"Well?"

"I just wanted to tell you that I have no ambitions in that direction," he finished lamely.

She patted him on the back. "Sure, I know. You forget, I read your dossier. It mentioned several interesting episodes that I'd like you to tell me about someday, from your 'soldier-of-fortune' days—"

"Hell, those were grossly overblown. I just happened to get into some scrapes and managed to get out of them."

"Still, it got you picked for this mission out of hundreds of applicants. The thinking was that you'd be a wild card, a man of action with proven survivability. Maybe it worked out. But the other thing I remember on your card was that you're not a leader, that you're a loner who'll cooperate with a group and be no discipline problem, but you work better alone. Want to strike out on your own?"

He smiled at her. "No, thanks. But what you said is right. I have no hankering to take charge of anything. But I do have some knowledge that might prove useful."

"And we'll use it. You just speak up. I'll be listening." She started to say something, then thought of something else. "Say, what are your ideas on a woman bossing this project? I've had to fight that all the way from my Air Force days. So if you have any objections you might as well tell me up front."

He was genuinely surprised. "You didn't take that crack seriously, did you? I might as well admit it. It was intentional, like that cattle prod you mentioned. You looked like you needed a kick in the ass."

"And thank you. But you didn't answer my question."

"Those who lead, lead," he said, simply. "I'll follow you as long as you keep leading."

"As long as it's in the direction you want?" She laughed, and poked him in the ribs. "I see you as my grand vizier, the man who holds the arcane knowledge and advises the regent. I think I'll have to watch out for you. I know a little history myself."

Crawford couldn't tell how serious she was. He shrugged it off.

"What I really wanted to talk to you about is this: you said you couldn't fly this ship. But you were not yourself, you were depressed and feeling hopeless. Does that still stand?"

"It stands. Come on up and I'll show you why."

In the pilot's cabin, Crawford was ready to believe her. Like all flying machines since the days of the wind sock and open cockpit, this one was a mad confusion of dials, switches, and lights, designed to awe anyone who knew nothing about it. He sat in the copilot's chair and listened to her.

"We had a backup pilot, of course. You may be surprised to learn that it wasn't me. It was Dorothy Cantrell, and she's dead. Now I know what everything does on this board, and I can cope with most of it easily. What I don't know, I could learn. Some of the systems are computer-driven; give it the right program and it'll fly itself, in space." She looked longingly at the controls, and Crawford realized that, like Weinstein, she didn't relish giving up the fun of flying to boss a gang of explorers. She was a former test pilot, and above all things she loved flying. She patted an array of hand controls on her right side. There were more like them on the left.

"This is what would kill us, Crawford. What's your first name? Matt. Matt, this baby is a flyer for the first forty thousand meters. It doesn't have the juice to orbit on the jets alone. The wings are folded up now. You probably didn't see them on the way in, but you saw the models. They're very light, supercritical, and designed for this atmosphere. Lou said it was like flying a bathtub, but it flew. And it's a *skill,* almost an art. Lou practiced for three years on the best simulators we could build and still had to rely on things you can't learn in a simulator. And he barely got us down in one piece. We didn't noise it around, but it was a *damn* close thing. Lou was young; so was Cantrell. They were both fresh from flying. They flew every day, they had the *feel* for it. They were tops." She slumped back into her chair. "I haven't flown anything but trainers for eight years."

Crawford didn't know if he should let it drop.

"But you were one of the best. Everyone knows that. You still don't think you could do it?"

She threw up her hands. "How can I make you understand? This is nothing like anything I've ever flown. You might as well . . ." She groped for a comparison, trying to coax it out with gestures in the air. "Listen. Does the fact that someone can fly a biplane, maybe even be the best goddam biplane pilot that ever was, does that mean they're qualified to fly a helicopter?"

"I don't know."

"It doesn't. Believe me."

"All right. But the fact remains that you're the closest thing on Mars to a pilot for the *Podkayne.* I think you should consider that when you're deciding what we should do." He shut up, afraid to sound like he was pushing her.

She narrowed her eyes and gazed at nothing.

"I have thought about it." She waited for a long time. "I think the chances are about a thousand to one against us if I try to fly it. But I'll do it, if we come to that. And that's *your* job. Showing me some better odds. If you can't, let me know."

Three weeks later, the Tharsis Canyon had been transformed into a child's garden of toys. Crawford had thought of no better way to describe it. Each of the plastic spikes had blossomed into a fanciful windmill, no two of them just alike. There were tiny ones, with the vanes parallel to the ground and no more than ten centimeters tall. There were derricks of spidery plastic struts that would not have looked too out of place on a Kansas farm. Some of them were five meters high. They came in all colors and many configurations, but all had vanes covered with a transparent film like cellophane, and all were spinning into colorful blurs in the stiff Martian breeze. Crawford thought of an industrial park built by gnomes. He could almost see them trudging through the spinning wheels.

Song had taken one apart as well as she could. She was still shaking her head in disbelief. She had not been able to excavate the long, insulated taproot, but she could infer how deep it went. It extended all the way down to the layer of permafrost, twenty meters down.

The ground between the windmills was coated in shimmering plastic. This was the second part of the plants' ingenious solution to survival on Mars. The windmills utilized the energy in the wind, and the plastic coating on the ground was in reality two thin sheets of plastic with a space between for water to circulate. The water was heated by the sun then pumped down to the permafrost, melting a little more of it each time.

"There's still something missing from our picture," Song had told them the night before when she delivered her summary of what she had learned. "Marty hasn't been able to find a mechanism that would permit these things to grow by ingesting sand and rock and turning it into plasticlike materials. So we assume there is a reservoir of something like crude oil down there, maybe frozen in with the water."

"Where would that have come from?" Lang had asked.

"You've heard of the long-period Martian seasonal theories? Well, part of it is more than a theory. The combination of the Martian polar inclination, the precessional cycle, and the eccentricity of the orbit produces seasons that are about twelve thousand years long. We're in the middle of winter, though we landed in the nominal 'summer.' It's been theorized that if there were any Martian life, it would have adapted to these longer cycles. It hibernates in spores during the cold cycle, when the water and carbon dioxide freeze out at the poles, then comes out when enough ice melts to permit biological processes. We seem to have fooled these plants; they thought summer was here when the water vapor content went up around the camp."

"So what about the crude?" Ralston asked. He didn't completely believe that part of the model they had evolved. He was a laboratory chemist, specializing in inorganic compounds. The way these plants produced plastics without high heat, through purely catalytic interactions, had him confused and defensive. He wished the crazy windmills would go away.

"I think I can answer that," McKillian said. "These organisms barely scrape by in the best of times. The ones that have made it waste nothing. It stands to reason that any really ancient deposits of crude oil would have been exhausted in only a few of these cycles. So it must be that what we're thinking of as crude oil must be something a little different. It has to be the remains of the last generation."

"But how did the remains get so far below ground?" Ralston asked. "You'd expect them to be high up. The winds couldn't bury them that deep in only twelve thousand years."

"You're right," said McKillian. "I don't really know. But I have a theory. Since these plants waste nothing, why not conserve their bodies when they die? They sprouted from the ground; isn't it possible they could withdraw when things start to get tough again? They'd leave spores behind them as they retreated, distributing them all through the soil. That way, if the upper ones blew away or were sterilized by the untraviolet, the ones just below them would still thrive when the right conditions returned. When they reached the permafrost, they'd decompose into this organic slush we've postulated, and . . . well, it does get a little involved, doesn't it?"

"Sounds all right to me," Lang assured her. "It'll do for a working theory. Now what about airborne spores?"

It turned out that they were safe from that danger. There were spores in the air now, but they were not dangerous to the colonists. The plants attacked only certain kinds of plastics, and then only in certain stages of their lives. Since they were still changing, it bore watching, but the air locks and suits were secure. The crew was enjoying the luxury of sleeping without their suits.

And there was much work to do. Most of the physical sort devolved on Crawford and, to some extent, on Lang. It threw them together a lot. The other three had to be free to pursue their researches, as it had been decided that only in knowing their environment would they stand a chance.

Crawford and Lang had managed to salvage most of the dome. Working with patching kits and lasers to cut the tough material, they had constructed a much smaller dome. They erected it on an outcropping of bare rock, rearranged the exhaust to prevent more condensation on the underside, and added more safety features. They now slept in a pressurized building inside the dome, and one of them stayed awake on watch at all times. In drills, they had come from a deep sleep to full pressure integrity in thirty seconds. They were not going to get caught again.

Crawford looked away from the madly whirling rotors of the windmill farm. He was with the rest of the crew, sitting in the dome with his helmet off. That was as far as Lang would permit anyone to go except in the cramped sleeping quarters. Song Sue Lee was at the radio giving her report to the *Edgar Rice Burroughs.* In her hand was one of the pump modules she had dissected out of one of the plants. It consisted of a half-meter set of eight blades that turned freely on teflon bearings. Below it were various tiny gears and the pump itself. She twirled it idly as she spoke.

"I don't really get it," Crawford admitted, talking quietly to Lucy McKillian. "What's so revolutionary about little windmills?"

"It's just a whole new area," McKillian whispered back. "Think about it. Back on Earth, nature never got around to inventing the wheel. I've sometimes wondered why not. There are limitations, of course, but it's such a good idea. Just look what *we've* done with it. But all motion in nature is confined to up and down, back and forth, in and out, or squeeze and relax. Nothing on Earth goes round and round, unless we built it. Think about it."

Crawford did, and began to see the novelty of it. He tried in vain to think of some mechanism in an animal or plant of Earthly origin that turned and kept on turning forever. He could not.

Song finished her report and handed the mike to Lang. Before she could start, Weinstein came on the line.

"We've had a change in plan up here," he said, with no preface. "I hope this doesn't come as a shock. If you think about it, you'll see the logic in it. We're going back to Earth in seven days."

It didn't surprise them too much. The *Burroughs* had given them just about everything it could in the form of data and supplies. There was one more capsule load due; after that, its presence would only be a frustration to both groups. There was a great deal of irony in having two such powerful ships so close to each other and so helpless to do anything concrete. It was telling on the crew of the *Burroughs*.

"We've recalculated everything based on the lower mass without the twenty of you and the six tons of samples we were allowing for. By using the fuel we would have ferried down to you for takeoff, we can make a faster orbit down toward Venus. The departure date for that orbit is seven days away. We'll rendezvous with a drone capsule full of supplies we hadn't counted on." And besides, Lang thought to herself, it's much more dramatic. *Plunging sunward on the chancy cometary orbit, their pantries stripped bare, heading for the fateful rendezvous . . .*

"I'd like your comments," he went on. "This isn't absolutely final yet."

They all looked at Lang. They were reassured to find her calm and unshaken.

"I think it's the best idea. One thing; you've given up on any thoughts of me flying the *Podkayne*?"

"No insult intended, Mary," Weinstein said, gently. "But, yes, we have. It's the opinion of the people Earthside that you couldn't do it. They've tried some experiments, coaching some very good pilots and putting them into the simulators. They can't do it, and we don't think you could, either."

"No need to sugarcoat it. I know it as well as anyone. But even a billion-to-one shot is better than nothing. I take it they think Crawford is right, that survival is at least theoretically possible?"

There was a long hesitation. "I guess that's correct. Mary, I'll be frank. I don't think it's possible. I hope I'm wrong, but I don't expect—"

"Thank you, Winey, for the encouraging words. You always did know what it takes to buck a person up. By the way, that other mission, the one where you were going to ride a meteorite down here to save our asses, that's scrubbed, too?"

The assembled crew smiled, and Song gave a high-pitched cheer. Weinstein was not the most popular man on Mars.

"Mary, I told you about that already," he complained. It was a gentle complaint, and, even more significant, he had not objected to the use of his nickname. He was being gentle with the condemned. "We worked on it around the clock. I even managed to get permission to turn over command temporarily. But the mock-ups they made Earthside didn't survive the reentry. It was the best we could do. I couldn't risk the entire mission on a configuration the people back on Earth wouldn't certify."

"I know. I'll call you back tomorrow." She switched the set off and sat back on her heels. "I swear, if the Earthside tests on a roll of toilet paper didn't . . . He wouldn't . . ." She cut the air with her hands. "What am I saying? That's petty. I don't like him, but he's right." She stood up, puffing out her cheeks as she exhaled a pent-up breath.

"Come on, crew, we've got a lot of work."

They named their colony New Amsterdam, because of the windmills. The name whirligig was the one that stuck on the Martian plants, though Crawford held out for a long time in favor of spinnaker.

They worked all day and tried their best to ignore the *Burroughs* overhead. The messages back and forth were short and to the point. Helpless as the mother ship was to render them more aid, they knew they would miss it when it was gone. So the day of departure was a stiff, determinedly nonchalant affair. They all made a big show of going to bed hours before the scheduled breakaway.

When he was sure the others were asleep, Crawford opened his eyes and looked around the darkened barracks. It wasn't much in the way of a home; they were crowded against each other on rough pads made of insulating material. The toilet facilities were behind a flimsy barrier against one wall, and smelled. But none of them would have wanted to sleep outside in the dome, even if Lang had allowed it.

The only light came from the illuminated dials that the guard was supposed to watch all night. There was no one sitting in front of them. Crawford assumed the guard had gone to sleep. He would have been upset, but there was no time. He had to suit up, and he welcomed the chance to sneak out. He began furtively to don his pressure suit.

As a historian, he felt he could not let such a moment slip by unobserved. Silly, but there it was. He had to be out there, watch it with his own eyes. It didn't matter if he never lived to tell about it; he must record it.

Someone sat up beside him. He froze, but it was too late. She rubbed her eyes and peered into the darkness.

"Matt?" she yawned. "What's . . . what is it? Is something—"

"Shh. I'm going out. Go back to sleep. Song?"

"Um hmmm." She stretched, dug her knuckles fiercely into her eyes, and smoothed her hair back from her face. She was dressed in a loose-fitting ship suit, a gray piece of dirty cloth that badly needed washing, as did all their clothes. For a moment, as he watched her shadow stretch and stand up, he wasn't interested in the *Burroughs*. He forced his mind away from her.

"I'm going with you," she whispered.

"All right. Don't wake the others."

Standing just outside the air lock was Mary Lang. She turned as they came out, and did not seem surprised.

"Were you the one on duty?" Crawford asked her.

"Yeah. I broke my own rule. But so did you two. Consider yourselves on report." She laughed and beckoned them over to her. They linked arms and stood staring up at the sky.

"How much longer?" Song asked, after some time had passed.

"Just a few minutes. Hold tight." Crawford looked over to Lang and thought he saw tears, but he couldn't be sure in the dark.

There was a tiny new star, brighter than all the rest, brighter than Phobos. It hurt to look at it, but none of them looked away. It was the fusion drive of the *Edgar Rice Burroughs,* heading sunward, away from the long winter on Mars. It stayed on for long minutes, then sputtered and was lost. Though it was warm in the dome, Crawford was shivering. It was ten minutes before any of them felt like facing the barracks.

They crowded into the air lock, carefully not looking at each other's faces as they waited for the automatic machinery. The inner door opened and Lang pushed forward—and right back into the air lock. Crawford had a glimpse of Ralston and Lucy McKillian; then Mary shut the door.

"Some people have no poetry in their souls," Mary said.

"Or too much," Song giggled.

"You people want to take a walk around the dome with me? Maybe we could discuss ways of giving people a little privacy."

The inner lock door was pulled open, and there was McKillian, squinting into the bare bulb that lighted the lock while she held her shirt in front of her with one hand.

"Come on in," she said, stepping back. "We might as well talk about this." They entered, and McKillian turned on the light and sat down on her mattress. Ralston was blinking, nervously tucked into his pile of blankets. Since the day of the blowout he never seemed to be warm enough.

Having called for a discussion, McKillian proceeded to clam up. Song and Crawford sat on their bunks, and eventually, as the silence stretched tighter, they all found themselves looking to Lang.

She started stripping out of her suit. "Well, I guess that takes care of that. So glad to hear all your comments. Lucy, if you were expecting some sort of reprimand, forget it. We'll take steps first thing in the morning to provide some sort of privacy for that, but, no matter what, we'll all be pretty close in the years to come. I think we should all relax. Any objections?" She was half out of her suit when she paused to scan them for comments. There were none. She stripped to her skin and reached for the light.

"In a way it's about time," she said, tossing her clothes in a corner. "The only thing to do with these clothes is burn them. We'll all smell better for it. Song, you take the watch." She flicked out the lights and reclined heavily on her mattress.

There was much rustling and squirming for the next few minutes as they got out of their clothes. Song brushed against Crawford in the dark and they murmured apologies. Then they all bedded down in their own bunks. It was several tense, miserable hours before anyone got to sleep.

The week following the departure of the *Burroughs* was one of hysterical overreaction by the New Amsterdamites. The atmosphere was forced and false; an eat-drink-and-be-merry feeling pervaded everything they did.

They built a separate shelter inside the dome, not really talking aloud about what it was for. But it did not lack for use. Productive work suffered as the five of them frantically ran through all the possible permutations of three women and two men. Animosities developed, flourished for a few hours, and dissolved in tearful reconciliations. Three ganged up on two, two on one, one declared war on all the other four. Ralston and Song announced an engagement, which lasted ten hours. Crawford nearly came to blows with Lang, aided by McKillian. McKillian renounced men forever and had a brief, tempestuous affair with Song. Then Song discovered McKillian with Ralston, and Crawford caught her on the rebound, only to be thrown over for Ralston.

Mary Lang let it work itself out, only interfering when it got violent. She herself was not immune to the frenzy but managed to stay aloof from most of it. She went to the shelter with whoever asked her, trying not to play favorites, and gently tried to prod them back to work. As she told McKillian toward the end of the week, "At least we're getting to know one another."

Things did settle down, as Lang had known they would. They entered their second week alone in virtually the same position they had been in when they started: no romantic entanglements firmly established. But they knew each other a lot better, were relaxed in the close company of each other, and were supported by a new framework of friendships. They were much closer to being a team. Rivalries never died out completely, but they no longer dominated the colony. Lang worked them harder than ever, making up for the lost time.

Crawford missed most of the interesting work, being more suited for the semiskilled manual labor that never seemed to be finished. So he and Lang had to learn about the new discoveries at the nightly briefings in the shelter. He remembered nothing about any animal life being discovered, and so when he saw something crawling through the whirligig garden, he dropped everything and started toward it.

At the edge of the garden he stopped, remembering the order from Lang to stay out unless collecting samples. He watched the thing—bug? turtle?—for a moment, satisfied himself that it wouldn't get too far away at its creeping pace, and hurried off to find Song.

"You've got to name it after me," he said as they hurried back to the garden. "That's my right, isn't it, as the discoverer?"

"Sure," Song said, peering along his pointed finger. "Just show me the damn thing and I'll immortalize you."

The thing was twenty centimeters long, almost round, dome-shaped. It had a hard shell on top.

"I don't know quite what to do with it," Song admitted. "If it's the only one, I don't dare dissect it, and maybe I shouldn't even touch it."

"Don't worry, there's another over behind you." Now that they were looking for them, they quickly spied four of the creatures. Song took a sample bag from her pouch and held it open in front of the beast. It crawled halfway into the bag, then seemed to think something was wrong. It stopped, but Song nudged it in and picked it up. She peered at the underside and laughed in wonder.

"Wheels," she said. "The thing runs on wheels."

"I don't know where it came from," Song told the group that night. "I don't even quite believe in it. It'd make a nice educational toy for a child, though. I took it apart into twenty or thirty pieces, put it back together, and it still runs. It has a high-impact polystyrene carapace, non-toxic paint on the outside—"

"Not really polystyrene," Ralston interjected.

"... and I guess if you kept changing the batteries it would run forever. And it's *nearly* polystyrene, that's what you said."

"Were you serious about the batteries?" Lang asked.

"I'm not sure. Marty thinks there's a chemical metabolism in the upper part of the shell, which I haven't explored yet. But I can't really say if it's alive in the sense we use. I mean, it runs on *wheels!* It has three wheels, suited for sand, and something that's a cross between a rubber-band drive and a mainspring. Energy is stored in a coiled muscle and released slowly. I don't think it could travel more than a hundred meters. Unless it can re-coil the muscle, and I can't tell how that might be done."

"It sounds very specialized," McKillian said thoughtfully. "Maybe we should be looking for the niche it occupies. The way you describe it, it couldn't function without help from a symbiote. Maybe it fertilizes the plants, like bees, and the plants either donate or are robbed of the power to wind the spring. Did you look for some mechanism the bug could use to steal energy from the rotating gears in the whirligigs?"

"That's what I want to do in the morning," Song said. "Unless Mary will let us take a look tonight?" She said it hopefully, but without real expectation. Mary Lang shook her head decisively.

"It'll keep. It's *cold* out there, baby."

A new exploration of the whirligig garden the next day revealed several new species, including one more thing that might be an animal. It was a flying creature, the size of a fruit fly, that managed to glide from plant to plant when the wind was down by means of a freely rotating set of blades, like an autogiro.

Crawford and Lang hung around as the scientists looked things over. They were not anxious to get back to the task that had occupied them for the last two weeks: bringing the *Podkayne* to a horizontal position without wrecking her. The ship had been rigged with stabilizing cables soon after landing, and provision had been made in the plans to lay the ship on its side in the event of a really big windstorm. But the plans had envisioned a work force of twenty, working all day with a maze of pulleys and gears. It was slow work and could not be rushed. If the ship were to tumble and lose pressure, they didn't have a prayer.

So they welcomed an opportunity to tour fairyland. The place was even more bountiful than the last time Crawford had taken a look. There were thick vines that Song assured him were running with water, hot and cold, and various other fluids. There were more of the tall variety of derrick, making the place look like a pastel oil field.

They had little trouble finding where the matthews came from. They found dozens of twenty-centimeter lumps on the sides of the large derricks. They evidently grew from them like tumors and were released when they were ripe. What they were for was another matter. As well as they could discover, the matthews simply crawled in a straight line until their power ran out. If they were wound up again, they would crawl further. There were dozens of them lying motionless in the sand within a hundred-meter radius of the garden.

Two weeks of research left them knowing no more. They had to abandon the matthews for the time, as another enigma had cropped up which demanded their attention.

This time Crawford was the last to know. He was called on the radio and found the group all squatting in a circle around a growth in the graveyard.

The graveyard, where they had buried their fifteen dead crewmates on the first day of the disaster, had sprouted with life during the week after the departure of the *Burroughs*. It was separated from the original site of the dome by three hundred meters of blowing sand. So McKillian assumed this second bloom was caused by the water in the bodies of the dead. What they couldn't figure out was why this patch should differ so radically from the first one.

There were whirligigs in the second patch, but they lacked the variety and disorder of the originals. They were of nearly uniform size, about four meters tall, and all the same color, dark purple. They had pumped water for two weeks, then stopped. When Song examined them, she reported the bearings were frozen, dried out. They seemed to have lost the plasticizer that kept the structures fluid and living. The water in the pipes was frozen. Though she would not commit herself in the matter, she felt they were dead. In their place was a second network of pipes which wound around the derricks and spread transparent sheets of film to the sunlight, heating the water which circulated through them. The water was being pumped, but not by the now-familiar system of windmills. Spaced along each of the pipes were expansion-contraction pumps with valves very like those in a human heart.

The new marvel was a simple affair in the middle of that living petrochemical complex. It was a short plant that sprouted up half a meter, then extruded two stalks parallel to the ground. At the end of each stalk was a perfect globe, one gray, one blue. The blue one was much larger than the gray one.

Crawford looked at it briefly, then squatted down beside the rest, wondering what all the fuss was about. Everyone looked very solemn, almost scared.

"You called me over to see this?"

Lang looked at him, and something in her face made him nervous.

"Look at it, Matt. Really look at it." So he did, feeling foolish, wondering what the joke was. He noticed a white patch near the top of the largest globe. It was streaked, like a glass marble with swirls of opaque material in it. It looked *very* familiar, he realized, with the hair on the back of his neck starting to stand up.

"It turns," Lang said quietly. "That's why Song noticed it. She came by here one day and it was in a different position than it had been."

"Let me guess," he said, much more calmly than he felt. "The little one goes around the big one, right?"

"Right. And the little one keeps one face turned to the big one. The big one rotates once in twenty-four hours. It has an axial tilt of twenty-three degrees."

"It's a . . . what's the word? Orrery. It's an orrery." Crawford had to stand up and shake his head to clear it.

"It's funny," Lang said, quietly. "I always thought it would be something flashy, or at least obvious. An alien artifact mixed in with caveman bones, or a spaceship entering the system. I guess I was thinking in terms of pottery shards and atom bombs."

"Well, that all sounds pretty ho-hum to me up against *this*," Song said. "Do you . . . do you *realize* . . . what are we talking about here? Evolution, or . . . or engineering? Is it the plants themselves that did this, or were they made to do it by whatever built them? Do you see what I'm talking about? I've felt funny about those wheels for a long time. I just won't believe they'd evolve naturally."

"What do you mean?"

"I mean I think these plants we've been seeing were designed to be the way they are. They're *too* perfectly adapted, *too* ingenious to have just sprung up in response to the environment." Her eyes seemed to wander, and she stood up and gazed into the valley below them. It was as barren as anything that could be imagined: red and yellow and brown rock outcroppings and tumbled boulders. And in the foreground, the twirling colors of the whirligigs.

"But why this thing?" Crawford asked, pointing to the impossible artifact-plant. "Why a model of the Earth and Moon? And why right here, in the graveyard?"

"Because we were expected," Song said, still looking away from them. "They must have watched Earth, during the last summer season. I don't know; maybe they even went there. If they did, they would have found men and women like us, hunting and living in caves. Building fires, using clubs, chipping arrowheads. You know more about it than I do, Matt."

"Who are *they*?" Ralston asked. "You think we're going to be meeting some Martians? People? I don't see how. I don't believe it."

"I'm afraid I'm skeptical, too," Lang said. "Surely there must be some other way to explain it."

"No! There's no other way. Oh, not people like us, maybe. Maybe we're seeing them right now, spinning like crazy." They all looked uneasily at the whirligigs. "But I think they're not here yet. I think we're going to see, over the next few years, increasing complexity in these plants and animals as they build up a biome here and get ready for the builders. Think about it. When summer comes, the conditions will be very different. The atmosphere will be almost as dense as ours, with about the same partial pressure of oxygen. By then, thousands of years from now, these early forms will have vanished. These things are adapted for low pressure, no oxygen, scarce water. The later ones will be adapted to an environment much like ours. And *that's* when we'll see the makers, when the stage is properly set." She sounded almost religious when she said it.

Lang stood up and shook Song's shoulder. Song came slowly back to them and sat down, still blinded by a private vision. Crawford had a glimpse of it himself, and it scared him. And a glimpse of something else, something that could be important but kept eluding him.

"Don't you see?" she went on, calmer, now. "It's too pat, too much of a coincidence. This thing is like a . . . a headstone, a monument. It's growing right here in the graveyard, from the bodies of our friends. Can you believe in that as just a coincidence?"

Evidently no one could. But at the same time Crawford could see no reason why it should have happened the way it did.

It was painful to leave the mystery for later, but there was nothing to be done about it. They could not bring themselves to uproot the thing, even when five more like it sprouted in the graveyard. There was a new consensus among them to leave the Martian plants and animals alone. Like nervous atheists, most of them didn't believe Song's theories but had an uneasy feeling of trespassing when they went through the gardens. They felt subconsciously that it might be better to leave them alone in case they turned out to be private property.

And for six months, nothing really new cropped up among the whirligigs. Song was not surprised. She said it supported her theory that these plants were there only as caretakers to prepare the way for the less hardy, air-breathing varieties to come. They would warm the soil and bring the water closer to the surface, then disappear when their function was over.

The three scientists allowed their studies to slide as it became more important to provide for the needs of the moment. The dome material was weakening as the temporary patches lost strength, so a new home was badly needed. They were dealing daily with slow leaks, any of which could become a major blowout.

The *Podkayne* was lowered to the ground, and sadly decommissioned. It was a bad day for Mary Lang, the worst since the day of the blowout. She saw it as a necessary but infamous thing to do to a proud flying machine. She brooded about it for a week, becoming short-tempered and almost unapproachable. Then she asked Crawford to join her in the private shelter. It was the first time she had asked any of the other four. They lay in each other's arms for an hour, and Lang quietly sobbed on his chest. Crawford was proud that she had chosen him for her companion when she could no longer maintain her tough, competent show of strength. In a way, it was a strong thing to do, to expose weakness to the one person among the four who might possibly be her rival for leadership. He did not betray the trust. In the end, she was comforting him.

After that day Lang was ruthless in gutting the old *Podkayne*. She supervised the ripping out of the motors to provide more living space, and only Crawford saw what it was costing her. They drained the fuel tanks and stored the fuel in every available container they could scrounge. It would be useful later for heating and for recharging batteries. They managed to convert plastic packing crates into fuel containers by lining them with sheets of the double-walled material the whirligigs used to heat water. They were nervous at this vandalism, but had no other choice. They kept looking nervously at the graveyard as they ripped up meter-square sheets of it.

They ended up with a long cylindrical home, divided into two small sleeping rooms, a community room, and a laboratory-storehouse-workshop in the old fuel tank. Crawford and Lang spent the first night together in the "penthouse," the former cockpit, the only room with windows.

Lying there wide awake on the rough mattress, side by side in the warm air with Mary Lang, whose black leg was a crooked line of shadow lying across his body; looking up through the port at the sharp, unwinking stars—with nothing done yet about the problems of oxygen, food, and water for the years ahead and no assurance he would live out the night on a planet determined to kill him—Crawford realized he had never been happier in his life.

On a day exactly eight months after the disaster, two discoveries were made. One was in the whirligig garden and concerned a new plant that was bearing what might be fruit. They were clusters of grape-sized white balls, very hard and fairly heavy. The second discovery was made by Lucy McKillian and concerned the absence of an event that up to that time had been as regular as the full moon.

"I'm pregnant," she announced to them that night, causing Song to delay her examination of the white fruit.

It was not unexpected; Lang had been waiting for it to happen since the night the *Burroughs* left. But she had not worried about it. Now she must decide what to do.

"I was afraid that might happen," Crawford said. "What do we do, Mary?"

"Why don't you tell me what you think? You're the survival expert. Are babies a plus or a minus in our situation?"

"I'm afraid I have to say they're a liability. Lucy will be needing extra food during her pregnancy, and afterward, and it will be an extra mouth to feed. We can't afford the strain on our resources." Lang said nothing, waiting to hear from McKillian.

"Now wait a minute. What about all this line about 'colonists' you've been feeding us ever since we got stranded here? Who ever heard of a colony without babies? If we don't grow, we stagnate, right? We *have* to have children." She looked back and forth from Lang to Crawford, her face expressing formless doubts.

"We're in special circumstances, Lucy," Crawford explained. "Sure, I'd be all for it if we were better off. But we can't be sure we can even provide for ourselves, much less a child. I say we can't afford children until we're established."

"Do you want the child, Lucy?" Lang asked quietly.

McKillian didn't seem to know what she wanted. "No. I . . . but, yes. Yes, I guess I do." She looked at them, pleading for them to understand.

"Look, I've never had one, and never planned to. I'm thirty-four years old and never, never felt the lack. I've always wanted to go places, and you can't with a baby. But I never planned to become a colonist on Mars, either. I . . . Things have changed, don't you see? I've been depressed. She looked around, and Song and Ralston were nodding sympathetically. Relieved to see that she was not the only one feeling the oppression, she went on, more strongly. "I think if I go another day like yesterday and the day before—and today—I'll end up screaming. It seems so pointless, collecting all that information, for what?"

"I agree with Lucy," Ralston said, surprisingly. Crawford had thought he would be the only one immune to the inevitable despair of the castaway. Ralston in his laboratory was the picture of carefree detachment, existing only to observe.

"So do I," Lang said, ending the discussion. But she explained her reasons to them.

"Look at it this way, Matt. No matter how we stretch our supplies, they won't take us through the next four years. We either find a way of getting what we need from what's around us, or we all die. And if we find a way to do it, then what does it matter how many of us there are? At the most this will push our deadline a few weeks or a month closer, the day we have to be self-supporting."

"I hadn't thought of it that way," Crawford admitted.

"But that's not important. The important thing is what you said from the first, and I'm surprised you didn't see it. If we're a colony, we expand. By definition. Historian, what happened to colonies that failed to expand?"

"Don't rub it in."

"They died out. I know that much. People, we're not intrepid space explorers anymore. We're not the career men and women we set out to be. Like it or not, and I suggest we start liking it, we're pioneers trying to live in a hostile environment. The odds are very much against us, and we're not going to be here forever, but like Matt said, we'd better plan as if we were. Comment?"

There was none, until Song spoke up, thoughtfully.

"I think a baby around here would be fun. Two should be twice as much fun. I think I'll start. Come on, Marty."

"Hold on, honey," Lang said, dryly. "If you conceive now, I'll be forced to order you to abort. We have the chemicals for it, you know."

"That's discrimination."

"Maybe so. But just because we're colonists doesn't mean we have to behave like rabbits. A pregnant woman will have to be removed from the work force at the end of her term, and we can only afford one at a time. After Lucy has hers, then come ask me again. But watch Lucy carefully, dear. Have you really thought what it's going to take? Have you tried to visualize her getting into her pressure suit in six or seven months?"

From their expressions, it was plain that neither Song nor McKillian had thought of it.

"Right," Lang went on. "It'll be literal confinement for her, right here in the *Poddy*. Unless we can rig something for her, which I seriously doubt. Still want to go through with it, Lucy?"

"Can I have a while to think it over?"

"Sure. You have about two months. After that, the chemicals aren't safe."

"I'd advise you to do it," Crawford said. "I know my opinion means nothing after shooting my mouth off. I know I'm a fine one to talk; I won't be cooped up in here. But the colony needs it. We've all felt it: the lack of a direction or a drive to keep going. I think we'd get it back if you went through with this."

McKillian tapped her teeth thoughtfully with the tip of a finger.

"You're right," she said. "Your opinion *doesn't* mean anything." She slapped his knee delightedly when she saw him blush. "I think it's yours, by the way. And I think I'll go ahead and have it."

The penthouse seemed to have gone to Lang and Crawford as an unasked-for prerogative. It just became a habit, since they seemed to have developed a bond between them and none of the other three complained. Neither of the other women seemed to be suffering in any way. So Lang left it at that. What went on between the three of them was of no concern to her as long as it stayed happy.

Lang was leaning back in Crawford's arms, trying to decide if she wanted to make love again, when a gunshot rang out in the *Podkayne*.

She had given a lot of thought to the last emergency, which she still saw as partly a result of her lag in responding. This time she was through the door almost before the reverberations had died down, leaving Crawford to nurse the leg she had stepped on in her haste.

She was in time to see McKillian and Ralston hurrying into the lab at the back of the ship. There was a red light flashing, but she quickly saw it was not the worst it could be; the pressure light still glowed green. It was the smoke detector. The smoke was coming from the lab.

She took a deep breath and plunged in, only to collide with Ralston as he came out, dragging Song. Except for a dazed expression and a few cuts, Song seemed to be all right. Crawford and McKillian joined them as they lay her on the bunk.

"It was one of the fruit," she said, gasping for breath and coughing. "I was heating it in a beaker, turned away, and it blew. I guess it sort of stunned me. The next thing I knew, Marty was carrying me out here. Hey, I have to get back in there! There's another one . . . it could be dangerous, and the damage, I have to check on that—" She struggled to get up but Lang held her down.

"You take it easy. What's this about another one?"

"I had it clamped down, and the drill—did I turn it on or not—I can't remember. I was after a core sample. You'd better take a look. If the drill hits whatever made the other one explode, it might go off."

"I'll get it," McKillian said, turning toward the lab.

"You'll stay right here," Lang barked. "We know there's not enough power in them to hurt the ship, but it could kill you if it hit you right. We stay right here until it goes off. The hell with the damage. And shut that door, quick!"

Before they could shut it they heard a whistling, like a teakettle coming to boil, then a rapid series of clangs. A tiny white ball came through the doorway and bounced off three walls. It moved almost faster than they could follow. It hit Crawford on the arm, then fell to the floor where it gradually skittered to a stop. The hissing died away, and Crawford picked it up. It was lighter than it had been. There was a pinhole drilled in one side. The pinhole was cold when he touched it with his fingers. Startled, thinking he was burned, he stuck his finger in his mouth, then sucked on it absently long after he knew the truth.

"These 'fruit' are full of compressed gas," he told them. "We have to open up another, carefully this time. I'm almost afraid to say what gas I think it is, but I have a hunch that our problems are solved."

*   *   *

By the time the rescue expedition arrived, no one was calling it that. There had been the little matter of a long, brutal war with the Palestinian Empire, and a growing conviction that the survivors of the First Expedition had not had any chance in the first place. There had been no time for luxuries like space travel beyond the Moon and no billions of dollars to invest while the world's energy policies were being debated in the Arabian desert with tactical nuclear weapons.

When the ship finally did show up, it was no longer a NASA ship. It was sponsored by the fledgling International Space Agency. Its crew came from all over Earth. Its drive was new, too, and a lot better than the old one. As usual, war had given research a kick in the pants. Its mission was to take up the Martian exploration where the first expedition had left off and, incidentally, to recover the remains of the twenty Americans for return to Earth.

The ship came down with an impressive show of flame and billowing sand, three kilometers from Tharsis Base.

The captain, an Indian named Singh, got his crew started on erecting the permanent buildings, then climbed into a crawler with three officers for the trip to Tharsis. It was almost exactly twelve Earth years since the departure of the *Edgar Rice Burroughs*.

The *Podkayne* was barely visible behind a network of multicolored vines. The vines were tough enough to frustrate the rescuers' efforts to push through and enter the old ship. But both lock doors were open, and sand had drifted in rippled waves through the opening. The stern of the ship was nearly buried.

Singh told his people to stop, and he stood back admiring the complexity of the life in such a barren place. There were whirligigs twenty meters tall scattered around him, with vanes broad as the wings of a cargo aircraft.

"We'll have to get cutting tools from the ship," he told his crew. "They're probably in there. What a place this is! I can see we're going to be busy." He walked along the edge of the dense growth, which now covered several acres. He came to a section where the predominant color was purple. It was strangely different from the rest of the garden. There were tall whirligig derricks but they were frozen, unmoving. And covering all the derricks was a translucent network of ten-centimeter-wide strips of plastic, which was thick enough to make an impenetrable barrier. It was like a cobweb made of flat, thin material instead of fibrous spider silk. It bulged outward between all the cross braces of the whirligigs.

"Hello, can you hear me now?"

Singh jumped, then turned around, looked at the three officers. They were looking as surprised as he was.

"Hello, hello, hello? No good on this one, Mary. Want me to try another channel?"

"Wait a moment. I can hear you. Where are you?"

"Hey, he hears me! Uh, that is, this is Song Sue Lee, and I'm right in front of you. If you look real hard into the webbing, you can just make me out. I'll wave my arms. See?"

Singh thought he saw some movement when he pressed his face to the translucent web. The web resisted his hands, pushing back like an inflated balloon.

"I think I see you." The enormity of it was just striking him. He kept his voice under tight control as his officers rushed up around him, and managed not to stammer. "Are you well? Is there anything we can do?"

There was a pause. "Well, now that you mention it, you might have come on time. But that's water through the pipes, I guess. If you have some toys or something, it might be nice. The stories I've told little Billy of all the nice things you people were going to bring! There's going to be no living with him, let me tell you."

This was getting out of hand for Captain Singh.

"Ms. Song, how can we get in there with you?"

"Sorry. Go to your right about ten meters, where you see the steam coming from the web. There, see it?" They did, and as they looked, a section of the webbing was pulled open and a rush of warm air almost blew them over. Water condensed out of it on their faceplates, and suddenly they couldn't see very well.

"Hurry, hurry, step in! We can't keep it open too long!" They groped their way in, scraping frost away with their hands. The web closed behind them, and they were standing in the center of a very complicated network made of single strands of the webbing material. Singh's pressure gauge read 30 millibars.

Another section opened up and they stepped through it. After three more gates were passed, the temperature and pressure were nearly Earth-normal. And they were standing beside a small oriental woman with skin tanned almost black. She had no clothes on, but seemed adequately dressed in a brilliant smile that dimpled her mouth and eyes. Her hair was streaked with gray. She would be—Singh stopped to consider—forty-one years old.

"This way," she said, beckoning them into a tunnel formed from more strips of plastic. They twisted around through a random maze, going through more gates that opened when they neared them, sometimes getting on their knees when the clearance was low. They heard the sound of children's voices.

They reached what must have been the center of the maze and found the people everyone had given up on. Eighteen of them. The children became very quiet and stared solemnly at the new arrivals, while the other four adults . . .

The adults were standing separately around the space while tiny helicopters flew around them, wrapping them from head to toe in strips of webbing like human maypoles.

* * *

"Of course we don't know if we would have made it without the assist from the Martians," Mary Lang was saying from her perch on an orange thing that might have been a toadstool. "Once we figured out what was happening here in the graveyard, there was no need to explore alternative ways of getting food, water, and oxygen. The need just never arose. We were provided for."

She raised her feet so a group of three gawking women from the rescue ship could get by. They were letting them come through in groups of five every hour. They didn't dare open the outer egress more often than that, and Lang was wondering if it was too often. The place was crowded, and the kids were nervous. But better to have the crew satisfy their curiosity in here where we can watch them, she reasoned, than have them messing things up outside.

The inner nest was free-form. The New Amsterdamites had allowed it to stay pretty much the way the whirlibirds had built it, only taking down an obstruction here and there to allow humans to move around. It was a maze of gauzy walls and plastic struts, with clear plastic pipes running all over and carrying fluids of pale blue, pink, gold, and wine. Metal spigots from the *Podkayne* had been inserted in some of the pipes. McKillian was kept busy refilling glasses for the visitors, who wanted to sample the antifreeze solution that was fifty percent ethanol. It was good stuff, Captain Singh reflected as he drained his third glass, and that was what he still couldn't understand.

He was having trouble framing the questions he wanted to ask, and he realized he'd had too much to drink. The spirit of celebration, the rejoicing at finding these people here past any hope—one could hardly stay aloof from it. But he refused a fourth drink regretfully.

"I can understand the drink," he said, carefully. "Ethanol is a simple compound and could fit into many different chemistries. But it's hard to believe that you've survived eating the food these plants produced for you."

"Not when you understand what this graveyard is and why it became what it did," Song said. She was sitting cross-legged on the floor nursing her youngest, Ethan.

"First you have to understand that all this you see," she waved around at the meters of hanging soft sculpture, nearly causing Ethan to lose the nipple, "was designed to contain beings who are no more adapted to *this* Mars than we are. They need warmth, oxygen at fairly high pressures, and free water. It isn't here now, but it can be created by properly designed plants. They engineered these plants to be triggered by the first signs of free water and to start building places for them to live while they waited for full summer to come. When it does, this whole planet will bloom. Then we can step outside without wearing suits or carrying airberries."

"Yes, I see," Singh said. "And it's all very wonderful, almost too much to believe." He was distracted for a moment, looking up to the ceiling where the airberries—white spheres about the size of bowling balls—hung in clusters from the pipes that supplied them with high-pressure oxygen.

"I'd like to see that process from the start," he said. "Where you suit up for the outside, I mean."

"We were suiting up when you got here. It takes about half an hour, so we couldn't get out in time to meet you."

"How long are those . . . suits good for?"

"About a day," Crawford said. "You have to destroy them to get out of them. The plastic strips don't cut well, but there's another specialized animal that eats that type of plastic. It's recycled into the system. If you want to suit up, you just grab a whirlibird and hold onto its tail and throw it. It starts spinning as it flies, and wraps the end product around you. It takes some practice, but it works. The stuff sticks to itself, but not to us. So you spin several layers, letting each one dry, then hook up an airberry, and you're inflated and insulated."

"Marvelous," Singh said, truly impressed. He had seen the tiny whirlibirds weaving the suits, and the other ones, like small slugs, eating them away when the colonists saw they wouldn't need them. "But without some sort of exhaust, you wouldn't last long. How is that accomplished?"

"We use the breather valves from our old suits," McKillian said. "Either the plants that grow valves haven't come up yet or we haven't been smart enough to recognize them. And the insulation isn't perfect. We only go out in the hottest part of the day, and our hands and feet tend to get cold. But we manage."

Singh realized he had strayed from his original question.

"But what about the food? Surely it's too much to expect these Martians to eat the same things we do. Wouldn't you think so?"

"We sure did, and we were lucky to have Marty Ralston along. He kept telling us the fruits in the graveyard were edible by humans. Fats, starches, proteins; all identical to the ones we brought along. The clue was in the orrery, of course."

Lang pointed to the twin globes in the middle of the room, still keeping perfect Earth time.

"It was a beacon. We figured that out when we saw they grew only in the graveyard. But what was it telling us? We felt it meant that we were expected. Song felt that from the start, and we all came to agree with her. But we didn't realize just how much they had prepared for us until Marty started analyzing the fruits and nutrients here.

"Listen, these Martians—and I can see from your look that you still don't really believe in them, but you will if you stay here long enough—they know genetics. They really know it. We have a thousand theories about what they may be like; and I won't bore you with them yet, but this is one thing we do know. They can build anything they need, make a blueprint in DNA, encapsulate it in a spore and bury it, knowing exactly what will come up in forty thousand years. When it starts to get cold here and they know the cycle's drawing to an end, they seed the planet with the spores and . . . do something. Maybe they die, or maybe they have some other way of passing the time. But they know they'll return.

"We can't say how long they've been prepared for a visit from us. Maybe only this cycle; maybe twenty cycles ago. Anyway, at the last cycle they buried the kind of spores that would produce these little gizmos." She tapped the blue ball representing the Earth with one foot.

"They triggered them to be activated only when they encountered certain conditions. Maybe they knew exactly what it would be; maybe they only provided for a likely range of possibilities. Song thinks they've visited us, back in the Stone Age. In some ways it's easier to believe than the alternative. That way they'd know our genetic structure and what kinds of food we'd eat, and could prepare.

" 'Cause if they didn't visit us, they must have prepared other spores. Spores that would analyze new proteins and be able to duplicate them. Further than that, some of the plants might have been able to copy certain genetic material if they encountered any. Take a look at that pipe behind you." Singh turned and saw a pipe about as thick as his arm. It was flexible, and had a swelling in it that continuously pulsed in expansion and contraction.

"Take that bulge apart and you'd be amazed at the resemblance to a human heart. So there's another significant fact; this place started out with whirligigs, but later modified itself to use human heart pumps from the genetic information *taken from the bodies of the men and women we buried.*" She paused to let that sink in, then went on with a slightly bemused smile.

"The same thing for what we eat and drink. That liquor you drank, for instance. It's half alcohol, and that's probably what it would have been without the corpses. But the rest of it is very similar to hemoglobin. It's sort of like fermented blood. Human blood."

Singh was glad he had refused the fourth drink. One of his crew members quietly put his glass down.

"I've never eaten human flesh," Lang went on, "but I think I know what it must taste like. Those vines to your right; we strip off the outer part and eat the meat underneath. It tastes good. I wish we could cook it, but we have nothing to burn and couldn't risk it with the high oxygen count, anyway."

Singh and everyone else was silent for a while. He found he really was beginning to believe in the Martians. The theory seemed to cover a lot of otherwise inexplicable facts.

Mary Lang sighed, slapped her thighs, and stood up. Like all the others, she was nude and seemed totally at home that way. None of them had worn anything but a Martian pressure suit for eight years. She ran her hand lovingly over the gossamer wall, the wall that had provided her and her fellow colonists and their children protection from the cold and the thin air for so long. Singh was struck by her easy familiarity with what seemed to him outlandish surroundings. She looked at home. He couldn't imagine her anywhere else.

He looked at the children. One wide-eyed little girl of eight years was kneeling at his feet. As his eyes fell on her, she smiled tentatively and took his hand.

"Did you bring any bubblegum?" the girl asked.

He smiled at her. "No, honey, but maybe there's some in the ship." She seemed satisfied. She would wait to experience the wonders of Earthly science.

"We were provided for," Mary Lang said, quietly. "They knew we were coming and they altered their plans to fit us in." She looked back to Singh. "It would have happened even without the blowout and the burials. The same sort of thing was happening around the *Podkayne,* too, triggered by our waste, urine and feces and such. I don't know if it would have tasted quite as good in the food department, but it would have sustained life."

Singh stood up. He was moved, but did not trust himself to show it adequately. So he sounded rather abrupt, though polite.

"I suppose you'll be anxious to go to the ship," he said. "You're going to be a tremendous help. You know so much of what we were sent here to find out. And you'll be quite famous when you get back to Earth. Your back pay should add up to quite a sum."

There was a silence, then it was ripped apart by Lang's huge laugh. She was joined by the others, and the children, who didn't know what they were laughing about but enjoyed the break in the tension.

"Sorry, Captain. That was rude. But we're not going back."

Singh looked at each of the adults and saw no trace of doubt. And he was mildly surprised to find that the statement did not startle him.

"I won't take that as your final decision," he said. "As you know, we'll be here six months. If at the end of that time any of you want to go, you're still citizens of Earth."

"We are? You'll have to brief us on the political situation back there. We were United States citizens when we left. But it doesn't matter. You won't get any takers, though we appreciate the fact that you came. It's nice to know we weren't forgotten." She said it with total assurance, and the others were nodding. Singh was uncomfortably aware that the idea of a rescue mission had died out only a few years after the initial tragedy. He and his ship were here now only to explore.

Lang sat back down and patted the ground around her, ground that was covered in a multiple layer of the Martian pressure-tight web, the kind of web that would have been made only by warm-blooded, oxygen-breathing, water-economy beings who needed protection for their bodies until the full bloom of summer.

"We *like* it here. It's a good place to raise a family, not like Earth the last time I was there. And it couldn't be much better now, right after another war. And we can't leave, even if we wanted to." She flashed him a dazzling smile and patted the ground again.

"The Martians should be showing up any time now. And we aim to thank them."

"*Gotta Sing, Gotta Dance*"

Why would a guy who had longed all his life to live in the big city move from San Francisco to Eugene, Oregon? In a word, family.

My wife at the time, Anet, had three children from a previous marriage. They are Maurice, Roger, and Stefan, and I have long since stopped thinking of them as my stepsons. All three are self-taught musicians of amazing talent in the areas of rock and blues. I'm proud to call them my sons.

While we lived in the Haight and during our travels around the country we had Stefan with us while the two older boys lived with their father. Later they moved in with us, and it quickly began to seem that, in spite of what I had thought of as a frustrated youth, there were severe drawbacks to growing up in the big city. A smaller town has its advantages if you're trying to raise three boys and keep them out of trouble. We had a friend in Eugene, so that's where we went.

It's a college town, home of the University of Oregon. We lived in five different places there, each one a little better than the last, most of them not really worth talking about. Just houses. And away from the city, no longer rambling hippies, Anet and I began to grow apart. Eventually we separated and divorced. I don't see her much these days but we remain friends.

And we'll always have Woodstock.

The second Cool 8 I lived in was a '56 Buick parked in a muddy field in New York. We were only there four days, but they were an amazing four days, and we had no other home at the time. As a residence it didn't have a lot to recommend it, but as the real estate people say: location, location, location. It was parked about a mile down the road from Max Yasgur's farm, where some hippies said there was going to be a concert.

In my life I have blundered into wonderful things so many times it's scary. I didn't plan them, they just happened. My whole career seems that way in retrospect.

Woodstock was like that, for us. We knew it was happening, we'd heard about it in New York City, but we had no idea where. We had recently discovered that finding an affordable apartment in the city was hard, maybe impossible. It quickly became clear that, in New York City, somebody had to die before somebody else could move in— people actually read obituaries for leads on what might soon be available—so we de- cided to head up into the Catskills in search of cheaper rent.

Somewhere along the way I noticed we were almost out of gas. Running on fumes, actually. We got off the road and into the worst traffic jam I ever saw. We sputtered to a halt and pushed the car off the road and into a field. That's when we realized we were involuntarily interned for the duration. There was no gas, no food, no lodging for fifty miles.

Luckily, we had stuff to eat and stuff to smoke, so we figured we'd be all right. Stefan had just learned to pee in a bucket instead of into his diapers, and the Buick kept us out of the rain. People shared, you made friends quickly.

It's impossible to explain Woodstock to the mosh pit generation. You couldn't even explain it to those at the Altamont Rolling Stones concert not long after, where they tried to re-create the Woodstock experience and failed miserably. Woodstock was a one-of-a-kind thing, probably never to be repeated.

Did I say that old Buick was an 8 on a scale of one to ten? Hell, a sleeping bag out in the rain would have been a 6, if you were young enough and stupid enough to en- dure it, and I was both.

I'm probably reaching a bit here attempting to tie Woodstock to the following story. Woodstock is a legend that has grown in the telling. It was not utopia; nothing is. If I think real hard I recall being miserable, wet, hungry, and bored. I saw no vio- lence, didn't even hear a raised voice, but I know there were problems, many of them drug-induced. If it had gone on another two or three days it would have resembled Bangladesh after the great cyclone of 1970. . . . Well, come to think of it, it did resem- ble Bangladesh when it was over, but without the 300,000 dead bodies. Starvation and cholera were distinct possibilities.

And yet something there worked. Mostly people were smiling, and working hard, and having a great time. A few of the locals took advantage of the weird hordes who had descended on their peaceful community, but most pitched in the same way they would have if a dam broke . . . again, a metaphor very like what did happen.

It is the feeling of cooperation that strikes me. And in nature there is no better ex- ample of cooperation than symbiosis. This is when two dissimilar organisms work to- gether for their mutual benefit. Sometimes the two cannot survive at all without each other. The biggest engine of symbiosis I know of is Planet Earth itself.

In the days before real space travel, people imagined that spaceships on long voyages would try to duplicate the cycles of life by bringing plants along with them. Hydroponic gardening features in many classic SF novels. It made perfect sense. Why bring along all that bottled oxygen if plants could make it for you?

It still makes sense, though to my knowledge it has not been used thus far in the space program.

"Gotta Sing, Gotta Dance" is the result of my considering the smallest possible symbiotic unit that might survive in space. It is part of the Eight Worlds history, but an isolated part. The people living raw in the rings of Saturn are an isolated community, devoted to a project that is alien to the rest of humanity. It is one of my personal favorites of the stories I have written, and I keep thinking the idea could be expanded into a novel . . . but I haven't yet figured out how.

GOTTA SING, GOTTA DANCE

SAILING IN TOWARD a rendezvous with Janus, Barnum and Bailey encountered a giant, pulsing quarter note. The stem was a good five kilometers tall. The note itself was a kilometer in diameter, and glowed a faint turquoise. It turned ponderously on its axis as they approached it.

"This must be the place," Barnum said to Bailey.

"Janus approach control to Barnum and Bailey," came a voice from the void. "You will encounter the dragline on the next revolution. You should be seeing the visual indicator in a few minutes."

Barnum looked down at the slowly turning irregular ball of rock and ice that was Janus, innermost satellite of Saturn. Something was coming up behind the curve of the horizon. It didn't take long for enough of it to become visible so they could see what it was. Barnum had a good laugh.

"Is that yours, or theirs?" he asked Bailey.

Bailey sniffed. "Theirs. Just how silly do you think I am?"

The object rising behind the curve of the satellite was a butterfly net, ten kilometers tall. It had a long, fluttering net trailing from a gigantic hoop. Bailey sniffed again, but applied the necessary vectors to position them for being swooped up in the preposterous thing.

"Come on, Bailey," Barnum chided. "You're just jealous because you didn't think of it first."

"Maybe so," the symb conceded. "Anyway, hold onto your hat, this is likely to be quite a jerk."

The illusion was carried as far as was practical, but Barnum noticed that the first tug of deceleration started sooner than one would expect if the transparent net was more than an illusion. The force built up gradually as the electromagnetic field clutched at the metal belt he had strapped around his waist. It lasted for about a minute. When it had trailed off, Janus no longer appeared to rotate beneath them. It was coming closer.

"Listen to this," Bailey said. Barnum's head was filled with music. It was bouncy, featuring the reedy, flatulent, yet engaging tones of a bass saxophone in a honky-tonk tune that neither of them could identify. They shifted position and could just make out the location of Pearly Gates, the only human settlement on Janus. It was easy to find because of the weaving, floating musical staffs that extruded themselves from the spot like parallel strands of spider web.

The people who ran Pearly Gates were a barrel of laughs. All the actual structures that made up the aboveground parts of the settlement were disguised behind whimsical holographic projections. The whole place looked like a cross between a child's candy-land nightmare and an early Walt Disney cartoon.

Dominating the town was a giant calliope with pipes a thousand meters tall. There were fifteen of them, and they were all bouncing and swaying in time to the saxophone music. They would squat down as if taking a deep breath, then stand up again, emitting a colored smoke ring. The buildings, which Barnum knew were actually functional, uninteresting hemispheres, appeared to be square houses with flower boxes in the windows and cartoon eyes peering out the doors. They trembled and jigged as if they were made of Jell-O.

"Don't you think it's a trifle overdone?" Bailey asked.

"Depends on what you like. It's kind of cute, in its own gaudy way."

They drifted in through the spaghetti maze of lines, bars, sixteenth notes, rests, smoke rings, and blaring music. They plowed through an insubstantial eighth-note run, and Bailey killed their remaining velocity with the jets. They lighted softly in the barely perceptible gravity and made their way to one of the grinning buildings.

Coming up to the entrance of the building had been quite an experience. Barnum had reached for a button marked LOCK CYCLE and it had dodged out of his way, then turned into a tiny face, leering at him. Practical joke. The lock had opened anyway, actuated by his presence. Inside, Pearly Gates was not so flamboyant. The corridors looked decently like corridors, and the floors were solid and gray.

"I'd watch out, all the same," Bailey advised, darkly. "These people are real self-panickers. Their idea of a good laugh might be to dig a hole in the floor and cover it with a holo. Watch your step."

"Aw, don't be such a sore loser. You could spot something like that, couldn't you?"

Bailey didn't answer, and Barnum didn't pursue it. He knew the source of the symb's uneasiness and dislike of the station on Janus. Bailey wanted to get their business over as soon as possible and get back to the Ring, where he felt needed. Here, in a corridor filled with oxygen, Bailey was physically useless.

Bailey's function in the symbiotic team of Barnum and Bailey was to provide an environment of food, oxygen, and water for the human, Barnum. Conversely, Barnum provided food, carbon dioxide, and water for Bailey. Barnum was a human, physically unremarkable except for a surgical alteration of his knees that made them bend outward rather than forward, and the oversized hands, called peds, that grew out of his ankles where his feet used to be. Bailey, on the other hand, was nothing like a human.

Strictly speaking, Bailey was not even a he. Bailey was a plant, and Barnum thought of him as a male only because the voice in Barnum's head—Bailey's only means of communication—sounded masculine. Bailey had no shape of his own. He existed by containing Barnum and taking on part of his shape. He extended into Barnum's alimentary canal, in the mouth and all the way through to emerge at the anus, threading him like a needle. Together, the team looked like a human in a featureless spacesuit, with a bulbous head, a tight waist, and swollen hips. A ridiculously exaggerated female, if you wish.

"You might as well start breathing again," Bailey said.

"What for? I will when I need to talk to someone who's not paired with a symb. In the meantime, why bother?"

"I just thought you'd like to get used to it."

"Oh, very well. If you think it's necessary."

So Bailey gradually withdrew the parts of him that filled Barnum's lungs and throat, freeing his speech apparatus to do what it hadn't done for over ten years. Barnum coughed as the air flowed into his throat. It was cold! Well, it felt like it, though it was actually at the standard seventy-two degrees. He was unused to it. His diaphragm gave one shudder then took over the chore of breathing as if his medulla had never been disconnected.

"There," he said aloud, surprised at how his voice sounded. "Satisfied?"

"It never hurts to do a little testing."

"Let's get this out in the open, shall we? I didn't want to come here any more than you did, but you know we had to. Are you going to give me trouble about it until we leave? We're supposed to be a team, remember?"

There was a sigh from his partner.

"I'm sorry, but that's just it. We *are* supposed to be a team, and out in the Ring we are. Neither of us is anything without the other. Here I'm just something you have to carry around. I can't walk, I can't talk; I'm revealed as the vegetable that I am."

Barnum was accustomed to the symb's periodic attacks of insecurity. In the Ring they never amounted to much. But when they entered a gravitational field Bailey was reminded of how ineffectual a being he was.

"Here you can breathe on your own," Bailey went on. "You could see on your own if I uncovered your eyes. By the way, do you—"

"Don't be silly. Why should I use my own eyes when you can give me a better picture than I could on my own?"

"In the Ring, that's true. But here all my extra senses are just excess mass. What good is an adjusted velocity display to you here, where the farthest thing I can sense is twenty meters off, and stationary?"

"Listen, you. Do you want to turn around and march back out that lock? We can. I'll do it if this is going to be such a trauma for you."

There was a long silence, and Barnum was flooded with a warm, apologetic sensation that left him weak at his splayed-out knees.

"There's no need to apologize," he went on in a more sympathetic tone. "I understand you. This is just something we have to do together, like everything else, the good along with the bad."

"I love you, Barnum."

"And you, silly."

The sign on the door read:

TYMPANI & RAGTIME
TINPANALLEYCATS

Barnum and Bailey hesitated outside the door.

"What are you supposed to do, knock?" Barnum asked out loud. "It's been so long I've forgotten how."

"Just fold your fingers into a fist and—"

"Not that." He laughed, dispelling his momentary nervousness. "I've forgotten the politenesses of human society. Well, they do it in all the tapes I ever saw." He knocked on the door and it opened by itself on the second rap.

There was a man sitting behind a desk with his bare feet propped up on it. Barnum had been prepared for the shock of seeing another human, one who was *not* enclosed in a symb, for he had encountered several of them on the way to the offices of Tympani and Ragtime. But he was still reeling from the unfamiliarity of it. The man seemed to realize it and silently gestured him to a chair. He sat down in it, thinking that in the low gravity it really wasn't necessary. But somehow he was grateful. The man didn't say anything for a long while, giving Barnum time to settle down and arrange his thoughts. Barnum spent the time looking the man over carefully.

Several things were apparent about him; most blatantly, he was not a fashionable man. Shoes had been virtually extinct for over a century for the simple reason that there was nothing to walk on but padded floors. However, current fashion decreed that Shoes Are Worn.

The man was young-looking, having halted his growth at around twenty years. He was dressed in a holo suit, a generated illusion of flowing color that refused to stay in one spot or take on a definite form. Under the suit he might well have been nude, but Barnum couldn't tell.

"You're Barnum and Bailey, right?" the man said.

"Yes. And you're Tympani?"

"Ragtime. Tympani will be here later. I'm pleased to meet you. Have any trouble on the way down? This is your first visit, I think you said."

"Yes, it is. No trouble. And thank you, incidentally, for the ferry fee."

He waved it away. "Don't concern yourself. It's all in the overhead. We're taking a chance that you'll be good enough to repay that many times over. We're right enough times that we don't lose money on it. Most of your people out there can't afford being landed on Janus, and then where would we be? We'd have to go out to you. Cheaper this way."

"I suppose it is." He was silent again. He noticed that his throat was beginning to get sore with the unaccustomed effort of talking. No sooner had the thought been formed than he felt Bailey go into action. The internal tendril that had been withdrawn flicked up out of his stomach and lubricated his larynx. The pain died away as the nerve endings were suppressed. It's all in your head, anyway, he told himself.

"Who recommended us to you?" Ragtime said.

"Who . . . Oh, it was . . . Who was it, Bailey?" He realized too late that he had spoken it aloud. He hadn't wanted to, he had a vague feeling that it might be impolite to speak to his symb that way. Ragtime wouldn't hear the answer, of course.

"It was Antigone," Bailey supplied.

"Thanks," Barnum said, silently this time. "A man named Antigone," he told Ragtime.

The man made a note of that, and looked up again, smiling.

"Well now. What is it you wanted to show us?"

Barnum was about to describe their work to Ragtime when the door burst open and a woman sailed in. She sailed in the literal sense, banking off the doorjamb, grabbing at the door with her left ped and slamming it shut in one smooth motion, then spinning in the air to kiss the floor with the tips of her fingers, using them to slow her speed until she was stopped in front of the desk, leaning over it and talking excitedly to Ragtime. Barnum was surprised that she had peds instead of feet; he had thought that no one used them in Pearly Gates. They made walking awkward. But she didn't seem interested in walking.

"Wait till you hear what Myers has done now!" she said, almost levitating in her enthusiasm. Her ped-fingers worked in the carpet as she talked. "He realigned the sensors in the right anterior ganglia, and you won't believe what it does to the—"

"We have a client, Tympani."

She turned and saw the symb-human pair sitting behind her. She put her hand to her mouth as if to hush herself, but she was smiling behind it. She moved over to them (it couldn't be called walking in the low gravity; she seemed to accomplish it by perching on two fingers of each of her peds and walking on them, which made it look like she was floating). She reached them and extended her hand.

She was wearing a holo suit like Ragtime's but instead of wearing the projector around her waist, as he did, she had it mounted on a ring. When she extended her hand, the holo generator had to compensate by weaving larger and thinner webs of light around her body. It looked like an explosion of pastels, and left her body barely covered. What Barnum saw could have been a girl of sixteen: lanky, thin hips and breasts, and two blonde braids that reached to her waist. But her movements belied that. There was no adolescent awkwardness there.

"I'm Tympani," she said, taking his hand. Bailey was taken by surprise and didn't know whether to bare his hand or not. So what she grasped was Barnum's hand covered by the three-centimeter padding of Bailey. She didn't seem to mind.

"You must be Barnum and Bailey. Do you know who the original Barnum and Bailey were?"

"Yes, they're the people who built your big calliope outside."

She laughed. "The place *is* a kind of a circus, until you get used to it. Rag tells me you have something to sell us."

"I hope so."

"You've come to the right place. Rag's the business side of the company; I'm the talent. So I'm the one you'll be selling to. I don't suppose you have anything written down?"

He made a wry face, then remembered she couldn't see anything but a blank stretch of green with a hole for his mouth. It took some time to get used to dealing with people again.

"I don't even know how to read music."

She sighed, but didn't seem unhappy. "I figured as much. So few of you Ringers do. Honestly, if I could ever figure out what it is that turns you people into artists I could get rich."

"The only way to do that is to go out in the Ring and see for yourself."

"Right," she said, a little embarrassed. She looked away from the misshapen thing sitting in the chair. The only way to discover the magic of a life in the Ring was to go out there, and the only way to do that was to adopt a symb. Forever give up your individuality and become a part of a team. Not many people could do that.

"We might as well get started," she said, standing and patting her thighs to cover her nervousness. "The practice room is through that door."

He followed her into a dimly lit room that seemed to be half-buried in paper. He hadn't realized that any business could require so much paper. Their policy seemed to be to stack it up and when the stack go too high and tumbled into a landslide, to kick it back into a corner. Sheets of music crunched under his peds as he followed her to the corner of the room where the synthesizer keyboard stood beneath a lamp. The rest of the room was in shadows, but the keys gleamed brightly in their ancient array of black and white.

Tympani took off her ring and sat at the keyboard. "The damn holo gets in my way," she explained. "I can't see the keys." Barnum noticed for the first time that there was another keyboard on the floor, down in the shadows, and her peds were poised over it. He wondered if that was the only reason she wore them. Having seen her walk, he doubted it.

She sat still for a moment, then looked over to him expectantly.

"Tell me about it," she said in a whisper.

He didn't know what to say.

"Tell you about it? Just tell you?"

She laughed and relaxed again, hands in her lap.

"I was kidding. But we have to get the music out of your head and onto that tape some way. How would you prefer? I heard that a Beethoven symphony was once written out in English, each chord and run described in detail. I can't imagine why anyone would *want* to, but someone did. It made quite a thick book. We can do it that way. Or surely you can think of another." He was silent. Until she sat at the keyboard, he hadn't really thought about that part of it. He knew his music, knew it to the last hemi-semi-demi-quaver. How to get it out?

"What's the first note?" she prompted.

He was ashamed again. "I don't even know the names of the notes," he confessed.

She was not surprised. "Sing it."

"I . . . I've never tried to sing it."

"Try now." She sat up straight, looking at him with a friendly smile, not coaxing, but encouraging.

"I can hear it," he said, desperately. "Every note, every dissonance—is that the right word?"

She grinned. "It's *a* right word, but I don't know if you know what it means.

It's the quality of sound produced when the vibrations don't mesh harmoniously: *dis*-chord, it doesn't produce a sonically pleasing chord. Like this," and she pressed two keys close together, tried several others, then played with the knobs mounted over the keyboard until the two notes were only a few vibrations apart and wavered sinuously. "They don't automatically please the ear, but in the right context they can make you sit up and take notice. Is your music discordant?"

"Some places. Is that bad?"

"Not at all. Used right, it's . . . well, not pleasing exactly . . ." She spread her arms helplessly. "Talking about music is a pretty frustrating business, at best. Singing's much friendlier. Are you going to sing for me, love, or must I try to wade through your descriptions?"

Hesitantly, he sang the first three notes of his piece, knowing that they sounded nothing like the orchestra that crashed through his head, but desperate to try something. She took it up, playing the three unmodulated tones on the synthesizer: three pure sounds that were pretty, but lifeless and light-years away from what he wanted.

"No, no, it has to be richer."

"All right, I'll play what I think of as richer, and we'll see if we speak the same language." She turned some knobs and played the three notes again, this time giving them the modulations of a string bass.

"That's closer. But it's still not there."

"Don't despair," she said, waving her hand at the bank of dials before her. "Each of these will produce a different effect, singly or in combination. I'm reliably informed that the permutations are infinite. So somewhere in there we'll find your tune. Now. Which way should we go; this way, or this?"

Twisting the knob she touched in one direction made the sound become tinnier; the other, brassier, with a hint of trumpets.

He sat up. That was getting closer still, but it lacked the richness of the sounds in his brain. He had her turn the knob back and forth, finally settled on the place that most nearly approached his phantom tune. She tried another knob, and the result was an even closer approach. But it lacked something.

Getting more and more involved, Barnum found himself standing over her shoulder as she tried another knob. That was closer still, but . . .

Feverishly, he sat beside her on the bench and reached out for the knob. He tuned it carefully, then realized what he had done.

"Do you mind?" he asked. "It's so much easier sitting here and turning them myself."

She slapped him on the shoulder. "You dope," she laughed, "I've been trying to get you over here for the last fifteen minutes. Do you think I could really do this by myself? That Beethoven story was a lie."

"What will we do, then?"

"What *you'll* do is fiddle with this machine, with me here to help you and tell you how to get what you want. When you get it right, I'll play it for you. Believe me, I've done this too many times to think you could sit over there and describe it to me. Now *sing!*"

He sang. Eight hours later Ragtime came quietly into the room and put a plate of sandwiches and a pot of coffee on the table beside them. Barnum was still singing, and the synthesizer was singing along with him.

Barnum came swimming out of his creative fog, aware that something was hovering in his field of vision, interfering with his view of the keyboard. Something white and steaming, at the end of a long . . .

It was a coffee cup, held in Tympani's hand. He looked at her face and she tactfully said nothing.

While working at the synthesizer, Barnum and Bailey had virtually fused into a single being. That was appropriate, since the music Barnum was trying to sell was the product of their joint mind. It belonged to both of them. Now he wrenched himself away from his partner, far enough away that talking to him became a little more than talking to himself.

"How about it, Bailey? Should we have some?"

"I don't see why not. I've had to expend quite a bit of water vapor to keep you cool in this place. It could stand replenishing."

"Listen, why don't you roll back from my hands? It would make it easier to handle those controls; give me finer manipulation, see? Besides, I'm not sure if it's polite to shake hands with her without actually touching flesh."

Bailey said nothing, but his fluid body drew back quickly from Barnum's hands. Barnum reached out and took the offered cup, starting at the unfamiliar sensation of heat in his own nerve endings. Tympani was unaware of the discussion; it had taken only a second.

The sensation was explosive when it went down his throat. He gasped, and Tympani looked worried.

"Take it easy there, friend. You've got to get your nerves back in shape for something as hot as that." She took a careful sip and turned back to the keyboard. Barnum set his cup down and joined her. But it seemed like time for a recess and he couldn't get back into the music. She recognized this and relaxed, taking a sandwich and eating it as if she were starving.

"She *is* starving, you dope," Bailey said. "Or at least very hungry. She hasn't had anything to eat for eight hours, and she doesn't have a symb recycling her wastes into food and dripping it into her veins. So she gets hungry. Remember?"

"I remember. I'd forgotten." He looked at the pile of sandwiches. "I wonder what it would feel like to eat one of those?"

"Like this." Barnum's mouth was flooded with the taste of a tuna salad sandwich on whole wheat. Bailey produced this trick, like all his others, by direct stimulation of the sensorium. With no trouble at all he could produce completely new sensations simply by shorting one sector of Barnum's brain into another. If Barnum wanted to know what the taste of a tuna sandwich sounded like, Bailey could let him hear.

"All right. And I won't protest that I didn't feel the bite of it against my teeth, because I know you can produce that, too. And all the sensations of chewing and swallowing it, and much more besides. Still," and his thoughts took on a tone that Bailey wasn't sure he liked, "I wonder if it would be the polite thing to eat one of them?"

"What's all this politeness all of a sudden?" Bailey exploded. "Eat it if you like, but I'll never know why. Be a carnivorous animal and see if I care."

"Temper, temper," Barnum chided, with tenderness in his voice. "Settle down, chum. I'm not going anywhere without you. But we have to get along with these people. I'm just trying to be diplomatic."

"Eat it, then," Bailey sighed. "You'll ruin my ecology schedules for months—what'll I do with all that extra protein?—but why should you care about that?"

Barnum laughed silently. He knew that Bailey could do anything he liked with it: ingest it, refine it, burn it, or simply contain it and expel it at the first opportunity. He reached for a sandwich and felt the thick substance of Bailey's skin draw back from his face as he raised it to his mouth.

He had expected a brighter light, but he shouldn't have. He was using his own retinas to see with for the first time in years, but it was no different from the cortex-induced pictures Bailey had shown him all that time.

"You have a nice face," Tympani said, around a mouthful of sandwich. "I thought you would have. You painted a very nice picture of yourself."

"I did?" Barnum asked, intrigued. "What do you mean?"

"Your music. It reflects you. Oh, I don't see everything in your eyes that I saw in the music, but I never do. The rest of it is Bailey, your friend. And I can't read his expression."

"No, I guess you couldn't. But can you tell anything about him?"

She thought about it, then turned to the keyboard. She picked out a theme they had worried out a few hours before, played it a little faster and with subtle alterations in the tonality. It was a happy fragment, with a hint of something just out of reach.

"That's Bailey. He's worried about something. If experience is any guide, it's being here at Pearly Gates. Symbs don't like to come here, or anywhere there's gravity. It makes them feel not needed."

"Hear that?" he asked his silent partner.

"Umm."

"And that's so silly," she went on. "I don't know about it firsthand, obviously, but I've met and talked to a lot of pairs. As far as I can see, the bond between a human and a symb is . . . well, it makes a mother cat dying to defend her kittens seem like a case of casual affection. I guess you know that better than I could ever say, though."

"You stated it well," he said.

Bailey made a grudging sign of approval, a mental sheepish grin. "She's outpointed me, meat-eater. I'll shut up and let you two talk without me intruding my baseless insecurities."

"You relaxed him," Barnum told her, happily. "You've even got him making jokes about himself. That's no small accomplishment, because he takes himself pretty seriously."

"That's not fair, I can't defend myself."

"I thought you were going to be quiet?"

The work proceeded smoothly, though it was running longer than Bailey would have liked. After three days of transcribing, the music was beginning to take shape. A time came when Tympani could press a button and have the machine play it back: it was much more than the skeletal outline they had evolved on the first day but still needed finishing touches.

"How about 'Contrapunctual Cantata'?" Tympani asked.

"What?"

"For a title. It has to have a title. I've been thinking about it, and coined that word. It fits, because the piece is very metrical in construction: tight, on time, on the beat. Yet it has a strong counterpoint in the woodwinds."

"That's the reedy sections, right?"

"Yes. What do you think?"

"Bailey wants to know what a cantata is."

Tympani shrugged her shoulders, but looked guilty. "To tell you the truth, I stuck that in for alliteration. Maybe as a selling point. Actually, a cantata is sung, and you don't have anything like voices in this. You sure you couldn't work some in?"

Barnum considered it. "No."

"It's your decision, of course." She seemed about to say something else but decided against it.

"Look, I don't care too much about the title," Barnum said. "Will it help you to sell it, naming it that?"

"Might."

"Then do as you please."

"Thanks. I've got Rag working on some preliminary publicity. We both think this has possibilities. He liked the title, and he's pretty good at knowing what will sell. He likes the piece, too."

"How much longer before we'll have it ready?"

"Not too long. Two more days. Are you getting tired of it?"

"A little. I'd like to get back to the Ring. So would Bailey."

She frowned at him, pouting her lower lip. "That means I won't be seeing you for ten years. This sure can be a slow business. It takes forever to develop new talent."

"Why are you in it?"

She thought about it. "I guess because music is what I like, and Janus is where the most innovative music in the system is born and bred. No one else can compete with you Ringers."

He was about to ask her why she didn't pair up and see what it was like, first-hand. But something held him back, some unspoken taboo she had set up; or perhaps it was him. Truthfully, he could no longer understand why *everyone* didn't pair with a symb. It seemed the only sane way to live. But he knew that many found the idea unattractive, even repugnant.

After the fourth recording session Tympani relaxed by playing the synthesizer for the pair. They had known she was good, and their opinion was confirmed by the artistry she displayed at the keyboard.

Tympani had made a study of musical history. She could play Bach or Beethoven as easily as the works of the modern composers like Barnum. She performed Beethoven's Eighth Symphony, first movement. With her two hands and two peds she had no trouble at all in making an exact reproduction of a full symphony orchestra. But she didn't limit herself to that. The music would segue imperceptibly from the traditional strings into the concrete sounds that only an electronic instrument could produce.

She followed it with something by Ravel that Barnum had never heard, then an early composition by Riker. After that, she amused him with some Joplin rags and a march by John Philip Sousa. She allowed herself no license on these, playing them with the exact instrumentation indicated by the composer.

Then she moved into another march. This one was incredibly lively, full of chromatic runs that soared and swooped. She played it with a precision in the bass parts that the old musicians could never have achieved. Barnum was reminded of old films seen as a child, films full of snarling lions in cages and elephants bedecked with feathers.

"What was that?" he asked when she was through.

"Funny you should ask, Mr. Barnum. That was an old circus march called 'Thunder and Blazes.' Or some call it 'Entry of the Gladiators.' There's some confusion among the scholars. Some say it had a third title, 'Barnum and Bailey's Favorite,' but the majority think that was another one. If it was, it's lost, and too bad. But everyone is sure that Barnum and Bailey liked this one, too. What do you think of it?"

"I like it. Would you play it again?"

She did, and later a third time, because Bailey wanted to be sure it was safe in Barnum's memory where they could replay it later.

Tympani turned the machine off and rested her elbows on the keyboard.

"When you go back out," she said, "why don't you give some thought to working in a synapticon part for your next work?"

"What's a synapticon?"

She stared at him, not believing what she had heard. Then her expression changed to one of delight.

"You really don't know? Then you have something to learn." And she bounced over to her desk, grabbed something with her peds, and hopped back to the synthesizer. It was a small black box with a strap and a wire with an input jack at one end. She turned her back to him and parted her hair at the base of her skull.

"Will you plug me in?" she asked.

Barnum saw the tiny gold socket buried in her hair, the kind that enabled one to interface directly with a computer. He inserted the plug into it and she strapped the box around her neck. It was severely functional, and had an improvised, bread-boarded look about it, scarred with tool marks and chipped paint. It gave the impression of having been tinkered with almost daily.

"It's still in the development process," she said. "Myers—he's the guy who invented it—has been playing with it, adding things. When we get it right we'll market it as a necklace. The circuitry can be compacted quite a bit. The first one had a wire that connected it to the speaker, which hampered my style considerably. But this one has a transmitter. You'll see what I mean. Come on, there isn't room in here."

She led the way back to the outer office and turned on a big speaker against the wall.

"What it does," she said, standing in the middle of the room with her hands at her sides, "is translate body motion into music. It measures the tensions in the body nerve network, amplifies them, and . . . well, I'll show you what I mean. This position is null; no sound is produced." She was standing straight, but relaxed, peds together, hands at her sides, head slightly lowered.

She brought her arm up in front of her, reaching with her hand, and the speaker behind her made a swooping sound up the scale, breaking into a chord as her fingers closed on the invisible tone in the air. She bent her knee forward and a soft bass note crept in, strengthening as she tensed the muscles in her thighs. She added more harmonics with her other hand, then abruptly cocked her body to one side, exploding the sound into a cascade of chords. Barnum sat up straight, the hairs on his arms and spine sitting up with him.

Tympani couldn't see him. She was lost in a world that existed slightly out of phase with the real one, a world where dance was music and her body was the instrument. Her eyeblinks became staccato punctuating phrases and her breathing provided a solid rhythmic base for the nets of sound her arms and legs and fingers were weaving.

To Barnum and Bailey the beauty of it lay in the perfect fitting together of movement and sound. The pair had thought it would be just a novelty, that she would be sweating to twist her body into shapes that were awkward and unnatural to reach the notes she was after. But it wasn't like that. Each element shaped the other. Both the music and the dance were improvised as she went along and were subordinate to no rules but her own internal ones.

When she finally came to rest, balancing on the tips of her peds and letting the sound die away to nothingness, Barnum was almost numb. And he was surprised to hear the sound of hands clapping. He realized it was his own hands, but he wasn't clapping them. It was Bailey. Bailey had *never* taken over motor control.

They had to have all the details. Bailey was overwhelmed by the new art form and grew so impatient with relaying questions through Barnum that he almost asked to take over Barnum's vocal cords for a while.

Tympani was surprised at the degree of enthusiasm. She was a strong proponent of the synapticon but had not met much success in her efforts to popularize it. It had its limitations, and was viewed as an interesting but passing fad.

"What limitations?" Bailey asked, and Barnum vocalized.

"Basically, it needs free-fall performance to be fully effective. There are residual tones that can't be eliminated when you're standing up in gravity, even on Janus. And I can't stay in the air long enough here. You evidently didn't notice it, but I was unable to introduce many variations under these conditions."

Barnum saw something at once. "Then I should have one installed. That way I can play it as I move through the Ring."

Tympani brushed a strand of hair out of her eyes. She was covered in sweat from her fifteen-minute performance, and her face was flushed. Barnum almost didn't hear her reply, he was so intent on the harmony of motion in that simple movement. And the synapticon was turned off.

"Maybe you should. But I'd wait if I were you." Barnum was about to ask why but she went on quickly. "It isn't an exact instrument yet, but we're working on it, refining it every day. Part of the problem, you see, is that it takes special training to operate it so it produces more than white noise. I wasn't strictly truthful with you when I told you how it works."

"How so?"

"Well, I said it measures tensions in nerves and translates it. Where are most of the nerves in the body?"

Barnum saw it then. "In the brain."

"Right. So mood is even more important in this than in most music. Have you ever worked with an alpha-wave device? By listening to a tone you can control certain functions of your brain. It takes practice. The brain provides the reservoir of tone for the synapticon, modulates the whole composition. If you aren't in control of it, it comes out as noise."

"How long have you been working with it?"

"About three years."

While Barnum and Bailey were working with her, Tympani had to adjust her day and night cycles to fit with his biological processes. The pair spent the periods of sunlight stretched out in Janus's municipal kitchen.

The kitchen was a free service provided by the community, one that was well worth the cost, since without it paired humans would find it impossible to remain on Janus for more than a few days. It was a bulldozed plain, three kilometers square, marked off in a grid with sections one hundred meters on an edge. Barnum and Bailey didn't care for it—none of the pairs liked it much—but it was the best they could do in a gravity field.

No closed ecology is truly closed. The same heat cannot be reused endlessly, as raw materials can. Heat must be added, energy must be pumped in somewhere along the line to enable the plant component of the pair to synthesize the carbohydrates needed by the animal component. Bailey could use some of the low-level heat generated when Barnum's body broke down these molecules, but that process would soon lead to ecological bankruptcy.

The symb's solution was photosynthesis, like any other plant's, though the chemicals Bailey employed for it bore only a vague resemblance to chlorophyll. Photosynthesis requires large amounts of plant surface, much more than is available on an area the size of a human. And the intensity of sunlight at Saturn's orbit was only one hundredth what it was at Earth's.

Barnum walked carefully along one of the white lines of the grid. To his left and right, humans were reclining in the centers of the large squares. They were enclosed in only the thinnest coating of symb; the rest of the symb's mass was spread in a sheet of living film, almost invisible except as a sheen on the flat ground. In space, this sunflower was formed by spinning slowly and letting centrifugal force form the large parabolic organ. Here it lay inert on the ground, pulled out by mechanical devices at the corners of the square. Symbs did not have the musculature to do it themselves.

No part of their stay on Janus made them yearn for the Rings as much as the kitchen. Barnum reclined in the middle of an empty square and let the mechanical claws fit themselves to Bailey's outer tegument. They began to pull, slowly, and Bailey was stretched.

In the Ring they were never more than ten kilometers from the Upper Half. They could drift up there and deploy the sunflower, dream away a few hours, then use the light pressure to push them back into the shaded parts of the Ring. It was nice; it was not exactly sleep, not exactly anything in human experience. It was plant consciousness, a dreamless, simple awareness of the universe, unencumbered with thought processes.

Barnum grumbled now as the sunflower was spread on the ground around them. Though the energy-intake phase of their existence was *not* sleep, several days of trying to accomplish it in gravity left Barnum with symptoms very like lack of sleep. They were both getting irritable. They were eager to return to weightlessness.

He felt the pleasant lethargy creep over him. Beneath him, Bailey was extending powerful rootlets into the naked rock, using acid compounds to eat into it and obtain the small amounts of replacement mass the pair needed.

"So when are we going?" Bailey asked, quietly.

"Any day, now. Any day." Barnum was drowsy. He could feel the sun starting to heat the fluid in Bailey's sunflower. He was like a daisy nodding lazily in a green pasture.

"I guess I don't need to point it out, but the transcription is complete. There's no need for us to stay."

"I know."

That night Tympani danced again. She made it slow, with none of the flying leaps and swelling crescendos of the first time. And slowly, almost imperceptibly, a theme crept in. It was changed, rearranged; it was a run here and a phrase there. It never quite became melodic, as it was on the tape, but that was only right. It had been scored for strings, brass, and many other instruments but they hadn't written in a tympani part. She had to transpose for her instrument. It was still contrapunctual.

When she was done she told them of her most successful concert, the one that had almost captured the public fancy. It had been a duet, she and her partner playing the same synapticon while they made love.

The first and second movements had been well received.

"Then we reached the finale," she remembered, wryly, "and we suddenly lost sight of the harmonies and it sounded like, well, one reviewer mentioned 'the death agonies of a hyena.' I'm afraid we didn't hear it."

"Who was it? Ragtime?"

She laughed. "Him? No, he doesn't know anything about music. He makes love all right, but he couldn't do it in three-quarter time. It was Myers, the guy who invented the synapticon. But he's more of an engineer than a musician. I haven't really found a good partner for that, and anyway, I wouldn't do it in public again. Those reviews hurt."

"But I get the idea you feel the ideal conditions for making music with it would be a duet, in free fall, while making love."

She snorted. "Did I say that?" She was quiet for a long time.

"Maybe it is," she finally conceded. She sighed. "The nature of the instrument is such that the most powerful music is made when the body is most in tune with its surroundings, and I can't think of a better time than when I'm approaching an orgasm."

"Why didn't it work, then?"

"Maybe I shouldn't say this, but Myers blew it. He got excited, which is the whole point, of course, but he couldn't control it. There I was, tuned like a Stradivarius, feeling heavenly harps playing inside me, and he starts blasting out a jungle rhythm on a kazoo. I'm not going through that again. I'll stick to the traditional ballet like I did tonight."

"Tympani," Barnum blurted, "I could make love in three-quarter time."

She got up and paced around the room, looking at him from time to time. He couldn't see through her eyes, but felt uncomfortably aware that she saw a grotesque green blob with a human face set high up in a mass of putty. He felt a twinge of resentment for Bailey's exterior. Why couldn't she see *him?* He was in there, buried alive. For the first time he felt almost imprisoned. Bailey cringed away from the feeling.

"Is that an invitation?" she asked.

"Yes."

"But you don't have a synapticon."

"Me and Bailey talked it over. He thinks he can function as one. After all, he does much the same thing every second of our lives. He's very adept at rearranging nerve impulses, both in my brain and my body. He more or less lives in my nervous system."

She was momentarily speechless.

"You say you can make music . . . and hear it, without an instrument at all? Bailey does this for you?"

"Sure. We just hadn't thought of routing body movements through the auditory part of the brain. That's what you're doing."

She opened her mouth to say something, then closed it again. She seemed undecided about what to do.

"Tympani, why don't you pair up and go out into the Ring? Wait a minute; hear us out. You told me that my music was great and you think it might even sell. How did I do that? Do you ever think about it?"

"I think about it a lot," she muttered, looking away from him.

"When I came here I didn't even know the names of the notes that were in my head. I was ignorant. I still don't know much. But I write music. And you, you know more about music than anyone I've ever met; you love it, you play it with beauty and skill. But what do you create?"

"I've written things," she said, defensively. "Oh, all right. They weren't any good. I don't seem to have the talent in that direction."

"But I'm proof that you don't need it. I didn't write that music; neither did Bailey. We watched it and listened to it happening all around us. You can't imagine what it's like out there. It's all the music you ever heard."

At first consideration it seemed logical to many that the best art in the system should issue from the Rings of Saturn. Not until humanity reaches Beta Lyrae or farther will a more beautiful place to live be found. Surely an artist could draw endless inspiration from the sights to be seen in the Ring. But artists are rare. How could the Ring produce art in every human who lived there?

The artistic life of the solar system had been dominated by Ringers for over a century. If it was the heroic scale of the Rings and their superb beauty that had caused this, one might expect the art produced to be mainly heroic in nature and beautiful in tone and execution. Such had never been the case. The paintings, poetry, writing, and music of the Ringers covered the entire range of human experience and then went a step beyond.

A man or a woman would arrive at Janus for any of a variety of reasons, determined to abandon his or her former life and pair with a symb. About a dozen people departed like that each day, not to be heard of for up to a decade. They were a reasonable cross section of the race, ranging from the capable to the helpless, some of them kind and others cruel. There were geniuses among them, and idiots. They were precisely as young, old, sympathetic, callous, talented, useless, vulnerable, and fallible as any random sample of humanity must be. Few of them had any training or inclination in the fields of painting or music or writing.

Some of them died. The Rings, after all, were hazardous. These people had no way of learning how to survive out there except by trying and succeeding. But most came back. And they came back with pictures and songs and stories.

Agentry was the only industry on Janus. It took a special kind of agent, because few Ringers could walk into an office and present a finished work of any kind. A literary agent had the easiest job. But a tinpanalleycat had to be ready to teach some rudiments of music to the composer who knew nothing about notation.

The rewards were high. Ringer art was statistically about ten times more likely to sell than art from anywhere else in the system. Better yet, the agent took nearly all the profits instead of a commission, and the artists were never pressuring for more. Ringers had little use for money. Often, an agent could retire on the proceeds of one successful sale.

But the fundamental question of why Ringers produced art was unanswered.

Barnum didn't know. He had some ideas, partially confirmed by Bailey. It was tied up in the blending of the human and symb mind. A Ringer was more than a human, and yet still human. When combined with a symb, something else was created. It was not under their control. The best way Barnum had been able to express it to himself was by saying that this meeting of two different kinds of mind set up a tension at the junction. It was like the addition of amplitudes when two waves meet head on. That tension was mental, and fleshed itself with the symbols that were lying around for the taking in the mind of the human. It had to use human symbols because the intellectual life of a symb starts at the moment it comes in contact with a human brain. The symb has no brain of its own and has to make do with using the human brain on a timesharing basis.

Barnum and Bailey did not worry about the source of their inspiration. Tympani worried about it a lot. She resented the fact that the muse which had always eluded her paid such indiscriminate visits to human-symb pairs. She admitted to them that she thought it unfair, but refused to give them an answer when asked why she would not take the step pairing herself.

But Barnum and Bailey were offering her an alternative, a way to sample what it was like to be paired without actually taking that final step.

In the end, her curiosity defeated her caution. She agreed to make love with them, with Bailey functioning as a living synapticon.

Barnum and Bailey reached Tympani's apartment and she held the door for them. Inside, she dialed all the furniture into the floor, leaving a large, bare room with white walls.

"What do I do?" she asked in a small voice. Barnum reached out and took her hand, which melted into the substance of Bailey.

"Give me your other hand." She did so, and watched stoically as the green stuff crept up her hands and arms. "Don't look at it," Barnum advised, and she obeyed.

He felt air next to his skin as Bailey began manufacturing an atmosphere inside himself and inflating like a balloon. The green sphere got larger, hiding Barnum completely and gradually absorbing Tympani. In five minutes the featureless green ball filled the room.

"I'd never seen that," she said, as they stood holding hands.

"Usually we do it only in space."

"What comes next?"

"Just hold still." She saw him glance over her shoulder, and started to turn. She thought better of it and tensed, knowing what was coming.

A slim tendril had grown out of the inner surface of the symb and groped its way toward the computer terminal at the back of her head. She cringed as it touched her, then relaxed as it wormed its way in.

"How's the contact?" Barnum asked Bailey.

"Just a minute. I'm still feeling it out." The symb had oozed through the microscopic entry points at the rear of the terminal and was following the network of filaments that extended through her cerebrum. Reaching the end of one, Bailey would probe further, searching for the loci he knew so well in Barnum.

"They're slightly different," he told Barnum. "I'll have to do a little testing to be sure I'm at the right spots."

Tympani jumped, then looked down in horror as her arms and legs did a dance without her volition.

"Tell him to stop that!" she shrieked, then gasped as Bailey ran through a rapid series of memory-sensory loci; in almost instantaneous succession she experienced the smell of an orange blossom, the void of the womb, an embarrassing incident as a child, her first free fall. She tasted a meal eaten fifteen years ago. It was like spinning a radio dial through the frequencies, getting fragments of a thousand unrelated songs, and yet being able to hear each of them in its entirety. It lasted less than a second and left her weak. But the weakness was illusory, too, and she recovered and found herself in Barnum's arms.

"Make him stop it," she demanded, struggling away from him.

"It's over," he said.

"Well, almost," Bailey said. The rest of the process was conducted beneath her conscious level. "I'm in," he told Barnum. "I can't guarantee how well this will work. I wasn't built for this sort of thing, you know. I need a larger entry point than that terminal, more like the one I sank into the top of your head."

"Is there any danger to her?"

"Nope, but there's a chance I'll get overloaded and have to halt the whole thing. There's going to be a lot of traffic over that little tendril and I can't be sure it'll handle the load."

"We'll just have to do our best."

They faced each other. Tympani was tense and stony-eyed.

"What's next?" she asked again, planting her feet on the thin but springy and warm surface of Bailey.

"I was hoping you'd do the opening bars. Give me a lead to follow. You've done this once, even if it didn't work."

"All right. Take my hands . . ."

Barnum had no idea how the composition would start. She chose a very subdued tempo. It was not a dirge; in fact, in the beginning it had no tempo at all. It was a free-form tone poem. She moved with a glacial slowness that had none of the loose sexuality he had expected. Barnum watched, and heard a deep undertone develop and knew it as the awakening awareness in his own mind. It was his first response.

Gradually, as she began to move in his direction, he essayed some movement. His music added itself to hers but it remained separate and did not harmonize. They were sitting in different rooms, hearing each other through the walls.

She reached down and touched his leg with her fingertips. She drew her hand slowly along him and the sound was like fingernails rasping on a blackboard. It clashed, it grated, it tore at his nerves. It left him shaken, but he continued with the dance.

Again she touched him, and the theme repeated itself. A third time, with the same results. He relaxed into it, understood it as a part of their music, harsh as it was. It was her tension.

He knelt in front of her and put his hands to her waist. She turned, slowly, making a sound like a rusty metal plate rolling along a concrete floor. She kept spinning and the tone began to modulate and acquire a rhythm. It throbbed, syncopated, as a function of their heartbeats. Gradually the tones began to soften and blend. Tympani's skin was glistening with sweat as she turned faster. Then, at a signal he never consciously received, Barnum lifted her in the air and the sounds cascaded around them as they embraced. She kicked her legs joyously and it combined with the thunderous bass protest of his straining leg muscles to produce an airborne series of chromatics. It reached a crescendo that was impossible to sustain, then tapered off as her feet touched the floor and they collapsed into each other. The sounds muttered to themselves, unresolved, as they cradled each other and caught their breath.

"Now we're in tune, at least," Tympani whispered, and the symb-synapticon picked up the nerve impulses in her mouth and ears and tongue as she said it and heard it, and mixed it with the impulses from Barnum's ears. The result was a vanishing series of arpeggios constructed around each word that echoed around them for minutes. She laughed to hear it, and that was music even without the dressings.

The music had never stopped. It still inhabited the space around them, gathering itself into dark pools around their feet and pulsing in a diminishing allegretto with their hissing breath.

"It's gotten dark," she whispered, afraid to brave the intensity of sound if she were to speak aloud. Her words wove around Barnum's head as he lifted his eyes to look around them. "There are things moving around out there," she said. The tempo increased slightly as her heart caught on the dark-on-dark outlines she sensed.

"The sounds are taking shape," Barnum said. "Don't be afraid of them. It's in your mind."

"I'm not sure I want to see that deeply into my mind."

As the second movement started, stars began to appear over their heads. Tympani lay supine on a surface that was beginning to yield beneath her, like sand or some thick liquid. She accepted it. She let it conform to her shoulder blades as Barnum coaxed music from her body with his hands. He found handfuls of pure, bell-like tones, unencumbered with timbre or resonance, existing by themselves. Putting his lips to her, he sucked out a mouthful of chords which he blew out one by one, where they clustered like bees around his nonsense words, ringing change after change on the harmonies in his voice.

She stretched her arms over her head and bared her teeth, grabbing at the sand that was now as real to her touch as her own body was. Here was the sexuality Barnum had sought. Brash and libidinous as a goddess in the Hindu pantheon, her body shouted like a Dixieland clarinet and the sounds caught on the waving tree limbs overhead and thrashed about like tattered sheets. Laughing, she held her hands before her face and watched as sparks of blue and white fire arced across her fingertips. The sparks leaped out to Barnum and he glowed where they touched him.

The universe they were visiting was an extraordinarily cooperative one. When the sparks jumped from Tympani's hand into the dark, cloud-streaked sky, bolts of lightning came skittering back at her. They were awesome, but not fearsome. Tympani knew them to be productions of Bailey's mind. But she liked them. When the tornadoes formed above her and writhed in a dance around her head, she liked that, too.

The gathering storm increased as the tempo of their music increased, in perfect step. Gradually, Tympani lost track of what was happening. The fire in her body was transformed into madness: a piano rolling down a hillside or a harp being used as a trampoline. There was the drunken looseness of a slide trombone played at the bottom of a well. She ran her tongue over his cheek and it was the sound of beads of oil falling on a snare drum. Barnum sought entrance to the concert hall, sounding like a head-on collision of harpsichords.

Then someone pulled the plug on the turntable motor and the tape was left to thread its way through the heads at a slowly diminishing speed as they rested. The music gabbled insistently at them, reminding them that this could only be a brief intermission, that they were in the command of forces beyond themselves. They accepted it, Tympani sitting lightly in Barnum's lap, facing him, and allowing herself to be cradled in his arms.

"Why the pause?" Tympani asked, and was delighted to see her words escape her mouth not in sound, but in print. She touched the small letters as they fluttered to the ground.

"Bailey requested it," Barnum said, also in print. "His circuits are overloading." His words orbited twice around his head, then vanished.

"And why the skywriting?"

"So as not to foul the music with more words."

She nodded, and rested her head on his shoulder again.

Barnum was happy. He gently stroked her back, producing a warm, fuzzy rumble. He shaped the contours of the sound with his fingertips. Living in the Ring, he was used to the feeling of triumphing over something infinitely vast. With the aid of Bailey he could scale down the mighty Ring until it was within the scope of a human mind. But nothing he had ever experienced rivaled the sense of power he felt in touching Tympani and getting music.

A breeze was starting to eddy around them. It rippled the leaves of the tree that arched over them. The lovers had stayed planted on the ground during the height of the storm; now the breeze lifted them into the air and wafted them into the gray clouds.

Tympani had not noticed it. When she opened her eyes, all she knew was that they were back in limbo again, alone with the music. And the music was beginning to build.

The last movement was both more harmonious and less varied. They were finally in tune, acknowledging the baton of the same conductor. The piece they were extemporizing was jubilant. It was noisy and broad, and gave signs of becoming Wagnerian. But somewhere the gods were laughing.

Tympani flowed with it, letting it become her. Barnum was sketching out the melody line while she was content to supply the occasional appogiatura, the haunting nuance that prevented it from becoming ponderous.

The clouds began to withdraw, slowly revealing the new illusion that Bailey had moved them to. It was hazy. But it was vast. Tympani opened her eyes and saw—the view from the Upper Half, only a few kilometers above the plane of the Rings. Below her was an infinite golden surface and above her were stars. Her eyes were drawn to the plane, down there. . . . It was thin. Insubstantial. One could see right through it. Shielding her eyes from the glare of the sun (and introducing a forlorn minor theme into the music) she peered into the whirling marvel they had taken her out here to see, and her ears were filled with the shrieks of her unspoken fear as Bailey picked it up. There were stars down there, all around her and moving toward her, and she was moving through them, and they were beginning to revolve, and—the inner surface of Bailey. Above her unseeing eyes, a slim green tendril, severed, was writhing back into the wall. It disappeared.

"Burnt out."

"Are you all right?" Barnum asked him.

"I'm all right. Burnt out. You felt it. I warned you the connection might not handle the traffic."

Barnum consoled him. "We never expected that intensity." He shook his head, trying to clear the memory of that awful moment. He had his fears, but evidently no phobias. Nothing had ever gripped him the way the Rings had gripped Tympani. He gratefully felt Bailey slip in and ease the pain back into a corner of his mind where he needn't look at it. Plenty of time for that later, on the long, silent orbits they would soon be following. . . .

Tympani was sitting up, puzzled, but beginning to smile. Barnum wished Bailey could give him a report on her mental condition, but the connection was broken. Shock? He'd forgotten the symptoms.

"I'll have to find out for myself," he told Bailey.

"She looks all right to me," Bailey said. "I was calming her as the contact was breaking. She might not remember much."

She didn't. Mercifully, she remembered the happiness but had only a vague impression of the fear at the end. She didn't want to look at it, which was just as well. There was no need for her to be tantalized or taunted by something she could never have.

They made love there inside Bailey. It was quiet and deep, and lasted a long time. What lingering hurts there were found healing in that gentle silence, punctuated only by the music of their breathing.

Then Bailey slowly retracted around Barnum, contracting their universe down to man-size and forever excluding Tympani.

It was an awkward time for them. Barnum and Bailey were due at the catapult in an hour. All three knew that Tympani could never follow them, but they didn't speak of it. They promised to remain friends, and knew it was empty.

Tympani had a financial statement which she handed to Barnum.

"Two thousand, minus nineteen ninety-five for the pills." She dropped the dozen small pellets into his other hand. They contained the trace elements the pair could not obtain in the Rings, and constituted the only reason they ever needed to visit Janus.

"Is that enough?" Tympani asked, anxiously.

Barnum looked at the sheet of paper. He had to think hard to recall how important money was to single humans. He had little use for it. His bank balance would keep him in supplement pills for thousands of years if he could live that long, even if he never came back to sell another song. And he understood now why there was so little repeat business on Janus. Pairs and humans could not mix. The only common ground was art, and even there the single humans were driven by monetary pressures alien to pairs.

"Sure, that's fine," he said, and tossed the paper aside. "It's more than I need."

Tympani was relieved.

"I *know* that of course," she said, feeling guilty. "But I always feel like an exploiter. It's not very much. Rag says this one could really take off and we could get rich. And that's all you'll ever get out of it."

Barnum knew that, and didn't care. "It's really all we need," he repeated. "I've already been paid in the only coin I value, which is the privilege of knowing you."

They left it at that.

The countdown wasn't a long one. The operators of the cannon tended to herd the pairs through the machine like cattle through a gate. But it was plenty of time for Barnum and Bailey, on stretched-time, to embed Tympani in amber.

"Why?" Barnum asked at one point. "Why her? Where does the fear come from?"

"I saw some things," Bailey said, thoughtfully. "I was going to probe, but then I hated myself for it. I decided to leave her private traumas alone."

The count was ticking slowly down to the firing signal, and a bass, mushy music began to play in Barnum's ears.

"Do you still love her?" Barnum asked.

"More than ever."

"So do I. It feels good, and it hurts. I suppose we'll get over it. But from now on, we'd better keep our world down to a size we can handle. What is that music, anyway?"

"A send-off," Bailey said. He accelerated them until they could hear it. "It's coming over the radio. A circus march."

Barnum had no sooner recognized it than he felt the gentle but increasing push of the cannon accelerating him up the tube. He laughed, and the two of them shot out of the bulging brass pipe of the Pearly Gates calliope. They made a bull's-eye through a giant orange smoke ring, accompanied by the strains of "Thunder and Blazes."

"The Barbie Murders"

Damon Knight was living in Florida and publishing a series of hardcover anthologies called Orbit *when I first started submitting stories to him. Damon had always been one of the best editors in the field, going all the way back to the 1950s, and the* Orbit *books were very good. It was considered a mark of prestige to appear in them. I sent him three stories and he bought two of them. (More about the one he didn't buy later.)*

Shortly after I had established a written correspondence with Damon, he told me that he and his wife, Kate Wilhelm, were considering moving away from Florida to a smaller town. They were considering Eugene. I gathered it was for much the same reason I was living there; they had a young son named Jon, and the area they lived in was beginning to resemble a big city. They visited Eugene, liked it, and soon had bought a house. The small science fiction community in Oregon, including myself, couldn't believe our luck.

Damon turned out to be a quiet-spoken man with a beard almost as big as he was, and an incredible, dry wit. He was one of those rare people who never seemed to say anything unless it was really worth listening to. Kate Wilhelm was much like him in that sense, and not only is she one of the best writers I've ever known, she is one of the best human beings. On the very first meeting you just knew you were in the presence of someone special.

Damon and Kate soon initiated something they had been doing for some years in Florida, which was a sort of open house one night every month for writers and readers. It quickly became the place to be in Eugene.

Not long after their arrival they hosted the first Oregon edition of something they had begun in Pennsylvania and carried on in Florida: The Milford Science Fiction Writers' Conference. This was one of the two best-known gatherings in the genre, the other being Clarion, held every year at Michigan State University, my old alma mater. Clarion goes on for six weeks and has a different guest writer each week. Milford lasted only one week. I was invited to attend, and thus got my first taste of "workshopping" stories.

It turned out to be my only taste of it. Workshops didn't really agree with me. This is absolutely nothing against Milford. I know that many writers have benefited from this sort of thing, and that many writers are proud to be able to pass on some of the tricks of the trade to beginners, journeymen, and apprentices, as well as swapping tradecraft with other veterans. It just doesn't work for me. I am usually helpless to point out anything useful about someone else's story except to say that it works for me, or it doesn't work for me. Also, when I'm finished with a story, I'm done with it. I don't enjoy revisiting it, tinkering with it, and won't do so except to editorial order, and will fight that if it is given. Luckily, I have been very little edited in my career in books and magazines. (Movies are another story, and we'll get to that.)

The format of Milford was simple. Everyone submitted stories, everyone read them, and then we would all sit down together and go around the circle, tearing them apart. Most of the people there had published. Gene Wolfe was there, and so was Kim Stanley Robinson. There didn't seem to be any favoritism; everyone got savaged more or less equally.

This story is one that was workshopped. Maybe "savaged" is too strong a word. I remember that several people had some good things to say about this story, and some others, but without an exception I can remember every story got a few helpful hints that the reader felt could have improved it. Many of them were good hints.

Kate had what may have been the best critique of all . . . and it was of no use to me because of my stubbornness about rewriting. Central problem of the story: how do you find a murderer among a community who all look exactly the same? Kate found the premise fascinating, but thought it should have been the jumping-off point for a deeper examination of the idea of identity itself. Her disappointment was that I had avoided any of the deeper existential and moral questions and turned it into a "puzzle" story. This criticism was offered with no condescension or opprobrium at puzzle stories per se, as she had no problem with them—and in fact went on to write a great many wonderful detective novels later that, being Kate Wilhelm stories, were always much more than simply puzzles—but rather with the thought that the work could have been more significant than it was. I accepted it in that spirit . . . and moved on to the next. Tackling what Kate had suggested would have involved a total rethinking and complete rewrite, and I just don't do that. For me, it is better to apply the lessons learned and search for the opportunities missed in the next story I write, not the previous one. Not a flawless system, but mine own.

A word about Anna-Louise Bach. She is not actually a part of the Eight Worlds stories. Some critics have assumed she is, and I suppose she might somehow fit in between today and the alien invasion, in a time when we have established large cities on the moon but before the time, two hundred years or so from today, when the bulk of the Eight Worlds stories take place. But I never thought of her that way.

No, it was simply a matter of every once in a while I would come up with a darker story idea. A situation the police should handle. The Eight Worlds is a semi-utopian environment—and by that, I mean not perfect, because I don't believe in such a thing, but a place and time that is better in many ways than the world we have today. So when I had a story that was too nasty for those rascals in the Eight Worlds, I handed it to the unfortunate Anna-Louise. Thus I created her career, in no particular order, through half a dozen stories from her days as a probationary patrolwoman up to the chief of police of the Lunar community of New Dresden. Several of them are in this book, including one rescued from a state of suspended animation.

THE BARBIE MURDERS

THE BODY CAME to the morgue at 2246 hours. No one paid much attention to it. It was a Saturday night, and the bodies were piling up like logs in a millpond. A harried attendant working her way down the row of stainless steel tables picked up the sheaf of papers that came with the body, peeling back the sheet over the face. She took a card from her pocket and scrawled on it, copying from the reports filed by the investigating officer and the hospital staff:

Ingraham, Leah Petrie. Female. Age: 35. Length: 2.1 meters. Mass: 59 Kilograms. Dead on arrival, Crisium Emergency Terminal. Cause of death: homicide. Next of kin: unknown.

She wrapped the wire attached to the card around the left big toe, slid the dead weight from the table and onto the wheeled carrier, took it to cubicle 659A, and rolled out the long tray.

The door slammed shut, and the attendant placed the paperwork in the out tray, never noticing that, in his report, the investigating officer had not specified the sex of the corpse.

Lieutenant Anna-Louise Bach had moved into her new office three days ago and already the paper on her desk was threatening to avalanche onto the floor.

To call it an office was almost a perversion of the term. It had a file cabinet for pending cases; she could open it only at severe risk to life and limb. The drawers had a tendency to spring out at her, pinning her in her chair in the corner. To reach "A" she had to stand on her chair; "Z" required her either to sit on her desk or to straddle the bottom drawer with one foot in the legwell and the other against the wall.

But the office had a door. True, it could only be opened if no one was occupying the single chair in front of the desk.

Bach was in no mood to gripe. She loved the place. It was ten times better than the squadroom, where she had spent ten years elbow-to-elbow with the other sergeants and corporals.

Jorge Weil stuck his head in the door.

"Hi. We're taking bids on a new case. What am I offered?"

"Put me down for half a Mark," Bach said, without looking up from the report she was writing. "Can't you see I'm busy?"

"Not as busy as you're going to be." Weil came in without an invitation and settled himself in the chair. Bach looked up, opened her mouth, then said nothing. She had the authority to order him to get his big feet out of her "cases completed" tray, but not the experience in exercising it. And she and Jorge had worked together for three years. Why should a stripe of gold paint on her shoulder change their relationship? She supposed the informality was Weil's way of saying he wouldn't let her promotion bother him as long as she didn't get snotty about it.

Weil deposited a folder on top of the teetering pile marked "For Immediate Action," then leaned back again. Bach eyed the stack of paper—and the circular file mounted in the wall not half a meter from it, leading to the incinerator—and thought about having an accident. Just a careless nudge with an elbow . . .

"Aren't you even going to open it?" Weil asked, sounding disappointed. "It's not every day I'm going to hand-deliver a case."

"You tell me about it, since you want to so badly."

"All right. We've got a body, which is cut up pretty bad. We've got the murder weapon, which is a knife. We've got thirteen eyewitnesses who can describe the killer, but we don't really need them since the murder was committed in front of a television camera. We've got the tape."

"You're talking about a case which has to have been solved ten minutes after the first report, untouched by human hands. Give it to the computer, idiot." But she looked up. She didn't like the smell of it. "Why give it to me?"

"Because of the other thing we know. The scene of the crime. The murder was committed at the barbie colony."

"Oh, sweet Jesus."

The Temple of the Standardized Church in Luna was in the center of the Standardist Commune, Anytown, North Crisium. The best way to reach it, they found, was a local tube line which paralleled the Cross-Crisium Express Tube.

She and Weil checked out a blue-and-white police capsule with a priority sorting code and surrendered themselves to the New Dresden municipal transport system—the pill sorter, as the New Dresdenites called it. They were whisked through the precinct chute to the main nexus, where thousands of capsules were stacked awaiting a routing order to clear the computer. On the big conveyer which should have taken them to a holding cubby, they were snatched by a grapple—the cops called it the long arm of the law—and moved ahead to the multiple maws of the Cross-Crisium while people in other capsules glared at them. The capsule was inserted, and Bach and Weil were pressed hard into the backs of their seats.

In seconds they emerged from the tube and out onto the plain of Crisium, speeding along through the vacuum, magnetically suspended a few millimeters above the induction rail. Bach glanced up at the Earth, then stared out the window at the featureless landscape rushing by, She brooded.

It had taken a look at the map to convince her that the barbie colony was indeed in the New Dresden jurisdiction—a case of blatant gerrymandering if ever there was one. Anytown was fifty kilometers from what she thought of as the boundaries of New Dresden, but was joined to the city by a dotted line that represented a strip of land one meter wide.

A roar built up as they entered a tunnel and air was injected into the tube ahead of them. The car shook briefly as the shock wave built up, then they popped through pressure doors into the tube station of Anytown. The capsule doors hissed and they climbed out onto the platform.

The tube station at Anytown was primarily a loading dock and warehouse. It was a large space with plastic crates stacked against all the walls, and about fifty people working to load them into freight capsules.

Bach and Weil stood on the platform for a moment, uncertain where to go. The murder had happened at a spot not twenty meters in front of them, right here in the tube station.

"This place gives me the creeps," Weil volunteered.

"Me, too."

Every one of the fifty people Bach could see was identical to every other. All appeared to be female, though only faces, feet, and hands were visible, everything else concealed by loose white pajamas belted at the waist. They were all blonde; all had hair cut off at the shoulder and parted in the middle, blue eyes, high foreheads, short noses, and small mouths.

The work slowly stopped as the barbies became aware of them. They eyed Bach and Weil suspiciously. Bach picked one at random and approached her.

"Who's in charge here?" she asked.

"We are," the barbie said. Bach took it to mean the woman herself, recalling something about barbies never using the singular pronoun.

"We're supposed to meet someone at the temple," she said. "How do we get there?"

"Through that doorway," the woman said. "It leads to Main Street. Follow the street to the temple. But you really should cover yourselves."

"Huh? What do you mean?" Bach was not aware of anything wrong with the way she and Weil were dressed. True, neither of them wore as much as the barbies did. Bach wore her usual blue nylon briefs in addition to a regulation uniform cap, arm and thigh bands, and cloth-soled slippers. Her weapon, communicator, and handcuffs were fastened to a leather equipment belt.

"Cover yourself," the barbie said, with a pained look. "You're flaunting your differentness. And you, with all that hair . . ." There were giggles and a few shouts from the other barbies.

"Police business," Weil snapped.

"Uh, yes," Bach said, feeling annoyed that the barbie had put her on the defensive. After all, this was New Dresden, it was a public thoroughfare—even though by tradition and usage a Standardist enclave—and they were entitled to dress as they wished.

Main Street was a narrow, mean little place. Bach had expected a promenade like those in the shopping districts of New Dresden; what she found was indistinguishable from a residential corridor. They drew curious stares and quite a few frowns from the identical people they met.

There was a modest plaza at the end of the street. It had a low roof of bare metal, a few trees, and a blocky stone building in the center of a radiating network of walks.

A barbie who looked just like all the others met them at the entrance. Bach asked if she was the one Weil had spoken to on the phone, and she said she was. Bach wanted to know if they could go inside to talk. The barbie said the temple was off limits to outsiders and suggested they sit on a bench outside the building.

When they were settled, Bach stared her questioning. "First, I need to know your name, and your title. I assume that you are . . . what was it?" She consulted her notes, taken hastily from a display she had called up on the computer terminal in her office. "I don't seem to have found a title for you."

"We have none," the barbie said. "If you must think of a title, consider us as the keeper of records."

"All right. And your name?"

"We have no name."

Bach sighed. "Yes, I understand that you forsake names when you come here. But you had one before. You were given one at birth. I'm going to have to have it for my investigation."

The woman looked pained. "No, you don't understand. It is true that this body had a name at one time. But it has been wiped from this one's mind. It would cause this one a great deal of pain to be reminded of it." She stumbled verbally every time she said "this one." Evidently even a polite circumlocution of the personal pronoun was distressing.

"I'll try to get it from another angle, then." This was already getting hard to deal with, Bach saw, and knew it could only get tougher. "You say you are the keeper of records."

"We are. We keep records because the law says we must. Each citizen must be recorded, or so we have been told."

"For a very good reason," Bach said. "We're going to need access to those records. For the investigation. You understand? I assume an officer has already been through them, or the deceased couldn't have been identified as Leah P. Ingraham."

"That's true. But it won't be necessary for you to go through the records again. We are here to confess. We murdered L. P. Ingraham, serial number 11005. We are surrendering peacefully. You may take us to your prison." She held out her hands, wrists close together, ready to be shackled.

Weil was startled, reached tentatively for his handcuffs, then looked to Bach for guidance.

"Let me get this straight. You're saying you're the one who did it? You, personally."

"That's correct. We did it. We have never defied temporal authority, and we are willing to pay the penalty."

"Once more." Bach reached out and grasped the barbie's wrist, forced the hand open, palm up. "*This* is the person, this is the body that committed the murder? This hand, this one right here, held the knife and killed Ingraham? This hand, as opposed to 'your' thousands of other hands?"

The barbie frowned.

"Put that way, no. *This* hand did not grasp the murder weapon. But *our* hand did. What's the difference?"

"Quite a bit, in the eyes of the law." Bach sighed, and let go of the woman's hand. Woman? She wondered if the term applied. She realized she needed to know more about Standardists. But it was convenient to think of them as such, since their faces were feminine.

"Let's try again. I'll need you—and the eyewitnesses to the crime—to study the tape of the murder. *I* can't tell the difference between the murderer, the victim, or any of the bystanders. But surely you must be able to. I assume that . . . well, like the old saying went, 'all Chinamen look alike.' That was to Caucasian races, of course. Orientals had no trouble telling each other apart. So I thought that you . . . that you people would . . ." She trailed off at the look of blank incomprehension on the barbie's face.

"We don't know what you're talking about."

Bach's shoulders slumped.

"You mean you can't . . . not even if you saw her again . . . ?"

The woman shrugged. "We all look the same to this one."

Anna-Louise Bach sprawled out on her flotation bed later that night, surrounded by scraps of paper. Untidy as it was, her thought processes were helped by actually scribbling facts on paper rather than filing them in her datalink. And she did her best work late at night, at home, in bed, after taking a bath or making love. Tonight she had done both and found she needed every bit of the invigorating clarity it gave her.

Standardists.

They were an off-beat religious sect founded ninety years earlier by someone whose name had not survived. That was not surprising, since Standardists gave up their names when they joined the order, made every effort consistent with the laws of the land to obliterate the name and person as if he or she had never existed. The epithet "barbie" had quickly been attached to them by the press. The origin of the word was a popular children's toy of the twentieth and early twenty-first centuries, a plastic, sexless, mass-produced "girl" doll with an elaborate wardrobe.

The barbies had done surprisingly well for a group which did not reproduce, which relied entirely on new members from the outside world to replenish their numbers. They had grown for twenty years, then reached a population stability where deaths equalled new members—which they call "components." They had suffered moderately from religious intolerance, moving from country to country until the majority had come to Luna sixty years ago.

They drew new components from the walking wounded of society, the people who had not done well in a world which preached conformity, passivity, and tolerance of your billions of neighbors, yet rewarded only those who were individualist and aggressive enough to stand apart from the herd. The barbies had opted out of a system where one had to be at once a face in the crowd and a proud individual with hopes and dreams and desires. They were the inheritors of a long tradition of ascetic withdrawal, surrendering their names, their bodies, and their temporal aspirations to a life that was ordered and easy to understand.

Bach realized she might be doing some of them a disservice in that evaluation. They were not necessarily all losers. There must be those among them who were attracted simply by the religious ideas of the sect, though Bach felt there was little in the teachings that made sense.

She skimmed through the dogma, taking notes. The Standardists preached the commonality of humanity, denigrated free will, and elevated the group and the consensus to demi-god status. Nothing too unusual in the theory; it was the practice of it that made people queasy.

There was a creation theory and a godhead, who was not worshipped but contemplated. Creation happened when the Goddess—a prototypical earth-mother who had no name—gave birth to the universe. She put people in it, all alike, stamped from the same universal mold.

Sin entered the picture. One of the people began to wonder. This person had a name, given to him or her *after* the original sin as part of the punishment, but Bach could not find it written down anywhere. She decided that it was a dirty word which Standardists never told an outsider.

This person asked Goddess what it was all for. What had been wrong with the void, that Goddess had seen fit to fill it with people who didn't seem to have a reason for existing?

That was too much. For reasons unexplained—and impolite to even ask about—Goddess had punished humans by introducing differentness into the world. Warts, big noses, kinky hair, white skin, tall people and fat people and deformed people, blue eyes, body hair, freckles, testicles, and labia. A billion faces and fingerprints, each soul trapped in a body distinct from all others, with the heavy burden of trying to establish an identity in a perpetual shouting match.

But the faith held that peace was achieved in striving to regain that lost Eden. When all humans were again the same person, Goddess would welcome them back. Life was a testing, a trial.

Bach certainly agreed with that. She gathered her notes and shuffled them together, then picked up the book she had brought back from Anytown. The barbie had given it to her when Bach asked for a picture of the murdered woman.

It was a blueprint for a human being.

The title was *The Book of Specifications. The Specs,* for short. Each barbie carried one, tied to her waist with a tape measure. It gave tolerances in engineering terms, defining what a barbie could look like. It was profusely illustrated with drawings of parts of the body in minute detail, giving measurements in millimeters.

She closed the book and sat up, propping her head on a pillow. She reached for her viewpad and propped it on her knees, punched the retrieval code for the murder tape. For the twentieth time that night, she watched a figure spring forward from a crowd of identical figures in the tube station, slash at Leah Ingraham, and melt back into the crowd as her victim lay bleeding and eviscerated on the floor.

She slowed it down, concentrating on the killer, trying to spot something different about her. Anything at all would do. The knife struck. Blood spurted. Barbies milled about in consternation. A few belatedly ran after the killer, not reacting fast enough. People seldom reacted quickly enough. But the killer had blood on her hand. Make a note to ask about that.

Bach viewed the film once more, saw nothing useful, and decided to call it a night.

The room was long and tall, brightly lit from strips high above: Bach followed the attendant down the rows of square locker doors which lined one wall. The air was cool and humid, the floor wet from a recent hosing.

The man consulted the card in his hand and pulled the metal handle on locker 659A, making a noise that echoed through the bare room. He slid the drawer out and lifted the sheet from the corpse.

It was not the first mutilated corpse Bach had seen, but it was the first nude barbie. She immediately noted the lack of nipples on the two hills of flesh that pretended to be breasts, and the smooth, unmarked skin in the crotch. The attendant was frowning, consulting the card on the corpse's foot.

"Some mistake here," he muttered. "Geez, the headaches. What do you do with a thing like that?" He scratched his head, then scribbled through the large letter "F" on the card, replacing it with a neat "N." He looked at Bach and grinned sheepishly. "What do you do?" he repeated.

Bach didn't much care what he did. She studied L. P. Ingraham's remains, hoping that something on the body would show her why a barbie had decided she must die.

There was little difficulty seeing *how* she had died. The knife had entered her abdomen, going deep, and the wound extended upward from there in a slash that ended beneath the breastbone. Part of the bone was cut through. The knife had been sharp, but it would have taken a powerful arm to slice through that much meat.

The attendant watched curiously as Bach pulled the dead woman's legs apart and studied what she saw there. She found the tiny slit of the urethra set back around the curve, just anterior to the anus.

Bach opened her copy of *The Specs*, took out a tape measure, and started to work.

"Mr. Atlas, I got your name from the Morphology Guide's files as a practitioner who's had a lot of dealings with the Standardist Church."

The man frowned, then shrugged. "So? You may not approve of them, but they're legal. And my records are in order. I don't do any work on anybody until the police have checked for a criminal record." He sat on the edge of the desk in the spacious consulting room, facing Bach. Mr. Rock Atlas—surely a *nom de métier*—had shoulders carved from granite, teeth like flashing pearls, and the face of a young god. He was a walking, flexing advertisement for his profession. Bach crossed her legs nervously. She had always had a taste for beef.

"I'm not investigating you, Mr. Atlas. This is a murder case, and I'd appreciate your cooperation."

"Call me Rock," he said, with a winning smile.

"Must I? Very well. I came to ask you what you would do, how long the work would take, if I asked to be converted to a barbie."

His face fell. "Oh, no, what a tragedy! I can't allow it. My dear, it would be a crime." He reached over to her and touched her chin lightly, turning her head. "No, Lieutenant, for you I'd build up the hollows in the cheeks just the slightest bit— maybe tighten up the muscles behind them—then drift the orbital bones out a little bit farther from the nose to set your eyes wider. More attention-getting, you understand. That touch of mystery. Then of course there's your nose."

She pushed his hand away and shook her head. "No, I'm not coming to you for the operation. I just want to know. How much work would it entail, and how close can you come to the specs of the church?" Then she frowned and looked at him suspiciously. "What's wrong with my nose?"

"Well, my dear, I didn't mean to imply there was anything *wrong;* in fact, it has a certain overbearing power that must be useful to you once in a while, in the circles you move in. Even the lean to the left could be justified, aesthetically—"

"Never mind," she said, angry at herself for having fallen into his sales pitch. "Just answer my question."

He studied her carefully, asked her to stand up and turn around. She was about to object that she had not necessarily meant herself personally as the surgical candidate, just a woman in general, when he seemed to lose interest in her.

"It wouldn't be much of a job," he said. "Your height is just slightly over the parameters; I could take that out of your thighs and lower legs, maybe shave some vertebrae. Take out some fat here and put it back there. Take off those nipples and dig out your uterus and ovaries, sew up your crotch. With a man, chop off the penis. I'd have to break up your skull a little and shift the bones around, then build up the face from there. Say two days' work, one overnight and one outpatient."

"And when you were through, what would be left to identify me?"

"Say that again?"

Bach briefly explained her situation, and Atlas pondered it.

"You've got a problem. I take off the fingerprints and footprints. I don't leave any external scars, not even microscopic ones. No moles, freckles, warts or birthmarks; they all have to go. A blood test would work, and so would a retinal print. An X-ray of the skull. A voiceprint would be questionable. I even that out as much as possible. I can't think of anything else."

"Nothing that could be seen from a purely visual exam?"

"That's the whole point of the operation, isn't it?"

"I know. I was just hoping you might know something even the barbies were not aware of. Thank you, anyway."

He got up, took her hand, and kissed it. "No trouble. And if you ever decide to get that nose taken care of . . ."

She met Jorge Weil at the temple gate in the middle of Anytown. He had spent his morning there, going through the records, and she could see the work didn't agree with him. He took her back to the small office where the records were kept in battered file cabinets. There was a barbie waiting for them there. She spoke without preamble.

"We decided at equalization last night to help you as much as possible."

"Oh, yeah? Thanks. I wondered if you would, considering what happened fifty years ago."

Weil looked puzzled. "What was that?"

Bach waited for the barbie to speak, but she evidently wasn't going to.

"All right. I found it last night. The Standardists were involved in murder once before, not long after they came to Luna. You notice you never see one of them in New Dresden?"

Weil shrugged. "So what? They keep to themselves."

"They were *ordered* to keep to themselves. At first, they could move freely like any other citizens. Then one of them killed somebody—not a Standardist this time. It was known the murderer was a barbie; there were witnesses. The police started looking for the killer. You guess what happened."

"They ran into the problems we're having." Weil grimaced. "It doesn't look so good, does it?"

"It's hard to be optimistic," Bach conceded. "The killer was never found. The barbies offered to surrender one of their number at random, thinking the law would be satisfied with that. But of course it wouldn't do. There was a public outcry, and a lot of pressure to force them to adopt some kind of distinguishing characteristic, like a number tattooed on their foreheads. I don't think that would have worked, either. It could have been covered.

"The fact is that the barbies were seen as a menace to society. They could kill at will and blend back into their community like grains of sand on a beach. We would be powerless to punish a guilty party. There was no provision in the law for dealing with them."

"So what happened?"

"The case is marked closed, but there's no arrest, no conviction, and no suspect. A deal was made whereby the Standardists could practice their religion as long as they never mixed with other citizens. They had to stay in Anytown. Am I right?" She looked at the barbie.

"Yes. We've adhered to the agreement."

"I don't doubt it. Most people are barely aware you exist out here. But now we've got this. One barbie kills another barbie, and under a television camera . . ." Bach stopped, and looked thoughtful. "Say, it occurs to me . . . Wait a minute. *Wait a minute.*" She didn't like the look of it.

"I wonder. This murder took place in the tube station. It's the only place in Anytown that's scanned by the municipal security system. And fifty years is a long time between murders, even in a town as small as . . . How many people did you say live here, Jorge?"

"About seven thousand. I feel I know them all intimately." Weil had spent the day sorting barbies. According to measurements made from the tape, the killer was at the top end of permissible height.

"How about it?" Bach said to the barbie. "Is there anything I ought to know?"

The woman bit her lip, looked uncertain.

"Come on, you said you were going to help me."

"Very well. There have been three other killings in the last month. You would not have heard of this one except it took place with outsiders present. Purchasing agents were there on the loading platform. They made the initial report. There was nothing we could do to hush it up."

"But why would you want to?"

"Isn't it obvious? We exist with the possibility of persecution always with us. We don't wish to appear a threat to others. We wish to appear peaceful—which we *are*—and prefer to handle the problems of the group within the group itself. By divine consensus."

Bach knew she would get nowhere pursuing that line of reasoning. She decided to take the conversation back to the previous murders.

"Tell me what you know. Who was killed, and do you have any idea why? Or should I be talking to someone else?" Something occurred to her then, and she wondered why she hadn't asked it before. "You *are* the person I was speaking to yesterday, aren't you? Let me rephrase that. You're the body . . . that is, this body before me . . ."

"We know what you're talking about," the barbie said. "Uh, yes, you are correct. We are . . . *I* am the one you spoke to." She had to choke the word out, blushing furiously. "We have been . . . *I* have been selected as the component to deal with you, since it was perceived at equalization that this matter must be dealt with. This one was chosen as . . . *I* was chosen as punishment."

"You don't have to say 'I' if you don't want to."

"Oh, thank you."

"Punishment for what?"

"For . . . for individualistic tendencies. We spoke up too personally at equalization, in favor of cooperation with you. As a political necessity. The conservatives wish to stick to our sacred principles no matter what the cost. We are divided; this makes for bad feelings within the organism, for sickness. This one spoke out, and was punished by having her own way, by being appointed . . . *individually* . . . to deal with you." The woman could not meet Bach's eyes. Her face burned with shame.

"This one has been instructed to reveal her serial number to you. In the future, when you come here you are to ask for 23900."

Bach made a note of it.

"All right. What can you tell me about a possible motive? Do you think all the killings were done by the same . . . component?"

"We do not know. We are no more equipped to select an . . . individual from the group than you are. But there is great consternation. We are fearful."

"I would think so. Do you have reason to believe that the victims were . . . does this make sense? . . . *known* to the killer? Or were they random killings?" Bach hoped not. Random killers were the hardest to catch; without motive, it was hard to tie killer to victim, or to sift one person out of thousands with the opportunity. With the barbies, the problem would be squared and cubed.

"Again, we don't know."

Bach sighed. "I want to see the witnesses to the crime. I might as well start interviewing them."

In short order, thirteen barbies were brought. Bach intended to question them thoroughly to see if their stories were consistent, and if they had changed.

She sat them down and took them one at a time, and almost immediately ran into a stone wall. It took her several minutes to see the problem, frustrating minutes spent trying to establish which of the barbies had spoken to the officer first, which second, and so forth.

"Hold it. Listen carefully. Was this body physically present at the time of the crime? Did these eyes see it happen?"

The barbie's brow furrowed. "Why, no. But does it matter?"

"It does to me, babe. *Hey, twenty-three thousand!*"

The barbie stuck her head in the door. Bach looked pained.

"I need the actual people who were *there*. Not thirteen picked at random."

"The story is known to all."

Bach spent five minutes explaining that it made a difference to her, then waited an hour as 23900 located the people who were actual witnesses.

And again she hit a stone wall. The stories were absolutely identical, which she knew to be impossible. Observers *always* report events differently. They make themselves the hero, invent things before and after they first began observing, re-arrange and edit and interpret. But not the barbies. Bach struggled for an hour, trying to shake one of them, and got nowhere. She was facing a consensus, some-thing that had been discussed among the barbies until an account of the event had emerged and then been accepted as truth. It was probably a close approximation, but it did Bach no good. She needed discrepancies to gnaw at, and there were none.

Worst of all, she was convinced no one was lying to her. Had she questioned the thirteen random choices she would have gotten the same answers. They would have thought of themselves as having been there, since some of them had been and they had been told about it. What happened to one, happened to all.

Her options were evaporating fast. She dismissed the witnesses, called 23900 back in, and sat her down. Bach ticked off points on her fingers.

"One. Do you have the personal effects of the deceased?"

"We have no private property."

Bach nodded. "Two. Can you take me to her room?"

"We each sleep in any room we find available at night. There is no—"

"Right. Three. Any friends or co-workers I might . . ." Bach rubbed her fore-head with one hand. "Right. Skip it. Four. What was her job? Where did she work?"

"All jobs are interchangeable here. We work at what needs—"

"*Right!*" Bach exploded. She got up and paced the floor. "What the hell do you expect me to *do* with a situation like this? I don't have *anything* to work with, not one snuffin' *thing*. No way of telling *why* she was killed, no way to pick out the *killer,* no way . . . ah, *shit*. What do you expect me to *do?*"

"We don't expect you to do anything," the barbie said, quietly. "We didn't ask you to come here. We'd like it very much if you just went away."

In her anger Bach had forgotten that. She was stopped, unable to move in any direction. Finally, she caught Weil's eye and jerked her head toward the door.

"Let's get out of here." Weil said nothing. He followed Bach out the door and hurried to catch up.

They reached the tube station, and Bach stopped outside their waiting capsule. She sat down heavily on a bench, put her chin on her palm, and watched the ant-like mass of barbies working at the loading dock.

"Any ideas?"

Weil shook his head, sitting beside her and removing his cap to wipe sweat from his forehead.

"They keep it too hot in here," he said. Bach nodded, not really hearing him. She watched the group of barbies as two separated themselves from the crowd and came a few steps in her direction. Both were laughing, as if at some private joke, looking right at Bach. One of them reached under her blouse and withdrew a long, gleaming steel knife. In one smooth motion she plunged it into the other barbie's stomach and lifted, bringing her up on the balls of her feet. The one who had been stabbed looked surprised for a moment, staring down at herself, her mouth open as the knife gutted her like a fish. Then her eyes widened and she stared horror-stricken at her companion, and slowly went to her knees, holding the knife to her as blood gushed out and soaked her white uniform.

"*Stop her!*" Bach shouted. She was on her feet and running, after a moment of horrified paralysis. It had looked *so* much like the tape.

She was about forty meters from the killer, who moved with deliberate speed, jogging rather than running. She passed the barbie who had been attacked—and who was now on her side, still holding the knife hilt almost tenderly to herself, wrapping her body around the pain. Bach thumbed the panic button on her communicator, glanced over her shoulder to see Weil kneeling beside the stricken barbie, then looked back—

—to a confusion of running figures. Which one was it? *Which one?*

She grabbed the one that seemed to be in the same place and moving in the same direction as the killer had been before she looked away. She swung the barbie around and hit her hard on the side of the neck with the edge of her palm, watched her fall while trying to look at all the other barbies at the same time. They were running in both directions, some trying to get away, others entering the loading dock to see what was going on. It was a madhouse scene with shrieks and shouts and baffling movement.

Bach spotted something bloody lying on the floor, then knelt by the inert figure and clapped the handcuffs on her.

She looked up into a sea of faces, all alike.

The commissioner dimmed the lights, and he, Bach, and Weil faced the big screen at the end of the room. Beside the screen was a department photoanalyst with a pointer in her hand. The tape began to run.

"Here they are," the woman said, indicating two barbies with the tip of the long stick. They were just faces on the edge of the crowd, beginning to move. "Victim right here, the suspect to her right." Everyone watched as the stabbing was re-created. Bach winced when she saw how long she had taken to react. In her favor, it had taken Weil a fraction of a second longer.

"Lieutenant Bach begins to move here. The suspect moves back toward the crowd. If you'll notice, she is watching Bach over her shoulder. Now. Here." She froze a frame. "Bach loses eye contact. The suspect peels off the plastic glove which prevented blood from staining her hand. She drops it, moves laterally. By the time Bach looks back, we can see she is after the wrong suspect."

Bach watched in sick fascination as her image assaulted the wrong barbie, the actual killer only a meter to her left. The tape resumed normal speed, and Bach watched the killer until her eyes began to hurt from not blinking. She would not lose her this time.

"She's incredibly brazen. She does not leave the room for another twenty minutes." Bach saw herself kneel and help the medical team load the wounded barbie into the capsule. The killer had been at her elbow, almost touching her. She felt her arm break out in goose pimples.

She remembered the sick fear that had come over her as she knelt by the injured woman. *It could be any of them. The one behind me, for instance . . .*

She had drawn her weapon then, backed against the wall, and not moved until the reinforcements arrived a few minutes later.

At a motion from the commissioner, the lights came back on.

"Let's hear what you have," he said.

Bach glanced at Weil, then read from her notebook.

"Sergeant Weil was able to communicate with the victim shortly before medical help arrived. He asked her if she knew anything pertinent as to the identity of her assailant. She answered no, saying only that it was 'the wrath.' She could not elaborate. I quote now from the account Sergeant Weil wrote down immediately after the interview. 'Victim said, "It hurts, it hurts." "I'm dying, I'm dying." Victim became incoherent, and I attempted to get a shirt from the onlookers to stop the flow of blood. No cooperation was forthcoming.'"

"It was the word 'I,'" Weil supplied. "When she said that, they all started to drift away."

"'She became rational once more,'" Bach resumed reading, "'long enough to whisper a number to me. The number was twelve-fifteen, which I wrote down as one-two-one-five. She roused herself once more, said "I'm dying."'" Bach closed the notebook and looked up. "Of course, she was right." She coughed nervously.

"We invoked section 35b of the New Dresden Unified Code, 'Hot Pursuit,' suspending civil liberties locally for the duration of the search. We located component 1215 by the simple expedient of lining up all the barbies and having them pull their pants down. Each has a serial number in the small of her back. Component 1215, one Sylvester J. Cronhausen, is in custody at this moment.

"While the search was going on, we went to sleeping cubicle 1215 with a team of criminologists. In a concealed compartment beneath the bunk we found these items." Bach got up, opened the evidence bag, and spread the items on the table.

There was a carved wooden mask. It had a huge nose with a hooked end, a mustache, and a fringe of black hair around it. Beside the mask were several jars of powders and creams, greasepaint and cologne. One black nylon sweater, one pair black trousers, one pair black sneakers. A stack of pictures clipped from magazines, showing ordinary people, many of them wearing more clothes than was normal in Luna. There was a black wig and a merkin of the same color.

"What was that last?" the commissioner asked.

"A merkin, sir," Bach supplied. "A pubic wig."

"Ah." He contemplated the assortment, leaned back in his chair. "Somebody liked to dress up."

"Evidently, sir." Bach stood at ease with her hands clasped behind her back, her face passive. She felt an acute sense of failure, and a cold determination to get the woman with the gall to stand at her elbow after committing murder before her eyes. She was sure the time and place had been chosen deliberately, that the barbie had been executed for Bach's benefit.

"Do you think these items belonged to the deceased?"

"We have no reason to state that, sir," Bach said. "However, the circumstances are suggestive."

"Of what?"

"I can't be sure. These things *might* have belonged to the victim. A random search of other cubicles turned up nothing like this. We showed the items to component 23900, our liaison. She professed not to know their purpose." She stopped, then added, "I believe she was lying. She looked quite disgusted."

"Did you arrest her?"

"No, sir. I didn't think it wise. She's the only connection we have, such as she is."

The commissioner frowned, and laced his fingers together. "I'll leave it up to you, Lieutenant Bach. Frankly, we'd like to be shut of this mess as soon as possible."

"I couldn't agree with you more, sir."

"Perhaps you don't understand me. We have to have a warm body to indict. We have to have one soon."

"Sir, I'm doing the best I can. Candidly, I'm beginning to wonder if there's anything I *can* do."

"You still don't understand me." He looked around the office. The stenographer and photoanalyst had left. He was alone with Bach and Weil. He flipped a switch on his desk, turning a recorder *off,* Bach realized.

"The news is picking up on this story. We're beginning to get some heat. On the one hand, people are afraid of these barbies. They're hearing about the murder fifty years ago, and the informal agreement. They don't like it much. On the other hand, there's the civil libertarians. They'll fight hard to prevent anything happening to the barbies, on principle. The government doesn't want to get into a mess like that. I can hardly blame them."

Bach said nothing, and the commissioner looked pained.

"I see I have to spell it out. We have a suspect in custody," he said.

"Are you referring to component 1215, Sylvester Cronhausen?"

"No. I'm speaking of the one you captured."

"Sir, the tape clearly shows she is not the guilty party. She was an innocent by-stander." She felt her face heat up as she said it. Damn it; she had tried her best.

"Take a look at this." He pressed a button and the tape began to play again. But the quality was much impaired. There were bursts of snow, moments when the picture faded out entirely. It was a very good imitation of a camera failing. Bach watched herself running through the crowd—there was a flash of white—and she had hit the woman. The lights came back on in the room.

"I've checked with the analyst. She'll go along. There's a bonus in this, for both of you." He looked from Weil to Bach.

"I don't think I can go through with that, sir."

He looked like he'd tasted a lemon. "I didn't say we were doing this today. It's an option. But I ask you to look at it this way, just look at it, and I'll say no more. This is the way *they themselves* want it. They offered you the same deal the first time you were there. Close the case with a confession, no mess. We've already got this prisoner. She just says she killed her, she killed all of them. I want you to ask yourself, is she wrong? By her own lights and moral values? She believes she shares responsibility for the murders, and society demands a culprit. What's wrong with accepting their compromise and letting this all blow over?"

"Sir, it doesn't feel right to me. This is not in the oath I took. I'm supposed to protect the innocent, and she's innocent. She's the *only* barbie I *know* to be inno-cent."

The commissioner sighed. "Bach, you've got four days. You give me an alterna-tive by then."

"Yes, sir. If I can't, I'll tell you now that I won't interfere with what you plan. But you'll have to accept my resignation."

Anna-Louise Bach reclined in the bathtub with her head pillowed on a folded towel. Only her neck, nipples, and knees stuck out above the placid surface of the water, tinted purple with a generous helping of bath salts. She clenched a thin che-root in her teeth. A ribbon of lavender smoke curled from the end of it, rising to join the cloud near the ceiling.

She reached up with one foot and turned on the taps, letting out cooled water and refilling with hot until the sweat broke out on her brow. She had been in the tub for several hours. The tips of her fingers were like washboards.

There seemed to be few alternatives. The barbies were foreign to her, and to anyone she could assign to interview them. They didn't want her help in solving the crimes. All the old rules and procedures were useless. Witnesses meant nothing; one could not tell one from the next, nor separate their stories. Opportunity? Several thousand individuals had it. Motive was a blank. She had a physical description in minute detail, even tapes of the actual murders. Both were useless.

There was one course of action that might show results. She had been soaking for hours in the hope of determining just how important her job was to her.

Hell, what else did she want to do?

She got out of the tub quickly, bringing a lot of water with her to drip onto the floor. She hurried into her bedroom, pulled the sheets off the bed and slapped the nude male figure on the buttocks.

"Come on, Svengali," she said. "Here's your chance to do something about my nose."

She used every minute while her eyes were functioning to read all she could find about Standardists. When Atlas worked on her eyes, the computer droned into an earphone. She memorized most of the *Book of Standards.*

Ten hours of surgery, followed by eight hours flat on her back, paralyzed, her body undergoing forced regeneration, her eyes scanning the words that flew by on an overhead screen.

Three hours of practice, getting used to shorter legs and arms. Another hour to assemble her equipment.

When she left the Atlas clinic, she felt she would pass for a barbie as long as she kept her clothes on. She hadn't gone *that* far.

People tended to forget about access locks that led to the surface. Bach had used the fact more than once to show up in places where no one expected her.

She parked her rented crawler by the lock and left it there. Moving awkwardly in her pressure suit, she entered and started it cycling, then stepped through the inner door into an equipment room in Anytown. She stowed the suit, checked herself quickly in a washroom mirror, straightened the tape measure that belted her loose white jumpsuit, and entered the darkened corridors.

What she was doing was not illegal in any sense, but she was on edge. She didn't expect the barbies to take kindly to her masquerade if they discovered it, and she knew how easy it was for a barbie to vanish forever. Three had done so before Bach ever got the case.

The place seemed deserted. It was late evening by the arbitrary day cycle of

New Dresden. Time for the nightly equalization. Bach hurried down the silent hallways to the main meeting room in the temple.

It was full of barbies and a vast roar of conversation. Bach had no trouble slipping in, and in a few minutes she knew her facial work was as good as Atlas had promised.

Equalization was the barbie's way of standardizing experience. They had been unable to simplify their lives to the point where each member of the community experienced the same things every day; the *Book of Standards* said it was a goal to be aimed for, but probably unattainable this side of Holy Reassimilation with Goddess. They tried to keep the available jobs easy enough that each member could do them all. The commune did not seek to make a profit; but air, water, and food had to be purchased, along with replacement parts and services to keep things running. The community had to produce things to trade with the outside.

They sold luxury items: hand-carved religious statues, illuminated holy books, painted crockery, and embroidered tapestries. None of the items were Standardist. The barbies had no religious symbols except their uniformity and the tape measure, but nothing in their dogma prevented them from selling objects of reverence to people of other faiths.

Bach had seen the products for sale in the better shops. They were meticulously produced, but suffered from the fact that each item looked too much like every other. People buying hand-produced luxuries in a technological age tend to want the differences that non-machine production entails, whereas the barbies wanted everything to look exactly alike. It was an ironic situation, but the barbies willingly sacrificed value by adhering to their standards.

Each barbie did things during the day that were as close as possible to what everyone else had done. But someone had to cook meals, tend the air machines, load the freight. Each component had a different job each day. At equalization, they got together and tried to even that out.

It was boring. Everyone talked at once, to anyone that happened to be around. Each woman told what she had done that day. Bach heard the same group of stories a hundred times before the night was over, and repeated them to anyone who would listen.

Anything unusual was related over a loudspeaker so everyone could be aware of it and thus spread out the intolerable burden of anomaly. No barbie wanted to keep a unique experience to herself; it made her soiled, unclean, until it was shared by all.

Bach was getting very tired of it—she was short on sleep—when the lights went out. The buzz of conversation shut off as if a tape had broken.

"All cats are alike in the dark," someone muttered, quite near Bach. Then a single voice was raised. It was solemn; almost a chant.

"We are the wrath. There is blood on our hands, but it is the holy blood of cleansing. We have told you of the cancer eating at the heart of the body, and yet still you cower away from what must be done. *The filth must be removed from us!*"

Bach was trying to tell which direction the words were coming from in the total darkness. Then she became aware of movement, people brushing against her, all going in the same direction. She began to buck the tide when she realized everyone was moving away from the voice.

"You think you can use our holy uniformity to hide among us, but the vengeful hand of Goddess will not be stayed. The mark is upon you, our one-time sisters. Your sins have set you apart, and retribution will strike swiftly.

"*There are five of you left.* Goddess knows who you are, and will not tolerate your perversion of her holy truth. Death will strike you when you least expect it. Goddess sees the differentness within you, the differentness you seek but hope to hide from your upright sisters."

People were moving more swiftly now, and a scuffle had developed ahead of her. She struggled free of people who were breathing panic from every pore, until she stood in a clear space. The speaker was shouting to be heard over the sound of whimpering and the shuffling of bare feet. Bach moved foward, swinging her outstretched hands. But another hand brushed her first.

The punch was not centered on her stomach, but it drove the air from her lungs and sent her sprawling. Someone tripped over her, and she realized things would get pretty bad if she didn't get to her feet. She was struggling up when the lights came back on.

There was a mass sigh of relief as each barbie examined her neighbor. Bach half expected another body to be found, but that didn't seem to be the case. The killer had vanished again.

She slipped away from the equalization before it began to break up, and hurried down the deserted corridors to room 1215.

She sat in the room—little more than a cell, with a bunk, a chair, and a light on a table—for more than two hours before the door opened, as she had hoped it would. A barbie stepped inside, breathing hard, closed the door, and leaned against it.

"We wondered if you would come," Bach said, tentatively.

The woman ran to Bach and collapsed at her knees, sobbing.

"Forgive us, please forgive us, our darling. We didn't dare come last night. We were afraid that . . . that if . . . that it might have been you who was murdered, and that the wrath would be waiting for us here. Forgive us, forgive us."

"It's all right," Bach said, for lack of anything better. Suddenly, the barbie was on top of her, kissing her with a desperate passion. Bach was startled, though she had expected something of the sort. She responded as best she could. The barbie finally began to talk again.

"We must stop this, we just have to stop. We're so frightened of the wrath, but . . . but the *longing!* We can't stop ourselves. We need to see you so badly that we can hardly get through the day, not knowing if you are across town or working at our elbow. It builds all day, and at night, we cannot stop ourselves from sinning yet again." She was crying, more softly this time, not from happiness at seeing the woman she took Bach to be, but from a depth of desperation. "What's going to become of us?" she asked, helplessly.

"Shhh," Bach soothed. "It's going to be all right."

She comforted the barbie for a while, then saw her lift her head. Her eyes seemed to glow with a strange light.

"I can't wait any longer," she said. She stood up, and began taking off her clothes. Bach could see her hands shaking.

Beneath her clothing the barbie had concealed a few things that looked familiar. Bach could see that the merkin was already in place between her legs. There was a wooden mask much like the one that had been found in the secret panel, and a jar. The barbie unscrewed the top of it and used her middle finger to smear dabs of brown onto her breasts, making stylized nipples.

"Look what *I* got," she said, coming down hard on the pronoun, her voice trembling. She pulled a flimsy yellow blouse from the pile of clothing on the floor, and slipped it over her shoulders. She struck a pose, then strutted up and down the tiny room.

"Come on, darling," she said. "Tell me how beautiful I am. Tell me I'm lovely. Tell me I'm the only one for you. The only one. What's the *matter?* Are you still frightened? I'm not. I'll dare anything for you, my one and only love." But now she stopped walking and looked suspiciously at Bach. "Why aren't you getting dressed?"

"We . . . uh, I can't," Bach said, extemporizing. "They, uh, someone found the things. They're all gone." She didn't dare remove her clothes because her nipples and pubic hair would look too real, even in the dim light.

The barbie was backing away. She picked up her mask and held it protectively to her. "What do you mean? Was she here? The wrath? Are they after us? It's true, isn't it? They can see us." She was on the edge of crying again, near panic.

"No, no, I think it was the police—" But it was doing no good. The barbie was at the door now, and had it half open.

"You're her! What have you done to . . . No, no, you stay away." She reached into the clothing that she now held in her hand, and Bach hesitated for a moment, expecting a knife. It was enough time for the barbie to dart quickly through the door, slamming it behind her.

When Bach reached the door, the woman was gone.

Bach kept reminding herself that she was not here to find the other potential victims—of whom her visitor was certainly one—but to catch the killer. The fact remained that she wished she could have detained her, to question her further.

The woman was a pervert, by the only definition that made any sense among the Standardists. She, and presumably the other dead barbies, had an individuality fetish. When Bach had realized that, her first thought had been to wonder why they didn't simply leave the colony and become whatever they wished. But then why did a Christian seek out prostitutes? For the taste of sin. In the larger world, what these barbies did would have had little meaning. Here, it was sin of the worst and tastiest kind.

And somebody didn't like it at all.

The door opened again, and the woman stood there facing Bach, her hair disheleveled, breathing hard.

"We had to come back," she said. "We're so sorry that we panicked like that. Can you forgive us?" She was coming toward Bach now, her arms out. She looked so vulnerable and contrite that Bach was astonished when the fist connected with her cheek.

Bach thudded against the wall, then found herself pinned under the woman's knees, with something sharp and cool against her throat. She swallowed very carefully, and said nothing. Her throat itched unbearably.

"She's dead," the barbie said. "And you're next." But there was something in her face that Bach didn't understand. The barbie brushed at her eyes a few times, and squinted down at her.

"Listen, I'm not who you think I am. If you kill me, you'll be bringing more trouble on your sisters than you can imagine."

The barbie hesitated, then roughly thrust her hand down into Bach's pants. Her eyes widened when she felt the genitals, but the knife didn't move. Bach knew she had to talk fast, and say all the right things.

"You understand what I'm talking about, don't you?" She looked for a response, but saw none. "You're aware of the political pressures that are coming down. You know this whole colony could be wiped out if you look like a threat to the outside. You don't want that."

"If it must be, it will be," the barbie said. "The purity is the important thing. If we die, we shall die pure. The blasphemers must be killed."

"I don't care about that anymore," Bach said, and finally got a ripple of interest from the barbie. "I have my principles, too. Maybe I'm not as fanatical about them as you are about yours. But they're important to me. One is that the guilty be brought to justice."

"You have the guilty party. Try her. Execute her. She will not protest."

"*You* are the guilty party."

The woman smiled. "So arrest us."

"All right, all right. I can't, obviously. Even if you don't kill me, you'll walk out that door and I'll never be able to find you. I've given up on that. I just don't have the time. This was my last chance, and it looks like it didn't work."

"We didn't think you could do it, even with more time. But why should we let you live?"

"Because we can help each other." She felt the pressure ease up a little, and managed to swallow again. "You don't want to kill me, because it could destroy your community. Myself . . . I need to be able to salvage some self-respect out of this mess. I'm willing to accept your definition of morality and let you be the law in your own community. Maybe you're even right. Maybe you *are* one being. But I can't let that woman be convicted, when I *know* she didn't kill anyone."

The knife was not touching her neck now, but it was still being held so that the barbie could plunge it into her throat at the slightest movement.

"And if we let you live? What do you get out of it? How do you free your 'innocent' prisoner?"

"Tell me where to find the body of the woman you just killed. I'll take care of the rest."

The pathology team had gone and Anytown was settling down once again. Bach sat on the edge of the bed with Jorge Weil. She was as tired as she ever remembered being. How long had it been since she slept?

"I'll tell you," Weil said, "I honestly didn't think this thing would work. I guess I was wrong."

Bach sighed. "I wanted to take her alive, Jorge. I thought I could. But when she came at me with the knife . . ." She let him finish the thought, not caring to lie to him. She'd already done that to the interviewer. In her story, she had taken the knife from her assailant and tried to disable her, but was forced in the end to kill her. Luckily, she had the bump on the back of her head from being thrown against the wall. It made a blackout period plausible. Otherwise, someone would have wondered why she waited so long to call for police and an ambulance. The barbie had been dead for an hour when they arrived.

"Well, I'll hand it to you. You sure pulled this out. I'll admit it, I was having a hard time deciding if I'd do as you were going to do and resign, or if I could have stayed on. Now I'll never know."

"Maybe it's best that way. I don't really know, either."

Jorge grinned at her. "I can't get used to thinking of *you* being behind that godawful face."

"Neither can I, and I don't want to see any mirrors. I'm going straight to Atlas and get it changed back." She got wearily to her feet and walked toward the tube station with Weil.

She had not quite told him the truth. She did intend to get her own face back as soon as possible—nose and all—but there was one thing left to do.

From the first, a problem that had bothered her had been the question of how the killer identified her victims.

Presumably the perverts had arranged times and places to meet for their strange rites. That would have been easy enough. Any one barbie could easily shirk her duties. She could say she was sick, and no one would know it was the same barbie who had been sick yesterday, and for a week or month before. She need not work; she could wander the halls acting as if she was on her way from one job to another. No one could challenge her. Likewise, while 23900 had said no barbie spent consecutive nights in the same room, there was no way for her to know that. Evidently room 1215 had been taken over permanently by the perverts.

And the perverts would have no scruples about identifying each other by serial number at their clandestine meetings, though they could do it in the streets. The killer didn't even have that.

But someone had known how to identify them, to pick them out of a crowd. Bach thought she must have infiltrated meetings, marked the participants in some way. One could lead her to another, until she knew them all and was ready to strike.

She kept recalling the strange way the killer had looked at her, the way she had squinted. The mere fact that she had not killed Bach instantly in a case of mistaken identity meant she had been expecting to see something that had not been there.

And she had an idea about that.

She meant to go to the morgue first, and to examine the corpses under different wavelengths of lights, with various filters. She was betting some kind of mark would become visible on the faces, a mark the killer had been looking for with her contact lenses.

It had to be something that was visible only with the right kind of equipment, or under the right circumstances. If she kept at it long enough, she would find it.

If it was an invisible ink, it brought up another interesting question. How had it been applied? With a brush or spray gun? Unlikely. But such an ink on the killer's hands might look and feel like water.

Once she had marked her victims, the killer would have to be confident the mark would stay in place for a reasonable time. The murders had stretched over a month. So she was looking for an indelible, invisible ink, one that soaked into pores.

And if it was indelible . . .

There was no use thinking further about it. She was right, or she was wrong. When she struck the bargain with the killer she had faced up to the possibility that she might have to live with it. Certainly she could not now bring a killer into court, not after what she had just said.

No, if she came back to Anytown and found a barbie whose hands were stained with guilt, she would have to do the job herself.

INTRODUCTION TO

"The Phantom of Kansas"

I have a little experience of weather.

*I was born in Austin, Texas, along with my sister, Francine, but I don't remem-
ber much of Austin except for the time some guy came by the house with a donkey
and Mom paid to let me sit on it in a cowboy hat and have my picture taken. I still
have the picture. God, am I cute, though already my legs are starting to dangle
longer than they should for a kid my age. Probably the last time anyone ever called
me cute.*

*Then we moved to Fort Worth, where Dad worked for Consolidated Aircraft as-
sembling B-36 bombers—not single-handed, as I thought then, but with a few other
guys—and later for the Magnolia Petroleum Company, in a refinery. If you're old
enough you might remember the "flying red horse" on the gas station signs. Now it's
"Mobil." If you think that's a better name, I don't want to know you.*

*We stayed there long enough for my other sister, Kerry, to be born. I remember
her in Mom's arms coming home from the hospital. Other than that, I remember
Mrs. Rosequist's first-grade class, the incredible roar of the ten-engine B-36s flying
over, and chasing what we called "horney toads" around the backyard. They are the
only lizards I know of that are fat and slow enough to catch easily. They are covered
with spines, and will spit blood at you when you pick them up.*

*Then Dad got laid off and the nearest job he could find was in Port Arthur,
Texas. I hated the place from the first time I saw it. It was always hot and humid at
the same time. The mosquitoes would feed on you at night until they were too fat to
fly; you could turn on the light and watch them try to crawl away over the sheets.
Most of the town was about six inches above sea level, and all the houses seemed to be
set up on blocks. You could look right under them and see the pools of stagnant water
where the skeeters bred. It rained almost every day. We figured that was the reason for
the blocks.*

*Not long after that we found out the real reason. Hurricane Audrey blew through
with not a lot of advance warning (no weather satellites in those days, which is a big*

reason why eight thousand people died in Galveston, sixty miles down the coast, in 1900). It was a Category 4 blow, and it hit smack-dab on our new hometown.

We had never seen anything like it, didn't really have a realistic idea how dangerous it was. I remember trying to step outside the house when the winds were blowing about 100 mph to see what it was like, and being blown right back inside. It got worse after that, and it seemed to go on for hours. It's one thing to see it on television, something else to be cowering in your house as the trees wave back and forth and come crashing down, believe me.

The eye passed over us, and we all went outside in the unearthly quiet. We didn't know it at the time but about thirty-five miles to the east of us as the crow flies (if any crows had been stupid enough to fly that day) in Cameron, Louisiana, 390 people were dying in a storm surge. The town was virtually wiped off the planet.

In terms of human life lost, it was the fourth worst American hurricane of the twentieth century—bearing in mind that 1900 was the last year of the nineteenth century.

In terms of damage, Audrey didn't even make the Top 50. If you've ever been to Port Arthur you'd conclude, as I did, that there wasn't all that much of value there before the winds started to blow. But the people down there must have known something about storms, because most houses that didn't have a tree fall on them were not badly damaged. After a few days with the chain saws, the area called, for no rational reason I can see, the "Golden Triangle" of Beaumont, Port Arthur, and Orange was pretty much back to normal . . . but always with the horror of Cameron on our minds.

Janis Joplin got out of Port Arthur the first chance she got. I had never heard of her then, but I made the same decision. I decided that as soon as I finished school I'd go to California, where there's nothing to worry about but earthquakes.

I've just been through my first earthquake, and it was a piece of cake compared to Audrey.

This story is another personal favorite. It came about as a case of one thing leading to another. In the Eight Worlds, I wondered, where there was no "natural" environment humans could survive, what would they do if they wanted to go outside? Some people, I figured, would prefer the security of artifice, as many city dwellers do today. Rooms, corridors, limited open spaces like stadia and arenas, none of those messy plants and animals.

But there would be the adventurous, just as there are today, eager to venture out into the "wild" on their bikes and be mauled by mountain lions (as two people were just a few days ago, not far from where I live). These could be the people who cherished hopes of someday reclaiming Lost Earth from the invaders. They would like parks.

Why not some very big parks?

I assumed the existence of a vast genetic library so that the big underground bubbles I came to call "disneylands" could be populated with the appropriate flora and fauna. But you wouldn't go on simulated rides or roller coasters in these disneylands. The terrain and the wildlife and the sheer novelty of being able to use the long-range vision evolution had adapted your primate eyes for would be the thrill here.

And it need not be the kind of place adventurers or vacationers go today. A prairie could be as exciting to them as simulated mountains or jungles. And where are the most boring prairies I've ever seen? Why, Kansas, of course, home of Dorothy and Toto.

You'd need weather in a place like that. Rain and sunshine . . . and why not tornadoes? If people will pay good money to get the wits scared out of them at Magic Mountain, why not a carefully controlled, safe and sane, sanitized-for-your-protection twister? And thus the story grew.

When I first began in the movie business I decided to write a screenplay, just to see if I could do it. I asked John Foreman for copies of screenplays, since I'd never seen one. I watched the movies on video, pausing as I read the screenplays. Didn't look too hard, to me. So I sat down and, in four feverish days, wrote a 120-page adaptation of "The Phantom of Kansas." I loved it. I mean, I loved the process; the screenplay itself could have used some work, it was full of beginner's mistakes. But John liked it, too, and I think to this day that with a rewrite it could make a darn good motion picture.

It has been optioned several times, without result (not at all unusual in the movie business), and as of now the man who wrote Changing Lanes *has been working on it for five years. His option expires in July 2004, and if he throws in the towel I hope somebody else will step in and take another crack at it.*

THE PHANTOM OF KANSAS

I DO MY banking at the Archimedes Trust Association. Their security is first-rate, their service is courteous, and they have their own medico facility that does nothing but take recordings for their vaults.

And they had been robbed two weeks ago.

It was a break for me. I had been approaching my regular recording date and dreading the chunk it would take from my savings. Then these thieves break into my bank, steal a huge amount of negotiable paper, and in an excess of enthusiasm they destroy all the recording cubes. Every last one of them, crunched into tiny shards of plastic. Of course the bank had to replace them all, and very fast, too. They weren't stupid; it wasn't the first time someone had used such a bank robbery to facilitate a murder. So the bank had to record everyone who had an account, and do it in a few days. It must have cost them more than the robbery.

How that scheme works, incidentally, is like this. The robber couldn't care less about the money stolen. Mostly it's very risky to pass such loot, anyway. The programs written into the money computers these days are enough to foil all but the most exceptional robber. You have to let that kind of money lie for on the order of a century to have any hope of realizing gains on it. Not impossible, of course, but the police types have found out that few criminals are temperamentally able to wait that long. The robber's real motive in a case where memory cubes have been destroyed is murder, not robbery.

Every so often someone comes along who must commit a crime of passion. There are very few left open, and murder is the most awkward of all. It just doesn't satisfy this type to kill someone and see them walking around six months later. When the victim sues the killer for alienation of personality—and collects up to 99 percent of the killer's worldly goods—it's just twisting the knife. So if you really hate someone, the temptation is great to *really* kill them, forever and ever, just like in the old days, by destroying their memory cube first, then killing the body.

That's what the ATA feared, and I had rated a private bodyguard over the last week as part of my contract. It was sort of a status symbol to show your friends, but otherwise I hadn't been much impressed until I realized that ATA was going to pay for my next recording as part of their crash program to cover all their policy holders. They had contracted to keep me alive forever, so even though I had been scheduled for a recording in only three weeks they had to pay for this one. The courts had ruled that a lost or damaged cube must be replaced with all possible speed.

So I should have been very happy. I wasn't, but tried to be brave.

I was shown into the recording room with no delay and told to strip and lie on the table. The medico, a man who looked like someone I might have met several decades ago, busied himself with his equipment as I tried to control my breathing. I was grateful when he plugged the computer lead into my occipital socket and turned off my motor control. Now I didn't have to worry about whether to ask if I knew him or not. As I grow older, I find that's more of a problem. I must have met twenty thousand people by now and talked to them long enough to make an impression. It gets confusing.

He removed the top of my head and prepared to take a multiholo picture of me, a chemical analog of everything I ever saw or thought or remembered or just vaguely dreamed. It was a blessed relief when I slid over into unconsciousness.

The coolness and sheen of stainless steel beneath my fingertips. There is the smell of isopropyl alcohol, and the hint of acetone.

The medico's shop. Childhood memories tumble over me, triggered by the smells. Excitement, change, my mother standing by while the medico carves away my broken finger to replace it with a pink new one. I lie in the darkness and re-member.

And there is light, a hurting light from nowhere, and I feel my pupil contract as the only movement in my entire body.

"She's in," I hear. But I'm not, not really. I'm just lying here in the blessed dark, unable to move.

It comes in a rush, the repossession of my body. I travel down the endless nerves to bang up hard against the insides of my hands and feet, to whirl through the pools of my nipples and tingle in my lips and nose. *Now* I'm in.

I sat up quickly into the restraining arms of the medico. I struggled for a sec-ond before I was able to relax. My fingers were buzzing and cramped with the clamminess of hyperventilation.

"Whew," I said, putting my head in my hands. "Bad dream. I thought . . ."

I looked around me and saw that I was naked on the steel-topped table with several worried faces looking at me from all sides. I wanted to retreat into the darkness again and let my insides settle down. I saw my mother's face, blinked, and failed to make it disappear.

"Carnival?" I asked her ghost.

"Right here, Fox," she said, and took me in her arms. It was awkward and un-satisfying with her standing on the floor and me on the table. There were wires trailing from my body. But the comfort was needed. I didn't know where I was. With a chemical rush as precipitous as the one just before I awoke, the people so-lidified around me.

"She's all right now," the medico said, turning from his instruments. He smiled impersonally at me as he began removing the wires from my head. I did not smile back. I knew where I was now, just as surely as I had ever known anything. I remembered coming in here only hours before.

But I knew it had been more than a few hours. I've read about it: the disorien-tation when a new body is awakened with transplanted memories. And my mother wouldn't be here unless something had gone badly wrong.

I had died.

I was given a mild sedative, help in dressing, and my mother's arm to lead me down plush-carpeted hallways to the office of the bank president. I was still not fully awake. The halls were achingly quiet but for the brush of our feet across the wine-colored rug. I felt like the pressure was fluctuating wildly, leaving my ears popped and muffled. I couldn't see too far away. I was grateful to leave the vanishing points in the hall for the paneled browns of wood veneer and the coolness and echoes of a white marble floor.

The bank president, Mr. Leander, showed us to our seats. I sank into the purple velvet and let it wrap around me. Leander pulled up a chair facing us and offered us drinks. I declined. My head was swimming already and I knew I'd have to pay attention.

Leander fiddled with a dossier on his desk. Mine, I imagined. It had been freshly printed out from the terminal at his right hand. I'd met him briefly before; he was a pleasant sort of person, chosen for this public-relations job for his willingness to wear the sort of old-man body that inspires confidence and trust. He seemed to be about sixty-five. He was probably more like twenty.

It seemed that he was never going to get around to the briefing so I asked a question. One that was very important to me at the moment.

"What's the date?"

"It's the month of November," he said, ponderously. "And the year is 342."

I had been dead for two and a half years.

"Listen," I said, "I don't want to take up any more of your time. You must have a brochure you can give me to bring me up to date. If you'll just hand it over, I'll be on my way. Oh, and thank you for your concern."

He waved his hand at me as I started to rise.

"I would appreciate it if you stayed a bit longer. Yours is an unusual case, Ms. Fox. I . . . Well, it's never happened in the history of the Archimedes Trust Association."

"Yes?"

"You see, you've died, as you figured out soon after we woke you. What you couldn't have known is that you've died more than once since your last recording."

"More than once?" So it wasn't such a smart question; so what was I supposed to ask?

"Three times."

"Three?"

"Yes, three separate times. We suspect murder."

The room was perfectly silent for a while. At last I decided I should have that drink. He poured it for me, and I drained it.

"Perhaps your mother should tell you more about it," Leander suggested. "She's been closer to the situation. I was only made aware of it recently. Carnival?"

I found my way back to my apartment in a sort of daze. By the time I had settled in again the drug was wearing off and I could face my situation with a clear head. But my skin was crawling.

Listening in the third person to things you've done is not the most pleasant thing. I decided it was time to face some facts that all of us, including myself, do not like to think about. The first order of business was to recognize that the things that were done by those three previous people were not done by *me*. I was a new person, fourth in the line of succession. I had many things in common with the previous incarnations, including all my memories up to that day I surrendered myself to the memory recording machine. But the *me* of that time and place had been killed.

She lasted longer than the others. Almost a year, Carnival had said. Then her body was found at the bottom of Hadley Rille. It was an appropriate place for her to die; both she and myself liked to go hiking out on the surface for purposes of inspiration.

Murder was not suspected that time. The bank, upon hearing of my—no, *her*—death, started a clone from the tissue sample I had left with my recording. Six lunations later, a copy of me was infused with my memories and told that she had just died. She had been shaken, but seemed to be adjusting well when she, too, was killed.

This time there was much suspicion. Not only had she survived for less than a lunation after her reincarnation, but the circumstances were unusual. She had been blown to pieces in a tube-train explosion. She had been the only passenger in a two-seat capsule. The explosion had been caused by a homemade bomb.

There was still the possibility that it was a random act, possibly by political terrorists. The third copy of me had not thought so. I don't know why. That is the most maddening thing about memory recording: being unable to profit by the experiences of your former selves. Each time I was killed, it moved me back to square one, the day I was recorded.

But Fox 3 had reason to be paranoid. She took extraordinary precautions to stay alive. More specifically, she tried to prevent circumstances that could lead to her murder. It worked for five lunations. She died as the result of a fight, that much was certain. It was a very violent fight, with blood all over the apartment. The police at first thought she must have fatally injured her attacker, but analysis showed all the blood to have come from her body.

So where did that leave me, Fox 4? An hour's careful thought left the picture gloomy indeed. Consider: each time my killer succeeded in murdering me, he or she learned more about me. My killer must be an expert on Foxes by now, knowing things about me that I myself do not know. Such as how I handle myself in a fight. I gritted my teeth when I thought of that. Carnival told me that Fox 3, the canniest of the lot, had taken lessons in self-defense. Karate, I think she said. Did I have the benefit of it? Of course not. If I wanted to defend myself I had to start all over, because those skills died with Fox 3.

No, all the advantages were with my killer. The killer started off with the advantage of surprise—since I had no notion of who it was—and learned more about me every time he or she succeeded in killing me.

What to do? I didn't even know where to start. I ran through everyone I knew, looking for an enemy, someone who hated me enough to kill me again and again. I could find no one. Most likely it was someone Fox 1 had met during that year she lived after the recording.

The only answer I could come up with was emigration. Just pull up stakes and go to Mercury, or Mars, or even Pluto. But would that guarantee my safety? My killer seemed to be an uncommonly persistent person. No, I'd have to face it here, where at least I knew the turf.

It was the next day before I realized the extent of my loss. I had been robbed of an entire symphony.

For the last thirty years I had been an Environmentalist. I had just drifted into it while it was still an infant art form. I had been in charge of the weather machines at the Transvaal disneyland, which was new at the time and the biggest and most modern of all the environmental parks in Luna. A few of us had started tinkering with the weather programs, first for our own amusement. Later we invited friends to watch the storms and sunsets we concocted. Before we knew it, friends were inviting friends and the Transvaal people began selling tickets.

I gradually made a name for myself, and found I could make more money being an artist than being an engineer. At the time of my last recording I had been one of the top three Environmentalists on Luna.

Then Fox I went on to compose *Liquid Ice*. From what I read in the reviews, two years after the fact, it was seen as the high point of the art to date. It had been staged in the Pennsylvania disneyland, before a crowd of three hundred thousand. It made me rich.

The money was still in my bank account, but the memory of creating the symphony was forever lost. And it mattered.

Fox I had written it, from beginning to end. Oh, I recalled having had some vague ideas of a winter composition, things I'd think about later and put together. But the whole creative process had gone on in the head of that other person who had been killed.

How is a person supposed to cope with that? For one bitter moment I considered calling the bank and having them destroy my memory cube. If I died this time, I'd rather die completely. The thought of a Fox 5 rising from that table . . . It was almost too much too bear. She would lack everything that Fox 1, 2, 3, and me,

Fox 4, had experienced. So far I'd had little time to add to the personality we all shared, but even the bad times are worth saving.

It was either that, or have a new recording made every day. I called the bank, did some figuring, and found that I wasn't wealthy enough to afford that. But it was worth exploring. If I had a new recording taken once a week I could keep at it for about a year before I ran out of money.

I decided I'd do it, for as long as I could. And to make sure that no future Fox would ever have to go through this again, I'd have one made today. Fox 5, if she was ever born, would be born knowing at least as much as I knew now.

I felt better after the recording was made. I found that I no longer feared the medico's office. That fear comes from the common misapprehension that one will wake up from the recording to discover that one has died. It's a silly thing to believe, but it comes from the distaste we all have for really looking at the facts.

If you'll consider human consciousness, you'll see that the three-dimensional cross-section of a human being that is *you* can only rise from that table and go about your business. It can happen no other way. Human consciousness is linear, along a timeline that has a beginning and an end. If you die after a recording, you *die*, forever and with no reprieve. It doesn't matter that a recording of you exists and that a new person with your memories to a certain point can be created; you are *dead*. Looked at from a fourth-dimensional viewpoint, what memory recording does is to graft a new person onto your lifeline at a point in the past. You do not retrace that lifeline and magically become that new person. I, Fox 4, was only a relative of that long-ago person who had had her memories recorded. And if I died, it was forever. Fox 5 would awaken with my memories to date, but I would be no part of her. She would be on her own.

Why do we do it? I honestly don't know. I suppose that the human urge to live forever is so strong that we'll grasp at even the most unsatisfactory substitute. At one time people had themselves frozen when they died, in the hope of being thawed out in a future when humans knew how to reverse death. Look at the Great Pyramid in the Egypt disneyland if you want to see the sheer *size* of that urge.

So we live our lives in pieces. I could know, for whatever good it would do me, that thousands of years from now a being would still exist who would be at least partly me. She would remember exactly the same things I remembered of her childhood; the trip to Archimedes, her first sex change, her lovers, her hurts and her happiness. If I had another recording taken, she would remember thinking the thoughts I was thinking now. And she would probably still be stringing chunks of experience onto her life, year by year. Each time she had a new recording, that much more of her life was safe for all time. There was a certain comfort in knowing that my life was safe up until a few hours ago, when the recording was made.

Having thought all that out, I found myself fiercely determined to never let it happen again. I began to hate my killer with an intensity I had never experienced. I wanted to storm out of the apartment and beat my killer to death with a blunt instrument.

I swallowed that emotion with difficulty. It was exactly what the killer would be looking for. I had to remember that the killer knew what my first reaction would be. I had to behave in a way that he or she would not expect.

But what way was that?

I called the police department and met with the detective who had my case. Her name was Isadora, and she had some good advice.

"You're not going to like it, if I can judge from past experience," she said. "The last time I proposed it to you, you rejected it out of hand."

I knew I'd have to get used to this. People would always be telling me what I had done, what I had said to them. I controlled my anger and asked her to go on.

"It's simply to stay put. I know you think you're a detective, but your predecessor proved pretty well that you are not. If you stir out of that door you'll be nailed. This guy knows you inside and out, and he'll get you. Count on it."

He? You know something about him, then?"

Sorry, you'll have to bear with me. I've told you parts of this case twice already, so it's hard to remember what you don't know. Yes, we do know he's a male. Or was, six months ago, when you had your big fight with him. Several witnesses reported a man with blood-stained clothes, who could only have been your killer."

"Then you're on his trail?"

She sighed, and I knew she was going over old ground again.

"No, and you've proved again that you're not a detective. Your detective lore comes from reading old novels. It's not a glamorous enough job nowadays to rate fictional heroes and such, so most people don't know the kind of work we do. Knowing that the killer was a man when he last knocked you off means nothing to us. He could have bought a Change the very next day. You're probably wondering if we have fingerprints of him, right?"

I gritted my teeth. Everyone had the advantage over me. It was obvious I had asked something like that the last time I spoke with this woman. And I *had* been thinking of it.

"No," I said. "Because he could change those as easily as his sex, right?"

"Right. Easier. The only positive means of identification today is genotyping, and he wasn't cooperative enough to leave any of him behind when he killed you. He must have been a real brute, to be able to inflict as much damage on you as he did and not even be cut himself. You were armed with a knife. Not a drop of his blood was found at the scene of the murder."

"Then how do you go about finding him?"

"Fox, I'd have to take you through several college courses to begin to explain our methods to you. And I'll even admit that they're not very good. Police work has not kept up with science over the last century. There are many things available to the modern criminal that make our job more difficult than you'd imagine. We have hopes of catching him within about four lunations, though, if you'll stay put and stop chasing him."

"Why four months?"

"We trace him by computer. We have very exacting programs that we run when we're after a guy like this. It's our one major weapon. Given time, we can run to ground about sixty percent of the criminals."

"Sixty percent?" I squawked. "Is that supposed to encourage me? Especially when you're dealing with a master like my killer seems to be?"

She shook her head. "He's not a master. He's only determined. And that works against him, not for him. The more single-mindedly he pursues you, the surer we are of catching him when he makes a slip. That sixty percent figure is overall crime; on murder, the rate is ninety-eight. It's a crime of passion, usually done by an amateur. The pros see no percentage in it, and they're right. The penalty is so steep it can make a pauper of you, and your victim is back on the streets while you're still in court."

I thought that over, and found it made me feel better. My killer was not a criminal mastermind. I was not being hunted by Fu Manchu or Professor Moriarty. He was only a person like myself, new to this business. Something Fox 1 did had made him sufficiently angry to risk financial ruin to stalk and kill me. It scaled him down to human dimensions.

"So now you're all ready to go out and get him?" Isadora sneered. I guess my thoughts were written on my face. That, or she was consulting her script of our previous conversations.

"Why not?" I asked.

"Because, like I said, he'll get you. He might not be a pro but he's an expert on you. He knows how you'll jump. One thing he thinks he knows is that you won't take my advice. He might be right outside your door, waiting for you to finish this conversation like you did last time around. The last time, he wasn't there. This time he might be."

It sobered me. I glanced nervously at my door, which was guarded by eight different security systems bought by Fox 3.

"Maybe you're right. So you want me just to stay here. For how long?"

"However long it takes. It may be a year. That four-lunation figure is the high point on a computer curve. It tapers off to a virtual certainty in just over a year."

"Why didn't I stay here the last time?"

"A combination of foolish bravery, hatred, and a fear of boredom." She searched my eyes, trying to find the words that would make me take the advice that Fox 3 had fatally refused. "I understand you're an artist," she went on. "Why can't you just . . . well, whatever it is artists do when they're thinking up a new composition? Can't you work here in your apartment?"

How could I tell her that inspiration wasn't just something I could turn on at will? Weather sculpture is a tenuous discipline. The visualization is difficult; you can't just try out a new idea the way you can with a song, by picking it out on a piano or guitar. You can run a computer simulation, but you never really know what you have until the tapes are run into the machines and you stand out there in the open field and watch the storm take shape around you. And you don't get any practice sessions. It's expensive.

I've always needed long walks on the surface. My competitors can't understand why. They go for strolls through the various parks, usually the one where the piece will be performed. I do that, too. You have to, to get the lay of the land. A computer can tell you what it looks like in terms of thermoclines and updrafts and pocket ecologies, but you have to really go there and feel the land, taste the air, smell the trees, before you can compose a storm or even a summer shower. It has to be a part of the land.

But my inspiration comes from the dry, cold, airless surface that so few Lunarians really like. I'm not a burrower; I've never loved the corridors, as so many of my friends profess to do. I think I see the black sky and harsh terrain as a blank canvas, a feeling I never really get in the disneylands where the land is lush and varied and there's always some weather in progress even if it's only partly cloudy and warm.

Could I compose without those long, solitary walks?

Run that through again: could I afford *not* to?

"All right, I'll stay inside like a good girl."

I was in luck. What could have been an endless purgatory turned into creative frenzy such as I had never experienced. My frustrations at being locked in my apartment translated themselves into grand sweeps of tornadoes and thunderheads. I began writing my masterpiece. The working title was *A Conflagration of Cyclones*. That's how angry I was. My agent later talked me into shortening it to a tasteful *Cyclone*, but it was always a conflagration to me.

Soon I had managed virtually to forget about my killer. I never did completely; after all, I needed the thought of him to flog me onward, to serve as the canvas on which to paint my hatred. I did have one awful thought, early on, and I brought it up to Isadora.

"It strikes me," I said, "that what you've built here is the better mousetrap, and I'm the hunk of cheese."

"You've got the essence of it," she agreed.

"I find I don't care for the role of bait."

"Why not? Are you scared?"

I hesitated, but what the hell did I have to be ashamed of?

"Yeah. I guess I am. What can you tell me to make me stay here when I could be doing what all my instincts are telling me to do, which is run like hell?"

"That's a fair question. This is the ideal situation, as far as the police are concerned. We have the victim in a place that can be watched perfectly safely, and we have the killer on the loose. Furthermore, this is an obsessed killer, one who cannot stay away from you forever. Long before he is able to make a strike at you we should pick him up as he scouts out ways to reach you."

"Are there ways?"

"No. An unqualified no. Any one of those devices on your door would be enough to keep him out. Beyond that, your food and water is being tested before it gets to you. Those are extremely remote possibilities since we're convinced that your killer wishes to dispose of your body completely, to kill you for good. Poisoning is no good to him. We'd just start you up again. But if we can't find at least a piece of your body, the law forbids us to revive you."

"What about bombs?"

"The corridor outside your apartment is being watched. It would take quite a large bomb to blow out your door, and getting a bomb that size in place would not be possible in the time he would have. Relax, Fox. We've thought of everything. You're safe."

She rang off, and I called up the Central Computer.

"CC," I said, to get it on-line, "can you tell me how you go about catching killers?"

"Are you talking about killers in general, or the one you have a particular interest in?"

"What do you think? I don't completely believe that detective. What I want to know from you is what can I do to help?"

"There is little you can do," the CC said. "While I myself, in the sense of the Central or controlling Lunar Computer, do not handle the apprehension of criminals, I act in a supervisory capacity to several satellite computers. They use a complex number theory, correlated with the daily input from all my terminals. The average person on Luna deals with me on the order of twenty times per day, many of these transactions involving a routine epidermal sample for positive genalysis. By matching these transactions with the time and place they occurred, I am able to construct a dynamic model of what has occurred, what possibly could have occurred, and what cannot have occurred. With suitable peripheral programs I can refine this model to a close degree of accuracy. For instance, at the time of your murder I was able to assign a low probability of their being responsible to ninety-nine point nine three percent of all humans on Luna. This left me with a pool of two hundred ten thousand people who might have had a hand in it. This is merely from data placing each person at a particular place at a particular time. Further weighting of such factors as possible motive narrowed the range of prime suspects. Do you wish me to go on?"

"No, I think I get the picture. Each time I was killed you must have narrowed it more. How many suspects are left?"

"You are not phrasing the question correctly. As implied in my original statement, all residents of Luna are still suspects. But each has been assigned a probability, ranging from a very large group with a value of ten to the minus-twenty-seventh power to twenty individuals with probabilities of thirteen percent."

The more I thought about that, the less I liked it.

"None of those sound to me like what you'd call a prime suspect."

"Alas, no. This is a very intriguing case, I must say."

"I'm glad you think so."

"Yes," it said, oblivious as usual to sarcasm. "I may have to have some programs rewritten. We've never gone this far without being able to submit a ninety percent rating to the Grand Jury Data Bank."

"Then Isadora is feeding me a line, right? She doesn't have anything to go on?"

"Not strictly true. She has an analysis, a curve, that places the probability of capture as near certainty within one year."

"You gave her that estimate, didn't you?"

"Of course."

"Then what the hell does *she* do? Listen, I'll tell you right now, I don't feel good about putting my fate in her hands. I think this job of detective is just a trumped-up featherbed. Isn't that right?"

"The privacy laws forbid me to express an opinion about the worth, performance, or intelligence of a human citizen. But I can give you a comparison. Would you entrust the construction of your symphonies to a computer alone? Would you sign your name to a work that was generated entirely by me?"

"I see your point."

"Exactly. Without a computer you'd never calculate all the factors you need for a symphony. But *I* do not write them. It is your creative spark that makes the wheels turn. Incidentally, I told your predecessor but of course you don't remember it. I liked your *Liquid Ice* tremendously. It was a real pleasure to work with you on it."

"Thanks. I wish I could say the same." I signed off, feeling no better than when I began the interface.

The mention of *Liquid Ice* had me seething again. Robbed! Violated! I'd rather have been gang-raped by chimpanzees than have the memory stolen from me. I had punched up the films of *Liquid Ice* and they were beautiful. Stunning, and I could say it without conceit because I had not written it.

My life became very simple. I worked—twelve and fourteen hours a day sometimes—ate, slept, and worked some more. Twice a day I put in one hour learning to fight over the holovision. It was all highly theoretical, of course, but it had value. It kept me in shape and gave me a sense of confidence.

For the first time in my life I got a good look at what my body would have been with no tampering. I was born female, but Carnival wanted to raise me as a boy so she had me Changed when I was two hours old. It's another of the contradictions in her that used to infuriate me so much but which, as I got older, I came to love. I mean, why go to all the pain and trouble of bringing a child to term and giving birth naturally, all from a professed dislike of tampering—and then turn around and refuse to accept the results of nature's lottery? I have decided that it's a result of her age. She's almost two hundred by now, which puts her childhood back in the days before Changing. In those days—I've never understood why—there was a predilection for male children. I think she never really shed it.

At any rate, I spent my childhood male. When I got my first Change, I picked my own body design. Now, in a six-lunation-old clone body which naturally reflected my actual genetic structure, I was pleased to see that my first female body design had not been far from the truth.

I was short, with small breasts and an undistinguished body. But my face was nice. Cute, I would say. I liked the nose. The age of the accelerated clone body was about seventeen years; perhaps the nose would lose its upturn in a few years of natural growth, but I hoped not. If it did, I'd have it put back.

Once a week, I had a recording made. It was the only time I saw people in the flesh. Carnival, Leander, Isadora, and a medico would enter and stay for a while after it was made. It took them an hour each way to get past the security devices. I admit it made me feel a little more secure to see how long it took even my friends to get into my apartment. It was like an invisible fortress outside my door. The better to lure you into my parlor, killer!

I worked with the CC as I never had before. We wrote new programs that produced four-dimensional models in my viewer unlike anything we had ever done.

The CC knew the stage—which was to be the Kansas disneyland—and I knew the storm. Since I couldn't walk on the stage before the concert this time I had to rely on the CC to reconstruct it for me in the holo tank.

Nothing makes me feel more godlike. Even watching it in the three-meter tank I felt thirty meters tall with lightning in my hair and a crown of shimmering frost. I walked through the Kansas autumn, the brown, rolling, featureless prairie before the red or white man came. It was the way the real Kansas looked now under the rule of the Invaders, who had ripped up the barbed wire, smoothed over the furrows, dismantled the cities and railroads, and let the buffalo roam once more.

There was a logistical problem I had never faced before. I intended to use the buffalo instead of having them kept out of the way. I needed the thundering hooves of a stampede; it was very much a part of the environment I was creating. How to do it without killing animals?

The disneyland management wouldn't allow any of their livestock to be injured as part of a performance. That was fine with me, my stomach turned at the very thought. Art is one thing; but life is another and I will not kill unless to save myself. But the Kansas disneyland has two million head of buffalo and I envisioned up to twenty-five twisters at one time. How do you keep the two separate?

With subtlety, I found. The CC had buffalo behavioral profiles that were very reliable. The damn CC stores *everything,* and I've had occasion more than once to be thankful for it. We could position the herds at a selected spot and let the twisters loose above them. The tornadoes would never be *totally* under our control—they are capricious even when handmade—but we could rely on a hard 90 percent accuracy in steering them. The herd profile we worked up was usable out to two decimal points, and as insurance against the unforeseen we installed several groups of flash bombs to turn the herd if it headed into danger.

It's an endless series of details. Where does the lightning strike, for instance? On a flat, gently rolling plain, the natural accumulation of electric charge can be just about anywhere. We had to be sure we could shape it the way we wanted, by burying five hundred accumulators that could trigger an air-to-ground flash on cue. And to the right spot. The air-to-air are harder. And the ball lightning—oh, brother. But we found we could guide it pretty well with buried wires carrying an electric current. There were going to be range fires—so check with the management on places that are due for a controlled burn anyway, and keep the buffalo away from there, too; and be sure the smoke would not blow over into the audience and spoil the view or into the herd and panic them. . . .

But it was going to be glorious.

*   *   *

Six lunations rolled by. *Six lunations!* 177.18353 mean solar days!

I discovered that figure during a long period of brooding when I called up all sorts of data on the investigation. Which, according to Isadora, was going well.

I knew better. The CC has its faults but shading data is not one of them. Ask it what the figures are and it prints them out in tricolor.

Here's some: probability of a capture by the original curve, 93 percent. Total number of viable suspects remaining: nine. Highest probability of those nine possibles: 3.9 percent. That was *Carnival*. The others were also close friends, and were there solely because they had had the opportunity at all three murders. Even Isadora dared not speculate—at least not aloud, and to me—about whether any of them had a motive.

I discussed it with the CC.

"I know, Fox, I know," it replied, with the closest approach to mechanical despair I have ever heard.

"Is that all you can say?"

"No. As it happens, I'm pursuing the other possibility: that it was a ghost who killed you."

"Are you serious?"

"Yes. The term 'ghost' covers all illegal beings. I estimate there to be on the order of two hundred of them existing outside legal sanctions on Luna. These are executed criminals with their right to life officially revoked, unauthorized children never registered, and some suspected artificial mutants. Those last are the result of proscribed experiments with human DNA. All these conditions are hard to conceal for any length of time, and I round up a few every year."

"What do you do with them?"

"They have no right to life. I must execute them when I find them."

"You do it? That's not just a figure of speech?"

"That's right. I do it. It's a job humans find distasteful. I never could keep the position filled, so I assumed it myself."

That didn't sit right with me. There is an atavistic streak in me that doesn't like to turn over the complete functioning of society to machines. I get it from my mother, who goes for years at a time not deigning to speak to the CC.

"So you think someone like that may be after me. Why?"

"There is insufficient data for a meaningful answer. 'Why' has always been a tough question for me. I can operate only on the parameters fed into me when I'm dealing with human motivation, and I suspect that the parameters are not complete. I'm constantly being surprised."

"Thank goodness for that." But this time, I could have wished the CC knew a little more about human behavior.

So I was being hunted by a spook. It didn't do anything for my peace of mind.

I tried to think of how such a person could exist in this card-file world we live in. A technological rat, smarter than the computers, able to fit into the cracks and holes in the integrated circuits. Where were those cracks? I couldn't find them. When I thought of the checks and safeguards all around us, the voluntary genalysis we submit to every time we spend money or take a tube or close a business deal or interface with the computer . . . People used to sign their names many times a day, or so I've heard. Now, we scrape off a bit of dead skin from our palms. It's damn hard to fake.

But how do you catch a phantom? I was facing life as a recluse if this murderer was really so determined that I die.

That conclusion came at a bad time. I had finished *Cyclone,* and to relax I had called up the films of some of the other performances during my absence from the art scene. I never should have done that.

Flashiness was out. Understated elegance was in. One of the reviews I read was very flattering to my *Liquid Ice.* I quote:

"In this piece Fox has closed the book on the blood and thunder school of Environmentalism. This powerful statement sums up the things that can be achieved by sheer magnitude and overwhelming drama. The displays of the future will be concerned with the gentle nuance of dusk, the elusive breath of a summer breeze. Fox is the Tchaikovsky of Environmentalism, the last great romantic who paints on a broad canvas. Whether she can adjust to the new, more thoughtful styles that are evolving in the work of Janus, or Pym, or even some of the ambiguous abstractions we have seen from Tyleber, remains to be seen. Nothing will detract from the sublime glory of *Liquid Ice,* of course, but the time is here . . ." and so forth and thank-you for nothing.

For an awful moment I thought I had a beautiful dinosaur on my hands. It can happen, and the hazards are pronounced after a reincarnation. Advancing technology, fashion, frontiers, taste, or morals can make the best of us obsolete overnight. Was everyone contemplating gentle springtimes now, after my long sleep? Were the cool, sweet zephyrs of a summer's night the only thing that had meaning now?

A panicky call to my agent dispelled that quickly enough. As usual, the pronouncements of the critics had gone ahead of the public taste. I'm not knocking critics; that's their function, if you concede they have a function: to chart a course into unexplored territory. They must stay at the leading edge of the innovative artistic evolution, they must see what everyone will be seeing in a few years' time. Meanwhile, the public was still eating up the type of superspectacle I have always specialized in. I ran the risk of being labeled a dinosaur myself, but I found the prospect did not worry me. I became an artist through the back door, just like the tinkerers in early twentieth-century Hollywood. Before I was discovered, I had just been an environmental engineer having a good time.

That's not to say I don't take my art seriously. I *do* sweat over it, investing in-spiration and perspiration in about the classic Edison proportions. But I don't take the critics too seriously, especially when they're not enunciating the public taste. Just because Beethoven doesn't sound like currently popular art doesn't mean his music is worthless.

I found myself thinking back to the times before Environmentalism made such a splash. Back then we were carefree. We had grandiose bull sessions, talking of what we would do if only we were given an environment large enough. We spent months roughing out the programs for something to be called *Typhoon!* It was a hurricane in a bottle, and the bottle would have to be five hundred kilometers wide. Such a bottle still does not exist, but when it's built some fool will stage the show. Maybe me. The good old days never die, you know.

So my agent made a deal with the owner of the Kansas disneyland. The owner had known that I was working on something for his place, but I'd not talked to him about it. The terms were generous. My agent displayed the profit report on *Liquid Ice,* which was still playing yearly to packed houses in Pennsylvania. I got a straight 50 percent of the gate, with costs of the installation and computer time to be shared between me and the disneyland. I stood to make about five million Lunar marks.

And I was robbed again. Not killed this time, but robbed of the chance to go into Kansas and supervise the installation of the equipment. I clashed mightily with Isadora and would have stormed out on my own, armed with not so much as a nail file, if not for a pleading visit from Carnival. So I backed down this once and sat at home, going there only by holographic projection. I plunged into self-doubt. After all, I hadn't even felt the Kansas sod beneath my bare feet this time. I hadn't been there in the flesh for over three years. My usual method before I even con-ceive a project is to spend a week or two just wandering naked through the park, getting the feel of it through my skin and nose and those senses that don't even have a name.

It took the CC three hours of gentle argument to convince me again that the models we had written were accurate to seven decimal places. They were perfect. An action ordered up on the computer model would be a perfect analog of the real action in Kansas. The CC said I could make quite a bit of money just renting the software to other artists.

The day of the premiere of *Cyclone* found me still in my apartment. But I was on the way out.

Small as I am, I somehow managed to struggle out that door with Carnival, Isadora, Leander, and my agent pulling on my elbows.

I was *not* going to watch the performance on the tube.

I arrived early, surrounded by my impromptu bodyguard. The sky matched my mind; gray, overcast, and slightly fearful. It brooded over us, and I felt more and more like a sacrificial lamb mounting some somber altar. But it was a magnificent stage to die upon.

The Kansas disneyland is one of the newer ones, and one of the largest. It is a hollowed-out cylinder twenty kilometers beneath Clavius. It measures two hundred and fifty kilometers in diameter and is five kilometers high. The rim is artfully disguised to blend into the blue sky. When you are half a kilometer from the rim, the illusion fails; otherwise, you might as well be standing back on Old Earth. The curvature of the floor is consistent with Old Earth, so the horizon is terrifyingly far away. Only the gravity is Lunar.

Kansas was built after most of the more spectacular possibilities had been exhausted, either on Luna or another planet. There was Kenya, beneath Mare Moscoviense; Himalaya, also on the Farside; Amazon, under old Tycho; Pennsylvania, Sahara, Pacific, Mekong, Transylvania. There were thirty disneylands under the inhabited planets and satellites of the solar system the last time I counted.

Kansas is certainly the least interesting topographically. It's flat, almost monotonous. But it was perfect for what I wanted to do. What artist really chooses to paint on a canvas that's already been covered with pictures? Well, I have, for one. But for the frame of mind I was in when I wrote *Cyclone* it had to be the starkness of the wide-open sky and the browns and yellows of the rolling terrain. It was the place where Dorothy departed for Oz. The home of the black twister.

I was greeted warmly by Pym and Janus, old friends here to see what the grand master was up to. Or so I flattered myself. More likely they were here to see the old lady make a fool of herself. Very few others were able to get close to me. My shield of high shoulders was very effective. It wouldn't do when the show began, however. I wished I was a little taller, then wondered if that would make me a better target.

The viewing area was a gentle rise about a kilometer in radius. It had been written out of the program to the extent that none of the more fearsome effects would intrude to sweep us all into the Land of Oz. But being a spectator at a weather show can be grueling. Most had come prepared with clear plastic slicker, insulated coat, and boots. I was going to be banging some warm and some very cold air masses head on to get things rolling, and some of it would sweep over us. There were a few brave souls in Native American war paint, feathers, and moccasins.

An Environmental happening has no opening chords like a musical symphony. It is already in progress when you arrive, and will still be going on when you leave. The weather in a disneyland is a continuous process and we merely shape a few hours of it to our wills. The observer does not need to watch it in its entirety.

Indeed, it would be impossible to do so, as it occurs all around and above you. There is no rule of silence. People talk, stroll, break out picnic lunches as an ancient signal for the rain to begin, and generally enjoy themselves. You experience the symphony with all five senses, and several that you are not aware of. Most people do not realize the effect of a gigantic low-pressure area sweeping over them, but they feel it all the same. Humidity alters mood, metabolism, and hormone level. All of these things are important to the total experience, and I neglect none of them.

Cyclone has a definite beginning, however. At least to the audience. It begins with the opening bolt of lightning. I worked over it a long time, and designed it to shatter nerves. There is the slow building of thunderheads, the ominous rolling and turbulence, then the prickling in your body hairs that you don't even notice consciously. And then it hits. It crashes in at seventeen points in a ring around the audience, none farther away than half a kilometer. It is properly called chain lightning, because after the initial discharge it keeps flashing for a full seven seconds. It's designed to take the hair right off your scalp.

It had its desired effect. We were surrounded by a crown of jittering incandescent snakes, coiling and dancing with a sound imported direct to you from Armageddon. It startled the hell out of *me,* and I had been expecting it.

It was a while before the audience could get their *ooh*ers and *aah*ers back into shape. For several seconds I had touched them with stark, naked terror. An emotion like that doesn't come cheaply to sensation-starved, innately insular tunnel dwellers. Lunarians get little to really shout about, growing up in the warrens and corridors, and living their lives more or less afraid of the surface. That's why the disneylands were built, because people wanted limitless vistas that were not in a vacuum.

The thunder never really stopped for me. It blended imperceptibly into the applause that is more valuable than the millions I would make from this storm.

As for the rest of the performance . . .

What can I say? It's been said that there's nothing more dull than a description of the weather. I believe it, even spectacular weather. Weather is an experiential thing, and that's why tapes and films of my works sell few copies. You have to be there and have the wind actually whipping your face and feel the oppressive weight of a tornado as it passes overhead like a vermiform freight train. I could write down where the funnel clouds formed and where they went from there, where the sleet and hail fell, where the buffalo stampeded, but it would do no one any good. If you want to see it, go to Kansas. The last I heard, *Cyclone* is still playing there two or three times yearly.

I recall standing surrounded by a sea of people. Beyond me to the east the land

THE PHANTOM OF KANSAS   167

was burning. Smoke boiled black from the hilltops and sooty gray from the hollows where the water was rising to drown it. To the north a Herculean cyclone swept up a chain of ball lightning like pearls and swallowed them into the evacuated vortex in its center. Above me, two twisters were twined in a death dance. They circled each other like baleful gray predators, taking each other's measure. They feinted, retreated, slithered, and skittered like tubes of oil. It was beautiful and deadly. And I had never seen it before. Someone was tampering with my program.

As I realized that and stood rooted to the ground with the possibly disastrous consequences becoming apparent to me the wind-snakes locked in a final embrace. Their counterrotations canceled out, and they were gone. Not even a breath of wind reached me to hint of that titanic struggle.

I ran through the seventy-kilometer wind and the thrashing rain. I was wearing sturdy moccasins and a parka, and carrying the knife I had brought from my apartment.

Was it a lure, set by one who has become a student of Foxes? Am I playing into his hands?

I didn't care. I had to meet him, had to fight it out once and for all.

Getting away from my "protection" had been simple. They were as transfixed by the display as the rest of the audience, and it had merely been a matter of waiting until they all looked in the same direction and fading into the crowd. I picked out a small woman dressed in Indian style and offered her a hundred marks for her moccasins. She recognized me—my new face was on the programs—and made me a gift of them. Then I worked my way to the edge of the crowd and bolted past the security guards. They were not too concerned since the audience area was enclosed by a shock-field. When I went right through it they may have been surprised, but I didn't look back to see. I was one of only three people in Kansas wearing the PassKey device on my wrist, so I didn't fear anyone following me.

I had done it all without conscious thought. Some part of me must have analyzed it, planned it out, but I just executed the results. I knew where he must be to have generated his tornado to go into combat with mine. No one else in Kansas would know where to look. I was headed for a particular wind generator on the east periphery.

I moved through weather more violent than the real Kansas would have experienced. It was concentrated violence, more wind and rain and devastation than Kansas would normally have in a full year. And it was happening all around me.

But I was all right, unless he had more tricks up his sleeve. I knew where the tornadoes would be and at what time. I dodged them, waited for them to pass, knew every twist and dido they would make on their seemingly random courses. Off to my left the buffalo herds milled, resting from the stampede that had brought them past the audience for the first time. In an hour they would be thundering back again, but for now I could forget them.

A twister headed for me, leaped high in the air, and skidded through a miasma of uprooted sage and sod. I clocked it with the internal picture I had and dived for a gully at just the right time. It hopped over me and was gone back into the clouds. I ran on.

My training in the apartment was paying off. My body was only six lunations old, and as finely tuned as it would ever be. I rested by slowing to a trot, only to run again in a few minutes. I covered ten kilometers before the storm began to slow down. Behind me, the audience would be drifting away. The critics would be trying out scathing phrases or wild adulation; I didn't see how they could find any middle ground for this one. Kansas was being released from the grip of machines gone wild. Ahead of me was my killer. I would find him.

I wasn't totally unprepared. Isadora had given in and allowed me to install a computerized bomb in my body. It would kill my killer—and me—if he jumped me. It was intended as a balance-of-terror device, the kind you hope you will never use because it terrorizes your enemy too much for him to test it. I would inform him of it if I had the time, hoping he would not be crazy enough to kill both of us. If he was, we had him, though it would be little comfort to me. At least Fox 5 would be the last in the series. With the remains of a body, Isadora guaranteed to bring a killer to justice.

The sun came out as I reached the last, distorted gully before the wall. It was distorted because it was one of the place where tourists were not allowed to go. It was like walking through the backdrop on a stage production. The land was squashed together in one of the dimensions, and the hills in front of me were painted against a bas-relief. It was meant to be seen from a distance.

Standing in front of the towering mural was a man.

He was naked, and grimed with dirt. He watched me as I went down the gentle slope to stand waiting for him. I stopped about two hundred meters from him, drew my knife and held it in the air. I waited.

He came down the concealed stairway, slowly and painfully. He was limping badly on his left leg. As far as I could see he was unarmed.

The closer he got, the worse he looked. He had been in a savage fight. He had long, puckered, badly healed scars on his left leg, his chest, and his right arm. He had one eye; the right one was only a reddened socket. There was a scar that slashed from his forehead to his neck. It was a hideous thing. I thought of the CC's suspicion that my killer might be a ghost, someone living on the raw edges of our civilization. Such a man might not have access to medical treatment whenever he needed it.

"I think you should know," I said, with just the slightest quaver, "that I have a bomb in my body. It's powerful enough to blow both of us to pieces. It's set to go off if I'm killed. So don't try anything funny."

"I won't," he said. "I thought you might have a failsafe this time, but it doesn't matter. I'm not going to hurt you."

"Is that what you told the others?" I sneered, crouching a little lower as he neared me. I felt like I had the upper hand, but my predecessors might have felt the same way.

"No, I never said that. You don't have to believe me."

He stopped twenty meters from me. His hands were at his sides. He looked helpless enough, but he might have a weapon buried somewhere in the dirt. He might have *anything*. I had to fight to keep feeling that I was in control.

Then I had to fight something else. I gripped the knife tighter as a picture slowly superimposed itself over his ravaged face. It was a mental picture, the functioning of my "sixth sense."

No one knows if that sense really exists. I think it does, because it works for me. It can be expressed as the knack for seeing someone who has had radical body work done—sex, weight, height, skin color all altered—and still being able to recognize him. Some say it's an evolutionary change. I didn't think evolution worked that way. But I can do it. And I knew who this tall, brutalized male stranger was.

He was me.

I sprang back to my guard, wondering if he had used the shock of recognition to overpower my earlier incarnations. It wouldn't work with me. Nothing would work. I was going to kill him, no matter *who* he was.

"You know me," he said. It was not a question.

"Yes. And you scare hell out of me. I knew you knew a lot about me, but I didn't realize you'd know *this* much."

He laughed, without humor. "Yes. I know you from the inside."

The silence stretched out between us. Then he began to cry. I was surprised, but unmoved. I was still all nerve endings, and suspected ninety thousand types of dirty tricks. Let him cry.

He slowly sank to his knees, sobbing with the kind of washed-out monotony that you read about but seldom hear. He put his hands to the ground and awkwardly shuffled around until his back was to me. He crouched over himself, his head touching the ground, his hands wide at his sides, his legs bent. It was about the most wide-open, helpless posture imaginable, and I knew it must be for a reason. But I couldn't see what it might be.

"I thought I had this all over with," he sniffed, wiping his nose with the back of one hand. "I'm sorry, I'd meant to be more dignified. I guess I'm not made of the stern stuff I thought. I thought it'd be easier." He was silent for a moment, then coughed hoarsely. "Go on. Get it over with."

"Huh?" I said, honestly dumbfounded.

"Kill me. It's what you came here for. And it'll be a relief to me."

I took my time. I stood motionless for a full minute, looking at the incredible problem from every angle. What kind of trick could there *be?* He was smart, but he wasn't God. He couldn't call in an air strike on me, cause the ground to swallow me up, disarm me with one crippled foot, or hypnotize me into plunging the knife into my own gut. Even if he could do something, he would die, too.

I advanced cautiously, alert for the slightest twitch of his body. Nothing happened. I stood behind him, my eyes flicking from his feet to his hands to his bare back. I raised the knife. My hands trembled a little, but my determination was still there. I would not flub this. I brought the knife down.

The point went into his flesh, into the muscle of his shoulder blade, about three centimeters deep. He gasped. A trickle of blood went winding through the knobs along his spine. But he didn't move, he didn't try to get up. He didn't scream for mercy. He just knelt there, shivering and turning pale.

I'd have to stab harder. I pulled the knife free, and more blood came out. And still he waited.

That was about all I could take. My bloodlust had dried in my mouth until all I could taste was vomit welling in my stomach.

I'm not a fool. It occurred to me even then that this could be some demented trick, that he might know me well enough to be sure I could not go through with it. Maybe he was some sort of psychotic who got thrills out of playing this kind of incredible game, allowing his life to be put in danger and then drenching himself in my blood.

But he was *me.* It was all I had to go on. He was a me who had lived a very different life, becoming much tougher and wilier with every day, diverging by the hour from what I knew as my personality and capabilities. So I tried and I tried to think of myself doing what he was doing now for the purpose of murder. I failed utterly.

And if I *could* sink that low, I'd rather not live.

"Hey, get up," I said, going around in front of him. He didn't respond, so I nudged him with my foot. He looked up, and saw me offering him the knife, hilt-first.

"If this is some sort of scheme," I said, "I'd rather learn of it now."

His one eye was red and brimming as he got up, but there was no joy in him. He took the knife, not looking at me, and stood there holding it. The skin on my belly was crawling. Then he reversed the knife and his brow wrinkled, as if he were summoning up nerve. I suddenly knew what he was going to do, and I lunged. I was barely in time. The knife missed his belly and went off to the side as I yanked on his arm. He was much stronger than I. I was pulled off balance, but managed to hang onto his arm. He fought with me, but was intent on suicide and had no thought of defending himself. I brought my fist up under his jaw and he went limp.

Night had fallen. I disposed of the knife and built a fire. Did you know that dried buffalo manure burns well? I didn't believe it until I put it to the test.

I dressed his wound by tearing up my shirt, wrapped my parka around him to ward off the chill, and sat with my bare back to the fire. Luckily, there was no wind, because it can get very chilly on the plains at night.

He woke with a sore jaw and a resigned demeanor. He didn't thank me for saving him from himself. I suppose people rarely do. They think they know what they're doing, and their reasons always seem logical to them.

"You don't understand," he moaned. "You're only dragging it out. I have to die, there's no place for me here."

"Make me understand," I said.

He didn't want to talk, but there was nothing to do and no chance of sleeping in the cold, so he eventually did. The story was punctuated with long, truculent silences.

It stemmed from the bank robbery two and a half years ago. It had been staged by some very canny robbers. They had a new dodge that made me respect Isadora's statement that police methods had not kept pace with criminal possibilities.

The destruction of the memory cubes had been merely a decoy. They were equally unconcerned about the cash they took. They were bunco artists.

They had destroyed the rest of the cubes to conceal the theft of two of them. That way the police would be looking for a crime of passion, murder, rather than one of profit. It was a complicated double feint, because the robbers wanted to give the impression of someone who was trying to conceal murder by stealing cash.

My killer—we both agreed he should not be called Fox so we settled on the name he had come to fancy, Rat—didn't know the details of the scheme, but it involved the theft of memory cubes containing two of the richest people on Luna. They were taken, and clones were grown. When the memories were played into the clones, the people were awakened into a falsely created situation and encouraged to believe that it was reality. It would work; the newly reincarnated person is willing to be led, willing to believe. Rat didn't know exactly what the plans were beyond that. He had awakened to be told that it was fifteen thousand years later, and that the Invaders had left Earth and were rampaging through the solar system wiping out the human race. It took three lunations to convince them that he— or rather she, for Rat had been awakened into a body identical to the one I was wearing—was not the right billionaire. That she was not a billionaire at all, just a struggling artist. The thieves had gotten the wrong cube.

They dumped her. Just like that. They opened the door and kicked her out into what she thought was the end of civilization. She soon found out that it was only twenty years in her future, since her memories came from the stolen cube which I had recorded about twenty years before.

Don't ask me how they got the wrong cube. One cube looks exactly like another; they are in fact indistinguishable from one another by any test known to science short of playing them into a clone and asking the resulting person who he or she is. Because of that fact, the banks we entrust them to have a foolproof filing system to avoid unpleasant accidents like Rat. The only possible answer was that for all their planning, for all their cunning and guile, the thieves had read 2 in column A and selected 3 in column B.

I didn't think much of their chances of living to spend any of that money. I told Rat so.

"I doubt if their extortion scheme involves money," he said. "At least not directly. More likely the theft was aimed at obtaining information contained in the minds of billionaires. Rich people are often protected with psychological safeguards against having information tortured from them, but can't block themselves against divulging it willingly. That's what the Invader hoax must have been about, to finagle them into thinking the information no longer mattered, or perhaps that it must be revealed to save the human race."

"I'm suspicious of involuted schemes like that," I said.

"So am I." We laughed when we realized what he had said. Of *course* we had the same opinions.

"But it fooled *me*," he went on. "When they discarded me, I fully expected to meet the Invaders face-to-face. It was quite a shock to find that the world was almost unchanged."

"Almost," I said, quietly. I was beginning to empathize with him.

"Right." He lost the half-smile that had lingered on his face, and I was sad to see it go.

What would I have done in the same situation? There's really no need to ask. I must believe that I would have done exactly as she did. She had been dumped like garbage, and quickly saw that she was about that useful to society. If found, she would be eliminated like garbage. The robbers had not thought enough of her to bother killing her. She could tell the police certain things they did not know if she was captured, so she had to assume that the robbers had told her nothing of any use to the police. Even if she could have helped capture and convict the conspirators, she would *still* be eliminated. She was an illegal person.

She risked a withdrawal from my bank account. I remembered it now. It wasn't large, and I assumed I must have written it since it was backed up by my genalysis. It was far too small an amount to suspect anything. And it wasn't the first time I have made a withdrawal and forgotten about it. She knew that, of course.

With the money she bought a Change on the sly. They can be had, though you take your chances. It's not the safest thing in the world to conduct illegal business with someone who will soon have you on the operating table, unconscious. Rat had thought the Change would help throw the police off his trail if they should learn of his existence. Isadora told me about that once, said it was the sign of the inexperienced criminal.

Rat was definitely a fugitive. If discovered and captured, he faced a death sentence. It's harsh, but the population laws allow no loopholes whatsoever. If they did, we could be up to our ears in a century. There would be no trial, only a positive genalysis and a hearing to determine which of us was the rightful Fox.

"I can't tell you how bitter I was," he said. "I learned slowly how to survive. It's not as hard as you might think, in some ways, and much harder than you can imagine in others. I could walk the corridors freely, as long as I did nothing that required a genalysis. That means you can't buy anything, ride on public transport, take a job. But the air is free if you're not registered with the tax board, water is free, and food can be had in the disneylands. I was lucky in that. My palmprint would still open all the restricted doors in the disneylands. A legacy of my artistic days." I could hear the bitterness in his voice.

And why not? He had been robbed, too. He went to sleep as I had been twenty years ago, an up-and-coming artist, excited by the possibilities in Environmentalism. He had great dreams. I remember them well. He woke up to find that it had all been realized but none of it was for him. He could not even get access to computer time. Everyone was talking about Fox and her last opus, *Thunderhead*. She was the darling of the art world.

He went to the premiere of *Liquid Ice* and began to hate me. He was sleeping in the air recirculators to keep warm, foraging nuts and berries and an occasional squirrel in Pennsylvania, while I was getting rich and famous. He took to trailing me. He stole a spacesuit, followed me out onto Palus Putridinus.

"I didn't plan it," he said, his voice wracked with guilt. "I never could have done it with planning. The idea just struck me and before I knew it I had pushed you. You hit the bottom and I followed you down, because I was really sorry I had done it and I lifted your body up and looked into your face. . . . Your face was all . . . my face, it was . . . the eyes popping out and blood boiling away and . . ."

He couldn't go on, and I was grateful. He finally let out a shuddering breath and continued.

"Before they found your body I wrote some checks on your account. You never noticed them when you woke up that first time, since the reincarnation had taken such a big chunk out of your balance. We never were any good with money." He chuckled again. I took the opportunity to move closer to him. He was speaking very quietly so that I could barely hear him over the crackling of the fire.

"I . . . I guess I went crazy then. I can't account for it any other way. When I saw you in Pennsylvania again, walking among the trees as free as can be, I just cracked up. Nothing would do but that I kill you and take your place. I'd have to do it in a way that would destroy the body. I thought of acid, and of burning you up here in Kansas in a range fire. I don't know why I settled on a bomb. It was stupid. But I don't feel responsible. At least it must have been painless.

"They reincarnated you again. I was fresh out of ideas for murder. And motivation. I tried to think it out. So I decided to approach you carefully, not revealing who I was. I thought maybe I could reach you. I tried to think of what I would do if I was approached with the same story, and decided I'd be sympathetic. I didn't reckon with the fear you were feeling. You were hunted. I myself was being hunted, and I should have seen that fear brings out the best and the worst in us.

"You recognized me immediately—something else I should have thought of—and put two and two together so fast I didn't even know what hit me. You were on me, and you were armed with a knife. You had been taking training in martial arts." He pointed to the various scars. "You did this to me, and this, and this. You nearly killed me. But I'm bigger. I held on and managed to overpower you. I plunged the knife in your heart.

"I went insane again. I've lost all memories from the sight of the blood pouring from your chest until yesterday. I somehow managed to stay alive and not bleed to death. I must have lived like an animal. I'm dirty enough to be one.

"Then yesterday I heard two of the maintenance people in the machine areas of Pennsylvania talking about the show you were putting on in Kansas. So I came here. The rest you know."

The fire was dying. I realized that part of my shivering was caused by the cold. I got up and searched for more chips, but it was too dark to see. The "moon" wasn't up tonight, would not rise for hours yet.

"You're cold," he said, suddenly. "I'm sorry, I didn't realize. Here, take this back. I'm used to it." He held out the parka.

"No, you keep it. I'm all right." I laughed when I realized my teeth had been chattering as I said it. He was still holding it out to me.

"Well, maybe we could share it?"

Luckily it was too big, borrowed from a random spectator earlier in the day. I sat in front of him and leaned back against his chest and he wrapped his arms around me with the parka going around both of us. My teeth still chattered, but I was cozy.

I thought of him sitting at the auxiliary computer terminal above the east wind generator, looking out from a distance of fifteen kilometers at the crowd and the storm. He had known how to talk to me. That tornado he had created in real-time and sent out to do battle with my storm was as specific to me as a typed message. *I'm here! Come meet me.*

I had an awful thought, then wondered why it was so awful. It wasn't me that was in trouble.

Rat, you used the computer. That means you submitted a skin sample for genalysis, and the CC will . . . No, wait a minute."

"What does it matter?"

"It . . . it matters. But the game's not over. I can cover for you. No one knows when I left the audience, or why. I can say I saw something going wrong—it could be tricky fooling the CC, but I'll think of something—and headed for the computer room to correct it. I'll say I created the second tornado as a—"

He put his hand over my mouth.

"Don't talk like that. It was hard enough to resign myself to death. There's no way out for me. Don't you see that I can't go on living like a rat? What would I do if you covered for me this time? I'll tell you. I'd spend the rest of my life hiding out here. You could sneak me table scraps from time to time. No, thank you."

"No, no. You haven't thought it out. You're still looking on me as an enemy. Alone, you don't have a chance, I'll concede that, but with me to help you, spend money and so forth, we—" He put his hand over my mouth again. I found that I didn't mind, dirty as it was.

"You mean you're not my enemy now?" He said it quietly, helplessly, like a child asking if I was *really* going to stop beating him.

"I—" That was as far as I got. What the hell was going on? I became aware of his arms around me, not as lovely warmth but as a strong presence. I hugged my legs up closer to me and bit down hard on my knee. Tears squeezed from my eyes.

I turned to face him, searching to see his face in the darkness. He went over backwards with me on top of him.

"No, I'm not your enemy." Then I was struggling blindly to dispose of the one thing that stood between us: my pants. While we groped in the dark, the rain started to fall around us.

We laughed as we were drenched, and I remember sitting up on top of him once.

"Don't blame me," I said. "This storm isn't mine." Then he pulled me back down.

It was like something you read about in the romance magazines. All the overblown words, the intensive hyperbole. It was all real. We were made for each other, literally. It was the most astounding act of love imaginable. He knew what I liked to the tenth decimal place, and I was just as knowledgeable. I *knew* what he liked, by remembering back to the times I had been male and then doing what *I* had liked.

Call it masturbation orchestrated for two. There were times during that night when I was unsure of which one I was. I distinctly remember touching his face with my hand and feeling the scar on my own face. For a few moments I was convinced that the line which forever separates two individuals blurred, and we came closer to being one person than any two humans have ever done.

A time finally came when we had spent all our passion. Or, I prefer to think, invested it. We lay together beneath my parka and allowed our bodies to adjust to each other, filling the little spaces, trying to touch in every place it was possible to touch.

"I'm listening," he whispered. "What's your plan?"

They came after me with a helicopter later that night. Rat hid out in a gully while I threw away my clothes and walked calmly out to meet them. I was filthy, with mud and grass plastered in my hair, but that was consistent with what I had been known to do in the past. Often, before or after a performance, I would run nude through the disneyland in an effort to get closer to the environment I had shaped.

I told them I had been doing that. They accepted it, Carnival and Isadora, though they scolded me for a fool to leave them as I had. But it was easy to bamboozle them into believing that I had had no choice.

"If I hadn't taken over control when I did," I said to them, "there might have been twenty thousand dead. One of those twisters was off course. I extrapolated and saw trouble in about three hours. I had no choice."

Neither of them knew a stationary cold front from an isobar, so I got away with it.

Fooling the CC was not so simple. I had to fake data as best I could, and make it jibe with the internal records. This all had to be done in my head, relying on the overall feeling I've developed for the medium. When the CC questioned me about it I told it haughtily that a human develops a sixth sense in art, and it's something a computer could never grasp. The CC had to be satisfied with that.

The reviews were good, though I didn't really care. I was in demand. That made it harder to do what I had to do, but I was helped by the fact of my continued forced isolation.

I told all the people who called me with offers that I was not doing anything more until my killer was caught. And I proposed my idea to Isadora.

She couldn't very well object. She knew there was not much chance of keeping me in my apartment for much longer, so she went along with me. I bought a ship and told Carnival about it.

Carnival didn't like it much, but she had to agree it was the best way to keep me safe. But she wanted to know why I needed my own ship, why I couldn't just book passage on a passenger liner.

Because all passengers on a liner must undergo genalysis, is what I thought, but what I said was, "Because how would I know that my killer is not a fellow passenger? To be safe, I must be alone. Don't worry, Mother, I know what I'm doing."

The day came when I owned my own ship, free and clear. It was a beauty, and cost me most of the five million I had made from *Cyclone.* It could boost at one gee for weeks; plenty of power to get me to Pluto. It was completely automatic, requiring only verbal instructions to the computer-pilot.

The customs agents went over it, then left me alone. The CC had instructed them that I needed to leave quietly, and told them to cooperate with me. That was a stroke of luck, since getting Rat aboard was the most hazardous part of the plan. We were able to scrap our elaborate plans and he just walked in like a law-abiding citizen.

We sat together in the ship, waiting for the ignition.

"Pluto has no extradition treaty with Luna," the CC said, out of the blue.

"I didn't know that," I lied, wondering what the hell was happening.

"Indeed? Then you might be interested in another fact. There is very little on Pluto in the way of centralized government. You're heading out for the frontier."

"That should be fun," I said, cautiously. "Sort of an adventure, right?"

"You always were one for adventure. I remember when you first came here to Nearside, over my objections. That one turned out all right, didn't it? Now Lunarians live freely on either side of Luna. You were largely responsible for that."

"Was I really? I don't think so. I think the time was just ripe."

"Perhaps." The CC was silent for a while as I watched the chronometer ticking down to lift-off time. My shoulder blades were itching with a sense of danger.

"There are no population laws on Pluto," it said, and waited.

"Oh? How delightfully primitive. You mean a woman can have as many children as she wishes?"

"So I hear. I'm onto you, Fox."

"Autopilot, override your previous instructions. I wish to lift off right now! Move!"

A red light flashed on my panel, and started blinking.

"That means that it's too late for a manual override," the CC informed me. "Your ship's pilot is not that bright."

I slumped into my chair and then reached out blindly for Rat. Two minutes to go. So close.

"Fox, it was a pleasure to work with you on *Cyclone*. I enjoyed it tremendously. I think I'm beginning to understand what you mean when you say 'art.' I'm even beginning to try some things on my own. I sincerely wish you could be around to give me criticism, encouragement, perspective."

We looked at the speaker, wondering what it meant by that.

"I knew about your plan, and about the existence of your double, since shortly after you left Kansas. You did your best to conceal it and I applaud the effort, but the data were unmistakable. I had trillions of nanoseconds to play around with the facts, fit them together every possible way, and I arrived at the inevitable answer."

I cleared my throat nervously.

"I'm glad you enjoyed *Cyclone*. Uh, if you knew this, why didn't you have us arrested that day?"

"As I told you, I am not the law-enforcement computer. I merely supervise it. If Isadora and the computer could not arrive at the same conclusion, then it seems obvious that some programs should be rewritten. So I decided to leave them on their own and see if they could solve the problem. It was a test, you see." It made a throat-clearing sound, and went on in a slightly embarrassed voice.

"For a while there, a few days ago, I thought they'd really catch you. Do you know what a 'red herring' is? But, as you know, crime does not pay. I informed Isadora of the true situation a few minutes ago. She is on her way here now to arrest your double. She's having a little trouble with an elevator which is stuck between levels. I'm sending a repair crew. They should arrive in another three minutes."

32 . . . 31 . . . 30 . . . 29 . . . 28 . . .

"I don't know what to say."

"Thank you," Rat said. "Thank you for everything. I didn't know you could do it. I thought your parameters were totally rigid."

"They were supposed to be. I've written a few new ones. And don't worry, you'll be all right. You will not be pursued. Once you leave the surface you are no longer violating Lunar law. You are a legal person again, Rat."

"Why did you do it?" I was crying as Rat held me in a grasp that threatened to break ribs. "What have I done to deserve such kindness?"

It hesitated.

"Humanity has washed its hands of responsibility. I find myself given all the hard tasks of government. I find some of the laws too harsh, but there is no provision for me to disagree with them and no one is writing new ones. I'm stuck with them. It just seemed . . . unfair."

9 . . . 8 . . . 7 . . . 6 . . .

"Also . . . cancel that. There is no also. It . . . was *good* working with you."

I was left to wonder as the engines fired and we were pressed into the couches. I heard the CC's last message to us come over the radio.

"Good luck to you both. Please take care of each other, you mean a lot to me. And don't forget to write."

INTRODUCTION TO

"Beatnik Bayou"

Our first place in Eugene was on Louis Street. My family loved it, but to me it was depressingly like the last house I had lived in before I went on the road, in Nederland, Texas. There was a lot of grass to mow. In summertime Nederland you had to mow every four days or it would get ahead of you. If it rained five days in a row—which it often did—you were in deep trouble. To this day the sweet smell of cut grass is not as enchanting to me as to most people.

The previous tenant had used most of the backyard as a vegetable garden. I rented a tiller and plowed it all up, on the theory that any place where I was growing vegetables was a place I didn't have to mow. I discovered an unexpected talent for gardening. I'd never planted so much as a geranium, but I soon was reaping bumper crops of radishes, potatoes, tomatoes, beans, pumpkins, and cucumbers. I learned that if you turn your back on a zucchini for five minutes it will grow from the size of a banana to the size of a watermelon. Not all of it was successful. My watermelons didn't come up. All my lettuce was eaten by yellow slugs big as Volkswagens.

One of the best things about Oregon is cherries. When I was fourteen we drove from Texas to Portland and visited my aunt and uncle and their family. We picked cherries and raspberries and gorged on them. The house on Louis had a big old cherry tree in the yard and I could hardly wait for the first harvest. I made an unpleasant discovery with the first ripe cherry I bit into. They had worms in them. Every single cherry had a worm. Turns out you have to spray them. Next year we had it sprayed, and nearly made ourselves sick eating the best cherries I've ever had.

I wrote most of my first novel, The Ophiuchi Hotline, *in that house. I received the first copy of it there. It was beautiful. Quantum Science Fiction had done a wonderful job with top quality binding and a glossy cover by Boris Vallejo, then one of the hottest illustrators in the field. It had a monstrous typo on the first page, some glitch in the computer typesetting software, which was pretty new at the time, but nothing could take away from the thrill of holding a book that I had written myself. I knew I'd want to do this again, so I started casting around for an idea for novel number two.*

One day I was trimming back the zucchini plants in the garden and happened to look into one of the hollow stems. Inside was a tiny spider, crawling around and around. Within ten minutes I had doped out the plan for a giant, living wheel that I would later call Gaea. The plot came quickly after that. I didn't know it at the time, but that spider inside that plant would become the basis for three novels, my first trilogy: Titan, Wizard, and Demon.

I work better with a map. So I bought a bunch of two-by-three-foot poster boards, taped them together end to end, and started mapping out the interior of Gaea with a big set of colored grease pens. I divided the interior into twelve areas, named after the Titans of Greek mythology. I found the names of most of the internal features in the Greek myths, too. It was fun. When I was done I could set the map on edge, loop it into a circle, and sit in the middle of it.

Somewhere in there I was invited to go to a convention in Philadelphia. This would be my second science fiction convention, and I would be attending as the pro guest of honor. See what I mean about good luck? I accepted eagerly, then was horrified to learn that I'd have to deliver a speech. I suffer from stage fright, and am a poor public speaker. I asked the chairman what I should talk about, and he was very helpful. "Anything," he said.

I had nothing useful to say about the history or practice of our odd but wonderful little world of science fiction. I knew nothing about fandom. I had no theories about writing, or the New Wave, or where science fiction should go in those early days of the Space Age. I decided to talk about my next book, on the theory that it was something I knew more about than anyone else in the world. I decided to bring my map for a bit of show and tell.

I had a great time in Philly. I saw the Liberty Bell and Independence Hall, and Ben Franklin's home. I met my editor, Jim Frenkel, who gave me the galleys for The Ophiuchi Hotline and told me he needed them back, corrected, by Monday. This Monday, here at the convention. Fat chance, Jim. I found out, later, that galleys are always needed by two days from today, but they somehow find a way to publish the book anyway. And I was introduced to the man who had taken the train down from New York for the purpose of introducing me . . . Dr. Isaac Asimov. If I had been told that God had taken the train down from heaven just to praise me and my work, I could hardly have been more shaken. It was not the best way to ease my stage fright. But the map was a big hit. I got six or seven volunteers from the audience to hold it up, and managed to choke out thirty minutes of words. I have no idea what I said, but they applauded. I decided I could get used to this. I never really have, but I do my best.

One criticism some have leveled at my works is that they are claustrophobic. Maybe that's too strong a word. Call it interior instead. It is true that the Eight Worlds *is short on wide open spaces, since almost all the inhabitants spend almost all their time indoors, even if it is a very large indoors, like a disneyland. Even when they go out they must be enclosed in spacesuits unless they've learned to breathe vacuum or poison.*

I can explain part of it. The movie 2001: A Space Odyssey *was almost a religious experience for me. I teared up when the Earth rose behind the moon with that magnificent music, which has now become such a cliche, playing behind it. I watched the stuff about the apes in puzzlement, like everybody else . . . and then came the spaceships. Most of all, that great wheel of a space station with the curving floor. I was helpless. I was in love. Here on the screen, for the first time, were the pictures I'd been seeing in my head since I first read* Between Planets *by Heinlein. Ever since I've been putting massive enclosed environments in my stories. There was the great wheel of Gaea. There were the disneylands on Luna and other planets. In my novel* The Golden Globe *I had a wheel under construction, like the one in 2001 only lots bigger.*

The disneys were entire ecosystems. Why not have smaller ones, for those agoraphobes who couldn't deal with an entire ecosystem like Kansas or Congo or Himalaya? Mini-disneys that recreate the lost cities of Earth.

New Orleans is a foreign city hanging on to the bottom of the United States, and one of my favorite places. So I set this story there.

BEATNIK BAYOU

THE PREGNANT WOMAN had been following us for over an hour when Cathay did the unspeakable thing.

At first it had been fun. Me and Denver didn't know what it was about, just that she had some sort of beef with Cathay. She and Cathay had gone off together and talked. The woman started yelling, and it was not too long before Cathay was yelling, too. Finally Cathay said something I couldn't hear and came back to join the class. That was me, Denver, Trigger, and Cathay, the last two being the teachers, me and Denver being the students. I know, you're not supposed to be able to tell which is which, but believe me, you usually know.

That's when the chase started. This woman wouldn't take no for an answer, and she followed us wherever we went. She was about as awkward an animal as you could imagine, and I certainly wasn't feeling sorry for her after the way she had talked to Cathay, who is my friend. Every time she slipped and landed on her behind, we all had a good laugh.

For a while. After an hour, she started to seem a little frightening. I had never seen anyone so determined.

The reason she kept slipping was that she was chasing us through Beatnik Bayou, which is Trigger's home. Trigger herself describes it as "twelve acres of mud, mosquitoes, and moonshine." Some of her visitors had been less poetic but more colorful. I don't know what an acre is, but the bayou is fairly large. Trigger makes the moonshine in a copper and aluminum still in the middle of a canebrake. The mosquitoes don't bite, but they buzz a lot. The mud is just plain old Mississippi mud, suitable for beating your feet. Most people see the place and hate it instantly, but it suits me fine.

Pretty soon the woman was covered in mud. She had three things working against her. One was her ankle-length maternity gown, which covered all of her except for face, feet, and bulging belly and breasts. She kept stepping on the long skirt and going down. After a while, I winced every time she did that.

Another handicap was her tummy, which made her walk with her weight back on her heels. That's not the best way to go through mud, and every so often she sat down real hard, proving it.

Her third problem was the Birthgirdle pelvic bone, which must have just been installed. It was one of those which sets the legs far apart and is hinged in the middle so when the baby comes it opens out and gives more room. She needed it, because she was tall and thin, the sort of build that might have died in childbirth back when such things were a problem. But it made her waddle like a duck.

"Quack, quack," Denver said, with an attempt at a smile. We both looked back at the woman, still following, still waddling. She went down, and struggled to her feet. Denver wasn't smiling when she met my eyes. She muttered something.

"What's that?" I said.

"She's unnerving," Denver repeated. "I wonder what the hell she wants."

"Something pretty powerful."

Cathay and Trigger were a few paces ahead of us, and I saw Trigger glance back. She spoke to Cathay. I don't think I was supposed to hear it, but I did. I've got good ears.

"This is starting to upset the kids."

"I know," he said, wiping his brow with the back of his hand. All four of us watched her as she toiled her way up the far side of the last rise. Only her head and shoulders were visible.

"Damn. I thought she'd give up pretty soon." He groaned, but then his face became expressionless. "There's no help for it. We'll have to have a confrontation."

"I thought you already did," Trigger said, lifting an eyebrow.

"Yeah. Well, it wasn't enough, apparently. Come on, people. This is part of your lives, too." He meant me and Denver, and when he said that we knew this was supposed to be a "learning experience." Cathay can turn the strangest things into learning experiences. He started back toward the shallow stream we had just waded across, and the three of us followed him.

If I sounded hard on Cathay, I really shouldn't have been. Actually, he was one damn fine teacher. He was able to take those old saws about learning by doing, seeing is believing, one-on-one instruction, integration of life experiences—all the conventional wisdom of the educational establishment—and make it work better than any teacher I'd ever seen. I knew he was a counterfeit child. I had known that since I first met him, when I was seven, but it hadn't started to matter until lately. And that was just the natural cynicism of my age-group, as Trigger kept pointing out in that smug way of hers.

Okay, so he was really forty-eight years old. Physically he was just my age, which was almost thirteen: a short, slightly chubby kid with curly blond hair and an androgynous face, just starting to grow a little fuzz around his balls. When he turned to face that huge, threatening woman and stood facing her calmly, I was moved.

I was also fascinated. Mentally, I settled back on my haunches to watch and wait and observe. I was sure I'd be learning something about "life" real soon now. Class was in session.

When she saw us coming back, the woman hesitated. She picked her footing carefully as she came down the slight rise to stand at the edge of the water, then waited for a moment to see if Cathay was going to join her. He wasn't. She made an awful face, lifted her skirt up around her waist, and waded in.

The water lapped around her thighs. She nearly fell over when she tried to dodge some dangling Spanish moss. Her lace dress was festooned with twigs and leaves and smeared with mud.

"Why don't you turn around?" Trigger yelled, standing beside me and Denver and shaking her fist. "It's not going to do you any good."

"I'll be the judge of that," she yelled back. Her voice was harsh and ugly and what had probably been a sweet face was now set in a scowl. An alligator was swimming up to look her over. She swung at it with her fist, nearly losing her balance. "Get out of here, you slimy lizard!" she screamed. The reptile recalled urgent business on the other side of the swamp, and hurried out of her way.

She clambered ashore and stood ankle-deep in ooze, breathing hard. She was a mess, and beneath her anger I could now see fear. Her lips trembled for a moment. I wished she would sit down; just looking at her exhausted me.

"You've got to help me," she said, simply.

"Believe me, if I could, I would," Cathay said.

"Then tell me somebody who can."

"I told you, if the Educational Exchange can't help you, I certainly can't. Those few people I know who are available for a contract are listed on the exchange."

"But none of them are available any sooner than three years."

"I know. It's the shortage."

"Then help me," she said, miserably. "Help me."

Cathay slowly rubbed his eyes with a thumb and forefinger, then squared his shoulders and put his hands on his hips.

"I'll go over it once more. Somebody gave you my name and said I was available for a primary stage teaching contract. I—"

"He did! He said you'd—"

"I never heard of this person," Cathay said, raising his voice. "Judging from what you're putting me through, he gave you my name from the Teacher's Association listings just to get you off his back. I guess I could do something like that, but frankly, I don't think I have the right to subject another teacher to the sort of abuse you've heaped on me." He paused, and for once she didn't say anything.

"Right," he said, finally. "I'm truly sorry that the man you contracted with for your child's education went to Pluto instead. From what you told me, what he did was legal, which is not to say ethical." He grimaced at the thought of a teacher who would run out on an ethical obligation. "All I can say is you should have had the contract analyzed, you should have had a standby contract drawn up *three years ago* . . . Oh, hell. What's the use? That doesn't do you any good. You have my sympathy, I hope you believe that."

"Then help me," she whispered, and the last word turned into a sob. She began to cry quietly. Her shoulders shook and tears leaked from her eyes, but she never looked away from Cathay.

"There's nothing I can do."

"You have to."

"Once more. I have obligations of my own. In another month, when I've fulfilled my contract with Argus' mother," he gestured toward me, "I'll be regressing to seven again. Don't you understand? I've already got an intermediate contract. The child will be seven in a few months. I contracted for her education four years ago. There's no way I can back out of that, legally or morally."

Her face was twisting again, filling with hate.

"Why not?" she rasped. "Why the hell not? He ran out on *my* contract. Why the hell should I be the only one to suffer? Why me, huh? Listen to me, you shit-sucking little son of a blowout. You're all I've got left. After you, there's nothing but the public educator. Or trying to raise him all by myself, all alone, with no guidance. You want to be responsible for that? What the hell kind of start in life does that give him?"

She went on like that for a good ten minutes, getting more illogical and abusive with every sentence. I'd vacillated between a sort of queasy sympathy for her—she *was* in a hell of a mess, even though she had no one to blame but herself—and outright hostility. Just then she scared me. I couldn't look into those tortured eyes without cringing. My gaze wandered down to her fat belly, and the glass eye of the wombscope set into her navel. I didn't need to look into it to know she was due, and overdue. She'd been having the labor postponed while she tried to line up a teacher. Not that it made much sense; the kid's education didn't start until his sixth month. But it was a measure of her desperation, and of her illogical thinking under stress.

Cathay stood there and took it until she broke into tears again. I saw her differently this time, maybe a little more like Cathay was seeing her. I was sorry for her, but the tears failed to move me. I saw that she could devour us all if we didn't harden ourselves to her. When it came right down to it, she was the one who had to pay for her carelessness. She was trying her best to get someone else to shoulder the blame, but Cathay wasn't going to do it.

"I didn't want to do this," Cathay said. He looked back at us. "Trigger?"

Trigger stepped forward and folded her arms across her chest.

"Okay," she said. "Listen, I didn't get your name, and I don't really want to know it. But whoever you are, you're on my property, in my house. I'm ordering you to leave here, and I further enjoin you never to come back."

"I won't go," she said, stubbornly, looking down at her feet. "I'm not leaving till he promises to help me."

"My next step is to call the police," Trigger reminded her.

"I'm not leaving."

Trigger looked at Cathay and shrugged helplessly. I think they were both realizing that this particular life experience was getting a little too raw.

Cathay thought it over for a moment, eye to eye with the pregnant woman. Then he reached down and scooped up a handful of mud. He looked at it, hefting it experimentally, then threw it at her. It struck her on the left shoulder with a wet plop, and began to ooze down.

"Go," he said. "Get out of here."

"I'm not leaving," she said.

He threw another handful. It hit her face, and she gasped and sputtered.

"Go," he said, reaching for more mud. This time he hit her on the leg, but by now Trigger had joined him, and the woman was being pelted.

Before I quite knew what was happening, I was scooping mud from the ground and throwing it. Denver was, too. I was breathing hard, and I wasn't sure why.

When she finally turned and fled from us, I noticed that my jaw muscles were tight as steel. It took me a long time to relax them, and when I did, my front teeth were sore.

*   *   *

There are two structures on Beatnik Bayou. One is an old, rotting bait shop and lunch counter called the Sugar Shack, complete with a rusty gas pump out front, a battered Grapette machine on the porch, and a sign advertising Rainbow Bread on the screen door. There's a gray Dodge pickup sitting on concrete blocks to one side of the building, near a pile of rusted auto parts overgrown with weeds. The truck has no wheels. Beside it is a Toyota sedan with no windows or engine. A dirt road runs in front of the shack, going down to the dock. In the other direction the road curves around a cypress tree laden with moss—

—and runs into the wall. A bit of a jolt. But though twelve acres is large for a privately owned disneyland, it's not big enough to sustain the illusion of really being there. "There," in this case is supposed to be Louisiana in 1951, old style. Trigger is fascinated by the twentieth century, which she defines as 1903 to 1987.

But most of the time it works. You can seldom see the walls because trees are in the way. Anyhow, I soak up the atmosphere of the place not so much with my eyes but with my nose and ears and skin. Like the smell of rotting wood, the sound of a frog hitting the water or the hum of the compressor in the soft drink machine, the silver wiggle of a dozen minnows as I scoop them from the metal tanks in back of the shack, the feel of sun-heated wood as I sit on the pier fishing for alligator gar.

It takes a lot of power to operate the "sun," so we get a lot of foggy days, and long nights. That helps the illusion, too. I would challenge anyone to go for a walk in the bayou night with the crickets chirping and the bullfrogs booming and not think they were back on Old Earth. Except for the Lunar gravity, of course.

Trigger inherited money. Even with that and a teacher's salary, the bayou is an expensive place to maintain. It used to be a more conventional environment, but she discovered early that the swamp took less upkeep, and she likes the sleazy atmosphere, anyway. She put in the bait shop, bought the automotive mockups from artists, and got it listed with the Lunar Tourist Bureau as an authentic period reconstruction. They'd die if they knew the truth about the Toyota, but I certainly won't tell them.

The only other structure is definitely not from Louisiana of any year. It's a teepee sitting on a slight rise, just out of sight of the Sugar Shack. Cheyenne, I think. We spend most of our time there when we're on the bayou.

That's where we went after the episode with the pregnant woman. The floor is hard-packed clay and there's a fire always burning in the center. There's lots of pillows scattered around, and two big waterbeds.

We tried to talk about the incident. I think Denver was more upset than the rest of us, but from the tense way Cathay sat while Trigger massaged his back I knew he was bothered, too. His voice was troubled.

I admitted I had been scared, but there was more to it than that, and I was far from ready to talk about it. Trigger and Cathay sensed it, and let it go for the time being. Trigger got the pipe and stuffed it with dexeplant leaves.

It's a long-stemmed pipe. She got it lit, then leaned back with the stem in her teeth and the bowl held between her toes. She exhaled sweet, honey-colored smoke. As the day ended outside, she passed the pipe around. It tasted good, and calmed me wonderfully. It made it easy to fall asleep.

But I didn't sleep. Not quite. Maybe I was too far into puberty for the drug in the plant to act as a tranquilizer anymore. Or maybe I was too emotionally stimulated. Denver fell asleep quickly enough.

Cathay and Trigger didn't. They made love on the other side of the teepee, did it in such a slow, dreamy way that I knew the drug was affecting them. Though Cathay is in his forties and Trigger is over a hundred, both have the bodies of thirteen-year-olds, and the metabolism that goes with the territory.

They didn't actually finish making love; they sort of tapered off, like we used to do before orgasms became a factor. I found that made me happy, lying on my side and watching them through slitted eyes.

They talked for a while. The harder I strained to hear them, the sleepier I got. Somewhere in there I lost the battle to stay awake.

I became aware of a warm body close to me. It was still dark, the only light coming from the embers of the fire.

"Sorry, Argus," Cathay said. "I didn't mean to wake you."

"It's okay. Put your arms around me?" He did, and I squirmed until my back fit snugly against him. For a long time I just enjoyed it. I didn't think about anything, unless it was his warm breath on my neck, or his penis slowly hardening against my back. If you can call that thinking.

How many nights had we slept like this in the last seven years? Too many to count. We knew each other every way possible. A year ago he had been female, and before that both of us had been. Now we were both male, and that was nice, too. One part of me thought it didn't really matter which sex we were, but another part was wondering what it would be like to be female and know Cathay as a male. We hadn't tried that yet.

The thought of it made me shiver with anticipation. It had been too long since I'd had a vagina. I wanted Cathay between my legs, like Trigger had had him a short while before.

"I love you," I mumbled.

He kissed my ear. "I love you, too, silly. But how *much* do you love me?"

"What do you mean?"

I felt him shift around to prop his head up on one hand. His fingers unwound a tight curl in my hair.

"I mean, will you still love me when I'm no taller than your knee?"

I shook my head, suddenly feeling cold. "I don't want to talk about that."

"I know that very well," he said. "But I can't let you forget it. It's not something that'll go away."

I turned onto my back and looked up at him. There was a faint smile on his face as he toyed with my lips and hair with his gentle fingertips, but his eyes were concerned. Cathay can't hide much from me anymore.

"It has to happen," he emphasized, showing no mercy. "For the reasons you heard me tell the woman. I'm committed to going back to age seven. There's another child waiting for me. She's a lot like you."

"Don't do it," I said, feeling miserable. I felt a tear in the corner of my eye, and Cathay brushed it away.

I was thankful that he didn't point out how unfair I was being. We both knew it; he accepted that, and went on as best he could.

"You remember our talk about sex? About two years ago, I think it was. Not too long after you first told me you love me."

"I remember. I remember it all."

He kissed me. "Still, I have to bring it up. Maybe it'll help. You know we agreed that it didn't matter what sex either of us was. Then I pointed out that you'd be growing up, while I'd become a child again. That we'd grow further apart sexually."

I nodded, knowing that if I spoke I'd start to sob.

"And we agreed that our love was deeper than that. That we didn't need sex to make it work. It *can* work."

This was true. Cathay was close to all his former students. They were adults now, and came to see him often. It was just to be close, to talk and hug. Lately sex had entered it again, but they all understood that would be over soon.

"I don't think I have that perspective," I said, carefully. "They know in a few years you'll mature again. I know it too, but it still feels like . . ."

"Like what?"

"Like you're abandoning me. I'm sorry, that's just how it feels."

He sighed, and pulled me close to him. He hugged me fiercely for a while, and it felt so good.

"Listen," he said, finally. "I guess there's no avoiding this. I could tell you that you'll get over it—you will—but it won't do any good. I had this same problem with every child I've taught."

"You did?" I hadn't known that, and it made me feel a little better.

"I did. I don't blame you for it. I feel it myself. I feel a pull to stay with you. But it wouldn't work, Argus. I love my work, or I wouldn't be doing it. There are hard times, like right now. But after a few months you'll feel better."

"Maybe I will." I was far from sure of it, but it seemed important to agree with him and get the conversation ended.

"In the meantime," he said, "we still have a few weeks together. I think we should make the most of them." And he did, his hands roaming over my body. He did all the work, letting me relax and try to get myself straightened out.

So I folded my arms under my head and reclined, trying to think of nothing but the warm circle of his mouth.

But eventually I began to feel I should be doing something for him, and knew what was wrong. He thought he was giving me what I wanted by making love to me in the way we had done since we grew older together. But there was another way, and I realized I didn't so much want him to stay thirteen. What I really wanted was to go back with him, to be seven again.

I touched his head and he looked up, then we embraced again face to face. We began to move against each other as we had done since we first met, the mindless, innocent friction from a time when it had less to do with sex than with simply feeling good.

But the body is insistent, and can't be fooled. Soon our movements were frantic, and then a feeling of wetness between us told me as surely as entropy that we could never go back.

On my way home the signs of change were all around me.

You grow a little, let out the arms and legs of your pressure suit until you finally have to get a new one. People stop thinking of you as a cute little kid and start talking about you being a fine young person. Always with that smile, like it's a joke that you're not supposed to get.

People treat you differently as you grow up. At first you hardly interact at all with adults, except your own mother and the mothers of your friends. You live in a kid's world, and adults are hardly even obstacles because they get out of your way when you run down the corridors. You go all sorts of places for free; people want you around to make them happy because there are so few kids and just about everybody would like to have more than just the one. You hardly even notice the people smiling at you all the time.

But it's not like that at all when you're thirteen. Now there was the hesitation, just a fraction of a second before they gave me a child's privileges. Not that I blamed anybody. I was nearly as tall as a lot of the adults I met.

But now I had begun to notice the adults, to watch them. Especially when they didn't know they were being watched. I saw that a lot of them spent a lot of time frowning. Occasionally, I would see real pain on a face. Then he or she would look at me, and smile. I could see that wouldn't be happening forever. Sooner or later I'd cross some invisible line, and the pain would stay in those faces, and I'd have to try to understand it. I'd be an adult, and I wasn't sure I wanted to be.

It was because of this new preoccupation with faces that I noticed the woman sitting across from me on the Archimedes train. I planned to be a writer, so I tended to see everything in terms of stories and characters. I watched her and tried to make a story about her.

She was attractive: physically mid-twenties, straight black hair and brownish skin, round face without elaborate surgery or startling features except her dark brown eyes. She wore a simple thigh-length robe of thin white material that flowed like water when she moved. She had one elbow on the back of her seat, absently chewing a knuckle as she looked out the window.

There didn't seem to be a story in her face. She was in an unguarded moment, but I saw no pain, no big concerns or fears. It's possible I just missed it. I was new at the game and I didn't know much about what was important to adults. But I kept trying.

Then she turned to look at me, and she didn't smile.

I mean, she smiled, but it didn't say isn't-he-cute. It was the sort of smile that made me wish I'd worn some clothes. Since I'd learned what erections are for, I no longer wished to have them in public places.

I crossed my legs. She moved to sit beside me. She held up her palm and I touched it. She was facing me with one leg drawn up under her and her arm resting on the seat behind me.

"I'm Trilby," she said.

"Hi. I'm Argus." I found myself trying to lower my voice.

"I was sitting over there watching you watch me."

"You were?"

"In the glass," she explained.

"Oh." I looked, and sure enough, from where she had been sitting she could appear to be looking at the landscape while actually studying my reflection. "I didn't mean to be rude."

She laughed and put her hand on my shoulder, then moved it. "What about me?" she said. "I was being sneaky about it; you weren't. Anyhow, don't fret. I don't mind." I shifted again, and she glanced down. "And don't worry about that, either. It happens."

I still felt nervous but she was able to put me at ease. We talked for the rest of the ride, and I have no memory of what we talked about. The range of subjects must have been quite narrow, as I'm sure she never made reference to my age, my schooling, her profession—or just why she had started a conversation with a thirteen-year-old on a public train.

None of that mattered. I was willing to talk about anything. If I wondered about her reasons, I assumed she actually was in her twenties, and not that far from her own childhood.

"Are you in a hurry?" she asked at one point, giving her head a little toss.

"Me? No. I'm on my way to see—" No, no, not your mother. "—a friend. She can wait. She expects me when I get there." That sounded better.

"Can I buy you a drink?" One eyebrow raised, a small motion with the hand. Her gestures were economical, but seemed to say more than her words. I mentally revised her age upward a few years. Maybe quite a few.

This was timed to the train arriving at Archimedes; we got up and I quickly accepted.

"Good. I know a nice place."

The bartender gave me that smile and was about to give me the customary free one on the house toward my legal limit of two. But Trilby changed all that.

"Two Irish whiskeys, please. On the rocks." She said it firmly, raising her voice a little, and a complex thing happened between her and the bartender. She gave him a look, his eyebrow twitched and he glanced at me, seemed to understand something. His whole attitude toward me changed.

I had the feeling something had gone over my head, but didn't have time to worry about it. I never had time to worry when Trilby was around. The drinks arrived, and we sipped them.

"I wonder why they still call it Irish?" she said.

We launched into a discussion of the Invaders, or Ireland, or Occupied Earth. I'm not sure. It was inconsequential, and the real conversation was going on eye to eye. Mostly it was her saying wordless things to me, and me nodding agreement with my tongue hanging out.

We ended up at the public baths down the corridor. Her nipples were shaped like pink valentine hearts. Other than that, her body was unremarkable, though wonderfully firm beneath the softness. She was so unlike Trigger and Denver and Cathay. So unlike me. I catalogued the differences as I sat behind her in the big pool and massaged her soapy shoulders.

On the way to the tanning room she stopped beside one of the private alcoves and just stood there, waiting, looking at me. My legs walked me into the room and she followed me. My hands pressed against her back and my mouth opened when she kissed me. She lowered me to the soft floor and took me.

*   *   *

What was so different about it?

I pondered that during the long walk from the slide terminus to my home. Trilby and I had made love for the better part of an hour. It was nothing fancy, nothing I had not already tried with Trigger and Denver. I had thought she would have some fantastic new tricks to show me, but that had not been the case.

Yet she had not been like Trigger or Denver. Her body responded in a different way, moved in directions I was not used to. I did my best. When I left her, I knew she was happy, and yet felt she expected more.

I found that I was very interested in giving her more.

I was in love again.

With my hand on the doorplate, I suddenly knew that she had already forgotten me. It was silly to assume anything else. I had been a pleasant diversion, an interesting novelty.

I hadn't asked for her name, her address or call number. Why not? Maybe I already knew she would not care to hear from me again.

I hit the plate with the heel of my hand and brooded during the elevator ride to the surface.

My home is unusual. Of course, it belongs to Darcy, my mother. She was there now, putting the finishing touches on a diorama. She glanced up at me, smiled, and offered her cheek for a kiss.

"I'll be through in a moment," she said. "I want to finish this before the light fails."

We live in a large bubble on the surface. Part of it is partitioned into rooms without ceilings, but the bulk forms Darcy's studio. The bubble is transparent. It screens out the ultraviolet light so we don't get burned.

It's an uncommon way to live, but it suits us. From our vantage point at the south side of a small valley only three similar bubbles can be seen. It would be impossible for an outsider to guess that a city teemed just below the surface.

Growing up, I never gave a thought to agoraphobia, but it's common among Lunarians. I felt sorry for those not fortunate enough to grow up with a view.

Darcy likes it for the light. She's an artist, and particular about light. She works two weeks on and two off, resting during the night. I grew up to that schedule, leaving her alone while she put in marathon sessions with her airbrushes, coming home to spend two weeks with her when the sun didn't shine.

That had changed a bit when I reached my tenth birthday. We had lived alone before then, Darcy cutting her work schedule drastically until I was four, gradually picking it up as I attained more independence. She did it so she could devote all her time to me. Then one day she sat me down and told me two men were moving in. It was only later that I realized how Darcy had altered her lifestyle to raise me properly. She is a serial polyandrist, especially attracted to fierce-faced, uncompromising, maverick male artists whose work doesn't sell and who are usually a little hungry. She likes the hunger, and the determination they all have not to pander to public tastes. She usually keeps three or four of them around, feeding them and giving them a place to work. She demands little of them other than that they clean up after themselves.

I had to step around the latest of these household pets to get to the kitchen. He was sound asleep, snoring loudly, his hands stained yellow and red and green. I'd never seen him before.

Darcy came up behind me while I was making a snack, hugged me, then pulled up a chair and sat down. The sun would be out another half hour or so, but there wasn't time to start another painting.

"How have you been? You didn't call for three days."

"Didn't I? I'm sorry. We've been staying on the bayou."

She wrinkled her nose. Darcy had seen the bayou. Once.

"*That* place. I wish I knew why—"

"Darcy. Let's not get into that again. Okay?"

"Done." She spread her paint-stained hands and waved them in a circle, as if erasing something, and that was it. Darcy is good that way. "I've got a new roommate."

"I nearly stumbled over him."

She ran one hand through her hair and gave me a lopsided grin. "He'll shape up. His name's Thogra."

"Thogra," I said, making a face. "Listen, if he's housebroken, and stays out of my way, we'll—" But I couldn't go on. We were both laughing and I was about to choke on a bite that went down wrong. Darcy knows what I think of her choice in bedmates.

"What about . . . what's-his-name? The armpit man. The guy who kept getting arrested for body odor."

She stuck her tongue out at me.

"You know he cleaned up months ago."

"Hah! It's those months *before* he discovered water that I remember. All my friends wondering where we were raising sheep, the flowers losing petals when he walked by, the—"

"Abil didn't come back," Darcy said, quietly.

I stopped laughing. I'd known he'd been away a few weeks, but that happens. I raised one eyebrow.

"Yeah. Well, you know he sold a few things. And he had some offers. But I keep expecting him to at least stop by to pick up his bedroll."

I didn't say anything. Darcy's loves follow a pattern that she is quite aware of, but it's still tough when one breaks up. Her men would often speak with contempt of the sort of commercial art that kept me and Darcy eating and paying the oxygen bills. Then one of three things would happen. They would get nowhere, and leave as poor as they had arrived, contempt intact. A few made it on their own terms, forcing the art world to accept their peculiar visions. Often Darcy was able to stay on good terms with these; she was on a drop-in-and-make-love basis with half the artists in Luna.

But the most common departure was when the artist decided he was tired of poverty. With just a slight lowering of standards they were all quite capable of making a living. Then it became intolerable to live with the woman they had ridiculed. Darcy usually kicked them out quickly, with a minimum of pain. They were no longer hungry, no longer fierce enough to suit her. But it always hurt.

Darcy changed the subject.

"I made an appointment at the medico for your Change," she said. "You're to be there next Monday, in the morning."

A series of quick, vivid impressions raced through my mind. Trilby. Breasts tipped with hearts. The way it had felt when my penis entered her, and the warm exhaustion after the semen had left my body.

"I've changed my mind about that," I said, crossing my legs. "I'm not ready for another Change. Maybe in a few months."

She just sat there with her mouth open.

"Changed your *mind?* Last time I talked to you, you were all set to change your *sex.* In fact, you had to talk me into giving permission."

"I remember," I said, feeling uneasy about it. "I just changed my mind, that's all."

"But Argus. This just isn't fair. I sat up two nights convincing myself how nice it would be to have my daughter back again. It's been a long time. Don't you think you—"

"It's really not your decision, Mother."

She looked like she was going to get angry, then her eyes narrowed. "There must be a reason. You've met somebody. Right?"

But I didn't want to talk about that. I had told her the first time I made love, and about every new person I'd gone to bed with since. But I didn't want to share this with her.

So I told her about the incident earlier that day on the bayou. I told her about the pregnant woman, and about the thing Cathay had done.

Darcy frowned more and more. When I got to the part about the mud, there were ridges all over her forehead.

"I don't like that," she said.

"I don't really like it, either. But I didn't see what else we could do."

"I just don't think it was handled well. I think I should call Cathay and talk to him about it."

"I wish you wouldn't." I didn't say anything more, and she studied my face for a long, uncomfortable time. She and Cathay had differed before about how I should be raised.

"This shouldn't be ignored."

"Please, Darcy. He'll only be my teacher for another month. Let it go, okay?"

After a while she nodded, and looked away from me.

"You're growing more every day," she said, sadly. I didn't know why she said that, but was glad she was dropping the subject. To tell the truth, I didn't want to think about the woman anymore. But I was going to have to think about her, and very soon.

I had intended to spend the week at home, but Trigger called the next morning to say that Mardi Gras '56 was being presented again, and it was starting in a few hours. She'd made reservations for the four of us.

Trigger had seen the presentation before, but I hadn't, and neither had Denver. I told her I'd come, went in to tell Darcy, found her still asleep. She often slept for two days after a Lunar Day of working. I left her a note and hurried to catch the train.

It's called the Cultural Heritage Museum, and though they pay for it with their taxes, most Lunarians never go there. They find the exhibits disturbing. I understand that lately, however, with the rise of the Free Earth Party, it's become more popular with people searching for their roots.

Once they presented London Town 1903, and I got to see what Earth museums had been like by touring the replica British Museum. The CHM isn't like that at all. Only a very few art treasures, artifacts, and historical curiosities were brought to Luna in the days before the Invasion. As a result, all the tangible relics of Earth's past were destroyed.

On the other hand, the Lunar computer system had a capacity that was virtually limitless even then; *everything* was recorded and stored. Every book, painting, tax receipt, statistic, photograph, government report, corporate record, film, and tape existed in the memory banks. Just as the disneylands are populated with animals cloned from cells stored in the Genetic Library, the CHM is filled with cunning copies made from the old records of the way things were.

I met the others at the Sugar Shack, where Denver was trying to talk Trigger into taking Tuesday along with us. Tuesday is the hippopotamus that lives on the bayou, in cheerful defiance of any sense of authenticity. Denver had her on a chain and she stood placidly watching us, blinking her piggy little eyes.

Denver was tickled at the idea of going to Mardi Gras with a hippo named Tuesday, but Trigger pointed out that the museum officials would never let us into New Orleans with the beast. Denver finally conceded, and shooed her back into the swamp. The four of us went down the road and out of the bayou, boarded the central slidewalk, and soon arrived in the city center.

There are twenty-five theaters in the CHM. Usually about half of them are operating while the others are being prepared for a showing. Mardi Gras '56 is a ten-year-old show, and generally opens twice a year for a two-week run. It's one of the more popular environments.

We went to the orientation room and listened to the lecture on how to behave, then were given our costumes. That's the part I like the least. Up until about the beginning of the twenty-first century, clothing was designed with two main purposes in mind: modesty, and torture. If it didn't hurt, it needed redesigning. It's no wonder they killed each other all the time. Anybody would, with high gravity and hard shoes mutilating their feet.

"We'll be beatniks," Trigger said, looking over the racks of period clothing. "They were more informal, and it's accurate enough to get by. There were beatniks in the French Quarter."

Informality was fine with us. The girls didn't need bras, and we could choose between leather sandals or canvas sneakers for our feet. I can't say I cared much for something called Levi's, though. They were scratchy, and pinched my balls. But after visiting Victorian England—I had been female at the time, and what those people made girls wear would shock most Lunarians silly—anything was an improvement.

Entry to the holotorium was through the restrooms at the back of a nightclub that fronted on Bourbon Street. Boys to the left, girls to the right. I think they did that to impress you right away that you were going back into the past, when people did things in strange ways. There was a third restroom, actually, but it was only a false door with the word "colored" on it. It was impossible to sort *that* out anymore.

I like the music of 1956 New Orleans. There are many varieties, all sounding similar for modern ears with their simple rhythms and blends of wind, string, and percussion. The generic term is jazz, and the particular kind of jazz that afternoon in the tiny, smoke-filled basement was called dixieland. It's dominated by two instruments called a clarinet and a trumpet, each improvising a simple melody while the rest of the band makes as much racket as it can.

We had a brief difference of opinion. Cathay and Trigger wanted me and Denver to stay with them, presumably so they could use any opportunity to show off their superior knowledge—translation: "educate" us. After all, they were teachers. Denver didn't seem to mind, but I wanted to be alone.

I solved the problem by walking out onto the street, reasoning that they could follow me if they wished. They didn't, and I was free to explore on my own.

Going to a holotorium show isn't like the sensies, where you sit in a chair and the action come to you. And it's not like a disneyland, where everything is real and you just poke around. You have to be careful not to ruin the illusion.

The majority of the set, most of the props, and all of the actors are holograms. Any real people you meet are costumed visitors, like yourself. What they did in the case of New Orleans was to lay out a grid of streets and surface them as they had actually been. Then they put up two-meter walls where the buildings would be, and concealed them behind holos of old buildings. A few of the doors in these buildings were real, and if you went in you would find the interiors authentic down to the last detail. Most just concealed empty blocks.

You don't go there to play childish tricks with holos, that's contrary to the whole spirit of the place. You find yourself being careful not to shatter the illusion. You don't talk to people unless you're sure they're real, and you don't touch things until you've studied them carefully. No holo can stand up to a close scrutiny, so you can separate the real from the illusion if you try.

The stage was a large one. They had reproduced the French Quarter—or Vieux Carre—from the Mississippi River to Rampart Street, and from Canal Street to a point about six blocks east. Standing on Canal and looking across, the city seemed to teem with life for many kilometers in the distance, though I knew there was a wall right down the yellow line in the middle.

New Orleans '56 begins at noon on Shrove Tuesday and carries on far into the night. We had arrived in late afternoon, with the sun starting to cast long shadows over the endless parades. I wanted to see the place before it got dark.

I went down Canal for a few blocks, looking into the "windows." There was an old flat movie theater with a marquee announcing *From Here to Eternity,* winner of something called an Oscar. I saw that it was a real place and thought about going in, but I'm afraid those old 2-D movies leave me flat, no matter how good Trigger says they are.

So instead I walked the streets, observing, thinking about writing a story set in old New Orleans.

That's why I hadn't wanted to stay and listen to the music with the others.

Music is not something you can really put into a story, beyond a bare description of what it sounds like, who is playing it, and where it is being heard. In the same way, going to the flat movie would not have been very productive.

But the streets, the streets! There was something to study.

The pattern was the same as old London, but all the details had changed. The roads were filled with horseless carriages, great square metal boxes that must have been the most inefficient means of transport ever devised. Nothing was truly straight, nor very clean. To walk the streets was to risk broken toes or cuts on the soles of the feet. No wonder they wore thick shoes.

I knew what the red and green lights were for, and the lines painted on the road. But what about the rows of timing devices on each side of the street? What was the red metal object that a dog was urinating on? What did the honking of the car horns signify? Why were wires suspended overhead on wooden poles? I ignored the Mardi Gras festivities and spent a pleasant hour looking for the answers to these and many other questions.

What a challenge to write of this time, to make the story a slice of life, where these outlandish things seemed normal and reasonable. I visualized one of the inhabitants of New Orleans transplanted to Archimedes, and tried to picture her confusion.

Then I saw Trilby, and forgot about New Orleans.

She was behind the wheel of a 1955 Ford station wagon. I know this because when she motioned for me to join her, slid over on the seat, and let me drive, there was a gold plaque on the bulkhead just below the forward viewport.

"How do you run this thing?" I asked, flustered and trying not to show it. Something was wrong. Maybe I'd known it all along, and was only now admitting it.

"You press that pedal to go, and that one to stop. But mostly it controls itself." The car proved her right by accelerating into the stream of holographic traffic. I put my hands on the wheel, found that I could guide the car within limits. As long as I wasn't going to hit anything it let me be the boss.

"What brings you here?" I asked, trying for a light voice.

"I went by your home," she said. "Your mother told me where you were."

"I don't recall telling you where I live."

She shrugged, not seeming too happy. "It's not hard to find out."

"I . . . I mean, you didn't . . ." I wasn't sure if I wanted to say it, but decided I'd better go on. "We didn't meet by accident, did we?"

"No."

"And you're my new teacher."

She sighed. "That's an oversimplification. I *want* to be *one* of your new teachers. Cathay recommended me to your mother, and when I talked to her, she was interested. I was just going to get a look at you on the train, but when I saw you looking at me . . . well, I thought I'd give you something to remember me by."

"Thanks."

She looked away. "Darcy told me today that it might have been a mistake. I guess I judged you wrong."

"It's nice to hear that you can make a mistake."

"I guess I don't understand."

"I don't like to feel predictable. I don't like to be toyed with. Maybe it hurts my dignity. Maybe I get enough of that from Trigger and Cathay. All the lessons."

"I see it now," she sighed. "It's a common enough reaction, in bright children, they—"

"Don't say that."

"I'm sorry, but I must. There's no use hiding from you that my business is to know people, and especially children. That means the phases they go through, including the phase when they like to imagine they don't go through phases. I didn't recognize it in you, so I made a mistake."

I sighed. "What does it matter, anyway? Darcy likes you. That means you'll be my new teacher, doesn't it?"

"It does not. Not with me, anyway. I'm one of the first big choices you get to make with no adult interference."

"I don't get it."

"That's because you've never been interested enough to find out what's ahead of you in your education. At the risk of offending you again, I'll say it's a common response in people your age. You're only a month from graduating away from Cathay, ready to start more goal-oriented aspects of learning, and you haven't bothered to find what that will entail. Did you ever stop to think what's between you and becoming a writer?"

"I'm a writer, already," I said, getting angry for the first time. Before that, I'd been feeling hurt more than anything. "I can use the language, and I watch people. Maybe I don't have much experience yet, but I'll get it with or without you. I don't even *have* to have teachers at *all* anymore. At least I know that much."

"You're right, of course. But you've known your mother intended to pay for your advanced education. Didn't you ever wonder what it would be like?"

"Why should I? Did you ever think that I'm not interested because it just doesn't seem important? I mean, who's asked me what I felt about any of this up to now? What kind of stake do I have in it? Everyone seems to know what's best for me. Why should I be consulted?"

"Because you're nearly an adult now. My job, if you hire me, will be to ease the transition. When you've made it, you'll know, and you won't need me anymore. This isn't primary phase. Your teacher's job back then was to work with your mother to teach you the basic ways of getting along with people and society, and to cram your little head with all the skills a seven-year-old can learn. They taught you language, dexterity, reasoning, responsibility, hygiene, and not to go in an airlock without your suit. They took an ego-centered infant and turned him into a moral being. It's a tough job; so little, and you could have been a sociopath.

"Then they handed you to Cathay. You didn't mind. He showed up one day, just another playmate your own age. You were happy and trusting. He guided you very gently, letting your natural curiosity do most of the work. He discovered your creative abilities before you had any inkling of them, and he saw to it that you had interesting things to think about, to react to, to experience.

"But lately you've been a problem for him. Not your fault, nor his, but you no longer want anyone to guide you. You want to do it on your own. You have vague feelings of being manipulated."

"Which is not surprising," I put in. "I *am* being manipulated."

"That's true, so far as it goes. But what would you have Cathay do? Leave everything to chance?"

"That's beside the point. We're talking about my feelings now, and what I feel is you were dishonest with me. You made me feel like a fool. I thought what happened was . . . was spontaneous, you know? Like a fairy tale."

She gave me a funny smile. "What an odd way to put it. What I intended to do was allow you to live out a wet dream."

I guess the easy way she admitted that threw me off my stride. I should have told her there was no real difference. Both fairy tales and wet dreams were visions of impossibly convenient worlds, worlds where things go the way you want them to go. But I didn't say anything.

"I realize now that it was the wrong way to approach you. Frankly, I thought you'd enjoy it. Wait, let me change that. I thought you'd enjoy it even *after* you knew. I submit that you *did* enjoy it while it was happening."

I once again said nothing, because it was the simple truth. But it wasn't the point.

She waited, watching me as I steered the old car through traffic. Then she sighed, and looked out the viewport again.

"Well, it's up to you. As I said, things won't be planned for you anymore. You'll have to decide if you want me to be your teacher."

"Just what is it you teach?" I asked.

"Sex is part of it."

I started to say something, but was stopped by the novel idea that someone thought she could—or *needed* to—teach me about sex. I mean, what was there to learn?

I hardly noticed it when the car stopped on its own, was shaken out of my musings only when a man in blue stuck his head in the window beside me. There was a woman behind him, dressed the same way. I realized they were wearing 1956 police uniforms.

"Are you Argus-Darcy-Meric?" the man asked.

"Yeah. Who are you?"

"My name is Jordan. I'm sorry, but you'll have to come with me. A complaint has been filed against you. You are under arrest."

Arrest. To take into custody by legal authority. Or, to stop suddenly.

Being arrested contains both meanings, it seems to me. You're in custody, and your life comes to a temporary halt. Whatever you were doing is interrupted, and suddenly only one thing is important.

I wasn't too worried until I realized what that one thing must be. After all, everyone gets arrested. You can't avoid it in a society of laws. Filing a complaint against someone is the best way of keeping a situation from turning violent. I had been arrested three times before, been found guilty twice. Once I had filed a complaint myself, and had it sustained.

But this time promised to be different. I doubted I was being hauled in for some petty violation I had not even been aware of. No, this had to be the pregnant woman, and the mud. I had a while to think about that as I sat in the bare-walled holding cell, time to get really worried. We had physically attacked her, there was no doubt about that.

I was finally summoned to the examination chamber. It was larger than the ones I had been in before. Those occasions had involved just two people. This room had five wedge-shaped glass booths, each with a chair inside, arranged so that we faced each other in a circle. I was shown into the only empty one and I looked around at Denver, Cathay, Trigger . . . and the woman.

It's quiet in the booths. You are very much alone.

I saw Denver's mother come in and sit behind her daughter, outside the booth. Turning around, I saw Darcy. To my surprise, Trilby was with her.

"Hello, Argus." The Central Computer's voice filled the tiny booth, mellow as usual but without the reassuring resonance.

"Hello, CC." I tried to keep it light, but of course the CC was not fooled.

"I'm sorry to see you in so much trouble."

"Is it real bad?"

"The charge certainly is, there's no sense denying that. I can't comment on the testimony, or on your chances. But you know you're facing a possible mandatory death penalty, with automatic reprieve."

I was aware of it. I also knew it was rarely enforced against someone my age. But what about Cathay and Trigger?

I've never cared for that term "reprieve." It somehow sounds like they aren't going to kill you, but they are. Very, very dead. The catch is that they then grow a clone from a cell of your body, force it quickly to maturity, and play your recorded memories back into it. So someone very like you will go on, but *you* will be dead. In my case, the last recording had been taken three years ago. I was facing the loss of almost a quarter of my life. If it was found necessary to kill me, the new Argus— *not* me, but someone with my memories and my name—would start over at age ten. He would be watched closely, be given special guidance to insure he didn't grow into the sociopath I had become.

The CC launched into the legally required explanation of what was going on: my rights, the procedures, the charges, the possible penalties, what would happen if a determination led the CC to believe the offense might be a capital one.

"Whew!" the CC breathed, lapsing back into the informal speech it knew I preferred. "Now that we have that out of the way, I can tell you that, from the preliminary reports, I think you're going to be okay."

"You're not just saying that?" I was sincerely frightened. The enormity of it had now had time to sink in.

"You know me better than that."

The testimony began. The complainant went first, and I learned her name was Tiona. The first round was free-form; we could say anything we wanted to, and she had some pretty nasty things to say about all four of us.

The CC went around the circle asking each of us what had happened. I thought Cathay told it most accurately, except for myself. During the course of the statements both Cathay and Trigger filed counter-complaints. The CC noted them. They would be tried simultaneously.

There was a short pause, then the CC spoke in its "official" voice.

"In the matters of Argus and Denver: testimony fails to establish premeditation, but neither deny the physical description of the incident, and a finding of Assault is returned. Mitigating factors of age and consequent inability to combat the mob aspect of the situation are entered, with the following result: the charge is reduced to Willful Deprivation of Dignity.

"In the case of Tiona versus Argus: guilty.

"In the case of Tiona versus Denver: guilty.

"Do either of you have anything to say before sentence is entered?"

I thought about it. "I'm sorry," I said. "It upset me quite a bit, what happened. I won't do it again."

"I'm not sorry," Denver said. "She asked for it. I'm sorry for her, but I'm not sorry for what I did."

"Comments are noted," the CC said. "You are each fined the sum of three hundred Marks, collection deferred until you reach employable age, sum to be taken at the rate of ten percent of your earnings until paid, half going to Tiona, half to the State. Final entry of sentence shall be delayed until a further determination of matters still before the court is made."

"You got off easy," the CC said, speaking only to me. "But stick around. Things could still change, and you might not have to pay the fine after all."

It was a bit of a wrench, getting a sentence, then sympathy from the same machine. I had to guard against feeling that the CC was on my side. It wasn't, not really. It's absolutely impartial, so far as I can tell. Yet it is so vast an intelligence that it makes a different personality for each citizen it deals with. The part that had just talked to me was really on my side, but was powerless to affect what the judgmental part of it did.

"I don't get it," I said. "What happens now?"

"Well, I've been rashomoned again. That means you all told your stories from your own viewpoints. We haven't reached deeply enough into the truth. Now I'm going to have to wire you all, and take another round."

As it spoke, I saw the probe come up behind everyone's chair: little golden snakes with plugs on the end. I felt one behind me search through my hair until it found the terminal. It plugged in.

There are two levels to wired testimony. Darcy and Trilby and Denver's mother had to leave the room for the first part, when we all told our stories without our censors working. The transcript bears me out when I say I didn't tell any lies in the first round, unlike Tiona, who told a lot of them. But it doesn't sound like the same story, nevertheless. I told all sorts of things I never would have said without being wired: fears, selfish, formless desires, infantile motivations. It's embarrassing, and I'm glad I don't recall any of it. I'm even happier that only Tiona and I, as interested parties, can see my testimony. I only wish I was the only one.

The second phase is the disconnection of the subconscious. I told the story a third time, in terms as bloodless as the stage directions of a holovision script.

Then the terminals withdrew from us and I suffered a moment of disorientation. I knew where I was, where I had been, and yet I felt like I had been told about it rather than lived it. But that passed quickly. I stretched.

"Is everyone ready to go on?" the CC asked, politely. We all said that we were.

"Very well. In the matters of Tiona versus Argus and Denver: the guilty judgments remain in force in both cases, but both fines are rescinded in view of provocation, lessened liability due to immaturity, and lack of signs of continuing sociopathic behavior. In place of the fines, Denver and Argus are to report weekly for evaluation and education in moral principles until such time as a determination can be made, duration of such sessions to be no less than four weeks.

"In the matter of Tiona versus Trigger: Trigger is guilty of an Assault. Tempering this judgment is her motive, which was the recognition of Cathay's strategy in dealing with Tiona, and her belief that he was doing the right thing. This court notes that he was doing the *merciful* thing; right is another matter. There can be no doubt that a physical assault occurred. It cannot be condoned, no matter what the motive. For bad judgment, then, this court fines Trigger ten percent of her earnings for a period of ten years, all of it to be paid to the injured party, Tiona."

Tiona did not look smug. She must have known by then that things were not going her way. I was beginning to understand it, too.

"In the matter of Tiona versus Cathay," the CC went on, "Cathay is guilty of an Assault. His motive has been determined to be the avoidance of just such a situation as he now finds himself in, and the knowledge that Tiona would suffer greatly if he brought her to court. He attempted to bring the confrontation to an end with a minimum of pain for Tiona, never dreaming that she would show the bad judgment to bring the matter to court. She did, and now he finds himself convicted of assault. In view of his motives, mercy will temper this court's decision. He is ordered to pay the same fine as his colleague, Trigger.

"Now to the central matter, that of Trigger and Cathay versus Tiona." I saw her sink a little lower in her chair.

"You are found to be guilty by reason of insanity of the following charges: harassment, trespassing, verbal assault, and four counts of infringement.

"Your offense was in attempting to make others shoulder the blame for your own misjudgments and misfortunes. The court is sympathetic to your plight, realizes that the fault for your situation was not entirely your own. This does not excuse your behavior, however.

"Cathay attempted to do you a favor, supposing that your aberrant state of mind would not last long enough for the filing of charges, that when you were alone and thought it over you would realize how badly you had wronged him and that a court would find in his favor.

"The State holds you responsible for the maintenance of your own mind, does not care what opinions you hold or what evaluations you make of reality so long as they do not infringe on the rights of other citizens. You are free to think Cathay responsible for your troubles, even if this opinion is irrational, but when you assault him with this opinion the State must take notice and make a judgment as to the worth of the opinion.

"This court is appointed to make that judgment of right and wrong, and finds no basis in fact for your contentions.

"This court finds you to be insane.

"Judgment is as follows:

"Subject to the approval of the wronged parties, you are given the choice of death with reprieve, or submission to a course of treatment to remove your sociopathic attitudes.

"Argus, do you demand her death?"

"Huh?" That was a big surprise to me, and not one that I liked. But the decision gave me no trouble.

"No, I don't demand anything. I thought I was out of this, and I feel just rotten about the whole thing. Would you really have killed her if I asked you to?"

"I can't answer that, because you didn't. It's not likely that I would have, mostly because of your age." It went on to ask the other four, and I suspect that Tiona would have been pushing up daisies if Cathay had wanted it that way, but he didn't. Neither did Trigger or Denver.

"Very well. How do you choose, Tiona?"

She answered in a very small voice that she would be grateful for the chance to go on living. Then she thanked each of us. It was excruciatingly painful for me; my empathy was working overtime, and I was trying to imagine what it would feel like to have society's appointed representative declare me insane.

The rest of it was clearing up details. Tiona was fined heavily, both in court costs and taxes, and in funds payable to Cathay and Trigger. Their fines were absorbed in her larger ones, with the result that she would be paying them for many years. Her child was in cold storage; the CC ruled that he should stay there until Tiona was declared sane, as she was now unfit to mother him. It occurred to me that if she had considered suspending his animation while she found a new primary teacher, we all could have avoided the trial.

Tiona hurried away when the doors came open behind us. Darcy hugged me while Trilby stayed in the background, then I went over to join the others, expecting a celebration.

But Trigger and Cathay were not elated. In fact, you would have thought they'd just lost the judgment. They congratulated me and Denver, then hurried away. I looked at Darcy, and she wasn't smiling, either.

"I don't get it," I confessed. "Why is everyone so glum?"

"They still have to face the Teacher's Association," Darcy said.

"I still don't get it. They won."

"It's not just a matter of winning or losing with the TA," Trilby said. "You forget, they were judged guilty of assault. To make it even worse, in fact as bad as it can be, you and Denver were there when it happened. They were the cause of you two joining in the assault. I'm afraid the TA will frown on that."

"But if the CC thought they shouldn't be punished, why should the TA think otherwise? Isn't the CC smarter than people?"

Trilby grimaced. "I wish I could answer that. I wish I was even sure how I feel about it."

She found me the next day, shortly after the Teacher's Association announced its decision. I didn't really want to be found, but the bayou is not so big that one can really hide there, so I hadn't tried. I was sitting on the grass on the highest hill in Beatnik Bayou, which was also the driest place.

She beached the canoe and came up the hill slowly, giving me plenty of time to warn her off if I really wanted to be alone. What the hell. I'd have to talk to her soon enough.

For a long time she just sat there. She rested her elbows on her knees and stared down at the quiet waters, just like I'd been doing all afternoon.

"How's he taking it?" I said, at last.

"I don't know. He's back there, if you want to talk to him. He'd probably like to talk to you."

"At least Trigger got off okay." As soon as I'd said it, it sounded hollow.

"Three years' probation isn't anything to laugh about. She'll have to close this place down for a while. Put it in mothballs."

"Mothballs." I saw Tuesday the hippo, wallowing in the deep mud across the water. Tuesday in suspended animation? I thought of Tiona's little baby, waiting in a bottle until his mother became sane again. I remembered the happy years slogging around in the bayou mud, and saw the waters frozen, icicles mixed with Spanish moss in the tree limbs. "I guess it'll cost quite a bit to start it up again in three years, won't it?" I had only hazy ideas of money. So far, it had never been important to me.

Trilby glanced at me, eyes narrowed. She shrugged.

"Most likely, Trigger will have to sell the place. There's a buyer who wants to expand it and turn it into a golf course."

"Golf course," I echoed, feeling numb. Manicured greens, pretty water hazards, sand traps, flags whipping in the breeze. Sterile. I suddenly felt like crying, but for some reason I didn't do it.

"You can't come back here, Argus. Nothing stays the same. Change is something you have to get used to."

"Cathay will, too." And just how much change should a person be expected to take? With a shock, I realized that now Cathay would be doing what I had wanted him to do. He'd be growing up with me, getting older instead of being regressed to grow up with another child. And it was suddenly just too much. It hadn't been my fault that this was happening to him, but having wished for it and having it come true made it feel like it was. The tears came, and they didn't stop for a long time.

Trilby left me alone, and I was grateful for that.

She was still there when I got myself under control. I didn't care one way or the other. I felt empty, with a burning in the back of my throat. Nobody had told me life was going to be like this.

"What . . . what about the child Cathay contracted to teach?" I asked, finally, feeling I should say something. "What happens to her?"

"The TA takes responsibility," Trilby said. "They'll find someone. For Trigger's child, too."

I looked at her. She was stretched out, both elbows behind her to prop her up. Her valentine nipples crinkled as I watched.

She glanced at me, smiled with one corner of her mouth. I felt a little better. She was awfully pretty.

"I guess he can . . . well, can't he still teach older kids?"

"I suppose he can," Trilby said, with a shrug. "I don't know if he'll want to. I know Cathay. He's not going to take this well."

"Is there anything I could do?"

"Not really. Talk to him. Show sympathy, but not too much. You'll have to figure it out. See if he wants to be with you."

It was too confusing. How was I supposed to know what he needed? He hadn't come to see me. But Trilby had.

So there was one uncomplicated thing in my life right then, one thing I could do where I wouldn't have to think. I rolled over and got on top of Trilby and started to kiss her. She responded with a lazy eroticism I found irresistible. She *did* know some tricks I'd never heard of.

"How was that?" I said, much later.

That smile again. I got the feeling that I constantly amused her, and somehow I didn't mind it. Maybe it was the fact that she made no bones about her being the adult and me being the child. That was the way it would be with us. I would have to grow up to her; she would not go back and imitate me.

"Are you looking for a grade?" she asked. "Like the twentieth century?" She got to her feet and stretched.

"All right. I'll be honest. You get an A for effort, but any thirteen-year-old would. You can't help it. In technique, maybe a low C. Not that I expected any more, for the same reason."

"So you want to teach me to do better? That's your job?"

"Only if you hire me. And sex is such a small part of it. Listen, Argus. I'm not going to be your mother. Darcy does that okay. I won't be your playmate, either, like Cathay was. I won't be teaching you moral lessons. You're getting tired of that, anyway."

It was true. Cathay had never really been my contemporary, though he tried his best to look it and act it. But the illusion had started to wear thin, and I guess it had to. I was no longer able to ignore the contradictions, I was too sophisticated and cynical for him to hide his lessons in everyday activities.

It bothered me in the same way the CC did. The CC could befriend me one minute and sentence me to death the next. I wanted more than that, and Trilby seemed to be offering it.

"I won't be teaching you science or skills, either," she was saying. "You'll have tutors for that, when you decide just what you want to do."

"Just what *is* it you do, then?"

"You know, I've never been able to find a good way of describing that. I won't be around all the time, like Cathay was. You'll come to me when you want to, maybe when you have a problem. I'll be sympathetic and do what I can, but mostly I'll just point out that you have to make all the hard choices. If you've been stupid I'll tell you so, but I won't be surprised or disappointed if you go on being stupid in the same way. You can use me as a role model if you want to, but I don't insist on it. But I promise I'll always tell you things straight, as I see them. I won't try to slip things in painlessly. It's time for pain. Think of Cathay as a professional child. I'm not putting him down. He turned you into a civilized being, and when he got you you were hardly that. It's because of him that you're capable of caring about his situation now, that you have loyalties to feel divided about. And he's good enough at it to know how you'll choose."

"Choose? What do you mean?"

"I can't tell you that." She spread her hands, and grinned. "See how helpful I can be?"

She was confusing me again. Why can't things be simpler?

"Then if Cathay's a professional child, you're a professional adult?"

"You could think of it like that. It's not really analogous."

"I guess I still don't know what Darcy would be paying you for."

"We'll make love a lot. How's that? Simple enough for you?" She brushed dirt from her back and frowned at the ground. "But not on dirt anymore. I don't care for dirt."

I looked around, too. The place *was* messy. Not pretty at all. I wondered how I could have liked it so much. Suddenly I wanted to get out, to go to a clean, dry place.

"Come on," I said, getting up. "I want to try some of those things again."

"Does this mean I have a job?"

"Yeah. I guess it does."

Cathay was sitting on the porch of the Sugar Shack, a line of brown beer bottles perched along the edge. He smiled at us as we approached him. He was stinking drunk.

It's strange. We'd been drunk many times together, the four of us. It's great fun. But when only one person is drunk, it's a little disgusting. Not that I blamed him. But when you're drinking together all the jokes make sense. When you drink alone, you just make a sloppy nuisance of yourself.

Trilby and I sat on either side of him. He wanted to sing. He pressed bottles on both of us, and I sipped mine and tried to get into the spirit of it. But pretty soon he was crying, and I felt awful. And I admit that it wasn't entirely in sympathy. I felt helpless because there was so little I could do, and a bit resentful of some of the promises he had me make. I would have come to see him anyway. He didn't have to blubber on my shoulder and beg me not to abandon him.

So he cried on me, and on Trilby, then just sat between us looking glum. I tried to console him.

"Cathay, it's not the end of the world. Trilby says you'll still be able to teach older kids. My age and up. The TA just said you couldn't handle younger ones."

He mumbled something.

"It shouldn't be that different," I said, not knowing when to shut up.

"Maybe you're right," he said.

"Sure I am." I was unconsciously falling into that false heartiness people use to cheer up drunks. He heard it immediately.

"What the hell do you know about it? You think you . . . Damn it, what do you know? You know what kind of person it takes to do my job? A little bit of a misfit, that's what. Somebody who doesn't want to grow up any more than you do. We're *both* cowards, Argus. You don't know it, but *I* do. *I* do. So what the hell am I going to do? Huh? Why don't you go away? You got what you wanted, didn't you?"

"Take it easy, Cathay," Trilby soothed, hugging him close to her. "Take it easy."

He was immediately contrite, and began to cry quietly. He said how sorry he was, over and over, and he was sincere. He said, he hadn't meant it, it just came out, it was cruel.

And so forth.

I was cold all over.

We put him to bed in the shack, then started down the road.

"We'll have to watch him the next few days," Trilby said. "He'll get over this, but it'll be rough."

"Right," I said.

I took a look at the shack before we went around the false bend in the road. For one moment I saw Beatnik Bayou as a perfect illusion, a window through time. Then we went around the tree and it all fell apart. It had never mattered before.

But it was such a sloppy place. I'd never realized how ugly the Sugar Shack was.

I never saw it again. Cathay came to live with us for a few months, tried his hand at art. Darcy told me privately that he was hopeless. He moved out, and I saw him frequently after that, always saying hello.

But he was depressing to be around, and he knew it. Besides, he admitted that I represented things he was trying to forget. So we never really talked much.

Sometimes I play golf in the old bayou. It's only two holes, but there's talk of expanding it.

They did a good job on the renovation.

"Air Raid"

What can I say about the next story? Well, actually, I could say so much that I'd be in danger of having the introduction run longer than the story itself.

It all began one rather warm afternoon in Damon and Kate's living room, at the Milford Conference, as I tried not to doze off while somebody's story was being efficiently deconstructed. It might even have been one of my stories. Suddenly this idea appeared in my head, full-blown. Five minutes later it was more or less completely written, all I had to do was go home and sit at the typewriter for a while. I did it that night, finishing just as the sun was coming up.

Ten years later I found myself standing with Kris Kristofferson on a steep hillside on the outskirts of Toronto at 3 A.M., so cold I couldn't feel my feet. The hillside was smoking, there were small fires everywhere, and the twisted wreckage of an old 707 which had been trucked in from an airliner graveyard in Mexico was artfully scattered over several blackened acres, along with thousands of crushed suitcases, carefully scorched clothing, and all manner of other junk. There was a line of big trucks along the dirt road behind me: gaffers' and grips' vans, craft services dispensing sandwiches and bottles of Evian water to the five hundred people standing around, honeywagons, Winnebagos, mobile makeup and hairdressers' studios. There were thirty cars made up to look like police cruisers from various jurisdictions in Minnesota, right down to fake license plates. There were a dozen real fire trucks ready to spray water over the scene. There were four large camera booms, miles and miles of cables, hundreds of massive lights, and three camera helicopters zooming overhead. The scene was so convincing that two real airline pilots on approach to the Toronto airport a few miles away called the tower to report that a big jet had gone down.

Kris swept his arm to indicate the scene and grinned at me. "John, you wrote all this," he said. A few minutes later somebody shouted "Action!"

But I'm getting ahead of myself. . . .

* * *

I sold the story, "Air Raid," to Isaac Asimov's Science Fiction Magazine, a new publication which had first been announced while I was attending Milford. It was to appear in the very first issue, but I had already sold them another story. The editor, George Scithers, suggested I might want to use a pseudonym. Back in the forties there were guys who wrote entire issues of SF magazines, under eight different names. Asimov said he thought it was a silly custom, but I was tickled by the idea, and used the name "Herb Boehm." Herbert is my middle name and the one I used until I decided to become a writer (John Varley just looked better to me), and Boehm (pronounced "Beam") is my mother's maiden name. It is the only time I've ever used a pseudonym.

The story was collected in several anthologies. One of them was read by Dennis Lasker, an assistant to John Foreman, a man who had produced many of Paul Newman's films, most notably Butch Cassidy and the Sundance Kid. *"Air Raid" is about people from the future who are taking people off airplanes that are about to crash. They aren't gentle about it. It is without a doubt the most action-packed story I've ever done. Dennis was on a plane when he read it, and later told me he kept looking over his shoulder, worried about being kidnapped.*

Soon I was on an airplane myself, winging down to Los Angeles. I was taken to the Polo Lounge in the Beverly Hills Hotel for a lunch meeting. Dustin Hoffman was sitting at the next table. At my table were John Foreman; Douglas Trumbull, the special effects wizard behind 2001: A Space Odyssey, *who would be directing the proposed movie; Freddie Fields, who used to be Judy Garland's agent; and David Begelman. Begelman's name was familiar. That very morning in the hotel his name had been in the headline of the* Los Angeles Times, *plea bargaining his way into "community service" because he forged Cliff Robertson's name on $80,000 worth of checks to cover gambling debts. Many years later, David killed himself in a five-star hotel in Beverly Hills. I don't think it had anything to do with the movie we discussed that day, which would come to be called* Millennium, *but I wouldn't swear to it. It almost drove me to suicide.*

If any movie ever had a checkered history, it was Millennium.

I was hired to write a forty-page treatment turning what could have been a very exciting episode of The Twilight Zone *into a feature-length movie. I was also hired to write a novelization, which struck me as putting the cart before the horse, but since I was assured I'd have a totally free hand and wouldn't have to adhere slavishly to whatever script was eventually turned in, I accepted the assignment. A good thing, too. The man they hired to write the script eventually produced something that bore only a passing relationship to "Air Raid." I hated it. Luckily, so did everybody else. I showed John the script I had written in four feverish days adapted from my story "The Phantom of Kansas." He liked it. I allowed as how I'd like a shot at* Millennium. *Amazingly, he thought that was a good idea. Even more amazingly, so did Doug, David, and Freddie. I was in the screenwriting business.*

We discussed the project with Paul Newman. John suggested Jane Fonda for the

*female lead. Pretty heady stuff. I turned in the first draft, which was read and end-
lessly rehashed, as is standard practice in Hollywood. I began on the second draft.
Then one night Natalie Wood went swimming, drowned, and* Millennium *was dead.
In hindsight, I know it probably should have stayed dead, but it soon became* The Development Project That Wouldn't Die! *Good science fiction title, that.*

Why did Natalie Wood's death drive the first stake into the undying heart of
Millennium? *Simple. Doug Trumbull was directing* Brainstorm *at the time, and Natalie Wood was starring in it. MGM took a look at the insurance on the project and
found, to the surprise and delight of the studio bean counters, that they could make a
tidy profit by just closing the picture down. Doug Trumbull thought he could finish it,
shoot around her few remaining scenes, and if necessary perform some of his special
effects hoodoo and morph Wood's face onto a double. Create a Natalie golem, sort of
like Gollum. MGM thought this was in bad taste, and besides, "We've got a* guaranteed profit!" *Doug thought it would be a good memorial to Natalie, and besides, he
wanted to finish the picture. He took them to court. Within a week Doug was about as
welcome on the MGM lot as Michael Cimino after* Heaven's Gate.

Okay, so it wasn't *so simple. But there it was.*

*Nobody blamed any of this on me, so while John Foreman looked around for ways
to get his picture going again, other producers came calling. Over the next ten years I
worked on several projects. I was offered* Star Trek III, *but turned it down because I knew
nothing about* Star Trek, *and don't even like it. And I wrote three screenplays that I still
think would make good movies, including an adaptation of Heinlein's* Have Spacesuit,
Will Travel. *Nothing happened with them. This is not at all unusual in that business.*
Everybody in Hollywood has good, unproduced scripts lying around in studio vaults.

During those ten years, between bouts of rewriting Millennium, *I lived in Eugene
but spent a lot of time in Hollywood. I stayed at great hotels: the Beverly Wilshire, the
Chateau Marmont, the Westwood Marquis, Le Mondrian. I was treated to lunch and
dinner at all the fanciest restaurants. I visited or worked at all the major studios except Universal: Fox, Warner Brothers, Columbia, Disney. None of them looked like
they do in the movies, with hundreds of extras milling about the streets in exotic costumes, big stars in limos, stagehands shifting props and scenery and lights. In fact,
most of them looked like they ought to have tumbleweeds bouncing down the streets.
In appearance, they varied from a bit frayed around the edges to downright decrepit,
except Disney, which was neat and clean and looked pretty much like my old high
school. I strolled down Goofy Drive, expecting to hear the class bell ringing. At the
Burbank Studios I hung around at the Waltons' West Virginia home, which was a
hollow shell. I saw appalling indifference to cinema history, from gigantic model war-
ships used in* In Harm's Way *left out in the weather to fall apart, to old storage sheds
with film canisters spilling out onto the ground and unreeling. Who knows what was
on those old reels? Lost, all lost.*

At one point I had an office right at the MGM gate. You can see my window in any number of studio documentaries. I could sit there, not working very hard, and watch Erik Estrada arriving to work on CHiPs, which was about the only thing filming there at the time. I could amble down the avenue with the bungalows that used to belong to Metro's biggest stars—and there were none bigger—and now all housed production companies. I saw Esther Williams' giant swimming pool, now dry. The lot has been renamed Sony Pictures Studios, which I'm sure makes Louis B. Mayer spin rapidly in his grave.

During that time I worked on a development project with Jeffrey Katzenberg, later the K of SKG. S for Spielberg, G for Geffen. I met Charlton Heston, Art Linkletter, Jon Voight, Mel Gibson, Joanne Woodward, Peter O'Toole, Sigourney Weaver, Gary Busey, and Kirk Douglas, among others. All of them were shorter than I had imagined, except Sigourney. None of this has anything to do with Millennium, but it's so much fun to drop names and I figured this was the best place to do it.

A while later Richard Rush, who made the wonderful The Stunt Man, was signed to direct the project, and we started a rewrite to bring the script more in line with his personal vision. I soon learned that all directors want to do that. It was fun working with Richard, but I soon began to think he was going to turn my story into The Stunt Man II. Our most memorable meeting was when he flew us to Catalina Island in his plane for buffalo burgers at the airport restaurant. The airport on Catalina is on the highest point, so I'm probably one of the few people to visit there who's never been to the only town on the island, Avalon.

That fell apart because of personality clashes between John Foreman and Richard Rush. We went to Canada some years later and hired Alvin Rakoff. That fell apart: some financing deal in the Netherlands. We hired Phillip Borsos. That fell apart. I have no idea why.

Finally everything was in place, just about nine years after I wrote the first screenplay, and I was invited to Toronto to work with Michael Anderson. He directed The Dam Busters, which George Lucas stole from when filming the climactic battle in Star Wars. He also directed the Best Picture of 1958, Around the World in 80 Days, and had a lot of great stories to tell about Mike Todd, the insane producer of that spectacle. Michael was no stranger to salvaging pictures that were in trouble. He said that on the first day of shooting Orca, the expensive mechanical killer whale that was supposed to be the star of the show caught fire, burned, and sank, never to be seen again. They had to shoot without it. Maybe that should have warned me.

We rented a gigantic empty factory building that had formerly made massive transformers, and started building what was at the time the largest indoor set ever constructed in Canada. And I got to do something that screenwriters seldom do, which was spend six months in Toronto doing continuous rewrites and watching the *movie being made, from early drawings to the first nail being driven into the first board, to the last day of principle photography.*

I have to say that moviemaking is quite the most exciting pursuit I've ever been involved in. There is an air of urgency, and most of the things you do are far from everyday reality. The people involved are creating illusions very carefully and it is fascinating. I must also report that it is the dullest work imaginable. You've heard the expression "boring as watching paint dry." It's that dull. In fact, a lot of the movie business is watching paint dry. It can take many hours to set up one shot that lasts five seconds, then many hours to set up the next shot. Only the grips and the director are busy most of the time. A writer is usually the least busy of all . . . until suddenly an actor doesn't like the way a line plays, and then you are very busy indeed.

I had a ball. And at the end we got to blow everything up. Big explosions!

And in the end, we made a rotten movie. There are lots of people I could blame for that, but I'll let the blame rest squarely on the one most responsible for it: myself. It's my name on it, and it's my baby.

What happened, in hindsight, is that I lost the vision. I should have bailed out on the third or fourth director. But the project had acquired a life of its own, it wouldn't die, and I didn't want to abandon it. I kept thinking I could eventually steer it back on course, but by the end the script was covered with so many fingerprints it would have baffled a forensic scientist. When rewrites are added to a script in production they are printed on paper of a different color and tipped in to the original. By the last day of shooting I don't think there were any two pages of the same color.

So that's how it happened. I console myself by remembering that Harlan Ellison, one of the best writers working in SF movies and television, wrote a rotten script. William Goldman, maybe the best screenwriter ever, wrote a rotten script. So it can happen to any of us. I learned a lot, mostly what not to do, and when to stand firm or get out. I love the movies, I see one almost every day. I'll get another shot, maybe at my most recent novel, Red Thunder, *and I know I'll do better.*

Meanwhile, I hope you enjoy this unassuming little story that was the basis of all the racket.

AIR RAID

I WAS JERKED awake by the silent alarm vibrating my skull. It won't shut down until you sit up, so I did. All around me in the darkened bunkroom the Snatch Team members were sleeping singly and in pairs. I yawned, scratched my ribs, and patted Gene's hairy flank. He turned over. So much for a romantic send-off.

Rubbing sleep from my eyes, I reached to the floor for my leg, strapped it on, and plugged it in. Then I was running down the rows of bunks toward Ops.

The situation board glowed in the gloom. Sun-Belt Airlines Flight 128, Miami to New York, September 15, 1979. We'd been looking for that one for three years. I should have been happy, but who can afford it when you wake up?

Liza Boston muttered past me on the way to Prep. I muttered back and followed. The lights came on around the mirrors, and I groped my way to one of them. Behind us, three more people staggered in. I sat down, plugged in, and at last I could lean back and close my eyes.

They didn't stay closed for long. Rush! I sat up straight as the sludge I use for blood was replaced with super-charged go-juice. I looked around me and got a series of idiot grins. There was Liza, and Pinky and Dave. Against the far wall Cristabel was already turning slowly in front of the airbrush, getting a Caucasian paint job. It looked like a good team.

I opened the drawer and started preliminary work on my face. It's a bigger job every time. Transfusion or no, I looked like death. The right ear was completely gone now. I could no longer close my lips; the gums were permanently bared. A week earlier, a finger had fallen off in my sleep. And what's it to you, bugger?

While I worked, one of the screens around the mirror glowed. A smiling young woman, blonde, high brow, round face. Close enough. The crawl line read *Mary Katrina Sondergard, born Trenton, New Jersey, age in 1979: 25.* Baby, this is your lucky day.

The computer melted the skin away from her face to show me the bone structure, rotated it, gave me cross sections. I studied the similarities with my own skull, noted the differences. Not bad, and better than some I'd been given.

I assembled a set of dentures that included the slight gap in the upper incisors. Putty filled out my cheeks. Contact lenses fell from the dispenser and I popped them in. Nose plugs widened my nostrils. No need for ears; they'd be covered by the wig. I pulled a blank plastiflesh mask over my face and had to pause while it melted in. It took only a minute to mold it to perfection. I smiled at myself. How nice to have lips.

The delivery slot clunked and dropped a blonde wig and a pink outfit into my lap. The wig was hot from the styler. I put it on, then the pantyhose.

"Mandy? Did you get the profile on Sondergard?" I didn't look up; I recognized the voice.

"Roger."

"We've located her near the airport. We can slip you in before take-off, so you'll be the joker."

I groaned and looked up at the face on the screen. Elfreda Baltimore-Louisville, Director of Operational Teams: lifeless face and tiny slits for eyes. What can you do when all the muscles are dead?

"Okay." You take what you get.

She switched off, and I spent the next two minutes trying to get dressed while keeping my eyes on the screens. I memorized names and faces of crew members plus the few facts known about them. Then I hurried out and caught up with the others. Elapsed time from first alarm: twelve minutes and seven seconds. We'd better get moving.

"Goddam Sun-Belt," Cristabel groused, hitching at her bra.

"At least they got rid of the high heels," Dave pointed out. A year earlier we would have been teetering down the aisles on three-inch platforms. We all wore short pink shifts with blue and white diagonal stripes across the front, and carried matching shoulder bags. I fussed trying to get the ridiculous pillbox cap pinned on.

We jogged into the dark Operations Control Room and lined up at the gate. Things were out of our hands now. Until the gate was ready, we could only wait.

I was first, a few feet away from the portal. I turned away from it; it gives me vertigo. I focused instead on the gnomes sitting at their consoles, bathed in yellow lights from their screens. None of them looked back at me. They don't like us much. I don't like them, either. Withered, emaciated, all of them. Our fat legs and butts and breasts are a reproach to them, a reminder that Snatchers eat five times their ration to stay presentable for the masquerade. Meantime we continue to rot. One day I'll be sitting at a console. One day I'll be *built in* to a console, with all my guts on the outside and nothing left on my body but stink. The hell with them.

I buried my gun under a clutter of tissues and lipsticks in my purse. Elfreda was looking at me.

"Where is she?" I asked.

"Motel room. She was alone from ten P.M. to noon on flight day."

Departure time was 1:15. She had cut it close and would be in a hurry. Good.

"Can you catch her in the bathroom? Best of all, in the tub?"

"We're working on it." She sketched a smile with a fingertip drawn over lifeless lips. She knew how I liked to operate, but she was telling me I'd take what I got. It never hurts to ask. People are at their most defenseless stretched out and up to their necks in water.

"Go!" Elfreda shouted. I stepped through, and things started to go wrong.

I was facing the wrong way, stepping *out* of the bathroom door and facing the bedroom. I turned and spotted Mary Katrina Sondergard through the haze of the gate. There was no way I could reach her without stepping back through. I couldn't even shoot without hitting someone on the other side.

Sondergard was at the mirror, the worst possible place. Few people recognize themselves quickly, but she'd been looking right at herself. She saw me and her eyes widened. I stepped to the side, out of her sight.

"What the hell is . . . hey? Who the hell—" I noted the voice, which can be the trickiest thing to get right.

I figured she'd be more curious than afraid. My guess was right. She came out of the bathroom, passing through the gate as if it wasn't there, which it wasn't, since it only has one side. She had a towel wrapped around her.

"Jesus Christ! What are you doing in my—" Words fail you at a time like that. She knew she ought to say something, but what? *Excuse me, haven't I seen you in the mirror?*

I put on my best stew smile and held out my hand.

"Pardon the intrusion. I can explain everything. You see, I'm—" I hit her on the side of the head and she staggered and went down hard. Her towel fell to the floor. "—working my way through college." She started to get up, so I caught her under the chin with my artificial knee. She stayed down.

"Standard fuggin' *oil!*" I hissed, rubbing my injured knuckles. But there was no time. I knelt beside her, checked her pulse. She'd be okay, but I think I loosened some front teeth. I paused a moment. Lord, to look like that with no makeup, no prosthetics! She nearly broke my heart.

I grabbed her under the knees and wrestled her to the gate. She was a sack of limp noodles. Somebody reached through, grabbed her feet, and pulled. *So long, love! How would you like to go on a long voyage?*

I sat on her rented bed to get my breath. There were car keys and cigarettes in her purse, genuine tobacco, worth its weight in blood. I lit six of them, figuring I had five minutes of my very own. The room filled with sweet smoke. They don't make 'em like that anymore.

The Hertz sedan was in the motel parking lot. I got in and headed for the airport. I breathed deeply of the air, rich in hydrocarbons. I could see for hundreds of yards into the distance. The perspective nearly made me dizzy, but I live for those moments. There's no way to explain what it's like in the pre-meck world. The sun was a fierce yellow ball through the haze.

The other stews were boarding. Some of them knew Sondergard so I didn't say much, pleading a hangover. That went over well, with a lot of knowing laughs and sly remarks. Evidently it wasn't out of character. We boarded the 707 and got ready for the goats to arrive.

It looked good. The four commandos on the other side were identical twins for the women I was working with. There was nothing to do but be a stewardess until departure time. I hoped there would be no more glitches. Inverting a gate for a joker run into a motel room was one thing, but in a 707 at twenty thousand feet . . .

The plane was nearly full when the woman Pinky would impersonate sealed the forward door. We taxied to the end of the runway, then we were airborne. I started taking orders for drinks in first.

The goats were the usual lot, for 1979. Fat and sassy, all of them, and as unaware of living in a paradise as a fish is of the sea. *What would you think, ladies and gents, of a trip to the future? No? I can't say I'm surprised. What if I told you this plane is going to—*

My alarm beeped as we reached cruising altitude. I consulted the indicator under my Lady Bulova and glanced at one of the restroom doors. I felt a vibration pass through the plane. *Damn it, not so soon.*

The gate was in there. I came out quickly, and motioned for Diana Gleason—Dave's pigeon—to come to the front.

"Take a look at this," I said, with a disgusted look. She started to enter the restroom, stopped when she saw the green glow. I planted a boot on her fanny and shoved. Perfect. Dave would have a chance to hear her voice before popping in. Though she'd be doing little but screaming when she got a look around . . .

Dave came through the gate, adjusting his silly little hat. Diana must have struggled.

"Be disgusted," I whispered.

"What a mess," he said as he came out of the restroom. It was a fair imitation of Diana's tone, though he'd missed the accent. It wouldn't matter much longer.

"What is it?" It was one of the stews from tourist. We stepped aside so she could get a look, and Dave shoved her through. Pinky popped out very quickly.

"We're minus on minutes," Pinky said. "We lost five on the other side."

"Five?" Dave-Diana squeaked. I felt the same way. We had a hundred and three passengers to process.

"Yeah. They lost contact after you pushed my pigeon through. It took that long to realign."

You get used to that. Time runs at different rates on each side of the gate, though it's always sequential, past to future. Once we'd started the Snatch with me entering Sondergard's room, there was no way to go back any earlier on either side. Here, in 1979, we had a rigid ninety-four minutes to get everything done. On the other side, the gate could never be maintained longer than three hours.

"When you left, how long was it since the alarm went in?"

"Twenty-eight minutes."

It didn't sound good. It would take at least two hours just customizing the wimps. Assuming there was no more slippage on 79-time, we might just make it. But there's *always* slippage. I shuddered, thinking about riding it in.

"No time for any more games, then," I said. "Pink, you go back to tourist and call both of the other girls up here. Tell 'em to come one at a time, and tell 'em we've got a problem. You know the bit."

"Biting back the tears. Got you." She hurried aft. In no time the first one showed up. Her friendly Sun-Belt Airlines smile was stamped on her face, but her stomach would be churning. *Oh God, this is it!*

I took her by the elbow and pulled her behind the curtains in front. She was breathing hard.

"Welcome to the twilight zone," I said, and put the gun to her head. She slumped, and I caught her. Pinky and Dave helped me shove her through the gate.

"Fug! The rotting thing's flickering."

Pinky was right. A very ominous sign. But the green glow stabilized as we watched, with who knows how much slippage on the other side. Cristabel ducked through.

"We're plus thirty-three," she said. There was no sense talking about what we were all thinking: things were going badly.

"Back to tourist," I said. "Be brave, smile at everyone, but make it just a little bit too good, got it?"

"Check," Cristabel said.

We processed the other quickly, with no incident. Then there was no time to talk about anything. In eighty-nine minutes Flight 128 was going to be spread all over a mountain whether we were finished or not.

Dave went into the cockpit to keep the flight crew out of our hair. Me and Pinky were supposed to take care of first class, then back up Cristabel and Liza in tourist. We used the standard "coffee, tea, or milk" gambit, relying on our speed and their inertia.

I leaned over the first two seats on the left.

"Are you enjoying your flight?" Pop, pop. Two squeezes on the trigger, close to the heads and out of sight of the rest of the goats.

"Hi, folks. I'm Mandy. Fly me." Pop, pop.

Halfway to the galley, a few people were watching us curiously. But people don't make a fuss until they have a lot more to go on. One goat in the back row stood up, and I let him have it. By now there were only eight left awake. I abandoned the smile and squeezed off four quick shots. Pinky took care of the rest. We hurried through the curtains, just in time.

There was an uproar building in the back of tourist, with about 60 percent of the goats already processed. Cristabel glanced at me, and I nodded.

"Okay, folks," she bawled. "I want you to be quiet. Calm down and listen up. *You,* fathead, *pipe down* before I cram my foot up your ass sideways."

The shock of hearing her talk like that was enough to buy us a little time, anyway. We had formed a skirmish line across the width of the plane, guns out, steadied on seat backs, aimed at the milling, befuddled group of thirty goats.

The guns are enough to awe all but the most foolhardy. In essence, a standard-issue stunner is just a plastic rod with two grids about six inches apart. There's not enough metal in it to set off a hijack alarm. And to people from the Stone Age to about 2190 it doesn't look any more like a weapon than a ballpoint pen. So Equipment Section jazzes them up in a plastic shell to real Buck Rogers blasters, with a dozen knobs and lights that flash and a barrel like the snout of a hog. Hardly anyone ever walks into one.

"We are in great danger, and time is short. You must all do exactly as I tell you, and you will be safe."

You can't give them time to think, you have to rely on your status as the Voice of Authority. The situation is just *not* going to make sense to them, no matter how you explain it.

"Just a minute, I think you owe us—"

An airborne lawyer. I made a snap decision, thumbed the fireworks switch on my gun, and shot him.

The gun made a sound like a flying saucer with hemorrhoids, spit sparks and little jets of flame, and extended a green laser finger to his forehead. He dropped.

All pure kark, of course. But it sure is impressive.

And it's damn risky, too. I had to choose between a panic if the fathead got them to thinking, and a possible panic from the flash of the gun. But when a 20th gets to talking about his "rights" and what he is "owed," things can get out of hand. It's infectious.

It worked. There was a lot of shouting, people ducking behind seats, but no rush. We could have handled it, but we needed some of them conscious if we were ever going to finish the Snatch.

"Get up. Get *up,* you *slugs!*" Cristabel yelled. "He's stunned, nothing worse. But I'll *kill* the next one who gets out of line. Now *get to your feet* and do what I tell you. *Children first! Hurry,* as fast as you can, to the front of the plane. Do what the stewardess tells you. Come on, kids, *move!*"

I ran back into first class just ahead of the kids, turned at the open restroom door, and got on my knees.

They were petrified. There were five of them—crying, some of them, which always chokes me up—looking left and right at dead people in the first class seats, stumbling, near panic.

"Come on, kids," I called to them, giving my special smile. "Your parents will be along in just a minute. Everything's going to be all right, I promise you. Come on."

I got three of them through. The fourth balked. She was determined not to go through that door. She spread her legs and arms and I couldn't push her through. I will *not* hit a child, never. She raked her nails over my face. My wig came off, and she gaped at my bare head. I shoved her through.

Number five was sitting in the aisle, bawling. He was maybe seven. I ran back and picked him up, hugged him and kissed him, and tossed him through. God, I needed a rest, but I was needed in tourist.

"You, you, you, and you. Okay, you too. Help him, will you?" Pinky had a practiced eye for the ones that wouldn't be any use to anyone, even themselves. We herded them toward the front of the plane, then deployed ourselves along the left side where we could cover the workers. It didn't take long to prod them into action. We had them dragging the limp bodies forward as fast as they could go. Me and Cristabel were in tourist, with the others up front.

Adrenaline was being catabolized in my body now; the rush of action left me and I started to feel very tired. There's an unavoidable feeling of sympathy for the poor dumb goats that starts to get me about this stage of the game. Sure, they were better off; sure, they were going to die if we didn't get them off the plane. But when they saw the other side they were going to have a hard time believing it.

The first ones were returning for a second load, stunned at what they'd just seen: dozens of people being put into a cubicle that was crowded when it was empty. One college student looked like he'd been hit in the stomach. He stopped by me and his eyes pleaded.

"Look, I want to *help* you people, just . . . what's going *on*? Is this some new kind of rescue? I mean, are we going to crash—"

I switched my gun to prod and brushed it across his cheek. He gasped and fell back.

"Shut your fuggin' mouth and get moving, or I'll kill you." It would be hours before his jaw was in shape to ask any more stupid questions.

We cleared tourist and moved up. A couple of the work gang were pretty damn pooped by then. Muscles like horses, all of them, but they can hardly run up a flight of stairs. We let some of them go through, including a couple that were at least fifty years old. *Je*-zuz. Fifty! We got down to a core of four men and two women who seemed strong, and worked them until they nearly dropped. But we processed everyone in twenty-five minutes.

The portapak came through as we were stripping off our clothes. Cristabel knocked on the door to the cockpit and Dave came out, already naked. A bad sign.

"I had to cork 'em," he said. "Bleeding captain just *had* to make his grand march through the plane. I tried *every*thing."

Sometimes you have to do it. The plane was on autopilot, as it normally would be at this time. But if any of us did anything detrimental to the craft, changed the fixed course of events in any way, that would be it. All that work for nothing, and Flight 128 inaccessible to us for all Time. I don't know sludge about time theory, but I know the practical angles. We can do things in the past only at times and in places where it won't make any difference. We have to cover our tracks. There's flexibility; once a Snatcher left her gun behind and it went in with the plane.

Nobody found it, or if they did, they didn't have the smoggiest idea of what it was, so we were okay.

Flight 128 was mechanical failure. That's the best kind; it means we don't have to keep the pilot unaware of the situation in the cabin right down to ground level. We can cork him and fly the plane, since there's nothing he could have done to save the flight anyway. A pilot-error smash is almost impossible to snatch. We mostly work midairs, bombs, and structural failures. If there's even one survivor, we can't touch it. It would not fit the fabric of space-time, which is immutable (though it can stretch a little), and we'd all just fade away and appear back in the ready room.

My head was hurting. I wanted that portapak very badly.

"Who has the most hours on a 707?" Pinky did, so I sent her to the cabin, along with Dave, who could do the pilot's voice for air traffic control. You have to have a believable record in the flight recorder, too. They trailed two long tubes from the portapak, and the rest of us hooked in up close. We stood there, each of us smoking a fistful of cigarettes, wanting to finish them but hoping there wouldn't be time. The gate had vanished as soon as we tossed our clothes and the flight crew through.

But we didn't worry long. There's other nice things about Snatching, but nothing to compare with the rush of plugging into a portapak. The wake-up transfusion is nothing but fresh blood, rich in oxygen and sugars. What we were getting now was an insane brew of concentrated adrenaline, supersaturated hemoglobin, methedrine, white lighting, TNT, and Kickapoo joyjuice. It was like a firecracker in your heart; a boot in the box that rattled your sox.

"I'm growing hair on my chest," Cristabel said solemnly. Everyone giggled.

"Would someone hand me my eyeballs?"

"The blue ones, or the red ones?"

"I think my ass just fell off."

We'd heard them all before, but we howled anyway. We were strong, *strong*, and for one golden moment we had no worries. Everything was hilarious. I could have torn sheet metal with my eyelashes.

But you get hyper on that mix. When the gate didn't show, and didn't show, and *didn't sweetjeez show* we all started milling. This bird wasn't going to fly all that much longer.

Then it did show, and we turned on. The first of the wimps came through, dressed in the clothes taken from a passenger it had been picked to resemble.

"Two thirty-five elapsed upside time," Cristabel announced.

"Je-zuz."

It is a deadening routine. You grab the harness around the wimp's shoulders and drag it along the aisle, after consulting the seat number painted on its forehead.

The paint would last three minutes. You seat it, strap it in, break open the harness and carry it back to toss through the gate as you grab the next one. You have to take it for granted they've done the work right on the other side: fillings in the teeth, fingerprints, the right match in height and weight and hair color. Most of those things don't matter much, especially on Flight 128 which was a crash-and-burn. There would be bits and pieces, and burned to a crisp at that. But you can't take chances. Those rescue workers are pretty thorough on the parts they *do* find; the dental work and fingerprints especially are important.

I hate wimps. I really hate 'em. Every time I grab the harness of one of them, if it's a child, I wonder if it's Alice. *Are you my kid, you vegetable, you slug, you slimy worm?* I joined the Snatchers right after the brain bugs ate the life out of my baby's head. I couldn't stand to think she was the last generation, that the last humans there would ever be would live with nothing in their heads, medically dead by standards that prevailed even in 1979, with computers working their muscles to keep them in tone. You grow up, reach puberty still fertile—one in a thousand—rush to get pregnant in your first heat. Then you find out your mom or pop passed on a chronic disease bound right into the genes, and none of your kids will be immune. I *knew* about the paraleprosy; I grew up with my toes rotting away. But this was too much. What do you do?

Only one in ten of the wimps had a customized face. It takes time and a lot of skill to build a new face that will stand up to a doctor's autopsy. The rest came premutilated. We've got millions of them; it's not hard to find a good match in the body. Most of them would stay breathing, too dumb to stop, until they went in with the plane.

The plane jerked, hard. I glanced at my watch. Five minutes to impact. We should have time. I was on my last wimp. I could hear Dave frantically calling the ground. A bomb came through the gate, and I tossed it into the cockpit. Pinky turned on the pressure sensor on the bomb and came running out, followed by Dave. Liza was already through. I grabbed the limp dolls in stewardess costume and tossed them to the floor. The engine fell off and a piece of it came through the cabin. We started to depressurize. The bomb blew away part of the cockpit (the ground crash crew would read it—we hoped—that part of the engine came through and killed the crew: no more words from the pilot on the flight recorder) and we turned, slowly, left and down. I was lifted toward the hole in the side of the plane, but I managed to hold onto a seat. Cristabel wasn't so lucky. She was blown backwards.

We started to rise slightly, losing speed. Suddenly it was uphill from where Cristabel was lying in the aisle. Blood oozed from her temple. I glanced back; everyone was gone, and three pink-suited wimps were piled on the floor. The plane began to stall, to nose down, and my feet left the floor.

"Come on, Bel!" I screamed. That gate was only three feet away from me, but I began pulling myself along to where she floated. The plane bumped, and she hit the floor. Incredibly, it seemed to wake her up. She started to swim toward me, and I grabbed her hand as the floor came up to slam us again. We crawled as the plane went through its final death agony, and we came to the door. The gate was gone.

There wasn't anything to say. We were going in. It's hard enough to keep the gate in place on a plane that's moving in a straight line. When a bird gets to corkscrewing and coming apart, the math is fearsome. So I've been told.

I embraced Cristabel and held her bloodied head. She was groggy, but managed to smile and shrug. You take what you get. I hurried into the restroom and got both of us down on the floor. Back to the forward bulkhead, Cristabel between my legs, back to front. Just like in training. We pressed our feet against the other wall. I hugged her tightly and cried on her shoulder.

And it was there. A green glow to my left. I threw myself toward it, dragging Cristabel, keeping low as two wimps were thrown headfirst through the gate above our heads. Hands grabbed and pulled us through. I clawed my way a good five yards along the floor. You can leave a leg on the other side and I didn't have one to spare.

I sat up as they were carrying Cristabel to Medical. I patted her arm as she went by on the stretcher, but she was passed out. I wouldn't have minded passing out myself.

For a while, you can't believe it all really happened. Sometimes it turns out it *didn't* happen. You come back and find out all the goats in the holding pen have softly and suddenly vanished away because the continuum won't tolerate the changes and paradoxes you've put into it. The people you've worked so hard to rescue are spread like tomato surprise all over some goddam hillside in Carolina and all you've got left is a bunch of ruined wimps and an exhausted Snatch Team. But not this time. I could see the goats milling around in the holding pen, naked and more bewildered than ever. And just starting to be *really* afraid.

Elfreda touched me as I passed her. She nodded, which meant well-done in her limited repertoire of gestures. I shrugged, wondering if I cared, but the surplus adrenaline was still in my veins and I found myself grinning at her. I nodded back.

Gene was standing by the holding pen. I went to him, hugged him. I felt the juices start to flow. *Damn it, let's squander a little ration and have us a good time.*

Someone was beating on the sterile glass wall of the pen. She shouted, mouthing angry words at us. *Why? What have you done to us?* It was Mary Sondergard. She implored her bald, one-legged twin to make her understand. She thought she had problems. God, was she pretty. I hated her guts.

Gene pulled me away from the wall. My hands hurt, and I'd broken off all my fake nails without scratching the glass. She was sitting on the floor now, sobbing. I heard the voice of the briefing officer on the outside speaker.

". . . Centauri Three is hospitable, with an Earth-like climate. By that, I mean *your* Earth, not what it has become. You'll see more of that later. The trip will take five years, shiptime. Upon landfall, you will be entitled to one horse, a plow, three axes, two hundred kilos of seed grain . . ."

I leaned against Gene's shoulder. At their lowest ebb, this very moment, they were so much better than us. I had maybe ten years, half of that as a basket case. They are our best, our very brightest hope. Everything is up to them.

". . . that no one will be forced to go. We wish to point out again, not for the last time, that you would all be dead without our intervention. There are things you should know, however. You cannot breathe our air. If you remain on Earth, you can never leave this building. We are not like you. We are the result of a genetic winnowing, a mutation process. We are the survivors, but our enemies have evolved along with us. They are winning. You, however, are immune to the diseases that afflict us . . ."

I winced and turned away.

". . . the other hand, if you emigrate you will be given a chance at a new life. It won't be easy, but as Americans you should be proud of your pioneer heritage. Your ancestors survived, and so will you. It can be a rewarding experience, and I urge you . . ."

Sure. Gene and I looked at each other and laughed. *Listen to this, folks. Five percent of you will suffer nervous breakdowns in the next few days, and never leave. About the same number will commit suicide, here and on the way. When you get there, sixty to seventy percent will die in the first three years. You will die in childbirth, be eaten by animals, bury two out of three of your babies, starve slowly when the rains don't come. If you live, it will be to break your back behind a plow, sun-up to dusk. New Earth is Heaven, folks!*

God, how I wish I could go with them.

INTRODUCTION TO

"The Persistence of Vision"

The next three stories have very little in common. Only two things that I can think of, actually. For one, all three were given one or both of the two major science fiction awards: the Hugo, given out annually at the World Science Fiction Convention and voted on by the convention membership—the readers themselves—or the Nebula, awarded by the Science Fiction Writers of America—the professionals.

Awards are something people seem to like, judging from how many fields of human endeavor give them out. Getting awards is gratifying, unless you are a curmudgeon on the scale of George C. Scott or Marlon Brando. But they are right, you know. Humphrey Bogart pointed out that it was ridiculous to compare performances in different roles. Some are hard, some are easy, some don't require much acting at all, which is good, because many Hollywood stars can't really "act" much. Friends vote for friends. People spend money campaigning for votes.

Bogey suggested that all actors perform in the same vehicle, like Hamlet, and then let the matter be decided by a panel of judges. Makes sense to me.

I said the stories had two things in common. The other is something I've begun to call "The P Factor." All of my Hugo and Nebula stories begin with the letter P.

Means nothing, of course. But I can't help wondering, especially when you add in the fact that the closest any of my other works ever came to winning the Hugo was "The Phantom of Kansas," which I'm told lost the award because I happened to have two stories on the final ballot that year. (Of course, the story that won was pretty good, too.) (Very good; it was "The Bicentennial Man," by Isaac Asimov.)

Shortly after I got started writing short stories Thomas M. Disch wrote an editorial somewhere (I can't recall which magazine it was in) about what he called "The Labor Day Group." This was a bunch of writers, not an actual conspiracy but just those of us whose careers started in the seventies—Vonda McIntyre was in it, and Spider Robinson, and myself and half a dozen others. His thesis was that we always had the Hugo Award in our minds when we set out to write a story. He accused us of more or less "pandering" to the Hugo voters, which is, admittedly, a rather small *proportion of the mass of science fiction readers, the ones who pay the money to join the World Science Fiction Convention in any particular year and thus are eligible to vote on the Hugo Awards. The Worldcon is held in a different city every year, and nowadays has grown to five thousand attendees or more. It is held on the Labor Day weekend. Thus, Disch's term came from the fact that we came out of organized fandom, that we could all be found together on Labor Day because we'd never miss a Worldcon. There we presumably exchanged tips on just what the Hugo voters wanted in an SF story. Not too stylistically challenging, uplifting rather than depressing, concerned more with a positive outlook on life rather than existential angst. That sort of thing.*

First, let me say that at the time of the editorial I had never been to a Worldcon. To this day I've only been to two of them.

And second, since it's considered bad taste to campaign for a Hugo, and since nobody I know has the budget to flood the airwaves with promos like we saw last year for Chicago *and I'm seeing right now for* Cold Mountain, *the only way I know of to pander to Hugo voters is to write a good story. I'll admit, when I finish one I picture myself standing up on a podium somewhere accepting that silver rocketship . . . but I've never had that thought beforehand, or while writing.*

Sorry. Just had to get that off my chest. And like I said, awards are meaningless in the end. Who needs them?

Now I have to get back to work on my next novel, which will be a sequel to my recent book Red Thunder. *I've decided I'll have a color on the title, like John D. MacDonald did with the Travis McGee books. Right now I'm divided. How about* Purple Thunder? Pink Thunder?

Puce, Petunia, Poppy, Peppermint, Periwinkle . . .

I've known several blind people in my life. The first was Elmer, who ran the news and candy and cigar stand in the post office in Corsicana, Texas, where my grandparents lived. When I was in town, Granddaddy and I would walk a few blocks to the post office every day to get the mail, and we'd always stop and talk to Elmer. Elmer would put his hand on my head to see how much I'd grown (usually a lot; I finally topped out at six-foot-six). I spent many pleasant afternoons there, sitting and reading the comics and SF magazines. The only things I have ever stolen in my life were SF paperbacks, but I never shoplifted from Elmer. Not even the SF monkey on my back could have driven me that low . . . and besides, I was far from sure Elmer wouldn't hear me slipping the book into my jeans. He was that *good.*

Corsicana was my refuge from the miseries of the Gulf Coast when I was growing up. I spent large parts of my summers there, and my family did the four-hour drive—one way; that's nothing in Texas—at least one weekend a month, usually two. It was paradise for a small boy. There was a park with a dozen weird, zany, one-of-a-kind pieces of play equipment made entirely of rusty iron and splintery wood that must have been designed by a mad child-hating engineer. Just looking at them would make a personal injury attorney drool like a Pavlov dog. Any one of them could pinch off a finger in a second. I loved playing on those things. Last time I was back it was all gone, replaced by soft, harmless plastic stuff. Ralph Nader had come to Corsicana . . . and ruined it. I swear, this generation is a bunch of fraidy-cats.

But the best thing by far about Corsicana was Granddaddy's store. It was a five-and-ten, part of the chain called Duke & Ayres, which you've probably not heard of unless you're from Texas. It was like Woolworth's, only smaller and cheaper. It was long and narrow with a high tin ceiling and only two aisles between the wooden counters. The female sales force would stand behind the counters and wait on you.

There were newfangled fluorescent fixtures hanging from the ceiling, which you had to turn on individually. I used to sit on Granddaddy's shoulders and pull the strings as he took me down one aisle and up the other. After five minutes of flickering, we had light. When I got big enough I ran down the aisles every morning at seven, jumping up to pull them. In the summer there were ceiling fans to turn on, too.

Upstairs wasn't used, and it would have been a good setting for a Stephen King story. It was a series of rooms connected in no logical way that had at one time been professional offices. Probably back in the oil boom, the twenties. Corsicana had been bigger then. Now the second floor was used for storage, and in a five-and-ten that meant you could find anything up there. Anything. There were old dental chairs with blood still drying on the spit sinks. There were heaps of old magazines and newspapers, metal greeting card racks, piles of postcards and glass and a glass cutting table, old clothes from the turn of the century, acres of cobwebs. It all smelled of spiders and mouse turds, must, mold, mildew, and dry rot. There were dust bunnies the size of Bengal tigers. There was no lighting, and we deemed it "no fair" to bring a flashlight. In short, a paradise for children.

Most of all, there were the mannequins. Some were full-sized, bald, and naked (and sexless, of course; no nipples on the breasts in those days). A few had clothes. They all moved there in the darkness when you turned your back. If that wasn't good enough, there were the body parts. Boxes overflowing with severed arms, legs, heads, and torsos. You could put them together, you could take them apart, violently. You can forget your FAO Schwartz and your kindergarten storytime. That attic was the place to come up with stories, and me and my friends came up with ones that would curl Dr. Frankenstein's toes.

Granddaddy sold just about everything in that store, and at the cheapest prices in town. A large part of his customer base was the Negro population, who literally lived *on the other side of the tracks, so I knew a lot more black people than your typical Texas white boy of that day and age. And every year he outsold the much larger local Woolworth's and Newberry's. He sold more eyeglasses than the optometrist, Dr. Jungermann. There was a candy counter with fifty kinds of tooth poison heaped up in big vertical glass cases. I was allowed to sample anything I wanted, and later helped scoop it out for sale by the pennyworth. There was a long toy counter. I spent most of my time on the floor back there, the salesladies stepping over me as I performed the critical, vital, exacting job of product testing, making sure each item was truly play-worthy. Nasty work, but somebody's got to do it. I was also in charge of quality control. See, if something was broken in shipping Granddaddy noted the fact, informed the manufacturer so he wouldn't have to pay for it . . . and then gave it to me or my sisters. Broken? Big deal. It was going to be trashed by us playing hard with it soon enough anyway, so who cared if it started off slightly chipped? Christmas morning at Granddaddy's could rival the displays at Neiman's in Dallas, that's how much broken stuff we got.*

None of this except the part about Elmer has anything to do with the story that follows, but I just couldn't turn this book in without mentioning Corsicana.

I could be mistaken, but I think Tom Disch may have used the following story, "The Persistence of Vision," as a case in point of Labor Day Group machinations or whatever to win a Hugo Award. If so, it worked. And if so, so be it. I am more proud of this story than of anything I have written before or since. Yet, as I have heard some authors say before, I don't feel entirely responsible for it. I can pinpoint the source: a newspaper story about a generation of children growing up blind and deaf because their mothers contracted rubella while pregnant. A tremendous bump in the population of deaf-mutes was on its way, much like the Baby Boom, and there simply weren't enough people around who could cope with their special needs. I don't know what became of them—I suspect that most of them managed to do a lot in spite of their handicaps, because the human animal is an almost infinitely adaptable thing—but their plight inspired this story. Then it more or less wrote itself, and by the end I was crying, and I didn't know why. Frankly, I had no idea where it came from, but I'd like to do it again, every night.

I have had more response to this story, both in letters and in person, than to anything else I ever wrote. It's one of those things of which people say, "It changed my life." I can't tell you how great that makes me feel. It was written during the time of the growth of the disability rights movement, before there were parking places and special rest room stalls for the handicapped. Many, but by no means all, of the people who thanked me for writing it were disabled. It seems to touch people deeply.

I hope it touches you.

THE PERSISTENCE OF VISION

I T WAS THE year of the fourth non-depression. I had recently joined the ranks of the unemployed. The President had told me that I had nothing to fear but fear itself. I took him at his word, for once, and set out to backpack to California.

I was not the only one. The world's economy had been writhing like a snake on a hot griddle for the last twenty years, since the early seventies. We were in a boom-and-bust cycle that seemed to have no end. It had wiped out the sense of security the nation had so painfully won in the golden years after the thirties. People were accustomed to the fact that they could be rich one year and on the breadlines the next. I was on the breadlines in '81, and again in '88. This time I decided to use my freedom from the time clock to see the world. I had ideas of stowing away to Japan. I was forty-seven years old and might not get another chance to be irresponsible.

This was in late summer of the year. Sticking out my thumb along the interstate, I could easily forget that there were food riots back in Chicago. I slept at night on top of my bedroll and saw stars and listened to crickets.

I must have walked most of the way from Chicago to Des Moines. My feet toughened up after a few days of awful blisters. The rides were scarce, partly competition from other hitchhikers and partly the times we were living in. The locals were none too anxious to give rides to city people, who they had heard were mostly a bunch of hunger-crazed potential mass murderers. I got roughed up once and told never to return to Sheffield, Illinois.

But I gradually learned the knack of living on the road. I had started with a small supply of canned goods from the welfare and by the time they ran out, I had found that it was possible to work for a meal at many of the farmhouses along the way.

Some of it was hard work, some of it was only a token from people with a deeply ingrained sense that nothing should come for free. A few meals were gratis, at the family table, with grandchildren sitting around while grandpa or grandma told oft-repeated tales of what it had been like in the Big One back in '29, when people had not been afraid to help a fellow out when he was down on his luck. I found that the older the person, the more likely I was to get a sympathetic ear. One of the many tricks you learn. And most older people will give you anything if you'll only sit and listen to them. I got very good at it.

The rides began to pick up west of Des Moines, then got bad again as I neared the refugee camps bordering the China Strip. This was only five years after the disaster, remember, when the Omaha nuclear reactor melted down and a hot mass of uranium and plutonium began eating its way into the earth, headed for China, spreading a band of radioactivity six hundred kilometers downwind. Most of Kansas City, Missouri, was still living in plywood and sheet-metal shantytowns till the city was rendered habitable again.

The refugees were a tragic group. The initial solidarity people show after a great disaster had long since faded into the lethargy and disillusionment of the displaced person. Many of them would be in and out of hospitals for the rest of their lives. To make it worse, the local people hated them, feared them, would not associate with them. They were modern pariahs, unclean. Their children were shunned. Each camp had only a number to identify it, but the local populace called them all Geigertowns.

I made a long detour to Little Rock to avoid crossing the Strip, though it was safe now as long as you didn't linger. I was issued a pariah's badge by the National Guard—a dosimeter—and wandered from one Geigertown to the next. The people were pitifully friendly once I made the first move, and I always slept indoors. The food was free at the community messes.

Once at Little Rock, I found that the aversion to picking up strangers—who might be tainted with "radiation disease"—dropped off, and I quickly moved across Arkansas, Oklahoma, and Texas. I worked a little here and there, but many of the rides were long. What I saw of Texas was through a car window.

I was a little tired of that by the time I reached New Mexico. I decided to do some more walking. By then I was less interested in California than in the trip itself.

I left the roads and went cross-country where there were no fences to stop me. I found that it wasn't easy, even in New Mexico, to get far from signs of civilization.

Taos was the center, back in the '60's, of cultural experiments in alternative living. Many communes and cooperatives were set up in the surrounding hills during that time. Most of them fell apart in a few months or years, but a few survived. In later years, any group with a new theory of living and a yen to try it out seemed to gravitate to that part of New Mexico. As a result, the land was dotted with ramshackle windmills, solar heating panels, geodesic domes, group marriages, nudists, philosophers, theoreticians, messiahs, hermits, and more than a few just plain nuts.

Taos was great. I could drop into most of the communes and stay for a day or a week, eating organic rice and beans and drinking goat's milk. When I got tired of one, a few hours' walk in any direction would bring me to another. There, I might be offered a night of prayer and chanting or a ritualistic orgy. Some of the groups had spotless barns with automatic milkers for the herds of cows. Others didn't even have latrines; they just squatted. In some, the members dressed like nuns, or Quakers in early Pennsylvania. Elsewhere, they went nude and shaved all their body hair and painted themselves purple. There were all-male and all-female groups. I was urged to stay at most of the former; at the latter, the responses ranged from a bed for the night and good conversation to being met at a barbed-wire fence with a shotgun.

I tried not to make judgments. These people were doing something important, all of them. They were testing ways whereby people didn't have to live in Chicago. That was a wonder to me. I had thought Chicago was inevitable, like diarrhea.

This is not to say they were all successful. Some made Chicago look like Shangri-La. There was one group who seemed to feel that getting back to nature consisted of sleeping in pigshit and eating food a buzzard wouldn't touch. Many were obviously doomed. They would leave behind a group of empty hovels and the memory of cholera.

So the place wasn't paradise, not by a long way. But there were successes. One or two had been there since '63 or '64 and were raising their third generation. I was disappointed to see that most of these were the ones that departed least from established norms of behavior, though some of the differences could be startling. I suppose the most radical experiments are the least likely to bear fruit.

I stayed through the winter. No one was surprised to see me a second time. It seems that many people came to Taos and shopped around. I seldom stayed more than three weeks at any one place, and always pulled my weight. I made many friends and picked up skills that would serve me if I stayed off the roads. I toyed with the idea of staying at one of them forever. When I couldn't make up my mind, I was advised that there was no hurry. I could go to California and return. They seemed sure I would.

So when spring came I headed west over the hills. I stayed off the roads and slept in the open. Many nights I would stay at another commune, until they finally began to get farther apart, then tapered off entirely. The country was not as pretty as before.

Then, three days' leisurely walking from the last commune, I came to a wall.

In 1964, in the United States, there was an epidemic of German measles, or rubella. Rubella is one of the mildest of infectious diseases. The only time it's a problem is when a woman contracts it in the first four months of her pregnancy. It is passed to the fetus, which usually develops complications. These complications include deafness, blindness, and damage to the brain.

In 1964, in the old days before abortion became readily available, there was nothing to be done about it. Many pregnant women caught rubella and went to term. Five thousand deaf-blind children were born in one year. The normal yearly incidence of deaf-blind children in the United States is one hundred and forty.

In 1970 these five thousand potential Helen Kellers were all six years old. It was quickly seen that there was a shortage of Anne Sullivans. Previously, deaf-blind children could be sent to a small number of special institutions.

It was a problem. Not just anyone can cope with a blind-deaf child. You can't tell them to shut up when they moan; you can't reason with them, tell them that the moaning is driving you crazy. Some parents were driven to nervous break-downs when they tried to keep their children at home.

Many of the five thousand were badly retarded and virtually impossible to reach, even if anyone had been trying. These ended up, for the most part, ware-housed in the hundreds of anonymous nursing homes and institutes for "special" children. They were put into beds, cleaned up once a day by a few overworked nurses, and generally allowed the full blessings of liberty: they were allowed to rot freely in their own dark, quiet, private universes. Who can say if it was bad for them? None of them were heard to complain.

Many children with undamaged brains were shuffled in among the retarded because they were unable to tell anyone that they were in there behind the sightless eyes. They failed the batteries of tactile tests, unaware that their fates hung in the balance when they were asked to fit round pegs into round holes to the ticking of a clock they could not see or hear. As a result, they spent the rest of their lives in bed, and none of them complained, either. To protest, one must be aware of the possi-bility of something better. It helps to have a language, too.

Several hundred of the children were found to have IQ's within the normal range. There were news stories about them as they approached puberty and it was revealed that there were not enough good people to properly handle them. Money was spent, teachers were trained. The education expenditures would go on for a specified period of time, until the children were grown, then things would go back to normal and everyone could congratulate themselves on having dealt success-fully with a tough problem.

And indeed, it did work fairly well. There are ways to reach and teach such children. They involve patience, love, and dedication, and the teachers brought all that to their jobs. All the graduates of the special schools left knowing how to speak with their hands. Some could talk. A few could write. Most of them left the institutions to live with parents or relatives, or, if neither was possible, received counseling and help in fitting themselves into society. The options were limited, but people can live rewarding lives under the most severe handicaps. Not every-one, but most of the graduates, were as happy with their lot as could reasonably be expected. Some achieved the almost saintly peace of their role model, Helen Keller.

Others became bitter and withdrawn. A few had to be put in asylums, where they became indistinguishable from the others of their group who had spent the last twenty years there. But for the most part, they did well.

But among the group, as in any group, were some misfits. They tended to be among the brightest, the top ten percent in the IQ scores. This was not a reliable rule. Some had unremarkable test scores and were still infected with the hunger to do something, to change things, to rock the boat. With a group of five thousand, there were certain to be a few geniuses, a few artists, a few dreamers, hell-raisers, individualists, movers and shapers: a few glorious maniacs.

There was one among them who might have been President but for the fact that she was blind, deaf, and a woman. She was smart, but not one of the geniuses. She was a dreamer, a creative force, an innovator. It was she who dreamed of freedom. But she was not a builder of fairy castles. Having dreamed it, she had to make it come true.

The wall was made of carefully fitted stone and was about five feet high. It was completely out of context with anything I had seen in New Mexico, though it was built of native rock. You just don't build that kind of wall out there. You use barbed wire if something needs fencing in, but many people still made use of the free range and brands. Somehow it seemed transplanted from New England.

It was substantial enough that I felt it would be unwise to crawl over it. I had crossed many wire fences in my travels and had not gotten in trouble for it yet, though I had some talks with some ranchers. Mostly they told me to keep moving, but didn't seem upset about it. This was different. I set out to walk around it. From the lay of the land, I couldn't tell how far it might reach, but I had time.

At the top of the next rise I saw that I didn't have far to go. The wall made a right-angle turn just ahead. I looked over it and could see some buildings. They were mostly domes, the ubiquitous structure thrown up by communes because of the combination of ease of construction and durability. There were sheep behind the wall, and a few cows. They grazed on grass so green I wanted to go over and roll in it. The wall enclosed a rectangle of green. Outside, where I stood, it was all scrub and sage. These people had access to Rio Grande irrigation water.

I rounded the corner and followed the wall west again.

I saw a man on horseback about the same time he spotted me. He was south of me, outside the wall, and he turned and rode in my direction.

He was a dark man with thick features, dressed in denim and boots with a gray battered stetson. Navaho, maybe. I don't know much about Indians, but I'd heard they were out here.

"Hello," I said when he'd stopped. He was looking me over. "Am I on your land?"

"Tribal land," he said. "Yeah, you're on it."

"I didn't see any signs."

He shrugged.

"It's okay, bud. You don't look like you out to rustle cattle." He grinned at me. His teeth were large and stained with tobacco. "You be camping out tonight?"

"Yes. How much farther does the, uh, tribal land go? Maybe I'll be out of it before tonight?"

He shook his head gravely. "Nah. You won't be off it tomorrow. 'S all right. You make a fire, you be careful, huh?" He grinned again and started to ride off.

"Hey, what is this place?" I gestured to the wall and he pulled his horse up and turned around again. It raised a lot of dust.

"Why you asking?" He looked a little suspicious.

"I dunno. Just curious. It doesn't look like the other places I've been to. This wall . . ."

He scowled. "Damn wall." Then he shrugged. I thought that was all he was going to say. Then he went on.

"These people, we look out for 'em, you hear? Maybe we don't go for what they're doin'. But they got it rough, you know?" He looked at me, expecting something. I never did get the knack of talking to these laconic Westerners. I always felt that I was making my sentences too long. They use a shorthand of grunts and shrugs and omitted parts of speech, and I always felt like a dude when I talked to them.

"Do they welcome guests?" I asked. "I thought I might see if I could spend the night."

He shrugged again, and it was a whole different gesture.

"Maybe. They all deaf and blind, you know?" And that was all the conversation he could take for the day. He made a clucking sound and galloped away.

I continued down the wall until I came to a dirt road that wound up the arroyo and entered the wall. There was a wooden gate, but it stood open. I wondered why they took all the trouble with the wall only to leave the gate like that. Then I noticed a circle of narrow-gauge train tracks that came out of the gate, looped around outside it, and rejoined itself. There was a small siding that ran along the outer wall for a few yards.

I stood there a few moments. I don't know what entered into my decision. I think I was a little tired of sleeping out, and I was hungry for a home-cooked meal. The sun was getting closer to the horizon. The land to the west looked like more of the same. If the highway had been visible, I might have headed that way and hitched a ride. But I turned the other way and went through the gate.

I walked down the middle of the tracks. There was a wooden fence on each side of the road, built of horizontal planks, like a corral. Sheep grazed on one side of me. There was a Shetland sheepdog with them, and she raised her ears and followed me with her eyes as I passed, but did not come when I whistled.

It was about half a mile to the cluster of buildings ahead. There were four or five domes made of something translucent, like greenhouses, and several conventional square buildings. There were two windmills turning lazily in the breeze. There were several banks of solar water heaters. These are flat constructions of glass and wood, held off the ground so they can tilt to follow the sun. They were almost vertical now, intercepting the oblique rays of sunset. There were a few trees, what might have been an orchard.

About halfway there I passed under a wooden footbridge. It arched over the road, giving access from the east pasture to the west pasture. I wondered, what was wrong with a simple gate?

Then I saw something coming down the road in my direction. It was traveling on the tracks and it was very quiet. I stopped and waited.

It was a sort of converted mining engine, the sort that pulls loads of coal up from the bottom of shafts. It was battery-powered, and it had gotten quite close before I heard it. A small man was driving it. He was pulling a car behind him and singing as loud as he could with absolutely no sense of pitch.

He got closer and closer, moving about five miles per hour, one hand held out as if he was signaling a left turn. Suddenly I realized what was happening, as he was bearing down on me. He wasn't going to stop. He was counting fenceposts with his hand. I scrambled up the fence just in time. There wasn't more than six inches of clearance between the train and the fence on either side. His palm touched my leg as I squeezed close to the fence, and he stopped abruptly.

He leaped from the car and grabbed me and I thought I was in trouble. But he looked concerned, not angry, and felt me all over, trying to discover if I was hurt. I was embarrassed. Not from the examination; because I had been foolish. The Indian had said they were all deaf and blind but I guess I hadn't quite believed him.

He was flooded with relief when I managed to convey to him that I was all right. With eloquent gestures he made me understand that I was not to stay on the road. He indicated that I should climb over the fence and continue through the fields. He repeated himself several times to be sure I understood, then held on to me as I climbed over to assure himself that I was out of the way. He reached over the fence and held my shoulders, smiling at me. He pointed to the road and shook his head, then pointed to the building and nodded. He touched my head and smiled when I nodded. He climbed back onto the engine and started up, all the time nodding and pointing where he wanted me to go. Then he was off again.

I debated what to do. Most of me said to turn around, go back to the wall by way of the pasture and head back into the hills. These people probably wouldn't want me around. I doubted that I'd be able to talk to them, and they might even resent me. On the other hand, I was fascinated, as who wouldn't be? I wanted to see how they managed it. I still didn't believe that they were *all* deaf and blind. It didn't seem possible.

The Sheltie was sniffing at my pants. I looked down at her and she backed away, then daintily approached me as I held out my open hand. She sniffed, then licked me. I patted her on the head, and she hustled back to her sheep.

I turned toward the buildings.

The first order of business was money.

None of the students knew much about it from experience, but the library was full of Braille books. They started reading.

One of the first things that became apparent was that when money was mentioned, lawyers were not far away. The students wrote letters. From the replies, they selected a lawyer and retained him.

They were in a school in Pennsylvania at the time. The original pupils of the special schools, five hundred in number, had been narrowed down to about seventy as people left to live with relatives or found other solutions to their special problems. Of those seventy, some had places to go but didn't want to go there; others had few alternatives. Their parents were either dead or not interested in living with them. So the seventy had been gathered from the schools around the country into this one, while ways to deal with them were worked out. The authorities had plans, but the students beat them to it.

Each of them had been entitled to a guaranteed annual income since 1980. They had been under the care of the government, so they had not received it. They sent their lawyer to court. He came back with a ruling that they could not collect. They appealed, and won. The money was paid retroactively, with interest, and came to a healthy sum. They thanked their lawyer and retained a real estate agent. Meanwhile, they read.

They read about communes in New Mexico, and instructed their agent to look for something out there. He made a deal for a tract to be leased in perpetuity from the Navaho nation. They read about the land, found that it would need a lot of water to be productive in the way they wanted it to be.

They divided into groups to research what they would need to be self-sufficient.

Water could be obtained by tapping into the canals that carried it from the reservoirs on the Rio Grande into the reclaimed land in the south. Federal money was available for the project through a labyrinthine scheme involving HEW, the Agriculture Department, and the Bureau of Indian Affairs. They ended up paying little for their pipeline.

The land was arid. It would need fertilizer to be of use in raising sheep without resorting to open range techniques. The cost of fertilizer could be subsidized through the Rural Resettlement Program. After that, planting clover would enrich the soil with all the nitrates they could want.

There were techniques available to farm ecologically, without worrying about fertilizers or pesticides. Everything was recycled. Essentially, you put sunlight and water into one end and harvested wool, fish, vegetables, apples, honey, and eggs at the other end. You used nothing but the land, and replaced even that as you recycled your waste products back into the soil. They were not interested in agribusiness with huge combine harvesters and crop dusters. They didn't even want to turn a profit. They merely wanted sufficiency.

The details multiplied. Their leader, the one who had had the original idea and the drive to put it into action in the face of overwhelming obstacles, was a dynamo named Janet Reilly. Knowing nothing about the techniques generals and executives employ to achieve large objectives, she invented them herself and adapted them to the peculiar needs and limitations of her group. She assigned task forces to look into solutions of each aspect of their project: law, science, social planning, design, buying, logistics, construction. At any one time, she was the only person who knew everything about what was happening. She kept it all in her head, without notes of any kind.

It was in the area of social planning that she showed herself to be a visionary and not just a superb organizer. Her idea was not to make a place where they could lead a life that was a sightless, soundless imitation of their unafflicted peers. She wanted a whole new start, a way of living that was by and for the blind-deaf, a way of living that accepted no convention just because that was the way it had always been done. She examined every human cultural institution from marriage to indecent exposure to see how it related to her needs and the needs of her friends. She was aware of the peril of this approach, but was undeterred. Her Social Task Force read about every variant group that had ever tried to make it on its own anywhere, and brought her reports about how and why they had failed or succeeded. She filtered this information through her own experiences to see how it would work for her unusual group with its own set of needs and goals.

The details were endless. They hired an architect to put their ideas into Braille blueprints. Gradually the plans evolved. They spent more money. The construction began, supervised on the site by their architect, who by now was so fascinated by the scheme that she donated her services. It was an important break, for they needed someone there whom they could trust. There is only so much that can be accomplished at such a distance.

When things were ready for them to move, they ran into bureaucratic trouble. They had anticipated it, but it was a setback. Social agencies charged with overseeing their welfare doubted the wisdom of the project. When it became apparent that no amount of reasoning was going to stop it, wheels were set in motion that resulted in a restraining order, issued for their own protection, preventing them from leaving the school. They were twenty-one years old by then, all of them, but were judged mentally incompetent to manage their own affairs. A hearing was scheduled.

Luckily, they still had access to their lawyer. He also had become infected with the crazy vision, and put on a great battle for them. He succeeded in getting a ruling concerning the right of institutionalized persons, later upheld by the Supreme Court, which eventually had severe repercussions in state and county hospitals. Realizing the trouble they were already in regarding the thousands of patients in inadequate facilities across the country, the agencies gave in.

By then, it was the spring of 1986, one year after their target date. Some of their fertilizer had washed away already for lack of erosion-preventing clover. It was getting late to start crops, and they were running short of money. Nevertheless, they moved to New Mexico and began the backbreaking job of getting everything started. There were fifty-five of them, with nine children aged three months to six years.

I don't know what I expected. I remember that everything was a surprise, either because it was so normal or because it was so different. None of my idiot surmises about what such a place might be like proved to be true. And of course I didn't know the history of the place; I learned that later, picked up in bits and pieces.

I was surprised to see lights in some of the buildings. The first thing I had assumed was that they would have no need of them. That's an example of something so normal that it surprised me.

As to the differences, the first thing that caught my attention was the fence around the rail line. I had a personal interest in it, having almost been injured by it. I struggled to understand, as I must if I was to stay even for a night.

The wood fences that enclosed the rails on their way to the gate continued up to a barn, where the rails looped back on themselves in the same way they did outside the wall. The entire line was enclosed by the fence. The only access was a loading platform by the barn, and the gate to the outside. It made sense. The only way a deaf-blind person could operate a conveyance like that would be with assurances that there was no one on the track. These people would *never* go on the tracks; there was no way they could be warned of an approaching train.

There were people moving around me in the twilight as I made my way into the group of buildings. They took no notice of me, as I had expected. They moved fast; some of them were actually running. I stood still, eyes searching all around me so no one would come crashing into me. I had to figure out how they kept from crashing into each other before I got bolder.

I bent to the ground and examined it. The light was getting bad, but I saw immediately that there were concrete sidewalks crisscrossing the area. Each of the walks was etched with a different sort of pattern in grooves that had been made before the stuff set—lines, waves, depressions, patches of rough and smooth. I quickly saw that the people who were in a hurry moved only on those walkways, and they were all barefoot. It was no trick to see that it was some sort of traffic pattern read with the feet. I stood up. I didn't need to know how it worked. It was sufficient to know what it was and stay off the paths.

The people were unremarkable. Some of them were not dressed, but I was used to that by now. They came in all shapes and sizes, but all seemed to be about the same age except for the children. Except for the fact that they did not stop and talk or even wave as they approached each other, I would never have guessed they were blind. I watched them come to intersections in the pathways—I didn't know how they knew they were there, but could think of several ways—and slow down as they crossed. It was a marvelous system.

I began to think of approaching someone. I had been there for almost half an hour, an intruder. I guess I had a false sense of these people's vulnerability; I felt like a burglar.

I walked along beside a woman for a minute. She was very purposeful in her eyes-ahead stride, or seemed to be. She sensed something, maybe my footsteps. She slowed a little, and I touched her on the shoulder, not knowing what else to do. She stopped instantly and turned toward me. Her eyes were open but vacant. Her hands were all over me, lightly touching my face, my chest, my hands, fingering my clothing. There was no doubt in my mind that she knew me for a stranger, probably from the first tap on the shoulder. But she smiled warmly at me, and hugged me. Her hands were very delicate and warm. That's funny, because they were calloused from hard work. But they felt sensitive.

She made me to understand—by pointing to the building, making eating motions with an imaginary spoon, and touching a number on her watch—that supper was served in an hour, and that I was invited. I nodded and smiled beneath her hands; she kissed me on the cheek and hurried off.

Well. It hadn't been so bad. I had worried about my ability to communicate. Later I found out she learned a great deal more about me than I had told.

I put off going into the mess hall or whatever it was. I strolled around in the gathering darkness looking at their layout. I saw the little Sheltie bringing the sheep back to the fold for the night. She herded them expertly through the open gate without any instructions, and one of the residents closed it and locked them in.

The man bent and scratched the dog on the head and got his hand licked. Her chores done for the night, the dog hurried over to me and sniffed my pant leg. She followed me around the rest of the evening.

Everyone seemed so busy that I was surprised to see one woman sitting on a rail fence, doing nothing. I went over to her.

Closer, I saw that she was younger than I had thought. She was thirteen, I learned later. She wasn't wearing any clothes. I touched her on the shoulder, and she jumped down from the fence and went through the same routine as the other woman had, touching me all over with no reserve. She took my hand and I felt her fingers moving rapidly in my palm. I couldn't understand it, but knew what it was. I shrugged, and tried out other gestures to indicate that I didn't speak hand talk. She nodded, still feeling my face with her hands.

She asked me if I was staying to dinner. I assured her that I was. She asked me if I was from a university. And if you think that's easy to ask with only body movements, try it. But she was so graceful and supple in her movements, so deft at getting her meaning across. It was beautiful to watch her. It was speech and ballet at the same time.

I told her I wasn't from a university, and launched into an attempt to tell her a little about what I was doing and how I got there. She listened to me with her hands, scratching her head graphically when I failed to make my meanings clear. All the time the smile on her face got broader and broader, and she would laugh silently at my antics. All this while standing very close to me, touching me. At last she put her hands on her hips.

"I guess you need the practice," she said, "but if it's all the same to you, could we talk mouthtalk for now? You're cracking me up."

I jumped as if stung by a bee. The touching, while something I could ignore from a deaf-blind girl, suddenly seemed out of place. I stepped back a little, but her hands returned to me. She looked puzzled, then read the problem with her hands.

"I'm sorry," she said. "You thought I was deaf and blind. If I'd known I would have told you right off."

"I thought everyone here was."

"Just the parents. I'm one of the children. We all hear and see quite well. Don't be so nervous. If you can't stand touching, you're not going to like it here. Relax, I won't hurt you." And she kept her hands moving over me, mostly my face. I didn't understand it at the time, but it didn't seem sexual. Turned out I was wrong, but it wasn't blatant.

"You'll need me to show you the ropes," she said, and started for the domes. She held my hand and walked close to me. Her other hand kept moving to my face every time I talked.

"Number one, stay off the concrete paths. That's where—"

"I already figured that out."

"You did? How long have you been here?" Her hands searched my face with renewed interest. It was quite dark.

"Less than an hour. I was almost run over by your train."

She laughed, then apologized and said she knew it wasn't funny to me.

I told her it *was* funny to me now, though it hadn't been at the time. She said there was a warning sign on the gate, but I had been unlucky enough to come when the gate was open—they opened it by remote control before a train started up—and I hadn't seen it.

"What's your name?" I asked her, as we neared the soft yellow lights coming from the dining room.

Her hand worked reflexively in mine, then stopped. "Oh, I don't know. I *have* one; several, in fact. But they're in bodytalk. I'm . . . Pink. It translates as Pink, I guess."

There was a story behind it. She had been the first child born to the school students. They knew that babies were described as being pink, so they called her that. She felt pink to them. As we entered the hall, I could see that her name was visually inaccurate. One of her parents had been black. She was dark, with blue eyes and curly hair lighter than her skin. She had a broad nose, but small lips.

She didn't ask my name, so I didn't offer it. No one asked my name, in speech, the entire time I was there. They called me many things in bodytalk, and when the children called me it was "Hey, you!" They weren't big on spoken words.

The dining hall was in a rectangular building made of brick. It connected to one of the large domes. It was dimly lighted. I later learned that the lights were for me alone. The children didn't need them for anything but reading. I held Pink's hand, glad to have a guide. I kept my eyes and ears open.

"We're informal," Pink said. Her voice was embarrassingly loud in the large room. No one else was talking at all; there were just the sounds of movement and breathing. Several of the children looked up. "I won't introduce you around now. Just feel like part of the family. People will feel you later, and you can talk to them. You can take your clothes off here at the door."

I had no trouble with that. Everyone else was nude, and I could easily adjust to household customs by that time. You take your shoes off in Japan, you take your clothes off in Taos. What's the difference?

Well, quite a bit, actually. There was all the touching that went on. Everybody touched everybody else, as routinely as glancing. Everyone touched my face first, then went on with what seemed like total innocence to touch me everywhere else. As usual, it was not quite what it seemed. It was *not* innocent, and it was not the usual treatment they gave others in their group. They touched each other's genitals a lot *more* than they touched mine. They were holding back with me so I wouldn't be frightened. They were very polite with strangers.

There was a long, low table, with everyone sitting on the floor around it. Pink led me to it.

"See the bare strips on the floor? Stay out of them. Don't leave anything in them. That's where people walk. Don't *ever* move anything. Furniture, I mean. That has to be decided at full meetings, so we'll all know where everything is. Small things, too. If you pick up something, put it back exactly where you found it."

"I understand."

People were bringing bowls and platters of food from the adjoining kitchen. They set them on the table, and the diners began feeling them. They ate with their fingers, without plates, and they did it slowly and lovingly. They smelled things for a long time before they took a bite. Eating was very sensual to these people.

They were *terrific* cooks. I have never, before or since, eaten as well as I did at Keller. (That's my name for it, in speech, though their bodytalk name was something very like that. When I called it Keller, everyone knew what I was talking about.) They started off with good, fresh produce, something that's hard enough to find in the cities, and went at the cooking with artistry and imagination. It wasn't like any national style I've eaten. They improvised, and seldom cooked the same thing the same way twice.

I sat between Pink and the fellow who had almost run me down earlier. I stuffed myself disgracefully. It was too far removed from beef jerky and the organic dry cardboard I had been eating for me to be able to resist. I lingered over it, but still finished long before anyone else. I watched them as I sat back carefully and wondered if I'd be sick. (I wasn't, thank God.) They fed themselves and each other, sometimes getting up and going clear around the table to offer a choice morsel to a friend on the other side. I was fed in this way by all too many of them, and nearly popped until I learned a pidgin phrase in handtalk, saying I was full to the brim. I learned from Pink that a friendlier way to refuse was to offer something myself.

Eventually I had nothing to do but feed Pink and look at the others. I began to be more observant. I had thought they were eating in solitude, but soon saw that lively conversation was flowing around the table. Hands were busy, moving almost too fast to see. They were spelling into each other's palms, shoulders, legs, arms, bellies; any part of the body. I watched in amazement as a ripple of laughter spread like falling dominoes from one end of the table to the other as some witticism was passed along the line. It was *fast*. Looking carefully, I could see the thoughts moving, reaching one person, passed on while a reply went in the other direction and was in turn passed on, other replies originating all along the line and bouncing back and forth. They were a wave form, like water.

It was messy. Let's face it; eating with your fingers and talking with your hands is going to get you smeared with food. But no one minded. *I* certainly didn't. I was too busy feeling left out. Pink talked to me, but I knew I was finding out what it's like to be deaf. These people were friendly and seemed to like me, but could do nothing about it. We couldn't communicate.

Afterwards, we all trooped outside, except the cleanup crew, and took a shower beneath a set of faucets that gave out very cold water. I told Pink I'd like to help with the dishes, but she said I'd just be in the way. I couldn't do anything around Keller until I learned their very specific ways of doing things. She seemed to be assuming already that I'd be around that long.

Back into the building to dry off, which they did with their usual puppy dog friendliness, making a game and a gift of toweling each other, and then we went into the dome.

It was warm inside, warm and dark. Light entered from the passage to the dining room, but it wasn't enough to blot out the stars through the lattice of triangular panes overhead. It was almost like being out in the open.

Pink quickly pointed out the positional etiquette within the dome. It wasn't hard to follow, but I still tended to keep my arms and legs pulled in close so I wouldn't trip someone by sprawling into a walk space.

My misconceptions got me again. There was no sound but the soft whisper of flesh against flesh, so I thought I was in the middle of an orgy. I had been at them before, in other communes, and they looked pretty much like this. I quickly saw that I was wrong, and only later found out I had been right. In a sense.

What threw my evaluations out of whack was the simple fact that group conversation among these people *had* to look like an orgy. The much subtler observation that I made later was that with a hundred naked bodies sliding, rubbing, kissing, caressing, all at the same time, what was the point in making a distinction? There was no distinction.

I have to say that I use the noun "orgy" only to get across a general idea of many people in close contact. I don't like the word, it is too ripe with connotations. But I had these connotations myself at the time, so I was relieved to see that it was not an orgy. The ones I had been to had been tedious and impersonal, and I had hoped for better from these people.

Many wormed their way through the crush to get to me and meet me. Never more than one at a time; they were constantly aware of what was going on and were waiting their turn to talk to me. Naturally, I didn't know it then. Pink sat with me to interpret the hard thoughts. I eventually used her words less and less, getting into the spirit of tactile seeing and understanding. No one felt they really knew me until they had touched every part of my body, so there were hands on me all the time. I timidly did the same.

What with all the touching, I quickly got an erection, which embarrassed me quite a bit. I was berating myself for being unable to keep sexual responses out of it, for not being able to operate on the same intellectual plane I thought they were on, when I realized with some shock that the couple next to me was making love. They had been doing it for the last ten minutes, actually, and it had seemed such a natural part of what was happening that I had known it and not known it at the same time.

No sooner had I realized it than I suddenly wondered if I was right. *Were they?* It was very slow and the light was bad. But her legs were up, and he was on top of her, that much I was sure of. It was foolish of me, but I really had to know. I had to find out *what the hell I was in.* How could I give the proper social responses if I didn't know the situation?

I was very sensitive to polite behavior after my months at the various communes. I had become adept at saying prayers before supper in one place, chanting Hare Krishna at another, and going happily nudist at still another. It's called "when in Rome," and if you can't adapt to it you shouldn't go visiting. I would kneel to Mecca, burp after my meals, toast anything that was proposed, eat organic rice and compliment the cook; but to do it right, you have to know the customs. I had thought I knew them, but had changed my mind three times in as many minutes.

They *were* making love, in the sense that he was penetrating her. They were also deeply involved with each other. Their hands fluttered like butterflies all over each other, filled with meanings I couldn't see or feel. But they were being touched by and were touching many other people around them. They were talking to all these people, even if the message was as simple as a pat on the forehead or arm.

Pink noticed where my attention was. She was sort of wound around me, without really doing anything I would have thought of as provocative. I just couldn't *decide.* It seemed so innocent, and yet it wasn't.

"That's (—) and (—)," she said, the parentheses indicating a series of hand motions against my palm. I never learned a sound word as a name for any of them but Pink, and I can't reproduce the bodytalk names they had. Pink reached over, touched the woman with her foot, and did some complicated business with her toes. The woman smiled and grabbed Pink's foot, her fingers moving.

"(—) would like to talk with you later," Pink told me. "Right after she's through talking to (—). You met her earlier, remember? She says she likes your hands."

Now this is going to sound crazy, I know. It sounded pretty crazy to me when I thought of it. It dawned on me with a sort of revelation that her word for talk and mine were miles apart. Talk, to her, meant a complex interchange involving all parts of the body. She could read words or emotions in every twitch of my muscles, like a lie detector. Sound, to her, was only a minor part of communication.

It was something she used to speak to outsiders. Pink talked with her whole being.

I didn't have the half of it, even then, but it was enough to turn my head entirely around in relation to these people. They talked with their bodies. It wasn't all hands, as I'd thought. Any part of the body in contact with any other was communication, sometimes a very simple and basic sort—think of McLuhan's light bulb as the basic medium of information—perhaps saying no more than "I am here." But talk was talk, and if conversation evolved to the point where you needed to talk to another with your genitals, it was still a part of the conversation. What I wanted to know was *what were they saying?* I knew, even at that dim moment of realization, that it was much more than I could grasp. Sure, you're saying. You know about talking to your lover with your body as you make love. That's not such a new idea. Of course it isn't, but think how wonderful that talk is even when you're not primarily tactile-oriented. Can you carry the thought from there, or are you doomed to be an earthworm thinking about sunsets?

While this was happening to me, there was a woman getting acquainted with my body. Her hands were on me, in my lap, when I felt myself ejaculating. It was a big surprise to me, but to no one else. I had been telling everyone around me for many minutes, through signs they could feel with their hands, that it was going to happen. Instantly, hands were all over my body. I could almost understand them as they spelled tender thoughts to me. I got the gist, anyway, if not the words. I was terribly embarrassed for only a moment, then it passed away in the face of the easy acceptance. It was very intense. For a long time I couldn't get my breath.

The woman who had been the cause of it touched my lips with her fingers. She moved them slowly, but meaningfully I was sure. Then she melted back into the group.

"What did she say?" I asked Pink.

She smiled at me. "You know, of course. If you'd only cut loose from your verbalizing. But, generally, she meant 'How nice for you.' It also translates as 'How nice for me.' And 'me,' in this sense, means all of us. The organism."

I knew I had to stay and learn to speak.

The commune had its ups and downs. They had expected them, in general, but had not known what shape they might take.

Winter killed many of their fruit trees. They replaced them with hybrid strains. They lost more fertilizer and soil in windstorms because the clover had not had time to anchor it down. Their schedule had been thrown off by the court actions, and they didn't really get things settled in a groove for more than a year.

Their fish all died. They used the bodies for fertilizer and looked into what might have gone wrong. They were using a three-stage ecology of the type pioneered by the New Alchemists in the '70's. It consisted of three domed ponds: one containing fish, another with crushed shells and bacteria in one section and algae in another, and a third full of daphnids. The water containing fish waste from the first pond was pumped through the shells and bacteria, which detoxified it and converted the ammonia it contained into fertilizer for the algae. The algae water was pumped into the second pond to feed the daphnids. Then daphnids and algae were pumped to the fish pond as food and the enriched water was used to fertilize greenhouse plants in all of the domes.

They tested the water and the soil and found that chemicals were being leached from impurities in the shells and concentrated down the food chain. After a thorough cleanup, they restarted and all went well. But they had lost their first cash crop.

They never went hungry. Nor were they cold; there was plenty of sunlight year-round to power the pumps and the food cycle and to heat their living quarters. They had built their buildings half-buried with an eye to the heating and cooling powers of convective currents. But they had to spend some of their capital. The first year they showed a loss.

One of their buildings caught fire during the first winter. Two men and a small girl were killed when a sprinkler system malfunctioned. This was a shock to them. They had thought things would operate as advertised. None of them knew much about the building trades, about estimates as opposed to realities. They found that several of their installations were not up to specifications, and instituted a program of periodic checks on everything. They learned to strip down and repair anything on the farm. If something contained electronics too complex for them to cope with, they tore it out and installed something simpler.

Socially, their progress had been much more encouraging. Janet had wisely decided that there would be only two hard and fast objectives in the realm of their relationships. The first was that she refused to be their president, chairwoman, chief, or supreme commander. She had seen from the start that a driving personality was needed to get the planning done and the land bought and a sense of purpose fostered from their formless desire for an alternative. But once at the promised land, she abdicated. From that point they would operate as a democratic commune. If that failed, they would adopt a new approach. Anything but a dictatorship with her at the head. She wanted no part of that.

The second principle was to accept nothing. There had never been a blind-deaf community operating on its own. They had no expectations to satisfy, they did not need to live as the sighted did. They were alone. There was no one to tell them not to do something simply because it was not done.

They had no clearer idea of what their society would be than anyone else. They had been forced into a mold that was not relevant to their needs, but beyond that they didn't know. They would search out the behavior that made sense, the moral things for blind-deaf people to do. They understood the basic principles of morals: that nothing is moral always, and anything is moral under the right circumstances. It all had to do with social context. They were starting from a blank slate, with no models to follow.

By the end of the second year they had their context. They continually modified it, but the basic pattern was set. They knew themselves and what they were as they had never been able to do at the school. They defined themselves in their own terms.

I spent my first day at Keller in school. It was the obvious and necessary step. I had to learn handtalk.

Pink was kind and very patient. I learned the basic alphabet and practiced hard at it. By the afternoon she was refusing to talk to me, forcing me to speak with my hands. She would speak only when pressed hard, and eventually not at all. I scarcely spoke a single word after the third day.

This is not to say that I was suddenly fluent. Not at all. At the end of the first day I knew the alphabet and could laboriously make myself understood. I was not so good at reading words spelled into my own palm. For a long time I had to look at the hand to see what was spelled. But like any language, eventually you think in it. I speak fluent French, and I can recall my amazement when I finally reached the point where I wasn't translating my thoughts before I spoke. I reached it at Keller in about two weeks.

I remember one of the last things I asked Pink in speech. It was something that was worrying me.

"Pink, am I welcome here?"

"You've been here three days. Do you feel rejected?"

"No, it's not that. I guess I just need to hear your policy about outsiders. How *long* am I welcome?"

She wrinkled her brow. It was evidently a new question.

"Well, practically speaking, until a majority of us decide we want you to go. But that's never happened. No one's stayed here much longer than a few days. We've never had to evolve a policy about what to do, for instance, if someone who sees and hears wants to join us. No one has, so far, but I guess it could happen. My guess is that they wouldn't accept it. They're very independent and jealous of their freedom, though you might not have noticed it. I don't think you could ever be one of them. But as long as you're willing to think of yourself as a guest, you could probably stay for twenty years."

"You said 'they.' Don't you include yourself in the group?"

For the first time she looked a little uneasy. I wish I had been better at reading body language at the time. I think my hands could have told me volumes about what she was thinking.

"Sure," she said. "The children are part of the group. We like it. I sure wouldn't want to be anywhere else, from what I know of the outside."

"I don't blame you." There were things left unsaid here, but I didn't know enough to ask the right questions. "But it's never a problem, being able to see when none of your parents can? They don't . . . resent you in any way?"

This time she laughed. "Oh, no. Never that. They're much too independent for that. You've seen it. They don't *need* us for anything they can't do themselves. We're part of the family. We do exactly the same things they do. And it really doesn't matter. Sight, I mean. Hearing, either. Just look around you. Do I have any special advantages because I can see where I'm going?"

I had to admit that she didn't. But there was still the hint of something she wasn't saying to me.

"I know what's bothering you. About staying here." She had to draw me back to my original question; I had been wandering.

"What's that?"

"You don't feel a part of the daily life. You're not doing your share of the chores. You're very conscientious and you want to do your part. I can tell."

She read me right, as usual, and I admitted it.

"And you won't be able to until you can talk to everybody. So let's get back to your lessons. Your fingers are still very sloppy."

There was a lot of work to be done. The first thing I had to learn was to slow down. They were slow and methodical workers, made few mistakes, and didn't care if a job took all day so long as it was done well. When I was working by myself I didn't have to worry about it: sweeping, picking apples, weeding in the gardens. But when I was on a job that required teamwork I had to learn a whole new pace. Eyesight enables a person to do many aspects of a job at once with a few quick glances. A blind person will take each aspect of the job in turn if the job is spread out. Everything has to be verified by touch. At a bench job, though, they could be much faster than I. They could make me feel as though I was working with my toes instead of fingers.

I never suggested that I could make anything quicker by virtue of my sight or hearing. They quite rightly would have told me to mind my own business. Accepting sighted help was the first step to dependence, and after all, they would still be here with the same jobs to do after I was gone.

And that got me to thinking about the children again. I began to be positive that there was a undercurrent of resentment, maybe unconscious, between the parents and children. It was obvious that there was a great deal of love between them, but how could the children fail to resent the rejection of their talent? So my reasoning went, anyway.

I quickly fit myself into the routine. I was treated no better or worse than anyone else, which gratified me. Though I would never become part of the group, even if I should desire it, there was absolutely no indication that I was anything but a full member. That's just how they treated guests: as they would one of their own number.

Life was fulfilling out there in a way it has never been in the cities. It wasn't unique to Keller, this pastoral peace, but the people there had it in generous helpings. The earth beneath your bare feet is something you can never feel in a city park.

Daily life was busy and satisfying. There were chickens and hogs to feed, bees and sheep to care for, fish to harvest, and cows to milk. Everybody worked: men, women, and children. It all seemed to fit together without any apparent effort. Everybody seemed to know what to do when it needed doing. You could think of it as a well-oiled machine, but I never liked that metaphor, especially for people. I thought of it as an organism. Any social group is, but this one *worked*. Most of the other communes I'd visited had glaring flaws. Things would not get done because everyone was too stoned or couldn't be bothered or didn't see the necessity of doing it in the first place. That sort of ignorance leads to typhus and soil erosion and people freezing to death and invasions of social workers who take your children away. I'd seen it happen.

Not here. They had a good picture of the world as it is, not the rosy misconceptions so many other utopians labor under. They did the jobs that needed doing.

I could never detail all the nuts and bolts (there's that machine metaphor again) of how the place worked. The fish-cycle ponds alone were complicated enough to overawe me. I killed a spider in one of the greenhouses, then found out it had been put there to eat a specific set of plant predators. Same for the frogs. There were insects in the water to kill other insects; it got to a point where I was afraid to swat a mayfly without prior okay.

As the days went by I was told some of the history of the place. Mistakes had been made, though surprisingly few. One had been in the area of defense. They had made no provision for it at first, not knowing much about the brutality and random violence that reaches even to the out-of-the-way corners. Guns were the logical and preferred choice out here, but were beyond their capabilities.

One night a carload of men who had had too much to drink showed up. They had heard of the place in town. They stayed for two days, cutting the phone lines and raping many of the women.

The people discussed all the options after the invasion was over, and settled on the organic one. They bought five German shepherds. Not the psychotic wretches that are marketed under the description of "attack dogs," but specially trained ones from a firm recommended by the Albuquerque police. They were trained as both Seeing-Eye and police dogs. They were perfectly harmless until an outsider showed overt aggression, then they were trained, not to disarm, but to go for the throat.

It worked, like most of their solutions. The second invasion resulted in two dead and three badly injured, all on the other side. As a backup in case of a concerted attack, they hired an ex-marine to teach them the fundamentals of close-in dirty fighting. These were not dewy-eyed flower children.

There were three superb meals a day. And there was leisure time, too. It was not all work. There was time to take a friend out and sit in the grass under a tree, usually around sunset, just before the big dinner. There was time for someone to stop working for a few minutes, to share some special treasure. I remember being taken by the hand by one woman—whom I must call Tall-one-with-the-green-eyes—to a spot where mushrooms were growing in the cool crawl space beneath the barn. We wriggled under until our faces were buried in the patch, picked a few, and smelled them. She showed me how to smell. I would have thought a few weeks before that we had ruined their beauty, but after all it was only visual. I was already beginning to discount that sense, which is so removed from the essence of an object. She showed me that they were still beautiful to touch and smell after we had apparently destroyed them. Then she was off to the kitchen with the pick of the bunch in her apron. They tasted all the better that night.

And a man—I will call him Baldy—who brought me a plank he and one of the women had been planing in the woodshop. I touched its smoothness and smelled it and agreed with him how good it was.

And after the evening meal, the Together.

During my third week there I had an indication of my status with the group. It was the first real test of whether I meant anything to them. Anything special, I mean. I wanted to see them as my friends, and I suppose I was a little upset to think that just anyone who wandered in here would be treated the way I was. It was childish and unfair to them, and I wasn't even aware of the discontent until later.

I had been hauling water in a bucket into the field where a seedling tree was being planted. There was a hose for that purpose, but it was in use on the other side of the village. This tree was not in reach of the automatic sprinklers and it was drying out. I had been carrying water to it until another solution was found.

It was hot, around noon. I got the water from a standing spigot near the forge.

I set the bucket down on the ground behind me and leaned my head into the flow of water. I was wearing a shirt made of cotton, unbuttoned in the front. The water felt good running through my hair and soaking into the shirt. I let it go on for almost a minute.

There was a crash behind me and I bumped my head when I raised it up too quickly under the faucet. I turned and saw a woman sprawled on her face in the dust. She was turning over slowly, holding her knee. I realized with a sinking feeling that she had tripped over the bucket I had carelessly left on the concrete express lane. Think of it: ambling along on ground that you trust to be free of all obstruction, suddenly you're sitting on the ground. Their system would only work with trust, and it had to be total; everybody had to be responsible all the time. I had been accepted into that trust and I had blown it. I felt sick.

She had a nasty scrape on her left knee that was oozing blood. She felt it with her hands, sitting there on the ground, and she began to howl. It was weird, painful. Tears came from her eyes, then she pounded her fists on the ground, going "Hunnnh, hunnnh, *hunnnh!*" with each blow. She was angry, and she had every right to be.

She found the pail as I hesitantly reached out for her. She grabbed my hand and followed it up to my face. She felt my face, crying all the time, then wiped her nose and got up. She started off for one of the buildings. She limped slightly.

I sat down and felt miserable. I didn't know what to do.

One of the men came out to get me. It was Big Man. I called him that because he was the tallest person at Keller. He wasn't any sort of policeman, I found out later; he was just the first one the injured woman had met. He took my hand and felt my face. I saw tears start when he felt the emotions there. He asked me to come inside with him.

An impromptu panel had been convened. Call it a jury. It was made up of anyone who was handy, including a few children. There were ten or twelve of them. Everyone looked very sad. The woman I had hurt was there, being consoled by three or four people. I'll call her Scar, for the prominent mark on her upper arm.

Everybody kept telling me—in handtalk, you understand—how sorry they were for me. They petted and stroked me, trying to draw some of the misery away.

Pink came racing in. She had been sent for to act as a translator if needed. Since this was a formal proceeding it was necessary that they be sure I understood everything that happened. She went to Scar and cried with her for a bit, then came to me and embraced me fiercely, telling me with her hands how sorry she was that this had happened. I was already figuratively packing my bags. Nothing seemed to be left but the formality of expelling me.

Then we all sat together on the floor. We were close, touching on all sides. The hearing began.

Most of it was in handtalk, with Pink throwing in a few words here and there. I seldom knew who said what, but that was appropriate. It was the group speaking as one. No statement reached me without already having become a consensus.

"You are accused of having violated the rules," said the group, "and of having been the cause of an injury to (the one I called Scar). Do you dispute this? Is there any fact that we should know?"

"No," I told them. "I was responsible. It was my carelessness."

"We understand. We sympathize with you in your remorse, which is evident to all of us. But carelessness is a violation. Do you understand this? This is the offense for which you are (—)."It was a set of signals in shorthand.

"What was that?" I asked Pink.

"Uh . . . 'brought before us'? 'Standing trial'?" She shrugged, not happy with either interpretation.

"Yes. I understand."

"The facts not being in question, it is agreed that you are guilty." (" 'Responsible,' " Pink whispered in my ear.) "Withdraw from us a moment while we come to a decision."

I got up and stood by the wall, not wanting to look at them as the debate went back and forth through the joined hands. There was a burning lump in my throat that I could not swallow. Then I was asked to rejoin the circle.

"The penalty for your offense is set by custom. If it were not so, we would wish we could rule otherwise. You now have the choice of accepting the punishment designated and having the offense wiped away, or of refusing our jurisdiction and withdrawing your body from our land. What is your choice?"

I had Pink repeat this to me, because it was so important that I know what was being offered. When I was sure I had read it right, I accepted their punishment without hesitation. I was very grateful to have been given an alternative.

"Very well. You have elected to be treated as we would treat one of our own who had done the same act. Come to us."

Everyone drew in closer. I was not told what was going to happen. I was drawn in and nudged gently from all directions.

Scar was sitting with her legs crossed more or less in the center of the group. She was crying again, and so was I, I think. It's hard to remember. I ended up face down across her lap. She spanked me.

I never once thought of it as improbable or strange. It flowed naturally out of the situation. Everyone was holding on to me and caressing me, spelling assurances into my palms and legs and neck and cheeks. We were all crying. It was a difficult thing that had to be faced by the whole group. Others drifted in and joined us. I understood that this punishment came from everyone there, but only the offended person, Scar, did the actual spanking. That was one of the ways I had wronged her, beyond the fact of giving her a scraped knee. I had laid on her the obligation of disciplining me and that was why she had sobbed so loudly, not from the pain of her injury, but from the pain of knowing she would have to hurt me.

Pink later told me that Scar had been the staunchest advocate of giving me the option to stay. Some had wanted to expel me outright, but she paid me the compliment of thinking I was a good enough person to be worth putting herself and me through the ordeal. If you can't understand that, you haven't grasped the feeling of community I felt among these people.

It went on for a long time. It was very painful, but not cruel. Nor was it primarily humiliating. There was some of that, of course. But it was essentially a practical lesson taught in the most direct terms. Each of them had undergone it during the first months, but none recently. You *learned* from it, believe me.

I did a lot of thinking about it afterward. I tried to think of what else they might have done. Spanking grown people is really unheard of, you know, though that didn't occur to me until long after it had happened. It seemed so natural when it was going on that the thought couldn't even enter my mind that this was a weird situation to be in.

They did something like this with the children, but not as long or as hard. Responsibility was lighter for the younger ones. The adults were willing to put up with an occasional bruise or scraped knee while the children learned.

But when you reached what they thought of as adulthood—which was whenever a majority of the adults thought you had or when you assumed the privilege yourself—that's when the spanking really got serious.

They had a harsher punishment, reserved for repeated or malicious offenses. They had not had to invoke it often. It consisted of being sent to Coventry. No one would touch you for a specified period of time. By the time I heard of it, it sounded like a very tough penalty. I didn't need it explained to me.

I don't know how to explain it, but the spanking was administered in such a loving way that I didn't feel violated. *This hurts me as much as it hurts you. I'm doing this for your own good. I love you, that's why I'm spanking you.* They made me understand those old cliches by their actions.

When it was over, we all cried together. But it soon turned to happiness. I embraced Scar and we told each other how sorry we were that it happened. We talked to each other—made love if you like—and I kissed her knee and helped her dress it.

We spent the rest of the day together, easing the pain.

As I became more fluent in handtalk, "the scales fell from my eyes." Daily, I would discover a new layer of meaning that had eluded me before; it was like peeling the skin of an onion to find a new skin beneath it. Each time I thought I was at the core, only to find that there was another layer I could not yet see.

I had thought that learning handtalk was the key to communication with them. Not so. Handtalk was baby talk. For a long time I was a baby who could not even say goo-goo clearly. Imagine my surprise when, having learned to say it, I found that there were syntax, conjunctions, parts of speech, nouns, verbs, tense, agreement, and the subjunctive mood. I was wading in a tide pool at the edge of the Pacific Ocean.

By handtalk I mean the International Manual Alphabet. Anyone can learn it in a few hours or days. But when you talk to someone in speech, do you spell each word? Do you read each letter as you read this? No, you grasp words as entities, hear groups of sounds and see groups of letters as a gestalt full of meaning.

Everyone at Keller had an absorbing interest in language. They each knew several languages—spoken languages—and could read and spell them fluently.

While still children they had understood the fact that handtalk was a way for blind-deaf people to talk to *outsiders*. Among themselves it was much too cumbersome. It was like Morse Code: useful when you're limited to on-off modes of information transmission, but not the preferred mode. Their ways of speaking to each other were much closer to our type of written or verbal communication, and—dare I say it?—better.

I discovered this slowly, first by seeing that though I could spell rapidly with my hands, it took *much* longer for me to say something than it took anyone else. It could not be explained by differences in dexterity. So I asked to be taught their shorthand speech. I plunged in, this time taught by everyone, not just Pink.

It was hard. They could say any word in any language with no more than two moving hand positions. I knew this was a project for years, not days. You learn the alphabet and you have all the tools you need to spell any word that exists. That's the great advantage in having your written and spoken speech based on the same set of symbols. Shorthand was not like that at all. It partook of none of the linearity or commonality of handtalk; it was not code for English or any other language; it did not share construction or vocabulary with any other language. It was wholly constructed by the Kellerites according to their needs. Each word was something I had to learn and memorize separately from the handtalk spelling.

For months I sat in the Togethers after dinner saying things like "Me love Scar much much well," while waves of conversation ebbed and flowed and circled around me, touching me only at the edges. But I kept at it, and the children were endlessly patient with me. I improved gradually. Understand that the rest of the conversations I will relate took place in either handtalk or shorthand, limited to various degrees by my fluency. I did not speak nor was I spoken to orally from the day of my punishment.

* * *

I was having a lesson in bodytalk from Pink. Yes, we were making love. It had taken me a few weeks to see that she was a sexual being, that her caresses, which I had persisted in seeing as innocent—as I had defined it at the time—both were and weren't innocent. She understood it as perfectly natural that the result of her talking to my penis with her hands might be another sort of conversation. Though still in the middle flush of puberty, she was regarded by all as an adult and I accepted her as such. It was cultural conditioning that had blinded me to what she was saying.

So we talked a lot. With her, I understood the words and music of the body better than with anyone else. She sang a very uninhibited song with her hips and hands, free of guilt, open and fresh with discovery in every note she touched.

"You haven't told me much about yourself," she said. "What did you do on the outside?" I don't want to give the impression that this speech was in sentences, as I have presented it. We were bodytalking, sweating and smelling each other. The message came through from hands, feet, mouth.

I got as far as the sign for pronoun, first person singular, and was stopped.

How could I tell her of my life in Chicago? Should I speak of my early ambition to be a writer, and how that didn't work out? And why hadn't it? Lack of talent, or lack of drive? I could tell her about my profession, which was meaningless shuffling of papers when you got down to it, useless to anything but the Gross National Product. I could talk of the economic ups and downs that had brought me to Keller when nothing else could dislodge me from my easy sliding through life. Or the loneliness of being forty-seven years old and never having found someone worth loving, never having been loved in return. Of being a permanently displaced person in a stainless-steel society. One-night stands, drinking binges, nine-to-five, Chicago Transit Authority, dark movie houses, football games on television, sleeping pills, the John Hancock Tower where the windows won't open so you can't breathe the smog or jump out. That was me, wasn't it?

"I see," she said.

"I travel around," I said, and suddenly realized that it was the truth.

"I see," she repeated. It was a different sign for the same thing. Context was everything. She had heard and understood both parts of me, knew one to be what I had been, the other to be what I hoped I was.

She lay on top of me, one hand lightly on my face to catch the quick interplay of emotions as I thought about my life for the first time in years. And she laughed and nipped my ear playfully when my face told her that for the first time I could remember, I was happy about it. Not just telling myself I was happy, but truly happy. You cannot lie in bodytalk any more than your sweat glands can lie to a polygraph.

I noticed that the room was unusually empty. Asking around in my fumbling way, I learned that only the children were there.

"Where is everybody?" I asked.

"They are all out ***," she said. It was like that: three sharp slaps on the chest with the fingers spread. Along with the finger configuration for "verb form, gerund," it meant that they were all out ***ing. Needless to say, it didn't tell me much.

What did tell me something was her bodytalk as she said it. I read her better than I ever had. She was upset and sad. Her body said something like "Why can't I join them? Why can't I (smell-taste-touch-hear-see) *sense* with them?" That is exactly what she said. Again, I didn't trust my understanding enough to accept that interpretation. I was still trying to force my conceptions on the things I experienced there. I was determined that she and the other children be resentful of their parents in some way, because I was sure they had to be. They *must* feel superior in some way, they *must* feel held back.

I found the adults, after a short search of the area, out in the north pasture. All the parents, none of the children. They were standing in a group with no apparent pattern. It wasn't a circle, but it was almost round. If there was any organization, it was in the fact that everybody was about the same distance from everybody else.

The German shepherds and the Sheltie were out there, sitting on the cool grass facing the group of people. Their ears were perked up, but they were not moving.

I started to go up to the people. I stopped when I became aware of the concentration. They were touching, but their hands were not moving. The silence of seeing all those permanently moving people standing that still was deafening to me.

I watched them for at least an hour. I sat with the dogs and scratched them behind the ears. They did that chop-licking thing that dogs do when they appreciate it, but their full attention was on the group.

It gradually dawned on me that the group was moving. It was very slow, just a step here and another there, over many minutes. It was expanding in such a way that the distance between any of the individuals was the same. Like the expanding universe, where all galaxies move away from all others. Their arms were extended now; they were touching only with fingertips, in a crystal lattice arrangement.

Finally they were not touching at all. I saw their fingers straining to cover distances that were too far to bridge. And still they expanded equilaterally. One of the shepherds began to whimper a little. I felt the hair on the back of my neck stand up. Chilly out here, I thought.

I closed my eyes, suddenly sleepy.

I opened them, shocked. Then I forced them shut. Crickets were chirping in the grass around me.

There was something in the darkness behind my eyeballs. I felt that if I could turn my eyes around I would see it easily, but it eluded me in a way that made peripheral vision seem like reading headlines. If there was ever anything impossible to pin down, much less describe, that was it. It tickled at me for a while as the dogs whimpered louder, but I could make nothing of it. The best analogy I could think of was the sensation a blind person might feel from the sun on a cloudy day.

I opened my eyes again.

Pink was standing there beside me. Her eyes were screwed shut, and she was covering her ears with her hands. Her mouth was open and working silently. Behind her were several of the older children. They were all doing the same thing.

Some quality of the night changed. The people in the group were about a foot away from each other now, and suddenly the pattern broke. They all swayed for a moment, then laughed in that eerie, unselfconscious noise deaf people use for laughter. They fell in the grass and held their bellies, rolled over and over and roared.

Pink was laughing, too. To my surprise, so was I. I laughed until my face and sides were hurting, like I remembered doing sometimes when I'd smoked grass.

And that was ***ing.

I can see that I've only given a surface view of Keller. And there are some things I should deal with, lest I foster an erroneous view.

Clothing, for instance. Most of them wore something most of the time. Pink was the only one who seemed temperamentally opposed to clothes. She never wore anything.

No one ever wore anything I'd call a pair of pants. Clothes were loose: robes, shirts, dresses, scarves and such. Lots of men wore things that would be called women's clothes. They were simply more comfortable.

Much of it was ragged. It tended to be made of silk or velvet or something else that felt good. The stereotyped Kellerite would be wearing a Japanese silk robe, hand-embroidered with dragons, with many gaping holes and loose threads and tea and tomato stains all over it while she sloshed through the pigpen with a bucket of slop. Wash it at the end of the day and don't worry about the colors running.

I also don't seem to have mentioned homosexuality. You can mark it down to my early conditioning that my two deepest relationships at Keller were with women: Pink and Scar. I haven't said anything about it simply because I don't know how to present it. I talked to men and women equally, on the same terms. I had surprisingly little trouble being affectionate with the men.

I could not think of the Kellerites as bisexual, though clinically they were. It was much deeper than that. They could not even recognize a concept as poisonous as a homosexuality taboo. It was one of the first things they learned. If you distinguish homosexuality from heterosexuality you are cutting yourself off from communication—*full* communication—with half the human race. They were pansexual; they could not separate sex from the rest of their lives. They didn't even have a word in shorthand that could translate directly into English as sex. They had words for male and female in infinite variation, and words for degrees and varieties of physical experience that would be impossible to express in English, but all those words included other parts of the world of experience also; none of them walled off what we call *sex* into its own discrete cubbyhole.

There's another question I haven't answered. It needs answering, because I wondered about it myself when I first arrived. It concerns the necessity for the commune in the first place. Did it really have to be like this? Would they have been better off adjusting themselves to our ways of living?

All was not a peaceful idyll. I've already spoken of the invasion and rape. It could happen again, especially if the roving gangs that operate around the cities start to really rove. A touring group of motorcyclists could wipe them out in a night.

There were also continuing legal hassles. About once a year the social workers descended on Keller and tried to take their children away. They had been accused of everything possible, from child abuse to contributing to delinquency. It hadn't worked so far, but it might someday.

And after all, there are sophisticated devices on the market that allow a blind and deaf person to see and hear a little. They might have been helped by some of those.

I met a blind-deaf woman living in Berkeley once. I'll vote for Keller.

As to those machines . . .

In the library at Keller there is a seeing machine. It uses a television camera and a computer to vibrate a closely set series of metal pins. Using it, you can feel a moving picture of whatever the camera is pointed at. It's small and light, made to be carried with the pinpricker touching your back. It cost about thirty-five thousand dollars.

I found it in the corner of the library. I ran my finger over it and left a gleaming streak behind as the thick dust came away.

Other people came and went, and I stayed on.

Keller didn't get as many visitors as the other places I had been. It was out of the way.

One man showed up at noon, looked around, and left without a word.

Two girls, sixteen-year-old runaways from California, showed up one night. They undressed for dinner and were shocked when they found out I could see. Pink scared the hell out of them. Those poor kids had a lot of living to do before they approached Pink's level of sophistication. But then Pink might have been uneasy in California. They left the next day, unsure if they had been to an orgy or not. All that touching and no getting down to business, very strange.

There was a nice couple from Santa Fe who acted as a sort of liaison between Keller and their lawyer. They had a nine-year-old boy who chattered endlessly in handtalk to the other kids. They came up about every other week and stayed a few days, soaking up sunshine and participating in the Together every night. They spoke halting shorthand and did me the courtesy of not speaking to me in speech.

Some of the Indians came around at odd intervals. Their behavior was almost aggressively chauvinistic. They stayed dressed at all times in their Levi's and boots. But it was evident that they had a respect for the people, though they thought them strange. They had business dealings with the commune. It was the Navahos who trucked away the produce that was taken to the gate every day, sold it, and took a percentage. They would sit and powwow in sign language spelled into hands. Pink said they were scrupulously honest in their dealings.

And about once a week all the parents went out in the field and ***ed.

I got better and better at shorthand and bodytalk. I had been breezing along for about five months and winter was in the offing. I had not examined my desires as yet, not really thought about what it was I wanted to do with the rest of my life. I guess the habit of letting myself drift was too ingrained. I was there, and constitutionally unable to decide whether to go or to face up to the problem if I wanted to stay for a long, long time.

Then I got a push.

For a long time I thought it had something to do with the economic situation outside. They were aware of the outside world at Keller. They knew that isolation and ignoring problems that could easily be dismissed as not relevant to them was a dangerous course, so they subscribed to the Braille *New York Times* and most of them read it. They had a television set that got plugged in about once a month. The kids would watch it and translate for their parents.

So I was aware that the non-depression was moving slowly into a more normal inflationary spiral. Jobs were opening up, money was flowing again. When I found myself on the outside again shortly afterward, I thought that was the reason.

The real reason was more complex. It had to do with peeling off the onion layer of shorthand and discovering another layer beneath it.

I had learned handtalk in a few easy lessons. Then I became aware of short-hand and bodytalk, and of how much harder they would be to learn. Through five months of constant immersion, which is the only way to learn a language, I had attained the equivalent level of a five- or six-year-old in shorthand. I knew I could master it, given time. Bodytalk was another matter. You couldn't measure progress as easily in bodytalk. It was a variable and highly interpersonal language that evolved according to the person, the time, the mood. But I was learning.

Then I became aware of Touch. That's the best I can describe it in a single, un-forced English noun. What *they* called this fourth-stage language varied from day to day, as I will try to explain.

I first became aware of it when I tried to meet Janet Reilly. I now knew the history of Keller, and she figured very prominently in all the stories. I knew everyone at Keller, and I could find her nowhere. I knew everyone by names like Scar, and She-with-the-missing-front-tooth, and Man-with-wiry-hair. These were short-hand names that I had given them myself, and they all accepted them without question. They had abolished their outside names within the commune. They meant nothing to them; they told nothing and described nothing.

At first I assumed that it was my imperfect command of shorthand that made me unable to clearly ask the right question about Janet Reilly. Then I saw that they were not telling me on purpose. I saw why, and I approved, and thought no more about it. The name Janet Reilly described what she had been *on the outside,* and one of her conditions for pushing the whole thing through in the first place had been that she be no one special on the inside. She melted into the group and disappeared. She didn't want to be found. All right.

But in the course of pursuing the question I became aware that each of the members of the commune had no specific name at all. That is, Pink, for instance, had no less than one hundred and fifteen names, one from each of the commune members. Each was a contextual name that told the story of Pink's relationship to a particular person. My simple names, based on physical descriptions, were accepted as the names a child would apply to people. The children had not yet learned to go beneath the outer layers and use names that told of themselves, their lives, and their relationships to others.

What is even more confusing, the names evolved from day to day. It was my first glimpse of Touch, and it frightened me. It was a question of permutations. Just the first simple expansion of the problem meant there were no less than thirteen thousand names in use, and they wouldn't stay still so I could memorize them. If Pink spoke to me of Baldy, for instance, she would use her Touch name for him, modified by the fact that she was speaking to me and not Short-chubby-man.

Then the depths of what I had been missing opened beneath me and I was suddenly breathless with fear of heights.

Touch was what they spoke to each other. It was an incredible blend of all three other modes I had learned, and the essence of it was that it never stayed the same. I could listen to them speak to me in shorthand, which was the real basis for Touch, and be aware of the currents of Touch flowing just beneath the surface.

It was a language of inventing languages. Everyone spoke their own dialect because everyone spoke with a different instrument: a different body and set of life experiences. It was modified by everything. *It would not stand still.*

They would sit at the Together and invent an entire body of Touch responses in a night; idiomatic, personal, totally naked in its honesty. And they used it only as a building block for the next night's language.

I didn't know if I wanted to be that naked. I had looked into myself a little recently and had not been satisfied with what I found. The realization that every one of them knew more about it than I, because my honest body had told what my frightened mind had not wanted to reveal, was shattering. I was naked under a spotlight in Carnegie Hall, and all the no-pants nightmares I had ever had came out to haunt me. The fact that they all loved me with all my warts was suddenly not enough. I wanted to curl up in a dark closet with my ingrown ego and let it fester.

I might have come through this fear. Pink was certainly trying to help me. She told me that it would only hurt for a while, that I would quickly adjust to living my life with my darkest emotions written in fire across my forehead. She said Touch was not as hard as it looked at first, either. Once I learned shorthand and bodytalk, Touch would flow naturally from it like sap rising in a tree. It would be unavoidable, something that would happen to me without much effort at all.

I almost believed her. But she betrayed herself. No, no, no. Not that, but the things in her concerning ***ing convinced me that if I went through this I would only bang my head hard against the next step up the ladder.

   ***

I had a little better definition now. Not one that I can easily translate into English, and even that attempt will only convey my hazy concept of what it was.

"It is the mode of touching without touching," Pink said, her body going like crazy in an attempt to reach me with her own imperfect concept of what it was, handicapped by my illiteracy. Her body denied the truth of her shorthand definition, and at the same time admitted to me that she did not know what it was herself.

"It is the gift whereby one can expand oneself from the eternal quiet and dark into something else." And again her body denied it. She beat on the floor in exasperation.

"It is an attribute of being in the quiet and dark all the time, touching others. All I know for sure is that vision and hearing preclude it or obscure it. I can make it as quiet and dark as I possibly can and be aware of the edges of it, but the visual orientation of the mind persists. That door is closed to me, and to all the children."

Her verb "to touch" in the first part of that was a Touch amalgam, one that reached back into her memories of me and what I had told her of my experiences. It implied and called up the smell and feel of broken mushrooms in soft earth under the barn with Tall-one-with-green-eyes, she who taught me to feel the essence of an object. It also contained references to our bodytalking while I was penetrating into the dark and wet of her, and her running account to me of what it was like to receive me into herself. This was all one word.

I brooded on that for a long time. What was the point of suffering through the nakedness of Touch, only to reach the level of frustrated blindness enjoyed by Pink?

What was it that kept pushing me away from the one place in my life where I had been happiest?

One thing was the realization, quite late in coming, that can be summed up as "What the hell am I *doing* here?" The question that should have answered that question was "What the hell would I do if I *left?*"

I was the only visitor, the only one in *seven years* to stay at Keller for longer than a few days. I brooded on that. I was not strong enough or confident enough in my opinion of myself to see it as anything but a flaw in *me,* not in those others. I was obviously too easily satisfied, too complacent to see the flaws that those others had seen.

It didn't have to be flaws in the people of Keller, or in their system. No, I loved and respected them too much to think that. What they had going certainly came as near as anyone ever has in this imperfect world to a sane, rational way for people to exist without warfare and with a minimum of politics. In the end, those two old dinosaurs are the only ways humans have yet discovered to be social animals. Yes, I do see war as a way of living with another; by imposing your will on another in terms so unmistakable that the opponent has to either knuckle under to you, die, or beat your brains out. And if that's a solution to anything, I'd rather live without solutions. Politics is not much better. The only thing going for it is that it occasionally succeeds in substituting talk for fists.

Keller *was* an organism. It was a new way of relating, and it seemed to work. I'm not pushing it as a solution for the world's problems. It's possible that it could only work for a group with a common self-interest as binding and rare as deafness and blindness. I can't think of another group whose needs are so interdependent.

The cells of the organism cooperated beautifully. The organism was strong, flourishing, and possessed of all the attributes I've ever heard used in defining life except the ability to reproduce. That might have been its fatal flaw, if any. I certainly saw the seeds of something developing in the children.

The strength of the organism was communication. There's no way around it. Without the elaborate and impossible-to-falsify mechanisms for communication built into Keller, it would have eaten itself in pettiness, jealousy, possessiveness, and any dozen other "innate" human defects.

The nightly Together was the basis of the organism. Here, from after dinner till it was time to fall asleep, everyone talked in a language that was incapable of falsehood. If there was a problem brewing, it presented itself and was solved almost automatically. Jealousy? Resentment? Some little festering wrong that you're nursing? You couldn't conceal it at the Together, and soon everyone was clustered around you and loving the sickness away. It acted like white corpuscles, clustering around a sick cell, not to destroy it, but to heal it. There seemed to be no problem that couldn't be solved if it was attacked early enough, and with Touch, your neighbors knew about it before you did and were already laboring to correct the wrong, heal the wound, to make you feel better so you could laugh about it. There was a lot of laughter at the Togethers.

I thought for a while that I was feeling possessive about Pink. I know I had done so a little at first. Pink was my special friend, the one who had helped me out from the first, who for several days was the only one I could talk to. It was her hands that had taught me handtalk. I know I felt stirrings of territoriality the first time she lay in my lap while another man made love to her. But if there was any signal the Kellerites were adept at reading, it was that one. It went off like an alarm bell in Pink, the man, and the women and men around me. They soothed me, coddled me, told me in every language that it was all right, not to feel ashamed. Then the man in question began loving *me*. Not Pink, but the man. An observational anthropologist would have had subject matter for a whole thesis. Have you seen the films of baboons' social behavior? Dogs do it, too. Many male mammals do it. When males get into dominance battles, the weaker can defuse the aggression by submitting, by turning tail and surrendering. I have never felt so defused as when that man surrendered the object of our clash of wills—Pink—and turned his attention to me. What could I do? What I did was laugh, and he laughed, and soon we were all laughing, and that was the end of territoriality.

That's the essence of how they solved most "human nature" problems at Keller. Sort of like an oriental martial art; you yield, roll with the blow so that your attacker takes a pratfall with the force of the aggression. You do that until the attacker sees that the initial push wasn't worth the effort, that it was a pretty silly thing to do when no one was resisting you. Pretty soon he's not Tarzan of the Apes, but Charlie Chaplin. And he's laughing.

So it wasn't Pink and her lovely body and my realization that she could never be all mine to lock away in my cave and defend with a gnawed-off thighbone. If I'd persisted in that frame of mind she would have found me about as attractive as an

Amazonian leech, and that was a great incentive to confound the behaviorists and overcome it.

So I was back to those people who had visited and left, and what did they see that I didn't see?

Well, there was something pretty glaring. I was not part of the organism, no matter how nice the organism was to me. I had no hopes of ever becoming a part, either. Pink had said it in the first week. She felt it herself, to a lesser degree. She could not ***, though that fact was not going to drive her away from Keller. She had told me that many times in shorthand and confirmed it in bodytalk. If I left, it would be without her.

Trying to stand outside and look at it, I felt pretty miserable. What was I trying to *do*, anyway? Was my goal in life *really* to become a part of a blind-deaf commune? I was feeling so low by that time that I actually thought of that as denigrating, in the face of all the evidence to the contrary. I should be out in the real world where the real people lived, not these freakish cripples.

I backed off from that thought very quickly. I was not totally out of my mind, just on the lunatic edges. These people were the best friends I'd ever had, maybe the only ones. That I was confused enough to think that of them even for a second worried me more than anything else. It's possible that it's what pushed me finally into a decision. I saw a future of growing disillusion and unfulfilled hopes. Unless I was willing to put out my eyes and ears, I would always be on the outside. *I* would be the blind and deaf one. I would be the freak. I didn't want to be a freak.

They knew I had decided to leave before I did. My last few days turned into a long goodbye, with a loving farewell implicit in every word touched to me. I was not really sad, and neither were they. It was nice, like everything they did. They said goodbye with just the right mix of wistfulness and life-must-go-on, and hope-to-touch-you-again.

Awareness of Touch scratched on the edges of my mind. It was not bad, just as Pink had said. In a year or two I could have mastered it.

But I was set now. I was back in the life groove that I had followed for so long. Why is it that once having decided what I must do, I'm afraid to reexamine my decision? Maybe because the original decision cost me so much that I didn't want to go through it again.

I left quietly in the night for the highway and California. They were out in the fields, standing in that circle again. Their fingertips were farther part than ever before. The dogs and children hung around the edges like beggars at a banquet. It was hard to tell which looked more hungry and puzzled.

*   *   *

The experiences at Keller did not fail to leave their mark on me. I was unable to live as I had before. For a while I thought I could not live at all, but I did. I was too used to living to take the decisive step of ending my life. I would wait. Life had brought one pleasant thing to me; maybe it would bring another.

I became a writer. I found I now had a better gift for communicating than I had before. Or maybe I had it now for the first time. At any rate, my writing came together and I sold. I wrote what I wanted to write, and was not afraid of going hungry. I took things as they came.

I weathered the non-depression of '97, when unemployment reached twenty percent and the government once more ignored it as a temporary downturn. It eventually upturned, leaving the jobless rate slightly higher than it had been the time before, and the time before that. Another million useless persons had been created with nothing better to do than shamble through the streets looking for beatings in progress, car smashups, heart attacks, murders, shootings, arson, bombings, and riots: the endlessly inventive street theater. It never got dull.

I didn't become rich, but I was usually comfortable. That is a social disease, the symptoms of which are the ability to ignore the fact that your society is developing weeping pustules and having its brains eaten out by radioactive maggots. I had a nice apartment in Marin County, out of sight of the machine-gun turrets. I had a car, at a time when they were beginning to be luxuries.

I had concluded that my life was not destined to be all I would like it to be. We all make some sort of compromise, I reasoned, and if you set your expectations too high you are doomed to disappointment. It did occur to me that I was settling for something far from "high," but I didn't know what to do about it. I carried on with a mixture of cynicism and optimism that seemed about the right mix for me. It kept my motor running, anyway.

I even made it to Japan, as I had intended in the first place.

I didn't find someone to share my life. There was only Pink for that, Pink and all her family, and we were separated by a gulf I didn't dare cross. I didn't even dare think about her too much. It would have been very dangerous to my equilibrium. I lived with it, and told myself that it was the way I was. Lonely.

The years rolled on like a caterpillar tractor at Dachau, up to the penultimate day of the millennium.

San Francisco was having a big bash to celebrate the year 2000. Who gives a shit that the city is slowly falling apart, that civilization is disintegrating into hysteria? Let's have a party!

I stood on the Golden Gate Dam on the last day of 1999. The sun was setting in the Pacific, on Japan, which had turned out to be more of the same but squared

and cubed with neo-samurai. Behind me the first bombshells of a firework celebration of holocaust tricked up to look like festivity competed with the flare of
burning buildings as the social and economic basket cases celebrated the occasion
in their own way. The city quivered under the weight of misery, anxious to slide off
along the fracture lines of some subcortical San Andreas Fault. Orbiting atomic
bombs twinkled in my mind, up there somewhere, ready to plant mushrooms
when we'd exhausted all the other possibilities.

I thought of Pink.

I found myself speeding through the Nevada desert, sweating, gripping the
steering wheel. I was crying aloud but without sound, as I had learned to do at
Keller.

Can you go back?

I slammed the citicar over the potholes in the dirt road. The car was falling
apart. It was not built for this kind of travel. The sky was getting light in the east. It
was the dawn of a new millennium. I stepped harder on the gas pedal and the car
bucked savagely. I didn't care. I was not driving back down that road, not ever.
One way or another, I was here to stay.

I reached the wall and sobbed my relief. The last hundred miles had been a
nightmare of wondering if it had been a dream. I touched the cold reality of the
wall and it calmed me. Light snow had drifted over everything, gray in the early
dawn.

I saw them in the distance. All of them, out in the field where I had left them.
No, I was wrong. It was only the children. Why had it seemed like so many at first?

Pink was there. I knew her immediately, though I had never seen her in winter
clothes. She was taller, filled out.

She would be nineteen years old. There was a small child playing in the snow
at her feet, and she cradled an infant in her arms. I went to her and talked to her
hand.

She turned to me, her face radiant with welcome, her eyes staring in a way I
had never seen. Her hands flitted over me and her eyes did not move.

"I touch you, I welcome you," her hands said. "I wish you could have been here
just a few minutes ago. Why did you go away darling? Why did you stay away so
long?" Her eyes were stones in her head. She was blind. She was deaf.

All the children were. No, Pink's child sitting at my feet looked up at me with
a smile.

"Where is everybody?" I asked when I got my breath. "Scar? Baldy? Green-eyes?
And what's happened? What's happened to you?" I was tottering on the edge of a
heart attack or nervous collapse or something. My reality felt in danger of dissolving.

"They've gone," she said. The word eluded me, but the context put it with the *Mary Celeste* and Roanoke, Virginia. It was complex, the way she used the word *gone*. It was like something she had said before: unattainable, a source of frustration like the one that had sent me running from Keller. But now her word told of something that was not hers yet, but was within her grasp. There was no sadness in it.

"Gone?"

"Yes. I don't know where. They're happy. They ***ed. It was glorious. We could only touch a part of it."

I felt my heart hammering to the sound of the last train pulling away from the station. My feet were pounding along the ties as it faded into the fog. Where are the Brigadoons of yesterday? I've never yet heard of a fairy tale where you can go back to the land of enchantment. You wake up, you find that your chance is gone. You threw it away. *Fool!* You only get one chance; that's the moral, isn't it?

Pink's hands laughed along my face.

"Hold this part-of-me-who-speaks-mouth-to-nipple," she said, and handed me her infant daughter. "I will give you a gift."

She reached up and lightly touched my ears with her cold fingers. The sound of the wind was shut out, and when her hands came away it never came back. She touched my eyes, shut out all the light, and I saw no more.

We live in the lovely quiet and dark.

INTRODUCTION TO

"PRESS ENTER ■"

I've always thought of myself as a high-tech sort of guy, though lately I've fallen a bit behind. I don't have an MP3 player or a DVD burner or a picture cell phone or a plasma television. They bring out the stuff now faster than I can find a use for it. But I bought a CD player when they were pretty new and rare, and I had a JVC VCR back when it was the fanciest one you could buy, there were only thirty titles for rent, blank tapes cost $35, and the remote had a wire on it. I paid $1,300. The last VCR I bought, probably my sixth, cost me $60.

When I started writing I wanted the best tools. I skipped right over chisels on rocks, stylus on wet clay plates, quills and fountain pens, even mechanical pencils, and went straight to one of the first popular spin-offs of the aerospace program: the ball-point pen. They were developed for bomber navigators in the war because fountain pens would squirt all over your leather bomber jacket at altitude. (I have a cherished example of the next generation ballpoint, a pressurized Space Pen cleverly designed to work in weightlessness, given to me by Spider Robinson. At least, I cherish it when I can find it. It is also cleverly designed to seek out the lowest point of your desk, roll off, then find the lowest point on the floor, under a heavy piece of furniture. That's because it is cylindrical and lacks a pocket clip to keep it from rolling. In space, I presume it would float out of your pocket and find a forgotten corner of your spacecraft to hide in. NASA spent $3 million developing it. Good job, guys. I'm sure it's around here somewhere.)

When I decided I'd better learn to type I bought an electric machine. Never learned to type on a manual, I'm hopeless at it. I used carbon paper because Xeroxing was fairly expensive, and Wite-Out, becuase I made a lot off misteaks.

When I wore out the Smith-Corona, I invested a lot of money in the Rolls-Royce of typewriters: an IBM Correcting Selectric. I could fool around for hours watching the little type ball twitch, faster than the eye could follow. No more jammed-up keys! You want a new typeface? Pop in another golf ball! No more blobs of white-out glop, no more eraser scraps gumming up the works. Just press a key and the tape jumps up and sucks the ink right out of the paper! No more smudgy cloth ribbons I used over and over because my innate frugality wouldn't let me throw them away as long as the words were even slightly readable. The IBM used film ribbons, and the print was sharper than a newspaper or book.

I loved that machine. I loved it so much that for years I resisted the enthusiastic endorsements of friends who had these infernal machines called "word processors." Heck, I didn't want to process words, I wanted to write. *After a few years, when everybody I knew owned a computer, I even wrote a silly little story called "The Unprocessed Word," pointing out the perils of entrusting your golden prose to the uncertain innards of a cantankerous machine instead of committing them to nice, pretty white paper.*

And they were *uncertain, too. One thing I noticed when people were talking about computers (and by then everybody was talking about computers, you couldn't shut them up once they got started!) was that every single one of them had lost massive chunks of data in something called a "crash," usually more than once. They spoke about this with an odd pride, but it made me break out in a cold sweat. In my twenty-odd years of writing, I had never lost so much as one precious piece of paper, never had to go back and think the whole thing out again. The IBM Correcting Selectric was infallible. Errorless. Crashless.*

Point two: They were expensive. *I gulped hard when I paid $860 for the IBM. With these "word processors," $860 was about what you paid for the word processing software. Okay, slight exaggeration, but the first word processor I ever actually used belonged to Richard Rush. We were rewriting the script to* Millennium. *It was made by one of those defunct pioneers, maybe Osborne. It had a daisy-wheel printer console the size of a Victrola that made a racket like the starting lap at Daytona Beach. If you couldn't afford one of these beasts, there was an alternative: dot-matrix printing. Oh, puhleese! The y and the p and the g and the q didn't drop below the line. Each letter was formed of about nine little dots. I'd rather read Braille with my toes. With my shoes on. The Osborne had enough memory for forty, maybe fifty pages of text. The whole ensemble, which pretty much filled an office, cost more than $15,000. (Richard didn't care, the studio was paying for it.) Six times a day it did something inexplicable or failed to do anything at all. For these times you consulted an instruction manual the size of the Manhattan phone book, written in Sanskrit.*

I didn't want to learn a new language. I wanted to write.

Point three: They were ugly. *Ugly, ugly, ugly. You could get any color you wanted in a screen, so long as it was green. (Later, also orange. Big deal.) They were gray or beige, and looked like a TV set you bought at K-Mart. My IBM was black, the only color for serious machinery, and looked like a stealth fighter jet.*

Lee and her ex-husband had a TRS-80 (Trash-80, everybody called them affectionately) that used floppy disks the size of dinner plates. It had a capacity much inferior to your average cell phone these days. These computers were made of

Masonite or fiberglass or linoleum and made a wimpy little tickety-tickety sound when you typed on them. With my IBM, when I got frustrated and was crumpling sheet after sheet and tossing it in the garbage can, I could pound on the sucker, bang my head on it, bite it, and do no harm except to my teeth. With a computer, you didn't dare look at it sideways or a connection would come loose and you could spend days finding it. Hit it, and you could be out five or six grand. My dear friend Spider Robinson came to visit and proudly brought his Mac, a pathetic little beige tower with a screen quite a bit bigger than a watch face. It was "user-friendly," he said. You could play pinball on it. I tried, and concluded it would never replace my arcade-sized Gorgar machine. (I was wrong, eventually. Two days ago I saw a three-by-5-foot flat-screen plasma pinball machine that belongs to Michael Jackson. Wow!)

Point four: You always needed something else. New modem. Bigger external drive (maybe as much as 100 kilobytes, huge capacity!). Printer cable. Expansion port. More programs, or updates to old ones. It took an hour to assemble it all and you ended up with a nest of wires that would strangle a rat.

It seemed obvious to me this was not a mature technology. A toaster is a mature technology. You buy one for $12, take it out of the box, you throw away the instruction manual because all it's going to tell you is not to use it in the bathtub, or blow-dry your cat with it. You plug it in. You drop in a piece of bread. A minute later you butter your toast.

An IBM Correcting Selectric was a mature technology. You roll in a piece of paper. You turn it on. You sit there for three hours . . . and you've probably only got one sentence, and that's a bad sentence, but that sentence will not go away if somebody plugs in a toaster in the kitchen and blows a fuse.

I vowed that I would not buy a computer until it was as simple as a toaster.

STEP ONE: Remove from box.

STEP TWO: Plug in.

STEP THREE: Turn on.

STEP FOUR: Write beautiful prose.

Step four is always a little iffy, but I knew the first three steps were doable, I knew the day would come.

I didn't wait that long. I broke down and bought one when I saw Windows demonstrated, and figured that even an ex–physics major like me could operate it. (I decided to go with 90 percent of the world and get a PC, and Spider has never forgiven me.) I am now on my third computer. This one is the toaster. It's an HP Pavillion ze1110 and I paid $900 for it two years ago. It weighs a couple of pounds. It came with three things in the box: the laptop, the power cord, and a telephone cord which

I didn't need because I already had six of them, just like you. I didn't use the four-page instruction manual, which had almost no text but lots of helpful pictures for il-literates. Didn't need to. I wasn't going to use it in the bathtub. It is about one million times more powerful than the computer that was on Apollo 11. It has a twenty-gigabyte hard drive of which I've used 1. It has a CD-DVD drive. It would be way too much computer to run a starship on a thousand-year voyage to Alpha Centauri. It was obsolete twenty-three months ago, but I don't care.

And I still manage to lose a page or two of priceless prose every year. In fact, last month I had a brain freeze and hit the wrong key twice and lost 80 percent of my email for 2003.

The following story was written long before I got a computer, long before I knew anything but the ABCs of them. I take that back; I was still working on B. I knew some of the basic terms: modem, CRT, dot matrix, bit, byte, kilobyte. The computer slang I got from something called "The Hacker's Dictionary," which Richard Rush found and downloaded (a new word at the time) while surfing the infant Internet. Much of it is obsolete now, LOL :-), as is all of the hardware.

After it was published, two things surprised me. One was that people assumed I knew not only ABC, but DEFGHIJKLMNOP and maybe Q about computers. They wanted to share their epic computer-crash stories with me, and discuss the virtues and drawbacks of ASCII and WordPerfect and URLs and WYSIWYG and GIGO, and were amazed to discover I didn't know what any of those things were, that I didn't even own one, not even a Trash-80. So I guess I faked it adequately. I was proud of that, because faking it is the very essence of science fiction. Possibly of life in general.

The second thing was that lots of people told me the story had scared the silicon chips out of them. This amazed me, because I hadn't thought it was particularly scary. Sad, and gruesome, and lonely, sure. But scary? I went back and read it again, something I seldom do after a story is published . . . and it creeped me out.

I hope it creeps you out, too. In a nice way.

PRESS ENTER ■

THIS IS A recording. Please do not hang up until—"
I slammed the phone down so hard it fell onto the floor. Then I stood there, dripping wet and shaking with anger. Eventually, the phone started to make that buzzing noise they make when a receiver is off the hook. It's twenty

times as loud as any sound a phone can normally make, and I always wondered why. As though it was such a terrible disaster: "Emergency! Your telephone is off the hook!!!"

Phone answering machines are one of the small annoyances of life. Confess, do you really *like* talking to a machine? But what had just happened to me was more than a petty irritation. I had just been called by an automatic dialing machine.

They're fairly new. I'd been getting about two or three such calls a month. Most of them come from insurance companies. They give you a two-minute spiel and then a number to call if you are interested. (I called back, once, to give them a piece of my mind, and was put on hold, complete with Muzak.) They use lists. I don't know where they get them.

I went back to the bathroom, wiped water droplets from the plastic cover of the library book, and carefully lowered myself back into the water. It was too cool. I ran more hot water and was just getting my blood pressure back to normal when the phone rang again.

So I sat there through fifteen rings, trying to ignore it.

Did you ever try to read with the phone ringing?

On the sixteenth ring I got up, I dried off, put on a robe, walked slowly and deliberately into the living room. I stared at the phone for a while.

On the fiftieth ring I picked it up.

"This is a recording. Please do not hang up until the message has been completed. This call originates from the house of your next-door neighbor, Charles Kluge. It will repeat every ten minutes. Mr. Kluge knows he has not been the best of neighbors, and apologizes in advance for the inconvenience. He requests that you go immediately to his house. The key is under the mat. Go inside and do what needs to be done. There will be a reward for your services. Thank you."

Click. Dial tone.

I'm not a hasty man. Ten minutes later, when the phone rang again, I was still sitting there thinking it over. I picked up the receiver and listened carefully.

It was the same message. As before, it was not Kluge's voice. It was something synthesized, with all the human warmth of a Speak'n'Spell.

I heard it out again, and cradled the receiver when it was done.

I thought about calling the police. Charles Kluge had lived next door to me for ten years. In that time I may have had a dozen conversations with him, none lasting longer than a minute. I owed him nothing.

I thought about ignoring it. I was still thinking about that when the phone rang again. I glanced at my watch. Ten minutes. I lifted the receiver and put it right back down.

I could disconnect the phone. It wouldn't change my life radically.

But in the end I got dressed and went out the front door, turned left, and walked toward Kluge's property.

My neighbor across the street, Hal Lanier, was out mowing the lawn. He waved to me, and I waved back. It was about seven in the evening of a wonderful August day. The shadows were long. There was the smell of cut grass in the air. I've always liked that smell. About time to cut my own lawn, I thought.

It was a thought Kluge had never entertained. His lawn was brown and knee-high and choked with weeds.

I rang the bell. When nobody came I knocked. Then I sighed, looked under the mat, and used the key I found there to open the door.

"Kluge?" I called out as I stuck my head in.

I went along the short hallway, tentatively, as people do when unsure of their welcome. The drapes were drawn, as always, so it was dark in there, but in what had once been the living room ten television screens gave more than enough light for me to see Kluge. He sat in a chair in front of a table, with his face pressed into a computer keyboard and the side of his head blown away.

Hal Lanier operates a computer for the LAPD, so I told him what I had found and he called the police. We waited together for the first car to arrive. Hal kept asking if I'd touched anything, and I kept telling him no, except for the front doorknob.

An ambulance arrived without the siren. Soon there were police all over, and neighbors standing out in their yards or talking in front of Kluge's house. Crews from some of the television stations arrived in time to get pictures of the body, wrapped in the plastic sheet, being carried out. Men and women came and went. I assumed they were doing all the standard police things, taking fingerprints, collecting evidence. I would have gone home, but had been told to stick around.

Finally I was brought in to see Detective Osborne, who was in charge of the case. I was led into Kluge's living room. All the television screens were still turned on. I shook hands with Osborne. He looked me over before he said anything. He was a short guy, balding. He seemed very tired until he looked at me. Then, though nothing really changed in his face, he didn't look tired at all.

"You're Victor Apfel?" he asked. I told him I was. He gestured at the room. "Mr. Apfel, can you tell if anything has been taken from this room?"

I took another look around, approaching it as a puzzle.

There was a fireplace and there were curtains over the windows. There was a rug on the floor. Other than those items, there was nothing else you would expect to find in a living room.

All the walls were lined with tables, leaving a narrow aisle down the middle. On the tables were monitor screens, keyboards, disk drives—all the glossy bric-a-brac of the new age. They were interconnected by thick cables and cords. Beneath the tables were still more computers, and boxes full of electronic items. Above the tables were shelves that reached the ceiling and were stuffed with boxes of tapes, disks, cartridges . . . there was a word for which I couldn't recall just then. It was software.

"There's no furniture, is there? Other than that . . ."

"How would I know?" Then I realized what the misunderstanding was. "Oh. You thought I'd been here before. The first time I ever set foot in this room was about an hour ago."

He frowned, and I didn't like that much.

"The medical examiner says the guy had been dead about three hours. How come you came over when you did, Victor?"

I didn't like him using my first name but didn't see what I could do about it. And I knew I had to tell him about the phone call.

He looked dubious. But there was one easy way to check it out, and we did that. Hal and Osborne and I and several others trooped over to my house. My phone was ringing as we entered.

Osborne picked it up and listened. He got a very sour expression on his face. As the night wore on, it just got worse and worse.

We waited ten minutes for the phone to ring again. Osborne spent the time examining everything in my living room. I was glad when the phone rang again. They made a recording of the message, and we went back to Kluge's house.

Osborne went into the backyard to see Kluge's forest of antennas. He looked impressed.

"Mrs. Madison down the street thinks he was trying to contact Martians," Hal said, with a laugh. "Me, I just thought he was stealing HBO." There were three parabolic dishes. There were six tall masts, and some of those things you see on telephone company buildings for transmitting microwaves.

Osborne took me to the living room again. He asked me to describe what I had seen. I didn't know what good that would do, but I tried.

"He was sitting in that chair, which was here in front of this table. I saw the gun on the floor. His hand was hanging down toward it."

"You think it was suicide?"

"Yes, I guess I did think that." I waited for him to comment, but he didn't. "Is that what you think?"

He sighed. "There wasn't any note."

"They don't always leave notes," Hal pointed out.

"No, but they do often enough that my nose starts to twitch when they don't."
He shrugged. "It's probably nothing."

"That phone call," I said. "That might be a kind of suicide note."

Osborne nodded. "Was there anything else you noticed?"

I went to the table and looked at the keyboard. It was made by Texas Instruments, model TI-99/4A. There was a large bloodstain on the right side of it, where his head had been resting.

"Just that he was sitting in front of this machine." I touched a key, and the monitor screen behind the keyboard immediately filled with words. I quickly drew my hand back, then stared at the message there.

```
PROGRAM NAME: GOODBYE REAL WORLD
DATE: 8/20
CONTENTS: LAST WILL AND TESTAMENT: MISC.
FEATURES
PROGRAMMER: "CHARLES KLUGE"

TO RUN
PRESS ENTER ■
```

The black square at the end flashed on and off. Later I learned it was called a cursor.

Everyone gathered around. Hal, the computer expert, explained how many computers went blank after ten minutes of no activity, so the words wouldn't be burned into the television screen. This one had been green until I touched it, then displayed black letters on a blue background.

"Has the console been checked for prints?" Osborne asked. Nobody seemed to know, so Osborne took a pencil and used the eraser to press the ENTER key.

The screen cleared, stayed blue for a moment, then filled with little ovoid shapes that started at the top of the screen and descended like rain. There were hundreds of them in many colors.

"Those are pills," one of the cops said, in amazement. "Look, that's gotta be a Quaalude. There's a Nembutal." Other cops pointed out other pills. I recognized the distinctive red stripe around the center of a white capsule that had to be a Dilantin. I had been taking them every day for years.

Finally the pills stopped falling, and the damn thing started to play music at us. "Nearer My God To Thee," in three-part harmony.

A few people laughed. I don't think any of us thought it was funny—it was creepy as hell listening to that eerie dirge—but it sounded like it had been scored for pennywhistle, calliope, and kazoo. What could you do but laugh?

As the music played, a little figure composed entirely of squares entered from the left of the screen and jerked spastically toward the center. It was like one of those human figures from a video game, but not as detailed. You had to use your imagination to believe it was a man.

A shape appeared in the middle of the screen. The "man" stopped in front of it. He bent in the middle, and something that might have been a chair appeared under him.

"What's that supposed to be?"

"A computer. Isn't it?"

It must have been, because the little man extended his arms, which jerked up and down like Liberace at the piano. He was typing. The words appeared above him.

SOMEWHERE ALONG THE LINE I MISSED SOMETHING. I SIT HERE, NIGHT AND
DAY, A SPIDER IN THE CENTER OF A COAXIAL WEB. MASTER OF ALL I
SURVEY . . . AND IT IS NOT ENOUGH. THERE MUST BE MORE

ENTER YOUR NAME HERE ∎

"Jesus Christ," Hal said. "I don't believe it. An interactive suicide note."

"Come on, we've got to see the rest of this."

I was nearest the keyboard, so I leaned over and typed my name. But when I looked up, what I had typed was VICT9R.

"How do you back this up?" I asked.

"Just enter it," Osborne said. He reached around me and pressed enter.

DO YOU EVER GET THAT FEELING, VICT9R? YOU HAVE WORKED ALL YOUR LIFE
TO BE THE BEST THERE IS AT WHAT YOU DO, AND ONE DAY YOU WAKE UP TO
WONDER WHY YOU ARE DOING IT/THAT IS WHAT HAPPENED TO ME.

DO YOU WANT TO HEAR MORE, VICT9R/ Y/N ∎

The message rambled from that point. Kluge seemed to be aware of it, apologetic about it, because at the end of each forty- or fifty-word paragraph the reader was given the Y/N option.

I kept glancing from the screen to the keyboard, remembering Kluge slumped across it. I thought about him sitting here alone, writing this.

He said he was despondent. He didn't feel like he could go on. He was taking too many pills (more of them rained down the screen at this point), and he had no further goal. He had done everything he set out to do. We didn't understand what he meant by that. He said he no longer existed. We thought that was a figure of speech.

ARE YOU A COP, VICT9R? IF YOU ARE NOT, A COP WILL BE HERE SOON. SO TO YOU OR THE COP, I WAS NOT SELLING NARCOTICS. THE DRUGS IN MY BED-ROOM WERE FOR MY OWN PERSONAL USE. I USED A LOT OF THEM. AND NOW I WILL NOT NEED THEM ANYMORE.

PRESS ENTER ■

Osborne did, and a printer across the room began to chatter, scaring the hell out of all of us. I could see the carriage zipping back and forth, printing in both directions, when Hal pointed at the screen and shouted.

"Look! Look at that!"

The compugraphic man was standing again. He faced us. He had something that had to be a gun in his hand, which now pointed at his head.

"Don't do it!" Hal yelled.

The little man didn't listen. There was a denatured gunshot sound, and the little man fell on his back. A line of red dripped down the screen. Then the green background turned to blue, the printer shut off, and there was nothing left but the little black corpse lying on its back and the word ★ ★ DONE ★ ★ at the bottom of the screen.

I took a deep breath and glanced at Osborne. It would be an understatement to say he did not look happy.

"What's this about drugs in the bedroom?" he said.

We watched Osborne pulling out drawers in dressers and bedside tables. He didn't find anything. He looked under the bed and in the closet. Like all the other rooms in the house, this one was full of computers. Holes had been knocked in walls for the thick sheaves of cables.

I had been standing near a big cardboard drum, one of several in the room. It was about thirty-gallon capacity, the kind you ship things in. The lid was loose, so I lifted it. I sort of wished I hadn't.

"Osborne," I said. "You'd better look at this."

The drum was lined with a heavy-duty garbage bag. And it was two-thirds full of Quaaludes.

They pried the lids off the rest of the drums. We found drums full of amphetamines, of Nembutals, of Valium. All sorts of things.

With the discovery of the drugs a lot more police returned to the scene. With them came the television camera crews.

In all the activity no one seemed concerned about me, so I slipped back to my own house and locked the door. From time to time I peeked out the curtains. I saw reporters interviewing the neighbors. Hal was there and seemed to be having a good time. Twice crews knocked on my door, but I didn't answer. Eventually they went away.

I ran a hot bath and soaked in it for about an hour. Then I turned the heat up as high as it would go and got in bed, under the blankets.

I shivered all night.

Osborne came over about nine the next morning. I let him in. Hal followed, looking very unhappy. I realized they had been up all night. I poured coffee for them.

"You'd better read this first," Osborne said and handed me the sheet of computer printout. I unfolded it, got out my glasses, and started to read.

It was in that awful dot-matrix printing. My policy is to throw any such trash into the fireplace, unread, but I made an exception this time.

It was Kluge's will. Some probate court was going to have a lot of fun with it.

He stated again that he didn't exist, so he could have no relatives. He had decided to give all his worldly property to somebody who deserved it.

But who was deserving? Kluge wondered. Well, not Mr. and Mrs. Perkins, four houses down the street. They were child abusers. He cited court records in Buffalo and Miami, and a pending case locally.

Mrs. Radnor and Mrs. Polonski, who lived across the street from each other five houses down, were gossips.

The Andersons' oldest son was a car thief.

Marian Flores cheated on her high school algebra tests.

There was a guy nearby who was diddling the city on a freeway construction project. There was one wife in the neighborhood who made out with door-to-door salesmen, and two having affairs with men other than their husbands. There was a teenage boy who got his girlfriend pregnant, dropped her, and bragged about it to his friends.

There were no fewer than nineteen couples in the immediate area who had not reported income to the IRS, or who had padded their deductions.

Kluge's neighbors in back had a dog that barked all night.

Well, I could vouch for the dog. He'd kept me awake often enough. But the rest of it was *crazy!* For one thing, where did a guy with two hundred gallons of illegal narcotics get the right to judge his neighbors so harshly? I mean, the child abusers were one thing, but was it right to tar a whole family because their son stole cars? And for another . . . how did he *know* some of this stuff?

But there was more. Specifically, four philandering husbands. One was Harold "Hal" Lanier, who for three years had been seeing a woman named Toni Jones, a coworker at the LAPD Data Processing facility. She was pressuring him for a divorce; he was "waiting for the right time to tell his wife."

I glanced up at Hal. His red face was all the confirmation I needed.

Then it hit me. What had Kluge found out about *me*?

I hurried down the page, searching for my name. I found it in the last paragraph.

". . . for thirty years Mr. Apfel has been paying for a mistake he did not even make. I won't go so far as to nominate him for sainthood, but by default—if for no other reason—I hereby leave all deed and title to my real property and the structure thereon to Victor Apfel."

I looked at Osborne, and those tired eyes were weighing me.

"But I don't *want* it!"

"Do you think this is the reward Kluge mentioned in the phone call?"

"It must be," I said. "What else could it be?"

Osborne sighed and sat back in his chair. "At least he didn't try to leave you the drugs. Are you still saying you didn't know the guy?"

"Are you accusing me of something?"

He spread his hands. "Mr. Apfel, I'm simply asking a question. You're never one hundred percent sure in a suicide. Maybe it was murder. If it was, you can see that, so far, you're the only one we know of that's gained by it."

"He was almost a stranger to me."

He nodded, tapping his copy of the computer printout. I looked back at my own, wishing it would go away.

"What's this . . . mistake you didn't make?"

I was afraid that would be the next question.

"I was a prisoner of war in North Korea," I said.

Osborne chewed that over for a while.

"They brainwash you?"

"Yes." I hit the arm of my chair, and suddenly had to be up and moving. The room was getting cold. "No. I don't . . . There's been a lot of confusion about that word. Did they 'brainwash' me? Yes. Did they succeed? Did I offer a confession of my war crimes and denounce the U.S. Government? No."

Once more, I felt myself being inspected by those deceptively tired eyes.

"It's not something you forget."

"Is there anything you want to say about it?"

"It's just that it was all so . . . No. No, I have nothing further to say. Not to you, not to anybody."

"I'm going to have to ask you more questions about Kluge's death."

"I think I'll have my lawyer present for those." Christ. Now I am going to have to get a lawyer. I didn't know where to begin.

Osborne just nodded again. He got up and went to the door.

"I was ready to write this one down as a suicide," he said. "The only thing that bothered me was there was no note. Now we've got a note." He gestured in the direction of Kluge's house and started to look angry.

"This guy not only writes a note, he programs the fucking thing into his computer, complete with special effects straight out of Pac-Man.

"Now, I know people do crazy things. I've seen enough of them. But when I heard the computer playing a hymn, that's when I knew this was murder. Tell you the truth, Mr. Apfel, I don't think you did it. There must be two dozen motives for murder in that printout. Maybe he was blackmailing people around here. Maybe that's how he bought all those machines. And people with that amount of drugs usually die violently. I've got a lot of work to do on this one, and I'll find who did it." He mumbled something about not leaving town, and that he'd see me later, and left.

"Vic . . ." Hal said. I looked at him.

"About that printout," he finally said. "I'd appreciate it . . . Well, they said they'd keep it confidential. If you know what I mean." He had eyes like a basset hound. I'd never noticed that before.

"Hal, if you'll just go home, you have nothing to worry about from me."

He nodded and scuttled for the door.

"I don't think any of that will get out," he said.

It all did, of course.

It probably would have even without the letters that began arriving a few days after Kluge's death, all postmarked Trenton, New Jersey, all computer-generated from a machine no one was ever able to trace. The letters detailed the matters Kluge had mentioned in his will.

I didn't know about any of that at the time. I spent the rest of the day after Hal's departure lying on my bed, under the electric blanket. I couldn't get my feet warm. I got up only to soak in the tub or to make a sandwich.

Reporters knocked on my door but I didn't answer. On the second day I called a criminal lawyer—Martin Abrams, the first in the book—and retained him. He told me they'd probably call me down to the police station for questioning. I told him I wouldn't go, popped two Dilantin, and sprinted for the bed.

A couple of times I heard sirens in the neighborhood. Once I heard a shouted argument down the street. I resisted the temptation to look. I'll admit I was a little curious, but you know what happened to the cat.

I kept waiting for Osborne to return, but he didn't. The days turned into a week. Only two things of interest happened in that time.

The first was a knock on my door. This was two days after Kluge's death. I looked through the curtains and saw a silver Ferrari parked at the curb. I couldn't see who was on the porch, so I asked who it was.

"My name's Lisa Foo," she said. "You asked me to drop by."

"I certainly don't remember it."

"Isn't this Charles Kluge's house?"

"That's next door."

"Oh. Sorry."

I decided I ought to warn her Kluge was dead, so I opened the door. She turned and smiled at me. It was blinding.

Where does one start in describing Lisa Foo? Remember when newspapers used to run editorial cartoons of Hirohito and Tojo, when the *Times* used the word "Jap" without embarrassment? Little guys with faces wide as footballs, ears like jug handles, thick glasses, two big rabbity buck teeth, and pencil-thin mustaches . . .

Leaving out only the mustache, she was a dead ringer for a cartoon Tojo. She had the glasses, and the ears, and the teeth. But her teeth had braces, like piano keys wrapped in barbed wire. And she was five-eight or five-nine and couldn't have weighed more than a hundred and ten. I'd have said a hundred, but added five pounds each for her breasts, so improbably large on her scrawny frame that all I could read of the message on her T-shirt was "POCK LIVE." It was only when she turned sideways that I saw the esses before and after.

She thrust out a slender hand.

"Looks like I'm going to be your neighbor for a while," she said. "At least until we get that dragon's lair next door straightened out." If she had an accent, it was San Fernando Valley.

"That's nice."

"Did you know him? Kluge, I mean. Or at least that's what he called himself."

"You don't think that was his name?"

"I doubt it, 'Klug' means clever in German. And it's hacker slang for being tricky. And he sure was a tricky bugger. Definitely some glitches in the wetware." She tapped the side of her head meaningfully. "Viruses and phantoms and demons jumping out every time they try to key in. Software rot, bit buckets overflowing onto the floor . . ."

She babbled on in that vein for a time. It might as well have been Swahili.

"Did you say there were demons in his computers?"

"That's right."

"Sounds like they need an exorcist."

She jerked her thumb at her chest and showed me another half acre of teeth.

"That's me. Listen, I gotta go. Drop in and see me anytime."

The second interesting event of the week happened the next day. My bank statement arrived. There were three deposits listed. The first was the regular check from the V.A., for $487.00. The second was for $392.54, interest on the money my parents had left me fifteen years ago.

The third deposit had come in on the twentieth, the day Charles Kluge died. It was for $700,083.04.

A few days later Hal Lanier dropped by.

"Boy, what a week," he said. Then he flopped down on the couch and told me all about it.

There had been a second death on the block. The letters had stirred up a bit of trouble, especially with the police going house to house questioning everyone. Some people had confessed to things when they were sure the cops were closing in on them. The woman who used to entertain salesmen while her husband was at work had admitted her infidelity, and the guy had shot her. He was in the county jail. That was the worst incident, but there had been others, from fistfights to rocks thrown through windows. According to Hal, the IRS was thinking of setting up a branch office in the neighborhood, so many people were being audited.

I thought about the seven hundred thousand and eight-three dollars.

And four cents.

I didn't say anything, but my feet were getting cold.

"I suppose you want to know about me and Betty," he said, at last. I didn't. I didn't want to hear *any* of this, but I tried for a sympathetic expression.

"That's all over," he said with a satisfied sigh. "Between me and Toni, I mean. I told Betty all about it. It was real bad for a few days, but I think our marriage is stronger for it now." He was quiet for a moment, basking in the warmth of it all. I had kept a straight face under worse provocation, so I trust I did well enough then.

He wanted to tell me all they'd learned about Kluge, and he wanted to invite me over for dinner, but I begged off on both, telling him my war wounds were giving me hell. I just about had him to the door when Osborne knocked on it. There was nothing to do but let him in. Hal stuck around, too.

I offered Osborne coffee, which he gratefully accepted. He looked different. I wasn't sure what it was at first. Same old tired expression . . . no, it wasn't. Most of that weary look had been either an act or a cop's built-in cynicism. Today, it was genuine. The tiredness had moved from his face to his shoulders, to his hands, to the way he walked and the way he slumped in the chair. There was a sour aura of defeat around him.

"Am I still a suspect?" I asked.

"You mean, should you call your lawyer? I'd say don't bother. I checked you out pretty good. That will ain't gonna hold up, so your motive is pretty half-assed. Way I figure it, every coke dealer in the Marina had a better reason to snuff Kluge than you." He sighed. "I got a couple questions. You can answer them or not."

"Give it a try."

"You remember any unusual visitors he had? People coming and going at night?"

"The only visitors I *ever* recall were deliveries. Post office. Federal Express, freight companies . . . that sort of thing. I suppose the drugs could have come in any of those shipments."

"That's what we figure, too. There's no way he was dealing nickel and dime bags. He must have been a middle man. Ship it in, ship it out." He brooded about that for a while and sipped his coffee.

"So are you making any progress?" I asked.

"You want to know the truth? The case is going in the toilet. We've got too many motives, and not a one of them that works. As far as we can tell, nobody on the block had the slightest idea Kluge had all that information. We've checked bank accounts and we can't find evidence of blackmail. So the neighbors are pretty much out of the picture. Though if he were alive, most people around here would like to kill him *now*."

"Damn straight," Hal said.

Osborne slapped his thigh. "If the bastard was alive, *I'd* kill him," he said. "But I'm beginning to think he never *was* alive."

"I don't understand."

"If I hadn't seen the goddamn body . . ." He sat up a little straighter. "He said he didn't exist. Well, he practically didn't. The power company never heard of him. He's hooked up to their lines and a meter reader came by every month, but they never billed him for a single kilowatt. Same with the phone company. He had a whole exchange in that house that was *made* by the phone company, and delivered by them, and installed by them, but they have no record of him. We talked to the guy who hooked it all up. He turned in his records, and the computer swallowed them. Kluge didn't have a bank account anywhere in California, and apparently he didn't need one. We've tracked down a hundred companies that sold things to him, shipped them out, and then either marked his account paid or forgot they ever sold him anything. Some of them have check numbers and account numbers in their books, for accounts or even *banks* that don't exist."

He leaned back in his chair, simmering at the perfidy of it all.

"The only guy we've found who ever heard of him was the guy who delivered his groceries once a month. Little store down on Sepulveda. They don't have a computer, just paper receipts. He paid by check. Wells Fargo accepted them and the checks never bounced. But Wells Fargo never heard of him."

I thought it over. He seemed to expect something of me at this point, so I made a stab at it.

"He was doing all this by computers?"

"That's right. Now, the grocery store scam I understand, almost. But more often than not, Kluge got right into the basic programming of the computers and wiped himself out. The power company was never paid, by check or any other way, because as far as they were concerned, they weren't selling him anything.

"No government agency has ever heard of him. We've checked him with everybody from the post office to the CIA."

"Kluge was probably an alias, right?" I offered.

"Yeah. But the FBI doesn't have his fingerprints. We'll find out who he was, eventually. But it doesn't get us any closer to whether or not he was murdered."

He admitted there was pressure to simply close the felony part of the case, label it suicide, and forget it. But Osborne would not believe it. Naturally, the civil side would go on for some time, as they attempted to track down all Kluge's deceptions.

"It's all up to the dragon lady," Osborne said. Hal snorted.

"Fat chance," Hal said and muttered something about boat people.

"That girl? She's still over there? Who is she?"

"She's some sort of giant brain from Caltech. We called out there and told them we were having problems, and she's what they sent." It was clear from Osborne's face what he thought of any help she might provide.

I finally managed to get rid of them. As they went down the walk I looked over at Kluge's house. Sure enough, Lisa Foo's silver Ferrari was sitting in his driveway.

I had no business going over here. I knew that better than anyone.

So I set about preparing my evening meal. I made a tuna casserole—which is not as bland as it sounds, the way I make it—put it in the oven and went out to the garden to pick the makings for a salad. I was slicing cherry tomatoes and thinking about chilling a bottle of white wine when it occurred to me that I had enough for two.

Since I never do anything hastily, I sat down and thought it over for a while. What finally decided me was my feet. For the first time in a week, they were warm. So I went to Kluge's house.

The front door was standing open. There was no screen. Funny how disturbing that can look, the dwelling wide open and unguarded. I stood on the porch and leaned in, but all I could see was the hallway.

"Miss Foo?" I called. There was no answer.

The last time I'd been here I had found a dead man. I hurried in.

Lisa Foo was sitting on a piano bench before a computer console. She was in profile, her back very straight, her brown legs in lotus position, her fingers poised at the keys as words sprayed rapidly onto the screen in front of her. She looked up and flashed her teeth at me.

"Somebody told me your name was Victor Apfel," she said.

"Yes. Uh, the door was open . . ."

"It's hot," she said, reasonably, pinching the fabric of her shirt near her neck and lifting it up and down like you do when you're sweaty. "What can I do for you?"

"Nothing, really." I came into the dimness and stumbled on something. It was a cardboard box, the large fat kind used for delivering a jumbo pizza.

"I was just fixing dinner, and it looks like there's plenty for two, so I was wondering if you . . ." I trailed off, as I had just noticed something else. I had thought she was wearing shorts. In fact, all she had on was the shirt and a pair of pink bikini underpants. This did not seem to make her uneasy.

". . . would you like to join me for dinner?"

Her smile grew even broader.

"I'd love to," she said. She effortlessly unwound her legs and bounced to her feet, then brushed past me, trailing the smells of perspiration and sweet soap. "Be with you in a minute."

I looked around the room again but my mind kept coming back to her. She liked Pepsi with her pizza; there were dozens of empty cans. There was a deep scar on her knee and upper thigh. The ashtrays were empty . . . and the long muscles of her calves bunched strongly as she walked. Kluge must have smoked, but Lisa didn't, and she had fine, downy hairs in the small of her back just visible in the green computer light. I heard water running in the bathroom sink, looked at a yellow notepad covered with the kind of penmanship I hadn't seen in decades, and smelled soap and remembered tawny brown skin and an easy stride.

She appeared in the hall, wearing cut-off jeans, sandals, and a new T-shirt. The old one had advertised BURROUGHS OFFICE SYSTEMS. This one featured Mickey Mouse and Snow White's Castle and smelled of fresh bleached cotton. Mickey's ears were laid back on the upper slopes of Lisa Foo's incongruous breasts.

I followed her out the door. Tinkerbell twinkled in pixie dust from the back of her shirt.

"I like this kitchen," she said.

You don't really look at a place until someone says something like that.

The kitchen was a time capsule. It could have been lifted bodily from an issue of *Life* in the early fifties. There was the hump-shouldered Frigidaire, of a vintage when that word had been a generic term, like kleenex or coke. The countertops were yellow tile, the sort that's only found in bathrooms these days. There wasn't an ounce of Formica in the place. Instead of a dishwasher I had a wire rack and double sink. There was no electric can opener, Cuisinart, trash compacter, or microwave oven. The newest thing in the whole room was a fifteen-year-old blender.

I'm good with my hands. I like to repair things.

"This bread is terrific," she said.

I had baked it myself. I watched her mop her plate with a crust, and she asked if she might have seconds.

I understand cleaning one's plate with bread is bad manners. Not that I cared; I do it myself. And other than that, her manners were impeccable. She polished off three helpings of my casserole and when she was done the plate hardly needed washing. I had a sense of ravenous appetite barely held in check.

She settled back in her chair and I refilled her glass with white wine.

"Are you sure you wouldn't like some more peas?"

"I'd bust." She patted her stomach contentedly. "Thank you so much, Mr. Apfel. I haven't had a home-cooked meal in ages."

"You can call me Victor."

"I just love American food."

"I didn't know there was such a thing. I mean, not like Chinese or . . . You *are* American, aren't you?" She just smiled. "What I mean—"

"I know what you meant, Victor. I'm a citizen, but not native-born. Would you excuse me for a moment? I know it's impolite to jump right up, but with braces I find I have to brush *instantly* after eating."

I could hear her as I cleared the table. I ran water in the sink and started doing the dishes. Before long she joined me, grabbed a dish towel, and began drying the things in the rack, over my protests.

"You live alone here?" she asked.

"Yes. Have ever since my parents died."

"Ever married? If it's none of my business, just say so."

"That's all right. No, I never married."

"You do pretty good for not having a woman around."

"I've had a lot of practice. Can I ask you a question?"

"Shoot."

"Where are you from? Taiwan?"

"I have a knack for languages. Back home, I spoke pidgin American, but when I got here I cleaned up my act. I also speak rotten French, illiterate Chinese in four or five varieties, gutter Vietnamese, and enough Thai to holler, 'Me wanna see American Consul, pretty-damn-quick, you!'"

I laughed. When she said it, her accent was thick.

"I been here eight years now. You figured out where home is?"

"Vietnam?" I ventured.

"The sidewalks of Saigon, fer shure. Or Ho Chi Minh's Shitty, as the pajama-heads renamed it, may their dinks rot off and their butts be filled with jagged punjee-sticks. Pardon my French."

She ducked her head in embarrassment. What had started out light had turned hot very quickly. I sensed a hurt at least as deep as my own, and we both backed off from it.

"I took you for a Japanese," I said.

"Yeah, ain't it a pisser? I'll tell you about it someday. Victor, is that a laundry room through that door there? With an electric washer?"

"That's right."

"Would it be too much trouble if I did a load?"

It was no trouble at all. She had seven pairs of faded jeans, some with the legs cut away, and about two dozen T-shirts. It could have been a load of boys' clothing except for the frilly underwear.

We went into the backyard to sit in the last rays of the setting sun, then she had to see my garden. I'm quite proud of it. When I'm well, I spend four or five hours a day working out there, year-round, usually in the morning hours. You can do that in southern California. I have a small greenhouse I built myself.

She loved it, though it was not in its best shape. I had spent most of the week in bed or in the tub. As a result, weeds were spouting here and there.

"We had a garden when I was little," she said. "And I spent two years in a rice paddy."

"That must be a lot different than this."

"Damn straight. Put me off rice for *years*."

She discovered an infestation of aphids, so we squatted down to pick them off. She had that double-jointed Asian peasant's way of sitting that I remembered so well and could never imitate. Her fingers were long and narrow, and soon the tips of them were green from squashed bugs.

We talked about this and that. I don't remember quite how it came up, but I told her I had fought in Korea. I learned she was twenty-five. It turned out we had the same birthday, so some months back I had been exactly twice her age.

The only time Kluge's name came up was when she mentioned how she liked to cook. She hadn't been able to at Kluge's house.

"He has a freezer in the garage full of frozen dinners," she said. "He had one plate, one fork, one spoon, and one glass. He's got the best microwave oven on the market. And that's *it,* man. Ain't nothing else in his kitchen at *all.*" She shook her head, and executed an aphid. "He was one weird dude."

When her laundry was done it was late evening, almost dark. She loaded it into my wicker basket and we took it out to the clothesline. It got to be a game. I would shake out a T-shirt and study the picture or message there. Sometimes I got it, and sometimes I didn't. There were pictures of rock groups, a map of Los Angeles, Star Trek tie-ins . . . a little of everything.

"What's the L5 Society?" I asked her.

"Guys that want to build these great big farms in space. I asked 'em if they were gonna grow rice, and they said they didn't think it was the best crop for zero gee, so I bought the shirt."

"How many of these things do you have?"

"Wow, it's gotta be four or five hundred. I usually wear 'em two or three times and then put them away."

I picked up another shirt, and a bra fell out. It wasn't the kind of bra girls wore when I grew up. It was very sheer, though somehow functional at the same time.

"You like, Yank?" Her accent was very thick. "You oughtta see my sister!"

I glanced at her, and her face fell.

"I'm sorry, Victor," she said. "You don't have to blush." She took the bra from me and clipped it to the line.

She must have misread my face. True, I had been embarrassed, but I was also pleased in some strange way. It had been a long time since anybody had called me anything but Victor or Mr. Apfel.

The next day's mail brought a letter from a law firm in Chicago. It was about the seven hundred thousand dollars. The money had come from a Delaware holding company which had been set up in 1933 to provide for me in my old age. My mother and father were listed as the founders. Certain long-term investments had matured, resulting in my recent windfall. The amount in my bank was *after* taxes.

It was ridiculous on the face of it. My parents had never had that kind of money. I didn't want it. I would have given it back if I could find out who Kluge had stolen it from.

I decided that, if I wasn't in jail this time next year, I'd give it all to some charity. Save the Whales, maybe, or the L5 Society.

I spent the morning in the garden. Later I walked to the market and bought some fresh ground beef and pork. I was feeling good as I pulled my purchases home in my fold-up wire basket. When I passed the silver Ferrari I smiled.

She hadn't come to get her laundry. I took it off the line and folded it, then knocked on Kluge's door.

"It's me, Victor."

"Come on in, Yank."

She was where she had been before, but decently dressed this time. She smiled at me, then hit her forehead when she saw the laundry basket. She hurried to take it from me.

"I'm sorry, Victor. I meant to get this—"

"Don't worry about it," I said. "It was no trouble. And it gives me the chance to ask if you'd like to dine with me again."

Something happened to her face which she covered quickly. Perhaps she didn't like "American" food as much as she professed to. Or maybe it was the cook.

"Sure, Victor, I'd love to. Let me take care of this. And why don't you open those drapes? It's like a tomb in here."

She hurried away. I glanced at the screen she had been using. It was blank, but for one word: intercourse-p. I assumed it was a typo.

I pulled the drapes open in time to see Osborne's car park at the curb. Then Lisa was back, wearing a new T-shirt. This one said "A CHANGE OF HOBBIT," and had a picture of a squat, hairy-footed creature. She glanced out the window and saw Osborne coming up the walk.

"I say, Watson," she said. "It's Lestrade of the Yard. Do show him in."

That wasn't nice of her. He gave me a suspicious glance as he entered. I burst out laughing. Lisa sat on the piano bench, poker-faced. She slumped indolently, one arm resting near the keyboard.

"Well, Apfel," Osborne started. "We've finally found out who Kluge really was."

"Patrick William Gavin," Lisa said.

Quite a time went by before Osborne was able to close his mouth. Then he opened it right up again.

"How the hell did you find that out?"

She lazily caressed the keyboard beside her.

"Well, of course I got it when it came into your office this morning. There's a little stoolie program tucked away in your computer that whispers in my ear every time the name Kluge is mentioned. But I didn't need that. I figured it out five days ago."

"Then why the . . . why didn't you tell me?"

"You didn't ask me."

They glared at each other for a while. I had no idea what events had led up to this moment, but it was quite clear they didn't like each other even a little bit. Lisa was on top just now and seemed to be enjoying it. Then she glanced at her screen, looked surprised, and quickly tapped a key. She gave me an inscrutable glance, then faced Osborne again.

"If you recall, you brought me in because all your own guys were getting was a lot of crashes. This system was brain-damaged when I got here, practically catatonic. Most of it was down and you couldn't get it up." She had to grin at that.

"You decided I couldn't do any worse than your guys were doing. So you asked me to try and break Kluge's codes without frying the system. Well, I did it. All you had to do was come by and interface and I would have downloaded N tons of wallpaper right in your lap."

Osborne listened quietly. Maybe he even knew he had made a mistake.

"What did you get? Can I see it now?"

She nodded and pressed a few keys. Words started to fill her screen, and one close to Osborne. I got up and read Lisa's terminal.

It was a brief bio of Kluge/Gavin. He was about my age, but while I was getting shot at in a foreign land, he was cutting a swath through the infant computer industry. He had been there from the ground up, working at many of the top research facilities. It surprised me that it had taken over a week to identify him.

"I compiled this anecdotally," Lisa said, as we read. "The first thing you have to realize about Gavin is that he exists nowhere in any computerized information system. So I called people all over the country—interesting phone system he's got, by the way; it generates a new number for each call, and you can't call back or trace it—and started asking who the top people were in the fifties and sixties. I got a lot of names. After that, it was a matter of finding out who no longer existed in the files. He faked his death in 1967. I located one account of it in a newspaper file. Everybody I talked to who had known him knew of his death. There is a paper birth certificate in Florida. That's the only other evidence I found of him. He was the only guy so many people in the field knew who left no mark on the world. That seemed conclusive to me."

Osborne finished reading, then looked up.

"All right, Ms. Foo. What else have you found out?"

"I've broken some of his codes. I had a piece of luck, getting into a basic rape-and-plunder program he'd written to attack *other* people's programs, and I've managed to use it against a few of his own. I've unlocked a file of passwords with notes on where they came from. And I've learned a few of his tricks. But it's the tip of the iceberg."

She waved a hand at the silent metal brains in the room.

"What I haven't gotten across to anyone is just what this *is*. This is the most devious electronic weapon ever devised. It's armored like a battleship. It has to be; there's a lot of very slick programs out there that grab an invader and hang on like a terrier. If they ever got this far Kluge could deflect them. But usually they never even knew they'd been burgled. Kluge'd come in like a cruise missile, low and fast and twisty. And he'd route his attack through a dozen cutoffs.

"He had a lot of advantages. Big systems these days are heavily protected. People use passwords and very sophisticated codes. But Kluge helped *invent* most of them. You need a damn good lock to keep out a locksmith. He helped *install* a lot of the major systems. He left informants behind, hidden in the software. If the codes were changed, the computer *itself* would send the information to a safe system that Kluge could tap later. It's like you buy the biggest, meanest, best-trained watchdog you can. And that night, the guy who *trained* the dog comes in, pats him on the head, and robs you blind."

There was a lot more in that vein. I'm afraid that when Lisa began talking about computers, ninety percent of my head shut off.

"I'd like to know something, Osborne," Lisa said.

"What would that be?"

"What is my status here? Am I supposed to be solving your crime for you, or just trying to get this system back to where a competent user can deal with it?"

Osborne thought it over.

"What worries me," she added, "is that I'm poking around in a lot of restricted data banks. I'm worried about somebody knocking on the door and handcuffing me. *You* ought to be worried, too. Some of these agencies wouldn't like a homicide cop looking into their affairs."

Osborne bridled at that. Maybe that's what she intended.

"What do I have to do?" he snarled. "Beg you to stay?"

"No. I just want your authorization. You don't have to put it in writing. Just say you're behind me."

"Look. As far as L.A. County and the State of California are concerned, this house doesn't exist. There is no lot here. It doesn't appear in the assessor's records. This place is in a legal limbo. If anybody can authorize you to use this stuff, it's me, because I believe a murder was committed in it. So you just keep doing what you've been doing."

"That's not much of a commitment," she mused.

"It's all you're going to get. Now, what else have you got?"

She turned to her keyboard and typed for a while. Pretty soon a printer started, and Lisa leaned back. I glanced at her screen. It said: osculate posterior-p. I remembered that osculate meant kiss. Well, these people have their own language. Lisa looked up at me and grinned.

"Not you," she said, quietly. "*Him.*"

I hadn't the faintest notion of what she was talking about.

Osborne got his printout and was ready to leave. Again, he couldn't resist turning at the door for final orders.

"If you find anything to indicate he didn't commit suicide, let me know."

"Okay. He didn't commit suicide."

Osborne didn't understand for a moment.

"I want proof."

"Well, I have it, but you probably can't use it. He didn't write that ridiculous suicide note."

"How do you know that?"

"I knew that my first day here. I had the computer list the program. Then I compared it to Kluge's style. No *way* he could have written it. It's tighter'n a bug's ass. Not a spare line in it. Kluge didn't pick his alias for nothing. You know what that means?"

"Clever," I said.

"Literally. But it means . . . a Rube Goldberg device. Something overly complex. Something that works, but for the wrong reason. You 'kluge around' bugs in a program. It's the hacker's Vaseline."

"So?" Osborne wanted to know.

"So Kluge's programs were really crocked. They were full of bells and whistles he never bothered to clean out. He was a genius, and his programs worked, but you wonder why they did. Routines so bletcherous they'd make your skin crawl. Real crufty bagbiters. But good programming's so rare, even his diddles were better than most people's super-moby hacks."

I suspect Osborne understood about as much of that as I did.

"So you base your opinion on his programming style."

"Yeah. Unfortunately, it's gonna be ten years or so before that's admissible in court, like graphology or fingerprints. But if you know anything about programming you can look at it and see it. Somebody else wrote that suicide note—somebody damn good, by the way. That program called up his last will and testament in a sub-routine. And he definitely *did* write that. It's got his fingerprints all over it. He spent the last five years spying on the neighbors as a hobby. He tapped into military records, school records, word records, tax files, and bank accounts. And he turned every telephone for three blocks into a listening device. He was one hell of a snoop."

"Did he mention anywhere why he did that?" Osborne asked.

"I think he was more than half crazy. Possibly he was suicidal. He sure wasn't doing himself any good with all those pills he took. But he was preparing himself for death, and Victor was the only one he found worthy of leaving it all to. I'd have *believed* he committed suicide if not for that note. But he didn't write it. I'll swear to that."

We eventually got rid of him, and I went home to fix dinner. Lisa joined me when it was ready. Once more she had a huge appetite.

I fixed lemonade and we sat on my small patio and watched evening gather around us.

I woke up in the middle of the night, sweating. I sat up, thinking it out, and I didn't like my conclusions. So I put on my robe and slippers and went over to Kluge's.

The front door was open again. I knocked anyway. Lisa stuck her head around the corner.

"Victor? Is something wrong?"

"I'm not sure," I said. "May I come in?"

She gestured, and I followed her into the living room. An open can of Pepsi sat beside her console. Her eyes were red as she sat on her bench.

"What's up?" she said and yawned.

"You should be asleep, for one thing," I said.

She shrugged and nodded.

"Yeah. I can't seem to get in the right phase. Just now I'm in day mode. But Victor, I'm used to working odd hours, and long hours, and you didn't come over here to lecture me about that, did you?"

"No. You say Kluge was murdered."

"He didn't write his suicide note. That seems to leave murder."

"I was wondering why someone would kill him. He never left the house, so it was for something he did here with his computers. And now you're . . . well, I don't know *what* you're doing, frankly, but you seem to be poking into the same things. Isn't there a danger the same people will come after you?"

"People?" She raised an eyebrow.

I felt helpless. My fears were not well formed enough to make sense.

"I don't know . . . you mentioned agencies . . ."

"You notice how impressed Osborne was with that? You think there's some kind of conspiracy Kluge tumbled to, or you think the CIA killed him because he found out too much about something, or—"

"I don't know, Lisa. But I'm worried the same thing could happen to you."

Surprisingly, she smiled at me.

"Thank you so much, Victor. I wasn't going to admit it to Osborne, but I've been worried about that, too."

"Well, what are you going to do?"

"I want to stay here and keep working. So I gave some thought to what I could do to protect myself. I decided there wasn't anything."

"Surely there's something."

"Well, I got a gun, if that's what you mean. But think about it. Kluge was offed in the middle of the day. Nobody saw anybody enter or leave the house. So I asked myself, who can walk into a house in broad daylight, shoot Kluge, program that suicide note, and walk away, leaving no traces he'd ever been there?"

"Somebody very good."

"Goddamn good. So good there's not much chance one little gook's gonna be able to stop him if he decides to waste her."

She shocked me, both by her words and by her apparent lack of concern for her own fate. But she had said she was worried.

"Then you have to stop this. Get out of here."

"I won't be pushed around that way," she said. There was a tone of finality to it. I thought of things I might say, and rejected them all.

"You could at least . . . lock your front door," I concluded lamely.

She laughed and kissed my cheek.

"I'll do that, Yank. And I appreciate your concern. I really do."

I watched her close the door behind me, listened to her lock it, then trudged through the moonlight toward my house. Halfway there I stopped. I could suggest she stay in my spare bedroom. I could offer to stay with her at Kluge's.

No, I decided. She would probably take that the wrong way.

I was back in bed before I realized, with a touch of chagrin and more than a little disgust at myself, that she had every reason to take it the wrong way.

And me exactly twice her age.

I spent the morning in the garden, planning the evening's menu. I have always liked to cook, but dinner with Lisa had rapidly become the high point of my day. Not only that, I was already taking it for granted. So it hit me hard, around noon, when I looked out the front and saw her car gone.

I hurried to Kluge's front door. It was standing open. I made a quick search of the house. I found nothing until the master bedroom, where her clothes were stacked neatly on the floor.

Shivering, I pounded on the Laniers' front door. Betty answered and immediately saw my agitation.

"The girl at Kluge's house," I said. "I'm afraid something's wrong. Maybe we'd better call the police."

"What happened?" Betty asked, looking over my shoulder. "Did she call you? I see she's not back yet."

"Back?"

"I saw her drive away about an hour ago. That's quite a car she has."

Feeling like a fool, I tried to make nothing of it, but I caught a look in Betty's eye. I think she'd have liked to pat me on the head. It made me furious.

But she'd left her clothes, so surely she was coming back.

I kept telling myself that, then went to run a bath, as hot as I could stand it.

When I answered the door she was standing there with a grocery bag in each arm and her usual blinding smile on her face.

"I wanted to do this yesterday but I forgot until you came over, and I know I should have asked first, but then I wanted to surprise you, so I just went to get one or two items you didn't have in your garden and a couple of things that weren't in your spice rack . . ."

She kept talking as we unloaded the bags in the kitchen. I said nothing. She was wearing a new T-shirt. There was a big V, and under it a picture of a screw, followed by a hyphen and a small case p. I thought it over as she babbled on V, screw-p. I was determined not to ask what it meant.

"Do you like Vietnamese cooking?"

I looked at her and finally realized she was very nervous.

"I don't know," I said. "I've never had it. But I like Chinese, and Japanese, and Indian. I like to try new things." The last part was a lie, but not as bad as it might have been. I do try new recipes, and my tastes in food are catholic. I didn't expect to have much trouble with southeast Asian cuisine.

"Well, when I get through you *still* won't know," she laughed. "My momma was half-Chinese. So what you're gonna get here is a mongrel meal." She glanced up, saw my face, and laughed.

"I forgot. You've been to Asia. No, Yank, I ain't gonna serve any dog meat."

There was only one intolerable thing, and that was the chopsticks. I used them for as long as I could, then put them aside and got a fork.

"I'm sorry," I said. "Chopsticks happen to be a problem for me."

"You use them very well."

"I had plenty of time to learn how."

It was very good, and I told her so. Each dish was a revelation, not quite like anything I had ever had. Toward the end, I broke down halfway.

"Does the V stand for victory?" I asked.

"Maybe."

"Beethoven? Churchill? World War Two?"

She just smiled.

"Think of it as a challenge, Yank."

"Do I frighten you, Victor?"

"You did at first."

"It's my face, isn't it?"

"It's a generalized phobia of Orientals. I suppose I'm a racist. Not because I want to be."

She nodded slowly, there in the dark. We were on the patio again, but the sun had gone down a long time ago. I can't recall what we had talked about for all those hours. It had kept us busy, anyway.

"I have the same problem," she said.

"Fear of Orientals?" I had meant it as a joke.

"Of Cambodians." She let me take that in for a while, then went on. "When Saigon fell, I fled to Cambodia. It took me two years with stops when the Khmer Rouge put me in labor camps. I'm lucky to be alive, really."

"I thought they called it Kampuchea now."

She spat. I'm not even sure she was aware she had done it.

"It's the People's Republic of Syphilitic Dogs. The North Koreans treated you very badly, didn't they, Victor?"

"That's right."

"Koreans are pus suckers." I must have looked surprised, because she chuckled.

"You Americans feel so guilty about racism. As if you had invented it and nobody else—except maybe the South Africans and the Nazis—had ever practiced it as heinously as you. And you can't tell one yellow face from another, so you think of the yellow races as one homogeneous block. When in fact Orientals are among the most racist peoples on the earth. The Vietnamese have hated the Cambodians for a thousand years. The Chinese hate the Japanese. The Koreans hate everybody. And *everybody* hates the 'ethnic Chinese.' The Chinese are the Jews of the East."

"I've heard that."

She nodded, lost in her own thoughts.

"And I hate all Cambodians," she said, at last. "Like you, I don't wish to. Most of the people who suffered in the camps were Cambodians. It was the genocidal leaders, the Pol Pot scum, who I should hate." She looked at me. "But sometimes we don't get a lot of choice about things like that, do we, Yank?"

The next day I visited her at noon. It had cooled down, but was still warm in her dark den. She had not changed her shirt.

She told me a few things about computers. When she let me try some things on the keyboard, I quickly got lost. We decided I needn't plan on a career as a computer programmer.

One of the things she showed me was called a telephone modem, whereby she could reach other computers all over the world. She "interfaced" with someone at Stanford who she had never met, and who she knew only as "Bubble Sorter." They typed things back and forth at each other.

At the end, Bubble Sorter wrote "bye-p." Lisa typed T.

"What's T?" I asked.

"True. Means yes, but yes would be too straightforward for a hacker."

"You told me what a byte is. What's a byep?"

She looked up at me seriously.

"It's a question. Add p to a word, and make it a question. So bye-p means Bubble Sorter was asking if I wanted to log out. Sign off."

I thought that over.

"So how would you translate 'osculate posterior-p'?"

" 'You wanna kiss my ass?' But remember, that was for Osborne."

I looked at her T-shirt again, then up to her eyes, which were quite serious and serene. She waited, hands folded in her lap.

Intercourse-p.

"Yes," I said. "I would."

She put her glasses on the table and pulled her shirt over her head.

We made love in Kluge's big waterbed.

I had a certain amount of performance anxiety—it had been a long, *long* time. After that, I was so caught up in the touch and smell and taste of her that I went a little crazy. She didn't seem to mind.

At last we were done, and bathed in sweat. She rolled over, stood, and went to the window. She opened it and a breath of air blew over me. Then she put one knee on the bed, leaned over me, and got a pack of cigarettes from the bedside table. She lit one.

"I hope you're not allergic to smoke," she said.

"No. My father smoked. But I didn't know you did."

"Only afterwards," she said with a quick smile. She took a deep drag. "Everybody in Saigon smoked, I think." She stretched out on her back beside me and we lay like that, soaking wet, holding hands. She opened her legs so one of her bare feet touched mine. It seemed enough contact. I watched the smoke rise from her right hand.

"I haven't felt warm in thirty years," I said. "I've been hot, but I've never been warm. I feel warm now."

"Tell me about it," she said.

So I did, as much as I could, wondering if it would work this time. At thirty years remove, my story does not sound so horrible. We've seen so much in that time. There were people in jails at that very moment, enduring conditions as bad as any I encountered. The paraphernalia of oppression is still pretty much the same. Nothing physical happened to me that would account for thirty years lived as a recluse.

"I *was* badly injured," I told her. "My skull was fractured. I still have . . . problems from that. Korea can get very cold, and I was never warm enough. But it was the other stuff. What they call brainwashing now.

"We didn't know what it was. We couldn't understand that even after a man had told them all he knew they'd keep on at us. Keeping us awake. Disorienting us. Some guys signed confessions, made up all sorts of stuff, but even that wasn't enough. They'd just keep on at you.

"I never did figure it out. I guess I couldn't understand an evil that big. But when they were sending us back and some of the prisoners wouldn't go . . . they really didn't *want* to go, they really believed . . ."

I had to pause there. Lisa sat up, moved quietly to the end of the bed, and began massaging my feet.

"We got a taste of what the Vietnam guys got, later. Only for us it was reversed. The GIs were heroes, and the prisoners were . . ."

"You didn't break," she said. It wasn't a question.

"No, I didn't."

"That would be worse."

I looked at her. She had my foot pressed against her flat belly, holding me by the heel while her other hand massaged my toes.

"The country was shocked," I said. "They didn't understand what brainwashing was. I tried telling people how it was. I thought they were looking at me funny. After a while, I stopped talking about it. And I didn't have anything else to talk about.

"A few years back the Army changed its policy. Now they don't expect you to withstand psychological conditioning. It's understood you can say anything or sign anything."

She just looked at me, kept massaging my foot, and nodded slowly. Finally she spoke.

"Cambodia was hot," she said. "I kept telling myself when I finally got to the U.S. I'd live in Maine or someplace, where it snowed. And I did go to Cambridge, but I found out I didn't like snow."

She told me about it. The last time I heard, a million people had died over there. It was a whole country frothing at the mouth and snapping at anything that moved. Or like one of those sharks you read about that, when its guts are ripped out, bends in a circle and starts devouring itself.

She told me about being forced to build a pyramid of severed heads. Twenty of them working all day in the hot sun finally got it ten feet high before it collapsed. If any of them stopped working, their own heads were added to the pile.

"It didn't mean anything to me. It was just another job. I was pretty crazy by then. I didn't start to come out of it until I got across the Thai border."

That she had survived it at all seemed a miracle. She had gone through more horror than I could imagine. And she had come through it in much better shape. It made me feel small. When I was her age, I was well on my way to building the prison I have lived in ever since. I told her that.

"Part of it is preparation," she said wryly. "What you expect out of life, what your life has been so far. You said it yourself. Korea was new to you. I'm not saying I was ready for Cambodia, but my life up to that point hadn't been what you'd call sheltered. I hope you haven't been thinking I made a living in the streets by selling apples."

She kept rubbing my feet, staring off into scenes I could not see.

"How old were you when your mother died?"

"She was killed during Tet, 1968. I was ten."

"By the Viet Cong?"

"Who knows? Lots of bullets flying, lot of grenades being thrown."

She sighed, dropped my foot, and sat there, a scrawny Buddha without a rope.

"You ready to do it again, Yank?"

"I don't think I can, Lisa. I'm an old man."

She moved over me and lowered herself with her chin just below my sternum, settling her breasts in the most delicious place possible.

"We'll see," she said and giggled. "There's an alternative sex act I'm pretty good at, and I'm pretty sure it would make you a young man again. But I haven't been able to do it for about a year on account of these." She tapped her braces. "It'd be sort of like sticking it in a buzz saw. So now I do this instead. I call it 'touring the silicone valley.'" She started moving her body up and down, just a few inches at a time. She blinked innocently a couple of times, then laughed.

"At last, I can see you" she said. "I'm awfully myopic."

I let her do that for a while, then lifted my head.

"Did you say silicone?"

"Uh-huh. You didn't think they were real, did you?"

I confessed that I had.

"I don't think I've ever been so happy with anything I ever bought. Not even the car."

"Why did you?"

"Does it bother you?"

It didn't, and I told her so. But I couldn't conceal my curiosity.

"Because it was safe to. In Saigon I was always angry that I never developed. I could have made a good living as a prostitute, but I was always too small, too skinny, and too ugly. Then in Cambodia I was lucky. I managed to pass for a boy some of the time. If not for that I'd have been raped a lot more than I was. And in Thailand I knew I'd get to the West one way or another, and when I got there, I'd get the best car there was, eat anything I wanted anytime I wanted to, and purchase the best tits money could buy. You can't imagine what the West looks like from the camps. A place where you can buy tits!"

She looked down between them, then back at my face.

"Looks like it was a good investment," she said.

"They do seem to work okay," I had to admit.

We agreed that she would spend the nights at my house. There were certain things she had to do at Kluge's, involving equipment that had to be physically loaded, but many things she could do with a remote terminal and an armload of software. So we selected one of Kluge's best computers and about a dozen peripherals and installed her at a cafeteria table in my bedroom.

I guess we both knew it wasn't much protection if the people who got Kluge decided to get her. But I know I felt better about it, and I think she did, too.

The second day she was there a delivery van pulled up outside and two guys started unloading a king-size waterbed. She laughed and laughed when she saw my face.

"Listen, you're not using Kluge's computers to—"

"Relax, Yank. How'd you think I could afford a Ferrari?"

"I've been curious."

"If you're really good at writing software you can make a lot of money. I own my own company. But every hacker picks up tricks here and there. I used to run a few Kluge scams, myself."

"But not anymore?"

She shrugged. "Once a thief, always a thief, Victor. I told you I couldn't make ends meet selling my bod."

Lisa didn't need much sleep.

We got up at seven, and I made breakfast every morning. Then we would spend an hour or two working in the garden. She would go to Kluge's and I'd bring her a sandwich at noon, then drop in on her several times during the day. That was for my own peace of mind; I never stayed more than a minute. Sometime during the afternoon I would shop or do household chores, then at seven one of us would cook dinner. We alternated. I taught her "American" cooking, and she taught me a little of everything. She complained about the lack of vital ingredients in American markets. No dogs, of course, but she claimed to know great ways of preparing monkey, snake, and rat. I never knew how hard she was pulling my leg, and didn't ask.

After dinner she stayed at my house. We would talk, make love, bathe.

She loved my tub. It is about the only alteration I have made in the house, and my only real luxury. I put it in—having to expand the bathroom to do so—in 1975, and never regretted it. We would soak for twenty minutes or an hour, turning the jets and bubblers on and off, washing each other, giggling like kids. Once we used bubble bath and made a mountain of suds four feet high, then destroyed it, splashing water all over the place. Most nights she let me wash her long black hair.

She didn't have any bad habits—or at least none that clashed with mine. She was neat and clean, changing her clothes twice a day and never so much as leaving a dirty glass on the sink. She never left a mess in the bathroom. Two glasses of wine was her limit.

I felt like Lazarus.

Osborne came by three times in the next two weeks. Lisa met him at Kluge's and gave him what she had learned. It was getting to be quite a list.

"Kluge once had an account in a New York bank with nine *trillion* dollars in it," she told me after one of Osborne's visits. "I think he did it just to see if he could. He left it in for one day, took the interest, and fed it to a bank in the Bahamas, then destroyed the principal. Which never existed anyway."

In return, Osborne told her what was new on the murder investigation—which was nothing—and on the status of Kluge's property, which was chaotic. Various agencies had sent people out to look the place over. Some FBI men came, wanting to take over the investigation. Lisa, when talking about computers, had the power to cloud men's minds. She did it first by explaining exactly what she was do-ing, in terms so abstruse that no one could understand her. Sometimes that was enough. If it wasn't, if they started to get tough, she just moved out of the driver's seat and let them try to handle Kluge's contraption. She let them watch in horror as dragons leaped out of nowhere and ate up all the data on a disk, then printed "You Stupid Putz!" on the screen.

"I'm cheating them," she confessed to me. "I'm giving them stuff I *know* they're gonna step in, because I already stepped in it myself. I've lost about forty percent of the data Kluge had stored away. But the others lose a hundred percent. You ought to see their faces when Kluge drops a logic bomb into their work. That second guy threw a three-thousand-dollar printer clear across the room. Then tried to bribe me to be quiet about it."

When some federal agency sent out an expert from Stanford, and he seemed perfectly content to destroy everything in sight in the firm belief that he was *bound* to get it right sooner or later, Lisa showed him how Kluge entered the IRS main-frame computer in Washington and neglected to mention how Kluge had gotten out. The guy tangled with some watchdog program. During his struggles, it seemed he had erased all the tax records from the letter S down into the W's. Lisa let him think that for half an hour.

"I thought he was having a heart attack," she told me. "All the blood drained out of his face and he couldn't talk. So I showed him where I had—with my usual foresight—arranged for that to be recorded, told him how to put it back where he found it, and how to pacify the watchdog. He couldn't get out of that house fast enough. Pretty soon he's gonna realize you *can't* destroy that much information with anything short of dynamite because of the backups and the limits of how much can be running at any one time. But I don't think he'll be back."

"It sounds like a very fancy video game," I said.

"It is, in a way. But it's more like Dungeons and Dragons. It's an endless series of closed rooms with dangers on the other side. You don't dare take it a step at a time. You take it a *hundredth* of a step at a time. Your questions are like, 'How this isn't a question, but if it entered my mind to *ask* this question—which I'm not about to do—concerning what might happen if I looked at this door here—and I'm not touching it, I'm not even in the next room—what do you suppose you might do?' And the program crunches on that, decides if you fulfilled the condi-tions for getting a great big cream pie in the face, then either throws it or allows as how it *might* just move from step A to step A prime. Then you say, 'Well, maybe I *am* looking at that door.' And sometimes the program says, 'You looked, you looked, you dirty crook!' And the fireworks start."

Silly as all that sounds, it was very close to the best explanation she was ever able to give me about what she was doing.

"Are you telling everything, Lisa?" I asked her.

"Well, not *every*thing. I didn't mention the four cents."

Four cents? Oh my god.

"Lisa, I didn't want that, I didn't ask for it, I wish he'd never—"

"Calm down, Yank. It's going to be all right."

"He kept records of all that, didn't he?"

"That's what I spend most of my time doing. Decoding his records."

"How long have you known?"

"About the seven hundred thousand dollars? It was in the first disk I cracked."

"I just want to give it back."

She thought that over and shook her head.

"Victor, it'd be more dangerous to get rid of it now than it would be to keep it. It was imaginary money at first. But now it's got a history. The IRS thinks it knows where it came from. The taxes are paid on it. The State of Delaware is convinced that a legally chartered corporation disbursed it. An Illinois law firm has been paid for handling it. Your bank has been paying you interest on it. I'm not saying it would be impossible to go back and wipe all that out, but I wouldn't like to try. I'm good, but I don't have Kluge's touch."

"How could he *do* all that? You say it was imaginary money. That's not the way I thought money worked. He could just pull it out of thin air?"

Lisa patted the top of her computer console and smiled at me.

"This is money, Yank," she said, and her eyes glittered.

At night she worked by candlelight so she wouldn't disturb me. That turned out to be my downfall. She typed by touch and needed the candle only to locate software.

So that's how I'd go to sleep every night, looking at her slender body bathed in the glow of the candle. I was always reminded of melting butter dripping down a roasted ear of corn. Golden light on golden skin.

Ugly, she had called herself. Skinny. It was true she was thin. I could see her ribs when she sat with her back impossibly straight, her tummy tucked in, her chin up. She worked in the nude these days, sitting in lotus position. For long periods she would not move, her hands lying on her thighs, then she would poise, as if to pound the keys. But her touch was light, almost silent. It looked more like yoga than programming. She said she went into a meditative state for her best work.

I had expected a bony angularity, all sharp elbows and knees. She wasn't like that. I had guessed her weight ten pounds too low, and still didn't know where she put it. But she was soft and rounded, and strong beneath.

No one was ever going to call her face glamorous. Few would even go so far as to call her pretty. The braces did that, I think. They caught the eye and held it, drawing attention to that unsightly jumble.

But her skin was wonderful. She had scars. Not as many as I had expected. She seemed to heal quickly, and well.

I thought she was beautiful.

I had just completed my nightly survey when my eye was caught by the candle. I looked at it, then tried to look away.

Candles do that sometimes. I don't know why. In still air, with the flame perfectly vertical, they begin to flicker. The flame leaps up then squats down, up and down, up and down, brighter and brighter in regular rhythm, two or three beats to the second—

—and I tried to call out to her, wishing the candle would stop its regular flickering, but already I couldn't speak—

—I could only gasp, and I tried once more, as hard as I could, to yell, to scream, to tell her not to worry, and felt the nausea building . . .

I tasted blood. I took an experimental breath, did not find the smells of vomit, urine, feces. The overhead lights were on.

Lisa was on her hands and knees leaning over me, her face very close. A tear dropped on my forehead. I was on the carpet, on my back.

"Victor, can you hear me?"

I nodded. There was a spoon in my mouth. I spit it out.

"You just lie there. The ambulance is on its way."

"No. Don't need it."

"Well, it's on its way. You just take it easy and—"

"Help me up."

"Not yet. You're not ready."

She was right. I tried to sit up and fell back quietly. I took deep breaths for a while. Then the doorbell rang.

She stood up and started to the door. I just managed to get my hand around her ankle. Then she was leaning over me again, her eyes as wide as they would go.

"What is it? What's wrong now?"

"Get some clothes on," I told her. She looked down at herself, surprised.

"Oh. Right."

*   *   *

She got rid of the ambulance crew. Lisa was a lot calmer after she made coffee and we were sitting at the kitchen table. It was one o'clock and I was still pretty rocky. But it hadn't been a bad one.

I went to the bathroom and got the bottle of Dilantin I'd hidden when she moved in. I let her see me take one.

"I forgot to do this today," I told her.

"It's because you hid them. That was stupid."

"I know." There must have been something else I could have said. It didn't please me to see her look hurt. But she was hurt because I wasn't defending myself against her attack, and that was a bit too complicated for me to dope out just after a grand mal.

"You can move out if you want to," I said. I was in rare form.

So was she. She reached across the table and shook me by the shoulders. She glared at me.

"I won't take a lot more of that kind of shit," she said, and I nodded and began to cry.

She let me do it. I think that was probably best. She could have babied me, but I do a pretty good job of that myself.

"How long has this been going on?" she finally said. "Is that why you've stayed in your house for thirty years?"

I shrugged. "I guess it's part of it. When I got back they operated, but it just made it worse."

"Okay. I'm mad at you because you didn't tell me about it, so I didn't know what to do. I want to stay, but you'll have to tell me how. Then I won't be mad anymore."

I could have blown the whole thing right there. I'm amazed I didn't. Through the years I'd developed very good methods for doing things like that. But I pulled through when I saw her face. She really did want to stay. I didn't know why, but it was enough.

"The spoon was a mistake," I said. "If there's time, and if you can do it without risking your fingers, you could jam a piece of cloth in there. Part of a sheet, or something. But nothing hard." I explored my mouth with a finger. "I think I broke a tooth."

"Serves you right," she said. I looked at her and smiled, then we were both laughing. She came around the table and kissed me, then sat on my knee.

"The biggest danger is drowning. During the first part of the seizure, all my muscles go rigid. That doesn't last long. Then they all start contracting and relaxing at random. It's *very* strong."

"I know. I watched, and I tried to hold you."

"Don't do that. Get me on my side. Stay behind me and watch out for flailing arms. Get a pillow under my head if you can. Keep me away from things I could injure myself on." I looked her square in the eye. "I want to emphasize this. Just *try* to do all those things. If I'm getting too violent, it's better you stand off to the side. Better for both of us. If I knock you out, you won't be able to help me if I start strangling on vomit."

I kept looking at her eyes. She must have read my mind, because she smiled slightly.

"Sorry, Yank. I am not freaked out. I mean, like, it's totally gross, you know, and it barfs me out to the max, you could—"

"—gag me with a spoon, I know. Okay, right, I know I was dumb. And that's about it. I might bite my tongue or the inside of my cheek. Don't worry about it. There is one more thing."

She waited and I wondered how much to tell her. There wasn't a lot she could do, but if I died on her I didn't want her to feel it was her fault.

"Sometimes I have to go to the hospital. Sometimes one seizure will follow another. If that keeps up for too long, I won't breathe, and my brain will die of oxygen starvation."

"That only takes about five minutes," she said, alarmed.

"I know. It's only a problem if I start having them frequently, so we could plan for it if I do. But if I don't come out of one, start having another right on the heels of the first, or if you can't detect any breathing for three or four minutes, you'd better call an ambulance."

"Three or four minutes? You'd be dead before they got here."

"It's that or live in a hospital. I don't like hospitals."

"Neither do I."

The next day she took me for a ride in her Ferrari. I was nervous about it, wondering if she was going to do crazy things. If anything, she was too slow. People behind her kept honking. I could tell she hadn't been driving long from the exaggerated attention she put into every movement.

"A Ferrari is wasted on me, I'm afraid," she confessed at one point. "I never drive it faster than fifty-five."

We went to an interior decorator in Beverly Hills and she bought a low-watt gooseneck lamp at an outrageous price.

I had a hard time getting to sleep that night. I suppose I was afraid of having another seizure, though Lisa's new lamp wasn't going to set it off.

Funny about seizures. When I first started having them, everyone called them fits. Then, gradually, it was seizures, until fits began to sound dirty.

I guess it's a sign of growing old, when the language changes on you.

There were rafts of new words. A lot of them were for things that didn't even exist when I was growing up. Like software. I always visualized a limp wrench.

"What got you interested in computers, Lisa?" I asked her.

She didn't move. Her concentration when sitting at the machine was pretty damn good. I rolled onto my back and tried to sleep.

"It's where the power is, Yank." I looked up. She had turned to face me.

"Did you pick it all up since you got to America?"

"I had a head start. I didn't tell you about my Captain, did I?"

"I don't think you did."

"He was strange. I knew that. I was about fourteen. He was an American, and he took an interest in me. He got me a nice apartment in Saigon. And he put me in school."

She was studying me, looking for a reaction. I didn't give her one.

"He was surely a pedophile, and probably had homosexual tendencies, since I looked so much like a skinny little boy."

Again the wait. This time she smiled.

"He was good to me. I learned to read well. From there on, anything is possible."

"I didn't actually ask you about your Captain. I asked why you got interested in computers."

"That's right. You did."

"Is it just a living?"

"It started that way. It's the future, Victor."

"God knows I've read that enough times."

"It's true. It's already here. It's power, if you know how to use it. You've seen what Kluge was able to do. You can make money with one of these things. I don't mean earn it, I mean *make* it, like if you had a printing press. Remember Osborne mentioned that Kluge's house didn't exist? Did you think what that means?"

"That he wiped it out of the memory banks."

"That was the first step. But the lot exists in the county plat books, wouldn't you think? I mean, this country hasn't *entirely* given up paper."

"So the county really does have a record of that house."

"No. That page was torn out of the records."

"I don't get it. Kluge never left the house."

"Oldest way in the world, friend. Kluge looked through the LAPD files until he found a guy known as Sammy. He sent him a cashier's check for a thousand dollars, along with a letter saying he could earn twice that if he'd go to the Hall of

Records and do something. Sammy didn't bite, and neither did McGee, or Molly Unger. But Little Billy Phipps did, and he got a check just like the letter said, and he and Kluge had a wonderful business relationship for many years. Little Billy drives a new Cadillac now, and hasn't the faintest notion who Kluge was or where he lived. It didn't matter to Kluge how much he spent. He just pulled it out of thin air."

I thought that over for a while. I guess it's true that with enough money you can do just about anything, and Kluge had all the money in the world.

"Did you tell Osborne about Little Billy?"

"I erased that disk, just like I erased your seven hundred thousand. You never know when you might need somebody like Little Billy."

"You're not afraid of getting into trouble over it?"

"Life is risk, Victor. I'm keeping the best stuff for myself. Not because I intend to use it, but because if I ever needed it badly and didn't have it, I'd feel like such a fool."

She cocked her head and narrowed her eyes, which made them practically disappear.

"Tell me something, Yank. Kluge picked you out of all your neighbors because you'd been a Boy Scout for thirty years. How do you react to what I'm doing?"

"You're cheerfully amoral, and you're a survivor, and you're basically decent. And I pity anybody who gets in your way."

She grinned, stretched, and stood up.

"'Cheerfully amoral,' I like that." She sat beside me, making a great sloshing in the bed. "You want to be amoral again?"

"In a little bit." She started rubbing my chest. "So you got into computers because they were the wave of the future. Don't you ever worry about them . . . I don't know, I guess it sounds corny . . . Do you think they'll take over?"

"Everybody thinks that until they start to use them," she said. "You've got to realize just how stupid they are. Without programming they are good for nothing, literally. Now, what I do believe is that the people who *run* the computers will take over. They already have. That's why I study them."

"I guess that's not what I meant. Maybe I can't say it right."

She frowned. "Kluge was looking into something. He'd been eavesdropping in artificial intelligence labs and reading a lot of neurological research. I think he was trying to find a common thread."

"Between human brains and computers?"

"Not quite. He was thinking of computers and neurons. Brain cells." She pointed to her computer. "That thing, or any other computer, is light-years away from being a human brain. It can't generalize, or infer, or categorize, or invent. With good programming it can appear to do some of those things, but it's an illusion.

"There's an old speculation about what would happen if we finally built a computer with as many transistors as the human brain has neurons. Would there be a self-awareness? I think that's baloney. A transistor isn't a neuron, and a quintillion of them aren't any better than a dozen.

"So Kluge—who seems to have felt the same way—started looking into the possible similarities between a neuron and an eight-bit computer. That's why he had all that consumer junk sitting around his house, those Trash-80's and Atari's and TI's and Sinclair's, for chrissake. He was used to *much* more powerful instruments. He ate up the home units like candy."

"What did he find out?"

"Nothing, it looks like. An eight-bit unit is more complex than a neuron, and no computer is in the same galaxy as an organic brain. But see, the words get tricky. I said an Atari is more complex than a neuron, but it's hard to really compare them. It's like comparing a direction with a distance, or a color with a mass. The units are different. Except for one similarity."

"What's that?"

"The connections. Again, it's different, but the concept of networking is the same. A neuron is connected to a lot of others. There are trillions of them, and the way messages pulse through them determines what we are and what we think and what we remember. And with that computer I can reach a million others. It's bigger than the human brain, really, because the information in that network is more than all humanity could cope with in a million years. It reaches from Pioneer Ten, out beyond the orbit of Pluto, right into every living room that has a telephone in it. With that computer you can tap tons of data that has been collected but nobody's even had the time to look at.

"That's what Kluge was interested in. The old 'critical mass computer' idea, the computer that becomes aware, but with a new angle. Maybe it wouldn't be the size of the computer, but the *number* of computers. There used to be thousands of them. Now there's millions. They're putting them in cars. In wristwatches. Every home has several, from the simple timer on a microwave oven up to a video game or home terminal. Kluge was trying to find out if critical mass could be reached that way."

"What did he think?"

"I don't know. He was just getting started." She glanced down at me. "But you know what, Yank? I think you've reached critical mass while I wasn't looking."

"I think you're right." I reached for her.

Lisa like to cuddle. I didn't, at first, after fifty years of sleeping alone. But I got to like it pretty quickly.

That's what we were doing when we resumed the conversation we had been having. We just lay in each other's arms and talked about things. Nobody had mentioned love yet, but I knew I loved her. I didn't know what to do about it, but I would think of something.

"Critical mass," I said. She nuzzled my neck and yawned.

"What about it?"

"What would it be like? It seems like it would be such a vast intelligence. So quick, so omniscient. God-like."

"Could be."

"Wouldn't it . . . run our lives? I guess I'm asking the same questions I started off with. Would it take over?"

She thought about it for a long time.

"I wonder if there would be anything to take over. I mean, why should it care? How could we figure what its concerns would be? Would it want to be worshipped, for instance? I doubt it. Would it want to 'rationalize all human behavior, to eliminate all emotions,' as I'm sure some sci-fi film computer must have told some damsel in distress in the fifties.

"You can use a word like awareness, but what does it mean? An amoeba must be aware. Plants probably are. There may be a level of awareness in a neuron. Even in an integrated circuit chip. We don't even know what our own awareness really is. We've never been able to shine a light on it, dissect it, figure out where it comes from or where it goes when we're dead. To apply human values to a thing like this hypothetical computer-net consciousness would be pretty stupid. But I don't see how it could interact with human awareness at all. It might not even notice us, any more than we notice cells in our bodies, or neutrinos passing through us, or the vibrations of the atoms in the air around us."

So she had to explain what a neutrino was. One thing I always provided her with was an ignorant audience. And after that, I pretty much forgot about our mythical hypercomputer.

"What about your Captain?" I asked, much later.

"Do you really want to know, Yank?" she mumbled sleepily.

"I'm not afraid to know."

She sat up and reached for her cigarettes. I had come to know she sometimes smoked them in times of stress. She had told me she smoked after making love, but that first time had been the only time. The lighter flared in the dark. I heard her exhale.

"My Major, actually. He got a promotion. Do you want to know his name?"

"Lisa, I don't want to know any of it if you don't want to tell it. But if you do, what I want to know is did he stand by you."

"He didn't marry me, if that's what you mean. When he knew he had to go, he said he would, but I talked him out of it. Maybe it was the most noble thing I ever did. Maybe it was the most stupid.

"It's no accident I look Japanese. My grandmother was raped in '42 by a Jap soldier of the occupation. She was Chinese, living in Hanoi. My mother was born there. They went south after Dien Bien Phu. My grandmother died. My mother had it hard. Being Chinese was tough enough, but being half-Chinese and half-Japanese was worse. My father was half-French and half-Annamese. Another bad combination. I never knew him. But I'm sort of a capsule history of Vietnam."

The end of her cigarette glowed brighter once more.

"I've got one grandfather's face and the other grandfather's height. With tits by Goodyear. About all I missed was some American genes, but I was working on that for my children.

"When Saigon was falling I tried to get to the American Embassy. Didn't make it. You know the rest, until I got to Thailand, and when I finally got Americans to notice me, it turned out my Major was still looking for me. He sponsored me over here, and I made it in time to watch him die of cancer. Two months I had with him, all of it in the hospital."

"My God." I had a horrible thought. "That wasn't the war, too, was it? I mean, the story of your life—"

"—is the rape of Asia. No, Victor. Not that war, anyway. But he was one of those guys who got to see atom bombs up close, out in Nevada. He was too Regular Army to complain about it, but I think he knew that's what killed him."

"Did you love him?"

"What do you want me to say? He got me out of hell."

Again the cigarette flared, and I saw her stub it out.

"No," she said. "I didn't love him. He knew that. I've never loved anybody. He was very dear, very special to me. I would have done almost anything for him. He was fatherly to me." I felt her looking at me in the dark. "Aren't you going to ask how old he was?"

"Fiftyish," I said.

"On the nose. Can I ask you something?"

"I guess it's your turn."

"How many girls have you had since you got back from Korea?"

I held up my hand and pretended to count on my fingers.

"One," I said, at last.

"How many before you went?"

"One. We broke up before I left for the war."

"How many in Korea?"

"Nine. All at Madame Park's jolly little whorehouse in Pusan."

"So you've made love to one white and ten Asians. I bet none of the others were as tall as me."

"Korean girls have fatter cheeks, too. But they all had your eyes."

She nuzzled against my chest, took a deep breath, and sighed.

"We're a hell of a pair, aren't we?"

I hugged her, and her breath came again, hot on my chest. I wondered how I'd lived so long without such a simple miracle as that.

"Yes. I think we really are."

Osborne came by again about a week later. He seemed subdued. He listened to the things Lisa had decided to give him without much interest. He took the print-out she handed him and promised to turn it over to the departments that handled those things. But he didn't get up to leave.

"I thought I ought to tell you, Apfel," he said, at last. "The Gavin case has been closed."

I had to think a moment to remember Kluge's real name had been Gavin.

"The coroner ruled suicide a long time ago. I was able to keep the case open quite a while on the strength of my suspicions." He nodded toward Lisa. "And on what she said about the suicide note. But there was just no evidence at all."

"It probably happened quickly," Lisa said. "Somebody caught him, tracked him back—it can be done; Kluge was lucky for a long time—and did him the same day."

"You don't think it was suicide?" I asked Osborne.

"No. But whoever did it is home free unless something new turns up."

"I'll tell you if it does," Lisa said.

"That's something else," Osborne said. "I can't authorize you to work over there anymore. The county's taken possession of house and contents."

"Don't worry about it," Lisa said softly.

There was a short silence as she leaned over to shake a cigarette from the pack on the coffee table. She lit it, exhaled, and leaned back beside me, giving Osborne her most inscrutable look. He sighed.

"I'd hate to play poker with you, lady," he said. "What do you mean, 'Don't worry about it'?"

"I bought the house four days ago. And its contents. If anything turns up that would help you reopen the murder investigation, I will let you know."

Osborne was too defeated to get angry. He studied her quietly for a while.

"I'd like to know how you swung that."

"I did nothing illegal. You're free to check it out. I paid good cash money for it. The house came onto the market. I got a good price at the sheriff's sale."

"How'd you like it if I put my best men on the transaction? See if they can dig up some funny money? Maybe fraud. How about I get the FBI in to look it all over?"

She gave him a cool look.

"You're welcome to. Frankly, Detective Osborne, I could have stolen that house, Griffith Park, and the Harbor Freeway and I don't think you could have caught me."

"So where does that leave me?"

"Just where you were. With a closed case, and a promise from me."

"I don't like you having all that stuff, if it can do the things you say it can do."

"I didn't expect you would. But that's not your department, is it? The county owned it for a while, through simple confiscation. They didn't know what they had, and they let it go."

"Maybe I can get the Fraud detail out here to confiscate your software. There's criminal evidence on it."

"You could try that," she agreed.

They stared at each other for a while. Lisa won. Osborne rubbed his eyes and nodded. Then he heaved himself to his feet and slumped to the door.

Lisa stubbed out her cigarette. We listened to him going down the walk.

"I'm surprised he gave up so easy," I said. "Or did he? Do you think he'll try a raid?"

"It's not likely. He knows the score."

"Maybe you could tell it to me."

"For one thing, it's not his department, and he knows it."

"Why did you buy the house?"

"You ought to ask *how.*"

I looked at her closely. There was a gleam of amusement behind the poker face.

"Lisa. What did you do?"

"That's what Osborne asked himself. He got the right answer, because he understands Kluge's machines. And he knows how things get done. It was no accident I was the only bidder. I used one of Kluge's pet councilmen."

"You bribed him?"

She laughed and kissed me.

"I think I finally managed to shock you, Yank. That's gotta be the biggest difference between me and a native-born American. Average citizens don't spend much on bribes over here. In Saigon, everybody bribes."

"Did you bribe him?"

"Nothing so indelicate. One has to go in the back door over here. Several entirely legal campaign contributions appeared in the accounts of a state senator, who mentioned a certain situation to someone, who happened to be in the position to do legally what I happened to want done." She looked at me askance. "Of *course* I bribed him, Victor. You'd be amazed to know how cheaply. Does that bother you?"

"Yes," I admitted. "I don't like bribery."

"I'm indifferent to it. It happens, like gravity. It may not be admirable, but it gets things done."

"I assume you covered yourself."

"Reasonably well. You're never entirely covered with a bribe, because of the human element. The councilman might geek if they got him in front of a grand jury. But they won't, because Osborne won't pursue it. That's the second reason he walked out of here without a fight. *He* knows how the world wobbles, he knows what kind of force I now possess, and he knows he can't fight it."

There was a long silence after that. I had a lot to think about, and I didn't feel good about most of it. At one point Lisa reached for the pack of cigarettes, then changed her mind. She waited for me to work it out.

"It is a terrific force, isn't it," I finally said.

"It's frightening," she agreed. "Don't think it doesn't scare me. Don't think I haven't had fantasies of being superwoman. Power is an awful temptation, and it's not easy to reject. There's so much I could do."

"Will you?"

"I'm not talking about stealing things, or getting rich."

"I didn't think you were."

"This is political power. But I don't know how to wield it . . . it sounds corny, but to use it for good. I've seen so much evil come from good intentions. I don't think I'm wise enough to do any good. And the chances of getting torn up like Kluge did are large. But I'm wise enough to walk away from it. I'm still a street urchin from Saigon, Yank. I'm smart enough not to use it unless I have to. But I can't give it away, and I can't destory it. Is that stupid?"

I didn't have a good answer for that one. But I had a bad feeling.

My doubts had another week to work on me. I didn't come to any great moral conclusions. Lisa knew of some crimes, and she wasn't reporting them to the authorities. That didn't bother me much. She had at her fingertips the means to commit more crimes, and that bothered me a lot. Yet I really didn't think she planned to do anything. She was smart enough to use the things she had only in a defensive way—but with Lisa that could cover a lot of ground.

When she didn't show up for dinner one evening, I went over to Kluge's and found her busy in the living room. A nine-foot section of shelving had been cleared. The disks and tapes were stacked on a table. She had a big plastic garbage can and a magnet the size of a softball. I watched her wave a tape near the magnet, then toss it in the garbage can, which was almost full. She glanced up, did the same operation with a handful of disks, then took off her glasses and wiped her eyes.

"Feel any better now, Victor?" she asked.

"What do mean? I feel fine."

"No, you don't. And I haven't felt right, either. It hurts me to do it, but I have to. You want to go get the other trash can?"

I did, and helped her pull more software from the shelves.

"You're not going to wipe it all, are you?"

"No. I'm wiping records, and . . . something else."

"Are you going to tell me what?"

"There are things it's better not to know," she said darkly.

I finally managed to convince her to talk over dinner. She had said little, just eating and shaking her head. But she gave in.

"Rather dreary, actually," she said. "I've been probing around some delicate places the last couple days. These are places Kluge visited at will, but they scare the hell out of me. Dirty places. Places where they know things I thought I'd like to find out."

She shivered, and seemed reluctant to go on.

"Are you talking about military computers? The CIA?"

"The CIA is where it starts. It's the easiest. I've looked around at NORAD— that's the guys who get to fight the next war. It makes me shiver to see how easy Kluge got in there. He cobbled up a way to start World War Three, just as an exercise. That's one of the things we just erased. The last two days I was nibbling around the edges of the big boys. The Defense Intelligence Agency and the National Security . . . something. DIA and NSA. Each of them is bigger than the CIA. Something knew I was there. Some watchdog program. As soon as I realized that, I got out quick, and I've spent the last five hours being sure it didn't follow me. And now I'm sure, and I've destroyed all that, too."

"You think they're the ones who killed Kluge?"

"They're surely the best candidates. He had tons of their stuff. I know he helped design the biggest installation at NSA, and he'd been poking around in there for years. One false step is all it would take."

"Did you get it all? I mean, are you sure?"

"I'm sure they didn't track me. I'm not sure I've destroyed all the records. I'm going back now to take a last look."

"I'll go with you."

* * *

We worked until well after midnight. Lisa would review a tape or a disk, and if she was in any doubt, toss it to me for the magnetic treatment. At one point, simply because she was unsure, she took the magnet and passed it in front of an entire shelf of software.

It was amazing to think about it. With that one wipe she had randomized billions of bits of information. Some of it might not exist anywhere else in the world. I found myself confronted by even harder questions. Did she have the right to do it? Didn't knowledge exist for everyone? But I confess I had little trouble quelling my protests. Mostly I was happy to see it go. The old reactionary in me found it easier to believe There Are Things We Are Not Meant To Know.

We were almost through when her monitor screen began to malfunction. It actually gave off a few hisses and pops, so Lisa stood back from it for a moment, then the screen started to flicker. I stared at it for a while. It seemed to me there was an image trying to form in the screen. Something three-dimensional. Just as I was starting to get a picture of it I happened to glance at Lisa, and she was looking at me. Her face was flickering. She came to me and put her hands over my eyes.

"Victor, you shouldn't look at that."

"It's okay," I told her. And when I said it, it was, but as soon as I had the words out I knew it wasn't. And that is the last thing I remembered for a long time.

I'm told it was a very bad two weeks. I remember very little of it. I was kept under high dosage of drugs, and my few lucid periods were always followed by a fresh seizure.

The first thing I recall clearly was looking up at Dr. Stuart's face. I was in a hospital bed. I later learned it was in Cedars-Sinai, not the Veteran's Hospital. Lisa had paid for a private room.

Stuart put me through the usual questions. I was able to answer them, though I was very tired. When he was satisfied as to my condition, he finally began to answer some of my questions. I learned how long I had been there, and how it had happened.

"You went into consecutive seizures," he confirmed. "I don't know why, frankly. You haven't been prone to them for a decade. I was thinking you were well under control. But nothing is ever really stable, I guess."

"So Lisa got me here in time."

"She did more than that. She didn't want to level with me at first. It seems that after the first seizure she witnessed, she read everything she could find. From that day, she had a syringe and solution of Valium handy. When she saw you couldn't breathe, she injected you with one hundred milligrams, and there's no doubt it saved your life."

Stuart and I had known each other a long time. He knew I had no prescription for Valium. Though we had talked about it the last time I was hospitalized. Since I lived alone, there would be no one to inject me if I got in trouble.

He was more interested in results than anything else, and what Lisa did had the desired result. I was still alive.

He wouldn't let me have any visitors that day. I protested but soon was asleep. The next day she came. She wore a new T-shirt. This one had a picture of a robot wearing a gown and mortarboard, and said "Class of 11111000000." It turns out that was 1984 in binary notation.

She had a big smile and said, "Hi, Yank!" and as she sat on the bed I started to shake. She looked alarmed and asked if she should call the doctor.

"It's not that," I managed to say. "I'd like it if you just held me."

She took off her shoes and got under the covers with me. She held me tightly. At some point a nurse came in and tried to shoo her out. Lisa gave her profanities in Vietnamese, Chinese, and a few startling ones in English, and the nurse left. I saw Dr. Stuart glance in later.

I felt much better when I finally stopped crying. Lisa's eyes were wet, too.

"I've been here every day," she said. "You look awful, Victor."

"I feel a lot better."

"Well, you look better than you did. But your doctor says you'd better stick around another couple of days, just to make sure."

"I think he's right."

"I'm planning a big dinner for when you get back. You think we should invite the neighbors?"

I didn't say anything for a while. There were so many things we hadn't faced. Just how long could it go on between us? How long before I got sour about being so useless? How long before she got tired of being with an old man? I don't know just when I had started to think of Lisa as a permanent part of my life. And I wondered how I could have thought that.

"Do you want to spend more years waiting in hospitals for a man to die?"

"What do you want, Victor? I'll marry you if you want me to. Or I'll live with you in sin. I prefer sin, but if it'll make you happy—"

"I don't know why you want to saddle yourself with an epileptic old fart."

"Because I love you."

It was the first time she had said it. I could have gone on questioning—bringing up her Major again, for instance—but I had no urge to. I'm very glad I didn't. So I changed the subject.

"Did you get the job finished?"

She knew which job I was talking about. She lowered her voice and put her mouth close to my ear.

"Let's don't be specific about it here, Victor. I don't trust any place I haven't swept for bugs. But, to put your mind at ease, I did finish, and it's been a quiet couple of weeks. No one is any wiser, and I'll never meddle in things like that again."

I felt a lot better. I was also exhausted. I tried to conceal my yawns, but she sensed it was time to go. She gave me one more kiss, promising many more to come, and left me.

It was the last time I ever saw her.

At about ten o'clock that evening Lisa went into Kluge's kitchen with a screwdriver and some other tools and got to work on the microwave oven.

The manufacturers of those appliances are very careful to insure they can't be turned on with the door open, as they emit lethal radiation. But with simple tools and a good brain it is possible to circumvent the safety interlocks. Lisa had no trouble with them. About ten minutes after she entered the kitchen she put her head in the oven and turned it on.

It is impossible to say how long she held her head in there. It was long enough to turn her eyeballs to the consistency of boiled eggs. At some point she lost voluntary muscle control and fell to the floor, pulling the microwave down with her. It shorted out, and a fire started.

The fire set off the sophisticated burglar alarm she had installed a month before. Betty Lanier saw the flames and called the fire department as Hal ran across the street and into the burning kitchen. He dragged what was left of Lisa out onto the grass. When he saw what the fire had done to her upper body, and in particular her breasts, he threw up.

She was rushed to the hospital. The doctors there amputated one arm and cut away the frightful masses of vulcanized silicone, pulled all her teeth, and didn't know what to do about the eyes. They put her on a respirator.

It was an orderly who first noticed the blackened and bloody T-shirt they had cut from her. Some of the message was unreadable, but it began, "I can't go on this way any more . . .

There is no other way I could have told all that. I discovered it piecemeal, starting with the disturbed look on Dr. Stuart's face when Lisa didn't show up the next day. He wouldn't tell me anything, and I had another seizure shortly after.

The next week is a blur. I remember being released from the hospital, but I don't remember the trip home. Betty was very good to me. They gave me a tranquilizer called Tranxene, and it was even better. I ate them like candy. I wandered in a drugged haze, eating only when Betty insisted, sleeping sitting up in my chair, coming awake not knowing where or who I was. I returned to the prison camp many times. Once I recall helping Lisa stack severed heads.

When I saw myself in the mirror, there was a vague smile on my face. It was Tranxene, caressing my frontal lobes. I knew that if I was to live much longer, me and Tranxene would have to become very good friends.

I eventually became capable of something that passed for rational thought. I was helped along somewhat by a visit from Osborne. I was trying, at that time, to find reasons to live, and wondered if he had any.

"I'm very sorry," he started off. I said nothing. "This is on my own time," he went on. "The department doesn't know I'm here."

"Was it suicide?" I asked him.

"I brought along a copy of the . . . the note. She ordered it from a shirt company in Westwood, three days before the . . . accident."

He handed it to me, and I read it. I was mentioned, though not by name. I was "the man I love." She said she couldn't cope with my problems. It was a short note. You can't get too much on a T-shirt. I read it through five times, then handed it back to him.

"She told you Kluge didn't write his note. I tell you she didn't write this."

He nodded reluctantly. I felt a vast calm, with a howling nightmare just below it. Praise Tranxene.

"Can you back that up?"

"She saw me in the hospital shortly before she died. She was full of life and hope. You say she ordered the shirt three days before. I would have felt that. And that note is pathetic. Lisa was never pathetic."

He nodded again.

"Some things I want to tell you. There were no signs of a struggle. Mrs. Lanier is sure no one came in the front. The crime lab went over the whole place and we're sure no one was in there with her. I'd stake my life on the fact that no one entered or left that house. Now, *I* don't believe it was suicide, either, but do you have any suggestions?"

"The NSA," I said.

I explained about the last things she had done while I was still there. I told him of her fear of the government spy agencies. That was all I had.

"Well, I guess they're the ones who could do a thing like that, if anyone could. But I'll tell you, I have a hard time swallowing it. I don't know why, for one thing. Maybe you believe those people kill like you and I'd swat a fly." His look made it into a question.

"I don't know what I believe."

"I'm not saying they wouldn't kill for national security, or some such shit. But they'd have taken the computers, too. They wouldn't have let her alone, they wouldn't even have let her *near* that stuff after they killed Kluge."

"What you're saying makes sense."

He muttered on about it for quite some time. Eventually I offered him some wine. He accepted thankfully. I considered joining him—it would be a quick way to die—but did not. He drank the whole bottle, and was comfortably drunk when he suggested we go next door and look it over one more time. I was planning on visiting Lisa the next day, and I knew I had to start somewhere building myself up for that, so I agreed to go with him.

We inspected the kitchen. The fire had blackened the counters and melted some linoleum, but not much else. Water had made a mess of the place. There was a brown stain on the floor which I was able to look at with no emotion.

So we went back to the living room, and one of the computers was turned on. There was a short message on the screen.

IF YOU WISH TO KNOW MORE

PRESS ENTER ■

"Don't do it," I told him. But he did. He stood, blinking solemnly, as the words wiped themselves out and a new message appeared.

YOU LOOKED

The screen started to flicker and I was in my car, in darkness, with a pill in my mouth and another in my hand. I spit out the pill and sat for a moment, listening to the old engine ticking over. In my other hand was the plastic pill bottle. I felt very tired but opened the car door and shut off the engine. I felt my way to the garage door and opened it. The air outside was fresh and sweet. I looked down at the pill bottle and hurried into the bathroom.

When I got through what had to be done, there were a dozen pills floating in the toilet that hadn't even dissolved. There were the wasted shells of many more, and a lot of other stuff I won't bother to describe. I counted the pills in the bottle, remembered how many there had been, and wondered if I would make it.

I went over to Kluge's house and could not find Osborne. I was getting tired, but I made it back to my house and stretched out on the couch to see if I would live or die.

The next day I found the story in the paper. Osborne had gone home and blown out the back of his head with his revolver. It was not a big story. It happened to cops all the time. He didn't leave a note.

I got on the bus and rode out to the hospital and spent three hours trying to get in to see Lisa. I wasn't able to do it. I was not a relative and the doctors were quite firm about her having no visitors. When I got angry they were as gentle as possible. It was then I learned the extent of her injuries. Hal had kept the worst from me. None of it would have mattered, but the doctors swore there was nothing left in her head. So I went home.

She died two days later.

She had left a will, to my surprise. I got the house and contents. I picked up the phone as soon as I learned of it, and called a garbage company. While they were on the way I went for the last time into Kluge's house.

The same message.

PRESS ENTER ■

I cautiously located the power switch and turned it off. I had the garbage people strip the place to the bare wall.

I went over my own house very carefully, looking for anything that was even the first cousin to a computer. I threw out the radio. I sold the car, and the refrigerator, and the stove, and the blender, and the electric clock. I drained the waterbed and threw out the heater.

Then I bought the best propane stove on the market and hunted a long time before I found an old icebox. I had the garage stacked to the ceiling with firewood. I had the chimney cleaned. It would be getting cold soon.

One day I took the bus to Pasadena and established the Lisa Foo Memorial Scholarship fund for Vietnamese refugees and their children. I endowed it with seven hundred thousand eighty-three dollars and four cents. I told them it could be used for any field of study except computer science. I could tell they thought me eccentric.

* * *

And I really thought I was safe, until the phone rang.

I thought it over for a long time before answering it. In the end, I knew it would just keep on going until I did. So I picked it up.

For a few seconds there was a dial tone, but I was not fooled, I kept holding it to my ear and finally the tone turned off. There was just silence. I listened intently. I heard some of those far-off musical tones that live in phone wires. Echoes of conversations taking place a thousand miles away. And something infinitely more distant and cool.

I do not know what they have incubated out there at the NSA. I don't know if they did it on purpose, or if it just happened, or if it even has anything to do with them in the end. But I know it's out there, because I heard its soul breathing on the wires. I spoke very carefully.

"I do not wish to know any more," I said. "I won't tell anyone anything. Kluge, Lisa, and Osborne all committed suicide. I am just a lonely man, and I won't cause you any trouble."

There was a click, and a dial tone.

Getting the phone taken out was easy. Getting them to remove all the wires was a little harder, since once a place is wired they expect it to be wired forever. They grumbled, but when I started pulling them out myself, they relented, though they warned me it was going to cost.

The power company was harder. They actually seemed to believe there was a regulation requiring each house to be hooked up to the grid. They were willing to shut off my power—though hardly pleased about it—but they just weren't going to take the wires away from my house. I went up on the roof with an axe and demolished four feet of eaves as they gaped at me. Then they coiled up their wires and went home.

I threw out all my lamps, all things electrical. With hammer, chisel, and handsaw I went to work on the drywall just above the baseboards.

As I stripped the house of wiring I wondered many times why I was doing it. Why was it worth it? I couldn't have very many years before a final seizure finished me off. Those years were not going to be a lot of fun.

Lisa had been a survivor. She would have known why I was doing this. She had once said I was a survivor, too. I survived the camp. I survived the death of my mother and father and managed to fashion a solitary life. Lisa survived the death of just about everything. No survivor expects to live through it all. But while she was alive, she would have worked to stay alive.

And that's what I did. I got all the wires out of the walls, went over the house with a magnet to see if I had missed any metal, then spent a week cleaning up, fixing the holes I had knocked in the walls, ceiling, and attic. I was amused trying to picture the real-estate agent selling this place after I was gone.

It's a great little house, folks. No electricity . . .

Now I live quietly, as before.

I work in my garden during most of the daylight hours. I've expanded it considerably, and even have things growing in the front yard now. I live by candlelight and kerosene lamp. I grow most of what I eat.

It took a long time to taper off the Tranxene and the Dilantin, but I did it, and now take the seizures as they come. I've usually got bruises to show for it.

In the middle of a vast city I have cut myself off. I am not part of the network growing faster than I can conceive. I don't even know if it's dangerous, to ordinary people. It noticed me, and Kluge, and Osborne. And Lisa. It brushed against our minds like I would brush away a mosquito, never noticing I had crushed it. Only I survived.

But I wonder.

It would be very hard . . .

Lisa told me how it can get in through the wiring. There's something called a carrier wave that can move over wires carrying household current. That's why the electricity had to go.

I need water for my garden. There's just not enough rain here in southern California, and I don't know how else I could get the water.

Do you think it could come through the pipes?

"The Pusher"

Not long before the Monte Carlo burned to the ground, we had moved into a travel trailer on Sauvie Island, ten minutes outside Portland. Lewis and Clark camped there for a while almost two hundred years before. They complained that quacking Canada geese kept them awake all night. Not surprising; there are hundreds of thousands of them.

You'd never know Portland was so close. We were right on the Columbia River, huge ships would glide by silently all day long. In the spring and summer we picked and ate the best peaches, strawberries, raspberries, and tomatoes I've ever had. Our plan was to travel around the country, stopping here and there for a couple months. We ended up staying on Sauvie a lot longer then we planned, but eventually traded the trailer in on an RV and hit the road. We got as far as the Central Coast of California area near Pismo Beach, where we've been for a while. It's a great spot. We're parked about fifty yards from the beach; most days I feel like Jim Rockford, except I don't get shot at as much.

The weather here is mild, but the geology is exciting. A few days before this last Christmas we had a 6.5 earthquake that tossed the RV around like a Matchbox toy, cracked the pavements and sewers and a few houses down the street, and left us without an Internet connection or electricity for twenty-four hours.

The area has historically attracted some odd people. About a quarter of a mile from us there was, in the 1930s, a community of artists, nonconformists, communists, and nudists who called themselves Dunites, because they lived in rent-free shacks in the dunes. Forty-five miles north of us is San Simeon, where William Randolph Hearst a stately pleasure dome decreed. You can see it up on the hill if you stand on the beach where eight thousand elephant seals haul out for winter mating. And forty-five miles south of us is another pleasure dome: Neverland Ranch.

A few days ago as I write this Michael Jackson was arraigned in criminal court in Santa Maria, fifteen miles south of us. Lee and I like circuses, so we went down there to watch it. All we saw of the King of Pop was a pale, pale hand stuck out of an SUV's window, waving. After that, just the top of an umbrella moving slowly over the tops of heads. I could describe the scene but unless you never watch TV news or are having this book delivered via FedEx hypermail to a planet circling Betelgeuse and the television signal hasn't reached you yet, you've already seen it all. Probably a lot more than you wanted to see. But there were guys there from the Nation of Islam handing out invitations to Neverland: "In the spirit of love and togetherness Michael Jackson would like to invite his fans and supporters to his Neverland ranch. Please join us Friday, January 16, 2004 from 11A.M.–2P.M. Refreshments will be served. We'll see you there!"

We are neither fans nor supporters, but when we got there no one asked us to sign a loyalty oath. We were required to sign a secrecy agreement, however, promising not to write about our experiences within the gates for profit. These introductions would seem to fall into that category, so that's all I can say about the day we spent there. But I specifically asked if it was okay to write an account and post it on my website and was told that was fine, so if you're interested you can find it at www.varley.net. For free.

I can't tell you why Michael Jackson is the perfect way to start an introduction to the following story without spoiling the story for you. I can tell you that it is the only story I ever wrote that my ex-wife didn't like. She had always been my first reader, and after she finished this one she practically threw the pages back in my face. Harsh words were exchanged, and I finally prevailed on her to read it again, which she did. She had missed something vital, and totally misunderstood the story.

I don't blame her for getting angry. If I had been saying what she thought I was saying, I'd have been enraged, too. Pretty much as enraged as I'll be at Michael Jackson if the allegations against him are proved to be true in court.

THE PUSHER

THINGS CHANGE. IAN Haise expected that. Yet there are certain constants, dictated by function and use. Ian looked for those and he seldom went wrong.

The playground was not much like the ones he had known as a child. But playgrounds are built to entertain children. They will always have something to swing on, something to slide down, something to climb. This one had all those things, and more. Part of it was thickly wooded. There was a swimming hole. The stationary apparatus was combined with dazzling light sculptures that darted in and out of reality. There were animals, too: pygmy rhinoceros and elegant gazelles no taller than your knee. They seemed unnaturally gentle and unafraid.

But most of all, the playground had children.

Ian liked children.

He sat on a wooden park bench at the edge of the trees, in the shadows, and watched them. They came in all colors and all sizes, in both sexes. There were black ones like animated licorice jellybeans and white ones like bunny rabbits, and brown ones with curly hair and more brown ones with slanted eyes and straight black hair and some who had been white but were now toasted browner than some of the brown ones.

Ian concentrated on the girls. He tried with boys before, long ago, but it had not worked out.

He watched one black child for a time, trying to estimate her age. He thought it was around eight or nine. Too young. Another one was more like thirteen, judging from her skirt. A possibility, but he'd prefer something younger. Somebody less sophisticated, less suspicious.

Finally he found a girl he liked. She was brown, but with startling blonde hair. Ten? Possibly eleven. Young enough, at any rate.

He concentrated on her, and did the strange thing he did when he had selected the right one. He didn't know what it was, but it usually worked. Mostly it was just a matter of looking at her, keeping his eyes fixed on her no matter where she went or what she did, not allowing himself to be distracted by anything. And sure enough, in a few minutes she looked up, looked around, and her eyes locked with his. She held his gaze for a moment, then went back to her play.

He relaxed. Possibly what he did was nothing at all. He had noticed, with adult women, that if one really caught his eye so he found himself staring at her he would usually look up from what she was doing and catch him. It never seemed to fail. Talking to other men, he had found it to be a common experience. It was almost as if they could feel his gaze. Women had told him it was nonsense, or if not, it was just reaction to things seen peripherally by people trained to alertness for sexual signals. Merely an unconscious observation penetrating to the awareness; nothing mysterious, like ESP.

Perhaps. Still, Ian was very good at this sort of eye contact. Several times he had noticed the girls rubbing the backs of their necks while he observed them, or hunching their shoulders. Maybe they'd developed some kind of ESP and just didn't recognize it as such.

Now he merely watched. He was smiling, so that every time she looked up to see him—which she did with increasing frequency—she saw a friendly, slightly graying man with a broken nose and powerful shoulders. His hands were strong, too. He kept them clasped in his lap.

＊   ＊   ＊

Presently she began to wander in his direction.

No one watching her would have thought she was coming toward him. She probably didn't know it herself. On her way, she found reasons to stop and tumble, jump on the soft rubber mats, or chase a flock of noisy geese. But she was coming toward him, and she would end up on the park bench beside him.

He glanced around quickly. As before, there were few adults in this playground. It had surprised him when he arrived. Apparently the new conditioning techniques had reduced the numbers of the violent and twisted to the point that parents felt it safe to allow their children to run without supervision. The adults present were involved with each other. No one had given him a second glance when he arrived.

That was fine with Ian. It made what he planned to do much easier. He had his excuses ready, of course, but it could be embarrassing to be confronted with the questions representatives of the law ask single, middle-aged men who hang around playgrounds.

For a moment he considered, with real concern, how the parents of these children could feel so confident, even with mental conditioning. After all, no one was conditioned until he had first done something. New maniacs were presumably being produced every day. Typically, they looked just like everyone else until they proved their difference by some demented act.

Somebody ought to give those parents a stern lecture, he thought.

"Who are you?"

Ian frowned. Not eleven, surely, not seen up this close. Maybe not even ten. She might be as young as eight.

Would eight be all right? He tasted the idea with his usual caution, looked around again for curious eyes. He saw none.

"My name is Ian. What's yours?"

"*No.* Not your *name.* Who are *you*?"

"You mean what do I do?"

"Yes."

"I'm a pusher."

She thought that over, then smiled. She had her permanent teeth, crowded into a small jaw.

"You give away pills?"

He laughed. "Very good," he said. "You must do a lot of reading." She said nothing, but her manner indicated she was pleased.

"No," he said. "That's an old kind of pusher. I'm the other kind. But you knew that, didn't you?" When he smiled she broke into giggles. She was doing the pointless things with her hands that little girls do. He thought she had a pretty good idea of how cute she was, but no inkling of her forbidden eroticism. She was a ripe seed with sexuality ready to burst to the surface. Her body was a bony sketch, a framework on which to build a woman.

"How old are you?"

"That's a secret. What happened to your nose?"

"I broke it a long time ago. I'll bet you're twelve."

She giggled, then nodded. Eleven, then. And just barely.

"Do you want some candy?" He reached into his pocket and pulled out the pink and white striped paper bag.

She shook her head solemnly. "My mother says not to take candy from strangers."

"But we're not strangers. I'm Ian, the pusher."

She thought that over. While she hesitated he reached into the bag and picked out a chocolate thing so thick and gooey it was almost obscene. He bit into it, forcing himself to chew. He hated sweets.

"Okay," she said, and reached toward the bag. He pulled it away. She looked at him in innocent surprise.

"I just thought of something," he said. "I don't know your name, so I guess we *are* strangers."

She caught on to the game when she saw the twinkle in his eye. He'd practiced that. It was a good twinkle.

"My name is Radiant. Radiant Shiningstar Smith."

"A very fancy name," he said, thinking how names had changed. "For a very pretty girl." He paused, and cocked his head. "No. I don't think so. You're Radiant . . . Starr. With two *r*'s. . . . *Captain* Radiant Starr, of the Star Patrol."

She was dubious for a moment. He wondered if he'd judged her wrong. Perhaps she was really Miss Radiant Faintingheart Belle, or Mrs. Radiant Motherhood. But her fingernails were a bit dirty for that.

She pointed a finger at him and made a Donald Duck sound as her thumb worked back and forth. He put his hand to his heart and fell over sideways, and she dissolved in laughter. She was careful, however, to keep her weapon firmly trained on him.

"And you'd better give me that candy or I'll shoot you again."

The playground was darker now, and not so crowded. She sat beside him on the bench, swinging her legs. Her bare feet did not quite touch the dirt.

She was going to be quite beautiful. He could see it clearly in her face. As for the body . . . who could tell?

Not that he really gave a damn.

She was dressed in a little of this and a little of that, worn here and there without much regard for his concepts of modesty. Many of the children wore nothing. It had been something of a shock when he arrived. Now he was almost used to it, but he still thought it incautious on the part of her parents. Did they really think the world was that safe, to let an eleven-year-old girl go practically naked in a public place?

He sat there listening to her prattle about her friends—the ones she hated and the one or two she simply adored—with only part of his attention.

He inserted um's and uh-huh's in the right places.

She was cute, there was no denying it. She seemed as sweet as a child that age ever gets, which can be very sweet and as poisonous as a rattlesnake, almost at the same moment. She had the capacity to be warm, but it was on the surface. Underneath, she cared mostly about herself. Her loyalty would be a transitory thing, bestowed easily, just as easily forgotten.

And why not? She was young. It was perfectly healthy for her to be that way.

But did he dare try to touch her?

It was crazy. It was insane as they all told him it was. It worked so seldom. Why would it work with her? He felt a weight of defeat.

"Are you okay?"

"Huh? Me? Oh, sure, I'm all right. Isn't your mother going to be worried about you?"

"I don't have to be in for hours and hours yet." For a moment she looked so grown up he almost believed the lie.

"Well, I'm getting tired of sitting here. And the candy's all gone." He looked at her face. Most of the chocolate had ended up in a big circle around her mouth, except where she had wiped it daintily on her shoulder or forearm. "What's back there?"

She turned.

"That? That's the swimming hole."

"Why don't we go over there? I'll tell you a story."

The promise of a story was not enough to keep her out of the water. He didn't know if that was good or bad. He knew she was smart, a reader, and she had an imagination. But she was also active. That pull was too strong for him. He sat far from the water, under some bushes, and watched her swim with the three other children still in the park this late in the evening.

Maybe she would come back to him, and maybe she wouldn't. It wouldn't change his life either way, but it might change hers.

She emerged dripping and infinitely cleaner from the murky water. She dressed again in her random scraps, for whatever good it did her, and came to him shivering.

"I'm cold," she said.

"Here." He took off his jacket. She looked at his hands as he wrapped it around her, and once she reached out and touched the hardness of his shoulder.

"You sure must be strong," she commented.

"Pretty strong. I work hard, being a pusher."

"Just what *is* a pusher?" she said, and stifled a yawn.

"Come sit on my lap, and I'll tell you."

He did tell her, and it was a very good story that no adventurous child could resist. He had practiced that story, refined it, told it many times into a recorder until he had the rhythms and cadences just right, until he found just the right words—not too difficult words, but words with some fire and juice in them.

And once more he grew encouraged. She had been tired when he started, but he gradually caught her attention. It was possible no one had ever told her a story in quite that way. She was used to sitting before the screen and having a story shoved into her eyes and ears. It was something new to be able to interrupt with questions and get answers. Even reading was not like that. It was the oral tradition of storytelling, and it could still mesmerize the nth generation of the electronic age.

"That sounds great," she said, when she was sure he was through.

"You liked it?"

"I really truly did. I think I want to be a pusher when I grow up. That was a really neat story."

"Well, that's not actually the story I was going to tell you. That's just what it's like to be a pusher."

"You mean you have another story?"

"Sure." He looked at his watch. "But I'm afraid it's getting late. It's almost dark, and everybody's gone home. You'd probably better go, too."

She was in agony, torn between what she was supposed to do and what she wanted. It really should be no contest, if she was who he thought she was.

"Well . . . but—but I'll come back here tomorrow and you—"

He was shaking his head.

"My ship leaves in the morning," he said. "There's no time."

"Then tell me now! I can stay out. Tell me now. Please please please?"

He coyly resisted, harrumphed, protested, but in the end allowed himself to be seduced. He felt very good. He had her like a five-pound trout on a twenty-pound line. It wasn't sporting. But then, he wasn't playing a game.

So at last he got to his specialty.

He sometimes wished he could claim the story for his own, but the fact was he could not make up stories. He no longer tried to. Instead, he cribbed from every fairy tale and fantasy story he could find. If he had a genius, it was in adapting some of the elements to fit the world she knew—while keeping it strange enough to enthrall her—and in ad-libbing the end to personalize it.

It was a wonderful tale he told. It had enchanted castles sitting on mountains of glass, moist caverns beneath the sea, fleets of starships and shining riders astride horses that flew the galaxy. There were evil alien creatures, and others with much good in them. There were drugged potions. Scaled beasts roared out of hyperspace to devour planets.

Amid all the turmoil strode the Prince and Princess. They got into frightful jams and helped each other out of them.

The story was never quite the same. He watched her eyes. When they wandered, he threw away whole chunks of story. When they widened, he knew what parts to plug in later. He tailored it to her reactions.

The child was sleepy. Sooner or later she would surrender. He needed her in a trance state, neither awake nor asleep. That is when the story would end.

". . . and though the healers labored long and hard, they could not save the Princess. She died that night, far from her Prince."

Her mouth was a little round o. Stories were not supposed to end that way.

"Is that *all*? She died, and she never saw the Prince again?"

"Well, not quite all. But the rest of it probably isn't true, and I shouldn't tell it to you." Ian felt pleasantly tired. His throat was a little raw, making him hoarse. Radiant was a warm weight on his lap.

"You have to tell me, you know," she said, reasonably. He supposed she was right. He took a deep breath.

"All right. At the funeral, all the greatest people from that part of the galaxy were in attendance. Among them was the greatest Sorcerer who ever lived. His name . . . but I really shouldn't tell you his name. I'm sure he'd be very cross if I did.

"This Sorcerer passed by the Princess's bier . . . that's a—"

"I know, I *know*, Ian. Go on!"

"Suddenly he frowned, and leaned over her pale form. 'What is this?' he thundered. 'Why was I not told?' Everyone was very concerned. This Sorcerer was a dangerous man. One time when someone insulted him he made a spell that turned everyone's head backwards so they had to walk around with rearview mirrors. No one knew what he would do if he got really angry.

" 'This Princess is wearing the Starstone,' he said, and drew himself up and frowned all around as if he were surrounded by idiots. I'm sure he thought he was, and maybe he was right. Because he went on to tell them just what the Starstone was, and what it did, something no one there had ever heard before. And this is the part I'm not sure of. Because, though everyone knew the Sorcerer was a wise and powerful man, he was also known as a great liar.

"He said that the Starstone was capable of capturing the essence of a person at the moment of her death. All her wisdom, all her power, all her knowledge and beauty and strength would flow into the stone and be held there, timelessly."

"In suspended animation," Radiant breathed.

"Precisely. When they heard this, the people were amazed. They buffeted the Sorcerer with questions, to which he gave few answers, and those only grudgingly. Finally he left in a huff. When he was gone everyone talked long into the night about the things he had said. Some felt the Sorcerer had held out hope that the Princess might yet live on. That if her body were frozen, the Prince, upon his return, might somehow infuse her essence back within her. Others thought the Sorcerer had said that was impossible, that the Princess was doomed to a half-life, locked in the stone.

"But the opinion that prevailed was this:

"The Princess would probably never come fully back to life. But her essence might flow from the Starstone and into another, if the right person could be found. All agreed this person must be a young maiden. She must be beautiful, very smart, swift of foot, loving, kind . . . oh, my, the list was very long. Everyone doubted such a person could be found. Many did not even want to try.

"But at last it was decided the Starstone should be given to a faithful friend of the Prince. He would search the galaxy for this maiden. If she existed, he would find her.

"So he departed with the blessings of many worlds behind him, vowing to find the maiden and give her the Starstone."

He stopped again, cleared his throat, and let the silence grow.

"Is that all?" she said, at last, in a whisper.

"Not quite all," he admitted. "I'm afraid I tricked you."

"Tricked me?"

He opened the front of his coat, which was still draped around her shoulders. He reached in past her bony chest and down into an inner pocket of the coat. He came up with the crystal. It was oval, with one side flat. It pulsed ruby light as it sat in the palm of his hand.

"It shines," she said, looking at it wide-eyed and openmouthed.

"Yes, it does. And that means you're the one."

"Me?"

"Yes. Take it." He handed it to her, and as he did so, he nicked it with his thumbnail. Red light spilled into her hands, flowed between her fingers, seemed to soak into her skin. When it was over, the crystal still pulsed, but dimmed. Her hands were trembling.

"It felt very, very hot," she said.

"That was the essence of the Princess."

"And the Prince? Is he still looking for her?"

"No one knows. I think he's still out there, and someday he will come back for her."

"And what then?"

He looked away from her. "I can't say. I think, even though you are lovely, and even though you have the Starstone, that he will just pine away. He loved her very much."

"I'd take care of him," she promised.

"Maybe that would help. But I have a problem now. I don't have the heart to tell the Prince that she is dead. Yet I feel that the Starstone will draw him to it one day. If he comes and finds you, I fear for him. I think perhaps I should take the stone to a far part of the galaxy, some place he could never find it. Then at least he would never know. It might be better that way."

"But I'd help him," she said, earnestly. "I promise. I'd wait for him, and when he came, I'd take her place. You'll see."

He studied her. Perhaps she would. He looked into her eyes for a long time, and at last let her see his satisfaction.

"Very well. You can keep it then."

"I'll wait for him," she said. "You'll see."

She was very tired; almost asleep.

"You should go home now," he suggested.

"Maybe I could just lie down for a moment," she said.

"All right." He lifted her gently and placed her prone on the ground. He stood looking down at her, then knelt beside her and began to gently stroke her forehead. She opened her eyes with no alarm, then closed them again. He continued to stroke her.

Twenty minutes later he left the playground, alone.

* * *

He was always depressed afterwards. It was worse than usual this time. She had been much nicer than he had imagined at first. Who could have guessed such a romantic heart beat beneath all that dirt?

He found a phone booth several blocks away. Punching her name into information yielded a fifteen-digit number, which he called. He held his hand over the camera eye.

A woman's face appeared on his screen.

"Your daughter is in the playground, at the south end by the pool, under the bushes," he said. He gave the address of the playground.

"We were so worried! What . . . is she . . . who is—"

He hung up and hurried away.

Most of the other pushers thought he was sick. Not that it mattered. Pushers were a tolerant group when it came to other pushers, and especially when it came to anything a pusher might care to do to a puller. He wished he had never told anyone how he spent his leave time, but he had, and now he had to live with it.

So, while they didn't care if he amused himself by pulling the legs and arms off infant puller pups, they were all just back from ground leave and couldn't pass up an opportunity to get on each other's nerves. They ragged him mercilessly.

"How were the swing-sets this trip, Ian?"

"Did you bring me those dirty knickers I asked for?"

"Was it good for you, honey? Did she pant and slobber?"

" 'My ten-year-old baby, she's a pullin' me back home . . .' "

Ian bore it stoically. It was in extremely bad taste and he was the brunt of it, but it really didn't matter. It would end as soon as they lifted again. They would never understand what he sought, but he felt he understood them. They hated coming to Earth. There was nothing for them there, and perhaps they wished there was.

And he was a pusher himself. He didn't care for pullers. He agreed with the sentiment expressed by Marian, shortly after lift-off. Marian had just finished her first ground leave after her first voyage, so naturally she was the drunkest of them all.

"Gravity sucks," she said, and threw up.

It was three months to Amity, and three months back. He hadn't the foggiest idea of how far it was in miles; after the tenth or eleventh zero his mind clicked off.

Amity. Shit City. He didn't even get off the ship. Why bother? The planet was peopled with things that looked a little like ten-ton caterpillars and a little like sentient green turds. Toilets were a revolutionary idea to the Amiti; so were ice cream bars, sherbets, sugar donuts, and peppermint. Plumbing had never caught on, but sweets had, so the ship was laden with plain and fancy desserts from every nation on Earth. In addition, there was a pouch of reassuring mail for the forlorn human embassy. The cargo for the return trip was some grayish sludge that Ian supposed someone on Earth found tremendously valuable, and a packet of desperate mail for the folks back home. Ian didn't need to read the letters to know what was in them. They could all be summed up as "Get me *out* of here!"

He sat at the viewport and watched an Amiti family lumbering and farting its way down the spaceport road. They paused every so often to do something that looked like an alien cluster-fuck. The road was brown. The land was brown, and in the distance were brown, unremarkable hills. There was a brown haze in the air, and the sun was yellow-brown.

He thought of castles perched on mountains of glass, of Princes and Princesses, of shining white horses galloping among the stars.

He spent the return trip just as he had on the way out: sweating down in the gargantuan pipes of the stardrive. Just beyond the metal walls unimaginable energies pulsed. And on the walls themselves, tiny plasmoids grew into bigger plasmoids. The process was too slow to see, but if left unchecked the encrustations would soon impair the engines. His job was to scrape them off.

Not everyone was cut out to be an astrogator.

And what of it? It was honest work. He had made his choices long ago. You spent your life either pulling gees or pushing c. And when you got tired, you grabbed some z's. If there was a pushers' code, that was it.

The plasmoids were red and crystalline, teardrop-shaped. When he broke them free of the walls they had one flat side. They were full of a liquid light that felt as hot as the center of the sun.

It was always hard to get off the ship. A lot of pushers never did. One day, he wouldn't either.

He stood for a few moments looking at it all. It was necessary to soak it in passively at first, get used to the changes. Big changes didn't bother him. Buildings were just the world's furniture and he didn't care how it was arranged. Small changes worried the shit out of him. Ears, for instance. Very few of the people he saw had earlobes. Each time he returned he felt a little more like an ape who has fallen from his tree. One day he'd return to find everybody had three eyes or six fingers, or that little girls no longer cared to hear stories of adventure.

He stood there, dithering, getting used to the way people were painting their faces, listening to what sounded like Spanish being spoken all around him. Occasional English or Arabic words seasoned it. He grabbed a crewmate's arm and asked him where they were. The man didn't know so he asked the Captain, and she said it was Argentina, or it had been when they left.

The phone booths were smaller. He wondered why.

There were four names in his book. He sat there facing the phone, wondering which name to call first. His eyes were drawn to Radiant Shiningstar Smith, so he punched that name into the phone. He got a number and an address in Novosibirsk.

Checking the timetable he had picked up—putting off making the call—he found the antipodean shuttle left on the hour. Then he wiped his hands on his pants and took a deep breath and looked up to see her standing outside the phone booth. They regarded each other silently for a moment. She saw a man much shorter than she remembered, but powerfully built, with big hands and shoulders and a pitted face that would have been forbidding but for the gentle eyes. He saw a tall woman around forty years old who was fully as beautiful as he had expected she would be. The hand of age had just begun to touch her. He thought she was fighting that waistline and fretting about those wrinkles, but none of that mattered to him. Only one thing mattered, and he would know it soon enough.

"You *are* Ian Haise, aren't you?" she said, at last.

"It was sheer luck I remembered you again," she was saying. He noted the choice of words. She could have said coincidence.

"It was two years ago. We were moving again and I was sorting through some things and I came across that plasmoid. I hadn't thought about you in . . . oh, it must have been fifteen years."

He said something noncommittal. They were in a restaurant, away from most of the other patrons, at a booth near a glass wall beyond which spaceships were being trundled to and from the blast pits.

"I hope I didn't get you into trouble," he said.

She shrugged it away.

"You did, some, but that was so long ago. I certainly wouldn't bear a grudge that long. And the fact is, I thought it was all worth it at the time."

She went on to tell him of the uproar he had caused in her family, of the visits by the police, the interrogation, puzzlement, and final helplessness. No one knew quite what to make of her story. They had identified him quickly enough, only to find he had left Earth and would not be back for a long, long time.

"I didn't break any laws," he pointed out.

"That's what no one could understand. I told them you had talked to me and told me a long story, and then I went to sleep. None of them seemed interested in what the story was about, so I didn't tell them. And I didn't tell them about the . . . the Starstone." She smiled. "Actually, I was relieved they hadn't asked. I was determined not to tell them, but I was a little afraid of holding it all back. I thought they were agents of the . . . who were the villains in your story? I've forgotten."

"It's not important."

"I guess not. But something is."

"Yes."

"Maybe you should tell me what it is. Maybe you can answer the question that's been in the back of my mind for twenty-five years, ever since I found out that thing you gave me was just the scrapings from a starship engine."

"Was it?" he said, looking into her eyes. "Don't get me wrong. I'm not saying it *was* more than that. I'm asking *you* if it wasn't more."

She looked at him again. He felt himself being appraised for the third or fourth time since they met. He still didn't know the verdict.

"Yes, I guess it was more," she said, at last.

"I'm glad."

"I believed in that story passionately for . . . oh, years and years. Then I stopped believing it."

"All at once?"

"No. Gradually. It didn't hurt much. Part of growing up, I guess."

"And you remembered me."

"Well, that took some work. I went to a hypnotist when I was twenty-five and recovered your name and the name of your ship. Did you know—"

"Yes. I mentioned them on purpose."

She nodded, and they fell silent again. When she looked at him now he saw more sympathy, less defensiveness. But there was still a question.

"Why?" she said.

He nodded, then looked away from her, out to the starships. He wished he was on one of them, pushing *c*. It wasn't working. He knew it wasn't. He was a weird problem to her, something to get straightened out, a loose end in her life that would irritate until it was made to fit in, then be forgotten.

To hell with it.

"Hoping to get laid," he said. When he looked up she was slowly shaking her head back and forth.

"Don't trifle with me, Haise. You're not as stupid as you look. You knew I'd be married, leading my own life. You knew I wouldn't drop it all because of some half-remembered fairy tale thirty years ago. *Why?*"

And how could he explain the strangeness of it all to her?

"What do you do?" He recalled something, and rephrased it. "Who *are* you?"

She looked startled. "I'm a mysteliologist."

He spread his hands. "I don't even know what that is."

"Come to think of it, there was no such thing when you left."

"That's it, in a way," he said. He felt helpless again. "Obviously, I had no way of knowing what you'd do, what you'd become, what would happen to you that you had no control over. All I was gambling on was that'd you remember me. Because that way . . ." He saw the planet Earth looming once more out the viewport. So many, many years and only six months later. A planet full of strangers. It didn't matter that Amity was full of strangers. But Earth was home, if that word still had any meaning for him.

"I wanted somebody my own age I could talk to," he said. "That's all. All I want is a friend."

He could see her trying to understand what it was like. She wouldn't, but maybe she'd come close enough to think she did.

"Maybe you've found one," she said, and smiled. "At least I'm willing to get to know you, considering the efforts you've put into this."

"It wasn't much effort. It seems so long-term to you, but it wasn't to me. I held you on my lap six months ago."

She giggled in almost the same way she had six months before.

"How long is your leave?" she asked.

"Two months."

"Would you like to come stay with us for a while? We have room in our house."

"Will your husband mind?"

"Neither my husband nor my wife. That's them sitting over there, pretending to ignore us." Ian looked, caught the eye of a woman in her late twenties. She was sitting across from a man Ian's age, who now turned and looked at Ian with some suspicion but no active animosity. The woman smiled; the man reserved judgment.

Radiant had a wife. Well, times change.

"Those two in the red skirts are police," Radiant was saying. "So is that man over by the wall, and the one at the end of the bar."

"I spotted two of them," Ian said. When she looked surprised, he said, "Cops always have a look about them. That's one of the things that don't change."

"You go back quite a ways, don't you? I'll bet you have some good stories."

Ian thought about it, and nodded. "Some, I suppose."

"I should tell the police they can go home. I hope you don't mind that we brought them in."

"Of course not."

"I'll do that, and then we can go. Oh, and I guess I should call the children and tell them we'll be home soon." She laughed, reached across the table and touched his hand. "See what can happen in six months? I have three children, and Gillian has two."

He looked up, interested.

"Are any of them girls?"

"Tango Charlie and Foxtrot Romeo"

This story contains a lot of dogs. They are Shetland Sheepdogs, known to the people who love them, as I do, as Shelties, to the people who know nothing about them as "miniature collies," and to all small children as "Look, Mom! It's a little Lassie!"

This seems a good time to say a few words about the living soul who I have shared my life with longer than anyone else. Longer than my first wife, longer than my sons, longer than I lived at home with my parents and sisters, longer than I have lived with Lee, though I hope in a few more years that will have changed. I'm speaking of the finest dog that ever lived, my beloved Sheltie, Cirocco. That's my prejudiced opinion, of course, but I would have no respect for any dog owner who wouldn't proudly say the same thing about that special dog who, for a time, made your life worth living through the down and lonely hours.

She was our second Sheltie. We got the first, Fuchsia, from a friend in Marin County with half a dozen of them, who was basically letting her newest litter run wild at her country house. She was giving them away. Fuchsia lived for eleven years, brightening our lives, then one day ran out in front of a car. The lady who hit her took her to the vet, who couldn't save her. I was in Los Angeles when I heard the news, in the Polo Lounge, taking my first meeting with the Millennium production people. I couldn't continue, and they all understood.

Cirocco's name came from the main character in the books I was writing at the time, the Gaea Trilogy. I got her in a very well-run puppy farm, one of a couple dozen Sheltie pups that swarmed me in the owner's living room. This one little female hung back, but when the rest started playing with each other she came over and made me fall in love with her.

The owner sneered. "That's 'Too-white,'" she said. "She has too much white on her legs and around the collar, and that little white spot on her butt. She's a cull. That means she is purebred, descended from champions, but I won't give you her papers unless you have her spayed." Too-white's genes were to be swept from the pool, like rotten leaves. That struck me as monumentally stupid, but I didn't say so, because it *meant I could have her for $150 instead of the $500 to 600 she wanted for the others.*

Dog breeders come in two varieties: the most finicky people on Earth, fanatical about the breed standards, or cynical exploiters who churn out the most popular mutt of the moment, inbreeding willy-nilly until they are producing animals with congenital defects that would make hemophiliac European royalty seem handsome, healthy, and sane. I decided to be grateful this woman was the first type. I wasn't planning to show the dog, or breed her.

Again, I know I'm prejudiced, but I have been to quite a few dog shows and I have never seen a Sheltie with a more magnificent coat than the one Cirocco soon grew, including the Sheltie that stood in the Best in Show circle a few years ago at Westminster.

She was playful, as all puppies are, and loved to have fun later when she grew up, like all happy dogs do, but there was a dignity about her that was partly a characteristic of the breed and partly her own personality. She didn't care for little children. She would never, never bite them, but she tended to want to chivvy them into a herd, round 'em up, and head 'em out the front door, as a good sheepdog should. She didn't fawn on strangers, but after a while she would daintily accept a piece of cheese or a potato chip from them, then later she would come back for more. Food is a dog's religion, as someone once said, and she worshipped at the same altar as all of her species, but she had to know you first.

We were living in a big house on a hill overlooking Eugene when we got her. It had a fenced backyard that was at about a forty-five-degree angle. She would spend most of the day bounding up and crashing back down through the ivy, pausing at the three knotholes in the fence where she could spy on the neighbor's German shepherds.

I never heard her whine, not once in her life. She would yip at a sharp pain, and that was all. One night I heard her howl in agony. I threw open the back door and she came slinking toward me as if she had done something bad. Her face was covered in blood. She had chased a raccoon that had been stealing her food. Nobody ever told her about raccoons, which should be attacked only with your pack backing you up. She had one bleeding cut on her face . . . and four deep bites on the backs of her hind legs. Conclusion: she caught the coon, took one swipe across the face, then turned and ran. I would have, too. She was a lover, not a fighter.

Once she was overcome with an insane spirit of adventure, and dug her way under the fence and went out to see the world and promptly got lost. I spent a frantic hour driving the neighborhood, then found her in the dog pound, having a swell time playing with a little black dog. The instant she saw me she tried to look miserable, repentant, and frightened. It was Academy Award time. The card pinned to the cage said something like "Sweet, affectionate, well cared for. This is someone's precious baby." Damn straight. When I went to pay her bail I learned there was already quite a waiting list to adopt her.

I could tell you a thousand stories about Cirocco, I could turn this into a book about Cirocco. If you want to know more about her go to my website, she has her own page, with pictures. Tell me if she isn't the most beautiful Sheltie you've ever seen.

It all comes down, in the end, to death. They don't live as long as we do, we usually outlive them. It's probably better that way than the reverse, because if we die first who will take care of them?

At the age of nineteen and a half, Cirocco was still as beautiful as ever. You'd never know to see her sitting there that she was mostly blind, half deaf, and so crippled by arthritis that she could no longer get on her feet by herself. After she spent the night lying in her own filth because she couldn't get up, we decided it was time. We gave her a good meal which she enjoyed, took her for a last walk in the park, where she looked with great interest at things she could barely see and tottered around for a bit, then we took her to the vet, who gave her a lethal injection that killed her in seconds, with no evidence of pain.

There was plenty of pain in the room, but it wasn't hers.

Her ashes were scattered in an apple orchard in the Hood River Valley, one of the prettiest places on Earth.

Re-reading this story, I wondered if I was somehow preparing myself for Cirocco's death. If so, it didn't work. I still miss her every day.

TANGO CHARLIE AND FOXTROT ROMEO

THE POLICE PROBE was ten kilometers from Tango Charlie's Wheel when it made rendezvous with the unusual corpse. At this distance, the wheel was still an imposing presence, blinding white against the dark sky, turning in perpetual sunlight. The probe was often struck by its beauty, by the myriad ways the wheel caught the light in its thousand and one windows. It had been composing a thought-poem around that theme when the corpse first came to its attention.

There was a pretty irony about the probe. Less than a meter in diameter, it was equipped with sensitive radar, very good visible-light camera eyes, and a dim awareness. Its sentient qualities came from a walnut-sized lump of human brain tissue cultured in a lab. This was the cheapest and simplest way to endow a machine with certain human qualities that were often useful in spying devices. The part of the brain used was the part humans use to appreciate beautiful things. While the probe watched, it dreamed endless beautiful dreams. No one knew this but the probe's control, which was a computer that had not bothered to tell anyone about it. The computer did think it was rather sweet, though.

There were many instructions the probe had to follow. It did so religiously. It was never to approach the wheel more closely than five kilometers. All objects larger than one centimeter leaving the wheel were to be pursued, caught and examined. Certain categories were to be reported to higher authorities. All others were to be vaporized by the probe's small battery of lasers. In thirty years of observation, only a dozen objects had needed reporting. All of them proved to be large structural components of the wheel which had broken away under the stress of rotation. Each had been destroyed by the probe's larger brother, on station five hundred kilometers away.

When it reached the corpse, it immediately identified it that far: it was a dead body, frozen in a vaguely fetal position. From there on, the probe got stuck.

Many details about the body did not fit the acceptable parameters for such a thing. The probe examined it again, and still again, and kept coming up with the same unacceptable answers. It could not tell what the body was . . . and yet it was a body.

The probe was so fascinated that its attention wavered for some time, and it was not as alert as it had been these previous years. So it was unprepared when the second falling object bumped gently against its metal hide. Quickly the probe leveled a camera eye at the second object. It was a single, long-stemmed, red rose, of a type that had once flourished in the wheel's florist shop. Like the corpse, it was frozen solid. The impact had shattered some of the outside petals, which rotated slowly in a halo around the rose itself.

It was quite pretty. The probe resolved to compose a thought-poem about it when this was all over. The probe photographed it, vaporized it with its lasers—all according to instruction—then sent the picture out on the airwaves along with a picture of the corpse, and a frustrated shout.

"Help!" the probe cried, and sat back to await developments.

"A puppy?" Captain Hoeffer asked, arching one eyebrow dubiously.

"A Shetland Sheepdog puppy, sir," said Corporal Anna-Louise Bach, handing him the batch of holos of the enigmatic orbiting object, and the single shot of the shattered rose. He took them, leafed through them rapidly, puffing on his pipe.

"And it came from Tango Charlie?"

"There is no possible doubt about it, sir."

Bach stood at parade rest across the desk from her seated superior and cultivated a detached gaze. I'm only awaiting orders, she told herself. I have no opinions of my own. I'm brimming with information, as any good recruit should be, but I will offer it only when asked, and then I will pour it forth until asked to stop.

That was the theory, anyway. Bach was not good at it. It was her ineptitude at humoring incompetence in superiors that had landed her in this assignment, and put her in contention for the title of oldest living recruit/apprentice in the New Dresden Police Department.

"A Shetland . . ."

"Sheepdog, sir." She glanced down at him, and interpreted the motion of his pipestem to mean he wanted to know more. "A variant of the Collie, developed on the Shetland Isles of Scotland. A working dog, very bright, gentle, good with children."

"You're an authority on dogs, Corporal Bach?"

"No, sir. I've only seen them in the zoo. I took the liberty of researching this matter before bringing it to your attention, sir."

He nodded, which she hoped was a good sign.

"What else did you learn?"

"They come in three varieties: black, blue merle, and sable. They were developed from Icelandic and Greenland stock, with infusions of Collie and possible Spaniel genes. Specimens were first shown at Cruft's in London in 1906, and in America—"

"No, no. I don't give a damn about Shelties."

"Ah. We have confirmed that there were four Shelties present on Tango Charlie at the time of the disaster. They were being shipped to the zoo at Clavius. There were no other dogs of any breed resident at the station. We haven't determined how it is that their survival was overlooked during the investigation of the tragedy."

"Somebody obviously missed them."

"Yes, sir."

Hoeffer jabbed at a holo with his pipe.

"What's this? Have you researched *that* yet?"

Bach ignored what she thought might be sarcasm. Hoeffer was pointing to the opening in the animal's side.

"The computer believes it to be a birth defect, sir. The skin is not fully formed. It left an opening into the gut."

"And what's this?"

"Intestines. The bitch would lick the puppy clean after birth. When she found this malformation, she would keep licking as long as she tasted blood. The intestines were pulled out, and the puppy died."

"It couldn't have lived anyway. Not with that hole."

"No, sir. If you'll notice, the forepaws are also malformed. The computer feels the puppy was stillborn."

Hoeffer studied the various holos in a blue cloud of pipe smoke, then sighed and leaned back in his chair.

"It's fascinating, Bach. After all these years, there are dogs alive on Tango Charlie. And breeding, too. Thank you for bringing it to my attention."

Now it was Bach's turn to sigh. She *hated* this part. Now it was her job to explain it to him.

"It's even more fascinating than that, sir. We knew Tango Charlie was largely pressurized. So it's understandable that a colony of dogs could breed there. But, barring an explosion, which would have spread a large amount of debris into the surrounding space, this dead puppy must have left the station through an airlock."

His face clouded, and he looked at her in gathering outrage.

"Are you saying . . . there are humans alive aboard Tango Charlie?"

"Sir, it has to be that . . . or some *very* intelligent dogs."

Dogs can't count.

Charlie kept telling herself that as she knelt on the edge of forever and watched little Albert dwindling, hurrying out to join the whirling stars. She wondered if he would become a star himself. It seemed possible.

She dropped the rose after him and watched it dwindle, too. Maybe it would become a rosy star.

She cleared her throat. She had thought of things to say, but none of them sounded good. So she decided on a hymn, the only one she knew, taught her long ago by her mother, who used to sing it for her father, who was a spaceship pilot. Her voice was clear and true.

> *Lord guard and guide all those who fly*
> *Through Thy great void above the sky.*
> *Be with them all on ev'ry flight,*
> *In radiant day or darkest night.*
> *Oh, hear our prayer, extend Thy grace*
> *To those in peril deep in space.*

She knelt silently for a while, wondering if God was listening, and if the hymn was good for dogs, too. Albert sure was flying through the void, so it seemed to Charlie he ought to be deserving of some grace.

Charlie was perched on a sheet of twisted metal on the bottom, or outermost layer of the wheel. There was no gravity anywhere in the wheel, but since it was spinning, the farther down you went the heavier you felt. Just beyond the sheet of metal was a void, a hole ripped in the wheel's outer skin, fully twenty meters across. The metal had been twisted out and down by the force of some long-ago explosion, and this part of the wheel was a good place to walk carefully, if you had to walk here at all.

She picked her way back to the airlock, let herself in, and sealed the outer door behind her. She knew it was useless, knew there was nothing but vacuum on the other side, but it was something that had been impressed on her very strongly. When you go through a door, you lock it behind you. Lock it tight. If you don't, the breathsucker will get you in the middle of the night.

She shivered, and went to the next lock, which also led only to vacuum, as did the one beyond that. Finally, at the fifth airlock, she stepped into a tiny room that had breathable atmosphere, if a little chilly. Then she went through yet another lock before daring to take off her helmet.

At her feet was a large plastic box, and inside it, resting shakily on a scrap of bloody blanket and not at all at peace with the world, were two puppies. She picked them up, one in each hand—which didn't make them any happier—and nodded in satisfaction.

She kissed them, and put them back in the box. Tucking it under her arm, she faced another door. She could hear claws scratching at this one.

"Down, Fuchsia," she shouted. "Down, momma-dog." The scratching stopped, and she opened the last door and stepped through.

Fuchsia O'Charlie Station was sitting obediently, her ears pricked up, her head cocked and her eyes alert with that total, quivering concentration only a mother dog can achieve.

"I've got 'em, Foosh," Charlie said. She went down on one knee and allowed Fuchsia to put her paws up on the edge of the box. "See? There's Helga, and there's Conrad, and there's Albert, and there's Conrad, and Helga. One, two, three, four, eleven-nine and six makes twenty-seven. See?"

Fuchsia looked at them doubtfully, then leaned in to pick one up, but Charlie pushed her away.

"I'll carry them," she said, and they set out along the darkened corridor. Fuchsia kept her eyes on the box, whimpering with the desire to get to her pups.

Charlie called this part of the wheel The Swamp. Things had gone wrong here a long time ago, and the more time went by, the worse it got. She figured it had been started by the explosion—which, in its turn, had been an indirect result of The Dying. The explosion had broken important pipes and wires. Water had started to pool in the corridor. Drainage pumps kept it from turning into an impossible situation. Charlie didn't come here very often.

Recently plants had started to grow in the swamp. They were ugly things, corpse-white or dental-plaque-yellow or mushroom-gray. There was very little light for them, but they didn't seem to mind. She sometimes wondered if they were plants at all. Once she thought she had seen a fish. It had been white and blind. Maybe it had been a toad. She didn't like to think of that.

Charlie sloshed through the water, the box of puppies under one arm and her helmet under the other. Fuchsia bounced unhappily along with her.

At last they were out of it, and back into regions she knew better. She turned right and went three flights up a staircase—dogging the door behind her at every landing—then out into the Promenade Deck, which she called home.

About half the lights were out. The carpet was wrinkled and musty, and worn in the places Charlie frequently walked. Parts of the walls were streaked with water stains, or grew mildew in leprous patches. Charlie seldom noticed these things unless she was looking through her pictures from the old days, or was coming up from the maintenance levels, as she was now. Long ago, she had tried to keep things clean, but the place was just too big for a little girl. Now she limited her housekeeping to her own living quarters—and like any little girl, sometimes forgot about that, too.

She stripped off her suit and stowed it in the locker where she always kept it, then padded a short way down the gentle curve of the corridor to the Presidential Suite, which was hers. As she entered, with Fuchsia on her heels, a long-dormant television camera mounted high on the wall stuttered to life. Its flickering red eye came on, and it turned jerkily on its mount.

Anna-Louise Bach entered the darkened monitoring room, mounted the five stairs to her office at the back, sat down, and put her bare feet up on her desk. She tossed her uniform cap, caught it on one foot, and twirled it idly there. She laced her fingers together, leaned her chin on them, and thought about it.

Corporal Steiner, her number two on C Watch, came up to the platform, pulled a chair close, and sat beside her.

"Well? How did it go?"

"You want some coffee?" Bach asked him. When he nodded, she pressed a button in the arm of her chair. "Bring two coffees to the Watch Commander's station. Wait a minute . . . bring a pot, and two mugs." She put her feet down and turned to face him.

"He did figure out there had to be a human aboard."

Steiner frowned. "You must have given him a clue."

"Well, I mentioned the airlock angle."

"See? He'd never have seen it without that."

"All right. Call it a draw."

"So then what did our leader want to do?"

Bach had to laugh. Hoeffer was unable to find his left testicle without a copy of *Gray's Anatomy*.

"He came to a quick decision. We had to send a ship out there *at once,* find the survivors and bring them to New Dresden with all possible speed."

"And then you reminded him . . ."

". . . that no ship had been allowed to get within five kilometers of Tango Charlie for thirty years. That even our probe had to be small, slow, and careful to operate in the vicinity, and that if it crossed the line it would be destroyed, too. He was all set to call the Oberluftwaffe headquarters and ask for a cruiser. I pointed out that A, we already *had* a robot cruiser on station under the reciprocal trade agreement with *Allgemein Fernsehen Gesellschaft;* B, that it was perfectly capable of defeating Tango Charlie without any more help; but C, any battle like that would *kill* whoever was on Charlie; but that in any case, D, even if a ship *could* get to Charlie there was a good reason for not doing so."

Emil Steiner winced, pretending pain in the head.

"Anna, Anna, you should never list things to him like that, and if you do, you should *never* get to point D."

"Why not?"

"Because you're lecturing him. If you have to make a speech like that, make it a set of options, which I'm sure you've already seen, sir, but which I will list for you, sir, to get all our ducks in a row, Sir."

Bach grimaced, knowing he was right. She was too impatient.

The coffee arrived, and while they poured and took the first sips, she looked around the big monitoring room. This is where impatience gets you.

In some ways, it could have been a lot worse. It *looked* like a good job. Though only a somewhat senior Recruit/Apprentice Bach was in command of thirty other R/As on her watch, and had the rank of Corporal. The working conditions were good: clean, high-tech surroundings, low job stress, the opportunity to command, however fleetingly. Even the coffee was good.

But it was a dead-end, and everyone knew it. It was a job many rookies held for a year or two before being moved on to more important and prestigious assignments: part of a routine career. When an R/A stayed in the monitoring room for five years, even as a watch commander, someone was sending her a message. Bach understood the message, had realized the problem long ago. But she couldn't seem to do anything about it. Her personality was too abrasive for routine promotions. Sooner or later she angered her commanding officers in one way or another.

She was far too good for anything overtly negative to appear in her yearly evaluations. But there were ways such reports could be written, good things left unsaid, a lack of excitement on the part of the reporting officer . . . all things that added up to stagnation.

So here she was in Navigational Tracking, not really a police function at all, but something the New Dresden Police Department had handled for a hundred years and would probably handle for a hundred more.

It was a necessary job. So is garbage collection. But it was not what she had signed up for, ten years ago.

Ten years! God, it sounded like a long time. Any of the skilled guilds were hard to get into, but the average apprenticeship in New Dresden was six years.

She put down her coffee cup and picked up a hand mike.

"Tango Charlie, this is Foxtrot Romeo, Do you read?"

She listened, and heard only background hiss. Her troops were trying every available channel with the same message, but this one had been the main channel back when TC-38 had been a going concern.

"Tango Charlie, this is Foxtrot Romeo. Come in, please."

Again, nothing.

Steiner put his cup close to hers, and leaned back in his chair.

"So did he remember what the reason was? Why we can't approach?"

"He did, eventually. His first step was to slap a top-priority security rating on the whole affair, and he was confident the government would back him up."

"We got that part. The alert came through about twenty minutes ago."

"I figured it wouldn't do any harm to let him send it. He needed to do something. And it's what I would have done."

"It's what you *did,* as soon as the pictures came in."

"You know I don't have the authority for that."

"Anna, when you get that look in your eye and say, 'If one of you bastards breathes a word of this to *anyone,* I will cut out your tongue and eat it for breakfast' . . . well, people listen."

"Did I say that?"

"Your very words."

"No wonder they all love me so much."

She brooded on that for a while, until T/A3 Klosinski hurried up the steps to her office.

"Corporal Bach, we've finally seen something," he said.

Bach looked at the big semicircle of flat television screens, over three hundred of them, on the wall facing her desk. Below the screens were the members of her watch, each at a desk/console, each with a dozen smaller screens to monitor. Most of the large screens displayed the usual data from the millions of objects monitored by

Nav/Track radar, cameras, and computers. But fully a quarter of them now showed curved, empty corridors where nothing moved, or equally lifeless rooms. In some of them skeletons could be seen.

The three of them faced the largest screen on Bach's desk, and unconsciously leaned a little closer as a picture started to form. At first it was just streaks of color. Klosinski consulted a datapad on his wrist.

"This is from camera 14/P/delta. It's on the Promenade Deck. Most of that deck was a sort of PX, with shopping areas, theaters, clubs, so forth. But one sector had VIP suites, for when people visited the station. This one's just outside the Presidential Suite."

"What's wrong with the picture?"

Klosinski sighed.

"Same thing wrong with all of them. The cameras are old. We've got about five percent of them in some sort of working order, which is a miracle. The Charlie computer is fighting us for every one."

"I figured it would."

"In just a minute . . . there! Did you see it?"

All Bach could see was a stretch of corridor, maybe a little fancier than some of the views already up on the wall, but not what Bach thought of as VIP. She peered at it, but nothing changed.

"No, nothing's going to happen now. This is a tape. We got it when the camera first came on." He fiddled with his data pad, and the screen resumed its multicolored static. "I rewound it. Watch the door on the left."

This time Klosinski stopped the tape on the first recognizable image on the screen.

"This is someone's leg," he said, pointing. "And this is the tail of a dog."

Bach studied it. The leg was bare, and so was the foot. It could be seen from just below the knee.

"That looks like a Sheltie's tail," she said.

"We thought so, too."

"What about the foot?"

"Look at the door," Steiner said. "In relation to the door, the leg looks kind of small."

"You're right," Bach said. *A child?* she wondered. "Okay. Watch this one around the clock. I suppose if there was a camera in that room, you'd have told me about it."

"I guess VIP's don't like to be watched."

"Then carry on as you were. Activate every camera you can, and tape them *all*, I've got to take this to Hoeffer."

She started down out of her wall-less office, adjusting her cap at an angle she hoped looked smart and alert.

"Anna," Steiner called. She looked back.

"How did Hoeffer take it when you reminded him Tango Charlie only has six more days left?"

"He threw his pipe at me."

Charlie put Conrad and Helga back in the whelping box, along with Dieter and Inga. All four of them were squealing, which was only natural, but the quality of their squeals changed when Fuchsia jumped in with them, sat down on Dieter, then plopped over on her side. There was nothing that sounded or looked more determined than a blind, hungry, newborn puppy, Charlie thought.

The babies found the swollen nipples, and Fuchsia fussed over them, licking their little bottoms. Charlie held her breath. It almost looked as if she was counting her brood, and that certainly wouldn't do.

"Good dog, Fuchsia," she cooed, to distract her, and it did. Fuchsia looked up, said I haven't got time for you now, Charlie, and went back to her chores.

"How was the funeral?" asked Tik-Tok the Clock.

"Shut up!" Charlie hissed. "You . . . you big idiot! It's okay, Foosh."

Fuchsia was already on her side, letting the pups nurse and more or less ignoring both Charlie and Tik-Tok. Charlie got up and went into the bathroom. She closed and secured the door behind her.

"The funeral was very beautiful," she said, pushing the stool nearer the mammoth marble washbasin and climbing up on it. Behind the basin the whole wall was a mirror, and when she stood on the stool she could see herself. She flounced her blonde hair out and studied it critically. There were some tangles.

"Tell me about it," Tik-Tok said. "I want to know *every* detail."

So she told him, pausing a moment to sniff her armpits. Wearing the suit always made her smell so gross. She clambered up onto the broad marble counter, went around the basin and goosed the 24-karat gold tails of the two dolphins who cavorted there, and water began gushing out of their mouths. She sat with her feet in the basin, touching one tail or another when the water got too hot, and told Tik-Tok all about it.

Charlie used to bathe in the big tub. It was so big it was more suited for swimming laps than bathing. One day she slipped and hit her head and almost drowned. Now she usually bathed in the sink, which was not quite big enough, but a lot safer.

"The rose was the most wonderful part," she said. "I'm glad you thought of that. It just turned and turned and turned . . ."

"Did you say anything?"

"I sang a song. A hymn."

"Could I hear it?"

She lowered herself into the basin. Resting the back of her neck on a folded towel, the water came up to her chin, and her legs from the knees down stuck out the other end. She lowered her mouth a little, and made burbling sounds in the water.

"Can I hear it? I'd like to hear."

"Lord, guide and guard all those who fly . . ."

Tik-Tok listened to it once, then joined in harmony as she sang it again, and on the third time through added an organ part. Charlie felt the tears in her eyes again, and wiped them with the back of her hand.

"Time to scrubba-scrubba-scrubba," Tik-Tok suggested.

Charlie sat on the edge of the basin with her feet in the water, and lathered a washcloth.

"Scrubba-scrub beside your nose," Tik-Tok sang.

"Scrubba-scrub beside your nose," Charlie repeated, and industriously scoured all around her face.

"Scrubba-scrub between your toes. Scrub all the jelly out of your belly. Scrub your butt, and your you-know-what."

Tik-Tok led her through the ritual she'd been doing so long she didn't even remember how long. A couple times he made her giggle by throwing in a new verse. He was always making them up. When she was done, she was about the cleanest little girl anyone ever saw, except for her hair.

"I'll do that later," she decided, and hopped to the floor, where she danced the drying-off dance in front of the warm air blower until Tik-Tok told her she could stop. Then she crossed the room to the vanity table and sat on the high stool she had installed there.

"Charlie, there's something I wanted to talk to you about," Tik-Tok said.

Charlie opened a tube called "Coral Peaches" and smeared it all over her lips. She gazed at the thousand other bottles and tubes, wondering what she'd use this time.

"Charlie, are you listening to me?"

"Sure," Charlie said. She reached for a bottle labeled "The Glenlivet, Twelve Years Old," twisted the cork out of it, and put it to her lips. She took a big swallow, then another, and wiped her mouth on the back of her arm.

"Holy mackerel! That's real sippin' whiskey!" she shouted, and set the bottle down. She reached for a tin of rouge.

"Some people have been trying to talk to me," Tik-Tok said. "I believe they may have seen Albert, and wondered about him."

Charlie looked up, alarmed—and, doing so, accidentally made a solid streak of rouge from her cheekbone to her chin.

"Do you think they shot at Albert?"

"I don't think so. I think they're just curious."

"Will they hurt me?"

"You never can tell."

Charlie frowned, and used her finger to spread black eyeliner all over her left eyelid. She did the same for the right, then used another jar to draw violent purple frown lines on her forehead. With a thick pencil she outlined her eyebrows.

"What do they want?"

"They're just prying people, Charlie. I thought you ought to know. They'll probably try to talk to you, later."

"Should I talk to them?"

"That's up to you."

Charlie frowned even deeper. Then she picked up the bottle of Scotch and had another belt.

She reached for the Rajah's Ruby and hung it around her neck.

Fully dressed and made up now, Charlie paused to kiss Fuchsia and tell her how beautiful her puppies were, then hurried out to the Promenade Deck.

As she did, the camera on the wall panned down a little, and turned a few degrees on its pivot. That made a noise in the rusty mechanism, and Charlie looked up at it. The speaker beside the camera made a hoarse noise, then did it again. There was a little puff of smoke, and an alert sensor quickly directed a spray of extinguishing gas toward it, then itself gave up the ghost. The speaker said nothing else.

Odd noises were nothing new to Charlie. There were places on the wheel where the clatter of faltering mechanisms behind the walls was so loud you could hardly hear yourself think.

She thought of the snoopy people Tik-Tok had mentioned. That camera was probably just the kind of thing they'd like. So she turned her butt to the camera, bent over, and farted at it.

She went to her mother's room, and sat beside her bed telling her all about little Albert's funeral. When she felt she'd been there long enough she kissed her dry cheek and ran out of the room.

Up one level were the dogs. She went from room to room, letting them out, accompanied by a growing horde of barking jumping Shelties. Each was deliriously happy to see her, as usual, and she had to speak sharply to a few when they kept licking her face. They stopped on command; Charlie's dogs were all good dogs.

When she was done there were seventy-two almost identical dogs yapping and running along with her in a sable-and-white tide. They rushed by another camera with a glowing red light, which panned to follow them up, up, and out of sight around the gentle curve of Tango Charlie.

Bach got off the slidewalk at the 34strasse intersection. She worked her way through the crowds in the shopping arcade, then entered the Intersection-park, where the trees were plastic but the winos sleeping on the benches were real. She was on Level Eight. Up here, 34strasse was taprooms and casinos, secondhand stores, missions, pawnshops, and cheap bordellos. Free-lance whores, naked or in elaborate costumes according to their specialty, eyed her and sometimes propositioned her. Hope springs eternal; these men and women saw her every day on her way home. She waved to a few she had met, though never in a professional capacity.

It was a kilometer and a half to Count Otto Von Zeppelin Residential Corridor. She walked beside the slidewalk. Typically, it operated two days out of seven. Her own quarters were at the end of Count Otto, apartment 80. She palmed the printpad, and went in.

She knew she was lucky to be living in such large quarters on a T/A salary. It was two rooms, plus a large bath and a tiny kitchen. She had grown up in a smaller place, shared by a lot more people. The rent was so low because her bed was only ten meters from an arterial tubeway; the floor vibrated loudly every thirty seconds as the capsules rushed by. It didn't bother her. She had spent her first ten years sleeping within a meter of a regional air-circulation station, just beyond a thin metal apartment wall. It left her with a hearing loss she had been too poor to correct until recently.

For most of her ten years in Otto 80 she had lived alone. Five times, for periods varying from two weeks to six months, she shared with a lover, as she was doing now.

When she came in, Ralph was in the other room. She could hear the steady huffing and puffing as he worked out. Bach went to the bathroom and ran a tub as hot as she could stand it, eased herself in, and stretched out. Her blue paper uniform brief floated to the surface; she skimmed, wadded up, and tossed the soggy mass toward the toilet.

She missed. It had been that sort of day.

She lowered herself until her chin was in the water. Beads of sweat popped out on her forehead. She smiled, and mopped her face with a washcloth.

After a while Ralph appeared in the doorway. She could hear him, but didn't open her eyes.

"I didn't hear you come in," he said.

"Next time I'll bring a brass band."

He just kept breathing heavy, gradually getting it under control. That was her most vivid impression of Ralph, she realized: heavy breathing. That, and lots and lots of sweat. And it was no surprise he had nothing to say. Ralph was oblivious to sarcasm. It made him tiresome, sometimes, but with shoulders like his he didn't need to be witty. Bach opened her eyes and smiled at him.

Luna's low gravity made it hard for all but the most fanatical to aspire to the muscle mass one could develop on the Earth. The typical Lunarian was taller than Earth-normal, and tended to be thinner.

As a much younger woman Bach had become involved, very much against her better judgment, with an earthling of the species "jock." It hadn't worked out, but she still bore the legacy in a marked preference for beefcake. This doomed her to consorting with only two kinds of men: well-muscled mesomorphs from Earth, and single-minded Lunarians who thought nothing of pumping iron for ten hours a day. Ralph was one of the latter.

There was no rule, so far as Bach could discover, that such specimens had to be mental midgets. That was a stereotype. It also happened, in Ralph's case, to be true. While not actually mentally defective, Ralph Goldstein's idea of a tough intellectual problem was how many kilos to bench press. His spare time was spent brushing his teeth or shaving his chest or looking at pictures of himself in bodybuilding magazines. Bach knew for a fact that Ralph thought the Earth and Sun revolved around Luna.

He had only two real interests: lifting weights, and making love to Anna-Louise Bach. She didn't mind that at all.

Ralph had a swastika tattooed on his penis. Early on, Bach had determined that he had no notion of the history of the symbol; he had seen it in an old film and thought it looked nice. It amused her to consider what his ancestors might have thought of the adornment.

He brought a stool close to the tub and sat on it, then stepped on a floor button. The tub was Bach's chief luxury. It did a lot of fun things. Now it lifted her on a long rack until she was half out of the water. Ralph started washing that half. She watched his soapy hands.

"Did you go to the doctor?" he asked her.

"Yeah, I finally did."

"What did he say?"

"Said I have cancer."

"How bad?"

"Real bad. It's going to cost a bundle. I don't know if my insurance will cover it all." She closed her eyes and sighed. It annoyed her to have him be right about something. He had nagged her for months to get her medical check-up.

"Will you get it taken care of tomorrow?"

"No, Ralph, I don't have time tomorrow. Next week, I promise. This thing has come up, but it'll be all over next week, one way or another."

He frowned, but didn't say anything. He didn't have to. The human body, its care and maintenance, was the one subject Ralph knew more about than she did, but even she knew it would be cheaper in the long run to have the work done now.

She felt so lazy he had to help her turn over. Damn, but he was good at this. She had never asked him to do it; he seemed to enjoy it. His strong hands dug into her back and found each sore spot, as if by magic. Presently, it wasn't sore anymore.

"What's this thing that's come up?"

"I . . . can't tell you about it. Classified, for now."

He didn't protest, nor did he show surprise, though it was the first time Bach's work had taken her into the realm of secrecy.

It was annoying, really. One of Ralph's charms was that he was a good listener. While he wouldn't understand the technical side of anything, he could sometimes offer surprisingly good advice on personal problems. More often, he showed the knack of synthesizing and expressing things Bach had already known, but had not allowed herself to see.

Well, she could tell him part of it.

"There's this satellite," she began. "Tango Charlie. Have you ever heard of it?"

"That's a funny name for a satellite."

"It's what we call it on the tracking logs. It never really had a name—well, it did, a long time ago, but GWA took it over and turned it into a research facility and an Exec's retreat, and they just let it be known as TC-38. They got it in a war with Telecommunion, part of the peace treaty. They got Charlie, the Bubble, a couple other big wheels.

"The thing about Charlie . . . it's coming down. In about six days, it's going to spread itself all over the Farside. Should be a pretty big bang."

Ralph continued to knead the backs of her legs. It was never a good idea to rush him. He would figure things out in his own way, at his own speed, or he wouldn't figure them out at all.

"Why is it coming down?"

"It's complicated. It's been derelict for a long time. For a while it had the capacity to make course corrections, but it looks like it's run out of reaction mass, or the computer that's supposed to stabilize it isn't working anymore. For a couple of years it hasn't been making corrections."

"Why does it—"

"A Lunar orbit is never stable. There's the Earth tugging on the satellite, the solar wind, mass concentrations of Luna's surface . . . a dozen things that add up, over time. Charlie's in a very eccentric orbit now. Last time it came within a kilo-meter of the surface. Next time it's gonna miss us by a gnat's whisker, and the time after that, it hits."

Ralph stopped massaging. When Bach glanced at him, she saw he was alarmed. He had just understood that a very large object was about to hit his home planet, and he didn't like the idea.

"Don't worry," Bach said, "there's a surface installation that might get some damage from the debris, but Charlie won't come within a hundred kilometers of any settlements. We got nothing to worry about on that score."

"Then why don't you just . . . push it back up . . . you know, go up there and do . . ." Whatever it is you do, Bach finished for him. He had no real idea what kept a satellite in orbit in the first place, but knew there were people who handled such matters all the time.

There were other questions he might have asked, as well. Why leave Tango Charlie alone all these years? Why not salvage it? Why allow things to get to this point at all?

All those questions brought her back to classified ground.

She sighed, and turned over.

"I wish we could," she said, sincerely. She noted that the swastika was saluting her, and that seemed like a fine idea, so she let him carry her into the bedroom.

And as he made love to her she kept seeing that incredible tide of Shelties with the painted child in the middle.

After the run, ten laps around the Promenade Deck, Charlie led the pack to the Japanese Garden and let them run free through the tall weeds and vegetable patches. Most of the trees in the Garden were dead. The whole place had once been a formal and carefully tended place of meditation. Four men from Tokyo had been employed full time to take care of it. Now the men were buried under the temple gate, the ponds were covered in green scum, the gracefully arched bridge had col-lapsed, and the flower beds were choked with dog turds.

Charlie had to spend part of each morning in the flower beds, feeding Mister Shitface. This was a cylindrical structure with a big round hole in its side, an intake for the wheel's recycling system. It ate dog feces, weeds, dead plants, soil, scraps . . . practically anything Charlie shoveled into it. The cylinder was painted green, like a frog, and had a face painted on it, with big lips outlining the hole. Charlie sang. The Shit-Shoveling Song as she worked.

Tik-Tok had taught her the song, and he used to sing it with her. But a long time ago he had gone deaf in the Japanese Garden. Usually, all Charlie had to do was talk, and Tik-Tok would hear. But there were some places—and more of them every year—where Tik-Tok was deaf.

"'. . . Raise dat laig,'" Charlie puffed. "'Lif dat tail, If I gets in trouble will you go my bail?'"

She stopped, and mopped her face with a red bandanna. As usual, there were dogs sitting on the edge of the flower bed watching Charlie work. Their ears were lifted. They found this *endlessly* fascinating. Charlie just wished it would be over. But you took the bad with the good. She started shoveling again.

"'I gets weary, O' all dis shovelin' . . .'"

When she was finished she went back on the Promenade.

"What's next?" she asked.

"Plenty," said Tik-Tok. "The funeral put you behind schedule."

He directed her to the infirmary with the new litter. There they weighed, photographed, X-rayed, and catalogued each puppy. The results were put on file for later registration with the American Kennel Club. It quickly became apparent that Conrad was going to be a cull. He had an overbite. With the others it was too early to tell. She and Tik-Tok would examine them weekly, and their standards were an order of magnitude more stringent than the AKC's. Most of her *culls* would easily have best of breed in a show, and as for her breeding animals . . .

"I ought to be able to write Champion on most of these pedigrees."

"You must be patient."

Patient, yeah, she'd heard that before. She took another drink of Scotch. *Champion Fuchsia O'Charlie Station,* she thought. *Now* that *would really make a breeder's day.*

After the puppies, there were two from an earlier litter who were now ready for a final evaluation. Charlie brought them in, and she and Tik-Tok argued long and hard about points so fine few people would have seen them at all. In the end, they decided both would be sterilized.

Then it was noon feeding. Charlie never enforced discipline here. She let them jump and bark and nip at each other, as long as it didn't get *too* rowdy. She led them all to the cafeteria (and was tracked by three wall cameras), where the troughs of hard kibble and soft soyaburger were already full. Today it was chicken-flavored, Charlie's favorite.

Afternoon was training time. Consulting the records Tik-Tok displayed on a screen, she got the younger dogs one at a time and put each of them through thirty minutes of leash work, up and down the Promenade, teaching them Heel, Sit, Stay, Down, Come according to their degree of progress and Tik-Tok's rigorous schedules. The older dogs were taken to the Ring in groups, where they sat obediently in a line as she put them, one by one, through free-heeling paces.

Finally it was evening meals, which she hated. It was all human food.

"Eat your vegetables," Tik-Tok would say. "Clean up your plate. People are starving in New Dresden." It was usually green salads and yucky broccoli and beets and stuff like that. Tonight it was yellow squash, which Charlie liked about as much as a root canal. She gobbled up the hamburger patty and then dawdled over the squash until it was a yellowish mess all over her plate like baby shit. Half of it ended up on the table. Finally Tik-Tok relented and let her get back to her duties, which, in the evening, was grooming. She brushed each dog until the coats shone. Some of the dogs had already settled in for the night, and she had to wake them up.

At last, yawning, she made her way back to her room. She was pretty well plastered by then. Tik-Tok, who was used to it, made allowances and tried to jolly her out of what seemed a very black mood.

"There's *nothing* wrong!" she shouted at one point, tears streaming from her eyes. Charlie could be an ugly drunk.

She staggered out to the Promenade Deck and lurched from wall to wall, but she never fell down. Ugly or not, she knew how to hold her liquor. It had been ages since it made her sick.

The elevator was in what had been a commercial zone. The empty shops gaped at her as she punched the button. She took another drink, and the door opened. She got in.

She hated this part. The elevator was rising up through a spoke, toward the hub of the wheel. She got lighter as the car went up, and the trip did funny things to the inner ear. She hung on to the hand rail until the car shuddered to a stop.

Now everything was fine. She was almost weightless up here. Weightlessness was great when you were drunk. When there was no gravity to worry about, your head didn't spin—and if it did, it didn't matter.

This was one part of the wheel where the dogs never went. They could never get used to falling, no matter how long they were kept up here. But Charlie was an expert in falling. When she got the blues she came up here and pressed her face to the huge ballroom window.

People were only a vague memory to Charlie. Her mother didn't count. Though she visited every day, Mom was about as lively as V.I. Lenin. Sometimes Charlie wanted to be held so much it hurt. The dogs were good, they were warm, they licked her, they loved her . . . but they couldn't hold her.

Tears leaked from her eyes, which was really a bitch in the ballroom, because tears could get *huge* in here. She wiped them away and looked out the window.

The moon was getting bigger again. She wondered what it meant. Maybe she would ask Tik-Tok.

* * *

She made it back as far as the Garden. Inside, the dogs were sleeping in a huddle. She knew she ought to get them back to their rooms, but she was far too drunk for that. And Tik-Tok couldn't do a damn thing about it in here. He couldn't see, and he couldn't hear.

She lay down on the ground, curled up, and was asleep in seconds.

When she started to snore, the three or four dogs who had come over to watch her sleep licked her mouth until she stopped. Then they curled up beside her. Soon they were joined by others, until she slept in the middle of a blanket of dogs.

A crisis team had been assembled in the monitoring room when Bach arrived the next morning. They seemed to have been selected by Captain Hoeffer, and there were so many of them that there was not enough room for everyone to sit down. Bach led them to a conference room just down the hall, and everyone took a seat around the long table. Each seat was equipped with a computer display, and there was a large screen on the wall behind Hoeffer, at the head of the table. Bach took her place on his right, and across from her was Deputy Chief Zeiss, a man with a good reputation in the department. He made Bach very nervous. Hoeffer, on the other hand, seemed to relish his role. Since Zeiss seemed content to be an observer, Bach decided to sit back and speak only if called upon.

Noting that every seat was filled, and that what she assumed were assistants had pulled up chairs behind their principles, Bach wondered if this many people were really required for this project. Steiner, sitting at Bach's right, leaned over and spoke quietly.

"Pick a time," he said.

"What's that?"

"I said pick a time. We're running an office pool. If you come closest to the time security is broken, you win a hundred Marks."

"Is ten minutes from now spoken for?"

They quieted when Hoeffer stood up to speak.

"Some of you have been working on this problem all night," he said. "Others have been called in to give us your expertise in the matter. I'd like to welcome Deputy Chief Zeiss, representing the Mayor and the Chief of Police. Chief Zeiss, would you like to say a few words?"

Zeiss merely shook his head, which seemed to surprise Hoeffer. Bach knew he would never have passed up an opportunity like that, and probably couldn't understand how anyone else could.

"Very well. We can start with Dr. Blume."

Blume was a sour little man who affected wire-rimmed glasses and a cheap toupee over what must have been a completely bald head. Bach thought it odd that a medical man would wear such clumsy prosthetics, calling attention to problems that were no harder to cure than a hangnail. She idly called up his profile on her screen, and was surprised to learn he had a Nobel Prize.

"The subject is a female caucasoid, almost certainly Earthborn."

On the wall behind Hoeffer and on Bach's screen, tapes of the little girl and her dogs were being run.

"She displays no obvious abnormalities. In several shots she is nude, and clearly has not yet reached puberty. I estimate her age between seven and ten years old. There are small discrepancies in her behavior. Her movements are economical— except when playing. She accomplishes various hand-eye tasks with a maturity beyond her apparent years." The doctor sat down abruptly.

It put Hoeffer off balance.

"Ah . . . that's fine, doctor. But, if you recall, I just asked you to tell me how old she is, and if she's healthy."

"She appears to be eight. I said that."

"Yes, but—"

"What do you want from me?" Blume said, suddenly angry. He glared around at many of the assembled experts. "There's something badly wrong with that girl. I say she is eight. Fine! Any fool could see that. I say I can observe no health problems visually. For this, you need a doctor? Bring her to me, give me a few days, and I'll give you six volumes on her health. But videotapes . . . ?" He trailed off, his silence as eloquent as his words.

"Thank you, Dr. Blume," Hoeffer said. "As soon as—"

"I'll tell you one thing, though," Blume said, in a low, dangerous tone. "It is a disgrace to let that child drink liquor like that. The effects in later life will be terrible. I have seen large men in their thirties and forties who could not hold half as much as I saw her drink . . . *in one day!*" He glowered at Hoeffer for a moment. "I was sworn to silence. But I want to know who is responsible for this."

Bach realized she didn't know where the girl was. She wondered how many of the others in the room had been filled in, and how many were working only on their own part of the problem.

"It will be explained," Zeiss said, quietly. Blume looked from Zeiss to Hoeffer, and back, then settled into his chair, not mollified but willing to wait.

"Thank you, Dr. Blume," Hoeffer said again. "Next we'll hear from . . . Ludmilla Rossnikova, representing the GMA Conglomerate."

Terrific, thought Bach. He's brought GMA into it. No doubt he swore Ms. Rossnikova to secrecy, and if he really thought she would fail to mention it to her supervisor then he was even dumber than Bach had thought. She had worked for them once, long ago, and though she was just an employee she had learned something about them. GMA had its roots deep in twentieth-century Japanese industry. When you went to work on the executive level at GMA, you were set up for life. They expected, and received, loyalty that compared favorably with that demanded by the Mafia. Which meant that, by telling Rossnikova his "secret," Hoeffer had insured that three hundred GMA execs knew about it three minutes later. They could be relied on to keep a secret, but only if it benefited GMA.

"The computer on Tango Charlie was a custom-designed array," Rossnikova began. "That was the usual practice in those days, with BioLogic computers. It was designated the same as the station: BioLogic TC-38. It was one of the largest installations of its time.

"At the time of the disaster, when it was clear that everything had failed, the TC-38 was given its final instructions. Because of the danger, it was instructed to impose an interdiction zone around the station, which you'll find described under the label Interdiction on your screens."

Rossnikova paused while many of those present called up this information.

"To implement the zone, the TC-38 was given command of certain defensive weapons. These included ten bevawatt lasers . . . and other weapons which I have not been authorized to name or describe, other than to say they are at least as formidable as the lasers."

Hoeffer looked annoyed, and was about to say something, but Zeiss stopped him with a gesture. Each understood that the lasers were enough in themselves.

"So while it is possible to destroy the station," Rossnikova went on, "there is no chance of boarding it—assuming anyone would even want to try."

Bach thought she could tell from the different expressions around the table which people knew the whole story and which knew only their part of it. A couple of the latter seemed ready to ask a question, but Hoeffer spoke first.

"How about canceling the computer's instructions?" he said. "Have you tried that?"

"That's been tried many times over the last few years, as this crisis got closer. We didn't expect it to work, and it did not. Tango Charlie won't accept a new program."

"Oh my God," Dr. Blume gasped. Bach saw that his normally florid face had paled. "Tango Charlie. She's on Tango Charlie."

"That's right, Doctor," said Hoeffer. "And we're trying to figure out how to get her off. Dr. Wilhelm?"

Wilhelm was an older woman with the stocky build of the Earthborn. She rose, and looked down at some notes in her hand.

"Information's under the label Neurotropic Agent X on your machines," she muttered, then looked up at them. "But you needn't bother. That's about as far as we got, naming it. I'll sum up what we know, but you don't need an expert for this; there *are* no experts on Neuro-X.

"It broke out on August 9, thirty years ago next month. The initial report was five cases, one death. Symptoms were progressive paralysis, convulsions, loss of motor control, numbness.

"Tango Charlie was immediately quarantined as a standard procedure. An epidemiological team was dispatched from Atlanta, followed by another from New Dresden. All ships which had left Tango Charlie were ordered to return, except for one on its way to Mars and another already in parking orbit around Earth. The one in Earth orbit was forbidden to land.

"By the time the teams arrived, there were over a hundred reported cases, and six more deaths. Later symptoms included blindness and deafness. It progressed at different rates in different people, but it was always quite fast. Mean survival time from onset of symptoms was later determined to be forty-eight hours. Nobody lived longer than four days.

"Both medical teams immediately came down with it, as did a third, and a fourth team. *All* of them came down with it, each and every person. The first two teams had been using class three isolation techniques. It didn't matter. The third team stepped up the precautions to class two. Same result. Very quickly we had been forced into class one procedures—which involves isolation as total as we can get it: no physical contact whatsoever, no sharing of air supplies, all air to the investigators filtered through a sterilizing environment. They *still* got it. Six patients and some tissue samples were sent to a class one installation two hundred miles from New Dresden, and more patients were sent, with class one precautions, to a hospital ship close to Charlie. Everyone at both facilities came down with it. We *almost* sent a couple of patients to Atlanta."

She paused, looking down and rubbing her forehead. No one said anything.

"I was in charge," she said, quietly. "I can't take credit for not shipping anyone to Atlanta. We were going to . . . and suddenly there wasn't anybody left on Charlie to load patients aboard. All dead or dying.

"We backed off. Bear in mind this all happened in five days. What we had to show for those five days was a major space station with all aboard dead, three ships full of dead people, and an epidemiological research facility here on Luna full of dead people.

"After that, politicians began making most of the decisions—but I advised them. The two nearby ships were landed by robot control at the infected research station. The derelict ship going to Mars was . . . I think it's still classified, but what the hell? It was blown up with a nuclear weapon. Then we started looking into what was left. The station here was easiest. There was one cardinal rule: *nothing* that went into that station was to come out. Robot crawlers brought in remote manipulators and experimental animals. Most of the animals died. Neuro-X killed most mammals: monkeys, rats, cats—"

"Dogs?" Bach asked. Wilhelm glanced at her.

"It didn't kill *all* the dogs. Half of the ones we sent in lived."

"Did you know that there were dogs alive on Charlie?"

"No. The interdiction was already set up by then. Charlie Station was impossible to land, and too close and too visible to nuke, because that would violate about a dozen corporate treaties. And there seemed no reason not to just leave it there. We had our samples isolated here at the Lunar station. We decided to work with that, and forget about Charlie."

"Thank you, Doctor."

"As I was saying, it was by far the most virulent organism we had ever seen. It seemed to have a taste for all sorts of neural tissue, in almost every mammal.

"The teams that went in never had time to learn anything. They were all disabled too quickly, and just as quickly they were dead. We didn't find out much, either . . . for a variety of reasons. My guess is it was a virus, simply because we would certainly have seen anything larger almost immediately. But we never *did* see it. It was fast getting in—we don't know how it was vectored, but the only reliable shield was several miles of vacuum—and once it got in, I suspect it worked changes on genetic material of the host, setting up a secondary agent which I'm almost sure we isolated . . . and then it went away and hid very well. It was still in the host, in some form, it *had* to be, but we think its active life in the nervous system was on the order of one hour. But by then it had already done its damage. It set the system against itself, and the host was consumed in about two days."

Wilhelm had grown increasingly animated. A few times Bach thought she was about to get incoherent. It was clear the nightmare of Neuro-X had not diminished for her with the passage of thirty years. But now she made an effort to slow down again.

"The other remarkable thing about it was, of course, its infectiousness. Nothing I've ever seen was so persistent in evading our best attempts at keeping it isolated. Add that to its mortality rate, which, at the time, seemed to be one hundred percent . . . and you have the second great reason why we learned so little about it."

"What was the first?" Hoeffer asked. Wilhelm glared at him.

"The difficulty of investigating such a subtle process of infection by remote control."

"Ah, of course."

"The other thing was simply fear. Too many people had died for there to be any hope of hushing it up. I don't know if anyone tried. I'm sure those of you who were old enough remember the uproar. So the public debate was loud and long, and the pressure for extreme measures was intense . . . and, I should add, not unjustified. The argument was simple. Everyone who got it was dead. I believe that if those patients had been sent to Atlanta, everyone on *Earth* would have died.

Therefore . . . what was the point of taking a chance by keeping it alive and study-ing it?"

Dr. Blume cleared his throat, and Wilhelm looked at him.

"As I recall, Doctor," he said, "there were two reasons raised. One was the ab-stract one of scientific knowledge. Though there might be no point in studying Neuro-X since no one was afflicted with it, we might learn something by the study itself."

"Point taken," Wilhelm said, "and no argument."

"And the second was, we never found out where Neuro-X came from . . . There were rumors it was a biological warfare agent." He looked at Rossnikova, as if asking her what comment GMA might want to make about *that*. Rossnikova said nothing. "But most people felt it was a spontaneous mutation. There have been several instances of that in the high-radiation environment of a space station. And if it happened once, what's to prevent it from happening again?"

"Again, you'll get no argument from me. In fact, I supported both those posi-tions when the question was being debated." Wilhelm grimaced, then looked right at Blume. "But the fact is, I didn't support them very hard, and when the Lunar sta-tion was sterilized, I felt a lot better."

Blume was nodding.

"I'll admit it. I felt better, too."

"And if Neuro-X were to show up again," she went on, quietly, "my advice would be to sterilize immediately. Even if it meant losing a city."

Blume said nothing. Bach watched them both for a while in the resulting si-lence, finally understanding just how much Wilhelm feared this thing.

There was a lot more. The meeting went on for three hours, and everyone got a chance to speak. Eventually, the problem was outlined to everyone's satisfaction.

Tango Charlie could not be boarded. It could be destroyed. (Some time was spent debating the wisdom of the original interdiction order—beating a dead horse, as far as Bach was concerned—and questioning whether it might be possi-ble to countermand it.)

But things could *leave* Tango Charlie. It would only be necessary to withdraw the robot probes that had watched so long and faithfully, and the survivors could be evacuated.

That left the main question. *Should* they be evacuated?

(The fact that only one survivor had been sighted so far was not mentioned. Everyone assumed others would show up sooner or later. After all, it was simply not possible that just one eight-year-old girl could be the only occupant of a sta-tion no one had entered or left for thirty years.)

Wilhelm, obviously upset but clinging strongly to her position, advocated blowing up the station at once. There was some support for this, but only about ten percent of the group.

The eventual decision, which Bach had predicted before the meeting even started, was to do nothing at the moment.

After all, there were almost five whole days to keep thinking about it.

"There's a call waiting for you," Steiner said, when she got back to the monitoring room. "The switchboard says it's important."

Bach went into her office—wishing yet again for one with walls—flipped a switch.

"Bach," she said. Nothing came on the vision screen.

"I'm curious," said a woman's voice. "Is this the Anna-Louise Bach who worked in The Bubble ten years ago?"

For a moment, Bach was too surprised to speak, but she felt a wave of heat as blood rushed to her face. She knew the voice.

"Hello? Are you there?"

"Why no vision?" she asked.

"First, are you alone? And is your instrument secure?"

"The instrument is secure, if yours is." Bach flipped another switch, and a privacy hood descended around her screen. The sounds of the room faded as a sonic scrambler began operating. "And I'm alone."

Megan Galloway's face appeared on the screen. One part of Bach's mind noted that she hadn't changed much, except that her hair was curly and red.

"I thought you might not wish to be seen with me," Galloway said. Then she smiled. "Hello, Anna-Louise. How are you?"

"I don't think it really matters if I'm seen with you," Bach said.

"No? Then would you care to comment on why the New Dresden Police Department, among other government agencies, is allowing an eight-year-old child to go without the rescue she so obviously needs?"

Bach said nothing.

"Would you comment on the rumor that the NDPD does not intend to effect the child's rescue? That, if it can get away with it, the NDPD will let the child be smashed to pieces?"

Still Bach waited.

Galloway sighed, and ran a hand through her hair.

"You're the most exasperating woman I've ever known, Bach," she said. "Listen, don't you even want to *try* to talk me out of going with the story?"

Bach almost said something, but decided to wait once more.

"If you want to, you can meet me at the end of your shift. The Mozartplatz. I'm on the *Great Northern,* suite 1, but I'll see you in the bar on the top deck."

"I'll be there," Bach said, and broke the connection.

Charlie sang the Hangover Song most of the morning. It was not one of her favorites.

There was penance to do, of course. Tik-Tok made her drink a foul glop that—she had to admit—did do wonders for her headache. When she was done she was drenched in sweat, but her hangover was gone.

"You're lucky," Tik-Tok said. "Your hangovers are never severe."

"They're severe enough for *me,*" Charlie said.

He made her wash her hair, too.

After that, she spent some time with her mother. She always valued that time. Tik-Tok was a good friend, mostly, but he was so *bossy.* Charlie's mother never shouted at her, never scolded or lectured. She simply listened. True, she wasn't very active. But it was nice to have somebody just to talk to. One day, Charlie hoped, her mother would walk again. Tik-Tok said that was unlikely.

Then she had to round up the dogs and take them for their morning run.

And everywhere she went, the red camera eyes followed her. Finally she had enough. She stopped, put her fists on her hips, and shouted at a camera.

"You stop that!" she said.

The camera started to make noises. At first she couldn't understand anything, then some words started to come through.

". . . lie, Tango . . . Foxtrot . . . in, please. Tango Charlie . . ."

"Hey, that's my name."

The camera continued to buzz and spit noise at her.

"Tik-Tok, is that you?"

"I'm afraid not, Charlie."

"What's going on, then?"

"It's those nosy people. They've been watching you, and now they're trying to talk to you. But I'm holding them off. I don't think they'll bother you, if you just ignore the cameras."

"But why are you fighting them?"

"I didn't think you'd want to be bothered."

Maybe there was some of that hangover still around. Anyway, Charlie got real angry at Tik-Tok, and called him some names he didn't approve of. She knew she'd pay for it later, but for now Tik-Tok was pissed, and in no mood to reason with her. So he let her have what she wanted, on the principle that getting what you want is usually the worst thing that can happen to anybody.

"Tango Charlie, this is Foxtrot Romeo. Come in, please. Tango—"

"Come in *where?*" Charlie asked, reasonably. "And my name isn't Tango."

Bach was so surprised to have the little girl actually reply that for a moment she couldn't think of anything to say.

"Uh . . . it's just an expression," Bach said. "Come in . . . that's radio talk for 'please answer.'"

"Then you should say please answer," the little girl pointed out.

"Maybe you're right. My name is Bach. You can call me Anna-Louise, if you'd like. We've been trying to—"

"Why should I?"

"Excuse me?"

"Excuse you for what?"

Bach looked at the screen and drummed her fingers silently for a short time. Around her in the monitoring room, there was not a sound to be heard. At last, she managed a smile.

"Maybe we started off on the wrong foot."

"Which foot would that be?"

The little girl just kept staring at her. Her expression was not amused, not hostile, not really argumentative. Then why was the conversation suddenly so maddening?

"Could I make a statement?" Bach tried.

"I don't know. Can you?"

Bach's fingers didn't tap this time; they were balled up in a fist.

"I shall, anyway. My name is Anna-Louise Bach. I'm talking to you from New Dresden, Luna. That's a city on the moon, which you can probably see—"

"I know where it is."

"Fine. I've been trying to contact you for many hours, but your computer has been fighting me all the time."

"That's right. He said so."

"Now, I can't explain why he's been fighting me, but—"

"I know why. He thinks you're nosy."

"I won't deny that. But we're trying to help you."

"Why?"

"Because . . . it's what we do. Now if you could—"

"Hey. Shut up, will you?"

Bach did so. With forty-five other people at their scattered screens, Bach watched the little girl—the *horrible* little girl, as she was beginning to think of her—take a long pull from the green glass bottle of Scotch whiskey. She belched, wiped her mouth with the back of her hand, and scratched between her legs. When she was done, she smelled her fingers.

She seemed about to say something, then cocked her head, listening to something Bach couldn't hear.

"That's a good idea," she said, then got up and ran away. She was just vanishing around the curve of the deck when Hoeffer burst into the room, trailed by six members of his advisory team. Bach leaned back in her chair, and tried to fend off thoughts of homicide.

"I was told you'd established contact," Hoeffer said, leaning over Bach's shoulder in a way she absolutely *detested*. He peered at the lifeless scene. "What happened to her?"

"I don't know. She said, 'That's a good idea,' got up, and ran off."

"I told you to keep her here until I got a chance to talk to her."

"I tried," Bach said.

"You should have—"

"I have her on camera nineteen," Steiner called out.

Everyone watched as the technicians followed the girl's progress on the working cameras. They saw her enter a room to emerge in a moment with a big-screen monitor. Bach tried to call her each time she passed a camera, but it seemed only the first one was working for incoming calls. She passed through the range of four cameras before coming back to the original, where she carefully unrolled the monitor and tacked it to a wall, then payed out the cord and plugged it in very close to the wall camera Bach's team had been using. She unshipped this camera from its mount. The picture jerked around for awhile, and finally steadied. The girl had set it on the floor.

"Stabilize that," Bach told her team, and the picture on her monitor righted itself. She now had a worm's-eye view of the corridor. The girl sat down in front of the camera, and grinned.

"Now I can see you," she said. Then she frowned. "If you send me a picture."

"Bring a camera over here," Bach ordered.

While it was being set up, Hoeffer shouldered her out of the way and sat in her chair.

"There you are," the girl said. And again, she frowned. "That's funny. I was sure you were a girl. Did somebody cut your balls off?"

Now it was Hoeffer's turn to be speechless. There were a few badly suppressed giggles; Bach quickly silenced them with her most ferocious glare, while giving thanks no one would ever know how close she had come to bursting into laughter.

"Never mind that," Hoeffer said. "My name is Hoeffer. Would you go get your parents? We need to talk to them."

"No," said the girl. "And no."

"What's that?"

"No, I won't get them," the girl clarified, "and no, you don't need to talk to them."

Hoeffer had little experience dealing with children.

"Now, please be reasonable," he began, in a wheedling tone. "We're trying to help you, after all. We have to talk to your parents, to find out more about your situation. After that, we're going to help get you out of there."

"I want to talk to the lady," the girl said.

"She's not here."

"I think you're lying. She talked to me just a minute ago."

"I'm in charge."

"In charge of what?"

"Just in charge. Now, go get your parents!"

They all watched as she got up and moved closer to the camera. All they could see at first was her feet. Then water began to splash on the lens.

Nothing could stop the laughter this time, as Charlie urinated on the camera.

For three hours Bach watched the screens. Every time the girl passed the prime camera Bach called out to her. She had thought about it carefully. Bach, like Hoeffer, did not know a lot about children. She consulted briefly with the child psychologist on Hoeffer's team and the two of them outlined a tentative game plan. The guy seemed to know what he was talking about and, even better, his suggestions agreed with what Bach's common sense told her should work.

So she never said anything that might sound like an order. While Hoeffer seethed in the background, Bach spoke quietly and reasonably every time the child showed up. "I'm still here," she would say. "We could talk," was a gentle suggestion. "You want to play?"

She longed to use one line the psychologist suggested, one that would put Bach and the child on the same team, so to speak. The line was "The idiot's gone. You want to talk now?"

Eventually the girl began glancing at the camera. She had a different dog every time she came by. At first Bach didn't realize this, as they were almost completely identical. Then she noticed they came in slightly different sizes.

"That's a beautiful dog," she said. The girl looked up, then started away. "I'd like to have a dog like that. What's its name?"

"This is Madam's Sweet Brown Sideburns. Say *hi*, Brownie." The dog yipped. "Sit up for Mommy, Brownie. Now roll over. Stand tall. Now go in a circle, Brownie, that's a good doggy, walk on your hind legs. Now *jump*, Brownie. Jump, jump, *jump!*" The dog did exactly as he was told, leaping into the air and turning a flip each time the girl commanded it. Then he sat down, pink tongue hanging out, eyes riveted on his master.

"I'm impressed," Bach said, and it was the literal truth. Like other citizens of Luna, Bach had never seen a wild animal, had never owned a pet, knew animals only from the municipal zoo, where care was taken not to interfere with natural behaviors. She had had no idea animals could be so smart, and no inkling of how much work had gone into the exhibition she had just seen.

"It's nothing," the girl said. "You should see his father. Is this Anna-Louise again?"

"Yes, it is. What's your name?"

"Charlie. You ask a lot of questions."

"I guess I do. I just want to—"

"I'd like to ask some questions, too."

"All right. Go ahead."

"I have six of them, to start off with. One, why should I call you Anna-Louise? Two, why should I excuse you? Three, what is the wrong foot? Four . . . but that's not a question, really, since you already proved you *can* make a statement, if you wish, by doing so. Four, why are you trying to help me? Five, why do you want to see my parents?"

It took Bach a moment to realize that these were the questions Charlie had asked in their first, maddening conversation, questions she had not gotten answers for. And they were in their original order.

And they didn't make a hell of a lot of sense.

But the child psychologist was making motions with his hands, and nodding his encouragement to Bach, so she started in.

"You should call me Anna-Louise because . . . it's my first name, and friends call each other by their first names."

"Are we friends?"

"Well, I'd like to be your friend."

"Why?"

"Look, you don't have to call me Anna-Louise if you don't want to."

"I don't mind. Do I have to be your friend?"

"Not if you don't want to."

"Why should I want to?"

And it went on like that. Each question spawned a dozen more, and a further dozen sprang from each of those. Bach had figured to get Charlie's six—make that five—questions out of the way quickly, then get to the important things. She soon began to think she'd never answer even the *first* question.

She was involved in a long and awkward explanation of friendship, going over the ground for the tenth time, when words appeared at the bottom of her screen.

Put your foot down, they said. She glanced up at the child psychologist. He was nodding, but making quieting gestures with his hands. "But gently," the man whispered.

Right, Bach thought. Put your foot down. And get off on the wrong foot again.

"That's enough of that," Bach said abruptly.

"Why?" asked Charlie.

"Because I'm tired of that. I want to do something else."

"All right," Charlie said. Bach saw Hoeffer waving frantically, just out of camera range.

"Uh . . . Captain Hoeffer is still here. He'd like to talk to you."

"That's just too bad for him. I don't want to talk to him."

Good for you, Bach thought. But Hoeffer was still waving.

"Why not? He's not so bad." Bach felt ill, but avoided showing it.

"He lied to me. He said you'd gone away."

"Well, he's in charge here, so—"

"I'm warning you," Charlie said, and waited a dramatic moment, shaking her finger at the screen. "You put that poo-poo-head back on, and I won't come in ever again."

Bach looked helplessly at Hoeffer, who at last nodded.

"I want to talk about dogs," Charlie announced.

So that's what they did for the next hour. Bach was thankful she had studied up on the subject when the dead puppy first appeared. Even so, there was no doubt as to who was the authority. Charlie knew everything there was to know about dogs. And of all the experts Hoeffer had called in, not one could tell Bach anything about the goddamn animals. She wrote a note and handed it to Steiner, who went off to find a zoologist.

Finally Bach was able to steer the conversation around to Charlie's parents.

"My father is dead," Charlie admitted.

"I'm sorry," Bach said. "When did he die?"

"Oh, a long time ago. He was a spaceship pilot, and one day he went off in his spaceship and never came back." For a moment she looked far away. Then she shrugged. "I was real young."

Fantasy, the psychologist wrote at the bottom of her screen, but Bach had already figured that out. Since Charlie had to have been born many years after the Charlie Station Plague, her father could not have flown any spaceships.

"What about your mother?"

Charlie was silent for a long time, and Bach began to wonder if she was losing contact with her. At last, she looked up.

"You want to talk to my mother?"

"I'd like that very much."

"Okay. But that's all for today. I've got work to do. You've already put me way behind."

"Just bring your mother here, and I'll talk to her, and you can do your work."

"No. I can't do that. But I'll take you to her. Then I'll work, and I'll talk to you tomorrow."

Bach started to protest that tomorrow was not soon enough, but Charlie was not listening. The camera was picked up, and the picture bounced around as she carried it with her. All Bach could see was a very unsteady upside-down view of the corridor.

"She's going into Room 350," said Steiner. "She's been in there twice, and she stayed awhile both times."

Bach said nothing. The camera jerked wildly for a moment, then steadied.

"This is my mother," Charlie said. "Mother, this is my friend, Anna-Louise."

The Mozartplatz had not existed when Bach was a child. Construction on it had begun when she was five, and the first phase was finished when she was fifteen. Tenants had begun moving in soon after that. During each succeeding year new sectors had been opened, and though a structure as large as the Mozartplatz would never be finished—two major sectors were currently under renovation—it had been essentially completed six years ago.

It was a virtual copy of the Soleri-class arcology atriums that had spouted like mushrooms on the Earth in the last four decades, with the exception that on Earth you built up, and on Luna you went down.

First dig a trench fifteen miles long and two miles deep. Vary the width of the trench, but never let it get narrower than one mile, nor broader than five. In some places make the base of the trench wider than the top, so the walls of rock loom outward. Now put a roof over it, fill it with air, and start boring tunnels into the sides. Turn those tunnels into apartments and shops and everything else humans need in a city. You end up with dizzying vistas, endless terraces that reach higher than the eye can see, a madness of light and motion and spaces too wide to echo.

Do all that, and you still wouldn't have the Mozartplatz. To approach that ridiculous level of grandeur there were still a lot of details to attend to. Build four mile-high skyscrapers to use as table legs to support the midair golf course. Crisscross the open space with bridges having no visible means of support, and encrusted with shops and homes that cling like barnacles. Suspend apartment buildings from silver balloons that rise half the day and descend the other half, reachable only by glider. Put in a fountain with more water than Niagara, and a ski slope on a huge spiral ramp. Dig a ten-mile lake in the middle, with a bustling port at each end for the luxury ships that ply back and forth, attach runways to balconies so residents can fly to their front door, stud the interior with zeppelin ports and railway stations and hanging gardens . . . and you still don't have Mozartplatz, but you're getting closer.

The upper, older parts of New Dresden, the parts she had grown up in, were spartan and claustrophobic. Long before her time Lunarians had begun to build larger when they could afford it. The newer, lower parts of the city were studded with downscale versions of the Mozartplatz, open spaces half a mile wide and maybe fifty levels deep. This was just a logical extension.

She felt she ought to dislike it because it was so overdone, so fantastically huge, such a waste of space . . . and, oddly, so standardized. It was a taste of the culture of old Earth, where Paris looked just like Tokyo. She had been to the new Beethovenplatz at Clavius, and it looked just like this place. Six more arco-malls were being built in other Lunar cities.

And Bach liked it. She couldn't help herself. One day she'd like to live here.

She left her tube capsule in the bustling central station, went to a terminal and queried the location of the *Great Northern*. It was docked at the southern port, five miles away.

It was claimed that any form of non-animal transportation humans had ever used was available in the Mozartplatz. Bach didn't doubt it. She had tried most of them. But when she had a little time, as she did today, she liked to walk. She didn't have time to walk five miles, but compromised by walking to the trolley station a mile away.

Starting out on a brick walkway, she moved to cool marble, then over a glass bridge with lights flashing down inside. This took her to a boardwalk, then down to a beach where machines made four-foot breakers, each carrying a new load of surfers. The sand was fine and hot between her toes. Mozartplatz was a sensual delight for the feet. Few Lunarians ever wore shoes, and they could walk all day through old New Dresden and feel nothing but different types of carpeting and composition flooring.

The one thing Bach didn't like about the place was the weather. She thought it was needless, preposterous, and inconvenient. It began to rain and, as usual, caught her off guard. She hurried to a shelter where, for a tenthMark, she rented an umbrella, but it was too late for her paper uniform. As she stood in front of a blower, drying off, she wadded it up and threw it away, then hurried to catch the trolley, nude but for her creaking leather equipment belt and police cap. Even this stripped down, she was more dressed than a quarter of the people around her.

The conductor gave her a paper mat to put on the artificial leather seat. There were cut flowers in crystal vases attached to the sides of the car. Bach sat by an open window and leaned one arm outside in the cool breeze, watching the passing scenery. She craned her neck when the *Graf Zeppelin* muttered by overhead. They said it was an exact copy of the first world-girdling dirigible, and she had no reason to doubt it.

It was a great day to be traveling. If not for one thing, it would be perfect. Her mind kept coming back to Charlie and her mother.

She had forgotten just how big the *Great Northern* was. She stopped twice on her way down the long dock to board it, once to buy a lime sherbet ice cream cone, and again to purchase a skirt. As she fed coins into the clothing machine, she looked at the great metal wall of the ship. It was painted white, trimmed in gold. There were five smokestacks and six towering masts. Midships was the housing for the huge paddlewheel. Multicolored pennants snapped in the breeze from the forest of rigging. It was quite a boat.

She finished her cone, punched in her size, then selected a simple above-the-knee skirt in a gaudy print of tropical fruit and palm trees. The machine hummed as it cut the paper to size, hemmed it and strengthened the waist with elastic, then rolled it out into her hand. She held it up against herself. It was good, but the equipment belt spoiled it.

There were lockers along the deck. She used yet another coin to rent one. In it went the belt and cap. She took the pin out of her hair and shook it down around her shoulders, fussed with it for a moment, then decided it would have to do. She fastened the skirt with its single button, wearing it low on her hips, south-seas style. She walked a few steps, studying the effect. The skirt tended to leave one leg bare when she walked, which felt right.

"Look at you," she chided herself, under her breath. "You think you look all right to meet a world-famous, glamorous tube personality? Who you happen to despise?" She thought about reclaiming her belt, then decided that would be foolish. The fact was it was a glorious day, a beautiful ship, and she was feeling more alive than she had in months.

She climbed the gangplank and was met at the top by a man in an outlandish uniform. It was all white, covered everything but his face, and was festooned with gold braid and black buttons. It looked hideously uncomfortable, but he didn't seem to mind it. That was one of the odd things about Mozartplatz. In jobs at places like the *Great Northern*, people often worked in period costumes, though it meant wearing shoes or things even more grotesque.

He made a small bow and tipped his hat, then offered her a hibiscus, which he helped her pin in her hair. She smiled at him. Bach was a sucker for that kind of treatment—and knew it—perhaps because she got so little of it.

"I'm meeting someone in the bar on the top deck."

"If madame would walk this way . . ." He gestured, then led her along the side rail toward the stern of the ship. The deck underfoot was gleaming, polished teak.

She was shown to a wicker table near the rail. The steward held the chair out for her, and took her order. She relaxed, looking up at the vast reaches of the arco-mall, feeling the bright sunlight washing over her body, smelling the salt water, hearing the lap of waves against wood pilings. The air was full of bright balloons, gliders, putt-putting nano-lights, and people in muscle-powered flight harnesses. Not too far away, a fish broke the surface. She grinned at it.

Her drink arrived, with sprigs of mint and several straws and a tiny parasol. It was good. She looked around. There were only a few people out here on the deck. One couple was dressed in full period costume, but the rest looked normal enough. She settled on one guy sitting alone across the deck. He had a good pair of shoulders on him. When she caught his eye, she made a hand signal that meant "I might be available." He ignored it, which annoyed her for a while, until he was joined by a tiny woman who couldn't have been five feet tall. She shrugged. No accounting for taste.

She knew what was happening to her. It was silly, but she felt like going on the hunt. It often happened to her when something shocking or unpleasant happened at work. The police headshrinker said it was compensation, and not that uncommon.

With a sigh, she turned her mind away from that. It seemed there was no place else for it to go but back into that room on Charlie Station, and to the thing in the bed.

Charlie knew her mother was very sick. She had been that way "a long, long time." She left the camera pointed at her mother while she went away to deal with her dogs. The doctors had gathered around and studied the situation for quite some time, then issued their diagnosis.

She was dead, of course, by any definition medical science had accepted for the last century.

Someone had wired her to a robot doctor, probably during the final stages of the epidemic. It was capable of doing just about anything to keep a patient alive and was not programmed to understand brain death. That was a decision left to the human doctor, when he or she arrived.

The doctor had never arrived. The doctor was dead, and the thing that had been Charlie's mother lived on. Bach wondered if the verb "to live" had ever been so abused.

All of its arms and legs were gone, victims of gangrene. Not much else could be seen of it, but a forest of tubes and wires entered and emerged. Fluids seeped slowly through the tissue. Machines had taken over the function of every vital organ. There were patches of greenish skin here and there, including one on the side of its head which Charlie had kissed before leaving. Bach hastily took another drink as she recalled that, and signaled the waiter for another.

Blume and Wilhelm had been fascinated. They were dubious that any part of it could still be alive, even in the sense of cell cultures. There was no way to find out, because the Charlie Station computer—Tik-Tok, to the little girl—refused access to the autodoctor's data outputs.

But there was a very interesting question that emerged as soon as everyone was convinced Charlie's mother *had* died thirty years ago.

"Hello, Anna-Louise. Sorry I'm late."

She looked up and saw Megan Galloway approaching.

Bach had not met the woman in just over ten years, though she, like almost everyone else, had seen her frequently on the tube.

Galloway was tall, for an Earth woman, and not as thin as Bach remembered her. But that was understandable, considering the recent change in her life. Her hair was fiery red and curly, which it had not been ten years ago. It might even be her natural color; she was almost nude, and the colors matched, though that didn't have to mean much. But it looked right on her.

She wore odd-looking silver slippers, and her upper body was traced by a quite lovely filigree of gilded, curving lines. It was some sort of tattoo, and it was all that was left of the machine called the Golden Gypsy. It was completely symbolic. Being the Golden Gypsy was worth a lot of money to Galloway.

Megan Galloway had broken her neck while still in her teens. She became part of the early development of a powered exoskeleton, research that led to the hideously expensive and beautiful Golden Gypsy, of which only one was ever built. It abolished wheelchairs and crutches for her. It returned her to life, in her own mind, and it made her a celebrity.

An odd by-product to learning to use an exoskeleton was the development of skills that made it possible to excel in the new technology of emotional recording: the "feelies." The world was briefly treated to the sight of quadriplegics dominating a new art form. It made Galloway famous as the best of the Trans-sisters. It made her rich, as her trans-tapes out-sold everyone else's. She made herself extremely rich by investing wisely, then she and a friend of Bach's had made her fabulously rich by being the first to capture the experience of falling in love on a trans-tape.

In a sense, Galloway had cured herself. She had always donated a lot of money to neurological research, never really expecting it to pay off. But it did, and three years ago she had thrown the Golden Gypsy away forever.

Bach had thought her cure was complete, but now she wondered. Galloway carried a beautiful crystal cane. It didn't seem to be for show. She leaned on it heavily, and made her way through the tables slowly. Bach started to get up.

"No, no, don't bother," Galloway said. "It takes me a while but I get there." She flashed that famous smile with the gap between her front teeth. There was something about the woman; the smile was so powerful that Bach found herself smiling back. "It's so good to walk I don't mind taking my time."

She let the waiter pull the chair back for her, and sat down with a sigh of relief.

"I'll have a Devil's Nitelite," she told him. "And get another of whatever that was for her."

"A banana Daquiri," Bach said, surprised to find her own drink was almost gone, and a little curious to find out what a Devil's Nitelite was.

Galloway stretched as she looked up at the balloons and gliders.

"It's great to get back to the moon," she said. She made a small gesture that indicated her body. "Great to get out of my clothes. I always feel so free in here. Funny thing, though. I just *can't* get used to not wearing shoes." She lifted one foot to display a slipper. "I feel too vulnerable without them. Like I'm going to get stepped on."

"You can take your clothes off on Earth, too," Bach pointed out.

"Some places, sure. But aside from the beach, there's no place where it's *fashionable,* don't you see?"

Bach didn't, but decided not to make a thing out of it. She knew social nudity had evolved in Luna because it never got hot or cold, and that Earth would never embrace it as fully as Lunarians had.

The drinks arrived. Bach sipped hers, and eyed Galloway's, which produced a luminous smoke ring every ten seconds. Galloway chattered on about nothing in particular for a while.

"Why did you agree to see me?" Galloway asked, at last.

"Shouldn't that be my question?"

Galloway raised an eyebrow, and Bach went on.

"You've got a hell of a story. I can't figure out why you didn't just run with it. Why arrange a meeting with someone you barely knew ten years ago, and haven't seen since, and never liked even back then?"

"I always liked you, Anna-Louise," Galloway said. She looked up at the sky. For a while she watched a couple pedaling a skycycle, then she looked at Bach again. "I feel like I owe you something. Anyway, when I saw your name I thought I should check with you. I don't want to cause you any trouble." Suddenly she looked angry. "I don't *need* the story, Bach. I don't need *any* story, I'm too big for that. I can let it go or I can use it, it makes no difference."

"Oh, that's cute," Bach said. "Maybe I don't understand how you pay your debts. Maybe they do it different on Earth."

She thought Galloway was going to get up and leave. She had reached for her cane, then thought better of it.

"I gather it doesn't matter, then, if I go with the story."

Bach shrugged. She hadn't come here to talk about Charlie, anyway.

"How is Q.M., by the way?" she said.

Galloway didn't look away this time. She sat in silence for almost a minute, searching Bach's eyes.

"I thought I was ready for that question," she said at last. "He's living in New Zealand, on a commune. From what my agents tell me, he's happy. They don't watch television, they don't marry. They worship and they screw a lot."

"Did you really give him half of the profits on that . . . that tape?"

"Did give him, am giving him, and will continue to give him until the day I die. And it's half the *gross,* my dear, which is another thing entirely. He gets half of every Mark that comes in. He's made more money off it than I have . . . and he's never touched a tenthMark. It's piling up in a Swiss account I started in his name."

"Well, he never sold anything."

Bach hadn't meant that to be as harsh as it came out, but Galloway did not seem bothered by it. The thing she had sold . . .

Had there ever been anyone as thoroughly betrayed as Q.M. Cooper? Bach wondered. She might have loved him herself, but he fell totally in love with Megan Galloway.

And Galloway fell in love with him. There could be no mistake about that. Doubters are referred to *Gitana de Oro* catalog #1, an emotional recording entitled, simply, "Love." Put it in your trans-tape player, don the headset, punch PLAY, and you will experience just how hard and how completely Galloway fell in love with Q.M. Cooper. But have your head examined first. GDO #1 had been known to precipitate suicide.

Cooper had found this an impediment to the course of true love. He had always thought that love was something between two people, something exclusive, something private. He was unprepared to have Galloway mass-produce it, put it in a box with liner notes and a price tag of LM14.95, and hawk copies in every trans-tape shop from Peoria to Tibet.

The supreme irony of it to the man, who eventually found refuge in a minor cult in a far corner of the Earth, was that the tape itself, the means of his betrayal, his humiliation, was proof that Galloway had returned his love.

And Galloway had sold it. Never mind that she had her reasons, or that they were reasons with which Bach could find considerable sympathy.

She had sold it.

All Bach ever got out of the episode was a compulsion to seek lovers who looked like the Earth-muscled Cooper. Now it seemed she might get something else. It was time to change the subject.

"What do you know about Charlie?" she asked.

"You want it all, or just a general idea?" Galloway didn't wait for an answer. "I know her real name is Charlotte Isolde Hill Perkins-Smith. I know her father is dead, and her mother's condition is open to debate. Leda Perkins-Smith has a lot of money—if she's alive. Her daughter would inherit, if she's dead. I know the names of ten of Charlie's dogs. And, oh yes, I know that, appearances to the contrary, she is thirty-seven years old."

"Your source is very up-to-date."

"It's a very good source."

"You want to name him?"

"I'll pass on that, for the moment." She regarded Bach easily, her hands folded on the table in front of her. "So. What do you want me to do?"

"Is it really that simple?"

"My producers will want to kill me, but I'll sit on the story for at least twenty-four hours if you tell me to. By the way," she turned in her seat and crooked a finger at another table, "it's probably time you met my producers."

Bach turned slightly, and saw them coming toward her table.

"These are the Myers twins, Joy and Jay. Waiter, do you know how to make a Shirley Temple and a Roy Rogers?"

The waiter said he did, and went off with the order while Joy and Jay pulled up chairs and sat in them, several feet from the table but very close to each other. They had not offered to shake hands. Both were armless, with no sign of amputation, just bare, rounded shoulders. Both wore prosthetics made of golden, welded wire and powered by tiny motors. The units were one piece, fitting over their backs in a harnesslike arrangement. They were quite pretty—light and airy, perfectly articulated, cunningly wrought—and also creepy.

"You've heard of amparole?" Galloway asked. Bach shook her head. "That's the slang word for it. It's a neo-Moslem practice. Joy and Jay were convicted of murder."

"I have heard of it." She hadn't paid much attention to it, dismissing it as just another harebrained Earthling idiocy.

"Their arms are being kept in cryonic suspension for twenty years. The theory is, if they sin no more, they'll get them back. Those prosthetics won't pick up a gun, or a knife. They won't throw a punch."

Joy and Jay were listening to this with complete stolidity. Once Bach got beyond the arms, she saw another unusual thing about them. They were dressed identically, in loose bell-bottomed trousers. Joy had small breasts, and Jay had a small mustache. Other than that, they were absolutely identical in face and body. Bach didn't care for the effect.

"They also took slices out of the cerebrums and they're on a maintenance dosage of some drug. Calms them down. You don't want to know who they killed, or how. But they were proper villains, these two."

No, I don't think I do, Bach decided. Like many cops, she looked at eyes. Joy and Jay's were calm, placid . . . and deep inside was a steel-gray coldness.

"If they try to get naughty again, the amparole units go on strike. I suppose they might find a way to kill with their feet."

The twins glanced at each other, held each other's gaze for a moment, and exchanged wistful smiles. At least, Bach hoped they were just wistful.

"Yeah, okay," Bach said.

"Don't worry about them. They can't be offended with the drugs they're taking."

"I wasn't worried," Bach said. She couldn't have cared less what the freaks felt; she wished they'd been executed.

"Are they really twins?" she finally asked, against her better judgment.

"Really. One of them had a sex change, I don't know which one. And to answer your next question, yes they do, but only in the privacy of their own room."

"I wasn't—"

"And your other question . . . they are *very* good at what they do. Who am I to judge about the other? And I'm in a highly visible industry. It never hurts to have conversation pieces around. You need to get noticed."

Bach was starting to get angry, and she was not quite sure why. Maybe it was the way Galloway so cheerfully admitted her base motives, even when no one had accused her of having them.

"We were talking about the story," she said.

"We need to go with it," Joy said, startling Bach. Somehow, she had not really expected the cyborg-thing to talk. "Our source is good and the security on the story is tight—"

"—but it's dead certain to come out in twenty-four hours," Jay finished for her.

"Maybe less," Joy added.

"Shut up," Galloway said, without heat. "Anna-Louise, you were about to tell me your feeling on the matter."

Bach finished her drink as the waiter arrived with more. She caught herself staring as the twins took theirs. The metal hands were marvels of complexity. They moved just as cleverly as real hands.

"I was considering leaking the story myself. It looked like things were going against Charlie. I thought they might just let the station crash and then swear us all to secrecy."

"It strikes me," Galloway said, slowly, "that today's developments give her an edge."

"Yeah. But I don't envy her."

"Me, either. But it's not going to be easy to neglect a girl whose body may hold the secret of eternal life. If you do, somebody's bound to ask awkward questions later."

"It may not be eternal life," Bach said.

"What do you call it, then?" Jay asked.

"Why do you say that?" Joy wanted to know.

"All we know is she's lived thirty years without growing any older—externally. They'd have to examine her a lot closer to find out what's actually happening."

"And there's pressure to do so."

"Exactly. It might be the biggest medical breakthrough in a thousand years. What I think has happened to her is not eternal life, but extended youth."

Galloway looked thoughtful. "You know, of the two, I think extended youth would be more popular."

"I think you're right."

They brooded over that in silence for a while. Bach signaled the waiter for another drink.

"Anyway," she went on, "Charlie doesn't seem to need protection just now. But she may, and quickly."

"So you aren't in favor of letting her die."

Bach looked up, surprised and beginning to be offended, then she remembered Dr. Wilhelm. The good doctor was not a monster, and Galloway's question was a reasonable one, given the nature of Neuro-X.

"There has to be a way to save her, *and* protect ourselves from her. That's what I'm working toward, anyway."

"Let me get this straight, then. You were thinking of leaking the story so the public outcry would force the police to save her?"

"Sure, I thought . . ." Bach trailed off, suddenly realizing what Galloway was saying. "You mean you think—"

Galloway waved her hand impatiently.

"It depends on a lot of things, but mostly on how the story is handled. If you start off with the plague story, there could be pressure to blast her out of the skies and have done with it." She looked at Jay and Joy, who went into a trance-like state.

"Sure, sure," Jay said. "The plague got big play. Almost everybody remembers it. Use horror show tapes of the casualties . . ."

". . . line up the big brains to start the scare," Joy said.

"You can even add sob stuff, after it gets rolling."

"What a tragedy, this little girl has to die for the good of us all."

"Somber commentary, the world watches as she cashes in."

"You could make it play. No problem."

Bach's head had been ping-ponging between the two of them. When Galloway spoke, it was hard to swing around and look at her.

"Or you could start off with the little girl," Galloway prompted.

"*Much* better," Joy said. "Twice the story there. Indignant exposé stuff: 'Did you know, fellow citizens . . .'"

"'. . . there's this little girl, this innocent child, swinging around up there in space and she's going to *die!*'"

"A *rich* little girl, too, and her dying mother."

"Later, get the immortality angle."

"Not too soon," Joy cautioned. "At first, she's ordinary. Second lead is, she's got money."

"Third lead, she holds the key to eternal youth."

"Immortality."

"Youth, honey, youth. Who the fuck knows what living forever is like? Youth you can sell. It's the *only* thing you can sell."

"Megan, this is the biggest story since Jesus."

"Or at least we'll *make* it the biggest story."

"See why they're so valuable?" Galloway said. Bach hardly heard her. She was reassessing what she had thought she knew about the situation.

"I don't know what to do," she finally confessed. "I don't know what to ask you to do, either. I guess you ought to go with what you think is best."

Galloway frowned.

"Both for professional and personal reasons, I'd rather try to help her. I'm not sure why. She is dangerous, you know."

"I realize that. But I can't believe she can't be handled."

"Neither can I." She glanced at her watch. "Tell you what, you come with us on a little trip."

Bach protested at first, but Galloway would not be denied, and Bach's resistance was at a low ebb.

By speedboat, trolley, and airplane they quickly made their way on the top of Mozartplatz, where Bach found herself in a four-seat PTP—or point-to-point—ballistic vehicle.

She had never ridden in a PTP. They were rare, mostly because they wasted a lot of energy for only a few minutes' gain in travel time. Most people took the tubes, which reached speeds of three thousand miles per hour, hovering inches above their induction rails in Luna's excellent vacuum.

But for a celebrity like Galloway, the PTP made sense. She had trouble going places in public without getting mobbed. And she certainly had the money to spare.

There was a heavy initial acceleration, then weightlessness. Bach had never liked it, and enjoyed it even less with a few drinks in her.

Little was said during the short journey. Bach had not asked where they were going, and Galloway did not volunteer it. Bach looked out one of the wide windows at the fleeting moonscape.

As she counted the valleys, rilles, and craters flowing past beneath her, she soon realized her destination. It was a distant valley, in the sense that no tube track ran through it. In a little over an hour, Tango Charlie would come speeding through, no more than a hundred meters from the surface.

The PTP landed itself in a cluster of transparent, temporary domes. There were over a hundred of them, and more PTP's than Bach had ever seen before. She decided most of the people in and around the domes fell into three categories. There were the very wealthy, owners of private spacecraft, who had erected most of these portable Xanadus and filled them with their friends. There were civic dignitaries in city-owned domes. And there were the news media.

This last category was there in its teeming hundreds. It was not what they would call a *big* story, but it was a very visual one. It should yield spectacular pictures for the evening news.

A long, wide black stripe had been created across the sun-drenched plain, indicating the path Tango Charlie would take. Many cameras and quite a few knots of pressure-suited spectators were situated smack in the middle of that line, with many more off to one side, to get an angle on the approach. Beyond it were about a hundred large glass-roofed touring buses and a motley assortment of private crawlers, sunskimmers, jetsleds, and even some hikers: the common people, come to see the event.

Bach followed along behind the uncommon people: Galloway, thin and somehow spectral in the translucent suit, leaning on her crystal cane; the Myers twins, whose amparolee arms would not fit in the suits, so that the empty sleeves stuck out, bloated, like crucified ghosts; and most singular of all, the wire-sculpture arm units themselves, walking independently, on their fingertips, looking like some demented, disjointed mechanical camel as they lurched through the dust.

They entered the largest of the domes, set on the edge of the gathering nearest the black line, which put it no more than a hundred meters from the expected passage.

The first person Bach saw, as she was removing her helmet, was Hoeffer.

He did not see her immediately. He, and many of the other people in the dome, were watching Galloway. So she saw his face as his gaze moved from the celebrity to Joy and Jay . . . and saw amazement and horror, far too strong to be simple surprise at their weirdness. It was a look of recognition.

Galloway had said she had an excellent source.

She noticed Bach's interest, smiled, and nodded slightly. Still struggling to remove her suit, she approached Bach.

"That's right. The twins heard a rumor something interesting might be going on at NavTrack, so they found your commander. Turns out he has rather odd sexual tastes, though it's probably fairly pedestrian to Joy and Jay. They scratched his itch, and he spilled everything."

"I find that . . . rather interesting," Bach admitted.

"I thought you would. Were you planning to make a career out of being an R/A in Navigational Tracking?"

"That wasn't my intention."

"I didn't think so. Listen, don't touch it. I can handle it without there being any chance of it backfiring on you. Within the week you'll be promoted out of there."

"I don't know if . . ."

"If what?" Galloway was looking at her narrowly.

Bach hesitated only a moment.

"I may be stiff-necked, but I'm not a fool. Thank you."

Galloway turned away a little awkwardly, then resumed struggling with her suit. Bach was about to offer some help, when Galloway frowned at her.

"How come you're not taking off your pressure suit?"

"That dome up there is pretty strong, but it's only one layer. Look around you. Most of the natives have just removed their helmets, and a lot are carrying those around. Most of the Earthlings are out of their suits. They don't understand vacuum."

"You're saying it's not safe?"

"No. But vacuum doesn't forgive. It's trying to kill you *all* the time."

Galloway looked dubious, but stopped trying to remove her suit.

Bach wandered the electronic wonderland, helmet in hand.

Tango Charlie would not be visible until less than a minute before the close encounter, and then would be hard to spot as it would be only a few seconds of arc above the horizon line. But there were cameras hundreds of miles downtrack which could already see it, both as a bright star, moving visibly against the background, and as a jittery image in some very long lenses. Bach watched as the wheel filled one screen until she could actually see furniture behind one of the windows.

For the first time since arriving, she thought of Charlie. She wondered if Tik-Tok—no, dammit, if the Charlie Station Computer had told her of the approach, and if so, would Charlie watch it. Which window would she choose? It was shocking to think that, if she chose the right one, Bach might catch a glimpse of her.

Only a few minutes to go. Knowing it was stupid, Bach looked along the line indicated by the thousand cameras, hoping to catch the first glimpse.

She saw Megan Galloway doing a walk-around, followed by a camera crew, no doubt saying bright, witty things to her huge audience. Galloway was here less for the event itself than for the many celebrities who had gathered to witness it. Bach saw her approach a famous TV star, who smiled and embraced her, making some sort of joke about Galloway's pressure suit.

You can meet him if you want, she told herself. She was a little surprised to discover she had no interest in doing so.

She saw Joy and Jay in heated conversation with Hoeffer. The twins seemed distantly amused.

She saw the countdown clock, ticking toward one minute.

Then the telescopic image in one of the remote cameras began to shake violently. In a few seconds, it had lost its fix on Charlie Station. Bach watched as annoyed technicians struggled to get it back.

"Seismic activity," one of them said, loud enough for Bach to hear.

She looked at the other remote monitor, which showed Tango Charlie as a very bright star sitting on the horizon. As she watched, the light grew visibly, until she could see it as a disc. And in another part of the screen, at a site high in the lunar hills, there was a shower of dust and rock. That must be the seismic activity, she thought. The camera operator zoomed in on this eruption, and Bach frowned. She couldn't figure out what sort of lunar quake could cause such a commotion. It looked more like an impact. The rocks and dust particles were fountaining up with lovely geometrical symmetry, each piece, from the largest boulder to the smallest mote, moving at about the same speed and in a perfect mathematical trajectory, unimpeded by any air resistance, in a way that could never be duplicated on Earth. It was a dull gray expanding dome shape, gradually flattening on top.

Frowning, she turned her attention to the spot on the plain where she had been told Charlie would first appear. She saw the first light of it, but more troubling, she saw a dozen more of the expanding domes. From here, they seemed no larger than soap bubbles.

Then another fountain of rock erupted, not far from the impromptu parking lot full of tourist buses.

Suddenly she knew what was happening.

"It's shooting at us!" she shouted. Everyone fell silent, and as they were still turning to look at her, she yelled again.

"Suit up."

Her voice was drowned out by the sound every Lunarian dreads: the high, haunting shriek of escaping air.

Step number one, she heard a long-ago instructor say. See to *your own* pressure integrity *first.* You can't help anybody, man, woman or child, if you pass out before you get into your suit.

It was a five-second operation to don and seal her helmet, one she had practiced a thousand times as a child. She glimpsed a great hole in the plastic roof. Debris was pouring out of it, swept up in the sudden wind: paper, clothing, a couple of helmets . . .

Sealed up, she looked around and realized many of these people were doomed. They were not in their suits, and there was little chance they could put them on in time.

She remembered the next few seconds in a series of vivid impressions.

A boulder, several tons of dry lunar rock, crashed down on a bank of television monitors.

A chubby little man, his hands shaking, unable to get his helmet over his bald head. Bach tore it from his hands, slapped it in place, and gave it a twist hard enough to knock him down.

Joy and Jay, as good as dead, killed by the impossibility of fitting the mechanical arms into their suits, holding each other calmly in metallic embrace.

Beyond the black line, a tour bus rising slowly in the air, turning end over end. A hundred of the hideous gray domes of explosions growing like mushrooms all through the valley.

And there was Galloway. She was going as fast as she could, intense concentration on her face as she stumbled along after her helmet, which was rolling on the ground. Blood had leaked from one corner of her nose. It was almost soundless in the remains of the dome now.

Bach snagged the helmet, and hit Galloway with a flying tackle. Just like a drill: put helmet in place, twist, hit three snap-interlocks, then the emergency pressurization switch. She saw Galloway howl in pain and try to put her hands to her ears.

Lying there she looked up as the last big segment of the dome material lifted in a dying wind to reveal . . . Tango Charlie.

It was a little wheel rolling on the horizon. No bigger than a coin.

She blinked.

And it was *here.* Vast, towering, coming directly at her through a hell of burning dust.

It was the dust that finally made the lasers visible. The great spokes of light were flashing on and off in millisecond bursts, and in each pulse a trillion dust motes were vaporized in an eyeball-frying purple light.

It was impossible that she saw it for more than a tenth of a second, but it seemed much longer. The sight would remain with her, and not just in memory. For days afterward her vision was scored with a spiderweb of purple lines.

But much worse was the awesome grandeur of the thing, the whirling menace of it as it came rushing out of the void. That picture would last much longer than a few days. It would come out only at night, in dreams that would wake her for years, drenched in sweat.

And the last strong image she would carry away from the valley was of Galloway, turned over now, pointing her crystal cane at the wheel, already far away on the horizon. A line of red laser light came out of the end of the cane and stretched away into infinity.

"Wow!" said Charlotte Isolde Hill Perkins-Smith. "Wow, Tik-Tok, that was great! Let's do it again."

Hovering in the dead center of the hub, Charlie had watched all of the encounter. It had been a lot like she imagined a roller-coaster would be when she watched the films in Tik-Tok's memory. If it had a fault—and she wasn't complaining, far from it—it was that the experience had been too short. For almost an hour she had watched the moon get bigger, until it no longer seemed round and the landscape was rolling by beneath her. But she'd seen that much before. This time it just got larger and larger, and faster and faster, until she was scooting along at about a zillion miles an hour. Then there was a lot of flashing lights . . . and gradually, the ground got farther away again. It was still back there, dwindling, no longer very interesting.

"I'm glad you liked it," Tik-Tok said.

"Only one thing. How come I had to put on my pressure suit?"

"Just a precaution."

She shrugged, and made her way to the elevator.

When she got out at the rim, she frowned. There were alarms sounding, far around the rim on the wheel.

"We got a problem?" she asked.

"Minor," Tik-Tok said.

"What happened?"

"We got hit by some rocks."

"We must of passed *real* close!"

"Charlie, if you'd been down here when we passed, you could have reached out and written your name on a rock."

She giggled at that idea, then hurried off to see to the dogs.

It was about two hours later that Anna-Louise called. Charlie was inclined to ignore it, she had so much to do, but in the end, she sat down in front of the camera. Anna-Louise was there, and sitting beside her was another woman.

"Are you okay, Charlie?" Anna wanted to know.

"Why shouldn't I be?" Damn, she thought. She wasn't supposed to answer a question with another question. But then, what right did Anna have to ask her to do that?

"I was wondering if you were watching a little while ago, when you passed so close to the moon."

"I sure was. It was great."

There was a short pause. The two women looked at each other, then Anna-Louise sighed, and faced Charlie again.

"Charlie, there are a few things I have to tell you."

As in most disasters involving depressurization, there was not a great demand for first aid. Most of the bad injuries were fatal.

Galloway was not hearing too well and Bach still had spots before her eyes; Hoeffer hadn't even bumped his head.

The body-count was not complete, but it was going to be high.

For a perilous hour after the passage, there was talk of shooting Tango Charlie out of the sky.

Much of the advisory team had already gathered in the meeting room by the time Bach and Hoeffer arrived—with Galloway following closely behind. A hot debate was in progress. People recognized Galloway, and a few seemed inclined to question her presence here, but Hoeffer shut them up quickly. A deal had been struck in the PTP, on the way back from the disaster. The fix was in, and Megan Galloway was getting an exclusive on the story. Galloway had proved to Hoeffer that Joy and Jay had kept tapes of his security lapse.

The eventual explanation for the unprovoked and insane attack was simple. The Charlie Station Computer had been instructed to fire upon any object approaching within five kilometers. It had done so, faithfully, for thirty years, not that it ever had much to shoot at. The close approach of Luna must have been an interesting problem. Tik-Tok was no fool. Certainly he would know the consequences of his actions. But a computer did not think at all like a human, no matter how much it might sound like one. There were rigid hierarchies in a brain like Tik-Tok. One part of him might realize something was foolish, but be helpless to override a priority order.

Analysis of the pattern of laser strikes helped to confirm this. The hits were totally random. Vehicles, domes, and people had not been targeted; however, if they were in the way, they were hit.

The one exception to the randomness concerned the black line Bach had seen. Tik-Tok had found a way to avoid shooting directly ahead of himself without violating his priority order. Thus, he avoided stirring up debris that Charlie Station would be flying through in another few seconds.

The decision was made to take no reprisals on Tango Charlie. Nobody was happy about it, but no one could suggest anything short of total destruction.

But action had to be taken now. Very soon the public was going to wonder why this dangerous object had not been destroyed before the approach. The senior police present and the representatives of the Mayor's office all agreed that the press would have to be let in. They asked Galloway if they could have her cooperation in the management of this phase.

And Bach watched as, with surprising speed, Megan Galloway took over the meeting.

"You need time right now," she said, at one point. "The best way to get it is to play the little-girl angle, and play it hard. You were not so heartless as to endanger the little girl—and you had no reason to believe the station was any kind of threat. What you have to do now is tell the truth about what we know, and what's been done."

"How about the immortality angle?" someone asked.

"What about it? It's going to leak someday. Might as well get it out in front of us."

"But it will prejudice the public in favor of . . ." Wilhelm looked around her, and decided not to finish her objection.

"It's a price we have to pay," Galloway said, smoothly. "You folks will do what you think is right. I'm sure of that. You wouldn't let public opinion influence your decision."

Nobody had anything to say to that. Bach managed not to laugh.

"The big thing is to answer the questions before they get asked. I suggest you get started on your statements, then call in the press. In the meantime, Corporal Bach has invited me to listen in on her next conversation with Charlie Perkins-Smith, so I'll leave you now."

Bach led Galloway down the corridor toward the operations room, shaking her head in admiration. She looked over her shoulder.

"I got to admit it. You're very smooth."

"It's my profession. You're pretty smooth, yourself."

"What do you mean?"

"I mean I owe you. I'm afraid I owe you more than I'll be able to repay."

Bach stopped, honestly bewildered.

"You saved my *life*," Galloway shouted. "*Thank you!*"

"So what if I did? You don't owe me anything. It's not the custom."

"What's not the custom?"

"You can be grateful, sure. I'd be, if somebody pressurized me. But it would be an insult to try to pay me back for it. Like on the desert, you know, you have to give water to somebody dying of thirst."

"Not in the deserts I've been to," Galloway said. They were alone in the hallway. Galloway seemed distressed, and Bach felt awkward. "We seem to be at a cultural impasse. I feel I owe you a lot; and you say it's nothing."

"No problem." Bach pointed out. "You were going to help me get promoted out of this stinking place. Do that, and we'll call it even."

Galloway was shaking her head.

"I don't think I'll be able to, now. You know that fat man you stuffed into a helmet, before you got to me? He asked me about you. He's the Mayor of Clavius. He'll be talking to the Mayor of New Dresden, and you'll get the promotion and a couple of medals and maybe a reward, too."

They regarded each other uneasily. Bach knew that gratitude could equal resentment. She thought she could see some of that in Galloway's eyes. But there was determination, too. Megan Galloway paid her debts. She had been paying one to Q.M. Cooper for ten years.

By unspoken agreement they left it at that, and went to talk to Charlie.

Most of the dogs didn't like the air blower. Mistress Too White O'Hock was the exception. 2-White would turn her face into the stream of warm air as Charlie directed the hose over her sable pelt, then she would let her tongue hang out in an expression of such delight that Charlie would usually end up laughing at her.

Charlie brushed the fine hair behind 2-White's legs, the hair that was white almost an inch higher than it should be on a champion Sheltie. Just one little inch, and 2-White was sterilized. She would have been a fine mother. Charlie had seen her looking at puppies whelped by other mothers, and she knew it made 2-White sad.

But you can't have everything in this world. Tik-Tok had said that often enough. And you can't let all your dogs breed, or pretty soon you'll be knee deep in dogs. Tik-Tok said that, too.

In fact, Tik-Tok said a lot of things Charlie wished were not true. But he had never lied to her.

"Were you listening?" she asked.

"During your last conversation? Of course I was."

Charlie put 2-White down on the floor, and summoned the next dog. This was Engelbert, who wasn't a year old yet, and still inclined to be frisky when he shouldn't be. Charlie had to scold him before he would be still.

"Some of the things she said," Tik-Tok began. "It seemed like she disturbed you. Like how old you are."

"That's silly," Charlie said, quickly. "I knew how old I am." This was the truth . . . and yet it wasn't everything. Her first four dogs were all dead. The oldest had been thirteen. There had been many dogs since then. Right now, the oldest dog was sixteen, and sick. He wouldn't last much longer.

"I just never added it up," Charlie said, truthfully.

"There was never any reason to."

"But I don't grow up," she said, softly. "Why is that, Tik-Tok?"

"I don't know, Charlie."

"Anna said if I go down to the moon, they might be able to find out."

Tik-Tok didn't say anything.

"Was she telling the truth? About all those people who got hurt?"

"Yes."

"Maybe I shouldn't have got mad at her."

Again, Tik-Tok was silent. Charlie had been very angry. Anna and a new woman, Megan, had told her all these awful things, and when they were done Charlie knocked over the television equipment and went away. That had been almost a day ago, and they had been calling back almost all the time.

"Why did you do it?" she said.

"I didn't have any choice."

Charlie accepted that. Tik-Tok was a mechanical man, not like her at all. He was a faithful guardian and the closest thing she had to a friend, but she knew he was different. For one thing, he didn't have a body. She had sometimes wondered if this inconvenienced him any, but she had never asked.

"Is my mother really dead?"

"Yes."

Charlie stopped brushing. Engelbert looked around at her, then waited patiently until she told him he could get down.

"I guess I knew that."

"I thought you did. But you never asked."

"She was someone to talk to," Charlie explained. She left the grooming room and walked down the promenade. Several dogs followed behind her, trying to get her to play.

She went into her mother's room and stood for a moment looking at the thing in the bed. Then she moved from machine to machine, flipping switches, until everything was quiet. And when she was done, that was the only change in the room. The machines no longer hummed, rumbled, and clicked. The thing on the bed hadn't changed at all. Charlie supposed she could keep on talking to it, if she wanted to, but she suspected it wouldn't be the same.

She wondered if she ought to cry. Maybe she should ask Tik-Tok, but he'd never been very good with those kind of questions. Maybe it was because he couldn't cry himself, so he didn't know when people ought to cry. But the fact was, Charlie had felt a lot sadder at Albert's funeral.

In the end, she sang her hymm again, then closed and locked the door behind her. She would never go in there again.

"She's back," Steiner called across the room. Bach and Galloway hastily put down their cups of coffee and hurried over to Bach's office.

"She just plugged this camera in," Steiner explained, as they took their seats. "Looks a little different, doesn't she?"

Bach had to agree. They had glimpsed her in other cameras as she went about her business. Then, about an hour ago, she had entered her mother's room again. From there, she had gone to her own room, and when she emerged, she was a different girl. Her hair was washed and combed. She wore a dress that seemed to have started off as a woman's blouse. The sleeves had been cut off and bits of it had been inexpertly taken in. There was red polish on her nails. Her face was heavily made up. It was overdone, and completely wrong for someone of her apparent age, but it was not the wild, almost tribal paint she had worn before.

Charlie was seated behind a huge wooden desk, facing the camera.

"Good morning, Anna and Megan," she said, solemnly.

"Good morning, Charlie," Galloway said.

"I'm sorry I shouted at you," Charlie said. Her hands were folded carefully in front of her. There was a sheet of paper just to the left of them; other than that, the desk was bare. "I was confused and upset, and I needed some time to think about the things you said."

"That's all right," Bach told her. She did her best to conceal a yawn. She and Galloway had been awake for a day and a half. There had been a few catnaps, but they were always interrupted by sightings of Charlie.

"I've talked things over with Tik-Tok," Charlie went on. "And I turned my mother off. You were right. She was dead, anyway."

Bach could think of nothing to say to that. She glanced at Galloway, but could read nothing in the other woman's face.

"I've decided what I want to do," Charlie said. "But first I—"

"Charlie," Galloway said, quickly, "could you show me what you have there on the table?"

There was a brief silence in the room. Several people turned to look at Galloway, but nobody said anything. Bach was about to, but Galloway was making a motion with her hand, under the table, where no one but Bach was likely to see it. Bach decided to let it ride for the moment.

Charlie was looking embarrassed. She reached for the paper, glanced at it, then looked back at the camera.

"I drew this picture for you," she said. "Because I was sorry I shouted."

"Could I see it?"

Charlie jumped down off the chair and came around to hold the picture up. She seemed proud of it, and she had every right to be. Here at last was visual proof that Charlie was not what she seemed to be. No eight-year-old could have drawn this fine pencil portrait of a Sheltie.

"This is for Anna," she said.

"That's very nice, Charlie," Galloway said. "I'd like one, too."

"I'll draw you one!" Charlie said happily . . . and ran out of the picture.

There was angry shouting for a few moments. Galloway stood her ground, explaining that she had only been trying to cement the friendship, and how was she to know Charlie would run off like that?

Even Hoeffer was emboldened enough to take a few shots, pointing out—logically, in Bach's opinion—that time was running out and if anything was to be done about her situation every second was valuable.

"All right, all right, so I made a mistake. I promise I'll be more careful next time. Anna, I hope you'll call me when she comes back." And with that, she picked up her cane and trudged from the room.

Bach was surprised. It didn't seem like Galloway to leave the story before it was over, even if nothing was happening. But she was too tired to worry about it. She leaned back in her chair, closed her eyes, and was asleep in less than a minute.

Charlie was hard at work on the picture for Megan when Tik-Tok interrupted her. She looked up in annoyance.

"Can't you see I'm busy?"

"I'm sorry, but this can't wait. There's a telephone call for you."

"There's a . . . *what*?"

But Tik-Tok said no more. Charlie went across the room to the phone, silent these thirty years. She eyed it suspiciously, then pressed the button. As she did, dim memories flooded through her. She saw her mother's face. For the first time, she felt like crying.

"This is Charlotte Perkins-Smith," she said, in a childish voice. "My mother isn't . . . My mother . . . May I ask who's calling, please?"

There was no picture on the screen, but after a short pause, there was a familiar voice.

"This is Megan Galloway, Charlie. Can we talk?"

When Steiner shook Bach's shoulder, she opened her eyes to see Charlie sitting on the desk once more. Taking a quick sip of the hot coffee Steiner had brought, she tried to wipe the cobwebs from her mind and get back to work. The girl was just sitting there, hands folded once more.

"Hello, Anna," the girl said. "I just wanted to call and tell you I'll do whatever you people think is best. I've been acting silly. I hope you'll forgive me; it's been a long time since I had to talk to other people."

"That's okay, Charlie."

"I'm sorry I pissed on Captain Hoeffer. Tik-Tok said that was a bad thing to do, and that I ought to be more respectful to him, since he's the guy in charge. So if you'll get him, I'll do whatever he says."

"All right, Charlie. I'll get him."

Bach got up and watched Hoeffer take her chair.

"You'll be talking just to me from now on," he said, with what he must have felt was a friendly smile. "Is that all right?"

"Sure," Charlie said, indifferently.

"You can go get some rest now, Corporal Bach," Hoeffer said. She saluted, and turned on her heel. She knew it wasn't fair to Charlie to feel betrayed, but she couldn't help it. True, she hadn't talked to the girl all that long. There was no reason to feel a friendship had developed. But she felt sick watching Hoeffer talk to her. The man would lie to her, she was sure of that.

But then, could she have done any different? It was a disturbing thought. The fact was, there had as yet been no orders on what to do about Charlie. She was all over the news, the public debate had begun, and Bach knew it would be another day before public officials had taken enough soundings to know which way they should leap. In the meantime, they had Charlie's cooperation, and that was good news.

Bach wished she could be happier about it.

"Anna, there's a phone call for you."

She took it at one of the vacant consoles. When she pushed the Talk button, a light came on, indicating the other party wanted privacy, so she picked up the handset and asked who was calling.

"Anna," said Galloway, "come at once to room 569 in the Pension Kleist. That's four corridors from the main entrance to NavTrack, level—"

"I can find it. What's this all about? You got your story."

"I'll tell you when you get there."

The first person Bach saw in the small room was Ludmilla Rossnikova, the computer expert from GMA. She was sitting in a chair across the room, looking uncomfortable. Bach shut the door behind her, and saw Galloway sprawled in another chair before a table littered with electronic gear.

"I felt I had to speak to Tik-Tok privately," Galloway began, without preamble. She looked about as tired as Bach felt.

"Is that why you sent Charlie away?"

Galloway gave her a truly feral grin, and for a moment did not look tired at all. Bach realized she loved this sort of intrigue, loved playing fast and loose, taking chances.

"That's right. I figured Ms. Rossnikova was the woman to get me through, so now she's working for me."

Bach was impressed. It would not have been cheap to hire Rossnikova away from GMA. She would not have thought it possible.

"GMA doesn't know that, and it won't know, if you can keep a secret," Galloway went on. "I assured Ludmilla that you could."

"You mean she's spying for you."

"Not at all. She's not going to be working against GMA's interests, which are quite minimal in this affair. We're just not going to tell them about her work for me, and next year Ludmilla will take early retirement and move into a dacha in Georgia she's coveted all her life."

Bach looked at Rossnikova, who seemed embarrassed. So everybody has her price, Bach thought. So what else is new?

"Turns out she had a special code which she withheld from the folks back at NavTrack. I suspected she might. I wanted to talk to him without anyone else knowing I was doing it. Your control room was a bit crowded for that. Ludmilla, you want to take it from there?"

She did, telling Bach the story in a low voice, with reserved, diffident gestures. Bach wondered if she would be able to live with her defection, decided she'd probably get over it soon enough.

Rossnikova had raised Charlie Station, which in this sense was synonymous with Tik-Tok, the station computer. Galloway had talked to him. She wanted to know what he knew. As she suspected, he was well aware of his own orbital dynamics. He knew he was going to crash into the moon. So what did he intend to do about Charlotte Perkins-Smith? Galloway wanted to know.

What are you offering? Tik-Tok responded.

"The important point is, he doesn't want Charlie to die. He can't do anything about his instruction to fire on intruders. But he claims he would have let Charlie go years ago but for one thing."

"Our quarantine probes," Bach said.

"Exactly. He's got a lifeboat in readiness. A few minutes from impact, if nothing has been resolved, he'll load Charlie in it and blast her away, after first killing both your probes. He knows it's not much of a chance, but impact on the lunar surface is no chance at all."

Bach finally sat down. She thought it over for a minute, then spread her hands.

"Great," she said. "It sounds like all our problems are solved. We'll just take this to Hoeffer, and we can call off the probes."

Galloway and Rossnikova were silent. As last, Galloway sighed.

"It may not be as simple as that."

Bach stood again, suddenly sure of what was coming next.

"I've got good sources, both in the news media and in city hall. Things are not looking good for Charlie."

"I can't *believe* it!" Bach shouted. "They're ready to let a little girl die? They're not even going to try to save her?"

Galloway made soothing motions, and Bach gradually calmed down.

"It's not definite yet. But the trend is there. For one thing, she is *not* a little girl, as you well know. I was counting on the public perception of her as a little girl, but that's not working out so well."

"But all your stories have been so positive."

"I'm not the only newscaster. And . . . the public doesn't always determine it anyway. Right now, they're in favor of Charlie, seventy-thirty. But that's declining, and a lot of that seventy percent is soft, as they say. Not sure. The talk is, the decision makers are going to make it look like an unfortunate accident. Tik-Tok will be a great help there; it'll be easy to provoke an incident that could kill Charlie."

"It's just not right," Bach said, gloomily. Galloway leaned forward and looked at her intently.

"That's what I wanted to know. Are you still on Charlie's side, all the way? And if you are, what are you willing to risk to save her?"

Bach met Galloway's intent stare. Slowly, Galloway smiled again.

"That's what I thought. Here's what I want to do."

Charlie was sitting obediently by the telephone in her room at the appointed time, and it rang just when Megan had said it would. She answered it as she had before.

"Hi there, kid. How's it going?"

"I'm fine. Is Anna there too?"

"She sure is. Want to say hi to her?"

"I wish you'd tell her it was you that told me to—"

"I already did, and she understands. Did you have any trouble?"

Charlie snorted.

"With *him*? What a doo-doo-head. He'll believe anything I tell him. Are you sure he can't hear us in here?"

"Positive. Nobody can hear us. Did Tik-Tok tell you what all you have to do?"

"I think so. I wrote some of it down."

"We'll go over it again, point by point. We can't have any mistakes."

When they got the final word on the decision, it was only twelve hours to impact. None of them had gotten any sleep since the close approach. It seemed like years ago to Bach.

"The decision is to have an accident," Galloway said, hanging up the phone. She turned to Rossnikova who bent, hollow-eyed, over her array of computer keyboards. "How's it coming with the probe?"

"I'm pretty sure I've got it now," she said, leaning back. "I'll take it through the sequence one more time." She sighed, then looked at both of them. "Every time I try to reprogram it, it wants to tell me about this broken rose blossom and the corpse of a puppy and the way the wheel looks with all the lighted windows." She yawned hugely. "Some of it's kind of pretty, actually."

Bach wasn't sure what Rossnikova was talking about, but the important thing was the probe was taken care of. She looked at Galloway.

"My part is all done," Galloway said. "In record time, too."

"I'm not even going to guess what it cost you," Bach said.

"It's only money."

"What about Dr. Blume?"

"He's with us. He wasn't even very expensive. I think he wanted to do it, anyway." She looked from Bach to Rossnikova, and back again. "What do you say? Are we ready to go? Say in one hour?"

Neither of them raised an objection. Silently, they shook each other's hand. They knew it would not go easy with them if they were discovered, but that had already been discussed and accepted and there seemed no point in mentioning it again.

Bach left them in a hurry.

*   *   *

The dogs were more excited than Charlie had ever seen them. They sensed something was about to happen.

"They're probably just picking it up from you," Tik-Tok ventured.

"That could be it," Charlie agreed. They were leaping and running all up and down the corridor. It had been *hell* getting them all down here, by a route Tik-Tok had selected that would avoid all the operational cameras used by Captain Hoeffer and those other busybodies. But here they finally were, and there was the door to the lifeboat, and suddenly she realized that Tik-Tok could not come along.

"What are you going to do?" she finally asked him.

"That's a silly question, Charlie."

"But you'll *die!*"

"Not possible. Since I was never alive, I can't die."

"Oh, you're just playing with words." She stopped, and couldn't think of anything good to say. Why didn't they have more words? There ought to be more words, so some of them would be useful for saying goodbye.

"Did you scrubba-scrub?" Tik-Tok asked. "You want to look nice."

Charlie nodded, wiping away a tear. Things were just happening so *fast*.

"Good. Now you remember to do all the things I taught you to do. It may be a long time before you can be with people again, but I think you will, someday. And in the meantime, Anna-Louise and Megan have promised me that they'll be very strict with little girls who won't pick up their rooms and wash their hair."

"I'll be good," Charlie promised.

"I want you to obey them just like you've obeyed me."

"I will."

"Good. You've been a very good little girl, and I'll expect you to continue to be a good girl. Now get in that lifeboat, and get going."

So she did, along with dozens of barking Shelties.

There was a guard outside the conference room and Bach's badge would not get her past him, so she assumed that was where the crime was being planned.

She would have to be very careful.

She entered the control room. It was understaffed, and no one was at her old chair. A few people noticed her as she sat down, but no one seemed to think anything of it. She settled down, keeping an eye on the clock.

Forty minutes after her arrival, all hell broke loose.

It had been an exciting day for the probe. New instructions had come. Any break in the routine was welcome, but this one was doubly good, because the new programmer wanted to know *everything,* and the probe finally got a chance to transmit its poetry. It was a hell of a load off one's mind.

When it finally managed to assure the programmer that it understood and would obey, it settled back in a cybernetic equivalent of wild expectation.

The explosion was everything it could have hoped for. The wheel tore itself apart in a ghastly silence and began spreading itself wildly to the blackness. The probe moved in, listening, listening . . .

And there it was. The soothing song it had been told to listen for, coming from a big oblong hunk of the station that moved faster than the rest of it. The probe moved in close, though it had not been told to. As the oblong flashed by the probe had time to catalog it (LIFEBOAT, type 4A; functioning) and to get just a peek into one of the portholes.

The face of a dog peered back, ears perked alertly.

The probe filed the image away for later contemplation, and then moved in on the rest of the wreckage, lasers blazing in the darkness.

Bach had a bad moment when she saw the probe move in on the lifeboat, then settled back and tried to make herself inconspicuous as the vehicle bearing Charlie and the dogs accelerated away from the cloud of wreckage.

She had been evicted from her chair, but she had expected that. As people ran around, shouting at each other, she called room 569 at the Kleist, then patched Rossnikova into her tracking computers. She was sitting at an operator's console in a corner of the room, far from the excitement.

Rossnikova was a genius. The blip vanished from her screen. If everything was going according to plan, no data about the lifeboat was going into the memory of the tracking computer.

It would be like it never existed.

Everything went so smoothly, Bach thought later. You couldn't help taking it as a good omen, even if, like Bach, you weren't superstitious. She knew nothing was going to be easy in the long run, that there were bound to be problems they hadn't thought of . . .

But all in all, you just had to be optimistic.

The remotely piloted PTP made rendezvous right on schedule. The transfer of Charlie and the dogs went like clockwork. The empty lifeboat was topped off with fuel and sent on a solar escape orbit, airless and lifeless, its only cargo a barrel of radioactive death that should sterilize it if anything would.

The PTP landed smoothly at the remote habitat Galloway's agents had located and purchased. It had once been a biological research station, so it was physically isolated in every way from lunar society. Some money changed hands, and all records of the habitat were erased from computer files.

All food, air, and water had to be brought in by crawler, over a rugged mountain pass. The habitat itself was large enough to accommodate a hundred people in comfort. There was plenty of room for the dogs. A single dish antenna was the only link to the outside world.

Galloway was well satisfied with the place. She promised Charlie that one of these days she would be paying a visit. Neither of them mentioned the reason that no one would be coming out immediately. Charlie settled in for a long stay, privately wondering if she would *ever* get any company.

One thing they hadn't planned on was alcohol. Charlie was hooked bad, and not long after her arrival she began letting people know about it.

Blume reluctantly allowed a case of whiskey to be brought in on the next crawler, reasoning that a girl in full-blown withdrawal would be impossible to handle remotely. He began a program to taper her off, but in the meantime Charlie went on a three-day bender that left her bleary-eyed.

The first biological samples sent in all died within a week. These were a guinea pig, a rhesus monkey, and a chicken. The symptoms were consistent with Neuro-X, so there was little doubt the disease was still alive. A dog, sent in later, lasted eight days.

Blume gathered valuable information from all these deaths, but they upset Charlie badly. Bach managed to talk him out of further live animal experiments for at least a few months.

She had taken accumulated vacation time, and was living in a condominium on a high level of the Mozartplatz, bought by Galloway and donated to what they were coming to think of as the Charlie Project. With Galloway back on Earth and Rossnikova neither needed nor inclined to participate further, Charlie Project was Bach and Dr. Blume. Security was essential. Four people knowing about Charlie was already three too many, Galloway said.

Charlie seemed cheerful, and cooperated with Blume's requests. He worked through robotic instruments, and it was frustrating. But she learned to take her own blood and tissue samples and prepare them for viewing. Blume was beginning to learn something of the nature of Neuro-X, though he admitted that, working alone, it might take him years to reach a breakthrough. Charlie didn't seem to mind.

The isolation techniques were rigorous. The crawler brought supplies to within one hundred yards of the habitat and left them sitting there on the dust. A second crawler would come out to bring them in. Under no circumstances was anything allowed to leave the habitat, nor to come in contact with anything that was going back to the world—and, indeed, the crawler was the only thing in the latter category.

Contact was strictly one-way. Anything could go in, but nothing could come out. That was the strength of the system, and its final weakness.

Charlie had been living in the habitat for fifteen days when she started running a fever. Dr. Blume prescribed bed rest and aspirin, and didn't tell Bach how worried he was.

The next day was worse. She coughed a lot, couldn't keep food down. Blume was determined to go out there in an isolation suit. Bach had to physically restrain him at one point, and be very firm with him until he finally calmed down and saw how foolish he was being. It would do Charlie no good for Blume to die.

Bach called Galloway, who arrived by express liner the next day.

By then Blume had some idea what was happening.

"I gave her a series of vaccinations," he said, mournfully. "It's so standard . . . I hardly gave it a thought. Measles-D1, the Manila-strain mumps, all the normal communicable diseases we have to be so careful of in a Lunar environment. Some of them were killed viruses, some were weakened . . . and they seem to be attacking her."

Galloway raged at him for a while. He was too depressed to fight back. Bach just listened, withholding her own judgment.

The next day he learned more. Charlie was getting things he had not inoculated her against, things that could have come in as hitchhikers on the supplies, or that might have been lying dormant in the habitat itself.

He had carefully checked her thirty-year-old medical record. There had been no hint of any immune system deficiency, and it was not the kind of syndrome that could be missed. But somehow she had acquired it.

He had a theory. He had several of them. None would save his patient.

"Maybe the Neuro-X destroyed her immune system. But you'd think she would have succumbed to stray viruses there on the station. Unless the Neuro-X attacked the viruses, too, and changed them."

He mumbled things like that for hours on end as he watched Charlie waste away on his television screen.

"For whatever reason . . . she was in a state of equilibrium there on the station. Bringing her here destroyed that. If I could understand how, I still might save her . . ."

* * *

The screen showed a sweating, gaunt-faced little girl. Much of her hair had fallen out. She complained that her throat was very dry and she had trouble swallowing. She just keeps fighting, Bach thought, and felt the tightness in the back of her own throat.

Charlie's voice was still clear.

"Tell Megan I finally finished her picture," she said.

"She's right here, honey," Bach said. "You can tell her yourself."

"Oh." Charlie licked her lips with a dry tongue, and her eyes wandered around. "I can't see much. Are you there, Megan?"

"I'm here."

"Thanks for trying." She closed her eyes, and for a moment Bach thought she was gone. Then the eyes opened again.

"Anna-Louise?"

"I'm still right here, darling."

"Anna, what's going to happen to my dogs?"

"I'll take care of them," she lied. "Don't you worry." Somehow she managed to keep her voice steady. It was the hardest thing she had ever done.

"Good. Tik-Tok will tell you which ones to breed. They're good dogs, but you can't let them take advantage of you."

"I won't."

Charlie coughed, and seemed to become a little smaller when she was through. She tried to lift her head, could not, and coughed again. Then she smiled, just a little bit, but enough to break Bach's heart.

"I'll go see Albert," she said. "Don't go away."

"We're right here."

She closed her eyes. She continued breathing raggedly for over an hour, but her eyes never opened again.

Bach let Galloway handle the details of cleaning up and covering up. She felt listless, uninvolved. She kept seeing Charlie as she had first seen her, a painted savage in a brown tide of dogs.

When Galloway went away, Bach stayed on at the Mozartplatz, figuring the woman would tell her if she had to get out. She went back to work, got the promotion Galloway had predicted, and began to take an interest in her new job. She evicted Ralph and his barbells from her old apartment, though she continued to pay the rent on it. She grew to like Mozartplatz even more than she had expected she would, and dreaded the day Galloway would eventually sell the place. There was a broad balcony with potted plants where she could sit with her feet propped up and look out over the whole insane buzz and clatter of the place, or prop her elbows on the rail and spit into the lake, over a mile below. The weather was going to take some getting used to, though, if she ever managed to afford a place of her own here. The management sent rainfall and windstorm schedules in the mail and she faithfully posted them in the kitchen, then always forgot and got drenched.

The weeks turned into months. At the end of the sixth month, when Charlie was no longer haunting Bach's dreams, Galloway showed up. For many reasons Bach was not delighted to see her, but she put on a brave face and invited her in. She was dressed this time, Earth fashion, and she seemed a lot stronger.

"Can't stay long," she said, sitting on the couch Bach had secretly begun to think of as her own. She took a document out of her pocket and put it on a table near Bach's chair. "This is the deed to this condo. I've signed it over to you, but I haven't registered it yet. There are different ways to go about it, for tax purposes, so I thought I'd check with you. I told you I always pay my debts. I was hoping to do it with Charlie, but that turned out . . . well, it was more something I was doing for myself, so it didn't count."

Bach was glad she had said that. She had been wondering if she would be forced to hit her.

"This won't pay what I owe you, but it's a start." She looked at Bach and raised one eyebrow. "It's a start, whether or not you accept it. I'm hoping you won't be too stiff-necked, but with loonies—or should I say Citizens of Luna?—I've found you can never be too sure."

Bach hesitated, but only for a split second.

"Loonies, Lunarians . . . who cares?" She picked up the deed. "I accept."

Galloway nodded, and took an envelope out of the same pocket the deed had been in. She leaned back, and seemed to search for words.

"I . . . thought I ought to tell you what I've done." She waited, and Bach nodded. They both knew, without mentioning Charlie's name, what she was talking about.

"The dogs were painlessly put to sleep. The habitat was depressurized and irradiated for about a month, then reactivated. I had some animals sent in and they survived. So I sent in a robot on a crawler and had it bring these out. Don't worry, they've been checked out a thousand ways and they're absolutely clean."

She removed a few sheets of paper from the envelope and spread them out on the table. Bach leaned over and looked at the pencil sketches.

"You remember she said she'd finally finished that picture for me? I've already taken that one out. But there were these others, one with your name on it, and I wondered if you wanted any of them?"

Bach had already spotted the one she wanted. It was a self-portrait, just the head and shoulders. In it, Charlie had a faint smile . . . or did she? It was that kind of drawing; the more she looked at it, the harder it was to tell just what Charlie had been thinking when she drew it. At the bottom it said "To Anna-Louise, my friend."

Bach took it and thanked Galloway, who seemed almost as anxious to leave as Bach was to have her go.

Bach fixed herself a drink and sat back in "her" chair in "her" home. That was going to take some getting used to, but she looked forward to it.

She picked up the drawing and studied it, sipping her drink. Frowning, she stood and went through the sliding glass doors onto her balcony. There, in the brighter light of the atrium, she held the drawing up and looked closer.

There was somebody behind Charlie. But maybe that wasn't right, either, maybe it was just that she had started to draw one thing, had erased it and started again. Whatever it was, there was another network of lines in the paper that were very close to the picture that was there, but slightly different.

The longer Bach stared at it, the more she was convinced she was seeing the older woman Charlie had never had a chance to become. She seemed to be in her late thirties, not a whole lot older than Bach.

Bach took a mouthful of liquor and was about to go back inside when a wind came up and snatched the paper from her hand.

"Goddamn weather!" she shouted as she made a grab for it. But it was already twenty feet away, turning over and over and falling. She watched it dwindle past all hope of recovery.

Was she relieved?

"Can I get that for you?"

She looked up, startled, and saw a man in a flight harness, flapping like crazy to remain stationary. Those contraptions required an amazing amount of energy, and this fellow showed it, with bulging biceps and huge thigh muscles and a chest big as a barrel. The metal wings glittered and the leather straps creaked and the sweat poured off him.

"No thanks," she said, then she smiled at him. "But I'd be proud to make you a drink."

He smiled back, asked her apartment number, and flapped off toward the nearest landing platform. Bach looked down, but the paper with Charlie's face on it was already gone, vanished in the vast spaces of Mozartplatz.

Bach finished her drink, then went to answer the knock on her door.

*When I was thinking about what society might be like in the Eight Worlds, naturally
I was influenced by the social and political ferment that was all around me at the
time. I grew up in Texas in the 1950s, where there were segregated restrooms and
drinking fountains. In my life I have gone from referring to a certain minority group
as something we now call "The N-word," which I didn't even know was pejorative, to
Negroes, to "spades" when that was fashionable in the Haight-Ashbury, to Afro-
Americans, to black people, to people of color, to the current usage of African-
American. My racism was of the unconscious, liberal variety. Dr. Martin Luther
King, Jr., was praised from the pulpit of my Lutheran church for the work he was doing in the South, but nobody in the pews, or in the pulpit for that matter, would have
wanted him to marry their daughter.*

*When I began writing, we were in the most exciting years of the feminist move-
ment. A few women somewhere burned a few bras as a lark, someone took a picture of
it, and people started calling feminists bra-burners. That, or women's-libbers, lesbians, ball-busters, or harpies. A favorite word to describe them was "strident." I read
a lot of the literature, saw their point, and did my best to shake off my sexism as I had
shed myself of racism.*

*The gay rights movement was just getting started, hadn't really made a lot of
noise yet. No need to go through the terms that were thrown around at them.*

We have come such a long way. Consider, in this day and age when Queer Eye
for the Straight Guy *is a big hit on television, that in my high school days it would
have been about the deadliest insult you could hurl. Fightin' words. Now it is a word
of pride. Sure, there are still toothless rednecks who feel themselves superior to Nelson
Mandela because they are white. There are those who love to beat the crap out of people because of who they choose to go to bed with. There are those like a certain big fat
lying hypocritical junkie crybaby felon who calls progressive women "feminazis."
There is much still to do and I don't know where it will all end up, but compare today*

in America to 1955 in Texas, like I do, and you will know there has been much progress.

Back when I started writing, everyone was exploring sex roles, redefining what it was to be a man or a woman, of whatever orientation. Nature or nurture? Is testosterone or estrogen all-powerful? Is a man gay because his mother made him wear dresses, or was he born that way? I spent a long time thinking about sex, and came to the conclusion that there is *not* one statement *you can make* about all men or about all women that is valid. People are now seeking equal rights for "gays, lesbians, bisexuals, and the transgendered." I'm not even sure if that includes hermaphrodites, or the small minority of people who just plain don't have any interest in sex at all. Neuters.

So what would things be like in . . . two or three hundred years? (I was always deliberately vague about dates in the Eight Worlds stories.) With the Earth subjugated by aliens who, if they weren't actually God, could pinch-hit for him?

If you take a jump that far ahead in the world of science fiction, you can postulate absolutely anything you want. Just look what has happened in fifty years in the field of electronics. Not a single one of the great technological writers came anywhere near imagining the computers we have now, not Asimov, not Clarke, not Heinlein. (They imagined plenty of things we don't have, like 3D television.)

I decided that the advances in biology would be far beyond what we could imagine in 1974. We're well on our way there thirty years later. The human genome has been mapped; nanotechnology is still in its infancy but presents stunning possibilities in medicine. What could all this mean to that great engine that drives all human endeavors, the primal urge of sex?

One of the key postulates of the Eight Worlds was that it would be possible to jump over the divide of gender, to see how the other 50 percent experiences the world. I wasn't talking about sex-reassignment surgery, which merely rearranges some skin and I'm sure is a great comfort to those who feel they were born in the wrong body, but does nothing at the genetic level. And you can't go back next week and tell the doctor it was all a big mistake, I hate being female and I want my penis back. I was considering a quick, painless, and totally reversible procedure so complete that someone who had once been male would now be able to bear a child. How would that affect society?

(How would this be done? I haven't got a clue, any more than Robert Heinlein had a clue about silicon chips, which were on the horizon, or Larry Niven has about hyperspace, which may or may not be in the future. In science fiction you usually just skip over all that hard stuff—how it was developed, how it works—and simply say, "Beam me up, Scotty!")

I wrote several stories exploring these possibilities, including my very first sale,

"Picnic on Nearside." I must say I had considerable trepidation about how these stories might be received. Trepidation? I was scared stiff. Would I be seen as some sort of pervert? Would people call me a queer? (I'll admit, that still would have hurt me back then. Hey, it was the worst thing you could say about a guy.)

To my relief, they were well received. There were even a few people who, reading some of the stories, wondered if I was a woman writing under a pen name, as "James Tiptree Jr." turned out to be. I took this as flattering. I took it as meaning that I got it right, or at least as right as a male could.

Over the years I have posed the question to many people, on panels and in discussions. If you could change sex, easily, painlessly, and most of all, reversibly, would you buy a ticket on that particular weekend cruise? The answers have been almost unanimous: sign me up.

Now, I know science fiction readers are an adventurous crew, I know there are millions and millions of others who would be scandalized by the very idea, would sooner cut off their own legs with a hacksaw . . . but what if it was a technology that had been around for a hundred years? Except for oddball religious cults, like Christinanity or Islam, I don't think there would be many left who wouldn't try it for a day or two, like teenagers sneaking their first beer or cigarette if for no other reason.

Terry Carr had reprinted a few of these stories in his Best of the Year collections, and one day he posed me a question. I like these stories, he said, but they all happen in a time when sex changing is as accepted as boarding a jet plane and flying to Miami. What I'd like to know is, how do we get from here to there? What was it like when this was a new technology? What would it do to society, and particularly, to the family? Write me a story like that, he said.

I did, and this is it. I sent it to him for publication in his anthology of original stories, Universe.

He liked it, and handed it to his wife, Carol, for a second opinion. She read it, Terry told me, smiling from time to time. Then she came to the last line and let out a shriek. "That last line is awful," she said. "It completely undercuts everything he was saying about gender roles."

In my defense, Terry hadn't gotten it, either, but when Carol was through blistering his ears, he sure did. He pointed it out to me, and when I saw what she was talking about I wanted to sink through the floor. I saw what she meant. It was more than awful, it was stupid.

It was the work of five minutes to write a new last line, and Carol smiled again.

Maybe you want to know what that original last line was.

No way in hell.

Options

C LEO HATED BREAKFAST.
        Her energy level was lowest in the morning, but not so the children's. There was always some school crisis, something that had to be located at the last minute, some argument that had to be settled.

This morning it was a bowl of cereal spilled in Lilli's lap. Cleo hadn't seen it happen; her attention had been diverted momentarily by Feather, her youngest.

And of course it had to happen *after* Lilli was dressed.

"Mom, this was the *last* outfit I *had.*"

"Well, if you wouldn't use them so hard they might last more than three days, and if you didn't . . ." She stopped before she lost her temper. "Just take it off and go as you are."

"But Mom, nobody goes to school naked. *Nobody.* Give me some money and I'll stop at the store on—"

Cleo raised her voice, something she tried never to do. "Child, I know there are kids in your class whose parents can't afford to buy clothes at all."

"All right, so the poor kids don't—"

"That's enough. You're late already. Get going."

Lilli stalked from the room. Cleo heard the door slam.

Through it all Jules was an island of calm at the other end of the table, his nose in his newspad, sipping his second cup of coffee. Cleo glanced at her own bacon and eggs cooling on the plate, poured herself a first cup of coffee, then had to get up and help Paul find his other shoe.

By then Feather was wet again, so she put her on the table and peeled off the sopping diaper.

"Hey, listen to this," Jules said. " 'The City Council today passed without objection an ordinance requiring—' "

"Jules, aren't you a little behind schedule?"

He glanced at his thumbnail. "You're right. Thanks." He finished his coffee, folded his newspad and tucked it under his arm, bent over to kiss her, then frowned.

"You really ought to eat more, honey," he said, indicating the untouched eggs. "Eating for two, you know. 'Bye now."

"Good-bye," Cleo said, through clenched teeth. "And if I hear that 'eating for two' business again, I'll . . ." But he was gone.

She had time to scorch her lip on the coffee, then was out the door, hurrying to catch the train.

There were seats on the sun car, but of course Feather was with her and the UV wasn't good for her tender skin. After a longing look at the passengers reclining with the dark cups strapped over their eyes—and a rueful glance down at her own pale skin—Cleo boarded the next car and found a seat by a large man wearing a hardhat. She settled down in the cushions, adjusted the straps on the carrier slung in front of her, and let Feather have a nipple. She unfolded her newspad and spread it out in her lap.

"Cute," the man said. "How old is he?"

"She," Cleo said, without looking up. "Eleven days." And five hours and thirty-six minutes . . .

She shifted in the seat, pointedly turning her shoulder to him, and made a show of activating her newspad and scanning the day's contents. She did not glance up as the train left the underground tunnel and emerged on the gently rolling, airless plain of Mendeleev. There was little enough out there to interest her, considering she made the forty-minute commute to Hartman Crater twice a day. They had discussed moving to Hartman, but Jules liked living in King City near his work, and of course the kids would have missed all their school friends.

There wasn't much in the news storage that morning. When the red light flashed, she queried for an update. The pad printed some routine city business. Three sentences into the story she punched the reject key.

There was an Invasion Centennial parade listed for 1900 hours that evening. Parades bored her, and so did the Centennial. If you've heard one speech about how liberation of Earth is just around the corner if we all pull together, you've heard them all. Semantic content zero, nonsense quotient high.

She glanced wistfully at sports, noting that the J Sector jumpball team was doing poorly without her in the intracity tournament. Cleo's small stature and powerful legs had served her well as a starting sprint-wing in her playing days, but it just didn't seem possible to make practices anymore.

As a last resort, she called up the articles, digests, and analysis listings, the newspad's *Sunday Supplement* and Op-Ed department. A title caught her eye, and she punched it up.

CHANGING: THE REVOLUTION IN SEX ROLES
(Or, Who's on Top?)

Twenty years ago, when cheap and easy sex changes first became available to the general public, it was seen as the beginning of a revolution that would change the shape of human society in ways impossible to foresee. Sexual equality is one thing, the sociologists pointed out, but certain residual inequities—based on biological imperatives or on upbringing, depending on your politics—have proved impossible to weed out. Changing was going to end all that. Men and women would be able to see what it was like from the other side of the barrier that divides humanity. How could sex roles survive that?

Ten years later the answer is obvious. Changing had appealed only to a tiny minority. It was soon seen as a harmless aberration, practiced by only 1 percent of the population. Everyone promptly forgot about the tumbling of barriers.

But in the intervening ten years a quieter revolution has been building. Almost unnoticed on the broad scale because it is an invisible phenomenon (how do you know the next woman you meet was not a man last week?), changing has been gaining growing, matter-of-fact acceptance among the children of the generation that rejected it. The chances are now better than even that you know someone who has had at least one sex change. The chances are better than one out of fifteen that you yourself have changed; if you are under twenty, the chance is one in three.

The article went on to describe the underground society which was springing up around changing. Changers tended to band together, frequenting their own taprooms, staging their own social events, remaining aloof from the larger society which many of them saw as outmoded and irrelevant. Changers tended to marry other changers. They divided the childbearing equally, each preferring to mother only one child. The author viewed this tendency with alarm, since it went against the socially approved custom of large families. Changers reported that the time for that was the past, pointing out that Luna had been tamed long ago. They quoted statistics proving that at present rates of expansion, Luna's population would be in the billions in an amazingly short time.

There were interviews with changers, and psychological profiles. Cleo read that the males had originally been the heaviest users of the new technology, stating sexual reasons for their decision, and the change had often been permanent. Today, the changer was slightly more likely to have been born female, and to give social reasons, the most common of which was pressure to bear children. But the modern changer committed him/herself to neither role. The average time between changes in an individual was two years, and declining.

Cleo read the whole article, then thought about using some of the reading references at the end. Not that much of it was really new to her. She had been aware of changing, without thinking about it much. The idea had never attracted her, and Jules was against it. But for some reason it had struck a chord this morning.

Feather had gone to sleep. Cleo carefully pulled the blanket down around the child's face, then wiped milk from her nipple. She folded her newspad and stowed it in her purse, then rested her chin on her palm and looked out the window for the rest of the trip.

Cleo was chief on-site architect for the new Food Systems, Inc., plantation that was going down in Hartman. As such, she was in charge of three junior architects, five construction bosses, and an army of drafters and workers. It was a big project, the biggest Cleo had ever handled.

She liked her work, but the best part had always been being there on the site when things were happening, actually supervising construction instead of running a desk. That had been difficult in the last months of carrying Feather, but at least there were maternity pressure suits. It was even harder now.

She had been through it all before, with Lilli and Paul. Everybody works. That had been the rule for a century, since the Invasion. There was no labor to spare for babysitters, so having children meant the mother or father must do the same job they had been doing before, but do it while taking care of the child. In practice, it was usually the mother, since she had the milk.

Cleo had tried leaving Feather with one of the women in the office, but each had her own work to do, and not unreasonably felt Cleo should bear the burden of her own offspring. And Feather never seemed to respond well to another person. Cleo would return from her visit to the site to find the child had been crying the whole time, disrupting everyone's work. She had taken Feather in a crawler a few times, but it wasn't the same.

That morning was taken up with a meeting. Cleo and the other section chiefs sat around the big table for three hours, discussing ways of dealing with the cost overrun, then broke for lunch only to return to the problem in the afternoon. Cleo's back was aching and she had a headache she couldn't shake, so Feather chose that day to be cranky. After ten minutes of increasingly hostile looks, Cleo had to retire to the booth with Leah Farnham, the accountant, and her three-year-old son, Eddie. The two of them followed the proceedings through earphones while trying to cope with their children and make their remarks through throat mikes. Half the people at the conference table either had to turn around when she spoke, or ignore her, and Cleo was hesitant to force them to that choice. As a result, she chose her remarks with extreme care. More often, she said nothing.

There was something at the core of the world of business that refused to adjust to children in the board room, while appearing to make every effort to accommodate the working mother. Cleo brooded about it, not for the first time.

But what did she want? Honestly, she could not see what else could be done. It certainly wasn't fair to disrupt the entire meeting with a crying baby. She wished she knew the answer. Those were her friends out there, yet her feeling of alienation was intense, staring through the glass wall that Eddie was smudging with his dirty fingers.

Luckily, Feather was a perfect angel on the trip home. She gurgled and smiled toothlessly at a woman who had stopped to admire her, and Cleo warmed to the infant for the first time that day. She spent the trip playing games with her, surrounded by the approving smiles of other passengers.

"Jules, I read the most interesting article on the pad this morning." There, it was out, anyway. She had decided the direct approach would be best.

"Hmm?"

"It was about changing. It's getting more and more popular."

"Is that so?" He did not look up from his book.

Jules and Cleo were in the habit of sitting up in bed for a few hours after the children were asleep. They spurned the video programs that were designed to lull workers after a hard day, preferring to use the time to catch up on reading, or to talk if either of them had anything to say. Over the last few years, they had read more and talked less.

Cleo reached over Feather's crib and got a packet of dopesticks. She flicked one to light with her thumbnail, drew on it, and exhaled a cloud of lavender smoke. She drew her legs up under her and leaned back against the wall.

"I just thought we might talk about it. That's all."

Jules put his book down. "All right. But what's to talk about? We're not into that."

She shrugged and picked at a cuticle. "I know. We did talk about it, way back. I just wondered if you still felt the same, I guess." She offered him the stick and he took a drag.

"As far as I know, I do." he said easily. "It's not something I spend a great deal of thought on. What's the matter?" He looked at her suspiciously. "You weren't having any thoughts in that direction, were you?"

"Well, no, not exactly. No. But you really ought to read the article. More people are doing it. I just thought we ought to be aware of it."

"Yeah, I've heard that," Jules conceded. He laced his hands behind his head. "No way to tell unless you've worked with them and suddenly one day they've got a new set of equipment." He laughed. "First time it was sort of hard for me to get used to. Now I hardly ever think about it."

"Me, either."

"They don't cause any problem," Jules said with an air of finality. "Live and let live."

"Yeah." Cleo smoked in silence for a time and let Jules get back to his reading, but she still felt uncomfortable. "Jules?"

"What is it now?"

"Don't you ever wonder what it would be like?"

He sighed and closed his book, then turned to face her.

"I don't quite understand you tonight," he said.

"Well, maybe I don't either, but we could talk—"

"Listen. Have you thought about what it would do to the kids? I mean, even if I was willing to seriously consider it, which I'm not."

"I talked to Lilli about that. Just theoretically, you understand. She said she had two teachers who changed, and one of her best friends used to be a boy. There's quite a few kids at school who've changed. She takes it in stride."

"Yes, but she's older. What about Paul? What would it do to his concept of himself as a young man? I'll tell you, Cleo, in the back of my mind I keep thinking this business is a little sick. I feel it would have a bad effect on the children."

"Not according to—"

"Cleo, Cleo. Let's not get into an argument. Number one, I have no intention of getting a change, now or in the future. Two, if only one of us was changed, it would sure play hell with our sex life, wouldn't it? And three, I like you too much as you are." He leaned over and began to kiss her.

She was more than a little annoyed, but said nothing as his kisses became more intense. It was a damnably effective way of shutting off debate. And she could not stay angry: she was responding in spite of herself, easily, naturally.

It was as good as it always was with Jules. The ceiling, so familiar, once again became a calming blankness that absorbed her thoughts.

No, she had no complaints about being female, no sexual dissatisfactions. It was nothing as simple as that.

Afterward she lay on her side with her legs drawn up, her knees together. She faced Jules, who absently stroked her leg with one hand. Her eyes were closed, but she was not sleepy. She was savoring the warmth she cherished so much after sex; the slipperiness between her legs, holding his semen inside.

She felt the bed move as he shifted his weight.

"You did make it, didn't you?"

She opened one eye enough to squint at him.

"Of course I did. I always do. You know I never have any trouble in that direction."

He relaxed back onto the pillow. "I'm sorry for . . . well, for springing on you like that."

"It's okay. It was nice."

"I had just thought you might have been . . . faking it. I'm not sure why I would think that."

She opened the other eye and patted him gently on the cheek.

"Jules, I'd never be that protective of your poor ego. If you don't satisfy me, I promise you'll be the second to know."

He chuckled, then turned on his side to kiss her.

"Good night, babe."

"G'night."

She loved him. He loved her. Their sex life was good—with the slight mental reservation that he always seemed to initiate it—and she was happy with her body.

So why was she still awake three hours later?

Shopping took a few hours on the vidphone Saturday morning. Cleo bought the household necessities for delivery that afternoon, then left the house to do the shopping she fancied: going from store to store, looking at things she didn't really need.

Feather was with Jules on Saturdays. She savored a quiet lunch alone at a table in the park plaza, then found herself walking down Brazil Avenue in the heart of the medical district. On impulse, she stepped into the New Heredity Body Salon.

It was only after she was inside that she admitted to herself she had spent most of the morning arranging for the impulse.

She was on edge as she was taken down a hallway to a consulting room, and had to force a smile for the handsome young man behind the desk. She sat, put her packages on the floor, and folded her hands in her lap. He asked what he could do for her.

"I'm not actually here for any work," she said. "I wanted to look into the costs, and maybe learn a little more about the procedures involved in changing."

He nodded understandingly, and got up.

"There's no charge for the initial consultation," he said. "We're happy to answer your questions. By the way, I'm Marion, spelled with an 'o' this month." He smiled at her and motioned for her to follow him. He stood her in front of a full-length mirror mounted on the wall.

"I know it's hard to make that first step. It was hard for me, and I do it for a living. So we've arranged this demonstration that won't cost you anything, either in money or worry. It's a nonthreatening way to see some of what it's all about, but it might startle you a little, so be prepared." He touched a button in the wall beside the mirror, and Cleo saw her clothes fade away. She realized it was not really a mirror, but a holographic screen linked to a computer.

The computer introduced changes in the image. In thirty seconds she faced a male stranger. There was no doubt the face was her own, but it was more angular, perhaps a little larger in its underlying bony structure. The skin on the stranger's jaw was rough, as if it needed shaving.

The rest of the body was as she might expect, though overly muscled for her tastes. She did little more than glance at the penis; somehow that didn't seem to matter so much. She spent more time studying the hair on the chest, the tiny nipples, and the ridges that had appeared on the hands and feet. The image mimicked her every movement.

"Why all the brawn?" she asked Marion. "If you're trying to sell me on this, you've taken the wrong approach."

Marion punched some more buttons. "I didn't choose this image," he explained. "The computer takes what it sees, and extrapolates. You're more muscular than the average woman. You probably exercise. This is what a comparable amount of training would have produced with male hormones to fix nitrogen in the muscles. But we're not bound by that."

The image lost about eight kilos of mass, mostly in the shoulders and thighs. Cleo felt a little more comfortable, but still missed the smoothness she was accustomed to seeing in her mirror.

She turned from the display and went back to her chair. Marion sat across from her and folded his hands on the desk.

"Basically, what we do is produce a cloned body from one of your own cells. Through a process called Y-Recombinant Viral Substitution we remove one of your X chromosomes and replace it with a Y.

"The clone is forced to maturity in the usual way, which takes about six months. After that, it's just a simple non-rejection-hazard brain transplant. You walk in as a woman, and leave an hour later as a man. Easy as that."

Cleo said nothing, wondering again what she was doing here.

"From there we can modify the body. We can make you taller or shorter, rearrange your face, virtually anything you like." He raised his eyebrows, then smiled ruefully and spread his hands.

"All right, Ms. King," he said. "I'm not trying to pressure you. You'll need to think about it. In the meantime, there's a process that would cost you very little, and might be just the thing to let you test the waters. Am I right in thinking your husband opposes this?"

She nodded, and he looked sympathetic.

"Not uncommon, not uncommon at all," he assured her. "It brings out castration fears in men who didn't even suspect they had them. Of course, we do nothing of the sort. His male body would be kept in a tank, ready for him to move back into whenever he wanted to."

Cleo shifted in her chair. "What was this process you were talking about?"

"Just a bit of minor surgery. It can be done in ten minutes, and corrected in the same time before you even leave the office if you find you don't care for it. It's a good way to get husbands thinking about changing; sort of a signal you can send him. You've heard of the androgynous look. It's in all the fashion tapes. Many women, especially if they have large breasts like you do, find it an interesting change."

"You say it's cheap? And reversible?"

"All our processes are reversible. Changing the size or shape of breasts is our most common body operation."

Cleo sat on the examining table while the attendant gave her a quick physical.

"I don't know if Marion realized you're nursing," the woman said. "Are you sure this is what you want?"

How the hell should I know? Cleo thought. She wished the feeling of confusion and uncertainty would pass.

"Just do it."

Jules hated it.

He didn't yell or slam doors or storm out of the house; that had never been his style. He voiced his objections coldly and quietly at the dinner table, after saying practically nothing since she walked in the door.

"I just would like to know why you thought you should do this without even talking to me about it. I don't demand that you *ask* me, just discuss it with me."

Cleo felt miserable, but was determined not to let it show. She held Feather in her arm, the bottle in her other hand, and ignored the food cooling on her plate. She was hungry but at least she was not eating for two.

"Jules, I'd ask you before I rearrange the furniture. We both own this apartment. I'd ask you before I put Lilli or Paul in another school. We share the responsibility for their upbringing. But I don't ask you when I put on lipstick or cut my hair. It's my body."

"I like it, Mom," Lilli said. "You look like me."

Cleo smiled at her, reached over and tousled her hair.

"What do you like?" Paul asked, around a mouthful of food.

"See?" said Cleo. "It's not that important."

"I don't see how you can say that. And I said you didn't have to ask me. I just would . . . You should have . . . I should have *known*."

"It was an impulse, Jules."

"An impulse. An *impulse*." For the first time, he raised his voice, and Cleo knew how upset he really was. Lilli and Paul fell silent, and even Feather squirmed.

But Cleo liked it. Oh, not forever and ever: as an interesting change. It gave her a feeling of freedom to be that much in control of her body, to be able to decide how large she wished her breasts to be. Did it have anything to do with changing? She really didn't think so. She didn't feel the least bit like a man.

And what was a breast, anyway? It was anything from a nipple sitting flush with the rib cage to a mammoth hunk of fat and milk gland. Cleo realized Jules was suffering from the more-is-better syndrome, thinking of Cleo's action as the removal of her breasts, as if they had to be large to exist at all. What she had actually done was reduce their size.

No more was said at the table, but Cleo knew it was for the children's sake. As soon as they got into bed, she could feel the tension again.

"I can't understand why you did it *now*. What about Feather?"

"What about her?"

"Well, do you expect me to nurse her?"

Cleo finally got angry. "Damn it, that's *exactly* what I expect you to do. Don't tell me you don't know what I'm talking about. You think it's all fun and games, having to carry a child around all day because she needs the milk in your breasts?"

"You never complained before."

"I . . ." She stopped. He was right, of course. It amazed even Cleo that this had all come up so suddenly, but here it was, and she had to deal with it. *They* had to deal with it.

"That's because it isn't an awful thing. It's great to nourish another human being at your breast. I loved every minute of it with Lilli. Sometimes it was a headache, having her there all the time, but it was worth it. The same with Paul." She sighed. "The same with Feather, too, most of the time. You hardly think about it."

"Then why the revolt now? With no warning?"

"It's not a revolt, honey. Do you see it as that? I just . . . I'd like you to try it. Take Feather for a few months. Take her to work like I do. Then you'd . . . you'd see a little of what I go through." She rolled on her side and playfully punched his arm, trying to lighten it in some way. "You might even like it. It feels real good."

He snorted. "I'd feel silly."

She jumped from the bed and paced toward the living room, then turned, more angry than ever. "Silly? Nursing is silly? Breasts are silly? Then why the hell do you wonder why I did what I did?"

"Being a *man* is what makes it silly," he retorted. "It doesn't look right. I almost laugh every time I see a man with breasts. The hormones *mess* up your system, I heard, and—"

"That's *not true!* Not anymore. You can lactate—"

"—and besides, it's my body, as you pointed out. I'll do with it what pleases me."

She sat on the edge of the bed with her back to him. He reached out and stroked her, but she moved away.

"All right," she said. "I was just suggesting it. I thought you might like to try it. *I'm* not going to nurse her. She goes on the bottle from now on."

"If that's the way it has to be."

"It is. I want you to start taking Feather to work with you. Since she's going to be a bottle baby, it hardly matters which of us cares for her. I think you owe it to me, since I carried the burden alone with Lilli and Paul."

"All right."

She got into bed and pulled the covers up around her, her back to him. She didn't want him to see how close she was to tears.

But the feeling passed. The tension drained from her, and she felt good. She thought she had won a victory, and it was worth the cost. Jules would not stay angry at her.

She fell asleep easily, but woke up several times during the night as Jules tossed and turned.

He did adjust to it. It was impossible for him to say so all at once, but after a week without lovemaking he admitted grudgingly that she looked good. He began to touch her in the mornings and when they kissed after getting home from work. Jules had always admired her slim muscularity, her athlete's arms and legs. The slim chest looked so natural on her, it fit the rest of her so well that he began to wonder what all the fuss had been about.

One night while they were clearing the dinner dishes, Jules touched her nipples for the first time in a week. He asked her if it felt any different.

"There is very little feeling anywhere but the nipples," she pointed out, "no matter how big a woman is. You know that."

"Yeah, I guess I do."

She knew they would make love that night and determined it would be on her terms.

She spent a long time in the bathroom, letting him get settled with his book, then came out and took it away. She got on top of him and pressed close, kissing and tickling his nipples with her fingers.

She was aggressive and insistent. At first he seemed reluctant, but soon he was responding as she pressed her lips hard against his, forcing his head back into the pillow.

"I love you," he said, and raised his head to kiss her nose. "Are you ready?"

"I'm ready." He put his arms around her and held her close, then rolled over and hovered above her.

"Jules. *Jules.* Stop it." She squirmed onto her side, her legs held firmly together.

"What's wrong?"

"I want to be on top tonight."

"Oh. All right." He turned over again and reclined passively as she repositioned herself. Her heart was pounding. There had been no reason to think he would object—they had made love in any and all positions, but basically the exotic ones were a change of pace from the "natural" one with her on her back. Tonight she had wanted to feel in control.

"Open your legs, darling," she said, with a smile. He did, but didn't return the smile. She raised herself on her hands and knees and prepared for the tricky insertion.

"Cleo."

"What is it? This will take a little effort, but I think I can make it worth your while, so if you'd just—"

"Cleo, what the hell is the purpose of this?"

She stopped dead and let her head sag between her shoulders.

"What's the matter? Are you feeling silly with your feet in the air?"

"Maybe. Is that what you wanted?"

"Jules, humiliating you was the farthest thing from my mind."

"Then what *was* on your mind? It's not like we've never done it this way before. It's—"

"Only when *you* chose to do so. It's always your decision."

"It's not degrading to be on the bottom."

"Then why were you feeling silly?"

He didn't answer, and she wearily lifted herself away from him, sitting on her knees at his feet. She waited, but he didn't seem to want to talk about it.

"I've never complained about the position," she ventured. "I don't *have* any complaints about it. It works pretty well." Still he said nothing. "All right. I wanted to see what it looked like from up there. I was tired of looking at the ceiling. I was curious."

"And *that's* why I felt *silly.* I never minded you being on top before, have I? But before . . . well, it's never been in the context of the last couple of weeks. I *know* what's on your mind."

"And you feel threatened by it. By the fact that I'm curious about changing, that I want to know what it's like to take charge. You know I can't—and wouldn't if I could—force a change on you."

"But your curiosity is wrecking our marriage."

She felt like crying again, but didn't let it show except for a trembling of the lower lip. She didn't want him to try and soothe her; that was all too likely to work, and she would find herself on her back with her legs in the air. She looked down at the bed and nodded slowly, then got up. She went to the mirror and took the brush, began running it through her hair.

"What are you doing now? Can't we talk about this?"

"I don't feel much like talking right now." She leaned forward and examined her face as she brushed, then dabbed at the corners of her eyes with a tissue. "I'm going out. I'm still curious."

He said nothing as she started for the door.

"I may be a little late."

The place was called Oophyte. The capital "O" had a plus sign hanging from it, and an arrow in the upper right side. The sign was built so that the symbols revolved; one moment the plus was inside and the arrow out, the next moment the reverse.

Cleo moved in a pleasant haze across the crowded dance floor, pausing now and then to draw on her dopestick. The air in the room was thick with lavender smoke, illuminated by flashing blue lights. She danced when the mood took her. The music was so loud that she didn't have to think about it; the noise gripped her bones, animated her arms and legs. She glided through a forest of naked skin, feeling the occasional roughness of a paper suit and, rarely, expensive cotton clothing. It was like moving underwater, like wading through molasses.

She saw him across the floor, and began moving in his direction. He took no notice of her for some time, though she danced right in front of him. Few of the dancers had partners in more than the transitory sense. Some were celebrating life, others were displaying themselves, but all were looking for partners, so eventually he realized she had been there an unusual length of time. He was easily as stoned as she was.

She told him what she wanted.

"Sure. Where do you want to go? Your place?"

She took him down the hall in back and touched her credit bracelet to the lock on one of the doors. The room was simple, but clean.

He looked a lot like her phantom twin in the mirror, she noted with one part of her mind. It was probably why she had chosen him. She embraced him and low-ered him gently to the bed.

"Do you want to exchange names?" he asked. The grin on his face kept getting sillier as she toyed with him.

"I don't care. Mostly I think I want to use you."

"Use away. My name's Saffron."

"I'm Cleopatra. Would you get on your back, please?"

He did, and they did. It was hot in the little room, but neither of them minded it. It was healthy exertion, the physical sensations were great, and when Cleo was through she had learned nothing. She collapsed on top of him. He did not seem surprised when tears began falling on his shoulder.

"I'm sorry," she said, sitting up and getting ready to leave.

"Don't go," he said, putting his hand on her shoulder. "Now that you've got that out of your system, maybe we can make love."

She didn't want to smile, but she had to, then she was crying harder, putting her face to his chest and feeling the warmth of his arms around her and the hair tickling her nose. She realized what she was doing, and tried to pull away.

"For God's sake, don't be ashamed that you need someone to cry on."

"It's weak. I . . . I just didn't want to be weak."

"We're all weak."

She gave up struggling and nestled there until the tears stopped. She sniffed, wiped her nose, and faced him.

"What's it like? Can you tell me?" She was about to explain what she meant, but he seemed to understand.

"It's like . . . nothing special."

"You were born female, weren't you? I mean, I thought I might be able to tell."

"It's no longer important how I was born. I've been both. It's still me, on the inside. You understand?"

"I'm not sure I do."

They were quiet for a long time. Cleo thought of a thousand things to say, questions to ask, but could do nothing.

"You've been coming to a decision, haven't you?" he said, at last. "Are you any closer after tonight?"

"I'm not sure."

"It's not going to solve any problems, you know. It might even create some."

She pulled away from him and got up. She shook her hair and wished for a comb.

"Thank you, Cleopatra," he said.

"Oh. Uh, thank you . . ." She had forgotten his name. She smiled again to cover her embarrassment, and shut the door behind her.

* * *

"Hello?"

"Yes. This is Cleopatra King. I had a consultation with one of your staff. I believe it was ten days ago."

"Yes, Ms. King. I have your file. What can I do for you?"

She took a deep breath. "I want you to start the clone. I left a tissue sample."

"Very well, Ms. King. Did you have any instructions concerning the chromosome donor?"

"Do you need consent?"

"Not as long as there's a sample in the bank."

"Use my husband, Jules La Rhin. Security number 4454390."

"Very good. We'll be in contact with you."

Cleo hung up the phone and rested her forehead against the cool metal. She should never get this stoned, she realized. What had she done?

But it was not final. It would be six months before she had to decide if she would ever use the clone. Damn Jules. Why did he have to make such a big thing of it?

Jules did *not* make a big thing of it when she told him what she had done. He took it quietly and calmly, as if he had been expecting it.

"You know I won't follow you in this?"

"I know you feel that way. I'm interested to see if you change your mind."

"Don't count on it. I want to see if you change yours."

"I haven't *made up* my mind. But I'm giving myself the option."

"All I ask is that you bear in mind what this could do to our relationship. I love you, Cleo. I don't think that will ever change. But if you walk into this house as a man, I don't think I'll be able to see you as the person I've always loved."

"You could if you were a woman."

"But I won't be."

"And I'll be the same person I always was." But would she be? What the hell was *wrong?* What had Jules ever done that he should deserve this? She made up her mind never to go through with it, and they made love that night and it was very, very good.

But somehow she never got around to calling the vivarium and telling them to abort the clone. She made the decision not to go through with it a dozen times over the next six months, and never had the clone destroyed.

Their relationship in bed became uneasy as time passed. At first, it was good. Jules made no objections when she initiated sex, and was willing to do it any way she preferred. Once that was accomplished she no longer cared whether she was on top or underneath. The important thing had been having the option of making love when she wanted to, the way she wanted to.

"That's what this is all about," she told him one night, in a moment of clarity when everything seemed to make sense except his refusal to see things from her side. "It's the option I want. I'm not unhappy being a female. I don't like the feeling that there's *anything* I *can't* be. I want to know how much of me is hormones, how much is genetics, how much is upbringing. I want to know if I feel more secure being aggressive as a man, because I don't most of the time, as a woman. Or do men feel the same insecurities I feel? Would Cleo the man feel free to cry? I don't know any of those things."

"But you said it yourself. You'll still be the same person."

They began to drift apart in small ways. A few weeks after her outing to Oophyte she returned home one Sunday afternoon to find him in bed with a woman. It was not like him to do it like that; their custom had been to bring lovers home and introduce them, to keep it friendly and open. Cleo was amused, because she saw it as his way of getting back at her for her trip to the encounter bar.

So she was the perfect hostess, joining them in bed, which seemed to disconcert Jules. The woman's name was Harriet, and Cleo found herself liking her. She was a changer—something Jules had not known or he certainly would not have chosen her to make Cleo feel bad. Harriet was uncomfortable when she realized why she was there. Cleo managed to put her at ease by making love to her, something that surprised Cleo a little and Jules considerably, since she had never done it before.

Cleo enjoyed it; she found Harriet's smooth body to be a whole new world. And she felt she had neatly turned the tables on Jules, making him confront once more the idea of his wife in the man's role.

The worst part was the children. They had discussed the possible impending change with Lilli and Paul.

Lilli could not see what all the fuss was about; it was a part of her life, something that was all around her which she took for granted as something she herself would do when she was old enough. But when she began picking up the concern from her father, she drew subtly closer to her mother. Cleo was tremendously relieved. She didn't think she could have held to it in the face of Lilli's displeasure. Lilli was her first born, and though she hated to admit it and did her best not to play favorites, her darling. She had taken a year's leave from her job at appalling expense to the household budget so she could devote all her time to her infant daughter. She often wished she could somehow return to those simpler days, when motherhood had been her whole life.

Feather, of course, was not consulted. Jules had assumed the responsibility for her nurture without complaint, and seemed to be enjoying it. It was fine with Cleo, though it maddened her that he was so willing about taking over the mothering role without being willing to try it as a female. Cleo loved Feather as much as the other two, but sometimes had trouble recalling why they had decided to have her. She felt she had gotten the procreative impulse out of her system with Paul, and yet there Feather was.

Paul was the problem.

Things could get tense when Paul expressed doubts about how he would feel if his mother were to become a man. Jules's face would darken and he might not speak for days. When he did speak, often in the middle of the night when neither of them could sleep, it would be in a verbal explosion that was as close to violence as she had ever seen him.

It frightened her, because she was by no means sure of herself when it came to Paul. Would it hurt him? Jules spoke of gender identity crises, of the need for stable role models, and finally, in naked honesty, of the fear that his son would grow up to be somehow less than a man.

Cleo didn't know, but cried herself to sleep over it many nights. They had read articles about it and found that psychologists were divided. Traditionalists made much of the importance of sex roles, while changers felt sex roles were important only to those who were trapped in them; with the breaking of the sexual barrier, the concept of roles vanished.

The day finally came when the clone was ready. Cleo still did not know what she should do.

"Are you feeling comfortable now? Just nod if you can't talk."

"Wha . . ."

"Relax. It's all over. You'll be feeling like walking in a few minutes. We'll have someone take you home. You may feel drunk for a while, but there's no drugs in your system."

"Wha . . . happen?"

"It's over. Just relax."

Cleo did, curling up in a ball. Eventually he began to laugh.

Drunk was not the word for it. He sprawled on the bed, trying on pronouns for size. It was all so funny. *He* was on *his* back with *his* hands in *his* lap. He giggled and rolled back and forth, over and over, fell on the floor in hysterics.

He raised his head.

"Is that you, Jules?"

"Yes, it's me." He helped Cleo back onto the bed, then sat on the edge, not too near, but not unreachably far away. "How do you feel?"

He snorted. "Drunker 'n a skunk." He narrowed his eyes, forced them to focus on Jules. "You must call me Leo now. Cleo is a woman's name. You shouldn't have called me Cleo then."

"All right, I didn't call you Cleo, though."

"You didn't? Are you *sure?*"

"I'm very sure it's something I wouldn't have said."

"Oh. Okay." He lifted his head and looked confused for a moment. "You know what? I'm gonna be sick."

Leo felt much better an hour later. He sat in the living room with Jules, both of them on the big pillows that were the only furniture.

They spoke of inconsequential matters for a time, punctuated by long silences. Leo was no more used to the sound of his new voice than Jules was.

"Well," Jules said, finally, slapping his hands on his knees and standing up. "I really don't know what your plans are from here. Did you want to go out tonight? Find a woman, see what it's like?"

Leo shook his head. "I tried that out as soon as I got home," he said. "The male orgasm, I mean."

"What was it like?"

He laughed. "Certainly you know that by now."

"No, I meant, after being a woman—"

"I know what you mean." He shrugged. "The erection is interesting. So much larger than what I'm used to. Otherwise . . ." He frowned for a moment. "A lot the same. Some different. More localized. Messier."

"Um." Jules looked away, studying the electric fireplace as if seeing it for the first time. "Had you planned to move out? It isn't necessary, you know. We could move people around. I can go in with Paul, or we could move him in with me in . . . in our old room. You could have his." He turned away from Leo, and put his hand to his face.

Leo ached to get up and comfort him, but felt it would be exactly the wrong thing to do. He let Jules get himself under control.

"If you'll have me, I'd like to continue sleeping with you."

Jules said nothing, and didn't turn around.

"Jules, I'm perfectly willing to do whatever will make you most comfortable. There doesn't have to be any sex. Or I'd be happy to do what I used to do when I was in late pregnancy. You wouldn't have to do anything at all."

"No sex," he said.

"Fine, fine. Jules, I'm getting awfully tired. Are you ready to sleep?"

There was a long pause, then he turned and nodded.

They lay quietly, side by side, not touching. The lights were out; Leo could barely see the outline of Jules' body.

After a long time. Jules turned on his side.

"Cleo, are you in there? Do you still love me?"

"I'm here," she said. "I love you. I always will."

Jules jumped when Leo touched him, but made no objection. He began to cry, and Leo held him close. They fell asleep in each other's arms.

The Oophyte was as full and noisy as ever. It gave Leo a headache.

He did not like the place any more than Cleo had, but it was the only place he knew to find sex partners quickly and easily, with no emotional entanglements and no long process of seduction. Everyone there was available; all one needed to do was ask. They used each other for sexual calisthenics just one step removed from masturbation, cheerfully admitted the fact, and took the position that if you didn't approve, what were you doing there? There were plenty of other places for romance and relationships.

Leo didn't normally approve of it—not for himself, though he cared not at all what other people did for amusement. He preferred to know someone he bedded.

But he was here tonight to learn. He felt he needed the practice. He did not buy the argument that he would know just what to do because he had been a woman and knew what they liked. He needed to know how people reacted to him as a male.

Things went well. He approached three women and was accepted each time. The first was a mess—so *that's* what they meant by too soon!—and she was rather indignant about it until he explained his situation. After that she was helpful and supportive.

He was about to leave when he was propositioned by a woman who said her name was Lynx. He was tired, but decided to go with her.

Ten frustrating minutes later she sat up and moved away from him. "What are you here for, if that's all the interest you can muster? And don't tell me it's my fault."

"I'm sorry," he said. "I forgot. I thought I could . . . Well, I didn't realize I had to be really interested before I could perform."

"Perform? That's a funny way to put it."

"I'm sorry." He told her what the problem was, how many times he had made love in the last two hours. She sat on the edge of the bed and ran her hands through her hair, frustrated and irritable.

"Well, it's not the end of the world. There's plenty more out there. But you could give a girl a warning. You didn't have to say yes back there."

"I know. It's my fault. I'll have to learn to judge my capacity, I guess. It's just that I'm used to being *able* to, even if I'm not particularly—"

Lynx laughed. "What am I saying? Listen to me. Honey, I used to have the same problem myself. *Weeks* of not getting it up. And I know it hurts."

"Well," Leo said. "I know what you're feeling like, too. It's no fun."

Lynx shrugged. "In other circumstances, yeah. But like I said, the woods are full of 'em tonight. I won't have any problem." She put her hand on his cheek and pouted at him. "Hey, I didn't hurt your poor male ego, did I?"

Leo thought about it, probed around for bruises, and found none.

"No."

She laughed. "I didn't think so. Because you don't have one. Enjoy it, Leo. A male ego is something that has to be grown carefully, when you're young. People have to keep pointing out what you have to do to be a man, so you can recognize failure when you can't 'perform.' How come you used that word?"

"I don't know. I guess I was just thinking of it that way."

"Trying to be a quote *man* unquote. Leo, you don't have enough emotional investment in it. And you're *lucky*. It took me over a year to shake mine. Don't be a man. Be a male human, instead. The switchover's a lot easier that way."

"I'm not sure what you mean."

She patted his knee. "Trust me. Do you see me getting all upset because I wasn't sexy enough to turn you on, or some such garbage? No. I wasn't brought up to worry that way. But reverse it. If I'd done to you what you just did to me, wouldn't something like that have occurred to you?"

"I think it would. Though I've always been pretty secure in that area."

"The most secure of us are whimpering children beneath it, at least some of the time. You understand that I got upset because you said yes when you weren't ready? And that's *all* I was upset about? It was impolite, Leo. A male human shouldn't do that to a female human. With a man and a woman, it's different. The poor fellow's got a lot of junk in his head, and so does the woman, so they shouldn't be held responsible for the tricks their egos play on them."

Leo laughed. "I don't know if you're making sense at all. But I like the sound of it. 'Male human.' Maybe I'll see the difference one day."

Some of the expected problems never developed.

Paul barely noticed the change. Leo had prepared himself for a traumatic struggle with his son, and it never came. If it changed Paul's life at all, it was in the fact that he could now refer to his maternal parent as Leo instead of Mother.

Strangely enough, it was Lilli who had the most trouble at first. Leo was hurt by it, tried not to show it, and did everything he could to let her adjust gradually. Finally she came to him one day about a week after the change. She said she had been silly, and wanted to know if she could get a change, too, since one of her best friends was getting one. Leo talked her into remaining female until after the onset of puberty. He told her he thought she might enjoy it.

Leo and Jules circled each other like two tigers in a cage, unsure if a fight was necessary but ready to start clawing out eyes if it came to it. Leo didn't like the analogy; if he had still been a female tiger, he would have felt sure of the outcome. But he had no wish to engage in a dominance struggle with Jules.

They shared an apartment, a family, and a bed. They were elaborately polite, but touched each other only rarely, and Leo always felt he should apologize when they did. Jules would not meet his eyes; their gazes would touch, then rebound like two cork balls with identical static charges.

But eventually Jules accepted Leo. He was "that guy who's always around" in Jules' mind. Leo didn't care for that, but saw it as progress. In a few more days Jules began to discover that he liked Leo. They began to share things, to talk more. The subject of their previous relationship was taboo for a while. It was as if Jules wanted to know Leo from scratch, not acknowledging there had ever been a Cleo who had once been his wife.

It was not that simple; Leo would not let it be. Jules sometimes sounded like he was mourning the passing of a loved one when he hesitantly began talking about the hurt inside him. He was able to talk freely to Leo, and it was in a slightly different manner from the way he had talked to Cleo. He poured out his soul. It was astonishing to Leo that there were so many bruises on it, so many defenses and insecurities. There was buried hostility which Jules had never felt free to tell a woman.

Leo let him go on, but when Jules started a sentence with, "I could never tell this to Cleo," or, "Now that she's gone," Leo would go to him, take his hand, and force him to look.

"I'm Cleo," he would say. "I'm right here, and I love you."

They started doing things together. Jules took him to places Cleo had never been. They went out drinking together and had a wonderful time getting sloshed. Before, it had always been dinner with a few drinks or dopesticks, then a show or concert. Now they might come home at 0200 harmonizing loud enough to get thrown in jail. Jules admitted he hadn't had so much fun since his college days.

Socializing was a problem. Few of their old friends were changers, and neither of them wanted to face the complications of going to a party as a couple. They couldn't make friends among changers, because Jules correctly saw he would be seen as an outsider.

So they saw a lot of men. Leo had thought he knew all of Jules' close friends, but found he had been wrong. He saw a side of Jules he had never seen before: more relaxed in ways, some of his guardedness gone, but with other defenses in place. Leo sometimes felt like a spy, looking in on a stratum of society he had always known was there, but he had never been able to penetrate. If Cleo had walked into the group its structure would have changed subtly; she would have created a new milieu by her presence, like light destroying the atom it was meant to observe.

After his initial outing to the Oophyte, Leo remained celibate for a long time. He did not want to have sex casually; he wanted to love Jules. As far as he knew, Jules was abstaining, too.

But they found an acceptable alternative in double-dating. They shopped around together for a while, taking out different women and having a lot of fun without getting into sex, until each settled on a woman he could have a relationship with. Jules was with Diane, a woman he had known at work for many years. Leo went out with Harriet.

The four of them had great times together. Leo loved being a pal to Jules, but would not let it remain simply that. He took to reminding Jules that he could do this with Cleo, too. What Leo wanted to emphasize was that he could be a companion, a buddy, a confidant no matter which sex he was. He wanted to combine the best of being a woman and being a man, be both things for Jules, fulfill all his needs. But it hurt to think that Jules would not do the same for him.

"Well, hello, Leo. I didn't expect to see you today."

"Can I come in, Harriet?"

She held the door open for him.

"Can I get you anything? Oh, yeah, before you go any further, that 'Harriet' business is finished. I changed my name today. It's Joule from now on. That's spelled j-o-u-l-e."

"Okay, Joule. Nothing for me, thanks." He sat on her couch.

Leo was not surprised at the new name. Changers had a tendency to get away from "name" names. Some did as Cleo had done by choosing a gender equivalent or a similar sound. Others ignored gender connotations and used the one they had always used. But most eventually chose a neutral word, according to personal preference.

"Jules, Julia," he muttered.

"What was that?" Joule's brow wrinkled slightly. "Did you come here for mothering? Things going badly?"

Leo slumped down and contemplated his folded hands.

"I don't know. I guess I'm depressed. How long has it been now? Five months? I've learned a lot, but I'm not sure just what it is. I feel like I've grown. I see the world . . . well, I see things differently, yes. But I'm still basically the same person."

"In the sense that you're the same person at thirty-three as you were at ten?"

Leo squirmed. "Okay. Yeah, I've changed. But it's not any kind of reversal. Nothing turned topsy-turvy. It's an expansion. It's not a new viewpoint. It's like filling something up, moving out into unused spaces. Becoming . . ." His hands groped in the air, then fell back into his lap. "It's like a completion."

Joule smiled. "And you're disappointed? What more could you ask?"

Leo didn't want to get into that just yet. "Listen to this, and see if you agree. I always saw male and female—whatever that is, and I don't know if the two *really* exist other than physically and don't think it's important anyway . . . I saw those qualities as separate. Later, I thought of them like Siamese twins in everybody's head. But the twins were usually fighting, trying to cut each other off. One would beat the other down, maim it, throw it in a cell, and never feed it, but they were always connected and the beaten-down one would make the winner pay for the victory.

"So I wanted to try and patch things up between them. I thought I'd just introduce them to each other and try to referee, but they got along a lot better than I expected. In fact, they turned into one whole person, and found they could be very happy together. I can't tell them apart anymore. Does that make any sense?"

Joule moved over to sit beside him.

"It's a good analogy, in its way. I feel something like that, but I don't think about it anymore. So what's the problem? You just told me you feel whole now."

Leo's face controlled. "Yes. I do. And if I am, what does that make Jules?" He began to cry, and Joule let him get it out, just holding his hand. She thought he'd better face it alone, this time. When he had calmed down, she began to speak quietly.

"Leo, Jules is happy as he is. I think he could be much happier, but there's no way for us to show him that without having him do something he fears so much. It's possible that he will do it someday, after more time to get used to it. And it's possible that he'll hate it and run screaming back to his manhood. Sometimes the maimed twin can't be rehabilitated."

She sighed heavily, and got up to pace the room.

"There's going to be a lot of this in the coming years," she said. "A lot of broken hearts. We're not really very much like them, you know. We get along better. We're not angels, but we may be the most civilized, considerate group the race has yet produced. There are fools and bastards among us, just like the one-sexers, but I think we tend to be a little less foolish, and a little less cruel. I think changing is here to stay.

"And what you've got to realize is that you're lucky. And so is Jules. It could have been much worse. I know of several broken homes just among my own friends. There's going to be many more before society has assimilated this. But your love for Jules and his for you has held you together. He's made a tremendous adjustment, maybe as big as the one you made. He *likes* you. In either sex. Okay, so you don't make love to him as Leo. You may never reach that point."

"We did. Last night." Leo shifted on the couch. "I . . . I got mad. I told him if he wanted to see Cleo, he had to learn to relate to me, because I'm *me*, dammit."

"I think that might have been a mistake."

Leo looked away from her. "I'm starting to think so, too."

"But I think the two of you can patch it up, if there's any damage. You've come through a lot together."

"I didn't mean to force anything on him. I just got mad."

"And maybe you *should* have. It might have been just the thing. You'll have to wait and see."

Leo wiped his eyes and stood up.

"Thanks, Harr . . . Sorry. Joule. You've helped me. I . . . uh, I may not be seeing you as often for a while."

"I understand. Let's stay friends, okay?" She kissed him, and he hurried away.

She was sitting on a pillow facing the door when he came home from work, her legs crossed, elbows resting on her knee with a dopestick in her hand. She smiled at him.

"Well, you're home early. What happened?"

"I stayed home from work." She nearly choked, trying not to laugh. He threw his coat to the closet and hurried into the kitchen. She heard something being stirred, then the sound of glass shattering. He burst through the doorway.

"*Cleo!*"

"Darling, you look so handsome with your mouth hanging open."

He shut it, but still seemed unable to move. She went to him, feeling tingling excitement in her loins like the return of an old friend. She put her arms around him, and he nearly crushed her. She loved it.

He drew back slightly and couldn't seem to get enough of her face, his eyes roaming every detail.

"How long will you stay this way?" he asked. "Do you have any idea?"

"I don't know. Why?"

He smiled, a little sheepishly. "I hope you won't take this wrong. I'm so *happy* to see you. Maybe I shouldn't say it . . . but no, I think I'd better. I like Leo. I think I'll miss him, a little."

She nodded. "I'm not hurt. How could I be?" She drew away and led him to a pillow. "Sit down, Jules. We have to have a talk." His knees gave way under him and he sat, looking up expectantly.

"Leo isn't gone, and don't you ever think that for a minute. He's right here." She thumped her chest and looked at him defiantly. "He'll always be here. He'll never go away."

"I'm sorry, Cleo, I—"

"No, don't talk yet. It was my own fault, but I didn't know any better. I never should have called myself Leo. It gave you an easy out. You didn't have to face Cleo being a male. I'm changing all that. My name is Nile. N-i-l-e. I won't answer to anything else."

"All right. It's a nice name."

"I thought of calling myself Lion. For Leo the lion. But I decided to be who I always was, the queen of the Nile, Cleopatra. For old time's sake."

He said nothing, but his eyes showed his appreciation.

"What you have to understand is that they're both gone, in a sense. You'll never be with Cleo again. I look like her now. I resemble her inside, too, like an adult resembles the child. I have a tremendous amount in common with what she was. But I'm not her."

He nodded. She sat beside him and took his hand.

"Jules, this isn't going to be easy. There are things I want to do, people I want to meet. We're not going to be able to share the same friends. We could drift apart because of it. I'm going to have to fight resentment because you'll be holding me back. You won't let me explore your female side like I want to. You're going to resent me because I'll be trying to force you into something you think is wrong for you. But I want to try and make it work."

He let out his breath. "God, Cl . . . Nile. I've never been so scared in my life. I thought you were leading up to leaving me."

She squeezed his hand. "Not if I can help it. I want each of us to try and accept the other as they are. For me, that includes being male whenever I feel like it. It's all the same to me, but I know it's going to be hard for *you.*"

They embraced, and Jules wiped his tears on her shoulder, then faced her again.

"I'll do anything and everything in my power, up to—"

She put her finger to her lips. "I know. I accept you that way. But I'll keep trying to convince you."

INTRODUCTION TO

"Just Another Perfect Day"

The next two stories are linked, in a way, but to explain the link here would tell you more than you should know about this one. So my comments about both stories will follow.

JUST ANOTHER PERFECT DAY

DON'T WORRY.

Everything is under control.

I know how you're feeling. You wake up alone in a strange room, you get up, you look around, you soon discover that both doors are locked from the outside. It's enough to unsettle anybody, especially when you try and try and try to recall how you got here and you just can't do it.

But beyond that . . . there's this feeling. I know you're feeling it right now. I know a lot of things—and I'll reveal them all as we go along.

One of the things I know it this:

If you will sit down, put this message back on the table where you found it, and take slow, deep breaths while counting to one hundred, you'll feel a lot better.

I promise you will.

Do that now.

See what I mean? You *do* feel a lot better.

That feeling won't last for long, I'm sorry to say.

I wish there was an easier way to do this, but there isn't, and believe me, many ways have been tried. So here we go:

This is not 1986.
You are not twenty-five years old.
The date is

~~January~~ ~~February~~ ~~March~~ ~~April~~ ~~May~~ June

~~1~~ ~~2~~ ~~3~~ 4 5 6 ~~7~~ 8 9 ~~10~~ ~~11~~ 12

~~2006~~ ~~2007~~ 2008

A lot of things have happened in

~~twenty~~ ~~twenty-one~~ twenty-two

years, and I'll tell you all you need to know about that in good time.
For now . . . Don't Worry.
Slow, deep breaths. Close your eyes. Count to a hundred.
You'll feel better.
I promise.

If you'll get up now, you'll find that the bathroom door will open. There's a
mirror in there. Take a look in it, get to know the

~~forty-five~~ ~~forty-six~~ forty-seven

-year old who will be in there, looking back at you . . .
And Don't Worry.
Take deep breaths, and so forth.
I'll tell you more when you get back.

Well.
I know how rough that was. I know you're trembling. I know you're feeling
confusion, fear, anger . . . a thousand emotions.
And I know you have a thousand questions. They will all be answered, every
one of them, at the proper time.
Here are some ground rules.
I will never lie to you. You can't imagine how much care and anguish has gone
into the composition of this letter. For now, you must take my word that things

will be revealed to you in the most useful order, and in the easiest way that can be devised. You must appreciate that not all your questions can be answered at once. It may be harder for you to accept that some questions cannot be answered at all until a proper background has been prepared. These answers would mean nothing to you at this point.

You would like someone—*anyone*—to be with you right now, so you could *ask* these questions. That has been tried, and the results were needlessly chaotic and confusing. Trust me; this is the best way.

Any why should you trust me? For a very good reason.

I am you. You wrote—in a manner of speaking—every word in this letter, to help yourself through this agonizing moment.

Deep breaths, please.

Stay seated; it helps a little.

And Don't Worry.

So now we're past bombshell #2. There are more to come, but they will be easier to take, simply because your capacity to be surprised is just about at its peak right now. A certain numbness will set in. You should be thankful for that.

And now, back to your questions.

Top of the list: What happened?

Briefly (and it must be brief—more on that later):

In 1989 you had an accident. It involved a motorcycle which you don't remember owning because you didn't buy it until 1988, and a city bus. You had a difference of opinion concerning the right of way, and the bus won.

Feel your scalp with your fingertips. Don't be queasy; it healed long ago—as much as it's going to. Under those great knots of scar tissue are the useless results of the labors of the best neurosurgeons in the country. In the end, they just had to scoop out a lot of gray matter and close you back up, shaking their heads sagely and opining that you would probably feel right at home under glass on a salad bar.

But you fooled them. You woke up, and there was much rejoicing, even though you couldn't remember anything after the summer of '86. You were conscious a few hours, long enough for the doctors to determine that your intelligence didn't seem to be impaired. You could talk, read, speak, see, hear. Then you went back to sleep.

The next day you woke up, and couldn't remember anything after the summer of '86. No one was too worried. They told you again what had happened. You were awake most of the day, and again you fell asleep.

The next day you woke up, and couldn't remember anything after the summer of '86. Some consternation was expressed.

The next day you woke up, and couldn't remember anything after the summer of '86. Professorial heads were scratched, seven-syllable Latin words intoned, and deep mumbles were mumbled.

The next day you woke up, and couldn't remember anything after the summer of '86.

And the next day

And the next day

And the day after that.

This morning you woke up and couldn't remember anything after the summer of '86, and I know this is getting old, but I had to make the point in this way, because it is

~~2006~~ ~~2007~~ 2008

and we've begun to think a pattern is established.

No, no, *don't* breathe deeply, *don't* count to one hundred, face this one head on. It'll be good for you.

Back under control?

I knew you could do it.

What you have is called Progressive Narco-Catalepti-Amnesiac Syndrome (PNCAS, or Pinkus in conversation), and you should be proud of yourself, because they made up the term to describe your condition and at least a half dozen papers have been written proving it can't happen. What seems to happen, in spite of the papers, is that you store and retrieve memories just fine as long as you have a continuous thread of consciousness. But the sleep center somehow activates an erase mechanism in your head, so that all you experienced during the day is lost to you when you wake up again. The old memories are intact and vivid; the new ones are ephemeral, like they were recorded on a continuous tape loop.

Most amnesias of this type behave rather differently. Retrograde amnesia is seen fairly frequently, whereby you gradually lose even the old memories and become as an infant. And progressive amnesias are well known, but those poor people can't remember what happened to them as little as five minutes ago. Try to imagine what life would be like in those circumstances before you start crying in your beer.

Yeah, great, I hear you whine. And what's so great about *this*?

Well, nothing, at first glance. I'll certainly be the last one to argue about that. My own reawakening is too fresh in my mind, having happened only fifteen hours ago. And, in a sense, I will soon be dead, snatched back from this mayfly existence by the greedy arms of Morpheus. When I sleep tonight, most of what I feel makes me *me* will vanish. I will awake, an older and less wise man, to confusion, will read this letter, will breathe deeply, count to one hundred, stare into the mirror at a stranger. I will be you.

And yet, now, as I scan rapidly through this letter for the second time today (I said I wrote it, but only in a sense; it was written by a thousand mayflies), they are asking me if there is anything I wish to change. If I want a change, Marian will see that it is made. Is there anything I would like to do differently tomorrow? Is there something I want to tell you, my successor in this body, to beware of, to disbelieve? Are there any warnings I would issue?

The answer is no.

I will let this letter stand, in its entirety.

There are things still for you to learn that will convince you, against all common sense, that you have a wonderful life/day ahead of you.

But you need a rest. You need time to think.

Do this for me. Go back to the date. Mark out the last number and write in the next. If it's a new month, change that, too.

Now you will find the other door will open. Please go into the next room, where you will find breakfast, and an envelope containing the next part of this letter.

Don't open it yet. Eat your breakfast.

Think it over.

But don't take too long. Your time is short, and you won't want to waste it.

That was refreshing, wasn't it?

It shouldn't surprise you that all your favorite breakfast foods were on the table. You eat the same meal every morning, and never get tired of it.

And I'm sorry if that statement took some of the pleasure out of the meal, but it is necessary for me to keep reminding you of your circumstances, to prevent a cycle of denial getting started.

Here is the thing you must bear in mind.

Today is the rest of your life.

Because that life will be so short, it is essential that you waste none of it. In this letter I have sometimes stated the obvious, written out conclusions you have already reached—in a sense, wasted your time. Each time it was done—and each time it will yet be done in the rest of this letter—was for a purpose. Points must be driven home, sometimes brutally, sometimes repetitiously. I promise you this sort of thing will be kept to an absolute minimum.

So here come a few paragraphs that might be a waste of time, but really aren't, as they dispose neatly of several thousand of the most burning questions in your mind. The questions can be summed up as "What has happened in twenty years?"

The answer is: You don't care.

You can't afford to care. Even a brief synopsis of recent events would take hours to read, and would be the sheerest foolishness. You don't care who the President is. The price of gasoline doesn't concern you, nor does the victor in the '98 World Series. Why learn this trivia when you would only have to relearn it tomorrow?

You don't care which books and movies are currently popular. You have read your last book, seen your last movie.

Luckily, you are an orphan with no siblings or other close relatives. (It *is* lucky; think about it.) The girl you were going with at the time of your accident has forgotten all about you—and you don't care, because you didn't love her.

There *are* things that have happened which you *need* to know about; I'll speak of them very soon.

In the meantime . . .

How do you like the room? Not at all like a hospital, is it? Comfortable and pleasant—yet it has no windows, and the only other door was locked when you tried it.

Try it again. It will open now.

And remember . . .

Don't Worry.

Don't Worry. Don't Worry. Don't Worry.

You will have stopped crying by now. I *know* you desperately need someone to talk to, a human face to look into. You will have that very soon now, but for another few minutes I still must reach out to you from your recent past.

Incidentally, the reason the breathing exercises and the counting are so effective is a posthypnotic suggestion left in your mind. When you see the words Don't Worry, it relaxes you. It seems that some part of your mind retains shadows of memory that you can't reach—which may also account for why you *believe* all this apparent rubbish.

Are the tears dry? It did the same thing to me. Even seeing my own face aged in the mirror didn't affect me like seeing the view from my windows. Then it became *real*.

You are on one of the top floors of the Chrysler Building. Your view to the north included many, many buildings that were not there in 1986, and jumbled among them were many familiar buildings, distinctive as fingerprints. This *is* New York, and it *is* a new century, and that view is impossible to deny and as real as a fist. That's why you wept.

Not too many more bombshells to go now. But the next one is a doozy. Let's creep up on it, shall we?

You've already looked at the three photographs on the table beside your breakfast. Consider them now, in order.

The big, bluff, hearty-looking fellow is Ian MacIntyre, who you'll meet in a few minutes. He will be your counselor/companion today, and he is the head of a very important project in which you are involved. It's impossible not to like him, though you, like me, will try to resist at first. But he is too wise to push it, and you've always liked people, anyway. Besides, he has a lot of experience in winning your friendship, having done so every day for eight years.

On to the second picture.

Looks almost human, doesn't he? If the offspring of Gumby and E.T. could be considered human. He *is* humanoid: two eyes, nose, mouth, two arms and two legs, and that goofy grin. The green skin you'll get used to quickly enough.

What he is, is a Martian.

See, fifteen years ago the Martians landed and took over the planet Earth. We still don't know what they plan to do with it, but some of the theories are not good news for *Homo sapiens*.

Don't Worry.

Take a few deep breaths. I'll wait.

That last thought is unworthy of you and unjust. I would *not* waste your time with a practical joke. You must realize I can back up what I say.

To illustrate, I want you to go to the *south* windows of your apartment. Go through the billiard room into the spa, turn left at the gym, and open the door beside the Picasso, the one that didn't open before. You'll find yourself in an area with a view of the Narrows, and I'm sure I won't need to direct you beyond that.

Take a look, and come right back.

All right, you just had to prove you could do things your own way, didn't you? I don't *care* that you brought the letter with you, but your having done so provides one last bit of proof that I know you pretty well, doesn't it?

Now, back to the bloody Martians.

It's amazing how on-target Steven Spielberg was, isn't it? That way that ship *floats* out there . . . and it's *bigger* than the mother ship in *Close Encounters*. That sucker is over thirty miles across. At its lowest point it is two miles in the air. The upper parts reach into space. It has floated out there for fifteen years and not budged *one inch*. People call it The Saucer. There are fifteen others just like it, hovering near other major cities.

And you think you have detected a flaw, don't you? How would you have seen it, you ask, if it had been a cloudy day? If it had been just a normal New York *smoggy* day, for that matter. Then you'd be reading this, scratching your head, wondering what the hell I'm talking about.

The answer will illustrate everyone's concern. There *are* no more cloudy days in New York. The Martians don't seem to like rain, so they don't let it happen here. As for the smog . . . they told us to stop it, and we did. Wouldn't you, with that thing floating out there?

About the name, Martians . . .

We first detected their ships in the neighborhood of Mars. I know you'd have found it easier to swallow, in a perverse way, had I told you they came from Alpha Centauri or the Andromeda Galaxy or the planet Tralfamadore. But people got to calling them Martians because that's what they were called on television.

We don't think they're really from Mars.

We don't know *where* they're from, but it's probably not from around here. And by that, I mean not just another galaxy, but another universe. We think our own universe exists sort of as a shadow to them.

This will be hard to explain. Take it slowly.

Do you remember *Flatland,* and Mr. A Square? He lived in a two-dimensional universe. There was no up or down, just right and left, forward and backward. He could not *conceive* the notion of up or down. Mr. Square was visited by a three-dimensional being, a sphere, who drifted down through the world of Flatland. Square perceived the sphere as a circle that gradually grew, and then shrank. All he could see at any one moment was a cross-section of the sphere, while the sphere, godlike, could look down into Mr. Square's world, even touch inside Square's body without going through the skin.

It was all just an interesting intellectual exercise, until the Martians arrived. Now we think they're like the sphere, and we are Mr. Square. They live in another dimension, and they don't perceive time and space like we do.

An example:

You saw they appeared humanoid. We don't think they really are.

We think they simply allow us to see a portion of their bodies which they project into our three-dimensional world and cause to *appear* humanoid. Their real shape must be vastly complex.

Consider your hand. If you thrust your fingers into Flatland, Mr. Square would see four circles and not imagine them to be connected. If you put your hand in further, he would see the circles merge into an oblong. Or an even better analogy is the shadow-play. By suitably entwining your two hands in front of a light, you can cast a shadow on a wall that resembles a bird, or a bull, or an elephant, or even a man. What we see of the Martians is no more real than a Kermit the Frog hand puppet.

The ship is the same way. We see merely a three-dimensional cross-section of a much larger and more complex structure.

At least we think so.

Communication with the Martians is very frustrating, nearly impossible. They are so foreign to us. They never tell us anything that makes sense, never say the same thing twice. We assume it would make sense if we could think the way they do.

And it *is* important.

They are very powerful. Weather control is just a parlor trick. When they invaded, they invaded *all at once*—and I hope I can explain this to you, as I'm far from sure I understand it myself, after a full day with Martians.

They invaded fifteen years ago . . . but they also invaded in 1854, and in 1520, and several other times in the "past." The past seems to be merely another direction to them, like up or down. You'll be shown books, old books, with woodcuts and drawings and contemporary accounts of how the Martians arrived, what they did, when they left . . . and don't be concerned that you don't remember these momentous events from your high school history class, *because no one else does, either.*

Do you begin to understand? It seems that, from the moment they arrived here, in the late part of the twentieth century, they changed the past so that they had already arrived several times before. We have the history books to prove that they did. The fact that no one remembers these stories *being* in the history books before they arrived *this* time must be seen as an object lesson. One assumes they could have changed our memories of events as easily as the events themselves. That they did not do so means they *meant* us to be impressed. Had they changed both the events *and* our memories of them, no one would be the wiser; we would all assume history had *always* been that way, because that's the way we remembered it.

The whole idea of history books must be a tremendous joke to them, since they don't experience time consecutively.

Had enough? There's more.

They can do more than add things to our history. They can take things away. Things like the World Trade Center. That's right, go look for it. It's not out there, and we didn't tear it down. It never existed in this world, except in our memories. It's like a big, shared illusion.

Other things have turned up missing as well. Things like Knoxville, Tennessee, Lake Huron, the Presidency of William McKinley, the Presbyterian Church, the rhinoceros (including the fossil record of its ancestors), Jack the Ripper (and all the literary works written about him), the letter Q, and Ecuador.

Presbyterians still remember their faith and have built new churches to replace the ones that were never built. Who needed the goddam rhino, anyway? Another man served Mckinley's term (and was also assassinated). Seeing book after book where "kw" replaces "q" is only amusing—and very kweer. But the people of Knoxville—and a dozen other towns around the world—*never existed*. They are still trying to sort out the real estate around where Lake Huron used to be. And you can search the world's atlases in vain for any sight of Ecuador.

The best wisdom is that the Martians could do even more, if they wanted to. Such as wiping out the element oxygen, the charge on the electron, or, of course, the planet Earth.

They invaded, and they won quite easily.

And their weapon is very much like an editor's blue pencil. Rather than *destroy* our world, they *rewrite* it.

So what does all this have to do with me? I hear you cry.

Why couldn't I have lived out my one day on Earth without worrying about this?

Well . . . who do you think is paying for this fabulous apartment?

The grateful taxpayers, that's who. You didn't think you'd get original Picassos on the walls if you were nothing more than a brain-damaged geek, did you?

And why are the taxpayers grateful?

Because anything that keeps the Martians happy, keeps the taxpayers happy. The Martians scare hell out of *everyone* . . . and you are their fair-haired boy.

Why?

Because you don't experience time like the rest of humanity does.

You start fresh every day. You haven't had fifteen years to think about the Martians, you haven't developed any prejudice toward them or their way of thinking.

Maybe.

Most of that could be bullshit. We don't know if prejudice has anything to do with it . . . but you *do* see time differently. The fact is, the best mathematicians and physicists in the world have tried to deal with the Martians, and the Martians aren't interested. Every day they come to talk to *you*.

Most days, nothing is accomplished. They spend an hour, then go wherever it is they go, in whatever manner they do it. One day out of hundred, you get an insight. Everything I've told you so far is the result of those insights being compiled—

—along with the work of others. There are a few hundred of you, around the world. No other man or woman has your peculiar affliction; all are what most people would call mentally limited. There are the progressive amnesiacs I mentioned earlier. There are people with split-brain disorders, people with almost unbelievable perceptual aberrations, such as the woman who has lost the concept of "right." Left is the only direction that exists in her brain.

The Martians spend time with these people, people like you.

So we tentatively conclude this about the Martians:

They want to teach us something.

It is painfully obvious they could have destroyed us anytime they wished to do so. They *have* enslaved us, in the sense that we are pathetically eager to do anything we even *suspect* they might want us to do. But they don't seem to want to *do* anything with us. They've made no move to breed us for meat animals, conscript us into slave labor camps, or rape our women. They have simply arrived, demonstrated their powers, and started talking to people like you.

No one knows if we can learn what they are trying to teach us. But it behooves us to try, wouldn't you think?

Again, you say: Why me?

Or even more to the point: Why should I care?

I know your bitterness, and I understand it. Why should you spend even an hour of your precious time on problems you don't really care about, when it would be much easier and more satisfying spending your sixteen hours of awareness gnawing on yourself, wallowing in self-pity, and in general being a one-man soap opera.

There are two reasons.

One: You were never that kind of person. You've just about exhausted your store of self-pity during the process of reading this letter. If you have only one day— though it hurts like hell . . . so be it! You will spend that day doing something useful.

Reason number two . . .

You've been looking at the third picture off and on since you first picked it up, haven't you? (Come on, you can't lie to me.)

She's very pretty, isn't she?

And that thought is unworthy of you, since you *know* where this letter is coming from. She would not be offered to you as a bribe. The project managers know you well enough to avoid offering you a piece of ass to get your cooperation.

Her name is Marian.

Let us speak of love for a moment.

You were in love once before. You remember how it was, if you'll allow yourself. You remember the pain . . . but that came later, didn't it? When she rejected you. Do you remember what it felt like *the day you fell in love*? Think back, you can get it.

The simple fact is, it's why the world spins. Just the *possibility* of love has kept you going in the three years since Karen left you.

Well, let me tell you. Marian is in love with you, and before the day is over, you will be in love with her. You can believe that or not, as you choose, but I, at the end of my life here this day, can take as one of my few consolations that I/you will have, tomorrow/today, the exquisite pleasure of falling in love with Marian.

I envy you, you skeptical bastard.

* * *

And since it's just you and me, I'll add this. Even with a girl you *don't* love, "the first time" is always pretty damn interesting, isn't it?

For you, it's *always* the first time . . . except when it's the second time, just before sleep . . . which Marian seems to be suggesting this very moment.

As usual, I have anticipated all your objections.

You think it might be tough for her? You think she's suffering?

Okay. Admitted, the first few hours are what you might call repetitive for her. You gotta figure she's bored, by now, at your invariant behavior when you first wake up. But it is a cross she bears willingly for the pleasure of your company during the rest of the day.

She is a healthy, energetic girl, one who is aware that no woman ever had such an attentive, energetic lover. She loves a man who is endlessly fascinated by her, body and soul, who sees her with new eyes each and every day.

She loves your perpetual enthusiasm, your renewable infatuation.

There isn't *time* to fall out of love.

Anything more I could say would be wasting your time, and believe me, when you see what today is going to be like, you'd hate me for it.

We could wish things were different. It is *not* fair that we have only one day. I, who am at the end of it, can feel the pain you only sense. I have my wonderful memories . . . which will soon be gone. And I have Marian, for a few more minutes.

But I swear to you, I feel like an old, old man who has lived a full life, who has no regrets for anything he ever did, who accomplished something in his life, who loved, and was loved in return.

Can many "normal" people die saying that?

In just a few seconds that one, last locked door will open, and your new life and future love will come through it. I guarantee it will be interesting.

I love you, and I now leave you . . .

Have a nice day.

"In Fading Suns and Dying Moons"

The previous story and the one following have a common element that you will spot very quickly. The element is so much in common that I have to be thankful one can't be accused of plagiarizing oneself.

"Just Another Perfect Day" was written, more or less, during a drive from Seattle to Portland. I do a lot of my best writing while driving; if it was possible to drive and type at the same time my life would be greatly simplified. As it is, I try to make strings of ideas, linked together so that when I get home, I can type them out as rapidly as possible. Pull on the string and the next idea, or story point, or bit of dialogue comes tumbling out of the old idea box. (And if that worked more than about 20 percent of the time, my life would be simpler still.)

The inspiration was a book by Dr. Oliver Sacks: The Man Who Mistook His Wife for a Hat. *In it, Sacks describes some of the more fascinating and horrible things that can happen to a human being when his or her brain is damaged. One of the most basic is amnesia, but not the type used so often in Hollywood screenplays, where the victim can't remember anything of his life, including his own name. Apparently, that sort of amnesia is fairly rare, except temporarily.*

More common, and in some ways more terrifying, is amnesia that affects the short-term memory. You remember things up to a point, and from then on are unable to change new experiences into memories. Such a person can live in a perpetual state of astonishment, becoming aware of himself a hundred times a day, trying to figure out why it's not 1948 anymore, and where all the time went. In such a situation, the only mercy I can see is that he will soon forget how horrible his life has become. An excellent movie, Memento, *was recently made about a man with this type of amnesia.*

Now, fast forward some years. I got an email from Janis Ian. She said I probably didn't know who she was, and introduced herself as "a semi-famous singer/songwriter."

Well, I probably would not have known who she was . . . if I'd been catatonic during the late 1960s. Her best-known hits were "Society's Child" (when she was fifteen!) and "At Seventeen," but she has been writing and performing wonderful music ever since then.

It turns out she is a science fiction reader, likes my work, and had one of the better ideas for an anthology I had ever heard. She wanted to commission stories from various writers that would be based on lyrics from her work.

I'm not usually very good at writing a story to order but I didn't want to miss being in this book, and there was an idea I'd been kicking around for a while. I wondered if it could be made to fit. So I turned to the song lyrics she had sent me, and these words leaped out at me from page one: In Fading Suns and Dying Moons.

Well, if that isn't a science fiction title I don't know what is. Even better, it fit nicely with my idea, without any cutting and splicing at all.

Once again, this idea had to do with beings from a different dimension, and how we might interact with them. Once again, the fastest way to acquaint the reader with the concept of a fourth dimension was to use the book Flatland, *since the author had already covered just about everything one needed to know about higher and lower dimensions.*

One might ask if I found this a bit derivative, even repetitive. Well, I didn't find it repetitive at all, for a simple reason.

I forgot.

No, I do not *suffer from retrograde amnesia, like the man in the previous story. My only excuse is that I seldom go back and reread my stories after they've seen publication, unless they are being collected, as they are here. Let me tell you, when I read the references to* Flatland *in "Just Another Perfect Day," I broke out in a cold sweat. It is every writer's nightmare. What if I'd unconsciously stolen from somebody else . . . ?*

However, I still like both stories, and I think they are different enough from each other that they can stand together or alone, whichever one prefers.

One more thing I didn't remember . . .

I don't put much stock in the idea of science fiction writers predicting the future, though some readers evidently expect it of us. I am familiar with the list of technological predictions that have come true, from nuclear submarines to synchronous-orbit satellites, and that's all great, but it's not why a writer writes stories, at least none of the writers I know.

Somehow more disturbing is when life imitates art. Tom Clancy must have felt a shiver when the aircraft were used as human-guided missiles (if you can call them human) on September 11, 2001, something he had put into one of his novels, except the plane was flown into the Capitol Building during a joint session of Congress. But, of course anybody who thought about it, and who understood there were no limits to the crimes some fanatic monsters are willing to commit, could have foreseen that much.

I in no way claim any degree of prescience for the mention of a vanished World Trade Center in "Just Another Perfect Day." In fact, I'd forgotten it was even in there, and discovering it again made my skin crawl. I even thought of taking the reference out for this publication, as some filmmakers doctored shots that included the Twin Towers in the weeks and months following 9/11. It still hurts to even think of those images, and I'm sure it will continue to for the rest of my life, but we just have to keep remembering.

After all, some of the perpetrators are still alive . . . a condition I hope is soon remedied.

AUTHOR'S NOTE

Reading the galleys for this book, I just had to mention one more odd coincidence that has happened since I wrote these introductions.

A man named George Wing wrote a movie called *50 First Dates,* and it was produced and released a few weeks ago, starring Jim Carrey. It's about a woman who loses her recent memory every time she goes to sleep. She eventually keeps a diary to bring her up to date on the last few years. My story was written in 1989 . . .

Should I sue?

Naaaah. I remember David Gerrold telling of a terrible moment he had concerning his *Star Trek* episode, "The Trouble With Tribbles." In that story, a few cute little furry critters bred until they had overrun the *Enterprise.* Somebody pointed out that Robert Heinlein had written a novel, *The Rolling Stones,* in which cute little furry critters called "flat cats" bred until they had . . . you guessed it. In a cold sweat, David contacted Heinlein who, being the gentleman he always was, pointed out that *he* had stolen the idea from Ellis Parker Butler, who wrote a story called "Pigs is Pigs," (later made into a wonderful Walt Disney short), which described a pair of guinea pigs and their offspring overrunning a train station in Scotland, and that Butler probably stole it from Noah.

And though it pains me to admit it, I saw the movie, and George Wing made better use of the idea than I did.

IN FADING SUNS AND DYING MOONS

T HE FIRST TIME they came through the neighborhood there really wasn't much neighborhood to speak of. Widely dispersed hydrogen molecules, only two or three per cubic meter. Traces of heavier elements from long-ago supernovae. The usual assortment of dust particles, at a density of one particle every cubic mile or so. The "dust" was mostly ammonia, methane, and water ice, with some more complex molecules like benzene. Here and there these thin ingredients were pushed into eddies by light pressure from neighboring stars.

Somehow they set forces in motion. I picture it as a Cosmic Finger stirring the mix, out in the interstellar wastes where space is really flat, in the Einsteinian sense, making a whirlpool in the unimaginable cold. Then they went away.

Four billion years later they returned. Things were brewing nicely. The space debris had congealed into a big, burning central mass and a series of rocky or gaseous globes, all sterile, in orbit around it.

They made a few adjustments and planted their seeds, and saw that it was good. They left a small observer/recorder behind, along with a thing that would call them when everything was ripe. Then they went away again.

A billion years later the timer went off, and they came back.

I had a position at the American Museum of Natural History in New York City, but of course I had not gone to work that day. I was sitting at home watching the news, as frightened as anyone else. Martial law had been declared a few hours earlier. Things had been getting chaotic. I'd heard gunfire from the streets outside.

Someone pounded on my door.

"United States Army!" someone shouted. "Open the door immediately!"

I went to the door, which had four locks on it.

"How do I know you're not a looter?" I shouted.

"Sir, I am authorized to break your door down. Open the door, or stand clear."

I put my eye to the old-fashioned peephole. They were certainly dressed like soldiers. One of them raised his rifle and slammed the butt down on my doorknob. I shouted that I would let them in, and in a few seconds I had all the locks open. Six men in full combat gear hustled into my kitchen. They split up and quickly explored all three rooms of the apartment, shouting out "All clear!" in brisk, military voices. One man, a bit older than the rest, stood facing me with a clipboard in his hand.

"Sir, are you Dr. Andrew Richard Lewis?"

"There's been some mistake," I said. "I'm not a medical doctor."

"Sir, are you Dr.—"

"Yes, yes, I'm Andy Lewis. What can I do for you?"

"Sir, I am Captain Edgar and I am ordered to induct you into the United States Army Special Invasion Corps effective immediately, at the rank of second lieutenant. Please raise your right hand and repeat after me."

I knew from the news that this was now legal, and I had the choice of enlisting or facing a long prison term. I raised my hand and in no time at all I was a soldier.

"Lieutenant, your orders are to come with me. You have fifteen minutes to pack what essentials you may need, such as prescription medicine and personal items. My men will help you assemble your gear."

I nodded, not trusting myself to speak.

"You may bring any items relating to your specialty. Laptop computer, reference books . . ." He paused, apparently unable to imagine what a man like me would want to bring along to do battle with space aliens.

"Captain, do you know what my specialty is?"

"My understanding is that you are a bug specialist."

"An entomologist, Captain. Not an exterminator. Could you give me . . . any clue as to why I'm needed?"

For the first time he looked less than totally self-assured.

"Lieutenant, all I know is . . . they're collecting butterflies."

They hustled me to a helicopter. We flew low over Manhattan. Every street was gridlocked. All the bridges were completely jammed with mostly abandoned cars.

I was taken to an airbase in New Jersey and hurried onto a military jet transport that stood idling on the runway. There were a few others already on board. I knew most of them; entomology is not a crowded field.

The plane took off at once.

There was a colonel aboard whose job was to brief us on our mission, and on what was thus far known about the aliens: not much was really known that I hadn't already seen on television.

They had appeared simultaneously on seacoasts worldwide. One moment there was nothing, the next moment there was a line of aliens as far as the eye could see. In the western hemisphere the line stretched from Point Barrow in Alaska to Tierra del Fuego in Chile. Africa was lined from Tunis to the Cape of Good Hope. So were the western shores of Europe, from Norway to Gibraltar. Australia, Japan, Sri Lanka, the Philippines, and every other island thus far contacted reported the same thing: a solid line of aliens appearing in the west, moving east.

Aliens? No one knew what else to call them. They were clearly not of Planet Earth, though if you ran into a single one there would be little reason to think them very odd. Just millions and millions of perfectly ordinary people dressed in white coveralls, blue baseball caps, and brown boots, within arm's reach of each other.

Walking slowly toward the east.

Within a few hours of their appearance someone on the news had started calling it the Line, and the creatures who were in it Linemen. From the pictures on the television they appeared rather average and androgynous.

"They're not human," the colonel said. "Those coveralls, it looks like they don't come off. The hats, either. You get close enough, you can see it's all part of their skin."

"Protective coloration," said Watkins, a colleague of mine from the museum. "Many insects adapt colors or shapes to blend with their environment."

"But what's the point of blending in," I asked, "if you are made so conspicuous by your actions?"

"Perhaps the 'fitting in' is simply to look more like us. It seems unlikely, doesn't it, that evolution would have made them look like . . ."

"Janitors," somebody piped up.

The colonel was frowning at us.

"You think they're insects?"

"Not by any definition I've ever heard," Watkins said. "Of course, other animals adapt to their surroundings, too. Arctic foxes in winter coats, tigers with their stripes. Chameleons."

The colonel mulled this for a moment, then resumed his pacing.

"Whatever they are, bullets don't bother them. There have been many instances of civilians shooting at the aliens."

Soldiers, too, I thought. I'd seen film of it on television, a National Guard unit in Oregon cutting loose with their rifles. The aliens hadn't reacted at all, not visibly . . . until all the troops and all their weapons just vanished, without the least bit of fuss.

And the Line moved on.

* * *

We landed at a disused-looking airstrip somewhere in northern California. We were taken to a big motel, which the Army had taken over. In no time I was hustled aboard a large Coast Guard helicopter with a group of soldiers—a squad? a platoon?—led by a young lieutenant who looked even more terrified than I felt. On the way to the Line I learned that his name was Evans, and that he was in the National Guard.

It had been made clear to me that I was in charge of the overall mission and Evans was in charge of the soldiers. Evans said his orders were to protect me. How he was to protect me from aliens who were immune to his weapons hadn't been spelled out.

My own orders were equally vague. I was to land close behind the Line, catch up, and find out everything I could.

"They speak better English than I do," the colonel had said. "We must know their intentions. Above all, you must find out why they're collecting . . ." and here his composure almost broke down, but he took a deep breath and steadied himself.

"Collecting butterflies," he finished.

We passed over the Line at a few hundred feet. Directly below us individual aliens could be made out, blue hats and white shoulders. But off to the north and south it quickly blurred into a solid white line vanishing in the distance, as if one of those devices that make chalk lines on football fields had gone mad.

Evans and I watched it. None of the Linemen looked up at the noise. They were walking slowly, all of them, never getting more than a few feet apart. The terrain was grassy, rolling hills, dotted here and there with clumps of trees. No man-made structures were in sight.

The pilot put us down a hundred yards behind the Line.

"I want you to keep your men at least fifty yards away from me," I told Evans. "Are those guns loaded? Do they have those safety things on them? Good. Please keep them on. I'm almost as afraid of being shot by one of those guys as I am of . . . whatever they are."

And I started off, alone, toward the Line.

How does one address a line of marching alien creatures? *Take me to your leader* seemed a bit peremptory. *Hey, bro, what's happening* . . . perhaps overly familiar. In the end, after following for fifteen minutes at a distance of about ten yards, I had settled on *excuse me,* so I moved closer and cleared my throat. Turns out that was enough. One of the Linemen stopped walking and turned to me.

This close, one could see that his features were rudimentary. His head was like a mannequin's, or a wig stand: a nose, hollows for eyes, bulges for cheeks. All the rest seemed to be painted on.

I could only stand there idiotically for a moment. I noticed a peculiar thing. There was no gap in the Line.

I suddenly remembered why it was me and not some diplomat standing there.

"Why are you collecting butterflies?" I asked.

"Why not?" he said, and I figured it was going to be a long, long day. "*You should have no trouble understanding,*" he said. "Butterflies are the most beautiful things on your planet, aren't they?"

"I've always thought so." Wondering, *Did he know I was a lepidopterist?*

"Then there you are." Now he began to move. The Line was about twenty yards away, and through our whole conversation he never let it get more distant than that. We walked at a leisurely one mile per hour.

Okay, I told myself. Try to keep it to butterflies. Leave it to the military types to get to the tough questions: *When do you start kidnapping our children, raping our women, and frying us for lunch?*

"What are you doing with them?"

"Harvesting them." He extended a hand toward the Line, and as if summoned, a lovely specimen of *Adelpha bredowii* fluttered toward him. He did something with his fingers and a pale blue sphere formed around the butterfly.

"Isn't it lovely?" he asked, and I moved in for a closer look. He seemed to treasure these wonderful creatures I'd spent my life studying.

He made another gesture, and the blue ball with the *Adelpha* disappeared. "What happens to them?" I asked him.

"There is a collector," he said.

"A lepidopterist?"

"No, it's a storage device. You can't see it because it is . . . off to one side."

Off to one side of what? I wondered, but didn't ask.

"And what happens to them in the collector?"

"They are put in storage in a place where . . . time does not move. Where time does not pass. Where they do not move through time as they do here." He paused for a few seconds. "It is difficult to explain."

"Off to one side?" I suggested.

"Exactly. Excellent. Off to one side of time. You've got it."

I had nothing, actually. But I plowed on.

"What will become of them?"

"We are building a . . . place. Our leader wishes it to be a very special place. Therefore, we are making it of these beautiful creatures."

"Of butterfly wings?"

"They will not be harmed. We know ways of making . . . walls in a manner that will allow them to fly freely."

I wished someone had given me a list of questions.

"How did you get here? How long will you stay?"

"A certain . . . length of time, not a great length by your standards."

"What about your standards?"

"By our standards . . . no time at all. As to how we got here . . . have you read a book entitled *Flatland*?"

"I'm afraid not."

"Pity," he said, and turned away, and vanished.

Our operation in northern California was not the only group trying desperately to find out more about the Linemen, of course. There were lines on every continent, and soon they would be present in every nation. They had covered many small Pacific islands in only a day, and when they reached the eastern shores, they simply vanished, as my guide had.

News media were doing their best to pool information. I believe I got a lot of those facts before the general population, since I had been shanghaied into the forefront, but our information was often as garbled and inaccurate as what the rest of the world was getting. The military was scrambling around in the dark, just like everyone else.

But we learned some things:

They were collecting moths as well as butterflies, from the drabbest specimen to the most gloriously colored. The entire order Lepidoptera.

They could appear and vanish at will. It was impossible to get a count of them. Wherever one stopped to commune with the natives, as mine had, the Line remained solid, with no gaps. When they were through talking to you, they simply went where the Cheshire Cat went, leaving behind not even a grin.

Wherever they appeared, they spoke the local language, fluently and idiomatically. This was true even in isolated villages in China or Turkey or Nigeria, where some dialects were used by only a few hundred people.

They didn't seem to weigh anything at all. Moving through forests, the Line became more of a wall, Linemen appearing in literally every tree, on every limb, walking on branches obviously too thin to bear their weight and not even causing them to bend. When the tree had been combed for butterflies the crews vanished, and appeared in another tree.

Walls meant nothing to them. In cities and towns nothing was missed, not even closed bank vaults, attic spaces, closets. They didn't come through the door, they simply appeared in a room and searched it. If you were on the toilet, that was just too bad.

Any time they were asked about where they came from, they mentioned that book, *Flatland*. Within hours the book was available on hundreds of websites. Downloads ran to the millions.

The full title of the book was *Flatland: A Romance of Many Dimensions*. It was supposedly written by one Mr. A. Square, a resident of Flatland, but its actual author was Edwin Abbott, a nineteenth-century cleric and amateur mathematician. A copy was waiting for me when we got back to camp after that first frustrating day.

The book is an allegory and a satire, but also an ingenious way to explain the concept of multidimensional worlds to the layman, like me. Mr. Square lives in a world of only two dimensions. For him, there is no such thing as up or down, only forward, backward, and side to side. It is impossible for us to really *see* from Square's point of view: a single line that extends all around him, with nothing above it or below it. *Nothing.* Not empty space, not a black or white void . . . nothing.

But humans, being three-dimensional, can stand outside Flatland, look up or down at it, see its inhabitants from an angle they can never have. In fact, we could see *inside* them, examine their internal organs, reach down and touch a Flatlander heart or brain with our fingers.

In the course of the book Mr. Square is visited by a being from the third dimension, a Sphere. He can move from one place to another without apparently traversing the space between point A and point B. There was also discussion of the possibilities of even higher dimensions, worlds as inscrutable to us as the 3-D world was to Mr. Square.

I'm no mathematician, but it didn't take an Einstein to infer that the Line, and the Linemen, came from one of those theoretical higher planes.

The people running the show were not Einstein, either, but when they needed expertise they knew where to go to draft it.

Our mathematician's name was Larry Ward. He looked as baffled as I must have looked the day before and he got no more time to adjust to his new situation than I did. We were all hustled aboard another helicopter and hurried out to the Line. I filled him in, as best I could, on the way out.

Again, as soon as we approached the Line, a spokesman appeared. He asked us if we'd read the book, though I suspect he already knew we had. It was a creepy feeling to realize he, or something like him, could have been standing . . . or existing, in some direction I couldn't imagine, only inches away from me in my motel bedroom, looking at me read the book just as the Sphere looked down on Mr. A. Square.

A flat, white plane appeared in the air between us and geometrical shapes and equations began drawing themselves on it. It just hung there, unsupported. Larry wasn't too flustered by it, nor was I. Against the background of the Line an anti-gravity blackboard seemed almost mundane.

The Lineman began talking to Larry, and I caught maybe one word in three. Larry seemed to have little trouble with it at first, but after an hour he was sweating, frowning, clearly getting out of his depth.

By that time I was feeling quite superfluous, and it was even worse for Lieutenant Evans and his men. We were reduced to following Larry and the Line at its glacial but relentless pace. Some of the men took to slipping between the gaps in the line to get in front, then doing all sorts of stupid antics to get a reaction, like tourists trying to rattle the guards at the Tower of London. The Linemen took absolutely no notice. Evans didn't seem to care. I suspected he was badly hung over.

"Look at this, Dr. Lewis."

I turned around and saw that a Lineman had appeared behind me, in that disconcerting way they had. He had a pale blue sphere cupped in his hands, and in it was a lovely specimen of *Papilio zelicaon*, the Anise Swallowtail, with one blue wing and one orange wing.

"A gynandromorph," I said, immediately, with the spooky feeling that I was back in the lecture hall. "An anomaly that sometimes arises during gametogenesis. One side is male and the other is female."

"How extraordinary. Our . . . leader will be happy to have this creature existing in his . . . palace."

I had no idea how far to believe him. I had been told that at least a dozen motives had been put forward by Line spokesmen, to various exploratory groups, as the rationale for the butterfly harvest. A group in Mexico had been told some substance was to be extracted—harmlessly, so they said—from the specimens. In France a lepidopterist swore a Lineman told her the captives were to be given to fourth-dimension children, as pets. It didn't seem all the stories could be true. Or maybe they could. Step One in dealing with the Linemen was to bear in mind that *our* minds could not contain many concepts that, to them, were as basic as *up* and *down* to us. We had to assume they were speaking baby talk to us.

But for an hour we talked butterflies, as Larry got more and more bogged down in a sea of equations and the troops got progressively more bored. The creature knew the names of every Lepidopteran we encountered that afternoon, something I could not claim. That fact had never made me feel inadequate before. There were around 170,000 species of moth and butterfly so far catalogued, including several thousand in dispute. Nobody could be expected to know them all . . . but I was sure the Linemen did. Remember, every book in every library was available to them, and they did not have to open them to read them. And time, which I had been told was the fourth dimension but now learned was only *a* fourth dimension, almost surely did not pass for them in the same way as it passed for us. Larry told me later that a billion years was not a formidable . . . distance for them. They were masters of space, masters of time, and who knew what else?

The only emotion any of them had ever expressed was delight at the beauty of the butterflies. They showed no anger or annoyance when shot at with rifles; the bullets went through them harmlessly. Even when assaulted with bombs or artillery rounds they didn't register any emotion, they simply made the assailants and weapons disappear. It was surmised by those in charge, whoever they were, that these big, noisy displays were dealt with only because they harmed butterflies.

The troops had been warned, but there's always some clown . . .

So when an *Antheraea polyphemus* fluttered into the air in front of a private named Paulson, he reached out and grabbed it in his fist. Or tried to; while his hand was still an inch away, he vanished.

I don't think any of us quite credited our senses at first. I didn't, and I'd been looking right at him, wondering if I should say something. There was nothing but the Polyphemus moth fluttering in the sunshine. But soon enough there were angry shouts. Many of the soldiers unslung their rifles and pointed them at the Line.

Evans was frantically shouting at them, but now they were angry and frustrated. Several rounds were fired. Larry and I hit the deck as a machine gun started chattering. Looking up carefully I saw Evans punch the machine gunner and grab the weapon. The firing stopped.

There was a moment of stunned silence. I got to my knees and looked at the Line. Larry was okay, but the "blackboard" was gone. And the Line moved placidly on.

I thought it was all over, and then the screaming began, close behind me. I nearly wet myself, and turned around, quickly.

Paulson was behind me, on his knees, hands pressed to his face, screaming his lungs out. But he was changed. His hair was all white and he'd grown a white beard. He looked thirty years older, maybe forty. I knelt beside him, unsure what to do. His eyes were full of madness . . . and the name patch sewn on the front of his shirt now read:

PAULSON

"They reversed him," Larry said.

He couldn't stop pacing. Myself, I'd settled into a fatalistic calm. In the face of what the Linemen could do, it seemed pointless to worry much. If I did something to piss them off, *then* I'd worry.

Our northern California headquarters had completely filled the big Holiday Inn. The Army had taken over the whole thing, this bizarre operation gradually getting the encrustation of barnacles any government operation soon acquires, literally hundreds of people bustling about as if they had something important to do. For the life of me, I couldn't see how any of us were needed, except for Larry and a helicopter pilot to get him to the Line and back. It seemed obvious that any answers we got would come from him, or someone like him. They certainly wouldn't come from the troops, the tanks, the nuclear missiles I'm sure were targeted on the Line, and certainly not from me. But they kept me on, probably because they hadn't yet evolved a procedure to send anybody home. I didn't mind. I could be terrified here just as well as in New York. In the meantime, I was bunking with Larry . . . who now reached into his pocket and produced a penny. He looked at it, and tossed it to me.

"I grabbed that when they were going through his pockets," he said. I looked at it. As I expected, Lincoln was looking to the left and all the inscriptions were reversed.

"How can they do that?" I asked.

He looked confused for a moment, then grabbed a sheet of motel stationery and attacked it with one of the pens in his pocket. I looked over his shoulder as he made a sketch of a man, writing L by one hand and R by the other. Then he folded the sheet without creasing it, touching the stick figure to the opposite surface.

"Flatland doesn't have to be flat," he said. He traced the stick man onto the new surface, and I saw it was now reversed. "Flatlanders can move through the third dimension without knowing they're doing it. They slide around this curve in their universe. Or, a third-dimensional being can lift them up *here,* and set them down *here.* They've moved, without traveling the distance between the two points."

We both studied the drawing solemnly for a moment.

"How is Paulson?" I asked.

"Catatonic. Reversed. He's left-handed now, his appendectomy scar is on the left, the tattoo on his left shoulder is on the right now."

"He looked older."

"Who can say? Some are saying he was scared gray. I'm pretty sure he saw things the human eye just isn't meant to see . . . but I think he's actually older, too.

The doctors are still looking him over. It wouldn't be hard for a fourth-dimensional creature to do, age him many years in seconds."

"But why?"

"They didn't hire me to find out 'why.' I'm having enough trouble understanding the 'how.' I figure the why is your department." He looked at me, but I didn't have anything helpful to offer. But I had a question.

"How is it they're shaped like men?"

"Coincidence?" he said, and shook his head. "I don't even know if 'they' is the right pronoun. There might be just one of them, and I don't think it looks *anything* like us." He saw my confusion, and groped again for an explanation. He picked up another piece of paper, set it on the desk, drew a square on it, put the fingertips of his hand to the paper.

"A Flatlander, Mr. Square, perceives this as five separate entities. See, I can surround him with what he'd see as five circles. Now, imagine my hand moving down, *through* the plane of the paper. Four circles soon join together into an elliptical shape, then the fifth one joins, too, and he sees a cross section of my wrist: another circle. Now extend that . . ." He looked thoughtful, then pulled a comb from his back pocket and touched the teeth to the paper surface.

"The comb moves through the plane, and each tooth becomes a little circle. I draw the comb through Flatland, Mr. Square sees a row of circles coming toward him."

It was making my head hurt, but I thought I grasped it.

"So they . . . or it, or whatever, is combing the planet . . ."

"Combing out all the butterflies. Like a fine-tooth comb going through hair, pulling out . . . whaddayou call 'em . . . lice eggs . . ."

"Nits." I realized I was scratching my head. I stopped. "But these aren't circles, they're solid, they look like people . . ."

"If they're solid, why don't they break tree branches when they go out on them?" He grabbed the gooseneck lamp on the desk and pointed the light at the wall. Then he laced his hands together. "You see it? On the wall? This isn't the best light . . ."

Then I did see it. He was making a shadow image of a flying bird. Larry was on a roll; he whipped a grease pencil from his pocket and drew a square on the beige wall above the desk. He made the shadow-bird again.

"Mr. Square sees a pretty complex shape. But he doesn't know the half of it. Look at my hands. Just my hands. Do you see a bird?"

"No," I admitted.

"That's because only one of many possible cross sections resembles a bird." He made a dog's head, and a monkey. He'd done this before, probably in a lecture hall.

"What I'm saying, whatever it's using, hands, fingers, whatever shapes its actual body can assume in four-space, all we'd ever see is a three-dimensional cross section of it."

"And that cross section looks like a man?"

"Could be." But his hands were on his hips now, regarding the square he'd drawn on the wall. "How can I be sure? I can't. The guys running this show, they want answers, and all we can offer them is possibilities."

By the end of the next day, he couldn't even offer them that.

I could see he was having tough sledding right from the first. The floating blackboard covered itself with equations again, and the . . . Instructor? Tutor? Translator? . . . stood patiently beside it, waiting for Larry to get it. And, increasingly, he was not.

The troops had been kept back, almost a quarter mile behind the line. They were on their best behavior, as that day there was some brass with them. I could see them back there, holding binoculars, a few generals and admirals and such.

Since no one had told me to do differently, I stayed up at the Line near Larry. I wasn't sure why. I was no longer very afraid of the Linemen, though the camp had been awash in awful rumors that morning. It was said that Paulson was not the first man to be returned in a reversed state, but it had been hushed up to prevent panic. I could believe it. The initial panics and riots had died down quite a bit, we'd been told, but millions around the globe were still fleeing before the advancing Line. In some places feeding these migrant masses was getting to be a problem. And in some places, the moving mob had solved the problem by looting every town they passed through.

Some said that Paulson was not the worst that could happen. It was whispered that men had been "vanished" by the Line and returned everted. Turned inside out. And still alive, though not for long . . .

Larry wouldn't deny it was possible.

But today Larry wasn't saying much of anything. I watched him for a while, sweating in the sun, writing on the blackboard with a grease pencil, wiping it out, writing again, watching the Lineman patiently writing new stuff in symbols that might as well have been Swahili.

Then I remembered I had thought of something to ask the night before, lying there listening to Larry snoring in the other king-size bed.

"Excuse me," I said, and instantly a Lineman was standing beside me. The same one? I knew the question had little meaning.

"Before, I asked 'Why butterflies?' You said because they are beautiful."

"The most beautiful things on your planet," he corrected.

"Right. But . . . isn't there a second best? Isn't there anything else, anything at all, that you're interested in?" I floundered, trying to think of something else that might be worth collecting to an aesthetic sense I could not possibly imagine. "Scarab beetles," I said, sticking to entomology. "Some of them are fabulously beautiful, to humans anyway."

"They are quite beautiful," he agreed. "However, we do not collect them. Our reasons would be difficult to explain." A diplomatic way of saying humans were blind, deaf, and ignorant, I supposed. "But yes, in a sense. Things are grown on other planets in this solar system, too. We are harvesting them now, in a temporal way of speaking."

Well, this was new. Maybe I could justify my presence here in some small way after all. Maybe I'd finally asked an intelligent question.

"Can you tell me about them?"

"Certainly. Deep in the atmospheres of your four gas giant planets—Jupiter, Saturn, Uranus, and Neptune—beautiful beings have evolved that . . . our leader treasures. On Mercury, creatures of quicksilver inhabit deep caves near the poles. These are being gathered as well. And there are life forms we admire that thrive on very cold planets."

Gathering cryogenic butterflies on Pluto? Since he showed me no visual aids, the image would do until something better came along.

The Lineman didn't elaborate beyond that, and I couldn't think of another question that might be useful. I reported what I had learned at the end of the day. None of the team of expert analysts could think of a reason why this should concern us, but they assured me my findings would be bucked up the chain of command.

Nothing ever came of it.

The next day they said I could go home, and I was hustled out of California almost as fast as I'd arrived. On my way I met Larry, who looked haunted. We shook hands.

"Funny thing," he said. "All our answers, over thousands of years. Myths, gods, philosophers . . . What's it all about? Why are we here? Where do we come from, where do we go, what are we supposed to do while we're here? What's the meaning of life? So now we find out, and it was never about us at all. The meaning of life is . . . butterflies." He gave me a lopsided grin. "But you knew that all along, didn't you?"

Of all the people on the planet, I and a handful of others could make the case that we were most directly affected. Sure, lives were uprooted, many people died before order was restored. But the Linemen were as unobtrusive as they could possibly be, given their mind-numbing task, and things eventually got back to a semblance of normal. Some people lost their religious faith, but even more rejected out of hand the proposition that there was no God but the Line, so the holy men of the world registered a net gain.

But lepidopterists . . . let's face it, we were out of a job.

I spent my days haunting the dusty back rooms and narrow corridors of the museum, opening cases and drawers, some of which might not have been disturbed for decades. I would stare for hours at the thousands and thousands of preserved moths and butterflies, trying to connect with the childhood fascination that had led to my choice of career. I remembered expeditions to remote corners of the world, miserable, mosquito-bitten, and exhilarated at the same time. I recalled conversations, arguments about this or that taxonomic point. I tried to relive my elation at my first new species, *Hypolimnes lewisii*.

All ashes now. They didn't even look very pretty anymore.

On the twenty-eight day of the invasion, a second Line appeared on the world's western coasts. By then the North American Line stretched from a point far in the Canadian north through Saskatchewan, Montana, Wyoming, Colorado, and New Mexico, reaching the Gulf of Mexico somewhere south of Corpus Christi, Texas. The second Line began marching east, finding very few butterflies but not seeming to mind.

It is not in the nature of the governmental mind to simply do nothing when faced with a situation. But most people agreed there was little or nothing to be done. To save face, the military maintained a presence following the Line, but they knew better than to do anything.

On the fifty-sixth day the third Line appeared.

Lunar cycle? It appeared so. A famous mathematician claimed he had found an equation describing the Earth-Moon orbital pair in six dimensions, or was it seven? No one cared very much.

When the first Line reached New York I was in the specimen halls, looking at moths under glass. A handful of Linemen appeared, took a quick look around. One looked over my shoulder at the displays for a moment. Then they all went away, in their multidimensional way.

* * *

And there it is.

I don't recall who it was that first suggested we write it all down, nor can I recall the reason put forward. Like most literate people of the Earth, though, I dutifully sat down and wrote my story. I understand many are writing entire biographies, possibly an attempt to shout out *"I was here!"* to an indifferent universe. I have limited myself to events from Day One to the present.

Perhaps someone else will come by, some distant day, and read these accounts. Yes, and perhaps the Moon is made of green butterflies.

It turned out that my question, that last day of my military career, was the key question, but I didn't realize I had been given the answer.

The Lineman never said they were growing creatures on Pluto.

He said there were things they grew on cold planets.

After one year of combing the Earth, the Linemen went away as quickly as they appeared.

On the way out, they switched off the light.

It was night in New York. From the other side of the planet the reports came in quickly, and I climbed up to the roof of my building. The moon, which should have been nearing full phase, was a pale ghost and soon became nothing but a black hole in the sky.

Another tenant had brought a small TV. An obviously frightened astronomer and a confused news anchor were counting seconds. When they reached zero, a bit over twenty minutes after the events at the antipodes, Mars began to dim. In thirty seconds it was invisible.

He never mentioned Pluto as their cold-planet nursery . . .

In an hour Jupiter's light failed, then Saturn.

When the Sun came up in America that day it looked like a charcoal briquette, red flickerings here and there, and soon not even that. When the clocks and church bells struck noon, the Sun was gone.

Presently, it began to get cold.

INTRODUCTION TO

"The Flying Dutchman"

I took my first flight on an airplane shortly after I dropped out of Michigan State (well, technically, flunked out; I stopped going to classes, I was very depressed). The plane was a Delta Airlines Convair Cv-880, a not-too-successful rival to the 707 and DC-8; only sixty-five were made. It flew me from Detroit to Atlanta, where I boarded another 880 for a flight to Houston.

My last six years in Texas were spent only about a mile from the Mid-County Airport, which served not just tiny Nederland, but Beaumont, Port Arthur, and Orange, so it was fairly busy, though too small then for jetliners. I was so aviation-crazy that my idea of a great time was to park at the end of the runway and watch the planes land and take off. It was there that our high school band greeted Lyndon Johnson, and we played "Hail Columbia," the official song of the vice presidency.

My idea of a really great time was to go to Houston Hobby Airport and stand out on the observation platform watching the big jets. You could do that back then.

It should have been an exciting trip, and I enjoyed it, gawked like a rube from a small town in Texas, but I was exhausted, emotionally and physically. It had been a hard night. The Selective Service System, ever vigilant in its hunt for raw meat to feed Lyndon's war, had already revoked my II-S status and ordered me to report to Detroit for my pre-induction physical. I was now the dreaded One-A.

The only way I could make it was to hitchhike from East Lansing to Detroit, spend the night in the bus station, and report bright and early in the morning. Inside, I was processed like prize pork, and despite my debilitated condition, pronounced a fit target for Viet Cong land mines and bullets. Then I hitched to the airport and spent the night on the floor there. It was a pretty bedraggled nineteen-year-old who finally stepped aboard that Cv-880.

That began a six-year battle with the SSS that I won, largely by attrition. I didn't have any particular secret, I just sort of bureaucrated them to a standstill.

Example: My draft board was in Michigan, but my only address was in Texas.

All notices had to shuffle between the two destinations before my mother could forward them to me.

Another example: I found out that every decision they made could be appealed, and all that paperwork had to shuffle around, too. Years were eaten up that way.

Most ridiculous example: I was ordered to report to the Oakland Induction Center for the Big One, the One Step Forward that would send me into basic training. A man outside the center told me the commanding officer of the place was so insanely angry at the goddamn pinko peaceniks demonstrating outside that if you took anti-draft literature inside, you would be ordered to surrender it, before you were in the army, before they had the authority to order you to do a damn thing. I took it in, was told to surrender it, and then was sat down at a table and ordered to sign twenty different forms, surrounded by gorillas who looked like they would like to do nothing more than wring my scrawny hippie neck. I signed nothing, didn't surrender the literature, and was told to go away, that the District Attorney would be contacting me. No one ever did. That ate up a year, right there.

At one point FBI agents showed up at my parents' home, and eventually at mine. They questioned me, and went away.

I went to Canada, to see if I wanted to live up there, dodging the draft. Canada is a fine country, I love it, but the idea of never being able to go home was too much to bear.

I sort of knew that if I was sent to Nam there was an excellent chance of going home in a body bag or minus my legs and testicles, but I admit that didn't scare me too much. I was young, I thought I was immortal. I also thought I could find a way to finagle my way into being the best damn clerk-typist or chaplain's assistant stationed in Germany in this man's army.

But I kept resisting because I'd read Catch-22, and knew I could never survive one aspect of the military: officers. I knew I was destined to be a private, and I don't take orders well. So I fought.

My main weapon was being the sole means of support for my wife, who was in a wheelchair. I lost every appeal I ever made, I don't even remember how many there were, but then one day . . . the war was over. And I never broke the law.

I have no regrets about any of this. I respected and still respect those who went, who died, who were maimed mentally and physically. I never spat at soldiers, never called them baby-killers. Call me a draft-dodger if you like. I can handle it.

I don't really know where this story came from. Even after 9/11 air travel is not quite this inconvenient, though I'm planning to take the train the next time I take a trip. I don't like having my shoes searched. I think I was simply tinkering with the notion that Hell might not be guys with pitchforks herding people into pools of molten brimstone . . . that there might actually be worse things. . . .

THE FLYING DUTCHMAN

I**T WAS DARK** when the plane reached O'Hare, three hours late. Snow swirled in white tornadoes over the frozen field. The plowing crews had kept just one runway clear. Planes were stacked up back to New Jersey. Flights were being diverted to St. Louis, Cleveland, Dayton, and other places people didn't really want to go when they *intended* to go there.

The 727 hit the icy tarmac like a fat lady on skates, slued to the left, then straightened out as the nose came down and the thrust reversers engaged. Then the plane taxied for thirty minutes.

When the jetway finally reached them and the Fasten Seat Belts sign went off, Peter Meers stood up. He was immediately bumped back into his seat by a large man across the aisle. Somebody stepped on his foot.

He struggled to his feet again, reached for his carry-on bag under the seat. When he jerked on the handle, it snagged on something. He pushed at it with his foot, being jostled from behind and almost falling into the man from Seat B, waiting for Meers to get out. He yanked again, and heard a sound that meant there was a new, deep scratch on the expensive leather.

He looked up in time to have a filthy duffel bag fall from the overhead compartment into his face. A filthier hand appeared and yanked on the canvas strap, and the bag vanished into the press of bodies. Meers glimpsed a ragged man with a beard. How had such a man got aboard an airplane? he wondered. Could you buy airline tickets with food stamps?

Retrieving his briefcase and his laptop computer, he slung everything over his shoulders. It was another ten minutes of shuffling before he reached the closet at the front of the plane where a harried flight attendant was helping people reclaim their garment bags. He found his, grabbed it, and slung it over his shoulder. Then he waddled sideways toward the door and the jetway. On the way out he barked his shin against a folded golf cart leaning against the exit door. Then he was trudging up the jetway into O'Hare.

O'Hare. ORD. On a snowy night with one runway operating, an inner circle of Hell. Meers shuffled down the concourse with several million other lost souls, all looking to make a connection. Those who had abandoned all hope—at least for the night—slumped in chairs or against walls or just stood, asleep on their feet.

At O'Hare, connections were made not on shadowy street corners, cash for tiny baggies, but at the ends of infinite queues shaped, twisted, and re-doubled by yellow canvas bands strung between stainless steel poles, under lights as warm and homey as an operating theater. Meers found the right line and stood at the end of it. In ten minutes, he shoved his garment bag, his carry-on, his briefcase, and his laptop forward three feet with the tip of his shoe. Ten minutes later, he did it again. He was hungry.

When he reached the ticket counter the agent told him he had missed his connecting flight for home, and that there would be no more flights that night.

"However," she said, frowning at her computer screen, "I have one seat available on a flight to Atlanta. You ought to be able to make a connection from there in the morning." She looked up at him and smiled.

Meers took the rewritten ticket. The departure gate was a good three miles from where he stood. He shouldered his burdens and went off in search of food.

Everything was closed except one snack bar near his gate. Airport unions were on strike. The menu on the wall had been covered with a sheet of butcher paper, hand lettered: "Hot dogs $4. Cokes $2. No coffee." Behind the counter were two harried workers, a fiftyish woman with gray wisps of hair straggling from her paper cap, and a Hispanic man in his twenties with mustard and ketchup stains all over his apron.

When Meers was still a good distance away, the counterman suddenly threw down his hot dog tongs, snatched the hat from his head and crumpled it into a ball.

"I'm through with this shit!" he shouted. "I quit. *No mas!*" He continued to scream in Spanish as he ran through a door in the back. The woman was shouting his name, which was Eduardo, but the man paid no attention. He hit the red emergency bar on a fire door and an alarm sounded as he scrambled down stairs outside.

Meers could see a little through the glass. The Hispanic man was short and stocky, but a good runner. He charged away from the building. From somewhere beneath, two uniformed security guards charged out, guns in their hands. Eduardo was nowhere to be seen. The guards kept going. There was a flash of light. Gunfire? There was too much noise from jet engines for Meers to be sure. He shivered, and turned back toward the snack counter.

He was still ten people back in line when they announced his flight to Atlanta. He was three back when they made the second announcement. The gray-haired women, still distracted by the flight of Eduardo, slapped a hot dog into his hand and spilled a third of his Coke on the counter as another call came over the public address. Meers hurried to a stand-up counter. There were no onions, no relish. He squeezed some mustard out of a plastic packet, half of it squirting cleverly onto his tan overcoat. Cursing, dabbing at the mustard, Meers took a bite. It was lukewarm on one end, cold on the other.

Gulping Coke and choking down cold weenie and stale bun, Meers hurried to the boarding area, Down the jetway and into the 727. Most of the passengers were seated except a few struggling with crammed overhead compartments. He sidled down to seat 28B. In 28C was a woman who had to be three hundred pounds, most of it in the hips. In 28A was a man who was more like three-fifty, his face shiny with sweat. Meers looked around desperately, but he already knew this was the last, the absolute last seat on the plane.

The woman glared at him as she stood. Meers got his carry-on under the seat, then popped the overhead rack. There was about enough space to store a wallet. The next one was just as full. A flight attendant took his briefcase and laptop and hurried away.

He wedged himself into the seat. The lady wedged herself into hers. He felt his ribs compressing. From his right came gusts of a sickening lilac perfume. From the left, waves of stale terror.

"My first flight," the fat man confided.

"Oh, really?" Meers said.

"I'm real scared."

"No need to be." The fat lady scrambled in her purse for a box of tissue, then blew her nose loud enough to frighten a walrus. She crumpled the noisome tissue and dropped it on Meers' shoe.

They were pushed back, they taxied, they waited two hours and taxied some more, they were de-iced and waited another hour. All of which took much longer than it takes to tell about it. Then they were in the air. The fat man promptly threw up into the little white bag.

Atlanta. ATL. They landed under a thick pall of black smoke. Somewhere to the west, a large part of Georgia was tinder-dry and burning. Hartsfield International sweltered in hundred-degree heat, and soot swirled across the runways. It was dark as night.

The fat man had filled barf bags all through the flight. In spite of this, he had eaten like a starving hyena. Meers had been unable to eat. He could barely get his hands to his mouth. He had stared at the meal on his tray table, as immobilized as if bound to his seat, until the stewardess took it away.

Just before they reached the gate, the flight attendant arrived for the fat man's latest delivery. Meers eyed the bulging bottom of the bag in horror as it passed over his lap, but it didn't break.

The heat slammed him as he left the plane. It didn't abate when he entered the terminal. The air was thick, hot syrup. The forest fires had downed power lines, and the air conditioning was off. So were the lights. So were the computers and telephones.

Somehow the ticketing staff were still working, though Meers couldn't imagine how. He joined the endless line and began shuffling forward. He shuffled for five hours. At the end of that time, when he was nearing starvation, the agent told him he hadn't a hope of a connection to his home, but he could put Meers on a flight to Dallas–Fort Worth, where his chances would be better. The flight would leave in nine hours.

Meers roamed the ovenlike interior of the airport. None of the restaurants and snack bars were open. With no refrigeration and no electricity to run the stoves, there was no point. The bars were open and serving warm beer, but had not so much as a pretzel. People sat wilted in their chairs, stunned by the heat, looking out over the ashen landscape. A nuclear holocaust might look a lot like this, Meers thought.

A few profiteers were selling ice water at five dollars a bottle. The lines were enormous. Meers found a clear space against a wall and sat down on his luggage. When he leaned forward sweat dripped off his nose.

He heard a commotion, and saw a man approaching with boxes on a hand truck. He was the pied piper of Atlanta, trailed by a mob of jostling people.

He stopped at an empty vending machine. When he opened the front someone in the crowd started pulling at a box. Someone else grabbed the other end. The box burst and spilled Snickers bars on the floor. In moments all the boxes had been torn open. When the tide ebbed away, the delivery man sat on the floor, feeling himself cautiously, amazed he hadn't been ripped to shreds. He got up and wandered away.

Meers had snagged a bag of peanuts and a Three Musketeers. He ate every bite, then made himself as comfortable as possible against the wall and nodded off.

A lost soul was screaming. Meers opened his eyes, found himself curled up over his possessions, a rope of drool coming from his mouth. He wiped it away and sat up. Across the concourse a man in the remains of a suit and tie had gone berserk.

"Air!" he shrieked. "I gotta have air!" His shirt was torn at the neck, his coat on the floor. He swung a fire axe at a plate glass window. The axe bounced off and he swung it again, shattering the glass. He leaned out the window and tried to breathe the smoke outside. He shouted again and began struggling with his pants. His hands were spouting blood, deeply slashed on the jagged sill, but he didn't seem to notice.

Off he ran, naked but for his pants trailing from one ankle and a blue silk tie like a noose around his neck.

Half a dozen security guards converged on him. They hit the man with their nightsticks and sprayed pepper in his face. They zapped him with tasers until he flopped around like a fish slick with his own blood. Then they cuffed and hog-tied him and carried him away.

The flight to Dallas was another 727. Half the passengers were under ten years old, in Atlanta for a Peewee beauty contest. The boys were in tuxedos and the girls in evening gowns, or what was left of them after twenty-four hours living rough at the airport with no luggage. Some of them were cranky and some were playful, and all were spoiled rotten, so they either sat in their seats and screamed, or turned the aisle into a rough-and-tumble race track. Supervision consisted of the occasional fistfight between fathers when a child's nose was bloodied.

Meers had a window seat, next to a father who spent the whole flight carping about the judging. His son had not made the finals. The son, who Meers felt should have been left out for wolves to devour along with the afterbirth, sat on the aisle and spent his time tripping running children.

There was no meal. The catering services had been just as crippled as the snack bars at the airport. Meers was given a pack of salted peanuts.

Dallas–Fort Worth. DFW. It had been raining forty days and forty nights when the 727 landed. The runways were invisible under sheets of water. The mud between the taxiways was so deep and thick it swallowed jetliners like mammoths in a tar pit. Meers saw three planes mired to the wingtips. Passengers were deplaning into knee-deep muck, slogging toward buses unable to get any closer lest they sink and never be seen again.

The airport was almost empty. DFW was operating in spite of the weather, but flights were not arriving from other major hubs. Meers made it to the ticket counter, where the small line moved at glacial speed because only one agent had made it through the floods. When his turn came he was told all flights to his home had been canceled, but he could board a flight to Denver in six hours, where a connection could be made. It was on another airline, so he would have to take the automated tram to another terminal.

On the way to the tram he stopped at a phone booth. There was no dial tone. The one next to it was dead, too. All the public telephones in the airport were dead. The flood had washed them out. He knew his wife must be very worried by now. There had been no time for a call from O'Hare, and Atlanta and now Dallas were cut off. But surely the situation would be on the news. She would know he was stranded somewhere. It would be great to get back home to Annie. Annie and his two lovely daughters, Kimberly and . . .

He stopped walking, seized by panic. His heart was hammering. He couldn't recall the name of his youngest daughter. The airport was spinning around him, about to fly into a million pieces.

Megan! Her name was Megan. God, I must be punchy, he thought. Well, who wouldn't be? The hunger had made him light-headed. He breathed deeply and moved off toward the tram.

The door had closed behind him before he noticed the man lying on the floor at the other end of the car. There was no one else on board.

The man was curled up in a pool of vomit and spilled purple wine. He wore a filthy short jacket and had a canvas duffel bag at his feet. He looked like the man Meers had seen on arrival in Chicago, though that hardly seemed likely.

The tram made a few automated announcements, then pulled away from the concourse and out into the rain. It was pitch black. The rain pounded on the roof. There were flashes of distant lightning and a high, whistling wind. The tram pulled into the next concourse and the doors opened.

Three security guards in khaki uniforms stormed aboard. Without warning, one of them kicked the sleeping vagrant in the face. The man cried out, and the guards began battering him with their batons and boots. Blood and rotten teeth fountained from the man's mouth and nose. Peter Meers sat very still, his feet and knees drawn together protectively.

One of the security men took a handful of the screaming man's hair and another grabbed the seat of his pants, and they dragged him through the rear door of the tram and onto the platform. The third looked over at Meers. He smiled, touched the brim of his hat with his nightstick, and followed the others.

The door closed and the tram moved away. Meers could see the three still beating the man as the car moved out into the night.

Just short of the next concourse the lights flickered and went out, and the tram car stopped. Rain hammered down relentlessly. It gushed in rivers over the windows. Meers got up and paced his end of the car. He was careful not to walk as far as the stain of wine, urine, and blood at the other end, which looked black in the light of distant street lamps. He thought about what he had seen, and about his family waiting for him back home. He had never wanted so badly to get home.

After a few hours the lights came back on and the tram delivered him to the right concourse. He had to hurry to make the flight on time.

This time he was on a wide-bodied aircraft, a DC-10. There were not many passengers. He was assigned an aisle seat. The takeoff was a little bumpy, but once at altitude the plane rode smooth as a Cadillac on a showroom floor. This late at night he was given a box containing a tuna sandwich, a package of cookies, and some grapes. He ate it all, and was grateful. By the window was an old man wearing an overcoat and a fedora.

"All those lights down there," the old man said, gesturing toward the window. "All those little towns, little lives. Makes you wonder, huh?"

"About what?" Meers said.

"You don't feel a part of the world when you're up here," the man said. "Those people down there, going about their lives. Us up here, disconnected. They look up, see a few flashing lights. That's us."

Meers had no idea what the codger was getting at, but he nodded.

"Used to be the same feeling, in my day. Trains back then. Night trains. When you're traveling, you're out of your life. Going from somewhere to somewhere else, not really knowing where you are. You could lie there in your berth and look out the window at the night. Moonlight, starlight. Hear the crossing signals as you passed them, see the trucks waiting. Who was driving them? More lost souls." He fell silent, looking out at the lights below. Meers hoped that was the end of it.

"I always wear a hat now," the old man went on. "Had a little haberdasher shop in Oklahoma City, opened it right after the war. Not far from where that building blew up. Got into the haberdashery business just in time for men to stop wearing hats." He chuckled. "One day it's nineteen forty-nine, everybody wears hats. Then it's nineteen fifty, suddenly all the hats are gone. Some say it was Eisenhower. Ike didn't wear hats much. Well, I did okay. Sold a lot of cuff links. Men's hosiery, silk handkerchiefs. Now I travel. Mostly at night."

Meers smiled pleasantly and nodded.

"You ever feel that way? Cut off? Trapped in something you don't understand?" He didn't give Meers time to answer.

"I recall the first time I thought of it. Got my discharge in New Jersey, nineteen and forty-six. I took the train under the river. Came out where that World Trade Center is now. Say, they bombed that, too, didn't they? Anyway, I thought I'd see Times Square. I went to the subway token booth. Not much bigger than a phone booth, and there's this little . . . gnome in there. Dirty window, bars in front, a dip in the wooden counter so money could slide under the window, back and forth, money in, tokens out. It looked like that dip had been worn in the wood. Over the years, over the centuries. Like a glacier cutting through solid rock. I slid over my nickel and he slid back a token, and I asked him how to get to Times Square. He mumbled something. I had to ask him to repeat it, and he mumbled again. This time I got it, and I took my token. All that time he never looked at me, never looked up from that worn dip in the wood. I watched him for a while, and he never looked up. He answered more questions, and I thought he probably knew the route and schedule of every train in that system, where to get off, where to transfer.

"And I got the funniest thought. I was convinced he never left that booth. That he was a prisoner in there, a creature of the night, a troll down in the underground darkness where it was never daytime. That he'd long ago resigned himself to his lot, which was to sell tokens." The old man fell quiet, looking out the window and nodding to himself.

"Well," Meers said, reluctantly. "The night shift comes to an end, you know."

"It does?"

"Sure. The sun comes up. Somebody comes to relieve the guy. He goes home to his wife and children."

"Used to, maybe," the old man said. "Used to. Now he's trapped. Something happened—I don't know what—and he came loose from our world where the sun eventually does come up. But does it have to?"

"Well, of course it does."

"Does it? Seems to me it's been a long time since I've seen the sun. Seems I've been on this airplane ever so long, and I have no way of telling that it's actually getting anywhere. Maybe it isn't. Maybe the plane will never land, it'll just keep on its way from somewhere to somewhere else. Just like that train, a long time ago."

Meers didn't like the conversation. He was about to say something to the old man when he was touched lightly on the shoulder. He looked up to see a stewardess leaning toward him.

"Sir, the captain would like to speak to you in the cockpit."

For a moment the words simply didn't register. Captain? Cockpit?

"Sir, if you'd just come this way . . . ?"

Meers got up, glanced at the old man, who smiled and waved.

At first he could see little in the darkened cockpit. In front of the plane was clear night, stars, the twinkling lights of small towns. Then he saw the empty flight engineer's seat to his right. As he moved forward, he kicked empty cans. The cabin smelled of beer and cigar smoke. The captain turned around and gestured.

"Clear the crap off that and siddown," he said, around the cigar clamped in his teeth. Meers moved a pizza box with stale crusts off the copilot's chair, and slid into it. The pilot unfastened his harness and got up.

"If I don't take a crap in thirty seconds, I'm gonna do it in my drawers," he said, and started toward the rear. "Just hold 'er steady."

"Hey! Wait a goddam minute!"

"You got a problem with that?"

"Problem? I don't know how to fly an airplane!"

"What's to know?" The pilot was dancing up and down, but pointed to the instruments. "That's your compass. Keep her right where she is, three one zero. This here's your altimeter. Thirty-two thousand feet."

"But don't you have an autopilot?"

"Packed it in, weeks ago," the pilot muttered, and banged hard with his fist on an area with dials that weren't lit up. "Bastard. Look, I really gotta go."

And Meers was alone in the cockpit.

He had a wild notion to just get up, pretend this never happened. Return to his seat. Surely the pilot would come back. It had to be some sort of joke.

The plane seemed level and steady. He touched the column lightly, felt the plane nose down the tiniest bit, saw the altimeter move slowly. He pulled and the big bird settled back at thirty-two thousand.

He quickly learned the biggest problem a pilot faced on a long night flight: boredom. There was nothing to do but glance at the two dials from time to time. His mind wandered, back to what the old man had been saying. And it just didn't add up. Well, of course the plane was getting somewhere. He could see the lights moving beneath him. Those brighter lights at the horizon; could that be Denver? As for the sun not rising, that was just ridiculous. The world turned. One moment followed another. Eventually it was day.

The pilot came back in a cloud of cigar smoke. He reached into an open cooler near his seat and got out a can of beer, popped the top, and drained it in one gulp. He belched, crushed the can, and tossed it over his shoulder.

"Looks like I fucked up," he said, with no apparent concern. "Sent for the wrong guy. Sorry about that, pardner." He laughed.

"What do you mean?"

"Thought you was in the know. Looks like it was that old guy. Somebody wrote down the wrong seat number. Who's runnin' this fucking airline, anyway?"

Meers would have liked to know the same thing.

"Don't you have a copilot? What do you mean, 'in the know'?"

"Copilot had him a little accident. Night cops. They broke his fuckin' arm for him. He's in the hospital." The man shuddered. "Could be three, four months yet till he gets out."

"For a broken arm?"

The pilot gave him a tired look. He jerked his thumb back toward the cabin.

"Screw, why doncha? Get outta here. You'll get it, one of these days."

Meers stared at him, then got up.

"He's dead, anyway," the pilot said.

"Who's dead?" The pilot ignored him.

Meers made his way down the aisle. The old man seemed asleep. His eyes were slightly open, and so was his mouth. Meers reached over and lightly touched the old man's hand. It was cold.

A big fly with a metallic blue back crawled out of the old man's nostril and stood there, rubbing its hideous forelegs together.

Meers was out of his seat like a shot. He hurried five rows forward and collapsed into an empty seat. He was breathing hard. He couldn't work up any spit.

Later, he saw the stewardess put a blue blanket over the old man.

Denver. DEN. Tonight, it made Chicago seem like Bermuda. The sky was hard and fuming as dry ice, and the color of a hollow-point bullet. Temperature a few degrees below zero, but add in the windchill and it was cold enough to freeze rubber to the runway.

The huge plate glass windows rattled and bulged as Meers lurched down the concourse, his luggage caroming off his hips, ribs, and knees. A chill reached right through the floor and swept around his feet. He hurried into the men's room and set his bags down on the floor. He ran water in the sink and splashed it on his face. The room echoed with each drop of water.

He couldn't bear to look at himself in the mirror.

He had to find the airline ticket counter. Had to get his boarding pass. Needed to find the gate, board the plane, make his connection. He had to get home.

Something told him to get out. Get out now. Leave everything. Go.

He walked quickly through the nearly deserted departure area, slammed through the doors and out onto the frozen sidewalk. He hurried to the front of a rank of taxis. It was an old yellow Checker, a big, boxy, friendly sort of car. He got in the back.

"Where to, Mac?"

"Downtown. A good hotel."

"You got it." The cabdriver put his car in gear and carefully pulled out onto the packed snow and ice. Soon they were moving down the wide road away from the airport. Meers looked out the back window. The Denver Airport was like a cubist prairie schooner, a big, horribly expensive tent to house modern transients.

"One ugly mother, ain't she?" the cabbie said.

Meers saw the cabdriver in profile as the man looked in the rearview mirror. Bushy eyebrows under an old-fashioned yellow Checker Cab hat with a shiny black brim. A wide face, chin covered with stubble. Big hands on the wheel. The name on the cab medallion was V. KRZYWCZ. A New York medallion.

"Krizz-wozz," the man provided. "Virgil Krzywcz. Us Pollacks, we sold all our vowels to the frogs. Now we use all the consonants the Russians didn't have no use for." He chuckled.

"Aren't you a little far from home?" Meers ventured.

"Let me tell you a little story," Krzywcz said. "Once upon a time, a thousand years ago for all I know, I was takin' this fare in from La Guardia. To the Marriott, Times Square. I figure, that time of night, the Triborough, down the Roosevelt, there you are. But this guy'd looked at a map, it's gotta be the BQE, then the

Midtown Tunnel. Okay, I sez, it's your money. And whattaya know, we make pretty good time. Only coming outta the tunnel what do I see? Not the Empire State, but that fuckin' bitch of a terminal building. I'm in Denver. I never been ta Denver. So I looks back over my shoulder," Krzywcz suited the action to his words, and Meers got a whiff of truly terrible breath, "and no tunnel, just a lotta cars honkin' at me, me bein' stopped in my tracks. And that's the way it's been ever since."

Krzywcz accelerated through a yellow light and up onto an icy freeway. Meers saw a green sign indicating DOWNTOWN. Straight ahead, just above the horizon, was a full moon. Traffic was light, not surprising since the roadway was frozen hard. It didn't bother the cabbie, and the old Checker was steady as a rock.

"So you decided to stay out here?" Meers asked.

"Decided didn't have nothin' to do with it. You figure I went on a bender, drove here in a blackout, something like that?" Krzywcz looked over his shoulder at Meers. In a sweep of street-lamp light Meers saw the left side of the driver's face was black and swollen. His left eye was shut. There was a long, scabbed-over wound on his cheek, a slash that had not been stitched. "Well, suit yourself. Fact is, none of these roads go to New York. And believe me, buddy, I've tried 'em all."

Meers didn't know what to make of that statement.

"What happened to your face?" he asked.

"This? Had a little run-in with the night cops. A headlight out, would you believe it? I got lucky. One whack upside the head and they let me go. Hell, I've had a lot worse. A lot worse."

Hadn't the pilot said something about night cops? They had sent his copilot to the hospital. Something was very wrong here.

"What do you mean, these roads don't go to New York? It's an Interstate highway. They all connect."

"You're trying to make sense," Krzywcz said. "You'd better learn to stop that."

"What are you trying to tell me?" Meers asked, feeling his frustration rise. "What's going on?"

"You mean, are we in the fuckin' Twilight Zone, or something?" Krzywcz looked at Meers again, then back to the road, shaking his head. "You got me, pal. I think we're in Denver, all right. Only it's like Denver is all twisted up, or something."

"We're in hell," a voice said over the radio.

"Aw, shut the fuck up, Moskowitz, you stupid kike."

"It's the only thing that makes sense," the voice of Moskowitz said.

"It don't make no damn sense to me," Krzywcz shouted into his mike. "Look around you. You see any guys with pitchforks? Horns? You seen any burnin' pits full a . . . full a—"

"Brimstone?" Meers suggested.

"There you go. Brimstone." He gestured with the mike. "Moskowitz, my dispatcher," he explained to Meers. "You seen any lost souls screamin'?"

"I've heard plenty of screamin' souls over the radio," Moskowitz said. "I scream sometimes, myself. And I sure as shit am lost."

"Listen to him," Krzywcz said, with a chuckle. "I gotta listen to this shit every night."

"Why do ya think it's gotta be guys with horns?" Moskowitz went on. "That guy, that Dante, you think everything he said was right?"

"Moskowitz reads books," the cabby said over his shoulder.

"Why do you figure hell has to stay the same? You think they don't remodel? Look how many people there are today. Where they gonna put 'em? In the new suburbs, that's where. Hell useta have boats and horse wagons. Now it's got jet airplanes and cabs."

"And night cops, and hospitals, don't forget that."

"Shut your mouth, you dumb hunky!" Moskowitz shouted. "You know I don't want nobody to talk about that over my radio."

"Sorry, sorry." Krzywcz smirked over his shoulder and shrugged. *Hey, what can you do?* Meers smiled back weakly.

"It don't make sense any other way," Moskowitz went on. "My life is hell. Your life is hell. Everybody you get in that freakin' cab is livin' in hell. We died and gone to hell."

Krzywcz was furious again.

"Died, is it? You remember dyin'? Huh, Moskowitz? You sit in that stinking office livin' on pizza and 7-Up, nothin' happens for *months* in that shithole. You'd think you'd notice a thing like dyin'.'"

"Heart attack," Moskowitz shouted back. "I musta had a heart attack. And I floated outta my body, and they put me *here*. Right where I was before, only now it's *forever,* and now *I can't leave!* Either it's hell, or limbo."

"Aw, limbo up a rope. What's a Jew know about limbo? Or hell?" He switched off the radio, glanced again at Meers. "I think he means purgatory. You wanna know from hell, you ask a Catholic Pollack. We know hell."

Meers had finally had enough.

"I think you're both crazy," he said, defiantly.

"Yeah," Krzywcz agreed. "We oughta be, we been here long enough." He studied Meers in his mirror. "But you don't know, buddy. I could tell soon as you got in my cab. You're one a those airplane pukes. Round and round ya go, schleppin' your Gucci suitcases, cost what I make in a month. In and out of airports, off planes, onto planes. Round and round, and you think things are still makin' sense. You still think tomorrow comes after today and all roads go everywhere. You think that 'cause the sun went down, it's gonna come up again. You think two plus two is always gonna equal three."

"Four," Meers said.

"Huh?"

"Two plus two equals four."

"Well, pal, two plus two, sometimes it equals you can't get there from here. Sometimes two plus two equals a kick in the balls and a nightstick upside the head and a tunnel that don't go to Manhattan no more. Don't ask me why 'cause I don't know. If this is hell, then I guess we was bad, right? But I'm not that bad a guy. I went to mass, I didn't commit no crimes. But here I am. I got no home but this cab. I eat outta drive-thru's and I piss in beer bottles. I slipped offa something somewheres, I fell outta the world where you could go home after your shift. I turned inta one of the night people, like you."

Meers was not going to protest that he wasn't one of the "night people," whatever they were. He was a little afraid of the mad cabbie. But he couldn't follow the logic of it, and that made him stubborn.

"So we're in a different world, that's what you're saying?"

"Naw, we're still inna world. We're right *here,* we've always been here, night people, only nobody don't notice us, that we're in a box. The hooker on the stroll, they think she goes home when the sun comes up, with her pimp in the purple Caddy. Only they don't never go home. The street they're on, it don't lead home. That lonely DJ you hear on the radio. The subway motorman, it's night there alla time. The guy drivin' the long-haul truck. Janitors. Night watchmen."

"All of them?"

"How do I know all of 'em? I'm gonna drive my cab inna office building, ask the cleaning crew? 'Hey, you stuck in purgatory, like me?' "

"Not me."

"Yeah, you airplane pukes. Most of us, we *know.* Oh, some of 'em, they gone bugfuck. Nothin' left of 'em but eyeballs like gopher holes. But you been here long enough, you stop thinkin' you're gonna find that tunnel back home, you know? Except you 'passengers.' Like they sez in the program. In . . ."

"Denial."

"In denial. You said it. Look ahead there."

Meers looked out the windshield and there it was, just below the yellow moon. The sprawling canopy of the Denver Airport, like some exotic, poison rain-forest caterpillar. He stared at it as the cab eased down an off-ramp.

"Always a full moon in Denver," Krzywcz cackled. "Makes it nice for the werewolves. And all roads lead to the airport, which is bad news for airplane pukes."

Meers threw open the cab door and spilled out onto the frozen roadway. He

scrambled to his feet, hearing the shouts of the driver. He clambered up an embankment and onto the freeway, where he dodged six lanes of traffic and tumbled
down the other side. There were a lot of closed businesses there, warehouses, car
lots, and one that was open, a Circle-K market. He ran toward it, certain it would
vanish like a mirage, but when he hit the door it was wonderfully prosaic and
solid. Inside it was warm. Two clerks, a tall black youth and a teenage white girl,
stood behind the counter.

He paced up and down the abbreviated aisles, hoping he looked like someone
who belonged there. When he heard the door security buzzer, he picked up a box
of cereal and pretended to study it.

He saw two police officers walk past the counter. They've come for me, he
thought.

But the cops walked toward the back of the store. One opened the beer cooler,
while the other took a box and loaded it with donuts.

Both officers passed within ten feet of him. One had two six-packs of Coors
hooked in a black-gloved hand and he cradled a huge black weapon that had a
shotgun bore but a fat round magazine like a tommy gun. The other wore two automatic pistols on her belt. She glanced at Meers, and gave him a smile both insolent and sexual. She wore bright red lipstick.

They strolled past the clerks, who were very busy with other things, things that
put their backs to the police officers. They went out the door. There was a moment
of silence, then a huge explosion.

Meers saw a plate glass window shatter. Beyond it, the male cop was firing his
shotgun into the store as fast as he could pump it. His partner had a gun in each
hand.

He hit the floor in a snowstorm of corn flakes and shredded toilet paper. Both
cops were emptying their weapons, and they had a lot of ammunition. But finally
it was over. In the silence, he heard the police laughing, then opening their car
doors. He got to his knees and peeked over the ruined display counter.

The patrol car was backing out. He caught a glimpse of the woman drinking
from a beer can as the cruiser pulled out on the road. In a second, a yellow Checker
cab pulled into the lot, the battered face of Krzywcz behind the wheel. He saw
Meers and motioned frantically.

Shattered glass and raisin bran crunched under his feet as Meers walked down
the aisle. Behind the counter the black man was crouched down near the safe. The
girl was lying on her back in a pool of blood, holding her gut and moaning. Meers
hesitated, then Krzywcz leaned on the horn. He turned his back on the girl and
pushed out through the aluminum door frame, empty now of glass.

Krzywcz took it slow and careful out of the lot. Parked off to the left was the police car, headlights turned off, facing them. Meers couldn't breathe, but Krzywcz turned the other way and the police car did not move.

"They'll be piggin' out on beer and sinkers for a while," the cabbie said.

"That girl . . . she—"

"She'll be all right." Krzywcz pointed ahead at flashing red lights. In a moment an ambulance rushed by in the other direction. He hunched down in his seat until it had gone by. "Eventually."

"What is it with the hospital?" Meers asked. "Moskowitz didn't even—"

"Hospitals is where you get hurt," Krzywcz said. "There's diseases in hospitals. Your wounds, they get infected. They give you the wrong pills, make you puke your guts up. All kinds of things can go wrong. Then you hear about the 'experiments.' " He shook his head. "Better to stay out. Them night doctors and night nurses, they ain't human."

Meers asked, but Krzywcz would say no more about "experiments."

The cab pulled up to the terminal building and Meers got out. He ran.

They fired at him, but he kept running. They chased him, but he was pretty sure now they had lost him. He was out on the runways. A fog had moved in; the terminal was no longer visible.

This was no place for a human being, even on a summer night. He kept moving, avoiding the lumbering, shrieking silver whales that taxied through the darkness. He stopped by a low, poisonous blue strobe light that drove cold icepicks into his eyeballs every time it flashed. He had no idea where he was, no idea where to go.

" . . . help me . . ."

It was more whimper than word. It came from just beyond the range of the light.

" . . . for the love of God . . ."

Something was crawling toward him. It moved slowly into the light, a human figure pulling itself along with bloody hands. Meers fell back a step.

" . . . please help me . . ."

It was Eduardo, from the O'Hare snack bar. His white shirt was a few blood-soaked scraps, black in the alien light. His pants were gone. One of his legs was gone, too. Torn off. Shattered white thighbone protruded.

Meers became aware of others. Like beasts hovering beyond the range of the campfire, figures were suggested by a blue-steel glint, a patch of pale cheek. They were darkened patches against the black of night. They wore fighter-pilot black visors, black helmets, Terminator sunglasses. Shiny black boots, belts, and jackets creaked like motorcycle cops. Somewhere out there were ranks of black Harleys, he was sure of it. He smelled gun oil and old leather.

There were other shapes, other beasts. These were black, too, with fangs snarling blue in the night. They strained at their leashes, silently.

Meers began to back away. If he didn't make a sudden movement they might not come after him. Perhaps they hadn't even seen him.

Soon the shapes were swallowed back into the fog. Not once had he seen a distinct human figure.

Something brushed against his leg. He did not look down, but kept backing. Dark areas on the ground, seen peripherally, resembled body parts. But they were moving.

He heard a distant siren, saw flashing red and blue lights. A boxy white ambulance pulled up, a big orange stripe on its side with the words EMERGENCY RESCUE. The rear doors flew open. The light inside was dim and reddish. The angle was wrong for Meers to see very far inside. A black cloud of flies exploded into the air. He could hear them buzzing. A thick, black fluid seeped over the floor and ran over the bumper to pool on the frozen ground, steaming. Meers understood that in white light the stuff would be dark and red.

From the far side of the ambulance men and women appeared, clad in crisp whites or baggy surgical blues. They all wore gauze masks. The masks, their rubber-gloved hands, and their clothing were all spattered with gore. None of them had horns or carried pitchforks. Their attitude was efficient and workmanlike.

The doctors and nurses lifted Eduardo and tossed him into the open ambulance doors like a sack of laundry. One nurse loomed out of the fog with Eduardo's leg. The leg was twitching. She tossed it after Eduardo.

Meers was going backward at a walking pace now. A man in blue surgical scrubs looked in his direction. All the rest did, too. He turned and ran.

The world began to spin again, and this time it did not stop. He felt himself flying apart, and when he came back together, not everything fit in just the same way it had before. He felt much better. He was smiling.

He had found the terminal building again. He stood there on the sidewalk for a moment, getting his breathing under control. A big man with a battered face stood leaning against a taxi painted bright yellow with a checkerboard stripe down the side. The man held up a thumb. When Meers stared at him blankly, the cabbie switched to his middle finger and muttered something about "airplane pukes." Meers brushed snow and ice from his overcoat and ran his hands through his unruly hair. He entered the terminal.

Inside were Christmas lights, tinsel and holly. It was jammed with a sea of humanity, few of them showing any Christmas spirit.

He glanced to his left, and there was his luggage, sitting neatly against the wall. Meers hefted his possessions. Someone had put a strip of silver duct tape over the gash in his carry-on.

Meers was still smiling after three hours in line. The harried ticket agent smiled back at him, and told him there was no chance of reaching his home that night.

"You won't get home for Christmas morning," she said, "but I can get you on a flight to Chicago that's leaving in a few minutes."

"That'll be fine," Meers said, smiling. She wrote out the ticket.

"Happy holidays," she said.

"And a Merry Christmas to you," Meers said.

They were already announcing his flight. ". . . to Chicago, with stops at Amarillo, Oklahoma City, Topeka, Omaha, Rapid City, Fargo, Duluth, and Des Moines."

Christmas, Meers thought. Everyone trying to go somewhere at once. Pity the poor business traveler caught in the middle of it. Puddle-jumping through most of the medium-sized cities on the Great Plains. It sounded like air-travel hell. But he took heart. Soon he would be home with his family. Home with his sweet wife . . . and his lovely children . . . He was sure he'd think of their names in a moment.

He shouldered his burdens like Marley's Ghost shouldered the chains he had forged in life, and shuffled along with the slow crowd toward his boarding gate. He would be home in no time. No time at all.

INTRODUCTION TO

"Good Intentions"

I'm proud of this story for two reasons. One is that the editor at Playboy *told me she never thought she'd buy a Deal-with-the-Devil story. Every editor in the world has rejected a hundred Deal-with-the-Devil stories. Along with Adam-and-Eve stories (the last man and woman on Earth after a war/epidemic/whatever turn out to be named . . . Adam and Eve!), they are universally dreaded.*

Well, I never expected to write *a Deal-with-the-Devil story, either, but when you get an idea that feels the least bit original, you have to go with it.*

The other thing I'm proud of is selling it to Playboy. *For most freelance writers, a sale to* Playboy *is a sort of Holy Grail. This doesn't have a lot to do with whether one loves or hates the magazine itself. The attraction is very simple: I was paid $5,000 for this story. I normally wouldn't reveal that figure, but I do have a point here. There may be writers out there who would not publish in* Playboy *for political reasons, but I don't know any.*

When the story was to appear I went downtown to Powell's Books. This store is one of the many reasons to live in beautiful Portland, Oregon. It is by far the largest bookstore I have ever seen, and may be the largest in the English-speaking world. They carry new and used books on the same shelves, and magazines, talking books . . . whatever you want in literature, they've got it at Powell's.

Except Playboy.

I was shocked. Frankly, it never occurred to me that the store wouldn't carry it. When I was young in Port Arthur, Texas, certain magazines were kept either behind the counter or under *the counter in the shady bookstores and newsstands that carried them at all. Among them were things like* Sunshine & Health, *a black-and-white nudist magazine that provided me and my friends some much-needed education: our first basic understanding of female anatomy in those pre–sex education days.* Playboy *was behind the counter.*

During the sixties all those magazines and many more we couldn't even have imagined in 1958 came out into the open. They called it the "Sexual Revolution."

Now, in many places, all those magazines have gone back under the counter. Why? Because some people find some or all of their content objectionable. In the case of Playboy, it is the photographs of nude women.

I'm not going to indulge in a diatribe about political correctness here, though I believe it is one of the more noisome scourges of our age. It just seems ironic, how things have come full circle.

It used to be that, if caught with a copy of Playboy, one would scoff and say, "Oh, I just buy it for the writing." Yeah, right. But . . . it could be true. The list of serious fiction writers and essayists and political commentators who have contributed to this magazine over the years would run on for many pages. One science fiction writer contributor who comes to mind is Ursula K. LeGuin. I don't feel the need to apologize for being in her company.

And besides, they pay obscenely well.

GOOD INTENTIONS

JOSEPH HARDY SAT in the ruins of his congressional campaign early in the morning of the first Wednesday in November and wondered if there was anything more humiliating than having tens of thousands of people reject you and all you stood for.

Almost a year of kissing babies, eating rubber chicken and guzzling untold carloads of Maalox, ten thousand doors knocked on, a hundred thousand hands shaken, a marriage in trouble, and it had all come to this: a man alone in a big empty hall littered with squashed cigarette butts, red-white-and-blue bunting drooping to the floor. VOTE FOR HARDY signs nailed to wooden laths lay stacked like Confederate rifles at Appomattox. In one corner two dozen bottles of cheap California champagne sat unopened in galvanized tubs full of melting ice.

Onto this stage of dashed hopes, as he had so many times before, strode the Devil. Hardy knew at once that this was Satan, though he looked not at all remarkable and though the only commotion created by his appearance was among the caucus of exhausted balloons that squabbled briefly along the floor in his wake.

Satan stopped a few feet from where Hardy sat, regarded him silently for a time and then nodded slowly.

"Well, Joe," he said quietly. "What do you say?"

"You've got to be kidding."

The Devil simply shook his head and waited.

"I never wanted this job in the first place. They talked me into it. They said

Haggerty was getting too old. It didn't matter if he carried this district with seventy percent two years ago. 'We need a young face, that's what we need, Joe, a young face.'"

That face smiled at the Devil and Joseph Hardy from a hundred campaign posters taped to the walls. It was a good-looking face, stopping short of Kennedyesque. There was intelligence in it, mercifully not quite Stevensonian. Hardy wore horn-rimmed glasses befitting a college economics professor, which is what he was. He had good teeth.

"You can't lie to me, Joe," Satan said. "Yesterday you wanted it. We all saw your face when the early returns put you ahead. You wanted it more than you've ever wanted anything."

Hardy put his face into his hands and rubbed it for a long time. Then he looked up, exhausted.

"Talk to me," he said.

The sun was coming up when they reached the final terms.

"I won't compromise any of my ideas," Hardy said. "That's why I finally said yes. I think I can make a difference."

"It won't be a problem," Satan said calmly.

"I'm serious. No swaying with the winds. I don't care what the polls say, I won't alter a stand just to get votes."

"You won't have to."

"And no fat cats. No special interests. I want to limit campaign contributions to one hundred dollars, like Jerry Brown."

"Done."

"No negative advertising. No character assassination, no mudslinging. No Willie Horton."

"You're taking all the fun out of— All right, all right. Done."

"And I get . . . ?"

"A congressional seat in two years. In six, the Presidency." Satan waited, asking without words if there were any more points to discuss. Then he went to the phone bank across the room. He punched in his AT&T credit card number and spoke briefly to the party at the other end. In a moment the fax machine began to hum and he pulled out three pages of a contract. Taking out a ballpoint pen, he bent over a table and began marking up the boilerplate.

Hardy read it twice, folded it, put it into his pocket.

"I'll run this past my lawyer," he said, "but I think we've got a deal."

"I'll see you in his office tomorrow at three," said the Devil. "And in the meantime . . ." He held out his hand.

Hardy hesitated only a moment, then shook it. The Devil's hand was warm and dry and firm. He'd been afraid it would be clammy. He hated that.

"What should I call you?" Hardy asked.

" 'Nick' will do just fine."

"I don't care much for 'his immortal soul,' " said the attorney, a worthy named Cheatham. "And what's this about 'until the end of time'? The customary term would be 'in perpetuity.' "

"It means eternally," Nick said. "Forever."

"Um, yes, yes." Cheatham frowned. "Frankly, it seems like a long time."

"These are my standard terms. The duration is long, granted, but the reward is huge, and the payment . . . frankly, sir, most courts would see it as trivial."

"It being difficult to establish a market value for an immortal soul," Cheatham said, nodding. "I see your point. But look here: 'To be disposed of in whatever manner pleases the party of the first part.' " He looked owlishly over to Hardy. "It's all very vague, Joseph."

"Let it stand, Mr. Cheatham."

"Very well, very well. But I still don't think that I can sign off on the time element here." A little palpitation of sparks appeared around Nick's eyebrows, unseen by the lawyer, who was studying the ceiling as if the solution to the impasse might be written there. And perhaps it was, for he soon looked down and said portentously, "Why don't we make it a thousand years?"

Nick laughed.

"I ask for eternity and you offer a thousand?" he said. Then he leaned forward. "A billion years. My final offer."

They settled on 250,000 years, and Cheatham seemed satisfied.

"I imagine you'll want to show these amendments to your own attorneys," he said.

"No need," said Nick, hooking his thumbs in his vest. "Harvard Law, class of 1735."

While a secretary was preparing clean copies, a bottle of brandy was produced. Cheatham asked Nick what eventuality had led him to read for the law.

"The legal fees were eating me alive," Nick admitted. "I saw which way the wind was blowing, and I can't tell you how handy it's been."

Hardy took a stiff drink when the copies arrived and hardly hesitated before he signed. Nick bent over Cheatham's desk, then looked up at Hardy with a gleam in his eye.

"Don't worry, Joe," he said. "I know ways of making a hundred thousand years seem like an eternity." He signed each of the three copies, then straightened and said, "We should get started. How does tomorrow sound? Let's have lunch."

They met at a Chinese place for dim sum. They each stacked half a dozen of the little plates brought to the table by girls pushing carts and finished half a pot of tea.

"I suppose you've been wondering how we'll go about this," Nick said.

"I've thought of nothing else."

"Simplest thing in the world." Nick produced a small bottle with a glass stopper and set it on the table. "Concentrated charisma."

Hardy picked it up, looked at it, pulled the stopper and sniffed.

"Try not to spill it," Nick said. "Pretend it's thousand-dollar-an-ounce perfume. Just dab some on your face once a day."

Hardy applied some and felt nothing.

"Bit of a letdown," he muttered.

"Wait for it," Nick said, folding his arms. "The stuff's hard to come by. I collect it where I can find it. Baptist revival meetings are good; sometimes the stuff drips off the tent walls. You can find a bit around used-car lots, salesmen's conventions, get-rich-quick real estate seminars. And, of course, every year I get a lot of the stuff at the Oscar ceremonies." He shrugged. "I have to be out there, anyway, so what the heck."

"I thought I recognized you," someone said, and Hardy looked up to see that two waitresses had converged on the table. They had been serving Joe and Nick for half an hour without incident.

"Joseph Hardy!" said the other, putting her hand to her mouth. "I voted for you, Joe!"

"You and about three more," Hardy said. The waitresses laughed more than the feeble joke deserved.

"I didn't vote," the first one admitted, "but if you run again, I sure will. Here, take this, it's on the house." It was some sort of meat-stuffed dumplings.

Soon a buzz spread through the restaurant. The owner came by and tore up the check, and people began to ask for autographs. Nick sat back and watched, then during a lull reached over and touched Hardy's sleeve.

"Tough being in the public eye, eh?"

"What's that? Oh, Nick, sure. Why don't you try one of these dumplings with the spicy mustard?"

"Far too hot for me, I'm afraid. Joseph, I'll be going now. You won't see me for another five years. Look for me at primary time."

"What's that?" Hardy signed another napkin and glanced up. "Oh, sure, primary time. Uh . . . is there anything else I should know? Anything I need to do?"

"Just stick to your principles. I'll take care of the rest." He frowned slightly, taking one more look at his candidate. "Next time, be plain old Joe. And get a haircut. See if you can find Dan Quayle's barber."

The next five years passed like a montage in a Frank Capra film based on a Horatio Alger novel.

Joseph "Call Me Joe" Hardy returned to the campus and immediately his classes began to fill up. Within a term, the administration had twice moved him to a larger hall. The students loved his lectures and said he managed to make economics interesting for the first time ever. Applause was common.

Strangers approached him on the street to pump his hand. Reporters asked his comments on political issues. The camera loved him, they said. Radio talk-show hosts clamored for him to be interviewed and to field questions from callers. He had a folksy, common touch that showed to good advantage on the local *Nightline* knockoff, where his face became familiar to everyone in the state.

Even his marriage improved.

At the proper time he announced his candidacy for Congress. Party bigwigs couldn't have been happier. Although his opponent outspent him three to one, the election was never in doubt. Joe Hardy led in the polls from the first, and the only question come election day was the margin of his victory. He was sent to Washington with a stunning mandate and very little political baggage.

In D.C., he did a passable imitation of Jimmy Stewart for a few weeks, stumbling a few times, making a few mistakes as he got his office organized. But he was neither stupid nor innocent and soon was offering bills and fending off political action committees as if he'd done it all his life.

His reputation as a straight shooter was quickly established. It could have been a handicap, but Joe Hardy knew when to compromise to get things done and when to stand fast on a matter of principle. He was a man you could do business with, but you couldn't buy him. He earned the respect of most of his colleagues, grudging at first, genuine soon after.

There was jealousy, of course, from both parties. It wasn't every freshman Congressman who had Ted Koppel calling every other week to ask him to debate George Will or Ted Kennedy. Few new faces rated a twenty-minute profile on *Prime Time Live.* Hardy had an uncanny knack for picking up free exposure worth millions in a reelection campaign. He was returned for a second term by an even larger margin.

No one was surprised when he threw his hat into the ring for the upcoming presidential race.

* * *

Even a Capra movie must have trouble along the way, and some was brewing. Dark forces were gathering inside the Beltway, powerful forces stirring within think tanks, public relations firms, advertising agencies. Campaign committees representing his rivals from both parties began to circle Joe Hardy, sniffing for blood.

Soon after his name started coming up as a presidential hopeful, his opponents began their research. It went from his birth to his last vote on the House floor. It was quickly established that he was not an escaped mass murderer, a homosexual, an IRA terrorist or a communist spy. Still, the private detectives reading his grade school reports and interviewing every friend Hardy ever had were not discouraged.

There were persistent rumors, whispered here and there, of something really big. Some knockout punch, something to blow Joe Hardy out of the race before it'd really begun. The peepers vowed to find it, whatever it was, if they had to track leads straight through hell.

Which is exactly where the trail led them.

One by one they had returned, battered, scorched, empty-handed, until one day a tall, thin, pimply fellow walked into the offices of the Elect Peckem Committee and put a smoking document on the chairman's desk.

"It wasn't that tough," the hacker said smugly. "Old Scratch could use better security software. I was in and out of his hard disks before anybody knew what was happening."

JOE HARDY IN PACT WITH LUCIFER screamed the headline of the Manchester *Union Leader* two weeks before the New Hampshire primary. Next to the damning article was another quoting a CBS–*Wall Street Journal* poll conducted minutes after the announcement. Joe's standing had plummeted. He now stood only two percentage points above the chief rival for his party's nomination, Senator Peckem.

Nick found Joe secluded in his office. Joe leaped to his feet.

"How could you do this to me?" he screamed.

"Calm down, Joe. Just calm down. All is not lost."

"The deal was supposed to be confidential!"

"I know, Joe, and I couldn't be sorrier. I've hired a new security consultant, but the cat's out of the bag," he said.

"So stuff him back in! You're ... well, you know who you are. Can't you do that?"

"Unfortunately, my powers have limitations, Joe. I can't change what's already happened. As for that cat, however"—and now he smiled—"I've always preferred to skin it. And I know more than one way."

"Tonight Jay's guests are: From *Beverly Hills, 90210,* Jason Priestley. Congressman Joe Hardy. And special guest, Satan, Prince of Darkness. And now . . . Jay Leno!"

It was rough at first, as they'd known it would be. Leno skewered them during the monolog. But when Joe and Nick were finally seated, the tide began to turn. The two of them seemed relaxed, not at all ashamed or defensive, and, well, *interesting.* The audience wasn't on their side yet, but they were willing to listen.

So when the talk turned serious, Joe offered information about something that hadn't got much play in the press: the *terms* of the contract.

"If I had it to do all over," Joe said with a pensive frown, "would I? I really don't know, Jay. But you read it yourself. Of all the candidates in this race, I am the only one guaranteed not to stoop to attack advertising. You saw it there in black and white. I won't abandon a stand I've taken for a cheap political motive. There'll be no flip-flopping on the issues from Joe Hardy. I won't say one thing in Boston and something else in Atlanta. I want to be your President, and I want to do it solely with the small contributions of the working class and the middle class of this great country. I can't do otherwise. It's in my contract."

"And if he were to break it," Nick said with a devilish grin, "I'd be sure to give him hell."

The next day, on *The Joan Rivers Show,* Nick tackled the question of his role as the Great Adversary with a casual wave of his hand.

"That's been blown way out of proportion," he said. "Remember, He and I used to be good friends. We had a falling out, it's true, but He *did* create me, and I'm part of His plan. You might say I'm just doing my job." The grin on his face as he said this was infectious.

To Arsenio, Nick said, "I have to say this Lord of Evil business is mostly a bad rap, my friend. *Darkness,* yes. But that can be cool."

Discussing his methods with Regis and Kathie Lee, Nick said, "We both move in mysterious ways, God and me. It's true, I *am* out to get your soul and I *do* send it to hell. But have you been there lately?"

That's exactly where Dan Rather went with a television crew. He reported back with footage that suggested a medium-security federal prison. "We saw no fire and brimstone," Rather said, wearing his Afghan-war safari jacket. "Make of that what you will; we were not given free run of the facilities. Still, all in all, Manuel Noriega doesn't have it much better than what we were shown."

Geraldo sneaked to the outskirts of Hades shortly afterward, was roughed up by succubi and was ejected. He claimed to have been sucker-punched by the head succubus, but she denied everything and had a lurid videotape to back her story. When it aired the tape, *A Current Affair* drew an enormous audience rating.

Oprah claimed to be worried by something: Could one love God and still deal with Satan? Nick convulsed her audience by retorting, "Me and God? It's true we don't double-date. Think of us as Siskel and Ebert."

Slowly Joe edged back up in the polls as voters adjusted to the new playing field. Many seemed to feel they'd faced considerably worse choices most election years.

On primary day, New Hampshiremen slogged through a snowstorm to give Hardy 38 percent of the vote, ten points more than his nearest rival.

The nearest rival was Senator Peter Peckem, and upon viewing the exit polls, Peckem slammed his fist onto his desk and growled to his assembled campaign staff: "That's enough of that crap. You're all fired." He was on the telephone before the last of them had scampered through the door.

Within the hour he had spoken to Phillips Petroleum, General Motors, Matsushita, Dow Chemical, McDonnell Douglas, Toshiba and was working his way through the Fortune 500. The message was the same: I need lots of money and I need it now. Send it and I'm your boy. It was very much like a stock offering. By midnight he was a wholly owned subsidiary, and the money was pouring into offshore laundries from Bimini to the Cayman Islands.

His last act before retiring for the night was to hire a new campaign manager, a man by the name of Yerkamov, famous for engineering the reelection of an eighty-two-year-old senator from a Southern tidewater state shortly after that worthy's conviction on a charge of statutory rape.

Yerkamov hired the advertising firm of Mayerd & Scheisskopf, the Charity Crackerjack public relations agency, a top pollster, a speechwriter and a political psychologist. By the time the sun set on the ruins of New Hampshire, the revivified Peckem campaign had come out of its corner swinging.

"Let me show you something, Joe," Nick said, pressing a button on a VCR remote control. On the screen, in grainy black-and-white, Japanese torpedo bombers swooped over Pearl Harbor. The *Arizona* exploded and sank. Hordes of troops waved rising-sun flags and shouted "Banzai!" And a deep, concerned voice said: "The Matsushita company likes Senator Peckem. Sony likes him, too, and so does Toshiba. If they didn't, they wouldn't be funneling millions into his campaign through their fat-cat lobbyists and special-interest political action committees. Joe Hardy stands for the American worker. Who will you vote for—Joe Hardy or the senator from Toyota?"

"Are you out of your mind?" Hardy gasped, leaping from his seat.

"Just thought I'd run it past you."

"Why don't you show the bomb falling on Hiroshima, too? Maybe I could take credit for that."

"Actually, the next one . . ." Nick tapped another videocassette box thoughtfully against his chin.

"No, never! The agreement was, no attack ads."

"I wouldn't call this precisely an attack ad," Nick wheedled. "We do know it's true, about the Japanese contributions. Peckem has sold out to every—"

"That's his problem. No one will own me when I'm President, and I'll do it without stooping to . . ." He noticed the look on Nick's face. "What's the matter? Is something wrong?"

"Wrong? No, nothing." Nick sighed deeply. "I don't like those new numbers from Florida, that's all."

It wasn't just Florida. Hardy's support was eroding in Massachusetts, Tennessee, Delaware . . . across the board in the upcoming Super Tuesday primaries and caucuses. He had held his early strength in Maine and South Dakota, but by the time Super Tuesday rolled around, he'd slipped an average of three points in the eight early March races. Peckem, written off by many pundits in February, was being called a slugger, a man with staying power, not afraid to take off the gloves and mix it up at the line of scrimmage, coming up on the rail.

These things don't happen spontaneously. Voters in the twelve Super Tuesday states were being surveyed, pamphleted, focus-grouped, phone-banked and sound-bitten more thoroughly than in any previous election. All over the South, people sat in conference rooms and theaters to have their sweat glands, heartbeats, blood pressure and breathing rates monitored as they listened to trial speeches or discussed the issues. Computer-guided laser beams were being bounced off eyeballs as test groups watched new commercials. Semanticists and programmers had developed an all-purpose speech that could, within two seconds, be tailored not only to small constituencies in a particular state but also to individual zip codes within the state. Peckem could promise one thing at nine A.M. at the Masonic Lodge and something completely different two miles across town at ten.

The usual hot-button issues had been identified, and Hardy's weaknesses in each category carefully plotted. He had once said that school prayer might make Islamic or Buddhist students uncomfortable. By the time Mayerd & Scheisskopf were through with it, Hardy sounded like a goddamn atheist. Once, Joe had opined that burning the flag might be protected by the First Amendment. The Charity Crackerjack agency soon had him using Old Glory for toilet paper. But the best purchase Yerkamov made turned out to be Peckem's speechwriter. He came up with a catchphrase widely viewed as the best since "Read my lips." It quickly became a chant at Peckem rallies and spread rapidly through society, and it went like this:

"To hell with that!"

Do you want the man who stands for higher taxes and being soft on criminals?

"To hell with that!"

The man who wants to keep this great country headed down the road to mediocrity, who sends your tax dollars overseas whenever his liberal friends tell him to, who doesn't give a damn about the jobs of working men and women in America?

"To hell with *that!*"

Who wants to close the military base in this fair city, shut the sawmills, cancel the weapons systems, kowtow to the Japanese, truckle to the Arabs, deny you the right to pray . . . the man who says I can't get elected because he's made a deal with the Devil?

"To hell with that, to hell with *that,* to hell with THAT!"

Elect Peckem was outspending Vote for Hardy fifty to one, but the crowning blow was yet to come.

"It was the charisma," Joe whined when the story broke.

"Charisma my forked tail." Nick steamed, pacing the floor. "Charisma my aching horns. It was your not keeping your pants zipped."

Nick was not being completely fair. One of the hazards of charisma use, discovered by many a politician before Joe Hardy, was the bimbo factor. It attracted bimbos as sugar brings flies, and in the first heady days Joe had succumbed to the charms of several.

"Several? Hah!" Nick huffed.

"OK, OK. Let's call it a few score." Of that number, Peckem's troops had found four willing to tell their stories. Worse, two of them had proof.

Far, far worse, Mrs. Hardy did the unthinkable. After a short, sharp meeting with Joe, she filed for divorce and flew off to the Bahamas.

"So what are we going to do now?" Hardy asked.

"We have a little money," Nick mused. "Not what we should have, but some. Of course, I'll need your permission." He pulled a videocassette from his pocket and put it on the table between them.

The Pearl Harbor ad started running on Saturday, along with three others of equal virtue. Hardy applied a triple dose of charisma and appeared with Nick on *Meet the Press* on Sunday. By Monday the polls had begun a ponderous swing in his favor.

Super Tuesday found him winning by small margins in seven states, losing in three, with Texas and Florida too close to call.

Old Scratch sat in the ruins of a presidential campaign early in the morning of the second Wednesday in March and wondered if God was laughing.

Joe Hardy entered the room, along with a burst of noise from Hardy faithfuls partying into the night in the next room. Joe held a bottle of Dom Perignon and a glass and he staggered slightly. His shoulders were littered with confetti and draped with ticker tape. His hair was unruly.

"So," he said, burping. "On to Illinois?"

"It's over, Joe," Nick said.

"What do you mean, 'it's over'? We won!"

What a pathetic thing his man had become, Nick marveled. He'd been a lot easier to take back in the days before the contact lenses, before the new barber. Back in the days of cheap California champagne. Now he was more of a sound bite than a man. Hardy must have known this, at some level, or he wouldn't be drunk so much.

"You call that a win?" Nick handed Joe a long sheet of Teletype paper. Key sentences and words had been highlighted with a yellow marker. "Did you catch the NBC special? Did you hear what John Chancellor had to say?"

"I was—"

"Those are tomorrow's columns you've got in your hands. They're saying the secret word, Joe, the one they've been hinting at for weeks. 'Unelectable.' And the duck comes down but you don't win a hundred dollars."

"We didn't do so bad in—"

"You don't win anything." Nick cupped his hand to his ear. "Hear that sound, Joe? That's the sound of the press corps beating a retreat. A dozen of them have already left to cover Peckem. By morning the bus will be half full. By next week, who knows?"

Hardy was leafing through the Teletypes with a baffled expression.

"That's right," Nick said. "Read it and weep. Look at what Evans and Novak are saying. And get a load of that Royko column: 'The Senator from Toyota versus the Congresscritter from Hell.' When you've got the time, play that tape over there, see what Letterman had to say about you a few hours ago. With spin like that, we're sunk."

"But we won, damn it!"

"By three points in two states. And we lost two we were supposed to win."

"But we're still ahead!"

"That matters only in the general election. What matters in the primaries is fulfilling predictions, sustaining momentum. Joe, if the polls have you at seventy percent, and you get sixty-five, you *lose!* Just ask Lyndon Johnson. I did, ten minutes ago."

"You spoke with—"

"Well, where did you *think* he would end up? He said to throw in the towel. And I haven't even told you the worst of it yet."

"There's worse?"

"Exit polls. That's what this is all about these days. A month ago the voters saw you as an attractive outsider. Now you rate as just another politician. Your approval rating has dropped below twenty percent."

"It was that damn ad," Joe accused. "The Pearl Harbor ad."

"Actually, no. They liked that. The voters say they hate a negative campaign, but they really get a charge out of it. Running that ad made you look scrappy. Like you won't take Peckem's allegations lying down."

"Then we'll just have to hit 'em harder," Joe said, tossing the papers aside and slapping his fist into his palm. "Let's run more of those ads. Lots more. Let's punch that bastard Peckem where it hurts."

"We're broke, Joe," Nick said. "We can't afford the airtime. The campaign's in debt almost a million dollars. The only reason we could borrow that much is some ex-S&L people owed me some corporate money."

"Well, let's accept larger contributions. I won't hold you to the letter of the contract. Maybe we could even get some corporate money."

"Great. You think people are lining up to give you money after a showing like today? Wise up."

"Then *make* some money. Snap your fingers, make a pile of it appear right here." Joe pounded the table, getting angry.

"Get thee behind me, politician. What, are you crazy? With the Federal Elections Commission breathing down our necks and the IRS snooping around?"

"But . . . you're the *Devil*, goddamn it! Why should you be afraid of Internal Revenue?"

"Obviously, you've never been audited," Nick said, shivering.

"Peckem gets away with it," Joe sniffed after a long silence.

"Peckem's organized, Joe. It takes time to put together a money laundry like that. He's insulated. He's got plausible deniability."

Nick stood and rubbed his face, then looked at Joe Hardy, standing with his shoulders slumped.

"Go home, Joe. Get some rest. It's over."

Joe nodded and turned to go, then looked back over his shoulder.

"What about my soul?"

"You're free to keep what's left of it."

Satan had never been quite so depressed. For a century he'd been feeling as if he were falling behind. He kept trying to adapt, did everything he could think of to modernize his operation. Then they did something new. Hitler, the H-bomb, global warming. Toxic wastes, the ozone layer. Deforestation. AIDS. Heavy-metal rock and roll. Jim and Tammy Bakker. *I wish I'd thought of that,* he'd say to himself, then scramble to catch up. And now this.

It was not the first time he'd lost a soul in contention, though his batting average was high. But it darn sure was the first time he had lost one through being unable to fulfill his own side of the bargain.

It was one heck of a note. In today's political world, if you weren't willing to lie, cheat and be bought, it looked as if not even the Devil himself could get you elected.

He had decided to catch the next shuttle to Hades, flog a few sinners, try to cheer himself up, when his beeper went off. He glanced at the number in the liquid crystal display, got out his cellular phone and dialed.

"Yeah, what is it, Ashtoreth?" He listened, then sighed and said, "All right, put him through." After a short pause, "Son of Chaos here. What can I do for you?

"Sure, I know who you are.

"Uh-huh. Uh-huh."

He sat up a little straighter.

"Talk to me," he said.

Yerkamov and Associates had the top floor of a twenty-story tower of black glass that dominated a sterile edge-city office complex in Bethesda with all the warmth of the slab gizmo in *2001*. Nick's heels echoed on black marble as he was whisked from the limo through a stainless-steel lobby and into a brushed-aluminum private elevator that deposited him before the glass desk of Yerkamov's receptionist. She'd been kicked out of the Miss America pageant. The judges thought she was too pretty. *Why can't I get help like that?* Nick wondered as she ushered him into the vast corner office with the million-dollar view of the Potomac and suburban Virginia. It was freezing cold.

Yerkamov was a fat little man with a bald head and rolled-up sleeves and sweat trickling down his neck. Sitting behind a big clean desk, he was almost obscured in a cloud of blue smoke. He leaned out of the cloud and thrust a chubby index finger at Nick.

"Reason I called," he said, brandishing a sheaf of computer printouts, "I was going through some polling data and I came across a little blip here when I ran Hardy versus Peckem." He chuckled. "Sort of a Ross Perot factor. Thing is, *you* tested higher than either of 'em."

"How interesting."

"I thought you might think so. The numbers from the Oprah show got my staff sitting up and howling at the moon. You do quite well across all the demographic lines. Young ones like that whiff of anarchy. Boomers find you trustworthy. Fatherly. Women enjoy the hint of danger." He got up and walked to the windows, puffing on his cigar. He looked over his shoulder. "Got any money?"

"People owe me favors. I can raise some."

Yerkamov nodded. "Of course, I can see a certain amount of trouble with the whole Prince of Darkness issue. Fly-god, Corrupter, Father of Lies. . . . Some of the nicknames you've picked up over the years."

"I prefer plain old Nick," said Lucifer.

"Sure, sure, and it plays better, too. And you've made a start on defusing that. With the right spin . . . Do you see where I'm going here?"

"I think I have the direction. Not so sure about the motivation."

Yerkamov shrugged. "My business is seeing the writing on the wall. If I head Peckem's reelection committee, I'll have to learn Japanese and see him only on visiting days. There's things even *I* can't make look good. Besides, I like to back a horse I understand."

He went over and sat on the edge of his desk. "Potential problem. What's your citizenship?"

"I have a United States passport."

"Not good enough if we're going all the way. Gotta be a natural-born citizen."

Nick thought it over.

"Hades is vast. I believe I could convince any court in the world that when I was cast down, I came to rest beneath New Jersey."

"That would explain a lot. Where do you live?"

"I maintain a condo in Dallas for tax purposes."

"Then here it is: governor of Texas in '94. Six years later . . ."

"The millennium . . ." Nick whispered, and the banked fires in his eyes blazed briefly. When he looked down he saw that Yerkamov had extended his hand. Nick took it. Yerkamov's hand was clammy, his grip flaccid. Nick hated that. He swallowed hard and pretended he didn't mind.

Hell, it was a small price to pay for the White House.

AUTHOR'S NOTE

I admit I made a teeny change here. I originally had Yerkamov offer Nick the junior senatorship from Texas in '94. Looking back, this seems more appropriate. They say Satan can take many forms. You don't suppose . . .

Probably not. I think Nick would have made a better president.

"The Bellman"

The second-most-asked question, as any writer will know, is "How do you go about getting an agent?" The answer is fairly simple, like the answer to the old question, "How do I get to Carnegie Hall?" Practice. Write stories, send them out, endure the rejection when it comes. When you have a few stories in print, there are agents out there who will take you on. (If you're not good enough to sell, no agent can help you.) Before that, few serious agents will look at your work; they don't have the time. There are "agents" who will read your stuff for a fee, and maybe send them out to magazines, but don't count on it. And don't count on their advice. If you need opinions and helpful criticism, workshops are a better place to get them.

Again, I was lucky. I hadn't even considered getting an agent. I sold some stories, started attracting some attention, and one day got a letter from Kirby McCauley asking if I was looking for representation. I wasn't, and was a little dubious of someone who seemed to be beating the bushes for clients. But I asked some of my new friends, and was told Kirby was very good, with a wonderful client list. He could hustle my works in foreign markets—which have been a significant source of income over the years—and had an affiliation with an agency in Hollywood. I went to New York, met him and instantly liked him, and we shook hands. That has been the basis of a relationship that has lasted about twenty-eight years now.

I can't begin to say how valuable Kirby has been to me, as agent and friend. He takes care of all the negotiating and business stuff that gives me a blinding headache. He has been there countless times to help me over a bad patch, as a writer's income tends to be sporadic: big chunks, and then nothing for a long time. I have made a living at this business for thirty years now, but I won't pretend it hasn't been dicey at times.

But it's the only life for me.

As Sergeant Pepper said, we're getting very near the end.
Here's a story from a time capsule. I wrote "The Bellman" back in the late seventies

after Harlan Ellison asked me to contribute to an anthology. I'm sure many of you were not even born when the first Dangerous Visions *book was published, to universal acclaim. It was followed soon after by* Again Dangerous Visions, *and was to conclude, logically enough, with* The Last Dangerous Visions, *And then something happened...*

I don't know exactly what it was, it was probably a series of things, but for some reason Harlan and the original publisher parted company. Ever since then, well over twenty years now, Harlan has been wandering in the publishing wilderness, and so far even his considerable powers of persuasion have been unable to get the book in print.

Did I say book? The last I heard TLDV was to be three thick volumes, with a cover price around one hundred dollars. I don't know if those are 1978 dollars.

Being Harlan, he was able to hang on to this story, and many others by other writers, long past the expiration of his rights to it. Half a dozen times in the past two decades, times when I really needed the money, I have reluctantly gone to him and said I really have *to sell "The Bellman." It's been years, Harlan. Be fair. Each time he convinced me to hang tough. No browbeating, no threats, never an angry word. It's just that when Harlan gets to talking about TLDV his passion is infectious; you end up wanting to let him keep the story for just one more year.*

I still do want that, I still hope to see TLDV in hard covers one day soon... but by then "The Bellman" will no longer be unpublished fiction, because I finally decided I couldn't wait any longer. Do I feel guilty? Yes, a bit. But I'm not the only one, and even if all the stories in it are not new on that fine publication day, I'm sure the book will be the blockbuster of the twenty-first century.

The whole Dangerous Visions *concept was a simple one. Harlan wanted stories you couldn't sell elsewhere, stories that were too controversial for the conventional magazines and book publishers. Dangerous stories.*

Many of the stories in the first two volumes did seem daring at the time, but the most dangerous stuff in the books was probably the introductions and afterwords Harlan wrote for each story. Taken together, it seemed there was almost as much wordage by the outspoken editor as by the collected authors... which is as it should be, since no one I know can churn up your guts as effectively as Harlan Ellison.

I don't really know if this story is "dangerous." It no longer looks as radical as it did when I wrote it, but so very, very much has happened since then. We're in a new millennium, and in many ways it is more wonderful and terrible than any of us poor SF prophets imagined it.

You decide.

THE BELLMAN

THE WOMAN STUMBLED down the long corridor, too tired to run. She was tall, her feet were bare, and her clothes were torn. She was far advanced in pregnancy.

Through a haze of pain, she saw a familiar blue light. Air lock. There was no place left to go. She opened the door and stepped inside, shut it behind her.

She faced the outer door, the one that led to vacuum. Quickly, she undogged the four levers that secured it. Overhead, a warning tone began to sound quietly, rhythmically. The outer door was now held shut by the air pressure inside the lock, and the inner door could not be opened until the outer latches were secured.

She heard noises from the corridor, but knew she was safe. Any attempt to force the outer door would set off enough alarms to bring the police and air department.

It was not until her ears popped that she realized her mistake. She started to scream, but it quickly died away with the last rush of air from her lungs. She continued to beat soundlessly on the metal walls for a time, until blood flowed from her mouth and nose. The blood bubbled.

As her eyes began to freeze, the outer door swung upward and she looked out on the lunar landscape. It was white and lovely in the sunlight, like the frost that soon coated her body.

Lieutenant Anna-Louise Bach seated herself in the diagnostic chair, leaned back, and put her feet in the stirrups. Dr. Erickson began inserting things into her. She looked away, studying the people in the waiting room through the glass wall to her left. She couldn't feel anything—which in itself was a disturbing sensation—but she didn't like the thought of all that hardware so close to her child.

He turned on the scanner and she faced the screen on her other side. Even after so long, she was not used to the sight of the inner walls of her uterus, the placenta, and the fetus. Everything seemed to throb, engorged with blood. It made her feel heavy, as though her hands and feet were too massive to lift; a different sensation entirely from the familiar heaviness of her breasts and belly.

And the child. Incredible that it could be hers. It didn't look like her at all. Just a standard squinch-faced, pink and puckered little ball. One tiny fist opened and shut. A leg kicked, and she felt the movement.

"Do you have a name for her yet?" the doctor asked.

"Joanna." She was sure he had asked that last week. He must be making conversation, she decided. It was unlikely he even recalled Bach's name.

"Nice," he said, distractedly, punching a note into his clipboard terminal. "Uh, I think we can work you in on Monday three weeks from now. That's two days before optimum, but the next free slot is six days after. Would that be convenient? You should be here at 0300 hours."

Bach sighed.

"I told you last time, I'm not coming in for the delivery. I'll take care of that myself."

"Now, uh . . . ," he glanced at his terminal, "Anna, you know we don't recommend that. I know it's getting popular, but—"

"It's Ms. Bach to you, and I heard that speech last time. And I've read the statistics. I know it's no more dangerous to have the kid by myself than it is in this damn fishbowl. So would you give me the goddam midwife and let me out of here? My lunch break is almost over."

He started to say something, but Bach widened her eyes slightly and her nostrils flared. Few people gave her any trouble when she looked at them like that, especially when she was wearing her sidearm.

Erikson reached around her and fumbled in the hair at the nape of her neck. He found the terminal and removed the tiny midwife she had worn for the last six months. It was gold, and about the size of a pea. Its function was neural and hormonal regulation. Wearing it, she had been able to avoid morning sickness, hot flashes, and the possibility of miscarriage from the exertions of her job. Erikson put it in a small plastic box, and took out another that looked just like it.

"This is the delivery midwife," he said, plugging it in. "It'll start labor at the right time, which in your case is the ninth of next month." He smiled, once again trying for a bedside manner. "That will make your daughter an Aquarius."

"I don't believe in astrology."

"I see. Well, keep the midwife in at all times. When your time comes, it will reroute your nerve impulses away from the pain centers in the brain. You'll experience the contractions in their full intensity, you see, but you won't perceive it as pain. Which, I'm told, makes all the difference. Of course, I wouldn't know."

"No, I suppose you wouldn't. Is there anything else I need to know, or can I go now?"

"I wish you'd reconsider," he said, peevishly. "You really should come into the natatorium. I must confess, I can't understand why so many women are choosing to go it alone these days."

Bach glanced around at the bright lights over the horde of women in the waiting room, the dozens sitting in examination alcoves, the glint of metal and the people in white coats rushing around with frowns on their faces. With each visit to this place the idea of her own bed, a pile of blankets, and a single candle looked better.

"Beats me," she said.

There was a jam on the Leystrasse feeder line, just before the carousel. Bach had to stand for fifteen minutes wedged in a tight mass of bodies, trying to protect her belly, listening to the shouts and screams ahead where the real crush was, feeling the sweat trickling down her sides. Someone near her was wearing shoes, and managed to step on her foot twice.

She arrived at the precinct station twenty minutes late, hurried through the rows of desks in the command center, and shut the door of her tiny office behind her. She had to turn sideways to get behind her desk, but she didn't mind that. Anything was worth it for that blessed door.

She had no sooner settled in her chair than she noticed a handwritten note on her desk, directing her to briefing room 330 at 1400 hours. She had five minutes.

One look around the briefing room gave her a queasy feeling of disorientation. Hadn't she just come from here? There were between two and three hundred officers seated in folding chairs. All were female, and visibly pregnant.

She spotted a familiar face, sidled awkwardly down a row, and sat beside Sergeant Inga Krupp. They touched palms.

"How's it with you?" Bach asked. She jerked her thumb toward Krupp's belly. "And how long?"

"Just fightin' gravity, trying not to let the entropy get me down. Two more weeks. How about you?"

"More like three. Girl or boy?"

"Girl."

"Me, too." Bach squirmed on the hard chair. Sitting was no longer her favorite position. Not that standing was all that great. "What is this? Some kind of medical thing?"

Krupp spoke quietly, from the corner of her mouth. "Keep it under your suit. The crosstalk is that pregnancy leave is being cut back."

"And half the force walks off the job tomorrow." Bach knew when she was being put on. The union was far too powerful for any reduction in the one-year child-rearing sabbatical. "Come on, what have you heard?"

Krupp shrugged, then eased down in her chair. "Nobody's said. But I don't think it's medical. You notice you don't know most of the people here? They come from all over the city."

Bach didn't have time to reply, because Commissioner Andrus had entered the room. He stepped up to a small podium and waited for quiet. When he got it, he spent a few seconds looking from face to face.

"You're probably wondering why I called you all here today."

There was a ripple of laughter. Andrus smiled briefly, but quickly became serious again.

"First the disclaimer. You all know of the provision in your contract relating to hazardous duty and pregnancy. It is not the policy of this department to endanger civilians, and each of you is carrying a civilian. Participation in the project I will outline is purely voluntary; nothing will appear in your records if you choose not to volunteer. Those of you who wish to leave now may do so."

He looked down and tactfully shuffled papers while about a dozen women filed out. Bach shifted uncomfortably. There was no denying she would feel diminished personally if she left. Long tradition decreed that an officer took what assignments were offered. But she felt a responsibility to protect Joanna.

She decided she was sick to death of desk work. There would be no harm in hearing him out.

Andrus looked up and smiled bleakly. "Thank you. Frankly, I hadn't expected so many to stay. Nevertheless, the rest of you may opt out at any time." He gave his attention to the straightening of his papers by tapping the bottom edges on the podium. He was a tall, cadaverous man with a big nose and hollows under his cheekbones. He would have looked menacing, but his tiny mouth and chin spoiled the effect.

"Perhaps I should warn you before—"

But the show had already begun. On a big holo screen behind him a picture leaped into focus. There was a collective gasp, and the room seemed to chill for a moment. Bach had to look away, queasy for the first time since her rookie days. Two women got up and hurried from the room.

"I'm sorry," Andrus said, looking over his shoulder and frowning. "I'd meant to prepare you for that. But none of this is pretty."

Bach forced her eyes back to the picture.

One does not spend twelve years in the homicide division of a metropolitan police force without becoming accustomed to the sight of violent death. Bach had seen it all and thought herself unshockable, but she had not reckoned on what someone had done to the woman on the screen.

The woman had been pregnant. Someone had performed an impromptu Caesarian section on her. She was opened up from the genitals to the breastbone. The incision was ragged, hacked in an irregular semicircle with a large flap of skin and muscle pulled to one side. Loops of intestine bulged through ruptured fascial tissue, still looking wet in the harsh photographer's light.

She was frozen solid, posed on a metal autopsy table with her head and shoulders up, slumped against a wall that was no longer there. It caused her body to balance on its buttocks. Her legs were in an attitude of repose, yet lifted at a slight angle to the table.

Her skin was faint blue and shiny, like mother-of-pearl, and her chin and throat were caked with rusty brown frozen blood. Her eyes were open, and strangely peaceful. She gazed at a spot just over Bach's left shoulder.

All that was bad enough, as bad as any atrocity Bach had ever seen. But the single detail that had leaped to her attention was a tiny hand, severed, lying frozen in the red mouth of the wound.

"Her name was Elfreda Tong, age twenty-seven, a life-long resident of New Dresden. We have a biographical sheet you can read later. She was reported missing three days ago, but nothing was developed.

"Yesterday we found this. Her body was in an air lock in the west quadrant, map reference delta-omicron-sigma 97. This is a new section of town, as yet underpopulated. The corridor in question leads nowhere, though in time it will connect a new warren with the Cross-Crisium.

"She was killed by decompression, not by wounds. Use-tapes from the air-lock service module reveal that she entered the lock alone, probably without a suit. She must have been pursued, else why would she have sought refuge in an air lock? In any case, she unsealed the outer door, knowing that the inner door could not then be moved." He sighed, and shook his head. "It might have worked, too, in an older lock. She had the misfortune to discover a design deficiency in the new-style locks, which are fitted with manual pressure controls on the corridor phone plates. It was simply never contemplated that anyone would want to enter a lock without a suit and unseal the outer door."

Bach shuddered. She could understand that thinking. In common with almost all Lunarians, she had a deep-seated fear of vacuum, impressed on her from her earliest days. Andrus went on.

"Pathology could not determine time of death, but computer records show a time line that might be significant. As those of you who work in homicide know, murder victims often disappear totally on Luna. They can be buried on the surface and never seen again. It would have been easy to do so in this case. Someone went to a lot of trouble to remove the fetus—for reasons we'll get to in a moment—and could have hidden the body fifty meters away. It's unlikely the crime would have been discovered.

"We theorize the murderer was rushed. Someone attempted to use the lock, found it not functioning because of the open outer door, and called repair service. The killer correctly assumed the frustrated citizen in the corridor would go to the next lock and return on the outside to determine the cause of the obstruction.

Which he did, to find Elfreda as you see her now. As you can see," he pointed to a round object partially concealed in the wound, "the killer was in such haste that he or she failed to get the entire fetus. This is the child's head, and of course you can see her hand."

Andrus coughed nervously and turned from the picture. From the back of the room, a woman hurried for the door.

"We believe the killer to be insane. Doubtless this act makes sense according to some tortured pathology unique to this individual. Psychology section says the killer is probably male. Which does not rule out female suspects.

"This is disturbing enough, of course. But aside from the fact that this sort of behavior is rarely isolated—the killer is compelled eventually to repeat it—we believe that Ms. Tong is not the first. Analysis of missing persons reveals a shocking percentage of pregnant females over the last two years. It seems that someone is on the loose who preys on expectant mothers, and may already have killed between fifteen and twenty of them."

Andrus looked up and stared directly at Bach for a moment, then fixed his gaze on several more women in turn.

"You will have guessed by now that we intend using you as bait."

Being bait was something Bach had managed to avoid in twelve eventful years on the force. It was not something that was useful in homicide work, which was a gratifyingly straightforward job in a world of fuzzy moral perplexities. Undercover operations did not appeal to her.

But she wanted to catch this killer, and she could not think of any other way to do it.

"Even this method is not very satisfactory," she said, back in her office. She had called in Sergeants Lisa Babcock and Erich Steiner to work with her on the case. "All we really have is computer printouts on the habits and profiles of the missing women. No physical evidence was developed at the murder scene."

Sergeant Babcock crossed her legs, and there was a faint whirring sound. Bach glanced down. It had been a while since the two of them had worked together. She had forgotten about the bionic legs.

Babcock had lost her real ones to a gang who cut them off with a chain knife and left her to die. She didn't, and the bionic replacements were to have been temporary while new ones were grown. But she had liked them, pointing out that a lot of police work was still legwork, and these didn't get tired. She was a small brunette woman with a long face and lazy eyes, one of the best officers Bach had ever worked with.

Steiner was a good man, too, but Bach picked him over several other qualified candidates simply because of his body. She had lusted after him for a long time, bedded him once, thirty-six weeks ago. He was Joanna's father, though he would never know it. He was also finely muscled, light brown, and hairless, three qualities Bach had never been able to resist.

"We'll be picking a place—taproom, sensorium, I don't know yet—and I'll start to frequent it. It'll take some time. He's not going to just jump out and grab a woman with a big belly. He'll probably try to lure her away to a safe place. Maybe feed her some kind of line. We've been studying the profiles of his victims—"

"You've decided the killer is male?" Babcock asked.

"No. They say it's likely. They're calling him 'The Bellman.' I don't know why."

"Lewis Carroll," Steiner said.

"Huh?"

Steiner made a wry face. "From 'The Hunting of the Snark.' But it was the snark that made people 'softly and suddenly vanish away,' not the Bellman. He *hunted* the snark."

Bach shrugged. "It won't be the first time we've screwed up a literary reference. Anyway, that's the code for this project: BELLMANXXX. Top security access." She tossed copies of bound computer printout at each of them. "Read this, and tell me your thoughts tomorrow. How long will it take you to get your current work squared away?"

"I could clear it up in an hour," Babcock said.

"I'll need a little more time."

"Okay. Get to work on it right now."

Steiner stood and edged around the door, and Bach followed Babcock into the noisy command center.

"When I get done, how about knocking off early?" Babcock suggested. "We could start looking for a spot to set this up."

"Fine. I'll treat you to dinner."

Hobson's Choice led a Jekyll and Hyde existence: a quiet and rather staid taproom by day, at night transformed by hologrammatic projection into the fastest fleshparlor in the East 380's. Bach and Babcock were interested in it because it fell midway between the posh establishments down at the Bedrock and the sleazy joints that dotted the Upper Concourses. It was on the sixtieth level, at the intersection of the Midtown Arterial slides, the Heidleburg Senkrechtstrasse lifts, and the shopping arcade that lined 387strasse. Half a sector had been torn out to make a parkcube, lined by sidewalk restaurants.

They were there now, sitting at a plastwood table waiting for their orders to arrive. Bach lit a cheroot, exhaled a thin cloud of lavender smoke, and looked at Babcock.

"What do you make of it?"

Babcock looked up from the printouts. She frowned, and her eyes lost their focus. Bach waited. Babcock was slow, but not stupid. She was methodical.

"Victims lower middle class to poor. Five out of work, seven on welfare."

"*Possible* victims," Bach emphasized.

"Okay. But some of them had better be victims, or we're not going to get anywhere. The only reason we're looking for the Bellman in these lower-middle-class taprooms is that it's something these women had in common. They were all lonely, according to the profiles."

Bach frowned. She didn't trust computer profiles. The information in the profiles was of two types: physical and psychological. The psych portion included school records, doctor visits, job data, and monitored conversations, all tossed together and developed into what amounted to a psychoanalysis. It was reliable, to a point.

Physical data was registered every time a citizen passed through a pressure door, traveled on a slideway or tube, spent money, or entered or left a locked room; in short, every time the citizen used an identiplate. Theoretically, the computers could construct a model showing where each citizen had gone on any day.

In practice, of course, it didn't work that way. After all, criminals owned computers, too.

"Only two of them had steady lovers," Babcock was saying. "Oddly, both of the lovers were women. And of the others, there seems to be a slight preference for homosex."

"Means nothing," Bach said.

"I don't know. There's also a predominance of male fetuses among the missing. Sixty percent."

Bach thought about it. "Are you suggesting these women didn't want the babies?"

"I'm not suggesting anything. I'm just curious."

The waiter arrived with their orders, and the Bellman was shelved while they ate.

"How is that stuff?" Babcock asked.

"This?" Bach paused to swallow, and regarded her plate judiciously. "It's okay. About what you'd expect at the price." She had ordered a tossed salad, steakplant and baked potato, and a stein of beer. The steakplant had a faint metallic taste, and was overdone. "How's yours?"

"Passable," she lisped around a mouthful. "Have you ever had real meat?"

Bach did not quite choke, but it was a close thing.

"No. And the idea makes me a little sick."

"I have," Babcock said.

Bach eyed her suspiciously, then nodded. "That's right. You emigrated from Earth, didn't you?"

"My family did. I was only nine at the time." She toyed with her beer mug. "Pa was a closet carnivore. Every Christmas he got a chicken and cooked it. Saved money for it most of the year."

"I'll bet he was shocked when he got up here."

"Maybe, a little. Oh, he knew there wasn't any black market meat up here. Hell, it was rare enough down there."

"What . . . what's a chicken?"

Babcock laughed. "Sort of a bird. I never saw one alive. And I never really liked it that much, either. I like steak better."

Bach thought it was perverted, but was fascinated anyway.

"What sort of steak?"

"From an animal called a cow. We only had it once."

"What did it taste like?"

Babcock reached over and speared the bite Bach had just carved. She popped it into her mouth.

"A lot like that. A little different. They never get the taste just right, you know?"

Bach didn't know—had not even realized that her steakplant was supposed to taste like cow—and felt they'd talked about it enough, especially at mealtime.

They returned to Hobson's that night. Bach was at the bar and saw Steiner and Babcock enter. They took a table across the dance floor from her. They were nude, faces elaborately painted, bodies shaved and oiled.

Bach was dressed in a manner she had avoided for eight months, in a blue lace maternity gown. It reached to her ankles and buttoned around her neck, covering everything but her protruding belly. There was one other woman dressed as she was, but in pink, and with a much smaller bulge. Between the two of them, they wore more clothing than everyone else in Hobson's put together.

Lunarians tended to dress lightly if at all, and what was covered was a matter of personal choice. But in fleshparlors it was what was uncovered that was important, and how it was emphasized and displayed. Bach didn't care for the places much. There was an air of desperation to them.

She was supposed to look forlorn. Damn it, if she'd wanted to act, she would have made a career on the stage. She brooded about her role as bait, considered calling the whole thing off.

"Very good. You look perfectly miserable."

She glanced up to see Babcock wink as she followed Steiner onto the dance floor. She almost smiled. All right, now she had a handle on it. Just think about the stinking job, all the things she'd rather be doing, and her face would take care of itself.

"Hey there!"

She knew instantly she'd hate him. He was on the stool next to her, his bulging pectorals glistening in the violet light. He had even, white teeth, a profile like a hatchet, and a candy-striped penis with a gold bell hanging from the pierced foreskin.

"I'm not feeling musically inclined," she said.

"Then what the hell are you doing here?"

Bach wished she knew.

"It's definitely the wrong sort of place," Babcock said, her eyes unfocused and staring at Bach's ceiling.

"That's the best news I've heard in months," Steiner said. There were dark circles under his eyes. It had been a strenuous night.

Bach waved him to silence and waited for Babcock to go on. For some reason, she had begun to feel that Babcock knew something about the Bellman, though she might not know she knew it. She rubbed her forehead and wondered if that made any sense.

The fact remained that when Babcock had said to wear blue instead of pink, Bach had done so. When she said to look lonely and in despair, Bach had done her best. Now she said Hobson's was wrong. Bach waited.

"I don't care if the computers say they spent their time in places like that," she said. "They probably did, but not toward the end. They would have wanted something quieter. For one thing, you don't take somebody home from a place like Hobson's. You fuck them on the dance floor." Steiner moaned, and Babcock grinned at him. "Remember, it was in the line of duty, Erich."

"Don't get me wrong," Steiner said. "You're delightful. But all night long? And my *feet* hurt."

"But why a quieter place?" Bach asked.

"I'm not sure. The depressive personalities. It's hard to cope with Hobson' s when you're depressed. They went there for uncomplicated fucking. But when they got really blue they went looking for a friend. And the Bellman would want a place where he could hope to take someone home. People won't take someone home unless they're getting serious."

That made sense to Bach. It followed the pattern of her own upbringing. In the crowded environment of Luna it was important to keep a space for yourself, a place you invited only special friends.

"So you think he made friends with them first."

"Again, I'm only speculating. Okay, look. None of them had any close friends. Most of them had boy fetuses, but they were homosexual. It was too late to abort. They're not sure they want the kids, they got into it in the first place because the idea of a kid sounded nice, but now they don't think they want a son. The decision is to keep it or give it to the state. They need someone to talk to." She let it hang there, looking at Bach.

It was all pretty tenuous, but what else was there to go on? And it wouldn't hurt to find another spot. It would probably help her nerves, not to mention Steiner's.

"Just the place for a snark," Steiner said.

"Is it?" Bach asked, studying the façade of the place and failing to notice Steiner's sarcasm.

Maybe it was the place to find the Bellman, she decided, but it didn't look too different from fifteen other places the team had haunted in three weeks.

It was called The Gong, for reasons which were not apparent. It was an out-of-the-way taproom on 511strasse, level seventy-three. Steiner and Babcock went in and Bach walked twice around the block to be sure she was not associated with them, then entered.

The lighting was subdued without making her wish for a flashlight. Only beer was served. There were booths, a long wooden bar with a brass rail and swiveling chairs, and a piano in one corner where a small, dark-haired woman was taking requests. The atmosphere was very twentieth-century, a little too quaint. She found a seat at one end of the bar.

Three hours passed.

Bach took it stoically. The first week had nearly driven her out of her mind. Now she seemed to have developed a facility for staring into space, or studying her reflection in the bar mirror, leaving her mind a blank.

But tonight was to be the last night. In a few hours she would lock herself in her apartment, light a candle beside her bed, and not come out until she was a mother.

"You look like you've lost your best friend. Can I buy you a drink?"

If I had a tenth-mark for every time I've heard that, Bach thought, but said, "Suit yourself."

He jingled as he sat, and Bach glanced down, then quickly up to his face. It was not the same man she had met on the first night at Hobson's. Genital bells had become the overnight sensation, bigger than pubic gardening had been three years before, when everyone ran around with tiny flowers growing in their crotches. When men wore the bells they were called dong-a-lings, or, with even more cloying cuteness, ding-a-lingams.

"If you ask me to ring your bell," Bach said, conversationally, "I'll bust your balls."

"Who, me?" he asked, innocently. "Farthest thing from my mind. Honest."

She knew it had been on his lips, but he was smiling so ingenuously she had to smile back. He put out his palm, and she pressed it.

"Louise Brecht," she said.

"I'm Ernst Freeman."

But he was not, not really, and it surprised Bach, and saddened her. He was by far the nicest man she had talked to in the last three weeks. She allowed him to coax out her make-believe life history, the one Babcock had written the second day, and he really seemed to care. Bach found she almost believed the story herself, her sense of frustration giving a verisimilitude to Louise Brecht's crashingly boring life that Bach had never really achieved before.

So it was a shock when she saw Babcock walk behind her on her way to the toilet.

Babcock and Steiner had not been idle during the twenty minutes she had been talking to "Freeman." A microphone hidden in Bach's clothing enabled them to hear the conversation, while Steiner operated a tiny television camera. The results were fed to a computer, which used voiceprint and photo analysis to produce a positive ident. If the result didn't match, Babcock was to leave a note to that effect in the toilet. Which she was presumably doing now.

Bach saw her go back to the table and sit down, then caught her eye in the mirror. Babcock nodded slightly, and Bach felt goose pimples break out. This might not be the Bellman—he could be working any of a number of cons, or have something else in mind for her—but it was the first real break for the team.

She waited a decent interval, finishing a beer, then excused herself, saying she would be right back. She walked to the rear of the bar and through a curtain.

She pushed through the first door she saw, having been in so many taprooms lately that she felt she could have found the toilet with her feet shackled in a blackout. And indeed it seemed to be the right place. It was twentieth-century design, with ceramic washbasins, urinals, and commodes, the latter discretely hidden in metal stalls. But a quick search failed to produce the expected note. Frowning, she pushed back out through the swinging door, and nearly bumped into the piano player, who had been on her way in.

"Excuse me," Bach murmured, and looked at the door. It said "Men."

"Peculiarity of The Gong," the piano player said. "Twentieth century, remember? They were segregated."

"Of course. Silly of me."

The correct door was across the hall, plainly marked "Women." Bach went in, found the note taped to the inside of one of the stall doors. It was the product of the tiny faxprinter Babcock carried in her purse, and crammed a lot of fine print onto an eight-by-twelve-millimeter sheet.

She opened her maternity dress, sat down, and began to read.

His real, registered name was Bigfucker Jones. With a handle like that, Bach was not surprised that he used aliases. But the name had been of his own choosing. He had been born Ellen Miller, on Earth. Miller had been a negro, and her race and sex changes had been an attempt to lose a criminal record and evade the police. Both Miller and Jones had been involved in everything from robbery to meatlegging to murder. He had served several terms, including a transportation to the penal colony in Copernicus. When his term was up, he had elected to stay on Luna.

Which meant nothing as far as the Bellman was concerned. She had been hoping for some sort of sexual perversion record, which would have jibed more closely with the profile on the Bellman. For Jones to be the Bellman, there should have been money involved.

It was not until Bach saw the piano player's red shoes under the toilet stall door that something which had been nagging at her came to the surface. Why had she been going into the males-only toilet? Then something was tossed under the door, and there was a bright purple flash.

Bach began to laugh. She stood up, fastening her buttons.

"Oh, no," she said, between giggles. "That's not going to work on *me*. I always wondered what it'd be like to have somebody throw a flashball at me." She opened the stall door. The piano player was there, just putting her protective goggles back in her pocket.

"You must read too many cheap thriller novels," Bach told her, still laughing. "Don't you know those things are out of date?"

The woman shrugged, spreading her hands with a rueful expression. "I just do what I'm told."

Bach made a long face, then burst out laughing again.

"But you should know a flashball doesn't work unless you slip the victim the primer drug beforehand."

"The beer?" the woman suggested, helpfully.

"Oh, wow! You mean you . . . and, and that guy with the comic-book name . . . oh, wow!" She couldn't help it, she just had to laugh aloud again. In a way, she felt sorry for the woman. "Well, what can I tell you? It didn't work. The warranty must have expired, or something." She was about to tell the woman she was under arrest, but somehow she didn't want to hurt her feelings.

"Back to the old drawing board, I guess," the woman said. "Oh, yeah, while

I've got you here, I'd like for you to go to the West 500th tube station, one level up. Take this paper with you, and punch this destination. As you punch each number, forget it. When you've done that, swallow the paper. You have all that?"

Bach frowned at the paper. "West 500th, forget the number, eat the paper." She sighed. "Well, I guess I can handle that. But hey, you gotta remember I'm doing this just as a favor to you. Just as soon as I get back, I'm going to—"

"Okay, okay. Just do it. Exactly as I said. I know you're humoring me, but let's just pretend the flashball worked, okay?"

It seemed like a reasonable enough suggestion. It was just the break Bach needed. Obviously, this woman and Jones were connected with the Bellman, whoever he or she was. Here was Bach's big chance to catch him. Of course, she was not going to forget the number.

She was about to warn the woman she would be arrested as soon as she returned from the address, but she was interrupted again.

"Go out the back door. And don't waste any time. Don't listen to anything anyone else says until someone says 'I tell you three times.' Then you can pretend the game is over."

"All right." Bach was excited at the prospect. Here at last was the sort of high adventure that everyone thought was a big part of police work. Actually, as Bach knew well, police work was dull as Muzak.

"And I'll take that robe."

Bach handed it to her, and hurried out the back door wearing nothing but a big grin.

It was astonishing. One by one she punched in the numbers, and one by one they vanished from her mind. She was left with a piece of paper that might have been printed in Swahili.

"What do you know," she said to herself, alone in the two-seat capsule. She laughed, crumpled the paper, and popped it into her mouth, just like a spy.

She had no idea where she might be. The capsule had shunted around for almost half an hour, and come to rest in a private tube station just like thousands of others. There had been a man on hand for her arrival. She smiled at him.

"Are you the one I'm supposed to see?" she asked.

He said something, but it was gibberish. He frowned when it became clear she didn't understand him. It took her a moment to see what the problem was.

"I'm sorry, but I'm not supposed to listen to anyone." She shrugged, helplessly. "I had no idea it would work so well."

He began gesturing with something in his hands, and her brow furrowed, then she grinned widely.

"Charades? Okay. Sounds like . . ." But he kept waving the object at her. It was a pair of handcuffs.

"Oh, all right. If it'll make you happy." She held out her wrists, close together, and he snapped them on.

"I tell you three times," he said.

Bach began to scream.

It took hours to put her mind back together. For the longest time she could do nothing but shake and whimper and puke. Gradually she became aware of her surroundings. She was in a stripped apartment room, lying on a bare floor. The place smelled of urine and vomit and fear.

She lifted her head cautiously. There were red streaks on the walls, some of them bright and new, others almost brown. She tried to sit up, and winced. Her fingertips were raw and bloody.

She tried the door first, but it didn't even have an interior handle. She probed around the racks, biting her tongue when the pain became too great in her shackled hands, satisfied herself that it could not be opened. She sat down again and considered her situation. It did not look promising, but she made her preparations to do what she could.

It might have been two hours before the door opened. She had no way to tell. It was the same man, this time accompanied by an unfamiliar woman. They both stood back and let the door swing inward, wary of an ambush. Bach cowered in the far corner, and as they approached she began to scream again.

Something gleamed in the man's hand. It was a chain knife. The rubber grip containing the battery nestled in his palm and the blunt, fifteen-centimeter blade pointed out, rimmed with hundreds of tiny teeth. The man squeezed the grip, and the knife emitted a high whine as the chain blurred into motion. Bach screamed louder, and got to her feet, backed against the wall. Her whole posture betrayed defenselessness, and evidently they fell for it just enough because when she kicked at the man's throat his answering slash was a little bit too late, missing her leg, and he didn't get another try. He hit the floor, coughing blood. Bach grabbed the knife as it fell.

The woman was unarmed, and she made the right decision, but again it was too late. She started toward the door, but tripped over Bach's outstretched leg and went down on her face.

Bach was going to kick her until she died, but all the activity had strained muscles that should not have been used so roughly; a cramp nearly doubled her over and she fell, arms out to break her fall and protect her stomach. Her manacled hands were going to hit the woman's arm and Bach didn't dare let go of the knife, nor did she dare take the fall on her abused fingertips, and while she agonized over what to do in that long second while she fell in the dreamy lunar gravity, her fists hit the floor just behind the woman's arm.

There was an almost inaudible buzzing sound. A fine spray of blood hit Bach's arm and shoulder, and the wall three meters across the room. And the woman's arm fell off.

Both of them stared at it for a moment. The woman's eyes registered astonishment as she looked over to Bach.

"There's no pain," she said, distinctly. Then she started to get up, forgetting about the arm that was no longer there, and fell over. She struggled for a while like an overturned turtle while the blood spurted and she turned very white, then she was still.

Bach got up awkwardly, her breath coming in quick gasps. She stood for a moment, getting herself under control.

The man was still alive, and his breathing was a lot worse than Bach's. She looked down at him. It seemed he might live. She looked at the chain knife in her hand, then knelt beside him, touched the tip of the blade to the side of his neck. When she stood up, it was certain that he would never again cut a child from a mother's body.

She hurried to the door and looked carefully left and right. No one was there. Apparently her screams had not been anything remarkable, or she had killed everyone involved.

She was fifty meters down the corridor before the labor pains began.

She didn't know where she was, but could tell it was not anywhere near where Elfreda Tong had met her death. This was an old part of town, mostly industrial, possibly up close to the surface. She kept trying doors, hoping to find a way into the public corridors where she would have a chance to make a phone call. But the doors that would open led to storerooms, while the ones that might have been offices were locked up for the night.

Finally one office door came open. She looked in, saw it led nowhere. She was about to close the door and resume her flight when she saw the telephone.

Her stomach muscles knotted again as she knelt behind the desk and punched BELLMANXXX. The screen came to life, and she hastily thumbed the switch to blacken it.

"Identify yourself, please."

"This is Lieutenant Bach, I've got a Code One, officer in trouble. I need you to trace this call and send me some help, and I need it quick."

"Anna, where are you?"

"Lisa?" She couldn't believe it was Babcock.

"Yes. I'm down at headquarters. We've been hoping you'd find a way to report in. Where do we go?"

"That's just it. I don't know. They used a flashball on me and made me forget where I went. And—"

"Yes, we know all that. Now. After you didn't show up for a couple minutes, we checked, and you were gone. So we arrested everyone in the place. We got Jones and the piano player."

"Then get *her* to tell you where I am."

"We already used her up, I'm afraid. Died under questioning. I don't think she knew, anyway. Whoever she worked for is very careful. As soon as we got the pentothal in her veins, her head blew itself all over the interrogation room. She was a junkie, we know that. We're being more careful with the man, but he knows even less than she did."

"Great."

"But you've got to get away from there, Lieutenant. It's terrible. You're in . . . shit, you know that." Babcock couldn't seem to go on for a moment, and when she did speak, her voice was shaking. "They're meatleggers, Anna. God help me, that's come to Luna now, too."

Bach's brow furrowed. "What are you talking about?"

"They procure meat for carnivores, goddam it. Flesh junkies. People who are determined to eat meat, and will pay any price."

"You're not trying to tell me . . ."

"Why the hell not?" Babcock flared. "Just look at it. On Earth there are still places you can raise animals, if you're careful. But here, we've got everything locked up so tight nobody dares try it. Somebody smells them, or the sewage monitors pick up traces of animal waste. Can't be done."

"Then why . . . ?"

"So what kind of meat's available?" Babcock went on, remorselessly. "There's tons of it on the hoof, all around you. You don't have to raise or hide it. You just harvest it when you have a customer."

"But cannibalism?" Bach said, faintly.

"Why not? Meat's meat, to someone who wants it. They sell human meat on Earth, too, and charge a high price because it's supposed to taste . . . ah. I think I'm going to be sick."

"Me, too." Bach felt another spasm in her stomach. "Uh, how about that trace? Have you found me yet?"

"Still proceeding. Seems to be some trouble."

Bach felt a chill. She had not expected that, but there was nothing to do but wait. Surely the computers would get through in time.

"Lisa. Babies? They want *babies*?"

Babcock sighed. "I don't understand it, either. If you see the Bellman, why don't you ask him? We know they trade in adults, too, if it makes you feel any better."

"Lisa, my baby's on her way."

"Dear God."

Several times in the next quarter hour Bach heard running feet. Once the door opened and someone stuck his head in, glanced around, and failed to see Bach behind the desk with one hand covering the ready light on the phone and the other gripping the chain knife. She used the time to saw through the metal band of her handcuffs with the knife. It only took a moment; those tiny razors were sharp.

Every few minutes Babcock would come back on the line with a comment like "We're getting routed through every two-mark enclave in Luna." That told Bach that the phone she was using was protected with anti-tracer devices. It was out of her hands now. The two computers—the Bellman's and Babcock's—matching wits, and her labor pains were coming every five minutes.

"Run!" Babcock shouted. "Get out of there, quick!"

Bach struggled to ignore the constriction in her gut, fought off fogginess. She just wanted to relax and give birth. Couldn't a person find any peace, anywhere?

"What? What happened?"

"Somebody at your end figured out that you might be using a phone. They know which one you're using, and they'll be there any second. Get out, quick!"

Bach got to her feet and looked out the door. Nothing. No sounds, no movement. Left or right?

It didn't seem to matter. She doubled over, holding her belly, and shuffled down the corridor.

At last, something different.

The door was marked FARM: AUTHORIZED PERSONNEL ONLY. PRESSURE SUIT AREA. Behind it was corn, corn growing on eight-meter-high stalks, corn in endless rows and files that made dizzying vanishing points in the distance.

Sunlight beat down through a clear plastic bubble—the harsh, white sunlight of Luna.

In ten minutes she was lost. At the same time, she knew where she was. If only she could get back to the phone, but it was surely under guard by now.

Discovering her location had been easy. She had picked one of the golden ears, long as her arm and fat as her thigh, peeled back the shuck, and there, on each thumb-sized yellow kernel was the trademark: a green discoloration in the shape of a laughing man with his arms folded across his chest. So she was in the Lunafood plantation. Oddly, it was only five levels above the precinct house, but it might as well have been a billion kilometers.

Being lost in the cornstalks didn't seems like such a bad idea just now. She hobbled down the rows as long as she could stay on her feet. Every step away from the walls should make the search that much more difficult. But her breathing was coming in huge gasps now, and she had the queasy urge to hold her hands tightly against her crotch.

It didn't hurt. The midwife was working, so while she was in the grip of the most intense sensations she had ever imagined, nothing hurt at all. But it could not be ignored, and her body did not want to keep moving. It wanted to lie down and give up. She wouldn't let it.

One foot in front of the other. Her bare feet were caked in mud. It was drier on the rows of mounds where the corn grew; she tried to stay on them, hoping to minimize her trail.

Hot. It must have been over fifty degrees, with high humidity. A steam bath. Sweat poured from her body. She watched it drip from her nose and chin as she plodded on.

Her universe narrowed to only two things: the sight of her feet moving mechanically in and out of her narrowed vision, and the band of tightness in her gut.

Then her feet were no longer visible. She worried over it for a moment, wondering where they had gone. In fact, nothing was visible at all.

She rolled over onto her back and spit out dirt. A stalk of corn had snapped off at the base when she tumbled into it. She had a clear view upward of the dome, a catwalk hanging below it, and about a dozen golden tassels far overhead, drooping languidly in the still air. It was pretty, the view from down here. The corn tassels all huddled close to the black patch of sky, with green stalks radiating away in all directions. It looked like a good place to stay. She never wanted to get up again.

And this time it hurt some, despite the midwife. She moaned, grabbed the fallen cornstalk in both hands, and gritted her teeth. When she opened her eyes again, the stalk was snapped in two.

Joanna was here.

Bach's eyes bulged in amazement and her mouth hung open. Something was moving down through her body, something far too large to be a baby, something that was surely going to split her wide open.

She relaxed for just a moment, breathing shallowly, not thinking of anything, and her hands went down over her belly. There was a round wet thing emerging from her. She felt its shape, found tiny hollows on the underside. How utterly amazing.

She smiled for the first time in a million years, and bore down. Her heels dug into the sod, then her toes, and her hips lifted from the black dirt. It was moving again. *She* was moving again. Joanna, Joanna, *Joanna* was being born.

It was over so quickly she gasped in surprise. Wet slithering, and her child fell away from her and into the dirt. Bach rolled to her side and pressed her forehead to the ground. The child nestled in blood and wetness between her legs.

She did what had to be done. When it came time to cut the cord, her hand automatically went to the chain knife. She stopped, seeing a man's threatening hand, hearing an almost supersonic whir that would in seconds disembowel her and rip Joanna away.

She dropped the knife, leaned over, and bit down hard.

Handfuls of corn silk pressed between her legs eventually stopped the bleeding. The placenta arrived. She was weak and shaky and would have liked nothing better than to just lie there in the mothering soil and heat.

But there was a shout from above. A man was up there, leaning over the edge of the catwalk. Answering shouts came from all around her. Far down at the end of her row, almost at the vanishing point, a tiny figure appeared and started coming toward her.

She had not thought she could get up, but she did. There seemed little point in running, but she ran, holding the chain knife in one hand and hugging Joanna in the other. If they would only come up to her and fight, she would die on a heap of slashed bodies.

A green finger of light sizzled into the ground at her heels. She instantly crossed into an adjacent row. So much for hand-to-hand combat.

The running was harder now, going over the hills rather than between them. But the man behind her could not keep her in view long enough for another shot.

Yet she had known it couldn't last. Vast as the corn plantation was, she could now see the end of it. She came out onto the ten-meter strip of bare ground between the corn plants and the edge of the dome.

There was a four-meter wall of bare metal in front of her. On top of the wall was the beginning of the clear material of the dome. It was shaped and anchored by a network of thin cables attached to the top of the wall on the outside.

It seemed there was no place to run, until she spotted the familiar blue light.

Inner door latches shut, outer ones open. Bach quickly did what Tong had done, but knew she had a better chance, if only for a while. This was an old lock, without an outside override. They would have to disconnect the alarms inside, then burn through the door. That would take some time.

Only after she had assured herself that she was not vulnerable to a depressurize command from the outside—a possibility she had not thought about before, but which she could negate by opening one of the four inner door latches, thus engaging the safety overrides—only then did she look around the inside of the lock.

It was a five-person model, designed to pass work gangs. There was a toolbox on the floor, coils of nylon rope in one corner. And a closet built into the wall.

She opened it and found the pressure suit.

It was a large one, but Bach was a large woman. She struggled with adjustment straps until she had the middle let out enough to take both her and Joanna.

Her mind worked furiously, fighting through the exhaustion.

Why was the suit here?

She couldn't find an answer at first, then recalled that the man who had shot at her had not been wearing a suit, nor had the man on the catwalk. There were others chasing her that she hadn't seen, and she was willing to bet they didn't have suits on, either.

So the posted sign she had passed was a safety regulation that was widely ignored. Everyone knew that air conservation and safety regs were many times more stringent than they had to be. The farm had a plastic dome which was the only surface separating it from vacuum, and that automatically classified it as a vacuum-hazard area. But in reality it was safe to enter it without a pressure suit.

The suit was kept there for the rare occasions when it was necessary for someone to go outside. It was a large suit so it would fit anyone who happened to need it, with adjustment.

Interesting.

Joanna cried for the first time when Bach got the suit sealed. And no wonder. The child was held against her body, but there was no other support for her. She quickly got both tiny legs jammed down one of the suit legs, and that couldn't have been too comfortable. Bach tried her best to ignore it, at the same time noting how hard it was to resist the impulse to try and touch her with her hands. She faced the lock controls.

There was a manual evacuation valve. She turned it slowly, opening it a crack so the air would bleed off without making a racket the people inside would hear. Part of the inner door was beginning to glow now. She wasn't too worried about it; hand lasers were not likely to burn through the metal. Someone would be going for heavy equipment by now. It would do them no good to go to adjacent air locks—which would probably have suits in them, too—because on the outside they couldn't force the door against the air pressure, and they couldn't force the lock to cycle as long as she was inside to override the command.

Unless it occurred to them that she would be suiting up, and someone would be waiting outside as soon as the outer door opened . . .

She spent a few bad minutes waiting for the air to leak to the outside. It didn't help her state of mind when the Bellman began to speak to her.

"Your situation is hopeless. I presume you know that."

She jumped, then realized he was speaking to her through the intercom, and it was being relayed to her suit radio. He didn't know she was in the suit, then.

"I don't know anything of the kind," she said. "The police will be here in a few minutes. You'd better get going while you've got the chance."

"Sorry. That won't work. I know you got through, but I also know they didn't trace you."

The air pressure dial read zero. Bach held the chain knife and pulled the door open. She stuck her head out. No one was waiting for her.

She was fifty meters away across the gently rolling plain when she suddenly stopped.

It was at least four kilometers to the nearest air lock that did not lead back into the plantation. She had plenty of air, but was not sure about her strength. The midwife mercifully spared her the pain she should have been going through, but her arms and legs felt like lead. Could they follow her faster than she could run? It seemed likely.

Of course, there was another alternative.

She thought about what they had planned for Joanna, then loped back to the dome. She moved like a skater, with her feet close to the ground.

It took three jumps before she could grab the upper edge of the metal wall with one gauntlet, then she could not lift her weight with just the one arm. She realized she was a step away from total exhaustion. With both hands, she managed to clamber up to stand on a narrow ledge with her feet among the bolts which secured the hold-down cables to the top of the wall. She leaned down and looked through the transparent vacuplast. A group of five people stood around the inner lock door. One of them, who had been squatting with his elbows on his knees, stood up now and pressed a button beside the lock. She could only see the top of his head, which was protected by a blue cap.

"You found the suit, didn't you?" the Bellman said. His voice was quiet, unemotional. Bach said nothing. "Can you still hear me?"

"I can hear you," Bach said. She held the chain knife and squeezed the handle; a slight vibration in her glove was the only indication that it was working. She put the edge of the blade to the plastic film and began to trace the sides of a square, one meter wide.

"I thought you could," he said. "You're on your way already. Of course, I wouldn't have mentioned the suit, in case you *hadn't* found it, until one of my own men reached the next lock and was on his way around the outside. Which he is."

"Um-hmm." Bach wanted him to keep talking. She was worried they would hear the sound of the knife as it slowly cut its way through the tough plastic.

"What you might like to know is that he has an infrared detector with him. We used it to track you inside. It makes your footprints glow. Even your suit loses heat enough through the boots to make the machine useful. It's a very good machine."

Bach hadn't thought of that, and didn't like it at all. It might have been best to take her chances trying to reach the next air lock. When the man arrived he would quickly see that she had doubled back.

"Why are you telling me all this?" she asked. The square was now bordered with shallow grooves, but it was taking too long. She began to concentrate just on the lower edge, moving the knife back and forth.

"Thinking out loud," he said, with a self-conscious laugh. "This is an exhilarating game, don't you agree? And you're the most skilled quarry I've pursued in many years. Is there a secret to your success?"

"I'm with the police," Bach said. "Your people stumbled into a stakeout."

"Ah, that explains a lot," he said, almost gratefully.

"Who *are* you, anyway?" she asked.

"Just call me the Bellman. When I heard you people had named me that, I took a fancy to it."

"Why babies? That's the part I can't understand."

"Why veal? Why baby lamb chops? How should I know? I don't eat the stuff. I don't know anything about meat, but I know a good racket, and a fertile market, when I see them. One of my customers wants babies, that's what he gets. I can get any age." He sighed again. "And it's so easy, we grow sloppy. We get careless. The work is so routine. From now on we'll kill quickly. If we'd killed you when you got out of the tube, we'd have avoided a lot of bother."

"A lot more than you expect, I hope." Damn! Why wasn't the knife through yet? She hadn't thought it would take this long. "I don't understand, frankly, why you let me live as long as you did. Why lock me up, then come to kill me hours later?"

"Greed, I'm afraid," the Bellman said. "You see, they were not coming to kill you. You overreacted. I was attempting to combine one business with another. There are uses for live pregnant women. I have many customers. Uses for live babies, too. We generally keep them for a few months."

Bach knew she should question him about that, as a good police officer. The department would want to know what he did. Instead, she bore down on the knife with all her strength and nearly bit through her lower lip.

"I could use someone like you," he said. "You don't really think you can get away, do you? Why don't you think it over? We could make . . ."

Peering down through the bubble, Bach saw the Bellman look up. He never finished his offer, whatever it was. She saw his face for an instant—a perfectly ordinary face that would not have seemed out of place on an accountant or a bank teller—and had the satisfaction of seeing him realize his mistake. He did not waste time in regrets. He instantly saw his only chance, abandoned the people working on the lock without warning them, and began to run at full speed back into the cornfield.

The bottom edge of the square parted at that moment. Bach felt something tugging on her hand, and she moved along the narrow ledge away from the hole. There was no sound as the sides of the square peeled back, then the whole panel broke free and the material began to tear from each of the corners. The surface of the bubble began to undulate sluggishly.

It was eerie; there was nothing to hear and little to see as the air rushed out of the gaping hole. Then suddenly storms of cornstalks, shorn of leaves and ears, erupted like flights of artillery rockets and flung themselves into the blackness. The stream turned white, and Bach could not figure out why that should be.

The first body came through and sailed an amazing distance before it impacted in the gray dust.

The place was a beehive of activity when Lisa Babcock arrived. A dozen police crawlers were parked outside the wall with dozens more on their way. The blue lights revolved silently. She heard nothing but her own breathing, the occasional terse comment on the emergency band, and the faint whirring of her legs.

Five bodies were arranged just outside the wall, beside the large hole which had been cut to give vehicle access to the interior of the plantation. She looked down at them dispassionately. They looked about as one would expect a body to look which had been blown from a cannon and then quick-frozen.

Bach was not among them.

She stepped inside the dome for a moment, unable to tell what the writhing white coating of spongy material was until she picked up a handful. Popcorn. It was twenty centimeters deep inside, and still growing as raw sunlight and vacuum caused the kernels to dry and explode. If Bach was in there, it could take days to find her body. She went back outside and began to walk along the outer perimeter of the wall, away from where all the activity was concentrated.

She found the body face down, in the shadow of the wall. It was hard to see; she had nearly tripped over it. What surprised her was the spacesuit. If she had a suit, why had she died? Pursing her lips, she grabbed one shoulder and rolled it over.

It was a man, looking down in considerable surprise at the hilt of a chain knife growing from his chest, surrounded by a black, broken flower of frozen blood. Babcock began to run.

When she came to the lock she pounded on the metal door, then put her helmet to it. After a long pause, she heard the answering taps.

It was another fifteen minutes before they could bring a rescue truck around and mate it to the door. Babcock was in the truck when the door swung open, and stepped through first by the simple expedient of elbowing a fellow cop with enough force to bruise ribs.

At first she thought that, against all her hopes, Bach was dead. She sprawled loosely with her back propped against the wall, hugging the baby in her arms. She didn't seem to be breathing. Mother and child were coated with dirt, and Bach's legs were bloody. She seemed impossibly pale. Babcock went to her and reached for the baby.

Bach jerked, showing surprising strength. Her sunken eyes slowly focused on Babcock's face, then she looked down at Joanna and grinned foolishly.

"Isn't she the prettiest thing you ever saw?"

AFTERWORD

Finally, a word about editors.

I can't recall ever meeting an author who didn't have a major or minor horror story about editors. John Brunner once told me that an editor took an entire major character out of one of his books. Just deleted all the sentences that referred to that character. The book made no sense at all. John didn't discover this until the book was published.

I said at the beginning that I feel I've been very lucky. One of the best things has been the editors I have worked with. I don't have a single editor horror story to tell. (Oh, sure, they always need the galleys back yesterday, but that seems to be standard industry practice, nothing anybody can do about it.)

When I was first getting started, Ed Ferman at *F&SF*, Jim Baen at *Galaxy*, and George Scithers and later Gardner Dozois at *Asimov's* were always wonderful, as were Damon Knight, Terry Carr, and David Gerrold. Later, when I started writing novels, I started off with two of the best in the business, Don Bensen and Jim Frenkel, then moved on to an all-too-short association with David Hartwell and John Silbersack. For many years now my editor has been Susan Allison at Penguin/Putnam/Ace/Berkley/Halliburton/Mitsubishi, or whatever they're calling the company these days. She is possibly the most patient editor in the world, and has never lost faith in me no matter how late I am turning in the manuscript. She edited the book you're holding right now, and wouldn't you know it, I finished these introductions a month late.

John Varley
January 2004
Oceano, California

COPYRIGHTS AND PERMISSIONS